CIRCLE OF BLOOD:

BOOKS 4 - 6

Other books by R. A. Steffan

The Last Vampire: Book One
The Last Vampire: Book Two
The Last Vampire: Book Three
The Last Vampire: Book Four
The Last Vampire: Book Five
The Last Vampire: Book Six

Vampire Bound: Book One
Vampire Bound: Book Two
Vampire Bound: Book Three
Vampire Bound: Book Four

Forsaken Fae: Book One
Forsaken Fae: Book Two
Forsaken Fae: Book Three

The Sixth Demon: Book One
The Sixth Demon: Book Two
The Sixth Demon: Book Three

The Complete Horse Mistress Collection
The Complete Lion Mistress Collection
The Complete Dragon Mistress Collection
The Complete Master of Hounds Collection

Antidote: Love and War, Book 1
Antigen: Love and War, Book 2
Antibody: Love and War, Book 3
Anthelion: Love and War, Book 4
Antagonist: Love and War, Book 5

CIRCLE OF BLOOD:

BOOKS 4 - 6

R. A. STEFFAN & JAELYNN WOOLF

Circle of Blood: Books 4 - 6

Copyright 2018 by R. A. Steffan

All rights reserved. Printed in the United States of America. No part of this book may be used or reproduced in any manner whatsoever without written permission except in the case of brief quotations embedded in critical articles or reviews.

This book is a work of fiction. Names, characters, businesses, organizations, places, events and incidents either are the product of the author's imagination or are used fictitiously. Any resemblance to actual persons, living or dead, events, or locales is entirely coincidental.

ISBN: 978-1-955073-47-9 (paperback)
ISBN: 978-1-955073-64-6 (hardcover)

Cover branding by Deranged Doctor Design

For information, contact the author at
http://www.rasteffan.com/contact/

Second Edition: December 2022

Introduction

This series contains graphic violence and explicit sexual content. It is intended for a mature audience.

TABLE OF CONTENTS

CIRCLE OF BLOOD BOOK FOUR:

LOVER'S ABSOLUTION

R. A. STEFFAN & JAELYNN WOOLF

ONE

"Oh, you have *got* to be shitting me," Xander said, as a dozen werewolves appeared in the mouth of the dead-end London alley.

"Sorry," said the dark-haired woman who'd lured him here on the pretext of helping her—apparently fictional—sister who had supposedly been attacked by a young boy with glowing eyes and fangs. She sounded genuinely sheepish as she jerked her chin at the man next to her, who was decked out in chains and ripped camo like some sort of cut-rate Mad Max reject. "He didn't think you'd come if you knew what we really were, vampire."

"Smarter than he looks, then," Xander observed, thinking privately that it wasn't a very high bar to reach. "Good to know."

The alpha werewolf's answering smile was thin and cruel. "You'd be amazed." He cocked his head. "No doubt you're getting ready to fly away home, little vamp, but you should hear what I have to tell you first. I've got something you want."

"You think so?" Xander asked, affecting boredom to cover his irritation at having fallen for a pretty woman's damsel-in-distress act. "What is it? Fleas? Kibbles? A squeaky toy? Maybe a nice, meaty bone?"

That cruel smile never wavered. "I've got that little baby vamp Manisha described to you, all chained up in iron shackles, so he can't get away. Interested, now?"

4

Yes. Of course he was interested now. Because if what the alpha was saying about holding a child vampire prisoner was true...

"God, I fucking hate werewolves," Xander told him, tone still conversational. "Have I mentioned that yet?"

"Oh, well. Off you flap, then," the leader said, making a shooing motion with one hand. "Nothing stopping you, is there? Not unless you want us to take you to see Junior first..."

Xander gritted his teeth, wanting nothing more at that moment than the human ability to crawl into a bottle, get blind, falling-down drunk, and never crawl back out.

"Fine, Fluffy," he grated. "You win. Take me to see this alleged vampire, and I won't brandish the rolled-up newspaper."

Fluffy's flat, hard eyes were starting to make Xander's skin crawl, quite honestly. But he held back any further insults as Fluffy shrugged a brawny shoulder.

"That's real magnanimous of you, mate," said the werewolf. "Best follow us, in that case. Dawn's coming soon. You wouldn't want to get a terminal case of sunburn, now would you?"

Actually, mate, Xander thought sourly, *you might be surprised. Lately, that prospect has been growing more appealing by the day.*

-o-o-o-

Manisha Sadhu was living a nightmare. With the green-eyed vampire and her other pack members in tow, she followed meekly behind Crank, the alpha werewolf. She and Sangye—the young boy she'd been meant to protect—had been handed to Crank like chattel a couple of weeks ago. Since then, he'd pretty much owned them both, body and soul. Before all this started, Manisha used to think she understood what reality was. She'd known evil existed in the world, of course—these days, you'd have to be blind, deaf, *and* stupid not to realize that evil existed in the world.

But… werewolves? Vampires?

Two weeks ago, she'd been a glorified nanny. No, even that was too generous. She was barely more than a housekeeper, included as part of the small retinue of people helping to hide Sangye in London. She'd been chosen for the position mostly because of her stint in British schools as a teenager and her distant family connections in the UK. After a roadside bomb in Tezpur killed Sangye's Regent and his teachers, he and his remaining retinue fled India for the West in hopes of finding less chaos there.

They should have known better. At first, it seemed that things might work out for them. They had a strong case to offer the Office of Tibet in London when they appealed for asylum, and they'd been awaiting official word while staying in a private house where they would not draw unwanted attention. Then came the terrible evening that would live in Manisha's dreams forever.

The sound of fists pounding on the door. A harsh shout to open up for the police. Bhuti, the most senior of Sangye's surviving teachers, had opened the door, saying that there must have been some mistake. Half a dozen black-clad men immediately swarmed in, breaking Bhuti's neck as Manisha watched in horror from the second story balcony.

She still remembered the smell that rose around the intruders like a cloud—in fact, some days she thought she would never be completely free of it. It was the smell of the grave. The smell of death. They moved quickly through the house, choked-off screams marking the senseless murders of the others who had been staying on the first floor.

Manisha ran into Sangye's bedroom and started yanking frantically at the window, trying without success to open it while his mother clasped the boy in her arms and attempted to keep him quiet. She'd hoped that if his mother Jampa held Manisha's legs while she lowered Sangye out by his hands, maybe the two of them could get the six-year-old down safely from the second story. But then it was too late.

One of the men kicked the flimsy bedroom door off its hinges even as Manisha searched around for something heavy enough to break the window's glass. Huge forms rushed in and overpowered them. She struggled, certain that she was about to be killed like the others. A cold laugh came from the open doorway.

"Oh, how utterly delectable," said a voice with an oily Eastern European accent. "You have truly outdone yourself, my Master."

The speaker was tall and broad-shouldered, dressed in sunglasses and a dark, tailored suit that contrasted sharply with the black military gear the other men were wearing. He also didn't appear to be conversing with anyone presently inside the room. A chill skittered its way up Manisha's spine.

Jampa was weeping now, straining toward her son. "Please," she begged in broken English. "Please, no! He is boy… just small boy!"

"Who are you?" Manisha snapped, trying not to gag at the stench now choking the bedroom. "I demand to know what agency or organization you represent!"

The man in the suit came closer, his sunglasses reflecting her frightened face in stereo.

"You *demand*?" he asked, clearly amused. "Well, if you *demand* it of me, then I will tell you that as far as you're concerned, I am here on behalf of the Ministry of Death."

A moan of fear escaped Jampa's throat, and she sagged in her captor's grip. From across the room, Sangye watched the man, wide-eyed, but still maintaining that otherworldly aura of calm and serenity that drew in everyone who met him.

"Why?" the boy asked simply.

The leader regarded him for a long moment, tilting his head as if to get a better look at him. "Because taking a bishop and a queen with a single move is far too tempting an opportunity to ignore." His attention shifted to the goon holding Manisha. "Cuff that one and take her outside to the van. If she doesn't keep quiet, gag her."

Her captor zip-tied Manisha's hands behind her back and dragged her down the stairs, past Bhuti's broken body, and outside to a waiting black van. Manisha clamped her lips together, not wanting to give the goon an excuse to gag her before they left the house. As soon as they were outside, though, she started shrieking like a banshee for help. Within a second, a meaty, stinking hand slapped across her mouth. She bit down hard on his clammy flesh, choking on the bile that tried to rise, but the man didn't even flinch.

He shoved her into the back of the van and stuffed a wad of cloth in her mouth, tying it in place to keep it there. Manisha's eyes watered, and she jammed herself into the corner, as far away from him as she could get. They stayed like that for what seemed like an age, even though it was probably no more than an hour—if that. Manisha's heart pounded, her head joining in with a throbbing rhythm as time dragged on.

Eventually, the van door opened again, and two more goons squeezed in with Sangye shackled between them. Manisha whimpered around the gag—heavy iron manacles bound the boy's wrists, ankles, and neck. He was fighting them with far more strength than a terrified child should possess; moving and flailing so much that Manisha couldn't get a proper look at him.

Jampa was conspicuously absent.

The goons clipped the heavy chains fastened to the shackles to solid steel rings welded to the van's frame. Manisha's guard situated himself on the bench opposite her in the other front corner of the cargo area. He drew a wicked-looking dagger of some dark metal. It looked like iron, as well, but… who made daggers out of iron? The other two guards released their grip on the chains and stepped quickly down from the back of the van, slamming the doors behind them.

Sangye stilled for an instant, and Manisha drew in a sharp breath when she saw his glowing red eyes in the near-darkness. As if the small noise had drawn his attention, he stared at her for the space of two heartbeats, and lunged. She shrieked in terrified surprise, the noise muffled by the gag. The heavy shackles pulled the boy to a stop less than an arm's length away from her as she scrabbled as far back into the corner as she could get.

The van was moving now. The intermittent sodium-yellow glow of streetlights streaming through the van's tiny, barred windows transformed Sangye's face into something monstrous. There was no recognition in his expression, and his teeth gnashed at the air as he strained toward her. She could see the wicked points of fangs glinting beneath his curled lips as his jaws chomped mindlessly on nothing.

The breath shook loose from her chest in a rush. Manisha started screaming again, the gag absorbing the sound with its smothering bulk. She screamed and screamed, and didn't stop screaming until the goons came back to drag Sangye away from her, still fighting to free himself from the shackles.

Whoever would have guessed that nightmarish van ride would only be the beginning? Suit-and-sunglasses had a guard haul her out after Sangye, and the black-clad men deposited them both in an abandoned basement. The place had been fitted with cells that would have been right at home in a dungeon somewhere, but the rest of the building looked like an old warehouse. She hadn't recognized any other buildings or landmarks during the brief trip from the van to the large double doors leading inside.

She was thrown into an empty cell, and from the horrible growling, choking noises nearby, Sangye had been dragged into the one next to her—probably still shackled, based on the casual way the guards exited and closed the door behind them. Manisha's knees went weak, and she sank down onto the filthy floor, tears squeezing from between her eyelids. She felt horribly lightheaded, and desperately thirsty as the cloth stuffed between her lips leached the moisture from her mouth.

Some time later, the door to her cell opened. She staggered clumsily to her feet, her balance thrown off by her bound hands. In the absence of any other viable plans, she charged toward the path to freedom. A ragged man with an unkempt gray beard grabbed her and held her with effortless strength as she kicked and struggled. Over his shoulder, she caught a glimpse of the Suit, his pasty face twisted in cold amusement behind the concealing dark glasses.

Graybeard dragged her back to the center of the cell, whirled her around in his grip, and buried his teeth in her shoulder, ripping out a chunk of her trapezius muscle. She screamed again, hoarse and muffled by choking cloth. Just as abruptly as he'd attacked, he let her fall to the ground. Pain exploded behind her eyes.

Manisha's consciousness wavered in and out, Graybeard's voice sounding like it was echoing through a tunnel as he growled, "Awright, now give me the damned money. Can't believe you talked me into turning a new bitch for Crank—that mangy bastard."

Her hearing faded, returning a moment later. "...sure this will make it a worthwhile venture for you. Now, leave." That was the Suit's voice, she thought dazedly.

A few more grumbled words, and then one set of footsteps came closer while another departed. A hand—soaked in so much aftershave she could hardly breathe without choking on it—pulled the gag from her mouth.

"*Why?*" she rasped, echoing Sangye's plaintive question from earlier. She could feel blood trickling down her shoulder to pool beneath her.

"Very simple," said the Suit. "You're one of the vampires' whores. I could sense it as soon as I got close to the boy. But your pet nightcrawler will hardly be able to reclaim you under the circumstances. Not now that you're a werewolf." He laughed. "It's so much more of a blow this way. Much better than simply killing you, only for you to be reborn yet again and return as a threat in a few short decades."

A *werewolf*? At the time, she'd tried to dismiss the nonsensical, unbelievable words. Now, some thirteen days later, she knew better. Something inside her had changed the moment she'd been bitten. She felt trapped here with the pack as surely as Sangye was trapped in his iron shackles, and her time was running out. The full moon was in two nights, and according to the others, once she'd transformed into a wolf for the first time, she would never be able to escape this curse.

Even now, the wolf trapped inside her drove her inexorably to stay with the pack. She could feel it cower and bare its throat whenever Crank so much as looked at her. If she had been alone, she knew she would have given into despair and stopped fighting. But it wasn't just herself that she needed to worry about.

Sangye was here, too.

Two

The day after their capture, Manisha heard Sangye weeping quietly in his cell. Crank came in not long after, supremely confident in his power over her as the alpha wolf. He'd cut the zip-tie binding her hands behind her back; given her food and water. Specifically, he'd given her a joint of some kind of raw meat still clinging to the bone. She'd fallen on it and torn it free in great chunks with her teeth.

Manisha was a vegetarian. She had been one her entire life.

But now, to her horror, she found that she was merely a wolf in human's clothing. After she'd eaten, Crank took her into Sangye's cell and told her to look after him. Told her that he was a vampire now, and would need to drink human blood. He carelessly informed her that he would have a homeless person or a runaway brought in, and instructed her to try and keep Sangye from killing them too fast when he fed.

Then he left, slamming the cell door behind him.

Sangye's face was smeared with rusty tear tracks that looked like old blood. "Kumari Sadhu?" he asked in a rasping voice, addressing her with the same respectful honorific he'd always used. "I have done something unforgivable."

It was so like his old demeanor that she didn't even think. She just stumbled forward and dropped to her knees, wrapping him up in her arms.

"No," she said, her voice sounding watery. "It's the men who took us who have done unforgivable things."

"You're hurt," Sangye murmured. "And you don't smell… right. What happened?"

The throbbing agony in her shoulder had faded to a dull ache with unnatural speed over the course of the hours she'd spent huddled in her cell. The wound should have been debilitating, left untreated as it had been. Yet she'd almost forgotten about it upon seeing Sangye.

"I'm all right," she managed. "Don't worry about it. Something has been… done to us, and I don't understand it. But I swear to you that I'll protect you and get us out of here somehow."

Even then, the fear she'd felt at the prospect of leaving this place—of disobeying the alpha werewolf who'd brought her food and told her to care for Sangye—made her realize that her words could well be a lie.

She told herself that going along with the leader was just smart strategy. She would ingratiate herself. Gain his trust. It only made sense, right? Inside, though, she worried that if and when an opportunity came, whatever shred of humanity she had left wouldn't be strong enough for her to take action. But she *had* to be strong enough. She had to be strong for Sangye. She'd just given him her word, after all.

As promised, Crank delivered a shaking teenage boy to the cell less than a day after he'd said he would. Sangye only closed his eyes and turned his head away, though Manisha could see the glint of fangs peeking out from under his upper lip in the harsh light of the naked bulb overhead. She had tried to share some of her meager ration of food and water with him, but he could barely choke it down. Anything he did manage to swallow came right back up.

At first, Crank was impatient. He slashed the kidnapped teen's arm with a switchblade and pressed the sluggishly bleeding cut against Sangye's mouth as his victim wailed and begged. Again and again, Sangye only turned away and clamped his lips together tightly. On the fourth day, he met the teenager's eyes with his glowing ones after refusing the blood. A moment later, the struggling adolescent went calm and still, the fear draining from him like water from cupped hands.

Crank gave Sangye a narrow-eyed stare and shrugged. "Suit yourself, pipsqueak," he said. "You'll give in before you starve to death, I'll wager."

Knowing Sangye as she did, Manisha wasn't so sure about that, but she kept her doubts to herself.

"Why are we keeping him here like this, anyway?" she asked, caught as always between the part of her that insisted the word 'we' was a part of her ruse to gain Crank's trust, and the part that thought it sounded quite natural to lump herself in with the other werewolves. "What do you need him for?"

"Bait," Crank said. "For a bigger fish." He smiled down at her and lifted a large, callused hand, brushing a strand of Manisha's hair back and hooking it over her ear.

And that was when she realized she had even more problems than she'd previously realized.

Though she felt hopelessly alone in her unfolding predicament, the reality was that the warehouse teemed with werewolves. The others in the pack came and talked with her sometimes. Really, she thought they came to gawp at Sangye, but at least they talked to her while they did it.

That was how she'd learned that unless the man who'd bitten her died before the next full moon, she'd be stuck as a werewolf forever once she'd undergone her first transformation. It was also how she learned that Crank used to have a lover—his mate, the others called her—but that she'd been killed a few months ago. The middle-aged woman who'd shared that particular bit of gossip had looked at Manisha with an air of speculation as she spoke.

And now Manisha knew why.

Crank started making little possessive gestures like that whenever he was around her over the next few days. Each time he did, the wolf in her preened, even as the human in her quailed. After the full moon, would she mindlessly fall into the arms of this creature who thought nothing of kidnapping innocents and keeping a six-year-old child manacled in a cell? Would the last trace of her free will be lost with the turning of the lunar month?

Desperation clawed at her, yet she was no closer to having a useful plan of escape than she'd been on the night Graybeard had torn a bloody chunk from her shoulder and changed her. She could try to run, fighting her new pack instincts all the way, but she didn't know where the key to Sangye's shackles was being kept. She had no way to free him from this place, and she feared that even if the police believed her far-fetched story, by the time she got anyone in the outside world to take action, Crank would simply have pulled up stakes and moved somewhere else.

And all that didn't even take Mr. Suit-and-Sunglasses into account. He'd known exactly where Sangye was being kept, even though the location of the private house where they were staying was supposedly secret. Add in the goons' military garb, and who knew whether the police and government could be trusted to help her in the first place?

The next morning, Crank called the pack together to talk to them.

"All right, you lot," he said, his voice booming around the empty warehouse. "We've got us another vamp to catch. My contact says one of the bloodsuckers is definitely in London. We need to find him and draw him here."

"Does your bloke know where he is?" asked one of the men—a grizzle-haired old grump who called himself Patch.

"Just that he's in this area," Crank said. "If Kovac gets close enough to pin down this nightcrawler's exact location, then the nightcrawler will be able to sense Kovac in turn, and he'll know he's being watched. It's up to us to stake out the likely spots where a freak might go to feel right at home. You all know the drill. We'll start looking tonight. And when we find him—" Crank's eyes fell on Manisha, pinning her, "—I want Brown Eyes here to draw him out into the open."

Manisha's heart beat faster. It was a test of her loyalty to the pack, she knew, and she probably didn't want to know what would happen if she failed it. But could it also be an opportunity in disguise? How crazy would she have to be to run away from werewolves, and straight into the arms of a vampire?

Yet… she'd held a vampire in her arms these last many nights. She'd held a small boy. He'd been turned into the ravenous monster she'd seen in the van, true. Now, though, he was to all appearances the same sweet child he'd been before. A serene, loving boy who refused to drink the blood of innocents even as he slowly starved to death.

"Why does this contact of yours want to catch vampires, anyway?" she asked.

Crank gave her a sour look. "No idea, luv. All I care about is that there's money and power at stake. Working with him is good for the pack, and if it's good for the pack, then it's what we do."

And so, several days later, that was how Manisha found herself marching back from a nightclub in Lambeth toward the warehouse in Battersea along with a dozen werewolves and one very brassed-off vampire. A note bearing a hastily scribbled plea for help burned a hole in her pocket. She'd spent the last hour second-guessing herself over the contents and handling of that note. She probably should have slipped the wad of paper to the vampire when she first approached him in the club, but she'd told herself she wanted to get a look at him first, and see if she could feel him out a bit before deciding whether or not to trust him.

Then she'd told herself that giving the note to him while they were still in the club would mess up Crank's plan and expose her, because she hadn't thought to write "play along" at the end of the short message. He'd have paused to read it, probably questioned her, and Manisha wasn't stupid enough to think that Crank didn't have someone in the club watching her every move.

On the walk to Battersea, she felt too exposed. The others were all around them. They'd see if she tried to pass something to him. And to make it worse, she still had no idea if she could even trust him or not. In the club, he'd been cold and brusque when he thought she was seeking help for her injured sister. When Crank and the others arrived, he'd been openly hostile.

But he'd also been completely un-cowed by Crank's presence. Indeed, he was the first person she'd seen who didn't show the alpha werewolf the slightest bit of deference. Or the slightest bit of respect, for that matter. Watching the vampire's careless disregard for the pack of werewolves hemming him in, Manisha had felt her pulse speed up, though she couldn't have said if it was with dread or excitement. Would this pale, handsome creature truly be powerful enough to back up his casual arrogance, if it came down to it?

Could he get Sangye away to safety somehow? Protect him from Crank and the others? She decided with sudden certainty that he was the best chance she was likely to get. She would have to beat back the cowering wolf inside her long enough for her human self to take this gamble.

Her chance came as they were descending the dark staircase leading to the warehouse basement. She positioned herself near the vampire, suddenly wishing that she had some sort of a background in either sleight of hand or pick-pocketing. He was understandably wary of his surroundings, his eyes glowing with an unnatural green light in the dim illumination.

Crank was ahead of them, not looking back, and the others were giving the vampire a healthy bubble of space inside the enclosed area. With a deep breath, Manisha eased the sloppily folded paper scrap out of her battered jeans, and tried to judge the best moment to slip it into his pocket.

He stiffened as her hand brushed the fabric of his tailored trousers, and her breath stuttered. God, how had she ever thought she could be subtle enough to pull off something like this? His hand darted out with inhuman speed, clasping her wrist in an uncompromising grip. Without warning, electricity jolted through her like she'd been struck by lightning. She gasped and jerked free, nearly tripping down the stairs in her haste.

She cast around with wide eyes. Panic gripped her throat as she became abruptly aware that every gaze in the stairwell was now pinned on her… and on the vampire who was standing two steps above her, staring down at her with shocked green eyes.

THREE

Xander's first thought when the jolt of raw power went through him was *no*. His second thought was also *no*. And his third thought was *oh, fuck no*.

All eyes were on the pair of them as they stood staring at each other in consternation. The woman recovered first. She surged up the steps separating them and slapped him full across the face with a strength that seemed less than werewolf, somehow, though it was certainly more than a human of her size should have been able to muster.

It was a toss-up what was more distracting—the shock of electricity as their skin connected, or the flare of pain as her nails dug furrows in his cheek. His hiss of surprise was unfeigned, but her strategy wasn't a bad one under the circumstances. Circumstances, he realized, which could hardly be worse. He'd felt her slip something into his trouser pocket, and now he could just about detect the crinkle of paper inside. A note?

There was no way to confirm it right now—Fluffy was already charging up the steps two at a time, his face locked in a scowl. The other werewolves looked on uncertainly.

"He tried to grab me!" his erstwhile damsel in distress accused, her mahogany eyes flashing fire.

With difficulty, Xander rallied his wits enough to play along with the game, even if he didn't know yet what the stakes were. Or what the rules were, come to that.

"She got too close," he said, in an approximation of the same cold, bored tone he'd used in the alley. "Keep your puppies under control, mate. This shirt is fucking *Versace*. I don't need someone shedding on it."

The werewolf alpha moved the woman aside—not gently, but also not with undue force—and then he was in Xander's face. Despite Xander being a step higher on the stairs, they were more or less eye-to-eye. Somewhat to his surprise, he felt testosterone-fueled anger rising in his chest at the open challenge from another male, even if it was a male from the wrong fucking species. The primitive reaction threatened to belie Xander's *cold, superior bastard* act, even though it would be the height of foolishness to engage with this prick in a stairwell while surrounded by ten other hostile-looking werewolves.

Still, the choice to dissipate into mist when a meaty hand closed on the front of the aforementioned Versace shirt was a shockingly difficult one to make in the face of his desire to start removing body parts instead. Or, at least, in the face of his desire to *attempt* removing body parts. Xander had never actually brawled with a two-meter-tall alpha werewolf before, and had no idea how the brute's strength would match up against a hundred-year-old vampire's.

This, he told himself very firmly, was obviously not the time or the place to find out, no matter what his instincts were screaming. He materialized at the base of the stairs, striving for *cool and unruffled* rather than *flustered, pissed off, and in desperate need of a drink*. Interestingly, he realized that the marks of the woman's nails on his left cheek had not immediately started to heal.

"Holding your little prisoner back here somewhere, are you?" he asked, as the flicker of a weak, vampiric presence teased his awareness. With an effort of will, he put aside the inconceivable revelation he'd just experienced a moment ago in favor of the thing he'd originally come here to investigate. Even so, he felt hyper-aware of the crinkling paper square nestled in his pocket... and of the female werewolf now emerging from the stairwell.

Xander didn't wait for Fluffy to answer, or for the others to catch up with him. The shadowy presence inside his mind was its own guide. He reached out mentally, moving toward it.

Can you hear me? he sent, and received a faint sense of confusion or query in reply.

The weakened vampire was in a cell near the far end of the underground level. Xander dissipated again, flowing through the small, barred window set in the heavy door. He reformed to find a boy of perhaps six or seven manacled to the concrete wall with iron. The child looked awful—emaciated and frightened. His dark eyes were defined by the graceful sweep of epicanthic folds, and his face would have been soft and round if not for the hollows under his cheeks.

Xander's immediate thought was, *his essence feels like Snag's...* but that was ridiculous. The child before him was freshly turned and desperately fragile—about as far from the millennia-old, silent head-case of a vampire he'd left back in Damascus in terms of age and power as it was possible to be.

"You're like me," the boy rasped in accented English.

"So it would seem," he said, a bit faintly. Outside the cell, he could hear cursing and the scraping of keys. "Quickly, now—I can feel that you need blood."

He crossed the distance separating them and offered his wrist. The boy's face twisted up.

"No," he whispered, to Xander's consternation.

"Why—" Xander began, only to be cut off when the door clanged open. Fluffy stood in the gap, an iron dagger held in one meaty paw. Behind him stood six other burly male werewolves, similarly armed.

"Get him," the alpha snarled, and lunged through the door.

Xander growled in frustration. "Oh, for god's sake—"

In the absence of intelligent alternatives, he dissipated for a third time and rushed toward the aboveground level of the warehouse before Fluffy could decide to do something predictable—like threatening the boy if Xander didn't return to human form.

I'll come back, I promise, he sent as he swirled away, adding, *hang in there, kid,* only to wince at the *faux pas* an instant later as he remembered the iron shackles.

There were several broken windows on the ground floor that no one had bothered to board up yet. Beyond them, the sun was poised to rise above London's jagged skyline. Since the alternative to making a run for it was to hover around the ceiling of the warehouse all day hiding from the mongrels, Xander flew a couple of blocks over, riding the wind currents and keeping to the shadows. Thankfully, he slipped through a ventilation pipe in a convenient office building before the first rays of sun could singe him.

Inside, he found a comfortable looking corner office, did a quick scout for security cameras, and reformed into solidity when he didn't find any. A couple of quick flicks drew the blinds across the large windows, cutting off the threat of the encroaching morning light. According to the clock on the wall, it was barely after five a.m. Figuring he was unlikely to be disturbed as long as he kept half an ear out for the maintenance staff, he flopped down in the desk chair.

Under the circumstances, leaving had clearly been the only reasonable thing to do. A long-buried streak of stubborn male ego had tried to goad him into attacking Fluffy in the stairwell. Now, the same stubborn streak insisted that leaving the woman and the boy behind felt an awful lot like running away with his tail between his legs.

In his defense, Xander had always enjoyed a good brawl—even more so, now that it would take a stake through the heart or decapitation to put him down and out for good. *At least, you enjoy it when the creatures you're brawling with aren't wearing the bodies of children while they shoot and hack at you,* noted the treacherous voice in the back of his mind, memories of his recent stint in Haiti floating to the surface.

That insidious little voice was one he'd spent decades quieting with whatever exotic chemicals he could find conveniently swimming in a nearby human's bloodstream. Unfortunately, the *better living through chemistry* option was off the table at the moment. His mouth twisted in displeasure. Pushing everything else to the side in favor of trying to figure out the current situation, he let out a sigh and kicked back to rest his feet on the edge of the desk. The note was still in his pocket. He pulled it out and unfolded it, examining it.

The paper was an irregular shape—dusty, torn on two edges, previously crumpled, and smelling faintly of werewolf. One side was covered with faded writing in pencil. It appeared to be someone's quick and dirty mathematical calculations, partially missing where the scrap had been torn from the larger page. He turned it over. The writing on the other side was much clearer, though it had been written with a cheap pen that was running out of ink.

THE CHILD AND I ARE BOTH PRISONERS PLEASE
HELP US GET AWAY—MEET ME IN THE SAME
ALLEY AS BEFORE AT MIDNIGHT TONIGHT

He tossed the paper onto the desk, once more drawn back to the elephant in the room. The one part of this fiasco that he really, *really* wasn't ready to acknowledge. The woman. She had been his—

No. He couldn't do anything about that right now. Practicality—that was the key.

So... stick to the practical parts. The proposed meeting didn't seem terribly likely to be a trap. And even if it was, no matter how many mongrels decided to show up to the party, he could always slip from their grasp the same way he'd done this morning—by flying away. If they had any fancier tricks to use on him, they'd have used them when they had him on their turf, surely. They didn't even appear to have firearms. If they had, they could have riddled him with bullets when they had the chance, in an attempt to weaken him too much for him to be able to transform into mist.

Given those facts, he'd lay odds that the note was genuine. His fingers grazed the four parallel scratches on his cheek—still open and raw more than half an hour after she'd struck him.

She'd been smart. Quick-thinking. *Beautiful*, his mind supplied without prompting.

A werewolf, he reminded himself sharply. *She'd been a fucking werewolf.*

And what the hell was he supposed to do about *that* tiny little wrinkle? He realized with a growl of irritation that he was—yet again—thinking about the one thing he didn't want to think about. He pulled out his mobile and powered it on.

There were three more messages from Tré's number waiting for him since their brief text exchange earlier. He chewed his lip for a moment, mulling over his options before he decided on a number and dialed. The call picked up on the fourth ring.

"Eris, mate," he said without preamble, "we've got a problem."

"*Xander?*" Eris sounded as though he'd just woken up. A sleepy, feminine murmur came from somewhere close by the phone's pickup, which in no way made something in Xander's chest go tight and achy. Eris cleared his throat and continued, "*Just a moment. Let me send Trynn to get the others.*"

Eris whispered something quietly to his mate. Xander gritted his teeth and very carefully did not listen closely enough to catch the details of the gentle exchange.

"*Oksana, Mason, and Duchess are in Singapore,*" Eris continued in a louder voice, sounding more awake now. "*You knew that, right? The rest of us are here, though. Tré said you were in London?*"

"Yes," Xander said tightly.

"*You shouldn't have gone off alone.*" There was more worry than censure in Eris' voice, but even so —

"Save it. I don't need another installment of the babysitting lecture right now."

There was a short pause.

"*You said there was a problem?*"

Xander let his feet fall back to the worn carpet and leaned forward, resting an elbow on the desk and pinching his thumb and forefinger around the bridge of his nose. "Yes, but I lied. There are actually two problems."

More silence.

He sighed. "Right. So… there's a little baby vampire trapped here, being held by a pack of werewolves. A young boy. The kid's maybe… seven years old or so? If that? Freshly turned, and weak. He's not feeding."

The voice on the other end of the line cursed sharply in Greek.

"They've got him shackled to a wall with iron, Eris," Xander continued. The phone was moving against his ear, and he realized that his hands were shaking. He gripped the mobile harder and pinched the bridge of his nose until it hurt. "It's obvious he's either too weak or not skilled enough yet to transform into mist and escape." He swallowed, trying to wet his dry throat. "I… *Christ.* I left him there."

Bugger. He hadn't actually meant to say that last part out loud.

The pause on Eris' end was shorter this time. *"Well, what else were you going to do, under the circumstances? Look. Just stay put, will you? Preferably somewhere you can keep the place they're holding him under surveillance — if you can do so safely. We'll come to you and go in en masse to retrieve him."*

"Can't—sorry," Xander said shortly. "Not unless you lot can crawl out of that hellhole you're wallowing in and get here in the next nineteen hours."

"Nineteen hours? Why nineteen hours?" Eris' response sounded wary.

Xander snorted. "I mentioned two problems, right? I sort of… ran into Eliza this morning."

"Eliza? Your mate? Xander, that's —"

"She's a werewolf," he interrupted. His stomach churned, as though saying the words aloud made it real somehow.

"She's — ?"

"A werewolf. You heard me." Xander paused, scrubbing at his closed eyelids. "And she's connected somehow to the boy. She managed to sneak a message to me this morning without the other mongrels noticing. She claims they're holding her there against her will. I'm supposed to meet her privately at midnight."

There was a small disturbance on Eris' end and a new voice spoke. *"Tovarăș."*

Xander ground his jaw. "Tré."

He could hear Tré draw breath to speak, only to hold it for a long moment.

"Nothing any of us say is going to sway you from your intended actions, I assume," he said eventually.

"No, it won't."

"We're still coming. We'll be there as soon as is practical."

"Of course." Xander dragged his mind back to logic. "So… somebody had better jot all this down. The boy is being held in the basement of the abandoned warehouse at the corner of Gwynne and Harroway Roads in Battersea. My meeting tonight is in the alley behind the back entrance of *Club Cirque*, under the arches off Lambeth Road. And I intend to return to the flat in Mayfair afterward. That's where you can meet me unless you hear otherwise."

The sound of an elevator door opening down the hall teased his hearing, followed by the squeak of metal wheels.

"Look," he told Tré, "I need to go. I'm squatting in someone's corner office, and I can hear a janitor's cart coming my way." His lip curled in distaste. "Nothing like the smell of lemony fresh disinfectant to lend a bit of bouquet to breakfast, I suppose. Maybe I can convince the bloke to sniff something interesting from an aerosol can before I drink him."

"Be careful tonight, Xander," Tré said, ignoring his foul-tempered grumbling. *"You'll help no one by doing something reckless."*

He scoffed. "Reckless? Me? These are *werewolves*, Tré. I can always fly away if things start to get too frisky." The janitor's cart was getting closer now, accompanied by the sound of cheerful, off-key whistling. "Sounds like breakfast is served. Let me know when the five of you are en route. I'll see you when you get here."

With a tap of his thumb, he disconnected the call. The door opened. Xander looked up to find a stooped, middle-aged man standing there staring at him from the doorway, open-mouthed and frozen with surprise.

"Morning, old chap," Xander said, his eyes glowing green. "I'll wager there aren't many people who can say this to someone who cleans public restrooms for a living, but I believe I've dealt with even more shit so far this morning than you have. Now, tell me… how would you like to make an easy twenty quid in the next five minutes?"

FOUR

Manisha didn't dare act like anything was out of the ordinary after her bizarre reaction to touching the vampire in the stairwell that morning. The day dragged by as she first pretended to nap with the other werewolves, and then busied herself trying unsuccessfully to convince Sangye to feed. She was worried for him. She was terrified for him, in fact, but she had no idea what to do beyond following through with her reckless plan to meet the vampire tonight.

What could possibly have caused that violent jolt when his skin had brushed hers? And again, when she'd struck him? It wasn't just the fact that he was a vampire, since she felt nothing of the sort when she touched Sangye. It hadn't only been a physical shock, either. The instant their hands connected, Manisha's past lives had flashed before her eyes fast enough to leave her dizzy.

Manisha had been raised in a culture where reincarnation was an accepted fact of life. Ever since she was a child, she'd had a clearer recollection than most people of her past existences. Many of them had been filled with troubles; a few had been short and undeniably tragic. One of them in particular had haunted her dreams on a regular basis when she was growing up. It was always hazy and unclear, yet *that* was the life which had leapt free from the background noise of centuries when the vampire grabbed her wrist.

She'd looked into his striking green eyes and felt the oddest flash of recognition… but then reality intruded. She did the first thing she could think of to throw

Crank and the others off the scent. She'd struck him full across the face.

She hadn't meant her nails to score red slashes into his pale, ivory-colored cheek. It was as though the wolf had taken over, curling her fingers into claws that tore flesh. Manisha shivered. Tonight was her last chance at salvation before the full moon tomorrow. Yet, she still didn't even know the name of the wolf who'd turned her, much less where he might be found or how he might be killed.

Even in that, she knew she was probably deluding herself. If she blinked and opened her eyes to find the gray-bearded werewolf standing before her and a gun with silver bullets in her hand, did she seriously think she'd be able to look her attacker in the eye and pull the trigger? Assuming the old chestnut about werewolves and silver bullets was even true.

All of this perfectly highlighted how pathetic she was. She'd been too squeamish and frightened to ask the other werewolves about their species' vulnerabilities. How could she possibly expect to be strong enough to take advantage of those vulnerabilities—if they even existed?

She'd watched a man—a *vampire*—vanish into a puff of mist and reappear seconds later. The rational world had been pulled from beneath her feet like a threadbare rug. The best she could hope for at this point was to find some kind of help for Sangye. If nothing else, he should be with his own kind. They would help him, wouldn't they? Surely other vampires wouldn't hold him in a cell, bound in heavy metal shackles that left blistering red marks on his skin like burns where they touched.

She would wait and sneak away, no matter how much the wolf in her whined and howled at the prospect of acting against the pack. Crank had no plans for them to search the city again tonight. From what she gathered, the pack leader was awaiting word from his so-called *contact* about what he should do next.

So, she bided her time, following the same schedule she'd fallen into over the past two weeks. Sleeping, eating, spending time with Sangye. Chatting about nothing of import with the others in the pack who were willing to talk with her. Avoiding Crank… though she thought she felt his cold gaze on her at several points throughout the day. She didn't look up; avoiding eye contact with him, just as her wolf insisted that she do.

Finally, at about ten o'clock at night, she slipped away. The warehouse door was padlocked, she knew, but it was more for appearances than anything, since the others all knew the combination. Besides, several of the ground floor windows were shattered. Crank didn't need locks to keep his pack members from wandering. They were *his pack*, after all. They weren't going any-where—not really.

It had taken her quite awhile to understand that concept properly. The others weren't prisoners. Well, they were—of a sort—but their prison was one that existed within, not without. The others came and went as they pleased unless the alpha needed them for some-thing. They submitted to him because he was the leader, and he was the leader because they submitted to him.

At any time, one of the other males could have attacked Crank and challenged his position as alpha of the pack. If the challenger won, he would become the new alpha. If he lost, Manisha suspected he would be dead soon afterward—Crank didn't strike her as the type to be forgiving of such a thing.

The point was, no one was *guarding* her, as such. Crank seemed supremely confident of her wolf's power over her human self, and of his power over her wolf. She was bound to the pack, and to him as alpha. He didn't think she was strong enough to fight those instincts.

Tonight, she was bound and determined to prove him wrong about that.

She waited until no one appeared to be paying her any particular attention. After heading casually toward the disgusting basement lavatory, she doubled back to the stairwell and kept to the shadows. She tiptoed up the stairs, every rustle of clothing and squeak of her shoes sounding amplified to her own ears.

Once on the ground level, she looked around nervously and headed straight for the nearest broken window, using her sleeve wrapped around her hand to remove enough of the jagged hunks of glass that she could shimmy through it without slicing herself to ribbons. Only when she was outside, her shoes crunching on broken glass, did she release the breath she'd been holding.

Wrong, wrong, stop, this is wrong, her instincts howled. She grit her teeth. *No*, she insisted. *What's wrong is chaining a little boy to a wall with shackles that burn his flesh. What's wrong is kidnapping and killing innocent people. Turning them into monsters!*

She realized with dismay that she was still standing by the open window like a statue, arguing silently with herself instead of running away. She turned and fled into the night.

-o-o-o-

Three more times, Manisha caught herself huddling in doorways or dark alleys, mentally debating her course of action. It was insidious, the way her mind was turning against itself, things inside her changing without her conscious awareness. On each occasion, some noise or movement at the corner of her eye would snap her back to her surroundings, and she would push that treacherous inner voice to one side so she could continue.

She'd thought she was leaving plenty of time to walk the six or so kilometers between Battersea and Lambeth, but her bouts of lapsing into a fugue state while she battled her instincts meant that she would have barely thirty minutes to spare by the time she arrived. She'd wanted to stake the place out for an hour or so… wait for the vampire to get there so she could watch him and try to gauge a bit more about him before she made herself known.

Would he come alone? Were there other vampires in London?

Yet again, her feet stumbled to a stop without her permission, while that crafty inner voice sowed fresh doubts about her course of action. She almost snarled aloud in frustration. Fortunately, the railway arch concealing the club entrance was within sight now. Anger propelled her the final few hundred meters—up to the next block, around the corner and into the warren of alleys beyond the rails.

A whiff of musky odor hit her nose, and large hands closed on her arms from both sides. She choked on a shriek, heart pounding, surprise stealing her breath. She hadn't heard a thing as they'd approached. Her eyes darted from one side to the other. Two of the males from Crank's pack held her securely between them. One was Tag—she'd spoken to him a few times, and he'd seemed a pleasant sort. She hadn't had much interaction with the red-haired man on her right, but she'd heard people call him Sawbones, and gathered he was one of Crank's most trusted lieutenants.

"Let me go!" she demanded, jerking her arms in their grip to no avail. Had they followed her all the way here without her even noticing? They must have done, and the thought sickened her.

"You shouldn't have run, Manisha," Tag said. She thought she detected a hint of regret beneath the words, but his manner was no-nonsense.

"I'm not Crank's property!" she nearly shouted. Her voice echoed around the dark alley, but there was no one nearby to hear it.

"Close enough to it," Sawbones growled.

Tag's voice was a bit calmer, but his grip on her arm never wavered. "It's complicated, pet. Things'll make more sense in a couple of days, once you've changed for the first time."

Sawbones gave her arm a little shake. "Who are you meeting here, girl? The vampire? Crank thought you might, after that scene at the warehouse," he said, his tone unyielding as his eyes bored into hers.

Manisha couldn't stop her gaze from sliding down and away, but she clamped her lips to keep the treacherous wolf from spilling everything to the sharp-eyed man staring down at her.

"Eh, why am I even bothering? Of course it's the vampire," Sawbones muttered, and shifted his attention to Tag. "She was obviously heading for the same dead-end alley from last night. Wait there for the bloodsucker, and give him the message like Crank said."

Tag looked nervous, but he just nodded and said, "Yeah, okay." The glance he threw Manisha as he let her arm go was a bit worried. A bit sad.

"You," Sawbones said, jerking her other arm roughly. "You're coming with me."

Her wolf wanted nothing more than to roll over in defeat, baring its neck. It was all she could do to plant her feet and glare at him. "What's to stop me from yelling *fire* or *rape* at the top of my lungs, you bastard?"

Sawbones snorted and gestured at the dark warren with his free hand. "Go right ahead. 'Round here, you'll probably just attract a crowd to watch."

She sucked in a breath, ready to take her chances, but he continued. "Oh, stop it. Save your damned breath, an' my ears while you're at it. Unless you want bad things to happen to your little vampy boy back at the warehouse, you'll keep your trap shut and come along quietly."

Manisha's heart stuttered.

"Crank gave you a chance, luv," Sawbones continued, "and you threw it in his face. He won't be too pleased. Best come back and take your lashes. Chances are he won't come down too hard on your pretty little arse since he's wanting you for a mate once you change over. But he doesn't like vamps, so I doubt he'll go so easy on the sprog if you raise a fuss and make trouble."

The fact that Crank had obviously been onto her since the scene in the stairwell felt like a lead weight in Manisha's stomach. She sagged, defeated. There was no point in trying to stall her captor—the vampire wasn't due to arrive for another half hour or more. There was no one here to help her. If she let Sawbones take her back to Crank, there would at least be a chance she could talk the alpha into punishing her personally rather than taking out his frustrations on Sangye.

Maybe if she played nice with him, she could eventually gain Crank's trust again. Find out what he was planning for Sangye with his mysterious contact in the black suit and sunglasses. Bide her time… wait for a better chance.

Yes, her wolf agreed. *That's right. Better to just go along with the pack.*

She cast a last, hopeless glance around the dingy surroundings, but there was no one here except her and her two captors.

"All right," she whispered, hating herself. "I'll come."

FIVE

The great barred owl was not the most inconspicuous sight in the sky over Lambeth at night, perhaps, but it was silent and sharp-eyed. Those two qualities were what Xander needed right now. The owl brought a different sort of awareness of one's surroundings than did a cloud of formless mist. And right now, he felt like a hunter.

He'd wanted to scope out the area around the meeting place before the woman — whom he refused to think of as Eliza — arrived. Courtesy of Murphy's Law, that plan culminated in Eris ringing him right as he'd been about to leave. The other vampire had passed on details of their travel itinerary, which was admittedly important information — but it had still detained Xander longer than he'd intended.

The others had managed to arrange a patchwork of private and public transport that would get them out of the beleaguered Middle East and into the UK before dawn on the day after tomorrow.

Hooray for them.

The practical upshot was that Xander reached the skies above *Club Cirque* with around twenty minutes to spare. Less than he would have liked, but thankfully still enough to get an owl's eye view of whatever awaited him before he committed to going through with the meeting. The gray buildings that formed the alleyways behind the back entrance of the club were mostly three stories tall or less, so it was easy enough to get a good look at the narrow passageways between them as he soared overhead. He rode the rising currents of warm air from the city below, his wings barely beating.

He traced the area, working his way from the outside in, scouting the maze with an eye toward identifying any obvious traps. The alleys were mostly devoid of any life larger than the occasional stray dog or cat. Rats darted here and there, scavenging through garbage. He noted two homeless people camped some distance from each other. Neither of them was particularly close to the cul-de-sac behind the *Cirque*. One of them was so old and emaciated that Xander discounted him as a threat. The other was a teenage girl, and while he could not discount her being a werewolf, she was poorly placed to attack, and unquestionably alone.

At last, with five minutes or so remaining before midnight, he flew over the meeting place itself. A single figure lounged against the wall near the alley mouth, arms folded as he scanned his surroundings. Almost certainly a werewolf; most definitely not Eliz—

Most definitely not the woman.

He tucked his wings and dove into the shadowed dead end, giving a couple of strong flaps to slow his descent and transforming to drop lightly onto his feet, standing across from the scruffy man.

The werewolf pushed away from the wall, his stance wary, but he did not immediately attack. Xander inhaled, scenting the air—one thing the owl was fairly useless at doing. Other wolves had been here. Not in this alley, but nearby. Their scents were already fading away, dissipating into the larger tapestry of London's back-alley stench. Still, he thought one of the mingled odors was the same one that had exploded in his nostrils when the woman struck him, leaving behind the four red lines that still decorated his face, unhealed nearly a full day later.

"Hello. You know, if you're supposed to be the trap, mate, your pack might want to consider bringing in a strategy consultant," Xander said, eyeing the slender, dark-haired man.

"Not a trap," said the werewolf. "Just a messenger. You're here for Manisha, right?"

"Manisha? Is that her name?" Xander asked. Something thin and wickedly sharp pricked at his heart, the point coated in a poisonous slurry of dread and old pain.

"She won't be coming," said the werewolf. "Crank says if you want to see her or the vampire kid alive, come to 314 Tedwin Mews in Stockwell at dusk tonight."

Xander grabbed the werewolf by his shirtfront and slammed him roughly against the alley wall before he could so much as blink. "Who the fuck is Crank?"

The lad—for that was what he was, not yet twenty and not long turned—paled under Xander's glowing green glare. To his credit, though, his voice didn't quake when he answered.

"You met him," he said. "The pack alpha."

"You mean Fluffy?" Xander grated. "I should've brought out the damned newspaper when I had the chance." His hand tightened, lifting the smaller man until his toes barely touched the ground. "Tell me, who did you piss off to get thrown under the bus like this?"

"When someone higher up in the pack tells you to do something, you do it."

Xander wished the little punk would fight back, and give him an excuse for violence. But he just hung there in Xander's grip, looking vaguely uncomfortable as the menacing silence stretched between them.

"Look," the werewolf said eventually, "I shouldn't tell you this. But if I were you, I'd just walk away. I don't claim to know why Crank's dragging us into this vampire shit, but I know it's bad news. So… just leave London, okay? Forget about the baby vamp. Forget about Manisha. Crank wants her for a mate once she's undergone her first full moon. That much I do know. I don't think he's really gonna kill her."

Unthinking rage the likes of which he couldn't remember feeling in decades flooded Xander's vision, turning it red. *"He wants her for what?"* he hissed, every word filled with deadly intent.

The werewolf obviously heard the threat of murder lurking behind the question, and his already pale face went chalky and bloodless. "I… I just meant—"

Xander realized with a jolt that he was about a second away from breaking the boy's neck. Which… might or might not be possible, since he was a werewolf, and which almost certainly wouldn't kill him. And, like a dimwit, Xander had neglected to return to his Mayfair flat after leaving the office building in Battersea at sunset. His flat… where the weapons collection in the spare bedroom contained, among other things, a case full of artistically wrought silver blades.

Xander could *probably* pummel the punk in his grip into the dirt, given that he was young, small, and in human form. But doing so would only be for the sake of dishing out pain. It wouldn't do a damned thing to change the situation. And, besides, the little sod had just given him free advice that would have been quite reasonable in other circumstances.

He forced the killing rage back into something a little more manageable. A moment later, the distant, nauseating wash of self-disgust that he usually quieted with chemical assistance reared its unwelcome head to fill the gap. Too bad chemical assistance wasn't going to be an option anytime soon.

He took a slow breath.

"Dusk, you said? To hell with that," he said. "You and I are taking a trip to Stockwell right the fuck now."

The werewolf gasped as Xander spun him around and pinned him face first against the wall with one arm twisted painfully up his back. "It won't make a difference," the kid mumbled into the filthy brickwork.

"Shut it," Xander replied, pulling his phone from his pocket to call up a map one-handed.

Stockwell had been a well-to-do hamlet at the edge of London when he'd still been human, but these days it was an uncomfortable mix of elegant old Victorian houses and grotty council estates. He'd not had much cause to spend time there, honestly. Making a quick decision, he used his larger frame to hold the werewolf in place while he hailed a ride on the Lyft app.

"Bloody Christ, I still miss Uber sometimes," he muttered. Then, louder, "Come on. Shift your mangy arse."

He manhandled the teenager toward the alley leading onto Carlisle Lane, keeping him in an unforgiving hammerlock with his arm twisted behind him. It was hit or miss whether dragging someone through the streets of South London like this in the middle of the night would cause any sort of problem, the way things were in the city these days. With the addition of a bit of vampiric suggestion, however, it became a complete non-issue.

Only two people bothered to give them a second look as Xander made his way to their pickup point at Carlisle and Royal Street. After a mental nudge convinced them that they had not, in fact, seen anything alarming, neither one gave Xander and his hostage a third look.

Similarly, when the white Nissan Leaf pulled up next to the curb, the look of startlement and dawning fear on the driver's face smoothed into serenity a moment later.

Xander might have been the youngest of the original vampires by about a century, but he'd always had a talent for mind control. Which… well. Everyone needed a hobby, right?

"Don't bother getting the door, luv. I've got it," he said grimly, and shoved his prisoner into the back seat—making a cursory attempt at not banging his head against the frame. There was no reason to dent such a shiny and eco-friendly car, after all.

Once they were all settled, the woman glanced back in the rearview mirror. "314 Tedwin Mews, right?" she asked. "In Stockwell?"

"Yes," Xander said. "Quick as you can, please."

The car rejoined the sporadic traffic, its electric engine eerily quiet. The driver filled the silence with idle chitchat about the latest bomb scares and riots, her chirpy tone at odds with both the circumstances and the subject matter.

The werewolf shot Xander a side-eyed glance. "So… you do realize that the hypnotism thing is creepy as hell, right?" he asked.

"Fuck off," Xander said evenly. "I'm a vampire. It's in the contract, hidden right down in the fine print."

His unwilling ride-share partner only shook his head, and turned away to look determinedly out the window as he said, "Like I told you, this isn't going to help anyone. The boy isn't gonna be there, and you can't do a damned thing for Manisha with the full moon coming." He glanced back at Xander with a hint of curiosity. "Assuming you even want to. What's that whole thing about, anyway? Do you two know each other or something?"

"Or something," Xander managed through a clenched jaw. "And like I mentioned before… *shut it.*"

The teenager shrugged and looked away again. Xander tried to tune out the driver's sensationalized recounting of the recent news stories about the so-called *zombie disease* in Syria. As if he didn't have enough on his plate right here in London, that shit in Damascus was going to reach a tipping point in the public consciousness one of these days, he knew. When it did, he had absolutely no clue what would happen… only that it would be Bad, with a capital *B*.

Finally, the interminable drive ended. "Nice to meet you both," the driver said pleasantly as she popped the door locks. "Have a nice day!"

Xander breathed out slowly through his nose and dragged the werewolf from the Nissan's back seat. Judging by the faded sign hanging off-kilter above the door, 314 Tedwin Mews had once been a butcher's shop. Now, it was boarded up and obviously abandoned. Clearly awaiting purchase by someone who cared enough to come and tear it down in favor of throwing up a Nando's or a KFC franchise… or something else equally horrible.

The boards sealing the front door shut had been pried free. It might have been the work of random looters, but Xander wouldn't have staked a single quid on that being the case. With the most fleeting of thoughts—quickly dismissed—that this might fall under the umbrella of actions Tré considered *reckless*, he marched his captive up to the damaged door and wrenched it open.

He could make out scuffling noises from the back of the darkened, gutted store. The noises stopped abruptly, most likely in response to the sound of the hinges on the front door shrieking. The place smelled of damp and rot. The skeletons of display shelving loomed in the shadows—some still upright, some leaning askew, and others knocked completely over, lying on the floor. At the back, a glass case ran nearly the width of the room. One end of it had been shattered, shards clinging to the frame.

As Xander's eyes adjusted, he could make out an interior door behind the counter leading to the back rooms. A sound came from beyond it. A human sound. Female. Frightened. Cut off by a lower male growl of irritation. His grip tightened on the arm of the werewolf he was holding.

"Look, mate," said the kid. "Seriously—you don't want to do this. Just turn around and walk away. It'll be better for everyone involved."

Xander didn't even bother replying. He dragged the boy forward, deeper into the store, ignoring the ghost of Tré's disapproving eyebrow looming in the back of his mind as his rage from earlier surged again. That rage was colder this time. More controlled. Which was probably a bad sign—not that he really gave a damn at the moment.

The door at the back opened onto a short hallway. There was an empty office on one side, the door hanging half off its hinges. Ahead, a pair of wider double doors gaped open, heavy and industrial looking, with darkness yawning beyond. Another werewolf stood in front of them, holding Eliz—

Holding… the woman. Manisha. His would-be damsel in distress from the club.

The male werewolf holding her was older than the wiry teenager whose arm Xander was still twisting against his back. Harder, too, by the look of it—both physically and mentally. A craggy-faced, ruddy-haired predator, even in human form. He glared at the boy in Xander's grip as they approached, rather than at Xander himself.

"What the hell, Tag?" the other werewolf asked in a low, rough voice.

Tag—who had stoically endured the best part of an hour as the hostage of a very pissed off vampire— flinched hard under the older man's angry gaze.

"Sorry. I… he…" the boy stammered.

"Your puppy gave me Fluffy's message, as instructed," Xander said, in hopes of moving things along, "but I didn't feel like cooling my heels until dusk."

"Son of a…" the older werewolf cursed under his breath.

Eliza's—*Manisha's*—eyes were pinned on Xander, wide and scared. "You came," she said, as if she couldn't quite believe it. "Please… you have to go to the warehouse. Save Sangye—"

"Quiet," her captor snapped. "You know the score, luv. You want the boy safe, you behave yourself and do as you're bid. Besides, I already told you what'll happen if you're on your own tonight, and you get loose around unsuspecting humans."

She opened her mouth as if to say something else, but the red-haired werewolf turned and shoved her hard, sending her staggering into the blackness beyond the steel doors. Xander heard her cry out as she fell, and his cold rage flared into a fiery, unthinking conflagration. He hurled Tag at his craggy faced pack-mate with inhuman strength.

The older werewolf stumbled back a step and tried to push the younger one off him, cursing viciously. But Xander had already shifted into mist, swirling past the confused tangle of limbs and re-forming. Placing himself squarely between his mate and the male who had dared to lay a hand on her. He stood, poised lightly on the balls of his feet, judging how much damage he'd have to do to put the two werewolves out of commission long enough for him to get Manisha away.

"Well," the red-haired veteran said philosophically, having righted himself on the other side of the entrance, "I s'pose that works, too."

At which point the double doors closed in Xander's face, solid and windowless, plunging the space around him into such complete darkness that even vampire eyes took a few moments to adjust.

"Erm…" he said, feeling suddenly as though he should have paid a bit more attention to the ghost of Tré's disapproving eyebrow looking down on him from above earlier.

Silence reigned for a beat, before a quiet female voice came from ground level a few feet away from him.

"It's a walk-in freezer. Crank ordered them to lock me in here for the full moon."

The depth of misery in that melodic voice pulled Xander the rest of the way back from the precipice of his unthinking fury, leaving him mired instead in a messy tangle of emotion that wavered between abject longing and utter panic.

"Are you hurt?" he asked, striving to modulate his tone into something approaching normality.

"Bruised knee, I think," she said, sounding unnaturally calm, "and my palms are scraped." Her dark silhouette—all he could make out in this lightless box of a room—eased into a seated position from the ungainly sprawl in which she'd landed. "I'm sorry," she continued. "Now you're trapped in here, too."

"I'm not the trapped one," Xander said, and scrubbed a palm over his face, trying to drag his wits out from under the avalanche of emotions that threatened to crush them into powder. "Okay, look. Here's the new plan. I'll nip outside and give those two the thrashing they so richly deserve, then come right back and get you out. Won't be two ticks."

"No, wait—" Manisha began, but Xander had already dissipated, shifting form before she could finish.

In a life as long as his, the occasional moment of abject humiliation such as this was unavoidable, but that didn't mean he wanted to wallow in it any longer than absolutely necessary. Fortunately, he thought as he circled the room, feeling for air currents, this particular abject humiliation was only a momentary detour for a vampire whose vaporous form could pass through the smallest gap.

Except… there didn't appear to be any air currents in here.

That didn't make sense, though. True, the industrial cooling units set into the wall were self-contained, recycling air that had already been cooled in the interest of efficiency, rather than bringing in warmer outside air. But even in an insulated cold room, there should be a vent tube somewhere. Otherwise, when the room's temperature went down and lowered the air pressure, it would form a vacuum that would make the doors almost impossible to open.

He let his form flow along the walls, looking for irregularities. For fuck's sake… the last thing his pride needed at this point was to have to re-form and pull up the flashlight app on his phone like some clueless wanker.

He found the air inlet on the third wall, close to the ceiling — a simple tube, little more than an inch in diameter. Still, there was no sense of air moving through it. He flowed down the tube, only to hit something soft and crumpled at the far end, where it ought to have exited the building's outer wall.

It was a wadded-up rag. Some complete *arsehole* had shoved a wadded-up rag into the only vent in the freezer.

He withdrew and let his form solidify, staring at the blank wall he could hardly make out in the dark.

Whether the werewolves had been smart and enterprising to plug the gap and make this place into a vampire prison, or whether it was as simple as the building's owner blocking the tube to keep mice and insects from getting in, the result was the same. Unless he somehow managed to batter down the heavy industrial doors, Xander was every bit as trapped as Manisha was. Trapped… with the woman he'd killed more than a hundred years ago, and whom he'd now also failed to protect from a pack of werewolves.

There was really only one reasonable response to the situation at this point.

"Bugger," he said, with feeling.

Six

"What's wrong?" Manisha asked. It was deeply unnerving to sit here in the dark, unable to see what was happening around her. Ever since she'd been bitten, her night vision had improved to an eerie degree, but this wasn't merely low light. It was *no* light. She brought her knees up to her chin and hugged them.

There was a rustle as the vampire trapped in the dark with her moved. When he spoke, his voice came from further away, as though he had retreated to stand as far as possible from her.

"The room's airtight. Not even mist can escape," he said in the monotone delivery of someone who was carefully locking away his reaction.

Manisha had come to understand what was behind that monotone rather intimately over the past couple of weeks. "Good," she said, in much the same tone.

He continued as though he hadn't heard her.

"Still, I suspect the lock on the doors wouldn't stand up to a sustained assault, though they might also have slid a bar through the handles to reinforce them—" He cut himself off, as if her reply had just registered. "Wait. What do you mean, *good*?"

She wrapped her arms a bit tighter around herself. "I imagine Sawbones will be guarding the entrance, at least until the full moon rises. Maybe Tag, too. If we escape, or if you attack them and they don't report in to Crank when they're supposed to, Crank will hurt Sangye to punish me."

She looked around, only uninterrupted darkness meeting her eyes, and gave a hollow laugh. It was a harsh, ugly sound. "At least the power's shut off. Otherwise, we'd both be icicles before long. This way, we just have to worry about running out of air."

"Breathing is mostly habit for vampires, rather than necessity," her companion said, still in that flat voice. "I expect what we exhale retains pretty much the same oxygen level as what we inhale. Still... I'll try to restrain myself as much as possible, as a precaution. It's no hardship, believe me—the bouquet in here leaves something to be desired."

"Yeah." The atmosphere in the stuffy, enclosed room still contained the echo of rotting meat. Manisha's stomach growled. She squeezed her eyes tightly shut, disgusted with her body's reaction.

She wondered if the vampire had heard the sound.

"If it helps, I doubt a lack of air can hurt you all that much, either," he went on. "Werewolves are notoriously difficult to kill."

Manisha swallowed. "You realize that if you're still locked in here when the moon rises tonight, I'll attack you."

"Vampires are also notoriously difficult to kill."

She shook her head, though she didn't know if he could see it. "I don't want to kill anyone. I don't want to hurt anyone." She paused. "Can you... could you do that thing where you turn into vapor? When I change, I mean? So I won't be able to do anything to you?"

Another faint rustle as he shifted position.

"If it comes to that—yes, I could." He sounded guarded. "But the better option would be for both of us to get out of here as soon as the rest of the wolves are distracted with... whatever werewolves do during the full moon."

A flash of dread made her shiver. "No. Please—you mustn't. Sawbones warned me that if I got near humans,

I'd kill them. Shifting form for the first time while separated from the pack… it means I'll be maddened. Out of control. That's the punishment Crank set for my plan to meet with you secretly."

A low noise of anger emerged from the darkness.

"God… I'm going to kill that bastard if it's the last thing I do," the vampire breathed, so softly she probably wouldn't have been able to make out the words without enhanced werewolf hearing.

"Promise me right now," she insisted, needing to make him understand. "*Promise* me that you won't let me get loose around humans, and that you won't let me hurt you."

The silence stretched for a painfully long time before he replied, "I give you my word that I won't let you hurt anyone."

"Including you," she insisted.

There was a soft sound of clothing whispering against skin, as if he'd shrugged. "I'm no martyr. Rather the opposite, in fact—and like I told you, I'm hard to damage. But we should still try to come up with an alternate plan before then."

As such things went, it was reassurance of a sort, she supposed. She scooted carefully back until she found a wall to lean against. She was exhausted, thirsty, and her head ached with a relentless dull, pounding throb. But the two of them also had quite a bit of time to pass before the moon rose the following evening.

"So," she asked, "if you're not a martyr, what are you exactly? *Who* are you?"

"You first," he countered in an arch tone. "Little Miss 'Please Help Me, My Sister was Attacked by a Vampire'."

She cringed, but refused to collapse into apologies. "Sangye is a vampire. You're a vampire. I thought playing along with Crank's plan to find you was my best chance to get help for him."

"You were being truthful about that part, then," he said evenly. "Why don't you tell me how you and the boy ended up in this mess."

Manisha took a deep breath, surprised by how much the idea of finally being able to unburden herself affected her. She let her shoulders slump, and everything she'd been holding inside poured out in a torrent of words.

Fleeing from India to London with Sangye and his retinue. The armed, black-clad police who weren't actually police. The horror of the van ride, with Sangye straining toward her in his shackles, teeth snapping mindlessly as he tried to get his jaws around her throat. Graybeard biting her. The man with the suit, smelling of death and aftershave as he told her she was *one of the vampires' whores*, and that she'd been turned into a werewolf.

"This man," her companion said, his normally velvet-lined voice gone hoarse, "did he give his name?"

"Crank called him Kovac," she said. "I guess they're still in fairly regular contact. I got the impression Crank was working for him."

A torrent of cursing foul enough to make her cheeks redden erupted from the other side of the room, only to be cut off abruptly.

"You know him, I take it?" she asked dryly, since that much was fairly obvious.

At first, she thought he might not reply. "Yes," he said eventually. "I know him. But I haven't sensed his presence, so he must not be staying in the immediate area." He seemed to shake himself free of the thought. "Okay, so you've told me who you are. Who is the boy? Royalty of some kind? Why was someone in Tezpur trying to kill him?"

Manisha hesitated for only a moment before making a leap of faith. Someone needed to know the truth, and as far as she was aware, she was the only one left who did.

"Sangye is believed by many to be the reincarnation of Tenzin Gyatso," she said, and heard the vampire inhale sharply. "Before the attack in India, he was slated for further testing by the Tibetan Lama Regent... in preparation for being confirmed as the fifteenth Dalai Lama."

Nothing moved in the silent, darkened room for a long beat.

"Please... *please* tell me you're joking," her companion said eventually.

A tiny bubble of reaction shook loose from the reservoir of hysteria lurking in Manisha's chest, making her shake.

"*Why would I joke about something like that?*" She pushed the hysteria back down and took a couple of deep breaths. "But the Lama Regent is dead now. Killed in the attack in Tezpur."

"The last Dalai Lama claimed before his death that he would not return," said the vampire. "He stated that the institution had served its purpose, and that he wanted to avoid political infighting with China over the process of naming a successor."

Manisha shrugged, not knowing if he could see the movement.

Her invisible companion made a frustrated noise. "He as much as said that any attempt to seat a fifteenth Dalai Lama would be a sure sign of a Chinese power play against Tibet," he continued, his voice rising. "And he died... what? Eight years ago, now? How old is the boy?"

"He died seven years ago, and Sangye is six," she said.

The sound of a body sliding down the wall to land with a soft, controlled *thump* reached her ears.

"Jesus Christ." The words were faint. "When I got near him, I remember thinking that his essence reminded me of Snag's. *Jesus tap-dancing Christ*. You're telling me… Bastian Kovac has a pack of werewolves holding the next Dalai Lama hostage… *and they've turned him into a fucking vampire.*"

SEVEN

How much of a sin would it be, Xander wondered, to batter down the freezer doors, pummel whatever werewolves were lurking outside into the dirt, drag Manisha someplace far, far away, and never look back? He couldn't even begin to speculate what Kovac and his demon puppet master could do with a broken spiritual icon in the shape of a six-year-old boy.

He didn't *want* to speculate. Yet his mind tossed a hundred questions into the air. What loved one had sacrificed their life for Sangye? A parent was the most obvious answer. Xander might not have had personal experience with loving parents, but no doubt many mothers and fathers would lay down their lives without a thought to save their children.

What was Manisha's connection to the boy? How had Kovac—or Bael—even located the child in the first place? Was Kovac behind the bombing in Tezpur? If so, had he been trying to kill Sangye, or force him into the open? Why give him to a pack of werewolves? What plan did Bael have for the boy when his aim up to this point had been to destroy vampires, not add to their ranks?

The barely audible sound of ragged breathing snapped Xander away from the cascade of questions, and toward the more immediate problem that he desperately didn't want to address.

Manisha. The reincarnation of lovely, blue-eyed Eliza, who had offered him her throat for the ripping, and whose death had saved the tattered remains of his worthless soul. Saved it, and condemned it in the very same instant.

He could scent her wavering emotional control beneath the freezer's sickly-sweet smell of old meat and the unmistakable musk of wolf—still faint, since she hadn't yet seen her first full moon. If he broke out of here right now, could he possibly find and kill the wolf who had turned her in the eighteen or so hours left before moonrise?

No. It was an impossible task. Based on what she'd told him, the werewolf who turned her had been from a different pack, and packs didn't usually rub up close together. Kovac probably had him brought in from some distant, sheep-infested moor for the sole purpose of turning her, and sent him off immediately afterward.

Crank wanted to mate her, and doubtless Kovac also wanted to see that happen. The very thought made Xander's hands itch to wrap around someone's throat and squeeze until the bones snapped. But an alpha werewolf wouldn't mate someone he'd sired, directly or indirectly. Crank's pack would be made up of the wolves he'd turned, and the wolves *they'd* turned.

So Kovac had made sure Manisha was sired by an unrelated pack leader. And the odds of Xander being able to track that werewolf down in the absence of any leads was essentially nonexistent. He couldn't save her from her fate.

Quelle surprise.

Not saving people from their fates was more or less the distillation of Xander's entire existence into a nutshell.

"I've told you my story, and Sangye's," said the object of his troubled thoughts. "Now tell me yours. Who are you, and why are Crank and this Kovac person after you?"

He could hear the telltale quaver in Manisha's voice, and sensed the effort she was putting forth to try and hide it. Absolute dread over what might happen if—when—her control finally crumbled nearly strangled him. He was trapped here with her. How would he respond to the emotional breakdown of the woman who had once been Eliza?

"*Well?*" she prodded. "I think I deserve that much, at least! And it's not as though we don't have time to fill."

Xander was still sitting against the grimy wall he'd slid down earlier. He pressed the heels of his hands into his eye sockets, scrubbing at his eyes until stars burst against the backs of his eyelids. Then he let his arms fall to rest limply on his knees.

"Call me Xander," he said eventually, aware of the utter insufficiency of the answer.

And just as Eliza wouldn't have let him get away with that, neither did Manisha.

"Xander is a name, not an explanation," she said, sounding combative.

He sighed. "What else would you like to know? I'm a vampire. I'm at least half of the reason why you'll be turning into a wolf this evening. Probably more. And I'm one of the worst people you'll ever meet. The good news is, you got your first slap in preemptively. Wise choice on that, by the way. So, does that about cover it?"

"No," she said without hesitation. "It doesn't. What was that jolt I felt when our skin touched? You felt it, too—I could tell. And it's not because you're a vampire. It's never happened when I've touched Sangye."

Bloody hell, but the woman had Eliza's stubbornness in spades. He gritted his teeth.

"That jolt can most succinctly be described as 'your shitty luck.' And also, a moot point, since you're a werewolf and I'm a vampire," he said, knowing he sounded like a complete arse. Which, along with not saving the people who mattered, was *also* Xander's entire existence in a nutshell.

"Touch me again," she said, and he heard her scramble to her feet across the room. "I want to feel it properly."

"No," he said, rising as well.

Alarm jangled along his nerves. As long as he didn't touch her, he could convince himself that what he said about their connection being a moot point was true. That it didn't matter, since Xander had been too late to save her. He had failed, and now she was a werewolf. Werewolves hated vampires. Vampires hated werewolves. Q.E.D., end of story.

Because if he couldn't convince himself of that fact… if it *wasn't* a moot point and it *did* still matter, then what in the hell was he supposed to do next?

She was walking toward him blindly, one arm out in front of her to feel her way across the empty room.

"Don't," he said. He could sidestep her. Use his superior vision to stay out of her reach, or even transform into vapor again. But both of those tactics would be so completely ridiculous and pathetic that if he employed them, he'd never be able to look at himself in a mirror again.

"Why not?" she asked, her tone growing angry. "What are you afraid of? What aren't you telling me?"

With a breath of irritation at himself, he pulled out his phone and turned on the flashlight app so she could see the room properly. He propped it carefully against the base of the wall, where it would light a larger area, and straightened to face her. She was disheveled. Frightened. Wide-eyed and wild looking.

Achingly beautiful.

The polar opposite of Eliza in so many ways — deep brown eyes instead of cornflower blue, straight black hair instead of copper curls. Her frame was short and curvy instead of tall and willowy. Meanwhile, the same stubborn, kind-hearted soul gazed out from that unfamiliar olive-skinned face.

Jesus. Who was he kidding? He was fucking well *doomed*.

"Your life is complicated enough as it is," he managed with some difficulty. "Do this, and it will become about a hundred times more complicated."

Those dark eyes flashed. "Then you should have told me what I wanted to know when I asked you."

A small hand reached for him, fingers brushing the four parallel scratches on his cheek. The wounds were finally closed now, though still red and angry with slowly healing scar tissue. He caught his breath sharply as lightning shocks raced along his nerves, moving outward from the point of contact, and had to clench his jaw to avoid jerking away from the sensation that was both right, and so very, very wrong.

-o-o-o-

The fact that Manisha was expecting it this time should have made the feeling of their skin touching less shocking. It didn't, and she couldn't stop the gasp that escaped her.

It really was like touching electricity — like the time when, as a teenager, she'd stupidly tried to use a pair of needle-nosed pliers to pry the metal base of a broken light bulb out of a lamp socket without unplugging it first. She wanted to jerk away, but she *couldn't* jerk away. The sensation was grating along her nerves, putting the wolf on edge, yet the idea of *not* feeling it was somehow even worse.

And then, the visions started. Again, a confusion of images from the distant past—from other lives— assaulted her. They blotted out the here and now. Just like last time, they raced past her awareness so fast she couldn't grasp them individually… only to crash to a stop at a single point, which came into crystalline focus for the first time.

It was the life she had dreamed about so often. The one she'd never quite been able to remember afterward.

-o-o-o-

She stood in the massive foyer, her heavy skirts twirling around as she twisted this way and that to take in the splendor of her surroundings. The oak staircase. The crystal chandeliers. The paneled ceiling far above her head. Marble and polished wood all around, every surface spotless.

"Am I dreaming?" she asked, her heart pounding madly against the snug confines of her boned corset.

Strong hands closed on her shoulders from behind. Her husband turned her to face him. He was as handsome as ever in his starched white shirt, dark waistcoat, tailored knee-length frock coat, and elegant cravat. His striking moss-green eyes met hers with their characteristic sharp glint of humor.

"Not dreaming," he said. "Do you like it, then? Because if so, it's yours. I can have the estate agent draw up the papers later today."

Eliza couldn't help the wholly unladylike grin that stole across her face, or the excitement that leapt in her chest. She'd grown up in a single rented room with her mother and five brothers, living hand to mouth after her father had died of consumption. When she'd fallen in love with the sly-eyed and quick-witted coal merchant's son at the end of the lane, she could never have guessed that a mere ten years later, she'd be married to a man who had built up a fortune from next to nothing. She would never have believed that she'd be standing in the foyer of a fashionable London mansion that was hers for the asking.

She'd started life as a destitute flower girl, and ended up the wife of a powerful mill owner who made more money in the space of a single month than she had expected to see cumulatively during her lifetime. She had so many plans now; so many dreams. There was so much she could do that she would never have been able to do before.

There was the women's suffrage movement. Prison reform. The Labouchere Amendment. She wanted to make a difference with all of it. To use her newfound wealth to help others. But would it be so terribly bad if she also lived in a beautiful house while she did those things?

She realized she was holding her breath. The low voice in her ear made her shiver deliciously, as it always did.

"We can afford it Eliza. I promise you. You'll still be able to slay your dragons. Besides, all those stuffy lords and ladies you'll be entertaining will take you a lot more seriously when your footmen show them into a fine drawing room, and the butler serves them expensive port."

There was a reason her husband had been able to build an empire out of a handful of farthings. It was because he was both terrifyingly intelligent and terrifyingly shrewd. He also had an annoying penchant for being right about things.

"I love it, Alexander," she said. "Please have the estate agent finalize the sale as soon as possible, so we can move in."

-o-o-o-

Green eyes closed against her touch as if in pain. That sharply handsome, eerily familiar face tipped to the side as the vampire leaned away from her fingers, breaking the contact between them.

She caught her breath as something slotted neatly into place inside her mind.

"Alexander Charles Grimshaw," she whispered. "You're him."

The vampire melted back into the shadows, beyond the reach of the arc of white light and dust motes that cut through the room.

"Alexander Grimshaw died well over a hundred years ago," he said. "Do yourself a favor. Don't try to remember him, and for god's sake don't mourn him."

"Oh. Oh, I see now! The man who captured me. Kovac," she continued, oblivious to his words. "He called me 'one of the vampires' whores.' In one of my past lives, I was your wife."

"Argh. Fucking *Buddhists*," he growled. "You could at least have the decency to sound shocked."

She shook her head, slowly lowering her hand from where it still hung in the air, suspended. "Why? Reincarnation is just a part of life. There's a whole industry in my homeland devoted to tracking down the reincarnations of people's loved ones. Look at me—I'm pledged to serve a child who is probably the next Dalai Lama."

"Except for the small point about him being a vampire now, and you being a werewolf," he said brutally.

A chill flowed down the length of her spine at the reminder of what awaited her this evening when the moon rose.

"So, is that what causes the shock when we touch?" she asked, trying to focus on the present instead. "The fact that we were connected in another life?"

"No," he said, still cloaking his features in the darkness.

"What, then?" she asked, frowning.

Silence. Until—

"You know, I'm not sure which would make me more of a bastard. Telling you now, or waiting for you to remember it on your own."

Manisha was generally a patient woman. But the restless beast inside her was eating away at her composure, its presence becoming harder and harder to ignore.

"Fine," she snapped. "You don't think I deserve a full explanation for everything that's been done to me over the past few weeks? Then get back over here so I can touch you again, and I'll bloody well figure it out for myself."

The shadows in the corner moved as he shifted uneasily in place.

She clenched her fists, feeling her control unraveling moment by moment. "I am scared out of my wits right now," she forced out, feeling the telltale burn of tears at the backs of her eyes. "I'm about to become a monster, and for all I know, a six-year-old boy is undergoing torture right now as some sort of twisted punishment for my actions. I'm trapped with a man from a past life who won't talk to me, I feel sick and weak and dizzy, and *I don't know what to do now.*"

A harsh breath came from the shadows, and that sharp-eyed face from the distant past emerged once more into the pale slash of light.

"I can't save you, Manisha," he said. "I'm the very last person you should come to for that."

She stared at him, seeing old pain looking back at her rather than the seamless armor he'd presented earlier.

"I think that may be the first truly honest thing you've said to me," she told him. A long breath escaped her. "It's all right. I'm beyond saving. I know that. What about Sangye, though?"

He swallowed, the shadow of his Adam's apple bobbing in the odd lighting from the mobile phone. "No one can undo what's been done to him."

"But will you get him away from Crank? From Kovac? Will you try to get him to safety?"

He paused as if choosing his words carefully. Manisha wished he would stop doing that. "I'm not sure there's such a thing as safety for any of us, now. I have allies, though. I've told them about the boy, and where he's currently being held. They will try to help him. Which reminds me…"

He picked up his phone and unlocked it, his rapid typing making the LED on the back waver crazily.

"What are you doing?"

"Texting them this address, so they'll have the information when they arrive. Unfortunately, they won't get here in time to do much for us tonight," he said. The flashlight app flicked off, plunging them into darkness again. "Sorry, but I need to conserve the battery."

"Don't worry about it," she said, even though the disorientation of the uninterrupted blackness made her already queasy stomach feel even worse. "So, your friends. They're also vampires? And they're coming here?"

"Yes, and yes," he said. "The ones who aren't halfway around the world are coming here, at any rate."

"Okay." That didn't do much to ease her immediate worries about what might be happening to Sangye, but at least other people with motivation to help him knew about his existence and location. If something happened to her and Alexander—or Xander, rather—maybe there would still be hope for him.

A new wave of dizziness made her waver on her feet. A hand appeared on her upper arm, steadying her, the thrum of power between them muted by the worn material of her jacket. She widened her stance, but her knees still trembled, threatening to give out.

"I... uh... really don't feel at all well," she said weakly. "Is that because of the full moon coming on?"

Xander's grip tightened. "I'm not sure. Probably." He urged her a few steps backward, until her back met one of the grimy, insulated wall panels. "Sit down. Try to get some rest. Maybe even some sleep. I expect you'll need it later." The last few words were grim.

She let him guide her down to sit on the floor with her back braced against the wall, as she had been earlier. She noticed that he was very careful not to let their bare skin touch, and that he retreated across the room again once she was settled.

"What's going to happen to me tonight?" she whispered. "I mean, exactly?"

"I can't answer that question," he said. "I've seen werewolves in human form, and I've seen werewolves in wolf form. I've never seen what happens in between the two forms."

She digested that for a moment. "You can transform yourself, though. What's it like for you? Does it hurt?"

"No," he said immediately. "No, it doesn't hurt. It was difficult to master at first, but now it comes quite naturally."

"Maybe it's natural and easy for werewolves, too," she said.

Inside her, the wolf growled and pushed against its restraints, impatient.

EIGHT

Xander let the silence stretch, unwilling to offer empty reassurance beyond what he'd already given her.

If her transformation were going to be easy, Crank wouldn't have ordered her locked up in here as a form of punishment. Sawbones wouldn't have warned her about killing humans, and he also wouldn't have evinced such satisfaction at trapping Xander in here with her.

That works, too, the red-haired werewolf had said in a philosophical tone as he slammed the door closed on them. There appeared to be little question that the other werewolves expected things inside their makeshift prison to turn ugly.

Buried rage at everything he was powerless to change was becoming so much a part of him these days that its resurgence was almost like the return of an old friend. Xander knew that fact should probably scare the ever-living fuck out of him. The problem was, it was usually easier to deal with the rage than to deal with the alternative.

He watched Manisha's dark silhouette as she removed her jacket and wadded it up to use as a rough pillow. Evidently, she intended to take his glib advice about getting some rest to heart. It worried him that she was already feeling ill with so many hours still to wait before moonrise.

"I don't know if I can sleep," she said, sounding thoroughly wretched.

It seemed that all of his quips, all of his wisecracks and smart-ass remarks had deserted him without a trace. "Try," he told her, in the absence of anything else to offer.

Silence fell again, and within a few minutes her breathing had evened out into sleep despite her protestations. He wished he could take even partial credit for that. The next twenty-four hours would look completely different if he could affect her mind with his mental powers. But, of course, he'd tried the moment she'd come toward him with her hand raised to touch him. His mental suggestion had no effect. Hell, there was no indication she'd even noticed the attempt.

They were both dark creatures, and his darkness held no sway over hers. He settled back in the corner and listened to her breathe.

The hours passed, broken only by Manisha's occasional restlessness. She was asleep again when his phone vibrated with a new text from Tré. It stated that he'd received the address of the old butcher's shop, but the five of them were delayed in Athens. Their new ETA would barely get them to Heathrow before the sun came up tomorrow. Which meant Xander couldn't expect the cavalry to charge in until the following dusk, at the earliest. Not unless he wanted the cavalry in question to arrive crispy-frittered from the sun.

He texted back his understanding and warned Tré that he would be powering his phone off to save the twenty-two percent of the battery he presently had left. Then, he leaned back against the wall and settled in to wait.

Hours passed.

Manisha's sleep was restless. Xander tried very hard not to speculate about the contents of her dreams. He judged that it must be late morning when the rhythm of her breathing changed from slumber to wakefulness. She didn't move or speak for several moments.

When she finally did, it was to say, "*Ah*," in the tone of someone who had just experienced a revelation. He tensed, waiting for the rest.

"I get it now," she said. Her voice was gravelly from sleep and lack of water. "We were married, but now you're a vampire and you look about the same age as you did back then. You killed me when you were turned, didn't you? Like Sangye killed his mother."

"What makes you assume that?" he asked, trying to postpone the inevitable.

"Is it true?" she countered.

"Yes. It's true," he said. "You looked up at me with those big blue eyes, told me that you trusted me completely, and I ripped your throat out with my teeth. I still remember the look of surprise on your face as you died. I remember it, and then I do my best to get so hammered that I can't remember my own name, much less yours. Easier said than done for a vampire."

She pondered that for a moment.

"That explains... quite a bit, really," she said, her tone musing.

He raised an eyebrow she couldn't see. "I did say you were smart to get your first slap in preemptively." She was silent for a bit. The pause ate at him. "No additional commentary to offer on what I just told you?" he couldn't help asking.

"What sort of commentary are you expecting?" she asked.

He crossed his arms, still hunched in the farthest corner from her. "The correct response is to express anger, and/or fear, and/or horror at the prospect of being trapped in a walk-in freezer with the man who brutally murdered you more than a century ago. Unless this is some kind of a werewolf thing?"

"Some kind of... werewolf thing?" This time, he could hear the faint bewilderment in her voice. "What are you talking about?"

He freed one hand to wave it in a frustrated gesture that encompassed her unnatural air of detachment. Of course, she couldn't see that, either. "The whole eerily calm and politely interested thing. You're supposed to be afraid now."

Even the beat of silence before she spoke sounded bemused. "I'm trapped in a freezer and I'm going to turn into a werewolf in a few hours. I'm bloody *terrified*. Is that not coming across? I thought I'd been pretty upfront about it."

"You're supposed to be afraid *of me* now," he clarified, unsure why he felt the need to belabor the issue to this degree.

"Oh," she said. "Right. Look… I'm sorry, but as things stand right now, you're pretty far down my list of concerns. I mean — I was stuck in the back of a van with Sangye right after he was turned into a vampire. If the chains he was shackled with had been a few centimeters longer, or if one of the bolts holding them had snapped, it's pretty clear he would have ripped me apart without batting an eyelash. But then by the next day, he was better — more or less back to his old self. Am I supposed to hold that van ride against him?"

Xander closed his eyes, wishing he could just rewind the last few minutes and not be having this conversation. "No. But… he didn't *actually hurt you*."

"I don't think that's really the point." He could hear the frustration creeping into her voice; hear the slow breath she took to try and contain it. "If becoming a vampire turns the *Dalai Lama* into a murderous ball of bloodlust, I think one can safely assume that it would turn *anyone* into a murderous ball of bloodlust. So unless you purposely sought out vampirism, knowing what it would entail—"

"*I didn't ask for any of this!*" he nearly shouted, only to clamp his jaw shut in horror against the torrent of enraged pain that suddenly tried to tear its way out of his chest.

This. *This* was why he didn't let anything real slip out from behind his facade without first wrapping it in a muffling blanket of sarcasm and defensive humor. He stood frozen in his corner, listening to the echoes fade.

"No," Manisha said evenly. "I didn't think you had."

And this was the part where he opened his mouth and apologized for being an arse. Except that the breath was locked in his chest; his lips and tongue lying paralyzed and useless.

"I'm going to try to sleep more," Manisha said. "I still feel really sick and weak."

"Yes. Good idea. You do that," he whispered. "I'll keep watch."

-o-o-o-

Sleeping—or, at least, dozing—worked until late afternoon. Time was meaningless inside the lightless box she shared with a bitter and wounded man whom she had once loved in another life. Time *should* have been meaningless, anyway—but the wolf knew that the full moon was coming, whether it could see the progress of the sun across the sky or not.

Restlessness eventually drew her to unsteady feet, and she paced the small space on wobbling knees. She felt like throwing up, but for one thing, doing so would only dehydrate her more, and for another, she didn't really want to have to navigate around a puddle of sick in the dark. Chills wracked her, which was ridiculous since the disused freezer had grown sweltering over the course of the last sixteen-plus hours.

"Is there anything I can do?" Xander asked quietly, without moving from his spot in the corner.

Part of her wanted to curl up in his arms and listen to that rich, velvet voice while he stroked her hair and told her that everything would be all right. The other part wanted to attack him and tear him into tiny pieces. The conflicting impulses infuriated her. She paused in her pacing, realizing that she was scratching her bare forearms hard enough to bloody them.

"I think you should change into mist now," she said, striving to keep the confusing tangle of neediness and anger out of her tone.

"It's still more than half an hour until moonrise," he said. "There's a bit of time left."

"That may be," she grated, "but I'm fighting a very strong urge to hit you right now."

He shifted position in the dark. "Don't feel bad. I'm told that's quite a common reaction to spending more than an hour or two at a time in my presence."

Her temper snapped. "*Is everything a joke to you*? Do you have any idea how much it scares me that I might hurt someone? Hurt *you*?"

"No, and yes," he said, his voice growing intense. "I killed you, remember? I know *exactly* what it feels like to come back to yourself with the blood of a loved one dripping down your chin."

"*So change!*" she yelled, and lunged toward the space where she thought he was standing. Strong hands caught her, ignoring the way her fingers clasped around his biceps like claws, nails digging into the fabric of his expensive shirt.

"I will," he promised, "when it's time."

Wolf and woman wavered between aggression and surrender for a breathless moment before she crumpled into him, feeling the low vibration of energy thrumming between them. It wasn't really an embrace, but he supported her as she shuddered against him, eyes wide open and dry of tears.

"I can't do this," she whispered. "I can't do this. *I can't do this.*"

The grip on her arms tightened. "I don't think it's something you do, Manisha," he said. Her cheek rested against him, and she rolled her head to press her ear to his chest and feel the rumble as he finished, "It just *is*, and you do your best to let it happen without fighting it."

They stayed like that for what seemed like an age, unmoving and unspeaking. The grating restlessness inside her grew into a physical ache, until her bones felt like they were covered in sandpaper, rasping against the muscles and sinews. She whimpered.

"It's almost moonrise," Xander said reluctantly.

"Please go," Manisha said, hating the quiver in her voice. "Change, I mean. Get away from me."

Stupidly, she was still clutching his arms even as she told him to leave her. Slick wetness coated her fingertips, and she realized with a lurch of her stomach that her fingernails had lengthened into claws and pierced his skin. The smell of blood tickled her nostrils. The wolf pricked up, scenting the air.

"*Namo Buddhaya!*" she cursed, wrenching her hands away. "Go. *Go!*"

He hesitated, but then said, "I'll be right here. Even if you can't see me—I'm here. It's just one night, Manisha. A single night, and then it's over."

Until the next full moon, she thought miserably. But she only nodded, the bones in her neck popping and crackling painfully.

The callused hands holding her did not fall away. They dissolved, and the sense of a solid body in front of her in the darkness disappeared between one breath and the next. A sharp pain rippled down the length of her spine, dropping her to her hands and knees. Panic sent her heart racing.

Agony spread from her gut outward, muscles seizing and tearing, bones and joints twisting impossibly. Manisha threw her head back and screamed until she thought her lungs would explode.

NINE

Manisha's scream of mortal agony echoed around the enclosed space, warping and echoing until it became a wolf's howl. The sonic vibrations danced through the space Xander occupied near the ceiling of the freezer, reflecting off the walls and buffeting him with an aria of tormented misery.

In this form, his physical senses were nearly useless, but his mental senses expanded to compensate. He wasn't sure if that was better or worse. He was aware of Manisha—of the wolf—twitching on the floor like a creature in its death throes. Instead of stilling though, the movements became more violent as time went on, her unfamiliar new body fighting to gain control of itself.

Within minutes, she was attempting to gain her feet, only to fall back to the ground over and over. Eventually, she stood braced on forepaws splayed widely apart, hind legs scrambling on the slick floor. She was a pack animal, trapped alone and at her most vulnerable, and Xander didn't need to be able to smell her panic in order to sense it.

Within an hour, the wolf was walking… prowling with stumbling steps around the square box in which she was trapped. Within two hours, her sniffing at corners became scrabbling, became whimpering, became howling, as her desperation to escape rose in tandem with the strength and coordination of her muscles.

By the third hour, she was hurling herself at the seam between the double doors, ripping at it with her claws. Xander wasn't entirely sure the doors would hold, nor was he entirely sure what to do if they didn't, given his glib promise earlier not to let her hurt any innocents.

The doors held.

There was no way to tell for certain, but he thought it must be nearing midnight when her demeanor changed again. The rage and fear that had been turned outward toward her prison suddenly focused inward. Like a rabid dog, Manisha turned on herself, teeth snapping and tearing at her own flanks. Yips and howls of pain rent the air. Madness permeated the small space like a sickly pall.

She tore at herself until she collapsed with exhaustion, only to stagger upright after a few minutes and do it all over again… over and over and over.

Xander hovered on the cusp of materializing and taking his chances at physically restraining her, only the knowledge that his corporeal presence would madden her further holding him back. He didn't know how strong she was, but the dents and gouges deforming the steel doors' interior surface spoke of strength no natural wolf would possess.

The odds were that he would not be able to restrain her—not without injuring her at least as badly as she was injuring herself. In fact, the odds were that they would both end up injured. But the morning would eventually come, bringing new dangers for both of them. He, at least, needed to try and be ready for what would come… afterward.

So Xander hovered throughout the night, as the soul of the woman he'd loved more than life or power or money shrieked in terrified agony. Inside him, the rage that had bubbled and simmered for more than a hundred years solidified into a solid mass that demanded its day of revenge. Revenge on Bael. On Bastian Kovac. On the wolves who dared touch his mate—who had dared even *look* at her. At that moment, Xander would gladly have tortured every goddamn one of them for the rest of his days.

He *hated*, like he'd never before hated in his long, miserable life.

No night had ever been as interminable as this one, he was certain.

When Manisha collapsed for the last time, her animal form shuddering and seizing as her limbs lengthened and her hide changed from thick fur to a smooth, naked, *human* expanse of skin, Xander rematerialized, feeling as exhausted as though he'd been the one fighting all night.

He immediately started tugging the buttons of his shirt free with shaking fingers. Manisha's clothing lay scattered in useless shreds around the dark room. He paused only long enough to power up his phone and turn on its light, propping it against the wall again so he could better assess the damage she'd done to herself.

Christ. Her sides were bruised and bleeding, torn by sharp teeth. Her skin was deathly pale, a gray cast beneath its usual olive-brown. He pulled off his shirt, intending to use it to cover her, and fell to his knees at her side. She was facedown, arms splayed and one leg hitched up to the side.

"Manisha." His voice was hoarse as he reached down to place a hand on her shoulder. "It's over now. It's *over*."

His fingertips closed around her warm flesh, and he was knocked on his arse the next instant as she exploded into motion, her eyes glowing yellow and her lips pulled back to reveal jagged teeth.

"Fucking *hell*—" Xander's curse was cut off when inhumanly strong hands closed around his throat and he was slammed onto his back on the gritty floor. He stared up at a figure whose body might have regained its usual shape, but whose mind was still caught between human and beast.

Shock immobilized him for the space of a heartbeat before he jammed a knee between their bodies and tried to buck her off without accidentally hurting her further. It was about as effective as trying to remove an industrial magnet from a steel beam with his fingernails. He gritted his teeth and pushed sideways instead. They grappled with each other, rolling around as they fought for dominance.

A crunch of glass came from beneath his shoulder as he slammed against the base of the wall. The LED on the phone flickered out, plunging them back into darkness. They rolled over again and Xander finally gained the upper hand, trapping Manisha beneath him.

She still hadn't released her grip on his throat. Unless she actually twisted his head *off*, she couldn't kill him by strangling him, but even after more than a century of functional immortality, his body still fought instinctive panic at the feeling of thumbs crushing his trachea.

He used his larger frame to pin her in place so he could rip her hands away, only to feel razor sharp teeth tear into his left forearm as he did so. The resulting curse lodged in his injured throat, which was already knitting itself back together while Manisha did her best to rip into whatever other parts of him she could reach. Xander tried to get a better angle to restrain her more fully, but she just used the moment to wriggle free like an eel and tackle him once more.

Teeth closed on the muscle running from his neck to his shoulder. He felt his fangs lengthen and his eyes burn with a vampiric glow, the darkness inside him rising in response to the attack by another dark creature. Manisha shook her head violently from side to side, tearing at his flesh. Blood ran down his arm in rivulets, and every higher brain function he still possessed shut down between one breath and the next. He hissed, plunging headfirst into a terrible, roiling swirl of mingled frustration and bloodlust.

Emphasis — god help him — on the *lust*.

Because Manisha was also grinding her body against his as she tore into him. And… well… he wasn't really making any concerted attempt to stop her. No — one of his hands was gripping her hip hard enough to bruise, while the other tangled in her heavy, dark hair and used the hold to jerk her head to the side. As his fangs sank into her neck, he tried to tell himself it was in the hopes that draining her blood would weaken her enough for them both to *calm the fuck down* for a minute — because if she kept doing what she was doing he was in real danger of coming in his pants like a goddamned teenager.

Xander made no bones about the fact that he'd done some seriously fucked-up shit in the last hundred and twenty years. Drinking werewolf blood while the werewolf in question dry-humped him into the concrete floor of a locked walk-in freezer arguably topped that list. But for some reason, the ever-present smell of wet dog no longer mattered. The fact that both of them were now bleeding freely from multiple wounds didn't matter. Nor did the fact that their guards might return and fling open the doors at any moment.

He knew the rather strange, dizzy sensation creeping over him as he swallowed mouthful after mouthful of Manisha's werewolf blood should be a giant red flag that this maybe wasn't the smartest idea he'd ever had. But Manisha's hands had stopped digging ragged furrows across his chest and ribcage in favor of ripping open his fly, and the only red he could see right now was the blood smeared across her naked body.

All right — that was actually a lie. There was also the red haze wafting across his vision as she grabbed his rock hard, aching cock and impaled herself on it, crying out in what might have been pain, pleasure, or both.

Xander growled against the flesh of her neck and thrust up into her blazing heat, no more able to stop himself than he could stop the tide or the orbital motion of the planets. His head was swimming. He released her throat with a gasp, letting his skull fall back with a solid thump against the floor. A predator's teeth sank into the flesh beneath his collarbone, which might have pissed him off rather a lot if she hadn't twisted her hips *just so* at the same time.

"*Fuck,*" he groaned, and dragged her off him with a sudden burst of strength.

This was supposed to be the part where he pushed her away; put some distance between them and tried to reason with her. Tried to coax her humanity back to the forefront. Instead, he wrestled her down and flipped her over onto her knees so he could enter her from behind. She keened and pushed her hips back to take him as deep as possible, drawing a rumbling growl from the depths of his chest that was utterly beyond his control.

Xander slammed into her, and she met him thrust for thrust, her cries growing into screams until her inner muscles clamped around his dick and she jerked out her climax, nearly sobbing with the strength of it. Xander had no room to comment—the noise he made as he followed her over the edge was not precisely what one would call *dignified*. The sensation was so intense that he suspected his vision had gone black, though in the lightless room there was no way to independently confirm the suspicion.

When the excruciating pleasure finally loosed its grip, he realized that the dizziness had grown exponentially worse in the interim. Manisha might have been feeling the same effects, because they collapsed to the side together in slow motion, panting hard in the stale air of the enclosed freezer. He slipped out of her warm body and shivered, flopping over to lie spread-eagled on his back as the room spun around him. Rational thought was still out of reach, but the vague feeling of having just done something hopelessly, *monumentally* stupid was creeping over his awareness, nonetheless.

"What—" she rasped, sounding fully human once more.

"… just happened?" he finished, staring blankly at the slowly spinning blackness above him.

Awkward didn't begin to describe the silence that followed.

"I feel really, *really* strange," she whispered hoarsely.

"Uh-huh," he agreed. "I'm right there with you, love."

Of course, that was the cue for one of the double doors to creak open, spilling a thin rectangle of weak light into the room. He and Manisha had fetched up in one of the far corners, and the illumination did not reach them.

"One of my men trapped the vampire in here with her." It was Fluffy, his voice sounding as though it were reaching Xander through a tunnel. "He'll be dead by now. She will have torn him to pieces during the blood rage. You want me to take her back to the warehouse and put her in with the boy again? He still won't feed from the humans we put in his cell."

The sense of a horribly familiar and unwelcome presence washed over Xander's reeling senses, even before a voice answered in a deep Eastern European drawl.

"Yes, yes. Do whatever it takes to make him feed," Bastian Kovac said carelessly. "The whelp is of no use to me if he's in a coma."

The double doors opened the rest of the way, illuminating the freezer's interior and silhouetting the two figures standing in the entrance.

"*Kovac.*" Rage drove Xander to his feet, but it was not enough to sustain him against the frightening sickness draining his strength. He took a single, staggering step and collapsed back to the floor.

Kovac peered down his nose at Xander. His image blurred, two more Kovacs appearing on either side of the original one, sliding in and out of focus for a moment before they merged back into a single figure.

"Dead, you say?" Kovac said with a sneer. "You're an idiot, Crank."

Crank shoved past him to stare down at Xander and Manisha. Xander saw the werewolf's eyes move from his bare chest to his ripped trousers. Saw his nostrils flare. The room reeked of sex and blood. He probably didn't even need werewolf senses to smell it.

"You might've knocked first, Fluffy," he slurred. "Is there no respect for people's privacy anymore?"

Even with his vision going dim and fuzzy again, Xander took a moment to relish the look of wide-eyed, apoplectic rage on Fluffy's face as he put two and two together.

"Tag! Sawbones!" the alpha roared. "Bring silver chains for the bitch, and iron for the bloodsucker!" He stepped closer, standing over Xander like an enraged pit bull. "I will fucking well make you suffer for this before you die."

Manisha lay unresponsive next to him — possibly out cold. Never mind the danger to himself — Xander knew that the potential danger to his mate made this the worst possible time to lose his tenuous hold on consciousness. Unfortunately, that didn't stop the whirling dizziness from stealing the last remnant of his sight, hearing, and rational thought, leaving him in comfortable darkness.

TEN

Cold metal encircled Xander's wrists, ankles and neck when he next regained awareness. Gashes and bite marks covered his upper body; many of them still open and bleeding sluggishly. The vertigo hadn't gone away, either; now, it threatened to make his gorge rise. He moved one arm from its uncomfortable twisted position, and it took a shocking amount of effort to do so. The iron shackle burning his skin with its metallic chill wasn't *that* heavy, surely.

Chains clanked with his ungainly attempt, and the movement of his arm was halted abruptly as the slack ran out. He swallowed, his dry throat clicking.

Manisha. She was in danger. He had to get to her. He *had* to —

With far too much difficulty, he peeled sticky eyelids open to reveal a fuzzy swirl of color that spun in lazy, nauseating circles around him.

The chains. Focus on the chains. He had to get out of them. Until he did that, he wasn't going anywhere.

Escape should have been a matter of such insignificance as to hardly be worth mentioning. A moment's thought, an application of will, and he would swirl away in a cloud of vapor. Hell, even the owl could slip free of them, though the heavy iron band around his neck might do some damage to delicate avian bones if he wasn't careful. He reached inward, attempting to gather the power at his center.

Nothing.

No rush of dematerialization. No clang of metal on concrete as the restraints fell free. He tried again. No flurry of wings and feathers followed.

Fuck.

He'd shifted form in the past while more seriously injured than this, he was certain. And yet, he couldn't remember ever feeling quite like he did right now, despite all the questionable things he'd imbibed through the medium of human blood during the course of his lifetime. He blinked rapidly, forcing his gritty eyes into something approaching focus.

The dizziness was disorientating, but his vision cleared enough for him to get a better idea of his surroundings. A moment later, he wished it hadn't. He was shackled to a heavy steel bike rack sunk into the pavement on which he was sprawled. Multi-story buildings crowded both sides of the narrow, deserted roadway. Plywood and boards covered fully half of the windows in his field of view. The whole area looked derelict.

And it was daylight.

His position at the edge of the pavement was still in shadow, but this was not the soft light of breaking dawn. It was the light of mid-morning. He squinted at the edge of the weak London sunlight illuminating the roadway, trying to force his vision to stop wavering. He stared fixedly at it for several moments, long enough to confirm that the edge of the shadow was, in fact, creeping inexorably toward him. He let his eyes slip closed and gritted his teeth, straining once more to force his body into transformation.

"Bloody… buggering…" he grated, and jerked at the chains, the movement as weak as a kitten's. "Son of a poxy whore!"

For the first time, real panic nibbled at the edges of his composure. He couldn't be trapped here like an ant under a sadistic child's magnifying glass, helpless and impotent and *useless* as the sunlight crept across the tarmac. Not when Manisha needed him.

"Hello!" he called, his voice raspy and not nearly as loud as he would have liked. "*Hello*! Is anyone about?"

There was no answer. And even if there had been... even if some human had come to investigate and he'd been able to mentally influence them, what did he expect them to do? Unless they just happened to be carrying around a heavy-duty hacksaw or a set of lockpicks, no human was going to be able to get him free of these damned chains.

"*Shite!*" he practically roared, and then collapsed into an undignified coughing fit as the shout dragged sandpaper over his parched throat.

He eyed the creeping sunlight again, trying to determine how much of its movement was due to the rising sun, and how much due to his swimming vision. What would the authorities make of it when someone eventually found him? As far as anyone knew, no vampire had ever been killed by sunlight... though all of them had been injured by it to various degrees at one point or another. And they all agreed that the sun's caress was just about the most painful sensation a vampire seemed capable of experiencing.

Would he be left as a burned corpse, or would the sun consume even his bones, leaving nothing behind but a smear of dust and ash? How much of the process would he have to experience in brilliant Technicolor before he lost consciousness?

And why couldn't he fucking *move*, or at least think properly? What the hell was wrong with him? Was Manisha suffering the same effects? It had seemed earlier that she might be, when Fluffy and that rotting stain on humanity Bastian Kovac had shown up.

Jesus... *Manisha*. He growled in frustration and tried to jerk against the chains again, but the effort only made gray fog swirl across his unsteady vision. When it cleared enough to see once more, the line of sunlight had jumped forward and was now only a few inches from his feet. He dragged his legs closer to his body and called out again, but this area was clearly deserted—a forgotten corner of the city that had been abandoned and left to rot as London's economy plummeted.

Twice more, he struggled against the chains until consciousness wavered, and when he came back to himself, the light was closer. He'd already shuffled around until he was as far into the dwindling shadows as the chains would allow, his limbs twisted uncomfortably.

Now, the shadow's edge lay perhaps two inches from his fingertips. He clenched the hand into a fist and closed his eyes, trying to center himself enough to reach out mentally. The others would be here in London by now, unless something else had detained them. Safely holed up someplace with a roof, presumably, and unable to venture forth in the daylight to help him even if they knew where he was—which they didn't.

Hell, who did he think he was kidding? *Xander* didn't even know where he was.

But if they were within mental range, he could at least tell them goodbye, and beg them to help Manisha and Sangye. He might not know where *he* was, but it had sounded like they were taking Manisha back to the warehouse in Battersea.

Perhaps unsurprisingly, focus was elusive. Xander thought he sensed the others as distant presences, but he could not solidify the connection. Even that small comfort was to be denied to him, it seemed.

It was probably for the best, he tried to tell himself. There was no telling how long he'd be able to maintain his mental shields. And while Xander was a selfish bastard and always had been, he wasn't selfish enough to force the others to experience his excruciating death vicariously.

I'm so sorry, Manisha, he thought. *I did warn you that I was the last person you should look to for salvation.*

He stared at his hand with eyes that slid in and out of focus. There was one final decision to be made, it seemed. Should he continue to cower here in the building's disappearing shade while the slow march of sunlight incinerated him an inch at a time? Or should he hurl himself into its path and be done with it faster?

He wavered, watching the sunlight close the final fraction of space to his balled-up hand. When he tried to tense his muscles, he discovered it was a moot point. He didn't have the strength to move. Trembling, breath trapped in his lungs, he lay there as the golden sunlight slid over his clenched knuckles.

Nothing happened.

He blinked.

Nothing continued to happen.

The light crept over his hand, warming the skin with a long-forgotten sensation that he had never thought to experience again. It slid over his wrist and up his forearm with a lover's silken caress, illuminating his deathly pale skin under a faint glow. He retraced its path upwards, to the fiery orb peeking over the rooftops, wishing his damned dizziness would subside enough for the sky to stop spinning.

"Huh. All right, then. Have to say, I really didn't see that one coming," he mumbled to no one in particular before promptly passing out like a snuffed candle, his body finally giving up the fight against the creeping weakness that dragged him down into blackness.

ELEVEN

Manisha experienced the trip back to the warehouse in Battersea as a series of disconnected snippets.

One moment, she was being dragged like a sack of grain between two large figures, something hard and cold burning into the skin of her wrists.

Then, she was in the back of a lorry, her battered and exhausted body jouncing with every bump in the road.

Time jumped, and Sawbones was looking down at her, an expression of displeasure or distaste twisting his craggy features as double vision made him waver in and out of focus.

Another jump. She was being manhandled again, her bare feet scraping painfully against the gritty pavement as the rust-stained white walls of the warehouse loomed ahead of her.

The next thing she knew, she was back in the familiar cell, lying on the floor, too weak to even sit up. A bucket of water splashed across her face and upper body, shockingly cold against her naked skin. She couldn't even raise the energy to splutter. She just laid there, muscles quaking with cold and weakness, and stared blankly at the blurry figures in front of her and the open cell door beyond.

"She's no use to anyone right now," said a disgusted voice. "Leave her to sleep it off for a few hours and try again."

Her arms were roughly dragged around, the cold metal around her wrists searing her skin a little deeper.

Chains clinked, feet stepped over her, and a moment later the door slammed shut. She lay there—cold, exposed, and helpless—and tried to understand what had happened to her.

"Are you there, Kumari Sadhu?" came a quiet voice from the other side of the thick wall. "Please. Please answer me."

She worked her throat, trying to swallow enough saliva to moisten it.

"I'm here," she said hoarsely, unsure if he'd be able to hear her. "It's all right, Sangye."

Of course, that was a lie. Nothing was all right, and she didn't know if it would ever be all right again. Bits and pieces of the past night and morning were started to organize themselves within her mind—a scattered jigsaw of memory, nightmare, and fevered imagining.

She was a werewolf. She had turned into a raging beast, and it had been horrific. Pure torment. Her wolf had been terrified. Desperate to get free—to escape the trap of the freezer and find its pack. To run. To hunt. To be with others of its kind.

She remembered the feeling as terror had given way to madness. The wolf wanted to rend flesh, and the only flesh within reach had been hers. Thank all that was holy Xander had agreed to stay out of her reach. She would have killed him—or killed herself in the attempt.

She'd thought at first that maybe her memory of what had happened next was a hallucination. For one thing, Xander's voice as he'd tried to comfort her had sounded completely different from its usual cold drawl.

Manisha, he'd said, his tone like roughened velvet. *It's over now. It's over.*

His callused fingers had felt so cool on her sweat-soaked, overheated skin. Her wolf had wanted to pounce on him—to try to make him yield, and see if he was strong enough to make her submit to him instead. Her heart pounded faster in a twisted tangle of shame and excitement as she remembered grabbing him by the throat… rubbing against him intimately… tearing at the maddening fabric that stood between her and the enticing expanse of cool flesh the she wanted so badly. That she *needed*.

Some tiny human part of her had been appalled by what was happening. She was *horrified* at herself. What she was doing was illegal. Immoral. Indefensible. Physical and sexual assault—two of the worst crimes one human being could perpetrate against another. But… neither of them was human anymore.

Still, she cringed as she remembered the way she'd practically *wallowed* in his blood. Some of it was still on her skin, for crying out loud, just as her blood was probably still on his.

He hadn't reacted with fear or horror at what she was doing, though. He hadn't even reacted with anger. At least, not exactly. No, he'd risen to the wolf's challenge, taken control, and given Manisha and her wolf exactly what they'd needed. The twin fang marks on the side of her neck throbbed with a deep, aching heat that echoed another part of her body that he had pierced. That heat helped drive back the awful chill of her wet skin against the bare, cold floor of the cell.

Manisha was far from being a blushing virgin, but the memory of what she and Xander had done to each other did bring a flush to her body despite the blood she'd lost. When the violent bloodlust had faded in the aftermath of a crashing orgasm, they'd both been in shock. A moment later, the doors had opened, and… then what? What had happened next? No matter how hard she tried to remember, all that came was the memory of terrible vertigo followed by darkness.

She had no idea where Xander was right now, or even if he was alive or dead. A thread of fresh panic wove its way into her consciousness. Since she was here, it meant Crank must have either come for her himself, or sent his lackeys to retrieve her. Either way, it would have been painfully obvious to whoever opened the door what had happened inside that stuffy freezer. She still reeked of sex and blood even after having been hit with a bucket of water.

Crank must have *completely lost his mind* when he found out. He'd wanted to be the one to mate her, after all.

Would he kill Xander and try to take her for himself regardless? The thought made her gorge rise. Before, her wolf had been resigned to the idea of him taking her as a mate, even though the human part of her had been repulsed. Now, the very thought of it brought red, animal rage roaring in its wake.

She would not accept Crank as her mate. She was *already* mated. She knew that her wolf would fight any such attempt to the death, regardless of the fact that Crank was bigger, stronger, and more dominant than she was. None of those things mattered to the wolf anymore. The wolf had mated another, and that was that. But was her mate still alive?

Vampires are notoriously difficult to kill, Xander had said. Even so, he'd seemed as weakened as she was in the aftermath of their rage and lust-fueled coupling. He wasn't indestructible. Vampires could apparently still die. Kovac's guards had carried iron daggers for a reason when they'd kidnapped her and Sangye. And if folklore was to be believed, vampires had other vulnerabilities, as well. Wooden stakes. Sunlight. Decapitation.

If Crank was set on killing Xander, he could probably manage to do it.

Yet, some completely irrational corner of her mind insisted that if he were dead, she would know it somehow. She would feel an absence—an empty gap that was supposed to be filled by a stunningly attractive, sarcastic English son of a bitch with a voice that could make the phonebook sound seductive and long-fingered hands whose gentleness belied his cool, sardonic facade.

No. She would work on the assumption that Xander was still alive. Besides, whether he was or he wasn't, his friends were supposedly coming for Sangye soon. She just had to hang on until then.

She needed a plan. She needed to stall for time. A large part of her wanted to wear her defiance like a cloak for Crank and the whole world to see, but that would not help keep her alive and Sangye safe. As much as the idea made her want to retch, it would be better to play innocent and pretend to go along with whatever Crank wanted. She would just have to hope that Crank wouldn't immediately try to claim her physically. because she knew that neither she nor the wolf would submit to that without a fight.

"Sangye," she croaked, "Try not to be afraid. I need to rest for a bit, but they'll bring me in to see you shortly, I think."

She thought she heard him reply, but exhaustion and queasiness were already pulling her down.

-0-0-0-

Movement outside of her cell brought her back to awareness. She was still in the same position, lying naked on the bare floor with her shackled arms chained to a heavy metal ring on the wall. She blinked rapidly until her vision cleared and looked at the manacles properly for the first time. They were a very light colored, shiny metal, and the skin of her wrists was bright red and blistered beneath them. Even the smallest motion made the metal burn like fire against her flesh, and she caught her breath.

She stared at the shackles. Were they… silver? They had that sort of pale white cast beneath the metallic sheen that reminded her of silver jewelry, certainly. And it made a certain kind of sense. Werewolves. Silver bullets. Maybe there *was* a kernel of truth to the old superstitions.

She thought silver was supposed to be a soft metal, and considered trying to get free from them. But she had a suspicion that the pain from trying to do so would send her right back into a dead faint.

The cell door opened, and Tag came in. He kept his eyes averted from her body, and cleared his throat nervously.

"Hey," he said. "Uh, I'm supposed to give you this and see how you're doing."

He held up a chunk of meat, and Manisha's stomach cramped with sudden hunger, its earlier nausea forgotten in an instant. Tag handed it over to her cautiously as she stretched out to take it from him. She tore into it with her teeth, her wolf silently daring him to comment.

He didn't.

Instead, he said, "Look… Crank is with that creepy Eastern European guy right now. He'll be coming for you after they're done, though. I'm gonna bring you a bucket of water and a rag. It might help if you, um, clean yourself up a bit before he gets here. He's, uh… he's pretty pissed."

Manisha swallowed a mouthful of mutton and pinned Tag with her gaze. He glanced at her, flushed a bit, and looked down again. Her wolf snarled in triumph, confident in her dominance over him.

"What happened to the vampire?" she asked, trying her best to keep her voice cold and clipped.

"I dunno," Tag muttered. "Crank had Sawbones get iron shackles for him, and then they talked for a minute but I couldn't hear what they were saying. Sawbones disappeared for a bit and came back in time to ride here with us in the lorry, but he didn't say anything to me about the vamp."

She nodded to indicate she'd heard and went back to the meat, ignoring his presence. He shifted his feet for a few seconds.

"I'll, um, just go and get that bucket, I guess," he said after a brief, awkward silence, and left the cell, shutting the door after him.

Manisha finished the mutton, feeling a bit stronger once she had, even though she wanted to tear the blasted shackles off of her burning wrists. Tag returned with the bucket as promised, and put it within her reach before hastily retreating from the cell.

For the first time, she was truly starting to understand the power of the pack structure—as if transforming for the first time had merged her humanity and her wolf into a single being, allowing her to tap into that power and finally understand it rather than simply being a victim to it. No matter what Crank wanted to believe, she was a mated alpha werewolf female now—and Tag, at least, could sense that.

She licked the last of the grease and meat juices from her fingers, tasting traces of Xander's blood on them as she did so. That faint, metallic saltiness filled her senses and unleashed a new craving in her belly, despite the meal she'd just finished. Without really examining what she was doing, she licked at the rust-colored stain on the back of her hand, feeling the dried blood explode across her tongue in a vibrant bouquet.

She pulled back, shocked. What… on… earth?

Her wolf perked up, snuffling at the scent of blood, and relaxed again as if to say that blood was good—but that *fresh* blood would be better. She lifted her fingers to brush at the aching fang marks in the sensitive skin at the side of her neck, and shivered. She had no idea what her unexpected reaction to blood meant, and she also didn't know enough about the strange new world into which she'd been thrust to speculate.

For now, she focused on cleaning herself up as best she could, while firmly pushing down the bizarre and frankly alarming urge to suck the pinkish stains from the worn cloth of the old rag she was using to wash.

Her goal was to remove as much of the smell of sex and Xander from her body as she could before Crank got here. Without soap and a proper shower, she suspected that was going to be a losing fight—but it couldn't hurt. If she was going to play the innocent victim, the fewer reminders Crank had of what had happened in the freezer, the better.

TWELVE

Crank came for her less than an hour later. She still felt awful; she still smelled faintly of blood and… other bodily fluids. And there was still an unpleasant gnawing sensation in her belly despite the meat she'd eaten. Her wolf still wanted to tear something's head off. All in all, this conversation was probably not going to go as smoothly as one might hope.

The alpha glared at her as the door slammed behind him. It took her a fraction longer than it should have to remember that she was supposed to look down submissively. Apparently, her wolf's attitude toward the pack leader had changed. She just hoped she could play the part of innocent victim well enough to fool him without relying on the wolf's social cues for guidance in how to act.

A tatty robe or wrap of some kind hit her in the chest and fell to the grimy floor.

"Put that on," Crank growled.

How am I supposed to get dressed when my wrists are chained to the wall, you half-wit? she thought irritably. But she swallowed down every last trace of her contempt before saying, "Could you please take my shackles off so I can do that, Crank?"

Crank grumbled something, but pulled a key out of his pocket and released the silver manacles one at a time. "If you try to run again, Manisha, things are going to get ugly. And it won't be your hide taking the lashing. It'll be the boy's."

Manisha kept her eyes down and nodded as though his words had cowed her. She pulled on the threadbare cover-up before she spoke.

"I won't run again. I'm sorry, Crank. I was scared, and I thought since Sangye was a vampire that maybe another vampire would help him. I won't make that mistake again. The bastard raped me while I was still disoriented from the transformation. I tried to fight him off, but he was so strong—"

Her wolf bristled at the fabrication, growling, and Manisha was right there with the animal, really. What kind of a person did it make her to be able to spout glib lies about such a thing? Of course, what kind of person did it make her that in reality, she'd been the one to assault *him*?

Mate, the wolf thought possessively. *Mine*.

No. She had to concentrate on survival now, for both her and Sangye. No matter how messed up this whole situation had become, the important thing was to hold on and stay alive. If she had to act like a lying, conniving, manipulative bitch to do that... well, so be it. She wasn't doing it just to save herself. She was doing it to save Sangye.

Crank's meaty hand tipped her chin up, and the touch made her skin crawl. Holding in the shudder that wanted to shake free, she glanced up at his angry gaze for only an instant before letting her eyes slide down and to the side again.

"Vampires are evil," Crank said in a hard tone. "That's why Kovac is trying to capture them—so he can put them down like the rabid animals they are. Sawbones shouldn't've trapped one of them in there with you. But you also shouldn't have let the filthy creature live. You should've killed him."

"I tried, Crank," she said, trying to inject as much pathos into the words as possible. "He was too strong."

He let her chin go abruptly, like he was suddenly disgusted with her. "I can't believe you let a vampire touch you like that. Jesus." He huffed out a disgruntled breath. "Kovac wants you to make the boy feed—no more pussyfooting around with it. But tonight, maybe I'll show you how a real man fucks a woman. Wipe those vampire handprints right off of your skin until you don't even remember what he did to you."

Nausea roiled in Manisha's aching gut as the wolf lunged inside her, battering at her mind and demanding she try to rip out this presumptuous male's throat. Tears burned against the backs of her eyes at the certain knowledge that if she couldn't get out of this mess by tonight, she was as good as dead. She would not submit to Crank, and he was too strong for her to win the fight. It was all she could do to nod agreeably, not looking up from the floor.

A large hand yanked her to unsteady feet. "C'mon. Kovac wants the brat to feed right away. No excuses."

As they entered the other cell, Manisha's chest ached upon seeing how frail and gaunt Sangye looked.

"Kumari?" he asked weakly. "Are you well?"

"I'm fine," she told him, knowing that she sounded very far from *fine*. "Sangye, please. You must feed today. You're growing very weak. Please… do it for me."

As if her words had been a signal, Bastian Kovac dragged a skinny teenage boy into the cell by the back of his neck. The boy's eyes seemed glazed and distant. He didn't speak or cry out when Kovac hurled him down at Sangye's feet. Almost immediately, the enclosed space filled with a reeking cloud of cologne and rot. It was all Manisha could do not to gag.

"Just…" She swallowed hard. "Just take a little. *Please*. Not enough to hurt him. Just enough to give you strength. Sangye, I'm scared for you."

Sangye closed his eyes. He looked dizzy, as though he were having trouble focusing. "I am sorry, Kumari

Sadhu. I cannot do as you ask." His eyes fluttered open, an unnatural glow emanating from their depths.

Manisha wasn't feeling too steady on her own feet, so she was unable to scramble away when Kovac strode over and dragged her backward, wrapping one thick-muscled arm around her neck. She gasped, then gagged at his stench pressed so close to her. Sangye's eyes glowed brighter, a look of anguish sliding over his hollow-cheeked face.

"I will make this very simple for you, whelp," said Kovac. "Drink the human's blood, or I will snap your nursemaid's neck and rip her head from her body. I assure you, that method of execution is highly effective on all creatures… even werewolves."

Manisha's breath was locked in her ribcage, leaving her powerless to say a word in either exhortation or denial. By contrast, Sangye's thin chest rose and fell like a bellows under the force of his emotions. She remembered Xander had said vampires didn't need to breathe, and hoped that hyperventilating like this wouldn't somehow hurt him. Kovac wrenched her head to the side, making her gasp in pain.

"I…" Sangye said faintly. "I… I can't…"

With that, his eyes rolled up in his head and he slumped bonelessly, held up only by the shackles around his wrists and throat.

Unconscious.

Manisha cried out and tried to lunge toward him despite Kovac's punishing grip. After a moment, Kovac made a noise of disgust and shoved her away. She stumbled to her knees near the teenager he had brought for Sangye to feed on. Staggering upright, she attempted to support Sangye in his chains, her stomach turning at the hissing sound as the iron bit into his flesh.

Crank dragged her away, and it was all Manisha could do not to turn on him then and there. But that would be suicide, she knew, and if she were dead, Sang-ye would be left all alone at the mercy of these evil men.

-o-o-o-

Bastian Kovac tilted his head to one side and scrutinized the unconscious vampire child through the dark lenses of his sunglasses.

"Disappointing," he observed philosophically. Unfortunately, the failure to get the whelp feeding was merely one among a number of things that were currently disappointing him. Perhaps it was finally time to do something about that situation.

"We can try again when he comes around," Crank muttered.

Yes, Kovac decided, *it was definitely time*.

He'd known when he'd first enlisted the help of London's werewolves that he would be surrounding himself with rampant stupidity, but the pack's leader had turned out to be even more of a simpleton than Kovac had originally expected. While the beast had managed to find and lure another of the vampires to this abandoned warehouse, that act was really the only thing he hadn't failed at doing.

There had been little question that the nightcrawler would be able to escape the werewolves after confirming the presence of the vampire child. That fact suited Kovac and his Master well enough, since it allowed him to contact his fellow bloodsuckers and draw the prey Kovac truly wanted into the net.

He needed the vampire called Snag.

With the woman Manisha now turned into a werewolf, she was safely out of her potential vampire mate's grasp. That meant neither of them posed any real threat to his Master at this point. Even with the temporary addition of the boy Sangye to the vampires' ranks, the prophesied Council of Thirteen was broken before it could ever form.

Now, it was almost time to win the war. Because the Mighty and Most High Bael was not at war with the vampires. He never had been. No, He was at war with the Angel Israfael. And to bring the Angel out of hiding so He could defeat her, He would need the oldest and most powerful of His failures—the vampire Snag.

The alpha werewolf was a fool. He'd held his rival—his sworn enemy—within his grip, weakened and helpless. And rather than kill the injured vampire, Crank had concocted a ridiculous plan for torture and revenge, ordering the nightcrawler chained in iron and left to burn in the sun.

Kovac had briefly considered forbidding the foolhardy endeavor and driving a stake through the creature's heart then and there. However, he'd sensed that the other vampires had arrived in the city, and changed his mind. The search for their endangered comrade would draw them into the open. If they managed to save him, he would lead them all right back here, into Bael's trap.

And if they didn't manage to save him? Well, it was reasonably likely the captured vampire had already given them the location of the warehouse, and they would still come. However, they would enter the battle distracted and upset after the tragic loss of one of their own. So, Kovac had allowed Crank his folly, quietly using his mental influence to ensure that the werewolf left behind as a guard and witness to the vampire's death wandered off as soon as the rest of them had gone.

Outside, the sun was going down. It was time to move the chess pieces into position.

"Take the woman back to her cell and shackle her again," he ordered.

"I want some time alone with her first," the alpha growled. "She and I have business."

Kovac saw the woman cringe at Crank's words, but he ignored it. "Later," he said carelessly.

Crank bristled, though he submitted under Kovac's flat stare, as Kovac had known he would. Grumbling, the alpha dragged the woman away from the vampire whelp, shaking her a bit when she tried to protest. The boy continued to hang limp in his shackles, oblivious to the burn of iron against his pale skin. Kovac turned his back on the child and followed Crank into the other cell, ensuring that the woman was secured in the silver shackles as he had directed.

"Leave the door open," he told Crank when the werewolf started to swing the heavy wood shut. "I want her to see this."

If the vampires were close enough to hear it, her screams of horror might draw them—especially if the one who'd once been her mate was still alive.

Crank's face furrowed in confusion. "What do you want her to see?" he asked stupidly.

"My Master's power," Kovac said, and closed his eyes.

He reached out, mentally prostrating himself before the might of Bael. Supplicating Him for the honor of His dark presence. The tiny hairs on Kovac's arms stood up as electricity crackled around the dingy basement, and Crank took an involuntary step back, looking around nervously.

"What the hell?" the werewolf asked, his fists clenching as though he could defend against the oncoming Darkness by punching it.

Kovac laughed, the sound growing high-pitched and unhinged as black, oily fog rolled into the warehouse through tiny cracks in the walls and floor.

"What is that?" the woman chained in silver cried from inside her cell. "What's happening—what are you doing?"

The dark mist billowed up around the werewolves, who choked and scrabbled at their own skin, trying to free themselves from the grip of the Darkness.

"What am I doing, whore?" Kovac asked, the words emerging almost gleeful. "Why, I am merely baiting the trap, preparing it in time for the prey to arrive."

THIRTEEN

When Xander next woke, Snag was crouched in the shadows a few feet away from him, sitting on his heels with his arms resting loosely across his knees. The old scarecrow's head was tilted to one side as he regarded Xander with a vaguely quizzical expression. Xander squeezed his eyes shut and blinked rapidly, trying to rid himself of the feeling that someone had glued emery powder to the insides of his eyelids.

The sun had made its passage across the open sky above while he'd lain insensible, and was now about to disappear behind the buildings on the opposite side of the road. Xander looked down at his bare torso, taking in unhealed wounds. His skin was flushed faintly pink with the sort of sunburn that afflicted careless humans at the beach, rather than the sort that turned vampires into charred meat.

Snag's deep, arresting mental voice interrupted his musings. *Little brother*, he asked conversationally, *what in the gods' names have you done?*

His tone carried the same sense of gentle chiding as a parent whose toddler had just jumped in a mud puddle, and Xander tried not to chafe under it.

"Snag—a little help here, mate?" he rasped. "If you wouldn't mind?"

Snag looked significantly at him, and then at the western sky, where the sun had not quite disappeared behind the roofline.

"Oh," Xander said, deflating. "Right."

Snag had never been what one might call a brilliant conversationalist, so Xander was a bit surprised when another question followed.

What attacked you? Your wounds are not healing properly.

Xander snorted and let his head fall back against the steel of the bike rack. With difficulty, he resisted the urge to smack his skull against it a couple more times for good measure.

"Ah-*woooo*!" he rasped, laying on as much irony as he could muster. "Werewolves of London..."

Silence greeted the quip.

"Never mind," he sighed. "Wrong audience. Damn it, I'd been saving that one for just the right moment, too." More of the past couple of days started to filter back into his consciousness, and he sobered. "Shit. *Shit.* Are the others here?"

He started shuffling around to the position he'd started in, which was now mostly in shadow. He felt Snag push awareness of his links with the others into his mind. Eris and Trynn, relatively nearby. Della and Tré, quite a distance away. Of course. They hadn't known where to find him once his captors had taken him away from the butcher's shop, so they'd split up.

Snag sent out a powerful, wordless call along the bond, and Xander nearly passed out again. "*Nngh,*" he groaned, trying very hard not to lose his stomach contents for the first time in more than a hundred twenty years. "Was that *really* necessary? Still feeling a bit delicate over here."

When he peeled open his eyelids again, Snag was at his side—the side with the shadows, obviously. One wiry arm extended within reach of Xander's fangs.

"I'm not sure blood loss is the problem, old chap," he rasped. "Something else is wrong with me, I think."

True, he'd lost blood, but not vast amounts, as evidenced by the fact that some of his wounds were still bleeding. Snag gave a mental shrug, as if to say, *do you have any better ideas*? Which, of course, Xander didn't, so he huffed a breath and bit into the pale skin he was offered.

Oddly enough, this was the first time he'd ever fed from Snag directly. And to be honest, up until recently he would have felt rather guilty in doing so, since the old ghoul never looked as though he had enough blood for himself, much less someone else. In the past few weeks, though, Snag had surprised them all by agreeing to feed from both Eris and Trynn. The difference that regular feeding had wrought in him was startling—his body, though still strikingly lean, was no longer skeletal, and his skin no longer resembled crackling parchment. A smattering of dark hair had even started to sprout on his eyebrows.

As Xander swallowed the first mouthful of that ancient blood, he took a moment to be grateful that Snag had been the one to find him. The old sod had been frighteningly powerful even when he seemed perpetually on the verge of becoming a petrified mummy. Now, his blood offered a kick like rocket fuel.

Xander's stomach wasn't too pleased about much of anything at that point, but the rest of him sure as hell appreciated the boost. His vision cleared and the world stopped spinning like a carnival ride. His skin itched as his flesh knitted back together. The trembling weakness in his limbs subsided.

There is a new kind of darkness residing within you, Snag observed as he pulled away.

Xander ignored the words and awkwardly wiped one manacled hand across his mouth. "Later. Bastian Kovac is here," he said, sounding more like himself. "He's got my mate. Which means that right now, we've got undead arse to kick." He took a breath and focused inward. "I still can't shift form. In the absence of the key to these shackles, I think we'll need to do this the old-fashioned way."

Snag's expression had hardened at the mention of Kovac's name. His gnarled fingers closed around the length of iron chain attached to Xander's wrist shackles. Xander winced at the sound of hissing and crackling as the iron burned Snag's skin, only to realize an instant later that it was not doing the same to him. In fact… it hadn't been burning him since he regained consciousness.

He put that tidbit away to ponder later, along with the part where he'd spent a few hours in direct sunlight with no real harm to show for it. Right now, there were more important things to worry about.

Coordinating mentally with Snag, he wrenched backward with all his might, his strength bolstered by the older vampire's. The iron chain snapped at its weakest link. They repeated the process with the chain shackling his legs, and finally his neck. Xander staggered to his feet without grace. He gathered up the lengths of hanging chain that were long enough to drag on the ground if he didn't, cursing both them and his inability to shift.

"Right. Where are we?" he snapped.

Snag sent him a mental snapshot of their location relative to the river, and he took a moment to orient himself against the mental map he had of his home city. Not far from Battersea, it appeared — thank god.

"The others can catch up with us on the way," he said, and took off at a run, heading for the first intersection where he could go west. Snag swirled into mist, pacing him. Xander cursed under his breath at the way the heavy shackles hampered his gait. If his sudden inability to shift was permanent, it was going to end up being a serious bitch.

They'd gone nearly four blocks through the deserted factory district before Xander heard the rumble of an elderly Vauxhall Astra in need of a tune-up heading in their direction. He stopped the car by the simple expedient of stepping into the roadway in front of it and raising one manacled hand, palm out.

Brakes squealed. Xander met the startled driver's eyes through the windscreen. Thankfully, he hadn't lost the ability to mentally influence humans, and thirty seconds later he was settling into the back seat. Snag materialized silently next to him as the Astra peeled out and did a U-turn, heading for Battersea as fast as the aging one-point-four-liter diesel would take them.

The journey could not have been more than two miles, but it seemed to take forever in the deepening dusk. A dark, winged shape swooped low enough to be visible through the window, and was joined a moment later by a second one, smaller and lighter-colored.

Xander? Eris' mental voice questioned.

Where are the others? Xander shot back, unwilling to take time for pleasantries.

Hello to you, too, came Trynn's dry voice. *Tré and Della started searching closer to your apartment and business headquarters. Nice digs, by the way. What does your company do? I never thought to ask before. Whatever it is, it's apparently pretty lucrative.*

Ask me when I'm not focused on the best way to turn a certain undead Slavic bastard into pulverized road kill, Xander growled.

Trynn immediately sobered. *You'll have to join the queue. Do we know what the hell Kovac's even doing here?*

Not a goddamned clue, beyond the obvious — trying to fuck our lives over more thoroughly than they've already been fucked. He clenched his jaw, remembering that there hadn't been a chance to pass on one very important piece of information to the others. *There's something you all need to know. This boy, he's not just some random kid.*

He took a breath.

Go on, Eris prompted.

Xander shook his head in frustration. *Sangye Rinchen was on his way to meet with the Tibetan Lama Regent when his motorcade was attacked in India.*

Snag's head whipped around, his dark eyes burning holes through Xander far more effectively than the sun had managed to do earlier.

The Lama Regent? Eris echoed. *You don't mean…*

Xander closed his eyes. *Yeah — I do mean. Manisha says Sangye is considered a candidate to be the fifteenth Dalai Lama.*

Complete silence fell across the link, broken only by the rough purr of the car's engine and the occasional honk of a horn as the mesmerized driver cut through traffic.

Then, Eris let out a string of mixed Latin and Cypriot Greek curses, creative and filthy enough that Xander was momentarily impressed despite the dire circumstances.

Do you realize what this means? Eris demanded, still sounding like he wanted to tear someone's head off.

I realize plenty, Xander snapped across the bond. *But right now, the only thing I give a tinker's damn about is the fact that Manisha has been in Kovac's hands for the better part of a day. I'm sure I don't have to remind everyone here what he managed to do to* you *during that length of time.*

That might have been a low blow, but it effectively drove home the point he was trying to make.

He could feel Trynn's simmering anger at the memory of what had happened to Eris after his ill-conceived reconnaissance mission into Kovac's territory outside of Damascus.

The others should be here soon, was all she said, as the Astra careened around a corner, ignoring a red light.

I'm not waiting. Xander would have crossed his arms stubbornly at that point, but the iron manacles made that impossible. Once again, he tried to reach into his center and transform his body into vapor. It had exactly the same effect as before—which was to say, none at all.

Wait. I felt that, Eris said with the mental equivalent of a frown. *Something else is wrong. What the hell happened to you?*

Snag raised a slow eyebrow at Xander as if to say, *this I have to hear.* Xander scowled at him. But… they were going to learn the details sooner or later, assuming they didn't all end up dead before dawn. And the information might end up being important, even though it was also embarrassing as fuck.

"I might or might not've been sexually assaulted by a half-turned werewolf in a way that also involved a fair amount of mutual biting and… uh… blood exchange," he muttered aloud, knowing the others would be able to pick it up through the bond.

Aaand… there was that dead silence again, exacerbated this time by the extremely odd expression Snag suddenly seemed to be wearing.

You bit a werewolf? Eris asked eventually, sounding almost insulted. *I thought you hated werewolves.*

"She bit me first!" he burst out, and then took a centering breath. *Look—she was out of control, and I thought draining her might calm her down.*

Uh-huh, Trynn drawled. *I bet that's what you tell all the girls.*

Shut up, Trynn. It… well. It sort of worked, he threw back sullenly. *Only now, I can't shift form, and I feel like two-day-old shit even after a double-shot of Snag's super espresso blood.*

Snag shot him another dark look.

Oh, Xander added. *And I, uh, spent several hours in direct sunlight with only a bit of a tan to show for it. Also, iron doesn't burn me anymore.*

Another beat of silence before Eris' rather shell-shocked response. *You… what, now?*

Xander was vaguely aware of Eris directing a question privately to Snag, probably double-checking his story, and of the older vampire's mental shrug of confirmation.

Whoa, Trynn said. *So, you can go out in daylight now? Seriously? Do you think it's permanent, or just some weird temporary thing?*

His teeth ground together. *How the hell should I know?*

Enough. We are close. Snag's commanding mental voice cut through the link.

Peering out the window, Xander confirmed that Snag was right. He wondered if that meant his companion could sense Sangye directly.

Yes, Snag confirmed. *I can.*

-o-o-o-

Manisha watched in terror through the open door of her cell as black mist swirled around the basement, choking the figures of the other werewolves. They cried out and writhed, clutching at their throats.

"No!" she shouted, ignoring the burning pain of the silver against her skin as she jerked against her chains. "Stop! *You're killing them!*"

She could just make out a low moan coming from Sangye in the cell next to hers. He was regaining consciousness. She struggled harder to get free, but the agonizing shock of the silver against her flesh threatened to send her to her knees. She subsided, panting.

"Kumari Sadhu!" Sangye called weakly. "What is it, what's happening?"

Just then, Crank appeared in the door of her cell, oily black fog coiled around his neck and body like tentacles.

"This is your fault! *Your fault!*" he roared, stumbling toward her. *"Why couldn't you just kill the fucker like you were supposed to!"*

He fell to the ground inches away from her, and a cry lodged in her throat as he scrabbled at the strangling fog, the light gradually fading from his accusing eyes until his arms flopped to the ground and lay limp.

This isn't because of me, she thought desperately, staring down at Crank's dead form. *It isn't me — it's the dark fog! Kovac's ancient evil! It isn't my fault!*

A tendril of the darkness unfurled, brushing her naked leg in a caress that burned as painfully as the silver. She clenched her eyes shut, suppressed tears making her chest jerk, and waited to die.

"Kumari Sadhu!" Sangye cried again, more fear in his voice this time. *"Kumari Sadhu!"*

"I'm sorry, Sangye," she whispered. "I tried. I tried to save us…"

Cool fingers grabbed her chin, reeking of cologne and decay. Her eyes flew open.

"Yes, so you did. That will probably be your last mistake," Bastian Kovac said in a low, intimate tone. "Never fear, though. My Master has one remaining use for you." He kicked Crank's corpse onto its side with one patent leather-clad foot. "Your pack leader was a fool. But you will still make highly effective bait for one vampire in particular… assuming his fellow nightcrawlers arrived in time to rescue him from the sun's rays."

Hatred leant Manisha a degree of courage she wouldn't otherwise have had, and she spit at Kovac's face, glaring into the reflective lenses of his dark glasses. The gob missed, hitting his shirt collar instead. He only let out a contemptuous huff of air through his nose, and released her chin with a disdainful little shove.

"Just like all the other vampires' whores," he said with a scornful sneer. "If your worthless cur of a lover does decide to show up, I'll make sure to let you watch as he dies in agony."

"Fuck you," Manisha whispered, her heart pounding against her chest as though trying to escape the cage of her ribs.

Kovac whipped out a perfectly folded pocket-handkerchief and wiped the gob of spit from his collar before tossing it at her feet. "I wouldn't stoop to dirty myself with your rotten hole, slut." He turned to the door, and the bodies littering the warehouse floor beyond. "Now, watch and learn."

He stretched out his arms, the tendons in his hands and fingers standing out as though he were lifting some invisible weight. His head fell back, lips curling into a rictus as power thrummed around the enclosed space.

"No..." Sangye moaned in the next cell, barely audible. "No, no, no..."

At Manisha's feet, Crank's corpse twitched and stirred. She gasped, trying to scramble backward even though she was already pressed against the wall. His eyes snapped open, lifeless and filmy. Limbs moving in a grotesque parody of life, the alpha werewolf rose to his feet and wavered for a moment, catching himself with a hand pressed to the wall on either side of her body. His huge frame towered over her; his dead eyes stared right through her. As she watched, aghast, a tiny droplet of drool trailed from the corner of his slack mouth.

Finally pushed beyond her limits, Manisha threw back her head and shrieked, again and again and again.

-o-o-o-

Xander met their unwitting chauffeur's glazed eyes in the rearview mirror. "Stop here," he told the man, unwilling to drag an innocent human any further into this mess. "Let us out, resume obeying the traffic laws, and drive back to where you found us. Then forget you ever saw us or stopped for us."

The Astra screeched to a halt. Xander was out of the vehicle an instant later, Snag swirling around him in a vaporous cloud as he, too, exited. Xander slammed the door behind him, and the car drove off sedately. A flurry of broad wings stirred the air on either side of him as Trynn and Eris dropped lightly to the ground in human form.

Eris raked his eyes up and down Xander's body once, and Xander could well imagine what he was seeing. No shirt, pink scars littering his body—still not completely faded even after drinking from Snag. Iron clamped around his wrists, ankles, and neck. Trousers held up by a single button that was hanging on by a thread—the ripped zipper having succumbed without protest to Manisha's assault in the freezer.

To his credit, all Eris said was, "Do you want me to see if I can pick the locks on those shackles? Trynn, have you got a hairpin or something?"

"Fuck the shackles," Xander said. "Come on."

"Wait," Eris said. "Weapons. We raided your flat."

"Guns won't be much use," he pointed out, impatient to be moving.

Trynn scowled at him, and pulled out a couple of daggers. "Give us a bit of credit, yeah? Werewolves. Silver. Even I've heard of that one. Though, do I really want to know why you keep a small arsenal of silver-bladed knives in your spare bedroom?"

He accepted the two sheathed daggers from her and a belt with half a dozen smaller throwing blades from Eris… which had the added benefit of reducing the likelihood that his battered trousers would end up around his ankles during a fight.

"London is one of the few major cities in the world with a standing werewolf population," he told Trynn.

"Just like in the song, huh?" she said.

His lips thinned. "Too late. I already used that one. Now, *come on.*"

They jogged quickly toward the warehouse. At least, he, Trynn, and Eris jogged, making Xander wish almost immediately that he'd let Eris take a stab at unlocking the damned shackles after all. Snag had vanished into mist again, not being a big one for traveling on foot.

They'd covered about half of the remaining distance when a piercing female scream of rage and horror nearly split Xander's skull in two. He staggered and nearly fell, catching himself on a hand and a knee, his other hand flying to clutch at his temple. A strong grip pulled him upright, but he shook it off, stumbling back a step.

"Manisha," he whispered.

"Xander," Eris said, "what is it? Are you in mental contact with her?"

Before he could formulate an answer, the scream came again, a noise containing all the terrified denial of someone witnessing a nightmare brought to life. Blood-hot rage welled up inside Xander like a volcanic eruption, demanding to be unleashed on whoever was responsible for making his mate sound like that. His limbs twisted as if his body could not contain the incandescent torrent of anger in its human form, and needed to become something else to accommodate it.

This was not the familiar morphing into winged flight or swirling vapor, however. It was something new. More powerful. More dangerous. He fell to all fours, the shackles falling from his wrists and ankles with a clatter. He was only vaguely aware of Eris snarling, "What the *hell*?" as he pressed Trynn protectively behind his body.

Xander threw back his head, and howled.

FOURTEEN

The wolf scrambled free of the shackles that had bound Xander's wrists and ankles in human form, his slender legs slipping out easily now. With a hard shake, he dislodged the heavy iron ring that hung around his neck. He fought his way loose from the torn remains of his trousers, the belt with the knives following them down to the ground.

The movement made him stagger sideways when his body didn't respond the way he was expecting, but he steadied himself stiffly on four splayed legs a moment later. His memory flashed back to Manisha struggling to gain control of her wolf form, and he knew he didn't have time for that. She had been panicked, and in physical agony. It was also the first experience she'd ever had with physical transformation.

Xander had been able to alter his form into something complete different for more than a century, and while he was fighting panic for Manisha after hearing her mental cry, becoming a wolf did not frighten him. Hell, anything that got him out of the manacles and lent him added running speed was peachy *fucking* keen with him right now.

Xander? Eris was still shielding Trynn behind him, though she was hopping up and down impatiently, trying to get a better look at him.

"What the hell just happened?" she asked. "Is that him?"

Snag had also graced them with his solid presence once more, staring at Xander warily from a few paces away.

Xander growled at them both mentally and aloud, needing a moment's quiet to get his new legs sorted out. Eris stiffened, and he realized that might not have been the most reassuring response to their expressions of shock.

Just give me a damned minute, will you? he sent instead. *I've never been a fucking quadruped before.*

Eris and Snag relaxed their wary stances, and Trynn wriggled free from Eris' protective hold to dart forward and retrieve the knife belt, strapping it around her waist since it was going to be fairly useless to Xander now.

"So… is this what happens when a werewolf bites a vampire?" she asked. "Because… well… *damn.*"

Xander was only vaguely aware of the rather pointed look that passed between Eris and Snag, since he was more focused on mastering basic locomotion.

"I'm not aware that anyone has been stupid enough to test the hypothesis before," Eris said. "But under the circumstances, I'm going to go with *yes.*"

Something prickled along Xander's awareness, and a moment later, two new presences materialized next to the others.

"What… on… *earth…?*" Della said faintly.

Tré blinked twice—for him, an expression of profound shock. Xander narrowed his eyes.

"Do I want to know?" Tré asked.

No, he sent.

"No," Eris confirmed.

"Yes," Trynn countered, "but not now. Xander, can you run?"

Xander trotted a few strides in the direction they needed to go. Rangy muscles propelled his long legs over the ground without effort, the rhythm quickly becoming natural. After a few moments he accelerated into a lope, and then a full run, aware of the others keeping pace with him in the air, borne aloft on silent, powerful wings.

Hurry, he urged. *Hurry!*

-o-o-o-

Manisha trembled in reaction as the cell door closed and locked with a solid click behind Kovac and the… *thing* that had been Crank. The black fog had receded, leaving the cell empty but for her. Tears squeezed from between her tightly closed eyelids, burning her cheeks as they slid down. Outside, she heard rustling and shuffling sounds as the others underwent the same gruesome transformation.

Tag.
Patch.
Gillian.
Penny.
Lilith.
Sawbones, and all the rest.

The entire pack—those who had treated her decently, those who had treated her poorly, and those who had more or less ignored her. All dead now. Worse than dead.

Manisha had heard the news reports coming out of Syria. BBC reporters calmly describing corpses crawling from the rubble; trying to make the appearance of rampaging undead berserkers sound like some kind of radiation sickness after the bomb had gone off in Damascus, rather than what it truly was. Her mind had rejected what she'd seen and heard at the time, when it was just some distant story on the television.

Now, it was right in front of her.

"Why do this?" Sangye asked, his pained voice coming from the other side of the wall separating them. "Why?"

She didn't dare try to answer him, certain that all she'd be able to get out would be angry, terrified sobbing rather than any kind of comfort or reassurance. She had an awful feeling she knew the answer to why Kovac had perpetrated this new crime against nature.

The vampires were coming. And if this truly were like what was happening in Damascus, they would be met by a pack of opponents who couldn't be stopped by gunfire or any other normal means of fighting. But these weren't normal humans to begin with. These were werewolves. Could they be stopped at all?

-o-o-o-

The area around the warehouse seemed strangely deserted when Xander and the other vampires approached. There was no sign of any werewolves guarding the area or keeping watch over the entrance points. Xander barely slowed as he bypassed the door where he'd been escorted into the building, what seemed like years ago—though in reality it had only been days. He raced around the perimeter until he came to a broken window boasting a large enough gap for his lupine body to fit through without getting sliced to pieces, and leapt. Broken glass cut into his tough paw pads as he landed on the other side, but he ignored the sting.

The others swirled through in vaporous form and followed his lead.

What kind of resistance are we looking at here? Tré asked.

Two-dozen werewolves, max, he growled. *Not all of them fighters.*

Kovac is inside, Eris said grimly.

Leave him to Snag, Tré insisted in an uncompromising tone. *That's an order.*

It was an order that Xander had no intention of following if he managed to get his fangs anywhere near Kovac's throat. He also suspected he'd be fighting off Trynn for the privilege of drawing first blood, but he said nothing.

Somewhat surprisingly, it was Snag who spoke next. *Undead nearby,* he warned.

Xander didn't slow, but he did cast his senses outward.

Shit. Snag was right, and Xander didn't know how the presence of Bael's mindless foot soldiers tied in to what was happening here. Still…

It's not the first time we've faced them, he pointed out, *and it won't be the last.*

His comrades materialized around him, flanking him with silver blades drawn. He led the way unerringly for the stairwell leading to the basement—the dark, claustrophobic space where Manisha's hand had brushed his as she slipped a crumpled note into his pocket, upending his life and crumbling the ground from underneath his feet.

I'm coming, Manisha, he thought, projecting as strongly as he could. *We're coming for you. Hold on.*

-o-o-o-

We're coming for you. Hold on.

The words echoed in Manisha's mind, making her breath catch. Were they a hallucination? Wishful thinking? Or did she dare believe that Xander was still alive? That he and the other vampires were here?

And if they were here, did they have any idea of what they were about to encounter?

If it wasn't a hallucination, she wondered if Xander would be able to hear her in his mind the way she'd just heard him. But she was too horrified to concentrate on clearing or projecting her thoughts right now, and had no real idea how to approach such a thing anyway. Instead, she strained her ears, hoping for some hint of what was happening outside.

The cell door next to hers opened and closed. *Sangye.* Her heart pounded as she heard Kovac's deep, rough laugh.

"It is almost time for you to perform your first service for my Master, whelp," he said, low and threatening.

"I will not serve your Master," Sangye replied in a quavering voice. "I will not serve you."

Manisha held her breath. More laughter. The rattle of chains.

"Oh, I think you will," Kovac said. "But for the moment, we do not require your cooperation, boy. Only your existence."

Sangye cried out in surprise—a sound like a startled bird.

"Sangye!" Manisha called. She lunged against the silver manacles holding her to the wall, and gasped at the pain as they bit into her sore wrists. "*Sangye!*"

"Yes, by all means, keep crying out in fear, whore," Kovac said, sounding amused. "Help draw your nightcrawler and his friends into the trap for me."

She snapped her jaw shut, fear and rage washing through her veins in equal measure. Beyond the cells, the sound of running feet echoed through the warehouse, followed by the snarl of a maddened wolf. That snarl wove through her chest, tugging at something inside—calling like to like. Though she could not have explained how she knew it, her wolf recognized the sound of its mate and returned a silent, answering howl.

The animal battered at her mind, trying to get free. Manisha reeled under the assault and dropped to her knees. Her eyes fell on the silver rings binding her wrists. She caught her breath, looking at them—realization hitting her all at once. The other werewolves had said nothing about the possibility of shifting form outside of the night of the full moon, but she could feel that the wolf inside her cared nothing for any of that.

Her wolf… wanted *out*.

As the sounds of battle erupted outside, Manisha narrowed her eyes at the silver shackles and let the animal take control. The wrenching transformation overtook her, less painful than it had been under the pull of the moon. Her body twisted, arms and hands changing into slender legs and paws that slipped free of the burning metal restraints, leaving her free.

The she-wolf shook her furry head, gaining balance and control quickly this time. Outside, her mate battled the undead specters of her former pack. She needed to be with him, fighting at his side, but the heavy door still stood between them. As she had done in the abandoned freezer, Manisha lunged at it, snarling in frustration and battering her body against the heavy wood.

-o-o-o-

Snag glided noiselessly into the shadowy basement, his senses spreading outward, unsurprised by what he found. Undead werewolves stood arrayed in the area beyond the stairwell's landing—a nightmare of his own making, now raised to a new level of horror by the power of Bael's darkness.

He felt realization sweep through his comrades; felt them hesitate… all except for Xander. The youngest and brashest of the Originals cared only for the fact that the lifeless figures stood between him and his mate. Which was as it should be—as long as that brashness didn't result in his death during a moment of distraction.

There were three presences in the warehouse who required Snag's immediate attention. The first was a wolf who still lived, and who shared the same strange tangle of powers that Xander now exhibited. He could hear her battering at the door of her prison, heedless of the damage to herself in the face of her need to join her mate.

An uncertain future awaited Snag behind the second locked door, but before he faced that future, he would at least do this for his friends. In front of him, Xander's powerful wolf-form slammed into the nearest puppet soldier, teeth and claws ripping. The others followed an instant later, outnumbered but determined.

Snag ignored the battle, effortlessly shifting into mist and slipping past the figures locked in mortal combat. Silver and iron blades flashed in the dim light. The warehouse was eerily silent except for Xander's growling and the answering howls emerging from behind the first door.

He rematerialized in front of the cell and examined the locking mechanism, ignoring the sounds of animal rage coming from within. The door itself was wood, but heavy and well seasoned. Even so, it was no match for a millennia-old vampire's focused strength.

He grasped the handle and set his feet, reaching inside himself. With a violent burst of controlled motion, he wrenched the door outward, splintering the wood around the metal bolt. It swung open on creaking hinges, disgorging a bristling blur of gray and white. Xander's mate headed straight for the undead werewolf he was battling and slammed into the creature's legs, downing it beneath a flurry of tearing fangs.

Snag had seen Xander's sense of the woman Manisha in his thoughts and memories—a gentle, loving person raised in a non-violent religion and possessed of a giving spirit. He hoped she would allow herself leniency for such violence against beings whose souls had already fled, leaving behind only empty shells. The path she now faced was difficult enough without the sort of guilt that he and the five other original vampires wore around their necks like millstones.

One of the werewolf husks stumbled toward him, its arms outstretched. Snag bared his fangs at it. The creature was too new for the stench of rot to have grown overpowering, but the reek of spiritual emptiness was just as grating to his acute senses. It reached for his throat and he thrust power outward, knocking it back a step.

There was only one thing to be done for such a creature in the absence of silver. Snag pounced, grabbing its skull in both hands and twisting with the same explosive strength he'd used to snap the lock on the door. There was a crack of bone… a wet, tearing sound… and the undead werewolf's head hit the concrete floor with a dull *thud* before rolling a short distance away. The body staggered forward a step, and Snag moved neatly out of its path. The arms jerked and waved as if for balance, then the large frame fell to its knees and toppled over. Its fingers continued to twitch as if attempting to drag itself toward him.

He ignored it in favor of doing a quick scan of the others, all of whom were still alive and fighting. *Beheading is effective*, he sent, noting that Xander and his werewolf mate had also had success with tearing off limbs until the torso could no longer locomote efficiently. Confident that they would look after each other and eventually prevail without him, Snag centered himself and turned to the second cell.

There was little question of what he would find inside.

He grasped the handle and the door swung open. Inside, Bael's chief minion awaited him, unruffled in his modern black suit and dark glasses, standing in the middle of the bare room with a dull-eyed, emaciated boy in his grip. A sword rested at the young vampire's throat. The child's mind hummed with unrealized power, held in check by his body's weakness and his own inexperience.

Snag knew what Eris believed about the boy, and he also knew that Eris was wrong. That knowledge made what he was about to do taste even bitterer than it would have otherwise—but he would do it nonetheless. One of the reasons Snag was a chess grandmaster was because he had learned that, in the end, the life of an innocent pawn was every bit as valuable as the life of a bishop, a knight, or a king.

He met Bastian Kovac's mirrored gaze impassively, and watched the slow smile spread across his undead face.

"Greetings, nightcrawler. Or perhaps I should call you Wolf Father instead?" said the puppet, his power rolling across the distance separating them to tangle with Snag's. Kovac laughed—an unpleasant sound—and continued. "No matter. Surrender yourself to my Master, or I will destroy the child."

The razor-sharp edge of the sword pressed harder against the boy's throat, tipping his head back. Behind him, Snag felt Eris register the words and jerk his head around, distracted from the opponent he was battling. An instant before the werewolf would have driven an iron blade through Eris' heart, Tré slammed into the undead creature, knocking it back a few steps.

I am sorry, my friend, Snag sent... the words for Eris alone. *You will understand why I did this in time.*

Blank incomprehension was his only reply, followed by shock as he silently walked into the cell. Oily black fog swirled up through the solid concrete of the floor, rising until it obscured all three of the cell's occupants. Snag closed his eyes as the old, well-remembered sensation of drowning in bitter acid overcame him. The last thing he heard was Eris' enraged cry echoing in his ears.

FIFTEEN

"**S**nag, *no!*" Eris roared, slashing viciously through his opponent's neck as Tré held its arms pinned.

He didn't even wait to see the body fall before hurling himself toward the open cells, desperation and denial coursing through his veins in equal measure.

Bael was *here*. The demon's power was rising from the earth beneath them in a poisonous mist, and Eris could feel the others becoming aware of the hated creature's presence as they focused on their remaining opponents with renewed determination.

Snag had disappeared inside the cell without a backward glance, but as Eris neared the door, he turned. His dark eyes met Eris' gaze for only a moment before black fog billowed around the three figures inside, obscuring them. A burst of power—Snag's? Bael's?—slammed Eris backwards. He hit the floor hard. By the time he rolled to his feet and lunged forward again, the cell was empty except for a few rapidly dissipating wisps of darkness.

SNAG! he called mentally, channeling every bit of psychic power he possessed into the silent shout.

There was no reply.

-o-o-o-

Xander heard Eris mentally cry out Snag's name, but he couldn't afford to split his attention now that he finally had Crank cornered. Well, he had what was left of Crank cornered, at any rate—which, if he were being honest with himself, was nothing at all except for a very large, very hard to destroy hunk of muscle and bone.

Bael and Kovac had made sure of that.

The newly born wolf in him raged at the lost chance to extract any meaningful revenge on his rival, but the cold-hearted bastard of a vampire in him was content to take out his frustrations on whatever was left over.

Blood dripped from the fur of Xander's chest where an iron dagger had opened his flesh, but what would once have been debilitating agony was now merely an annoyance. Crank swiped at him with one meaty fist and he ducked under the blow, twisting to snap his jaws around the werewolf's hamstring. His opponent staggered and tried to shake him off, but his wolf was well acquainted with the struggling of larger prey. He jerked his head back and forth, widening the wound and attempting to drag Crank off balance.

The taste of dead flesh and blood made his nose wrinkle. A wolf might tolerate carrion when nothing better was available, but it was beyond sickening to a vampire. Nevertheless, Crank stumbled under his assault and went down on one knee. Xander abandoned his hold in favor of slamming his full weight into Crank's midsection. Beefy arms closed around his canine body in a punishing bear hug as he tried to get teeth near Crank's throat.

Not for the first time in the last few minutes, he wished he'd had more time to gain familiarity with this new form before being thrown directly into battle. Still, he could appreciate good design when he was walking around in it, and the wolf was definitely a killing machine. He wriggled, that tender throat almost within reach... even though it felt like his ribs were about to crack.

In the next instant, another set of canine jaws clamped around one of Crank's arms and pulled. *Manisha.* As he twisted free from Crank's hold, Xander caught a glimpse of her elegant form—slender with thick gray and white fur, blood coating her muzzle and chest. He knew in a deeper, more human part of himself that there would be serious emotional repercussions for such a sweet, gentle human when she shifted back... assuming they both survived the night. But he couldn't help his instinctive animal reaction to seeing her in battle, tearing fearlessly at the man who had wronged her so badly.

Xander lunged for Crank's jugular and started ripping. It wouldn't be enough to put the undead werewolf down for the count, he knew—but it still felt *really fucking good*. When Crank's throat was a torn and bloody mess, he went to work on the arm Manisha wasn't currently tearing to shreds and efficiently severed the ligaments.

Crank's legs continued to kick out, but Xander ignored them. Using his weight to pin the large figure, he took a moment to turn his focus inward, feeling out the shape of this new transformative ability. With an application of will, he flipped the mental switch controlling it, and an instant later, he knelt straddling Crank in human form.

A quick glance around located Tré, and he snapped, "Tré! *Blade*!" He pinned Crank with on forearm pressed to his ruined throat, and lifted his other hand as Tré met his eyes. A dagger arced toward him, hilt first, and he snatched it out of the air. Manisha shied away from the glint of silver, but he was too intent on ending the fight to react to her flinch.

The blade slashed through Crank's neck, and when it hit bone, Xander grabbed Crank's skull and *wrenched*. The feel of vertebra snapping made him grit his teeth. A moment later, the head hit the ground nearby and the body beneath him subsided into weak twitching. He rolled free and ran an appreciative thumb over the flat of the antique silver blade, only to hiss in surprise as the metal burned his skin.

"Oh, my god. Are you fucking joking?" he asked the knife, as the implication set in. *Great.* One *tiny little incident of exchanging bodily fluids with a werewolf and he was no longer sensitive to iron, but to silver instead. Bloody typical.*

He took stock, aware that the others were finishing up as well. Setting the traitorous knife safely out of reach of any twitching undead limbs, he turned to Manisha, who was still in wolf form, shaking Crank's unresponsive body by the arm like a rag doll.

"Manisha," he said, trying to modulate his voice to something reassuring rather than murderous. "Manisha, It's over. He's finished. Come away."

He wasn't entirely sure what to expect when his arms closed around her furry shoulders. She growled and gave the body a final shake, but relented under his grip and backed away. Christ, she truly was beautiful; gray-furred, golden-eyed, and with the tips of her ears as black as though they'd been dipped in ink. Her wide eyes darted around the basement, looking for additional threats and finding them all eliminated.

"That's right," he said, still trying to calm her. "Come back, Manisha. Come back to me now. You can do it—look inside yourself and remember what being human feels like. You changed outside of the full moon. That means you can control this. I know you can."

She shivered in his grip. For a long moment, nothing happened, but then the body under his hands twisted and he was holding her human form, shuddering and gasping.

"I've got you," he said, turning her so he could pull her against his chest. "All right. I've got you."

Xander knew something big must have happened while he and the others were focused on not getting killed by rampaging undead werewolves. He'd felt a dark, powerful presence that he'd never wanted to feel again, and then Eris had completely lost his shit, calling out for Snag. Xander could think of a handful of possible scenarios that would cover the facts, all of them equally bad. This much was certain, though—Bael's noxious, much-hated presence had retreated back to whatever rock it usually lived under. He couldn't sense it anymore. Nor could he feel any hint whatsoever of Bastian Kovac, or the child Sangye.

Or of Snag.

As if she'd heard the boy's name echo inside his mind, Manisha murmured, "*Sangye...*" against his chest, and tried to push upright.

He attempted to steady her, but she was already pulling free and staggering to her feet. "I need to get him out of those shackles!" she said, ignoring both her nakedness and the blood coating her face and neck. "We have to get him away from here—"

"Manisha," he warned, rising shakily to join her.

It was too late, though. She'd already stumbled over to the second cell door, catching herself against the frame in a pose that mirrored Eris'.

"No," she whispered. "No, he can't be gone... he was *here*. No, no *no*—"

Her voice rose, the denials growing louder. Xander closed his hands over her shoulders from behind.

"We'll figure out what happened and find them," he said firmly, hoping that the words wouldn't end up being yet another bullet point entry on the long list of promises to her that he hadn't been able to keep. "Eris?" he prodded.

But Eris was still staring blankly into the empty cell, his fingers clenching the doorframe so hard Xander was surprised he hadn't splintered it. The sound of a female throat being cleared behind him drew his attention away. He looked over his shoulder to find Della pointedly not looking at him as she proffered her knee-length black leather jacket in his general direction.

"Thanks," he said distractedly, taking the clothing and gently placing it over Manisha's shaking shoulders. She gripped it around herself, but her eyes never moved from the place where Sangye had been.

"Oy! Little Lord Fauntleroy. Incoming," warned Trynn. A pair of bloodstained trousers slapped against Xander's shoulder, and he scrambled to catch them. "Put those on. No one wants to see the view your flashing us right now."

It was a testament to how far down the shitter they'd already circled that it didn't seem worth the effort to toss out a comeback to the casual insult. But, on a more practical note, Trynn also had the best chance of anyone here at dragging information out of Eris right now — and they needed to know what the hell was going on.

He put on the damned trousers, trying to ignore the fact that they'd just been pulled off a dead werewolf.

"Eris," Trynn said, grasping her mate's shoulder and pulling him around to look at her. "Hey, now. What just happened? I can't feel Snag anymore. What did that crazy bastard do?"

Eris blinked, as if coming back to himself. He took a breath as if to speak, but nothing emerged. Tré joined them. "Tell us what you saw, Eris. *Quickly*," he ordered.

With a slow shake of his head, Eris met their eyes in turn — all except Manisha's, who was still staring at the empty iron shackles hanging from the back wall of the cell.

"He just… walked right into Bael's hands," he said, as if he couldn't conceive of Snag ever doing such a thing. As if it had been a personal betrayal.

In Eris' defense, Xander was at something of a loss as well. They'd all worried for a long time that Snag's sanity was… tenuous. But he'd seemed to be getting *better* recently, not worse. Xander could picture precisely zero circumstances under which he would voluntarily give himself over to Bael. It was utterly unthinkable. Death would be preferable.

Hell, eternal torture would be preferable.

"What about Sangye?" Manisha asked softly. "Kovac was with him in this cell. Where did they go? How could they have just… disappeared like this?"

Eris took a deep breath. "Kovac was holding a sword to the boy's neck. He ordered Snag to surrender himself to Bael, and Snag just… *did it*." His eyes flew to Tré's, flashing gold. "We have to find him and get him back. We can't let him do this."

Suddenly, Manisha was in Eris' face, her eyes glowing just as brightly. "*Them*!" she snarled. "We have to get *them* back! I don't know who this other person you're talking about is, and I don't really care! But don't you dare ignore Sangye! He's just an innocent boy, and I… I was supposed to…"

Her chest started to hitch beneath the words. Xander clasped her upper arms from behind, easing her back a few steps, out of Eris' personal space.

"I was supposed to protect him," she managed as she dissolved into tears. Aching for her, he turned her around and pressed her against him so that her next words were muffled against his shoulder. "I swore I'd protect him…"

Xander rested a hand on her head, smoothing his palm over her tangled hair and saying nothing—painfully familiar with the realities of letting down those you loved.

Tré's deep voice filled the silence that followed. "Eris. Can you sense Snag or Kovac at all right now? Is there any indication of where they might currently be?" he asked, taking effortless command of the situation as he always did.

"No," Eris said in a hollow voice. "They were here, and then they were gone. There's nothing."

"Very well," Tré said, all cold practicality. "We have injuries, and we're also far too exposed here in unfamiliar territory. We'll regroup at the Mayfair flat, contact the others in Singapore, and decide what to do from there."

It took a few minutes searching among the werewolves' personal belongings to find a stash of extra clothing that fit Manisha, and another that would do for Xander long enough for them to get back to his flat. Fortunately, aside from the slash across his chest, Xander hadn't fared too badly in the fight, and Manisha only had scrapes and bruises.

Tré had a stab wound in one thigh that didn't seem to have hit anything terribly vital. Eris sported a nasty slice down the length of his upper arm from shoulder to elbow.

Neither Trynn nor Della had suffered anything serious in the fight, and a taste of their blood was enough to start their mates' injuries healing. On the negative side, the iron blades meant that it would take more time and energy than usual for them to recover completely. Xander waved off Trynn's offered wrist, knowing the blood Snag had given him earlier would help him heal before long without any additional feeding—especially since his body no longer reacted violently to iron.

Della and Trynn flew ahead to ready the flat for their arrival while the rest of them followed by taxi. They weren't a particularly salubrious looking bunch by that point, but apparently the cabbie had seen worse in recent months. He ran a jaded eye over them and shrugged, driving them the five miles to Mayfair without comment... or the need for hypnotism.

Xander couldn't deny the way his shoulders relaxed in relief as he led Manisha into the sprawling penthouse flat, arming the security system behind them once the door was closed and locked. The stark, gleaming panorama of glass and metal was the closest thing he had to a home of his own, even if he'd only really stayed here during fleeting business visits to London over the past few years.

People told him the flat was elegant, but he knew it was actually cold—a reflection of himself, and the farthest thing he'd been able to find from dark, ornate Victorian sensibilities. Right now, though, it was undoubtedly a refuge. Nothing short of Bael himself could reach them in here without Xander knowing about it first, and they had everything they could possibly need. The place was outfitted and stocked with nothing but the best.

The familiar surroundings were more than welcome, because he was frankly a bit freaked out at this point by Manisha's continued air of utter defeat. She'd wept quietly on the drive over, neither encouraging Xander nor resisting him as he tucked her against his side and stroked her hair, murmuring soothing nonsense that he knew did her no good.

Now, she seemed wrung out, acceding to his guiding arm around her shoulders and showing no reaction to what was happening around her. In a human, he would have called it shock. In a newly-turned werewolf who had exchanged an alarming amount of blood with a vampire and then had her entire life ripped apart in front of her eyes, he didn't know what to call it beyond *bad*.

"Spiked blood is on the top shelf of the refrigerator hidden in the pantry," he told the others. "Un-spiked blood is on the second shelf. You know where the guest bathroom is; there are robes and some spare clothing in the hall closet. Manisha and I will be in the master suite. We might be a while. The Wi-Fi password is *G3t-off-my-LAN!*, but I'd rather you waited until we get back before you Skype the three musketeers in Singapore. It's midmorning there anyway—they're probably asleep."

Tré nodded, his expression one of understanding. "Go. We're fine here. Take care of her, *tovarăş.*"

Xander threw him a look of gratitude, and guided Manisha deeper into the flat on dragging feet. He knew there were a hundred things he should be focusing on—a thousand questions they needed answered—but right now, he couldn't spare a single thought for any of it.

He couldn't spare thought for anything except the woman in his arms.

Sixteen

The feeling of strong arms leading her slowly through an unfamiliar maze of rooms barely penetrated Manisha's cloak of misery. Her wolf wanted to howl—to cry out its pain to the world. She felt it urging her to shift again, and while a part of her wondered if the bitter loss of Sangye would hurt less if she gave into its demands, the larger part of her knew she would need her human wits to face whatever came next.

Right now, though, it was all she could do to face putting one foot in front of the other. Had it not been for Xander's grip on her shoulders, she was quite certain she would have sunk down into a pathetic heap on the floor and never moved again.

The conversation between the others had flowed over her, not really sticking, but she gathered they were somewhere the vampires considered safe, at least for now. The pristine, tastefully staged surroundings could not have been more different from the grungy warehouse basement with its converted holding cells, mouse-infested walls, and overflowing toilet.

After rattling off the string of instructions to his friends, Xander had been silent as he led her deeper into the elegant apartment. They passed through a bedroom with a king-sized bed decked out in black, white, and dove gray. She had a brief impression of expensive modern art hanging on the walls.

Double doors led into a spacious bathroom arranged around the centerpiece of a huge, clear glass walk-in shower. He guided her to the far wall and settled her down on the closed lid of the toilet, kneeling in front of her. His hands closed around hers, squeezing. She stared down at their tangled fingers, her gaze unfocused… and *ached* for everything she'd lost.

"Manisha," he said, in that low, velvet-wrapped voice, "look at me. You're safe now. Nothing will happen to you here."

She lifted her eyes until they met his moss-green gaze. His brows drew together.

"Do you trust me?" he asked.

The silence stretched, and finally her muddled brain realized that he was waiting for her to answer the question. Did she trust him?

He had come for her. In fact, he'd done every single thing she'd asked of him. She'd slapped him… attempted to throttle him in the throes of bloodlust… practically *raped* him—and he'd still risked his life to try to save her and Sangye.

A callused hand cradled her cheek. "Stop," he said. "Look—I'll concede the slap and the attempted strangulation, but you did *not* 'practically rape' me. I'll grant you, it wasn't the most carefully negotiated BDSM scene I've ever participated in. For once, though, I was the sober one in the equation—so I think you've got more room for complaint there than I do. Now, answer the question, Manisha."

She had to think for a moment to remember what she was supposed to be answering. "I trust you," she whispered.

Some of the tension in his bearing drained away. "Good."

"How did you know what I was thinking just now?" she asked, though the question emerged flat. "And before, when I thought I heard you in my head in the warehouse."

"We're two dark creatures who have shared each others' blood," he answered without hesitation. "It's a bit spotty right now, admittedly, but that means there's a mental bond between us. Look inside yourself. Can you feel it?"

She tried to look inside herself, but there was only emptiness. She shook her head slowly.

"I don't know what to do now," she said in a hollow tone. "What do I do now?"

The hollowness flowed down into her stomach, making it cramp.

"Now, we get you cleaned up," Xander told her firmly. "Or rather, we'll get both of us cleaned up, I suppose… but you first." He lifted her hand and pressed a kiss to her knuckles before settling it in her lap and rising. She watched him move around the bathroom, setting out clean towels and starting the water running in the cavernous shower.

With a sudden jolt, she realized that she hadn't had a hot shower in *weeks*. Without giving it another thought, she started pulling off the ill-fitting, borrowed clothes Xander's friends had found for her and tossing them away. She was shuffling out of the threadbare leggings when Xander turned back to her. He paused, but didn't look away or blush. After a brief flicker downwards, he focused his gaze squarely on her face and moved toward her as if to assist her.

Tired of feeling helpless, she ignored his outstretched hand, only for her knees to give way the moment she stood and tried to take a step under her own power. He was there before she could hit the ground, catching her and keeping her upright.

"Let me help," he said quietly. "Unless you'd rather shift—it'd be easier to stay upright on four legs than two, I imagine. And I can always clean the dog hair out of the shower drain later."

She shook her head and let him support her over to the shower. Steam billowed out as he swung the door open on silent hinges. He didn't remove his own clothing beyond toeing off the too-large, borrowed boots; he just half-walked and half-carried her into the warm spray of water, ignoring the way it soaked the ratty t-shirt and military-style khakis he'd taken from the warehouse.

The stinging spray of droplets against her filthy, blood-encrusted skin was like nirvana. Her knees crumpled again, but rather than holding her upright, Xander controlled their descent until they were both sitting against the glass wall. She turned into him, all of her pride and self-respect apparently having fled the moment she saw the empty cell where Sangye should have been.

As he had done before, Xander sheltered her against his body without a word. She let her long hair fall over her face like a curtain. He rubbed a hand along her spine with long, sure strokes as the hot water pelted her, driving back the chill that had settled over her soul.

Evidently, the wolf lived too firmly in the moment to hold onto that much hurt when her mate's arms were around her and his lips were pressed against the crown of her head. The animal slowly settled, even as Manisha's human mind continued to worry at the feelings of grief and failure.

"Shh," Xander said. "Listen to the wolf on this one. Let it all go for a few minutes and just rest. I'll hold onto it for you in the mean time—I promise. We're not abandoning them. We're just regrouping."

Manisha still wasn't sure how to feel about the idea of him being able to see her thoughts—though at least it saved her the energy of trying to talk right now. This time, when she looked inside herself, she thought she could almost feel the sense of him inside her mind. A cool, reflective surface, hiding troubled depths beneath.

"All right," she murmured against his skin, watching through a gap in her hair as the rivulets of water running toward the drain turned slowly from rusty brown to clear.

It was such a relief to set everything aside for a little while. To simply exist, here in this warm, steamy haven with strong arms holding her. She drifted for what seemed like a very long time, though the water showed no signs of cooling. Xander stretched out an arm, reaching for something, and a moment later a soft cloth lathered soap over her skin as he scrubbed at her gently.

She let him work without reacting except to move this way and that as he guided her around so he could reach all of her. His touch was thorough without being salacious, and the wolf rumbled in satisfaction under the casual intimacy of the situation. By the time the last of the grime was gone from her skin, there wasn't an ounce of tension left in her muscles. He tucked her soaking hair behind her ear and stroked her cheek with his fingertips, coaxing her eyes to open and meet his.

"Back with me now?" he asked, trying on a brief twitch of a smile that didn't manage to cover the rather lost expression lurking behind his gaze.

She blinked, not quite ready to face what awaited them beyond the steamy glass walls.

"There's… uh… there's some shampoo here if you want it. And conditioner," he said. "If you're all right on your own for a minute, I should give myself a quick scrub, too. Unless, you know, you'd rather I help you out so you can get dried off first. You could lie down for a bit while I—"

"No," she said, her voice emerging raspy. "Go on. I'm fine right here."

Fine maybe wasn't the word. Her stomach was cramping again, a strange, gnawing sensation that grew worse as he nodded his understanding and helped her prop herself against the wall, the shampoo and conditioner bottles within easy reach. When he straightened away, moving to the other end of the large space and turning his back, that strange hunger pressed her to get up and follow him.

She pushed down the impulse and tried to focus on washing her filthy, tangled hair. Still, she couldn't help sending glances his way as he pulled off the soaked black t-shirt, revealing the rippling muscles of his back. He reached up and turned on a second showerhead, then set to work efficiently washing himself as best he could with the ill-fitting trousers still hanging low on his hips.

Feeling slightly revived, she rinsed her hair and worked conditioner into it, picking through the worst of the tangles with her fingers while trying to ignore the empty hole yawning in her stomach.

The wolf grumbled, discontent.

-o-o-o-

Xander steeled himself to turn around again. It was a kind of torture, having Manisha here like this. Caring for her, as though he had some right to this intimacy with a woman whose life he had destroyed not once, but twice now.

How did he expect to be able to help her find Sang-ye when the boy had not only been whisked away without a trace, but had been whisked away by *Bael himself*? It appeared now that not even Snag could stand against the demon's power. And if Snag couldn't resist, the rest of them had about as much chance in this fight as a snowball had in hell.

He shoved the thoughts aside and let the spray run over his face, washing everything away. When he blinked the water out of his eyes and turned around, it was to find Manisha standing only a step away from him. His brows drew together—he hadn't even heard her move.

She looked frighteningly pale beneath her rich olive complexion, and her eyes were fevered. He tried to get a sense of her through the faint connection running between them, only to be hit with the echo of a strong spasm that nearly doubled her over. His hands shot out to steady her, a fresh stab of fear piercing him.

Was she hurt? Ill? It had almost felt like—

She clutched at her stomach, grimacing up at him. "Please… something's wrong. I n-need—"

Understanding flooded him, and he gripped her shoulders harder.

"Blood," he said. "Oh, my god. I drained you, and you bit me. And now you're craving blood."

Her eyes glowed yellow. "It hurts," she whispered. "I—I can't…"

He didn't even think. He pulled her flush against his body, bending down a bit so that her lips brushed the juncture of his neck and shoulder. She gasped and tried to twist her head away, but he lifted a hand to the back of her head.

"*Manisha*," he said. "Drink. You've been fighting the cravings for a while now, haven't you? You're weak. You need blood. Christ… why didn't I realize—?"

She made a broken noise and an instant later, sharp teeth pierced his neck. His eyes slipped closed as she drew his blood inside herself, and he struggled to keep his traitorous cock under control. *Not the time,* he told himself firmly. Even so, he thought a moan might've slipped free… or maybe that had only been in his head.

Because the bond between them was flaring into life now, a supernova compared to the dim little dwarf star he'd glimpsed earlier.

What am I doing so good no no mustn't no stop need you so much please please no I can't be alone like this anymore what's wrong with me—?

Manisha. Enough, he told her. *You're not alone anymore. Can you feel me in your mind now?*

A thread of surprise wove through her growing hysteria. *What? How—*

He stroked his fingers over the wet, heavy mass of her hair. The fangs buried in his neck sank deeper, and the strong pull of her mouth against his flesh might as well have been reaching down the length of his body to tug directly on his balls.

He struggled to keep that fact from coloring his voice as he said, "I told you. We shared blood. Now you're strengthening the link even more."

I asked you not to let me hurt you! she raged, even as her body latched on more tightly to his. *I practically begged you! I can't control what I'm doing—*

A lovely, light-headed feeling was beginning to wash over him—one that he suspected would be utterly sublime to experience while his cock was buried inside her to the hilt.

No, Xander, he reminded himself. *Bad vampire. Down, boy.*

He huffed a breath that might have been self-deprecating laughter. "You can't hurt me by draining my blood, love. I'm a vampire. If I pass out on you, just nip into the kitchen and grab a bottle of red from the fridge. Pour it down my throat and I'll be good as new afterward—promise."

He swallowed, feeling the movement of her fangs against his flesh as his throat bobbed. *And if you think this is hurting me,* he added, *you're not paying close enough attention to the link.*

He felt her focus turn further inward. He could tell the moment when she truly felt him—felt his body's response—rather than merely hearing his words. She jerked away from him with a gasp of surprise, leaving him reeling a bit at the sudden loss. Steadying himself with a hand against the glass enclosure, he blinked at her through the spray of hot water, watching as she tried to file this new bit of information in with all the other things whirling around in her head like a file cabinet full of papers caught in a hurricane.

"You don't have to stop, you know," he said. "Not until the cravings are sated. Unless you'd rather I went and got you a bottle to drink from instead of a vein?"

She was breathing hard, and it was a considerable struggle to keep his eyes on her face rather than watching the way rivulets of water trickled down the golden-brown expanse of her heaving breasts. It became even harder when he noticed the way her eyes were tracing the path of the blood trickling from his neck as it mixed with the shower water and ran down his chest.

Manisha lifted fingertips to her bottom lip, dabbing at the smear of his blood that clung there. He found he couldn't look away from the glistening red mark.

"I, um… no. I think…" She paused, sucking the last traces of blood from her lip. Xander could see that her teeth were once again human-flat as she continued, "I think I'm all right now. In fact, I don't feel nearly as weak and out-of-it as I did before. What's happening to me?"

"The same thing that's happening to me, I gather," he said. "Only in reverse. We need to talk to the others. As far as I know, a werewolf has never bitten a vampire before. Or vice versa."

She pressed the heel of her hand to her forehead as if fighting a headache. "This is crazy," she muttered.

He quirked an eyebrow. "Yes. Welcome to my world."

Manisha shook her head. A moment later, she seemed to take in her surroundings properly for the first time since they had arrived at the flat. Her cheeks darkened.

He tore his eyes away from her with difficulty. "I'll get you a towel and a robe," he said. "Stay here. I won't be a minute."

Xander slipped out of the shower before he could talk himself into staying, and closed the door behind him. The glass walls were covered with steam, blocking her view, so he stripped off the borrowed trousers and tossed them into the Japanese soaking tub set against the side wall. After drying off and donning a robe, he took a towel from the warming rack and draped a second robe over his arm.

Rapping his knuckles lightly on the outside of the glass, he waited for the water to turn off and the door to swing open partway so he could hand the towel to her without looking. Then he hung the robe from the corner of the open shower door.

"There's a comb on the vanity," he said. "Clean toothbrushes in the top left drawer under the sink. Help yourself to anything in the flat, and if you can't find something, ask. I'll be right outside. When you're done, we'll go speak with the others and figure out our next move."

Call me if you need anything, he added, and left before she could formulate any kind of an answer, either silently or aloud.

Xander closed the bathroom door and leaned back against it, putting up enough of a mental shield to hide his thoughts from her while still ensuring that he would feel it if she was in any distress.

Bloody, buggering hell. Where did he get off thinking he had the right to treat her like this—to treat her as if she was his? She didn't know the first thing about him; had no reason to trust him and every reason not to.

He pushed away from the door, and the resulting mild dizziness catapulted his mind right back to the feeling of her fangs piercing him, her lips pressing against the tender skin of his throat as she drank him down. For a vampire, it was foreplay, but for her, it was probably some serious horror movie shit—another nightmare come to life. And that *still* completely ignored the fact that he had no real idea what the two of them had done to each other.

It appeared he was now a vampire who could survive direct sunlight, but shifted into the form of a wolf instead of mist or an owl, and was burned by silver. While she was a werewolf who craved blood and could change her form outside of the full moon. It made no sense. And it also made perfect sense.

He dressed quickly, unwilling to face the others without donning at least the appearance of his usual armor beforehand. Manisha emerged into the bedroom a short time later, the robe tied snugly around her body and her damp hair plaited in a messy braid that hung nearly to her waist. Xander wanted to run his fingers through that long, silky hair. He wanted to see what it looked like spread across a pillow like a dark halo. He wanted to erase that hollow, haunted look from her eyes.

He was so, *so* fucked.

"I can try and find you some clothes that fit," he offered.

"Will we be leaving here tonight?" she asked.

He shook his head. "I shouldn't think so. Like Tré said, we need to regroup and decide what we're going to do before we run off half-cocked."

"Then the robe is fine," she said. Silence stretched, and it seemed she was deciding whether or not to say something else. "Do you think Sangye is dead?" she asked eventually, the words emerging all in a rush.

He shook his head. "No. I don't."

She examined his face for a long moment. "Are you just saying that to keep from upsetting me?"

He stepped into her space so he could look down at her, not even aware that he was doing it until he'd already moved. "Not at all." He paused, trying to organize his thoughts into words. "Bael turned Sangye *purposely*. He's never done that before. The rest of us... we were his mistakes. His goal these past long years has been to destroy vampires, not add to our ranks. He must have had a reason for that."

Her eyebrows drew together, a furrow forming in the skin between them. "Bael? Is that the name of Kovac's master? The ancient evil he serves?"

The vitriolic burn of Xander's hatred coiled in his gut. "Yes. The demon that tried to make us into his soulless puppets, and instead turned us into what we are now. You may have seen dark mist swirling around Snag and Sangye when they were taken. That mist is the physical manifestation of his power."

Her eyes slipped closed. "That's what destroyed the werewolves and made them into undead... *things*. I felt it touch me. It was like acid; I thought I was going to die."

The thought of Bael touching the woman standing before him was like a stake through his chest. His hands closed around her arms, startling her into looking up at him again.

"We're devoted to stopping him, Manisha—no matter what it takes," he said hoarsely. "Bael's defeat is our one and only purpose in life. I'm just sorry you got caught up in it."

Her lips pressed together in a firm line. "Until this happened, I had never before in my life felt the desire to kill someone."

Xander's shields slipped, and for a moment he felt their mutual hatred of Bael flow together like blood and water mixing.

"I have a feeling it won't be as straightforward as simple killing," he said. "But whatever happens, you are one of us now. So is Sangye—and we look after our own. You're not alone in this. We're all in it together, to the bitter end."

She took a deep breath and let it out. "Let's go talk to the others."

Seventeen

Manisha followed Xander back to the flat's spacious sitting room, the floor smooth and warm under her bare feet. Not surprisingly, the others had gotten themselves cleaned up while she was busy having a meltdown in Xander's luxurious shower.

She looked at the other vampires properly for the first time—two couples, all four of them strikingly attractive in different ways. One of the men was pale-skinned, with high Slavic cheekbones, a serious brow, and unusual silver-gray eyes beneath dark hair. Next to him sat a woman about Manisha's height or a bit shorter, with a riot of wavy chestnut hair and the sort of curves that would make any man look twice.

Another woman sat cross-legged on a second couch. Her black hair was close cropped at the sides with a longer forelock falling across her forehead. She was taller and built a bit boyishly, though her full lips and the delicate brows arched over her intelligent eyes still marked her as a very striking woman.

A second man—the one Manisha vaguely remembered yelling at earlier—paced restlessly around the open, airy space. Dark, wavy hair on the long side of fashionable framed sharply drawn Mediterranean features. His brown eyes were flat and angry.

Xander ushered her further into the room, and all four vampires looked at her.

"Manisha," Xander said, "may I present Della, Tré, Eris, and Trynn. Try not to hold their long history of voluntary association with me against them."

Tré rose, and offered a precise bow of the head that you might expect to see from old world aristocracy in a movie. "A pleasure," he said in a deep, Eastern European accent.

The woman named Della rose as well, and came forward to clasp Manisha's hand in a brief handshake. "Hi," she said, her voice a broad American drawl. "It's nice to meet you."

"Horrible circumstances notwithstanding, of course. Unfortunately, we tend to get those a lot," added the dark-haired woman, Trynn. Rather than rise and shake Manisha's hand, she smiled tightly and gestured to another of the elegant couches scattered around the large space. "Make yourself comfortable. I expect we've got quite a bit to discuss."

"That we do," said the other man—Eris. His tone was grim. She thought maybe he was Greek, but mostly what struck her was the aura of age and barely leashed power crackling around him like invisible sparks.

It made the wolf restless and put Manisha on edge, but she only nodded and said, "All right," before taking a seat on the empty couch Trynn had indicated.

Xander followed her and sank down to sit on the floor near her legs, bracing his back against the edge of the couch and stretching. She heard a series of pops as his spine cracked, and he relaxed into a slouch, close to her but not touching. Tré and Della returned to their previous seats, while Eris circled around to stand behind Trynn and rest his hands on the back of the sofa, still looking twitchy.

"Before we get into the rest of it," Xander said, "I need to pick your brains on something."

"Oh? You mean the small matter of you being impervious to sunlight and unexpectedly shifting into a wolf?" Eris asked. "I was wondering when you'd ask."

Manisha felt a glimmer of irritation that didn't belong to her pricking inside her head. That mental link…

was going to take some serious getting used to. It had implications that she wasn't quite ready to examine too closely.

"Manisha bit me while she was in mid-transformation," Xander said very precisely, clipping the words off one at a time, "and I bit her in an attempt to weaken her enough that she could assert her humanity over the wolf. There was a fairly significant exchange of... bodily fluids... and we both became quite ill afterward."

Eris muttered something in a language Manisha didn't recognize. Xander lifted his chin, but didn't move from his loose sprawl otherwise.

"Eris, mate," he said, "I get that your knickers are in a twist over Snag. But right now, I need a peek into that encyclopedia you keep locked up inside your two-thousand-year-old skull. I do *not*—" He paused, emphasizing the word. "—need you judging me under your breath in Cypriot. Which I do, in fact, speak."

Della was frowning. "Wait. So, you think that by sharing Manisha's blood, you've become... what? Part werewolf?"

"That's what I'm hoping the bookworm can answer," Xander said. "Though it's not just me that's affected, it's both of us."

Eris' dark eyes flicked over them, a hint of gold lurking behind them. "Tell me exactly what you've both experienced since then."

Xander gestured at her in a clear *ladies first* gesture.

Manisha cleared her throat, looking around at the interested gazes nervously. "It was right after my first transformation. The moon was setting, and Xander got close to me too soon. I... uh... I attacked him. When I came back to myself properly, I felt really dizzy and weak. I must've passed out. The werewolves took me back to the warehouse and chained me up with what I'm pretty sure were silver shackles."

"Did the metal burn your skin?" Eris asked, all business now.

She nodded. "Yes, it was awful. After I woke up, they brought me some meat. I was ravenous, and after I ate it I felt a bit stronger. But… there was also blood on my skin, and I wanted to lick it off. I remember thinking that fresh blood would have been even better."

Eris' eyebrows went up. "So you wanted both food and blood? And the meat didn't make you feel ill?"

"Yes, I wanted both," she said. "And, no, eating didn't make me feel sick."

"Are you still craving blood?" Eris asked.

Manisha felt her cheeks heat, and shot a glance at the top of Xander's head.

"She was craving it, yes," Xander said evenly. "She's not anymore."

His fingers reached up to brush the side of his neck, where Manisha could just make out red marks and bruising. The others' attention focused on the movement, and Eris nodded.

"Right," he said. "Xander, have you tried eating solid food?"

Xander made a vague noise of disgust. "No, I have not. Unlike Oksana, I don't enjoy putting my body through that. Speaking of which, we should Skype the Singapore brigade now so we don't have to go over the ugly details of this debacle twice."

Tré spoke up. "I'll do that. Are your passwords still the same?"

"Yes."

Tré made a noise of disapproval. "Your IT division would be appalled, *tovarăş*." He left the room and returned a moment later with a sleek laptop. "While I set up the call, you should check to see if you can tolerate human food now. I assume you have some around for… visitors?"

Something about the way he said it, combined with what Manisha thought she knew of Xander, made her think he was looking for a polite way to say *one-night stands*. Which should not have made her hackles rise, but did anyway.

Xander grunted and pushed to his feet. "Yeah, I think there's some microwave chicken tikka masala in the freezer."

"Classy," Trynn observed.

"Shut up," Xander told her.

Trynn snorted. Manisha's stomach rumbled audibly.

The corner of Xander's mouth twitched before his gaze landed on her, and softened. "Hungry again? I can heat up two portions."

She looked down. "I'm a vegetarian," she said bitterly. "Or at least, I was. But all the werewolves gave me after I was turned was meat. Most of which was fucking *raw*."

Della made a noise of combined sympathy and anger.

"Jesus," said Trynn. "What a bunch of bastards. Eris, does she have to eat meat just because she's a werewolf?"

Manisha raised her head to look at Trynn's mate, who lifted one shoulder in a shrug. "I've no idea, though I expect the wolf will dictate at least some of her physical requirements." His dark eyes met hers. "What are your feelings about fish and shellfish? Or about hunting small game while in the form of the wolf?"

She mulled it over for a few moments. "I'm not sure. Though I suppose I find the idea of eating shellfish is a bit less upsetting than gnawing on something's leg bone." She shuddered. "Or of pouncing on some poor, unsuspecting rabbit and breaking its neck in my jaws."

Della shifted position. "You know, the last Dalai Lama wasn't totally vegetarian. I remember reading that in an interview."

Manisha tried to smile at her despite the pang that went through her at the reminder of Sangye. "Yes. I know. Lots of Tibetan Buddhists aren't. Differing schools of thought. It's how I was raised, though."

"I'm fairly sure there's some pasta with scallops in the freezer, along with the chicken," Xander said. "I can at least offer you protein without a central nervous system. We can experiment more with your diet when you're not quite so busy recovering from... well... everything."

'*We* can experiment.' It should have sounded presumptuous. So why did the words make her wolf want to roll over and rub her back all over Xander's plush area rug?

"Okay. Thanks," she said. When he'd disappeared into the kitchen, she took a deep breath. "So, I'm really the first werewolf to bite a vampire? Or, you know, vice versa? Bully for me, I guess."

Eris arched a heavy eyebrow, his already dark expression hardening even further. "Well... yes and no," he said.

"Oh, *come on*, Eris! What the bloody hell is that supposed to mean?" Xander called from the kitchen, the ding of a microwave being set following the words.

"Let's wait for the Singapore call to go through, and get the others up to speed," Eris said. "I only want to tell this once."

A few moments later, Tré set the laptop on the coffee table facing the largest of the couches. The others clustered around it, and after a quick round of greetings with the newcomers, Tré ran through a succinct recap of recent events. Manisha crept around until she could see the screen, where a pretty black woman and a pale-skinned blonde who looked like a runway model sat with a pleasant-faced white man with sandy brown hair and blue eyes.

The microwave dinged again, and Xander emerged with two steaming plastic trays and a couple of elegant silver forks. She eyed the forks warily.

"It's stainless, not the good silver," he assured her, handing her one along with the tray of pasta. The food smelled ridiculously good for something that had just been removed from a cardboard box and microwaved.

Xander perched himself on the arm of the sofa, within range of the laptop's camera.

"Xander. We leave you alone for *one week*, mon chou…" said the blonde woman.

"Hello to you, too, Duchess," Xander said, and lifted a forkful of chicken to his nose. He winced, but gamely took a tiny taste.

And immediately spat it out.

"Problem?" asked the black woman. "And here I thought you might finally have seen the light."

"Yeah, that's a great big *no*," he said, and took the tray back into the kitchen.

Manisha dug into her pasta, the wolf seeming quite content with both the scallops and the creamy noodles with bits of broccoli mixed in.

"So," Xander continued upon returning, "not a completely equal exchange of characteristics, then."

The man on the laptop screen tapped his chin for a moment before speaking in a pleasant Australian accent. "That makes sense, though. Scientifically speaking, grafting werewolf abilities onto a vampire wouldn't necessarily have the same results as grafting vampire abilities onto a werewolf."

"Cheers, Ozzie," said Xander, "and kudos for being able to say both 'vampires' and 'werewolves' in the same sentence without flinching. I'm impressed."

"I'm a quick learner," the man replied in a dry tone.

"Strictly speaking," Eris said in a low voice, "they're all vampire traits, originally."

Xander crossed his arms. "Okay, enough. You seem to think the whole 'being cryptic' thing makes you look cool, and it really, *really* doesn't. You've been hinting around something all evening, and it's driving me batty. Which, I hasten to add, is neither a vampire nor a werewolf trait—thank you *so* much, Bram Stoker."

Manisha was starting to understand that engaging in endless quips was Xander's way of dealing with things that were unpleasant or emotional. Even though she couldn't feel the strange mental bond with him at all right now, she got the sense that he was rattled, and that, in turn, made *her* feel rattled.

Eris straightened from where he'd been leaning his hands on the back of the sofa. "To explain," he said, "I'm going to need to break a confidence."

The blonde woman on the laptop screen tilted her head like a bird. "Why? Is this to do with Snag?" she asked.

Trynn craned around to look at her mate with interest. "Is it?"

"It is, yes," Eris said. "Under the circumstances, it's directly relevant. And it's not as though he's here for me to ask permission." His voice grew tight on the last sentence.

EIGHTEEN

Eris turned to look at Manisha. "Snag is the oldest vampire in existence. The first vampire Bael ever made, unless another exists that we haven't found, or who was killed before the rest of us were turned. He was born in Egypt, south of what is now Cairo, in the year 2650 BCE or thereabouts—as far as I've been able to determine, at any rate. Snag has no knowledge of, or real interest in, his exact age."

Manisha tried to rein in her shock, even as Tré looked at Eris curiously.

"How do you know all of this?" the silver-eyed vampire asked. "In the centuries I've known him, I have never heard him speak of his past in any detail."

Trynn crossed her arms and glared at Tré. "Yeah? You know, if the rest of you talked to him more and didn't treat him like some kind of a freak, maybe he'd open up more to you in turn."

"He is a freak, Trynn," Xander said evenly. "We're all freaks, here—some of us more than others. And, I'm sorry, but Snag has always been firmly on the 'more' end of the spectrum."

Trynn inhaled as if to argue, but Eris spoke first.

"I know these things about Snag because I'm the one who stumbled across his petrified body in an underground tomb in 326 AD. And, yes, because I made the effort to cultivate his friendship over the course of the intervening centuries."

His expression darkened again, but he shook it off.

"He has always been different than the rest of us. More powerful. But also, more… damaged. He won't speak of what happened when he was turned. However, what the rest of you may not appreciate is that, in the almost forty-seven hundred years since he emerged from his initial bloodlust, he never once fed from a human until the day a few months ago when he helped me turn Trynn."

Trynn's eyes flew to her mate in surprise, and Eris rested a hand on her shoulder. A shocked silence settled across the room.

Manisha wasn't clear about what this had to do with werewolves, or with her and Xander, but it was undeniably difficult to take in. "If he's a vampire, and he's more than four thousand years old but has never hunted humans… how is he still alive?" she asked.

"He fed from Eris," Tré said slowly, "but only barely enough to keep himself functioning. More recently, he has fed from Trynn as well."

"Mostly because I never stopped nagging him about it," Trynn put in.

"However, that does not account for the almost three millennia after he was turned, but before you found him, Eris," Tré continued. "It seems unlikely that he could have survived that long without any blood whatsoever."

"I didn't say he survived without blood—although he did spend much of that period in a petrified, coma-like state brought on by starvation. That was how I found him, and he had been sealed inside his tomb for a very long time."

Xander tensed beside her. "But you said…"

"I said," Eris continued, "that he never fed from a human."

"Son of a bitch," Xander said. "This had better not be heading where I think it's heading, Eris."

Eris only stared at him.

"Go on," Tré prompted.

Eris let out a deep breath. "Snag ruled a minor city-state, and was something of a gadfly to the pharaoh at the time. After he was turned, several of Snag's former soldiers managed to subdue him and drag him before the priests while he was still weakened. The priests performed powerful spells on him to keep him that way."

The black woman on the laptop screen inhaled sharply. "Those scars on his body," she said, "some of them are symbols of power common across several ancient religions."

"Yes," Eris agreed. "The priests weakened him enough that he was unable to overpower them or shift form. Then, his former subjects presented him as a gift to the pharaoh, hoping to curry favor and avoid war now that they were leaderless. The pharaoh was happy enough to have his old adversary as a prisoner, and amused himself for several years by putting Snag in the arena with wild animals as a sort of spectacle."

The others looked grim. Della looked positively ill.

"Oh my god," she breathed. "He killed the animals and drank from them?"

"Rather than attack humans, yes," Eris said.

"The first time I saw him," Della said faintly, "I noticed that some of his scars looked like branded symbols, and the rest looked like—"

"Claw marks," Trynn finished for her, wincing. "Yeah. *Fuck.*"

Manisha thought she had a pretty good idea where this was going now.

Eris continued, "They threw him in with anything they could find that had fangs, claws, and a vicious temper. There was usually enough blood shed on both sides to entertain the crowds, but of course none of the animals could overcome him. He always killed them in the end. At least... he killed them until one day when the arena guards dragged a huge golden wolf out of the fighting pit, only to discover that it was stunned rather than dead."

"He drank from a wolf, but didn't kill it," Xander said flatly. "And… let me guess…"

Eris nodded. "It had bitten him, as well. The beast woke up and savaged one of the guards before escaping. A few days later, it started coming into the city at night, attacking people until someone finally managed to chop its head off."

"And those people it attacked turned into werewolves," Manisha said, feeling as ill as Della looked. "He *made* werewolves. By accident."

"As you say." Eris rubbed at the bridge of his nose. "After one of the surviving guards came in to throw the wolf's head at his feet and tell him what happened, Snag just… gave up. He stopped feeding at all; let the animals maul him until it wasn't enough of a show for the pharaoh's taste anymore. When he finally grew too weak to heal, he lapsed into a death-like state and his enemies sealed him in an underground tomb."

"And that's where you found him," Xander said flatly. "Three thousand years later."

"A human would have assumed he was a mummy," Eris said. "But even after all that time, I could still sense him inside my mind. It was the moment when I first discovered that I was not alone in the world."

Manisha shivered, imagining what it would be like to believe you were the only one of your kind in existence.

"How does any of this help, though?" she asked. "This vampire… this being who is responsible for making me what I am… is trapped somewhere with Sangye and a demon who wants us all dead. So now what?"

She rubbed her temples, wishing she could stop the pounding in her head somehow. After a few moments, she let her arms fall to her sides, a hollow laugh escaping her. "This is nuts. And you want to know what's even more ironic?"

Xander looked at her, concern lurking behind his green eyes.

"Sangye also refused to drink human blood," she continued. "At least… afterward. I can't say it for certain, but I'm fairly sure he must have killed his mother in the bloodlust right after he was, uh, changed."

"It is likely," Tré said in a heavy voice. "It's the willing sacrifice of a loved one's life that thwarts Bael's power, making his intended victim into a vampire rather than an undead puppet."

She nodded, thinking of Eliza Grimshaw, Xander's wife. About the woman Manisha had once been. "Jampa—Sangye's mother—would have given her life for him in a heartbeat. Of that, I have no doubt."

Manisha closed her eyes, remembering Sangye's monstrous demeanor as he'd snapped his jaws at her in a mindless killing frenzy, held back from ripping out her throat only by the iron chains shackling him.

She continued, "After they threw us into the cells at the warehouse, he seemed to come back to himself. And from that moment forward, he refused to feed even when Crank dangled bound humans right in front of his face." Tears began to burn behind her eyes, and she tried to blink them back. "The bastard tried everything he could think of. Cutting their flesh and waving the blood right under Sangye's nose… threatening to torture or murder them if he wouldn't feed."

An arm closed around her shoulders, but she kept staring forward blankly, her vision starting to blur.

"But… Sangye would just look at Crank in that quiet way he had, and tell him that he couldn't stop Crank from committing whatever violence he was intent on. And when the homeless kids Crank brought in for him started to panic or scream or cry, he'd meet their gaze, and his eyes would start to glow. He'd tell them not to be afraid; to go to sleep and that everything would be all right. And… they would do it. They would do exactly what he said."

She realized that her voice was shaking, and tears were sliding down her cheeks. The arm held her tighter.

"Xander, mate—" The Australian voice came from the laptop speakers, calm and sober. " —your lady friend needs someplace quiet, a shoulder to lean on, and a few hours' sleep. Doctor's orders."

"On it," said the quiet voice at her side.

"We still need to come up with a strategy—" Eris began.

Tré cut him off. "We need to rest and heal. Right now, we have no information to work with. Unless you can sense Snag's location?"

Eris' spine stiffened. Trynn looked up at him and said, "What if you tried to, I don't know… meditate for a bit first? Clear your mind, and then try to contact him again? Maybe the two of us together could do it."

Xander led Manisha away before she could hear Eris' response, heading back down the hallway to the luxurious master suite. She let herself be guided, suddenly feeling exhausted beyond measure. She was still crying, and the prospect of giving in fully to the wracking sobs that wanted to shake free of her chest was more than she could bear right now. She just wanted it all to go away for a bit. She needed… not to feel like this. She needed that desperately.

The bedroom door closed behind them, and Xander turned her so she was facing him, his hands bracketing her shoulders. She felt the barrier he'd erected earlier in his mind slide lower, his thoughts brushing up against hers as if to assess her state of mind.

"I'm going to make a suggestion," he said, "which you are free to ignore. In a minute, I'm going to shift into my wolf for a while. I think things will be easier for you if you do the same. Animals are… simpler, in many ways. Curl up on the bed. Sleep for a bit. Shed on the comforter and give my housekeeping service something to wonder about the next time they come. I'll keep watch and wake you if anything important happens."

She blinked up at him stupidly, but he only leaned down to press his lips to her forehead before letting her go and slipping into the bathroom. A moment later, the huge male wolf who'd fought at her side in the warehouse padded out, its green eyes full of depths she couldn't bring herself to plumb right now.

It sat at her feet, obviously ready to stand guard just as Xander had promised. The animal sharing Manisha's body and mind surged up, suddenly desperate to get free. To get to its mate. Fresh tears fell. How had all of this just… *happened*? The wolf was an entirely new part of her, appearing from nowhere like a puzzle piece that needed to be slotted into place before she could be whole again.

And she had no idea how to do that.

She hadn't asked for this. But what was the alternative? She was the reincarnation of Xander's lost love, whether she'd asked to be or not. Her wolf was mated to his now, whether she'd asked for it or not. And all this time, he'd been—

He'd been a perfect gentleman, ever since the night of the full moon. More than that—he'd been her wisecracking English knight in tarnished armor. Rushing to her rescue. Trying to hold her broken pieces together even when she could feel through the link that doing so was cracking his brittle facade into smaller and smaller shards.

He'd opened his home to her. Opened a vein for her. And the wolf inside her needed to get to him *right now*, like she needed her next breath.

Still weeping softly, Manisha untied her robe and let it fall, dropping to all fours beside the pile of thick terrycloth as her body twisted and changed. With a surge of relief, she rushed forward to lick and nuzzle at her mate's jaw, even as she whimpered her distress over the loss of Sangye and her fear about the future.

Her mate slung a front paw over her shoulder and lapped at her cheek with slow, reassuring strokes. Manisha flopped down, tangling their bodies together, and rolled onto her side. A feeling of safety and protection flooded her as Xander curled himself around her, still licking her fur with the same soothing rhythm. She pressed her body more fully against his comforting warmth, letting her human grief and worry float away into the ether.

He'd been right. The wolf lived only in the moment. Manisha was warm. Her belly was full. The male with whom she'd bonded was next to her, keeping watch against the night. Everything else could wait until she was rested. Her eyes slipped closed, the human bedroom replaced by visions of open fields at night, full of interesting smells and the scampering of small prey animals.

Manisha slept, her legs twitching with small movements as she dreamed of running side by side with her mate—the sky a wide, black expanse above them, shot through with stars.

Nineteen

It was still dark when a hand stroked over her skull and down her spine, waking her. Even though he was in his human form now, the wolf still recognized her mate. She yawned in contentment, jaw cracking. Muscles pulled deliciously beneath her skin as she indulged in a slow, full-body stretch.

"Manisha," he said, "*Christ*. I've just realized something. It's important. We need to talk to the others again."

The fuzzy cloth covering she'd worn earlier in human form reappeared, draping across her body.

"Come back to me now," he said, and shook his head. "Good god. I can't believe we've all been such idiots."

The manic edge beneath his words was enough to rouse her human sensibilities, and the wolf reluctantly stepped aside. Her body rippled and changed, leaving Manisha sprawled inelegantly on the floor at the foot of Xander's bed where the wolf had fallen asleep.

"What's wrong?" she mumbled, feeling dull and befuddled.

He helped her wrap the robe around herself properly. "Many, many things," he said, frowning. "But I realized a few minutes ago that we've all been shown up by a six-year-old. Well, a six-year-old and a terrifying old scarecrow who I always thought was one slip away from becoming humanity's second-worst nightmare."

She blinked at him, trying to bring her brain back online. "Look—I'm sorry, but I have absolutely no idea what you're trying to say."

His mouth ticked up as though he were attempting to smile, but his brows were still drawn together in a frown. "That's because you already said it. Not your fault that the rest of us weren't paying attention. Neither Snag nor Sangye ever drank human blood, except for the initial bloodlust where they had no control."

She still wasn't getting it, but she let him help her to her feet and lead her out by the hand.

"I've summoned the others," he was saying. "They should be trying to get Oksana, Mason, and Duchess back on the line, though it'll be daytime in Singapore so they may be asleep."

"Um… okay?" she said, following him back to the living area, where the others were also trailing in with varying expressions of curiosity and grogginess.

"What's up?" Della asked, pushing her sleep-tangled hair back from her face. She flopped down on the nearest sofa and raised an eyebrow at Xander's obvious agitation.

"Let the others get here first," Xander said, urging Manisha to join her on the couch and turning to pace restlessly around the room.

Eris and Trynn arrived next. Manisha couldn't help noticing that Eris looked like death warmed over—pale and exhausted, with dark circles under his eyes. Trynn wasn't faring much better.

Finally, Tré crossed the room to place the laptop in front of them. The blonde woman, Duchess, was alone on the screen this time.

"Where are Mason and Oksana?" Xander asked.

"Sleeping," Duchess said, looking perfectly put together right down to her blood-red lipstick. "I didn't want to wake them until I knew what was happening."

"Get them," Xander insisted. "Everyone needs to hear this."

She lifted a sculpted brow, and tilted her head, her eyes going distant for a moment. "Very well. They're on their way, *mon chou*. While we're waiting, please take a deep breath. You're making me twitchy, and I'm half a world away."

Xander stopped pacing, but the tension in his spine did not subside. After a brief wait, the Australian doctor and the sweet-faced black woman, Oksana, came into camera range and sat down, obviously freshly awoken.

"What's wrong?" Oksana asked.

Xander sat down next to Manisha, his knee jiggling restlessly. "We're all fools, that's what's wrong."

There was a beat of silence, before Trynn said, "A little clarification here, maybe?"

Xander sucked in a breath and let it flow out, as if trying to marshal his words. "We've been fighting this battle against Bael, but we've been throwing him boxes full of ammunition to use against us at the same time." He ran a hand through his hair in frustration. "A *six-year-old* figured this out, for Christ's sake—and we didn't. Snag figured it out millennia ago, and if we find him in one piece I'm going to kick his bony arse for not spelling it out to the rest of us."

"Xander…" Tré said.

Xander shot to his feet again, too wired to stay still. "Right—sorry. It's so *obvious*, though. *You can't fight evil when you're stealing people's blood and preying on them.* You can't be the good guys under those circumstances, not even when you're stealing their blood from them very nicely and politely. Don't you see? We're part of the very darkness we're trying to fight!"

Manisha blinked, finally understanding what he was getting at. She knew, though, that she didn't have enough of a view into their world to truly offer an opinion. Which wasn't true for the others, clearly.

"Oh, my god," Oksana said softly.

"Too long without drinking blood," Tré said, "and we won't be fighting anyone or anything, Xander. You know that."

Xander shook his head in frustration. "Listen, though. Della. Trynn. Mason. Have any of you drunk blood from innocents yet?"

"No," Della said. "I just… haven't been able to face that, yet."

"No," Trynn echoed. "Only from Eris. Oh—and once from Oksana, when I got hurt in Damascus."

There was a short pause. "Yes. I… drank from my brother," said Mason.

Xander cocked an eyebrow. "Did he offer first?"

"Well, of course," Mason said. "I would hardly have done it otherwise."

"Good," said Xander. "That's good."

Tré frowned at him. "Is it? *Tovarăş*, our mates can only indulge in their preference not to hunt if some of us feed from humans. And when we are feeding another vampire, we must hunt more often than if we were only providing for ourselves. The same thing goes for Snag. Eris is providing for both him and Trynn." His pale eyes met Manisha's for a moment before moving back to Xander. "And as to the boy, if he has been starving himself, he will eventually become too weak to function. I'm afraid I fail to understand the point you're making."

Trynn looked uncertain. "I mean… I suppose we could try stealing from blood banks instead of hunting, but…"

Della shook her head. "But that's even worse. Being drained by a vampire doesn't do any lasting harm to a person. But the blood supply is always tight, and when someone needs a transfusion, it's usually life threatening. We'd be stealing from those in real need."

"No." The voice came from the laptop speakers—Oksana. "That's not what he means, is it, Xander?"

Xander mustered a faint twitch of a smile for her. "Score one for the snack food addict," he said, relief coloring his tone. "Now, please tell me I'm not crazy."

Duchess snorted.

"No comment," said Oksana, "but I won't hold it against you in this case. It's a frighteningly valid point."

Mason raised his eyebrows. "You're thinking about the girls in Haiti, aren't you?"

Xander nodded. "Yes. The girls in Haiti. And your brother."

Oksana nodded as well.

"What girls in Haiti?" Della asked in confusion.

Oksana smiled. "When we were preparing to rescue the children, the mambo we were staying with brought in some volunteers from the village. Haitians are more aware of the supernatural—and more comfortable with it—than many cultures. The three girls who came knew what we were and offered their blood freely."

"Their siblings were among the kidnapping victims," Mason added. "They wanted to help get them back in whatever way they could."

Tré looked between them. "So, you're proposing… what?"

"I'm proposing that we stop doing evil things when we're supposed to be fighting evil," Xander said.

Manisha spoke up. "Do you think you can find other people who would willingly offer blood? I mean, do you have friends who know about you being vampires, or—?"

"No," Eris said flatly. "We don't."

"Yes," Mason contradicted, "we do. Maybe not many. But I already told you that my brother Jackson knows. His wife does, too, though she's understandably still a bit wary of us. And a colleague of mine, Dr. Belawen."

"There are several people in Haiti," Oksana added. "Mama Lovelie, the girls we already talked about, and a retired healer in the same village."

"Madame Francine, in New Orleans," Della added.

"And a former employee of hers named Madeleine," Xander mused. "Though she may well be a werewolf by now."

Manisha looked at him sharply.

"Voluntarily," he was quick to add. "The man she was in love with became a werewolf, and she followed him."

She couldn't imagine anyone signing up for such a thing voluntarily, but she let it go.

"As interesting as this is," Duchess said, "pursuing it would be a logistical nightmare."

"It's hardly our biggest concern right now," Eris said tightly.

There was a beat, and then Della said, "Well, I think it's a good idea." The words were quiet, and she didn't look at the rest of them, her eyes fixed firmly on her hands lying folded in her lap.

"I agree," Oksana put in immediately.

Several of the others were looking at Tré, who seemed to be the de facto leader of the group. Tré, in turn, was looking at Xander.

"You have more to say on this matter, I think," he said, holding Xander's gaze steadily. "So, *tovarăş*—convince me."

-o-o-o-

Xander met his best friend's disconcerting pale gaze, and tried not to think about what he was poised to reveal. There were things about him that none of them knew; things that the selfish part of him would much rather keep hidden in the dark. But he'd had an epiphany earlier tonight—one that the others hadn't caught up with yet, it was clear.

He didn't let his gaze waver as he said, "I think I finally understand the true nature of the war in which we're embroiled, Tré. And it's not the war we thought we'd signed up for."

Tré nodded slowly. "Very well. Explain that to us."

He tore his eyes away and ran a hand through his hair, agitated. Unable to keep still, he started to pace again, a few steps in one direction, a few steps in the other, trying not to think about the bottles of spiked blood in the hidden refrigerator, only a room away.

"Right. So. We've been looking at this as a fight. A battle where Bael throws things at us and we fight them off. Bombs. Riots. Undead soldiers. He attacks and we counter. Sometimes we think we've won, sometimes we know we've lost, and along the way we pick up more soldiers, hoping that if we can get the magic number thirteen, it will somehow change the rules of the game."

"The prophecy about the Council of Thirteen is the only hope of victory we've been able to find," Eris grated, sounding like he was nearing the end of his tether.

Xander's jaw clenched, but he forced himself not to rise to the bait. Not to let things devolve into sniping and avoidance the way he normally would.

"Yes," he said. "But, Eris, it's a battle between Light and Darkness. If we're supposed to be on the side of Light, why are we fighting with guns and knives and claws and fangs? Why are we allowing the Darkness to dictate the terms of the battle?"

He paused to let the words sink in.

Duchess' voice emerged from the laptop speakers. "Xander. We are vampires. We are all dark creatures. Darkness is woven into our very natures."

And that was the perfect segue into the thing he didn't want to talk about. The desire for a few pints of blood containing something in the illegal opioid or narcotic family grew stronger, making his palms itch.

"It is," he agreed. "For some of us, it's woven more deeply than others. But we have true innocents among our numbers now, as well. A child of six? A pediatric doctor who volunteers in fucking *war zones*? A trio of women whose only crime was trying to live their lives, hurting no one?"

Xander looked at Tré again—a man as close to him as a brother. Noble to a fault, but not a saint. Not after six centuries walking the Earth. He looked at Duchess—the ice queen who had spent hundreds of years punishing herself for a crime she'd never shared with any of them. At Eris, the professional art thief and tomb raider. Oksana, who had ripped her own leg off and dug free of the grave she'd been buried in, savaging an innocent teenager who'd been left there to keep watch.

"One day soon," he said, "the nature of this war is going to change, and all of our darkness is going to be dragged forward into the light. Don't you get it? It's *spiritual warfare*. And I choose, right here and now, to pull my darkness into the light on my own terms."

Xander realized, with a faint feeling of shock, that his hands were physically trembling. He tucked them under his arms and kept pacing. His goddamned shields were wavering, too. He could feel Manisha's curiosity and concern brushing up against his senses.

Then Tré's grounding mental voice. *We already know each other's darkness, old friend. There is no need to dwell on it, surely.*

But he shook his head, speaking aloud since his friends in Singapore were too far away for him to link with them mentally. "No. There are things about me none of you know. Things that will change the way you view me, and rightfully so. I don't know if those things can ever be balanced out, but I have been a parasite since long before I ever became a bloodsucker. And that, at least, is going to have to change. Starting today."

He heard Manisha draw in a breath and recognized that he'd been wrong earlier—there was one person here who already knew about the sins of his past. The sharp stab of pain he felt in response to that realization was irrational. She would have remembered sooner or later what sort of creature her wolf had bonded to, and he might as well face her disgust at the same time he faced all of the others'.

He wondered if any of them would still call him friend an hour from now. Duchess, maybe, he thought. Or perhaps not, given her soft spot for children. Eris, he was even less sure of—they barely tolerated each other at the best of times. And if he thought too closely about either Tré or Oksana turning their backs on him, he'd talk himself right out of this bloody madness before he even started.

Oddly, he found himself wishing Snag were here. Snag had seen some shit. There probably wasn't much *anyone* could come up with that would shock Snag.

Tell them. It was Manisha's voice. *I think you're right about this war.*

He swallowed and closed his eyes.

TWENTY

Manisha realized what Xander was working up to all at once, dream images bubbling up in her mind from the distant past. *Oh.* No wonder he was upset.

The reality of what it meant to be on the front lines of a war between good and evil suddenly pulled into sharp focus before her eyes. It was no surprise that none of the others had looked at it in such a way before. It simply wasn't human nature—or vampire nature, she suspected—to react to a blatantly physical attack by asking how one could become a better person. No, it was human—or vampire—nature to defend against the attack and fight back in kind.

Tell them, she urged Xander silently, convinced in this moment that he had discovered an important key to what was happening around them. *I think you're right about this war.*

She could feel his tightly controlled distress over what he assumed her reaction would be. Her reaction, and the others'. But he wasn't taking into account that she had been a part of his secret shame, too. Perhaps not as she was today—as Manisha—but that long-ago lifetime as Eliza was still part of her karma. She would be a hypocrite if she condemned Xander without also condemning herself.

And if his friends condemned him? She could feel her wolf bristle, ready to defend its mate against any threat—even if that threat came from those he thought of as family. Manisha couldn't control the others' reactions, but she could ensure that Xander didn't face them alone.

She saw his throat bob and his eyes slip closed. A moment later, he began to speak in a flat, faraway tone.

"You're all content to hand matters of finance over to me," he said. "To let me be the one to worry about making enough money to provide what we need, so we can travel at a moment's notice… live wherever we need to live… surround ourselves with comfort when we're not busy fighting for our lives." He gestured around the extravagant penthouse flat.

Tré cocked his head. "You have a talent for business, Xander. You always have. It only makes sense to utilize it."

"A talent for business," Xander echoed softly. "A talent gained by pulling myself out of the gutter a farthing at a time, beginning when I was thirteen years old—the youngest son of a struggling coal merchant. Ten years later, I was one of the richest men in London. Tell me… do you think I managed that feat without climbing over the broken bodies of those less ruthless than I was?"

There was a beat of silence before Eris said, "We've all done things we're not proud of, Xander. What's your point?"

"When I was thirteen, I stole half of my mother's savings—a handful of pennies—and used it to buy waste cotton from a local mill. Anything with defects that I could get my hands on, I sold at a profit to private seamstresses who couldn't afford first-quality bolts. By the time I was fifteen, I had standing contracts with a dozen mills to take their seconds and overages at a discounted price.

"When I was eighteen, I started brokering deals with orphanages. I arranged for them to *apprentice* any children between the ages of eleven and fourteen to the cotton mills in exchange for a percentage of the wage savings the owners enjoyed as a result. When I was twenty, I talked a doddering old banker into giving me a loan and bought my first mill."

The room was perfectly still. Manisha closed her eyes, reliving hazy half-memories of touring the newly completed bunkhouses next to the textile factory where the orphans—the so-called apprentices—slept in shifts when they weren't working.

"I worked those children twelve hours a day, six days a week, and the adult employees fourteen hours a day. I paid the orphans three shillings a week, and the orphanage took half of that. My overseers sent the smallest children to crawl inside the machinery for cleaning and repair. The conditions were horrible. Within three years, I'd purchased nine more mills, thanks to my knack for keeping labor costs so low and productivity so high.

"Meanwhile, I lived in a stylish mansion with Eliza and a bevy of servants, surrounded by luxury. A parasite living off the sweat and labor of children, spending my days finding new loopholes in the pathetic excuses for labor laws that were all they had to protect them."

Movement on the laptop screen drew Manisha's eye. Duchess rose silently and disappeared from the camera's view. Manisha felt a sharp ache cut through Xander's chest as she left without a word, but he continued to speak.

"I lived that life of ease right up until the night a demon decided that either my money or my ruthlessness might be valuable to him. Bael recognized my blighted soul for exactly what it was, and turned me into a leech of the far more literal variety. If thinking about it in those terms didn't make me want to stake myself, it would probably be fucking hilarious."

He turned away abruptly and walked into the kitchen. A moment later, he crossed to the hallway leading back to the bedrooms, pausing with his hand on the wall. The other held a glass bottle, its contents the deepest crimson.

"So," he said, not looking back at them, "if you want to know why I, at least, need to stop being a literal parasite on humanity… that's why. Now, I just have to figure out if I know any humans who give enough of a shit about me to open a vein for this particular cut-rate Count Dracula."

With that, he disappeared into the back of the flat, leaving a heavy pall of silence behind him.

"Shit," Mason said, his voice sounding flat and shocked over the computer's speakers.

There was another long stretch of nothing. Manisha let more of the hazy images from the past slide across her mind, thinking back to those days spent in a world a hundred years before she'd been born.

"Tré…" Oksana's soft voice emerged from the screen.

The silver-eyed leader roused himself from his introspection. "Yes," he said. "I'm going, Oksana." He looked around, meeting each of their eyes in turn. "It was a different time. In many ways, that does not excuse it. But childhood was not the same in the past as it is today. In my village, boys and girls as young as four worked the fields from dawn until dusk, and no one would ever have thought to question it. It simply… *was*."

Eris nodded. "Yes. The past was… a different world. A grimmer world. As children, we either worked, or our families starved."

Tré rose and headed after Xander. Manisha quickly scrambled up to follow him, meeting his eyes with a challenging gaze. "I'm going with you."

He assessed her for a beat before speaking. "And what will you say to him? Whether you realize it or not, Manisha, you hold the sharpened stake he talked about in your hand right now."

She narrowed her eyes at him, the wolf rumbling a warning at him in her mind. "Unlike the rest of you, I was there with him—living in that beautiful mansion. So, I'll take whatever portion of blame my spirit deserves, and then I'll remind him of some of the things he so carefully left out while he was so busy painting himself in the worst possible light."

Tré lifted his chin, regarding her, and then nodded his approval. "Very well. Come on, then."

-o-o-o-

They found Xander in the master bedroom, sprawled in a high-backed chair. He was holding the bottle in one hand, turning it slowly back and forth, staring at the facets in the crimson liquid as though he might find the secrets of the universe reflected therein. He did not look up as they entered.

Manisha marched over and took the bottle from him, setting it on the low table next to his chair. He looked up at her warily, his eyes flicking over her shoulder to Tré, and then back to focus on a point near her chin—not meeting her gaze.

Not really thinking before she moved, she darted a hand out and twisted it in his neatly pressed collar, pulling him forward and bending down until their lips met. He froze in surprise, and she shivered minutely at the frisson as their skin touched—so different now than the sharp, shocking jolt she'd felt when his hand had first brushed hers in the warehouse stairwell.

He made a noise into the kiss, quiet and startled. For a moment, he melted into her—only to catch himself, stiffening and pulling away carefully. Cautious green eyes lifted to meet hers.

"Why?" he asked, the word emerging chary and guarded.

She could feel him in her mind… feel that cold, reflective surface that meant he was shielding his thoughts from her. The smooth mirror was rippling now, though, struck glass resonating like a tuning fork. Manisha loosened her grip on his shirt and placed her hand on the center of his chest, palm flat. Following some newly awakened instinct, she did the same thing mentally, pressing her thoughts against the glass barrier he held between them.

The mirror shattered, brilliant shards raining down.

Beyond, she felt the buzz of conflicted emotions, the itch of an addict resisting the siren lure of self-medication, the pain of someone who had never and would never extend to himself the same forgiveness and leniency he offered those he cared about. She also felt the echo of his bonds with the others — most notably, the man in the room with them now.

We are still here, tovarăş, Tré said, his mental voice every bit as deep and reassuring as his physical one. *Do you think you mean so little to us that the sins of your past would make a difference in our regard for you?*

Manisha let her fingertips slide away from his chest as Xander curled forward in the chair, ducking his face. His hand covered his eyes for a moment, and it was shaking. Then he scrubbed at his forehead and straightened. He looked… fragile. Every bit as much in danger of shattering as his mental barriers had been.

"If I'm right about this war," he said hoarsely, "I may be a liability you'd do better without, Tré. Even if Duchess decides to forgive me for what I did when I was human, there may not be enough lipstick in the world to dress up this particular swine in time for the party."

"You're talking drivel," Manisha snapped, and pressed hazy images into his mind.

Alexander Grimshaw, paying doctors out of his own pocket to treat his employees when they were sick or injured… slipping his workers money off the books to deal with family emergencies… stocking the orphans' lodgings with books and toys… hiring tutors to school them on their days off.

Tré huffed in the background. *Of course. Why am I not surprised in the least?* he sent through the bond.

Xander surged to his feet, as if he couldn't bear to sit still while those memories slipped into his mind.

"Tiny dribs and drabs of benevolence to act as a balm for my pricking conscience," he snarled. "Meaningless tokens!"

She blocked his path before he could start pacing again. "*Meaningless*? I doubt they were meaningless to the people receiving them!"

"Oh? Do you know what would make that argument valid?" he shot back, biting off the words. "What would make that argument valid was if I had kept only as much money to live on as I paid to the lowest of my employees. Had I done that, and reinvested everything else in the people who worked and toiled and slaved for me, those mills might not have been the hellholes that they were. *But I didn't.*"

"But *we* didn't, you mean," Manisha said. "You weren't the only one to benefit from the money made by those mills."

He waved off the words. "You're *not Eliza*. Manisha, you have never at any point in your life had the slightest control of or influence over what happened more than a century ago. Hell, given the social mores of the time, Eliza didn't have a whole lot of influence over it, either."

"You think so?" Manisha asked. "Because I distinctly remember being asked if I wanted to own a beautiful London mansion, and I remember how simple it was to justify answering 'yes' to myself."

"*Enough,* you two." Tré's words cut through the standoff, dragging both of their attention to him. "None of this can be changed. Everyone who ever worked for you back then is dead, Xander. Most of them have been dead for a very long time. You were a human being who did both good and evil in the world. So were we all."

Xander fell back into the chair again. "Fuck you, Tré. You're so goddamned noble it makes me want to puke. You always have been."

Tré seemed unperturbed by the casual abuse, only raising an eyebrow. "Hardly. I was raised the privileged child of a nobleman, taught from the time I could crawl that I had more worth than the people around me. A lesson I absorbed wholeheartedly, and put into practice with everyone I knew. Had I survived to take my father's position, who knows what damage I could have done. But I didn't survive, and neither did you. We were attacked by Bael. We will never know how those lives would have turned out."

"And now you both fight to save the world from darkness, even though the darkness has already tried to claim you," Manisha added.

"Yes," Tré said. "We do."

TWENTY-ONE

The door creaked open. "Yup. That all sounds about right to me," Trynn said.

The others followed. Eris fetched up against the doorframe, his arms crossed. Della was carrying the laptop. She slipped past him into the room and set it on the neatly made bed.

Oksana was still on the Skype call, though Mason had gone.

"Xander," she said kindly.

He looked at the screen. "Oksana. Did Ozzie do a runner as well, then?"

"He went to talk to Duchess." She regarded him fondly through the camera. "You know how she gets when children are involved, *ti mwen*. She'll eventually come around, and realize what the rest of us already know."

"And what's that?" Xander asked, sounding tired.

Her voice was gentle. "That everyone makes mistakes, and everyone deserves an opportunity for redemption."

Manisha decided that she liked Xander's friends.

Trynn made herself comfortable leaning against the bed's headboard. "Hey, that reminds me. You still never told me what your current company does, Xander. What exactly is paying for all these chartered helicopters and penthouse apartments?"

A soft laugh came from the laptop.

Trynn peered around to look at the screen. "What's so funny?"

Oksana shook her head. "Ah, you'll see. Tell her, Xander."

That was enough to make Manisha curious as well.

"Photovoltaic cells, mostly," he muttered.

She got the joke at the same moment Trynn did, judging by the other woman's startled bark of laughter. "Oh my god," Trynn said. "You run a vampire-controlled *solar panel* company?"

Della's expression was priceless, and Manisha suspected hers was as well.

"We're branching out into wind turbine technology, too," Xander said under his breath.

"Perhaps now you'll finally be able to inspect your products while they're in use," Tré suggested. "Without succumbing to horrific burn injuries in the process, I mean."

Eris made a frustrated sound. "As heartwarming as all of this is, we have other things to worry about right now. The rest of this is just a distraction."

Manisha turned to look at him, and so did the others. His arms were crossed tightly; his body language tense. He really did look awful, and she wondered if he'd spent the hours since they first retired trying to mentally contact this ancient vampire friend of his who'd surrendered himself to their enemy. They stared at him, and he stared back, frustration and more than a hint of anger behind his gold-flecked brown gaze.

"I keep asking myself why the rest of you aren't more focused on what really matters, here," he said.

"We are focused on several things that matter, Eris," Tré said mildly. "Chief among those, the fact that we have no actionable leads, and that we are in need of a few hours, at least, to recuperate from injuries and exhaustion."

"Have you truly not made the connection?" Eris pushed away from the wall and uncrossed his arms. "This child — Sangye — *does not have a mate.*"

"What are you talking about?" Manisha asked, Eris' combative manner still rubbing her wolf the wrong way. "He's six years old!"

"And you said his mother sacrificed herself for him?" Eris asked.

It took a moment to work out what he meant, but she remembered them saying that it was the willing sacrifice of a loved one that made a vampire, earlier when they'd been talking about Sangye's refusal to drink human blood.

"Yes, that's right," she said warily. "At least, I think that's what must have happened."

Eris looked at the others again, a furrow between his brows. "Don't you *see*? Sangye killed his mother only a short time ago. Even if her spirit were to be immediately reincarnated, she wouldn't be born for months."

"Oh," Xander said blankly. "*Oh.* Son of a *bitch.*"

"Yes. Things are clearly coming to a head. Look around. There are nine of us." Eris gestured around the room, the movement encompassing the laptop and the vampires on the other end of the Skype call. "Add in Duchess' mate. Snag. Snag's mate. That's twelve. And an unattached boy with no spiritual connection to a living person—"

"Makes thirteen." Xander ran a hand through his hair. "Bloody hell."

Manisha looked between them, noting that the others looked a bit shell-shocked, too. "You said something earlier about the number thirteen. Something about a... prophecy?"

"The Council of Thirteen," Della said quietly. "It's supposedly the only thing that can stand against Bael's darkness."

"There were six original vampires," Tré explained. "Those of us who were turned by Bael over the course of several millennia. For a long time, we assumed that there were other vampires and we simply had not found them… or perhaps they had once existed but had been destroyed."

Della took up the thread again. "This prophecy pops up in a few different places, but the gist is that the Council will be made up of thirteen of Bael's greatest failures and that once it comes together, it will be able to fight him."

A small shock went through her as she did the math. "Wait. So you think *I'm* part of this somehow?" She shook her head, trying to clear it. "And… what's that part about 'greatest failures'?"

"You are Xander's mate," Tré said, not unkindly. "The reincarnation of the soul who saved him through a willing sacrifice."

Her eyes flew to Xander, but he was looking down and would not meet her gaze.

"As for the failure part," Trynn said. "Bael was originally trying to turn our mates into puppets—creatures like Bastian Kovac who would exist only to do his bidding." Her voice went rough with hatred on the name, and Manisha's wolf growled in solidarity. "But Bael discounted the power of love. Instead of mindless servants, he ended up with vampires who hate him with every fiber of their beings. Who will stop at nothing to see him destroyed."

Della's hazel eyes snapped. "And it's not just the original vampires. We are also his failures. He thought we were dead. He discounted us. But death wasn't enough to keep our souls apart from the ones we love. We came back, and we found those we'd lost."

Her words made something in Manisha's chest ache for a moment before it settled into place and eased. There was a terrible and beautiful sort of symmetry to what she had just been told.

Eris met her eyes and spoke. "Bael tried to remove you from the chessboard by making you into a were-wolf—bait for Xander that he could chase, but never truly possess. Yet even in that, he failed. After all these countless years, he still has no conception of the true power of love. It is foreign to him—impenetrable and unknowable."

The feeling of possessive satisfaction she felt upon hearing those words was pure wolf. When she turned glowing eyes back to Xander, it was to find him looking up at her with an expression of painful hope and longing on his haggard features. As their eyes met, though, he tore his gaze free and looked away again.

"I dragged you into this by virtue of my very existence—and for that, I'm sorry," he said. "None of us asked for this, but I don't think that there's any way for us to escape it now."

"I don't want to escape it," she said. "I want to find Sangye and this other vampire friend of yours. And then I want us to stop this creature who delights in spreading pain and darkness across the world."

This time, their eyes locked and held. Green light flared behind Xander's gaze.

"Good," Tré said from behind her. "Now, we just need to decide our next step. Eris? I assume you and Trynn attempted to reach Snag again? Did you have any success?"

With difficulty, Manisha dragged her attention away from Xander and back to the conversation.

Eris shook his head in frustration. "There's nothing. No trace, no sense of his existence."

"Which merely means that he is not nearby, correct?" Tré asked. "Not that he is necessarily dead."

"Yes, that's correct."

Oksana spoke. "I still think that Xander is onto something. Perhaps we should all meet somewhere that we can find humans willing to feed us voluntarily. Which, right now, probably means either here in Singapore, or back in Haiti."

Mason and Duchess reappeared in camera range and rejoined her. The blonde woman appeared pale, but composed.

"I disagree on the subject of devoting large amounts of effort toward finding volunteers to feed us," Duchess said evenly. "If the option is readily available, that's fine. Otherwise, it puts us at too much of a tactical disadvantage."

"I agree." That was Eris. "I don't have time to devote to wild theories when Snag and the boy are in Bael's hands. I also have no intention of jetting halfway around the world when the most logical place to start a search is near the area where they went missing."

Tré lifted his chin and drew everyone in with his gaze. "Very well. Both arguments have merit. Xander, if those of us who are already here were to start searching outward from the UK and into Western Europe, would there be any option for those who wish to stop hunting and only drink blood that is freely given?"

Xander looked utterly exhausted, but he drew his shoulders back and nodded. "Possibly. I'll start trying to find employees inside HelioTeque who can be trusted with the truth." He scrubbed a hand across his eyes. "One thing about it—if they lose their shit when they find out their boss is a vampire, I can always mesmerize them into forgetting it again."

"Mind-whammy to the rescue," Trynn muttered.

Manisha wondered with a jolt if her new thirst for blood meant she would also be able to influence humans' minds, as she'd seen Sangye do to the hapless teenagers Crank had dragged in for him to feed on. She blinked free of the startling thought and focused on the matter at hand.

"I have relatives in Swansea," she said in a hesitant voice. "They're not particularly close—second and third cousins, mostly—but they do at least know who I am. It's conceivable that if I told them what happened with

Sangye, they'd help. Of course, it's also conceivable they'd run screaming in the other direction." She shrugged.

"It's worth a try," Tré said. "Those of us who are already here will start our search outward from London. Duchess... Oksana... Mason... do you intend to join us?"

Duchess shook her head. "Not immediately. There are reports coming out of Malaysia that are... unsettling. Singapore is a good base of operations from which to monitor things for a few more weeks."

"But do contact us right away if you learn anything new about Snag or Sangye, obviously," Oksana added. "Travel in this area is relatively undisrupted—so far, at least, and we can get to you pretty fast if we need to."

"In that case," Tré said, "is everyone agreed on this general course of action?"

There were shrugs and expressions of agreement, including a tight nod from Eris, who still looked deeply unhappy. Tré's silver gaze played over Xander for a moment before coming to rest on Manisha.

Do you two wish some time alone? The words whispered quietly inside her mind.

She recognized the leader's mental voice, and got the impression that the question had only been for her and Xander to hear.

Xander's brow furrowed. *I'm not sure that's a good—*

Yes, she thought as clearly and loudly as she could, cutting him off—only to flush when Eris, Trynn, and Della snapped around to look at her. *Whoops.*

"Don't feel bad," Trynn said. "I nearly shouted Eris' ear off when I was trying to learn that trick. But, yeah, when you project that loudly we can all hear it. So... yes to what, exactly?"

"Yes, it would be best if the rest of us returned to our hotel before dawn, and left these two in peace," Tré answered, saving Manisha the added embarrassment.

"There is still time if we leave now, and we can reconvene here tonight, once we've all had a chance to rest properly."

The tense line of Xander's shoulders eased. "Take some of the bottled blood with you, if you want. I won't be getting more using the methods I have in the past, but since it's already here, there's no further ethical stain involved in drinking it. Pouring it down the drain would only make it a waste on top of everything else."

"No argument here. Dibs on one of the spiked bottles," Trynn said tiredly.

"We'll leave you lot to it, then," Mason said from the laptop. "Keep us posted. And Xander? Chin up, mate. You may be an arsehole, but you're still *our* arsehole."

"I'm choking up over here, Ozzie," Xander said.

After a brief round of farewells, the Singapore contingent signed off. A few moments later the others were gathering bottles from the fridge and heading out. Della paused and wrapped Manisha in a brief, one-armed hug. Caught by surprise, she hugged back, realizing with a pang how long it had been since she'd had any female friends who just… did things like that.

My pack, the wolf insisted.

Her eyes squeezed shut as Della murmured, "Hang in there, okay? The world sucks… but you two still found each other despite the odds. Grab onto the good things and hold tight. Don't let go."

"Thanks," Manisha whispered.

Trynn gave her a pat on the shoulder and a sympathetic smile as well, and then the pair of women returned to Tré and Eris' sides. Tré gave Manisha a solemn nod, and even Eris dipped his chin in farewell before the group disappeared through the door. The flat seemed very quiet once their footsteps had faded into silence.

TWENTY-TWO

"You never answered my question, you know," Xander said quietly, once they were alone.

Manisha blinked at him, hoping it was only the combination of exhaustion and mental overload that was making her feel stupid. "What question is that?" she asked.

Rather than answer, he walked into the kitchen and returned a moment later with a bottle, which he pressed into her hands. "Here, drink this. The mental confusion and that gnawing feeling you're trying to ignore means the cravings are about to return. You should learn to recognize when your body needs blood." He made an awkward gesture toward the bottle. "Don't worry. This is the un-spiked stuff."

Her mouth started to water, and she swallowed hard. "*What question?*" she repeated, trying to focus on him and not the draw of the red liquid in her hand.

His lips pressed together, and he replied, "Drink that first, and then I'll tell you."

She unscrewed the cap, and as soon as the smell hit her nostrils, her fangs lengthened, poking the insides of her cheeks. Her stomach cramped. She lifted the bottle to her lips cautiously. The first drop touched her tongue, and her vision went blurry. When she came back to herself, the bottle was empty and she was licking around the opening, trying to get her tongue inside as low growling noises emerged from her throat.

Shocked, she jerked her head back and let the glass container drop as though it had suddenly become red hot. A hand darted out to catch it neatly before it could shatter on the pristine tile floor.

"Shit!" she gasped, staggering back a couple of steps. "What did I just—?"

"The first few days can be a bit overwhelming. Try not to worry about it. In a pinch, you can always drink from me if there isn't a bottle to hand."

He wasn't looking at her, instead pretending to examine the bottle's label. She could only imagine what she'd looked like—an animal trying to lick up every last drop of gore—snarling over its prize. Humiliation flooded her, growing even deeper when she remembered that there was a very good chance the man standing in front of her could hear every thought running through her head. He must think she was pathetic… must be wondering why he'd ever let this pitiful, out-of-control freak of nature through his doors—

"No, Manisha." The words, spoken aloud, broke through her litany of self-recrimination. "That's… really not the direction my thoughts were taking…"

She looked at him, still mute, and he huffed out a sharp breath.

"Sorry," he said. "I'd assumed you'd figured it out by now. You drew the short straw and ended up with the perverted vampire. I'd apologize for it again, but I'm afraid it's pretty much hard-wired in at this point."

Manisha stared, trying to decide if he was being honest or just trying to make her feel better. Belatedly, it occurred to her to look inward, through the link—which she did, just in time to detect a flash of discomfort from him.

"I could, er, probably call Tré and Della back if you'd be more comfortable staying with them…" he said.

With difficulty, she shook off her embarrassment over her lapse of control.

"Why? Are you trying to get rid of me?" she asked.

I'm trying to protect you, you stubborn woman. Something about the faint air of desperation lurking under the words made her think he hadn't intended her to hear them. This was confirmed a moment later, when he said, "I'm trying to do the right thing, that's all. Several people over the years have intimated that I should try it sometime. This seemed like the perfect opportunity."

"You still haven't told me what question I didn't answer," she reminded him.

He turned and set the bottle carefully on the bar that separated the kitchen from the living area. "You kissed me. Afterward, I asked you why, and you didn't answer."

Surprise threaded through her. *I did an awful lot more than kiss you when we were trapped in the freezer, and you barely batted an eyelash,* she thought.

He glanced at her sideways. "You were out of your head at the time," he said, "and you didn't know me from Adam."

"My wolf knew you," she said.

"*You* didn't know what sort of… person I was. But now you do. And you still kissed me again."

"My wolf knows you, even now."

The growing intensity of his green gaze made something jump, low in her stomach. Inside her, the wolf stretched and pricked its ears.

"Why are you still here, Manisha?" he asked, tone vehement… as though the answer were vitally important to him. *Why haven't you run away from me yet?* echoed silently in the background.

Behind her stretched the crumbled bridge of her life, its broken pieces toppled into a bottomless ravine, irretrievable. Ahead of her stood a man with hand outstretched, offering her a strong arm to pull her onto the stony ledge of the future. Others might have seen a monster. They might have seen a cold, sharp-witted bastard.

Her wolf saw its mate. And Manisha—

She saw the man who had come for her when she was in danger. Who had held her in his arms like a cracked treasure, gluing her broken pieces together and propping her up until she was strong enough to stand on her own again. Who had done all those things while harboring the utter certainty that she would flee in horror the moment she remembered their shared past; her life—and death—as his beloved Eliza.

"I'm here because our souls are connected," she said, the truth of the words weaving around her like a spell even as she spoke them. "I'm here because we belong together."

An instant later, her face was cradled in Xander's hands, and he was kissing her like he wanted to drink her down... as though her breath was the finest wine. In the back of her mind, she heard a desperate whisper. *Please, please, please, for the love of god, don't let me wake up from this and find it was only a drug-fueled hallucination.*

Something about that mental whisper nearly shattered her heart, and she wrapped herself around him, deepening the kiss. The wolf inside her rumbled in satisfaction at the rightness of the feeling. She realized distantly that the low, animal noise was actually vibrating up from her chest, and decided she didn't care. If he hadn't been put off by her practically tongue-fucking a wine bottle to get at the dregs of blood inside, she figured he could probably handle her growling at him.

Manisha, love, he thought very clearly and distinctly, pressing their bodies together until she could feel his hard length pressing into the crease of her hip, *you really have no idea.*

She stopped fighting and let the wolf lead, pulling away from his lips in favor of trailing biting kisses and licks along his strong jaw line. His hands slipped from her cheeks to her hair, and he buried his fingers in the thick mass. Shivers of lightning trailed across her scalp and down her spine, a combination of the strange spark running between them and the intimacy of the touch.

He nuzzled her cheek as she ran her lips over his face and neck. The absolute *rightness* of this feeling washed through her like a warm tide. Everything else in her life right now was wrong, frightening, and painful. The eightfold path of her religious upbringing seemed like a distant mirage, unreachable—retreating further into the distance with every step she took toward it. But here, now, with Xander's hands wrapped in her hair and his body pressing against hers from chest to knees, she could breathe, if only for a moment.

He eased her head back a few centimeters until he could rest their foreheads together. Her eyes slipped closed, her mind going blissfully blank for one precious, much-needed moment as her heated flesh pressed against his cool skin.

Just for a little while, she needed this. She needed this respite so very badly, before they once more had to face a world drowning in darkness. Maybe Xander needed it, too, because his mind was quiet even though the mirrored barrier protecting his thoughts was nowhere to be found. All she could sense was a deep, still pool of gratitude, not a ripple marring its perfect surface.

She marveled. A lifetime of daily meditation, and it was here—standing in a vampire's embrace in the short space of time between one crisis and the next—that she finally found true stillness.

"Come outside with me," he whispered into the air between them. "The sun is about to rise, and I want to watch it with you."

She nodded, a tiny movement that she knew he would feel since they were still resting forehead to forehead. "I'd like that," she murmured. How often had she wondered over the past few weeks whether she would survive to see the next sunrise?

Perhaps he heard the thought, because one of his hands dropped to encircle her shoulders and hold her tight against him. She rested there for another moment before pulling back so she could look up at him. "Come on, then. Show me London at dawn."

The large room at the end of the hall was a study, and one wall was dominated by a sliding glass door that led onto an east-facing terrace. The open space was furnished with potted plants covered in night-blooming flowers. An assortment of chairs was arranged around three sides of a small table, with a chaise lounge on the fourth side that faced out over the city. Manisha tangled her fingers with Xander's and led him to the wall at the edge of the large balcony, undeniably enchanted by their surroundings.

It was still dark out, but streaks of orange and pink painted the eastern horizon. She scanned the London cityscape, lit by millions of lights.

"Where are we?" she asked breathlessly. "Mayfair, right?"

She scanned the skyline, finding the distinctive outline of The Shard in the distance, perhaps two or three kilometers away. She craned a bit to see further to the right, where the London Eye and Big Ben could be seen much closer to them.

Xander was a solid presence behind her left shoulder. He lifted an arm, pointing almost straight ahead. "That's Trafalgar Square, with the National Gallery just a bit north of it." His finger tracked a few degrees to the left. "There's Piccadilly Circus… and just beyond that, the theater district."

She stared into the gradually lightening gray dawn for a few minutes before closing her eyes, casting her mind back to memories that both were and were not hers.

"Where was our house before?" she asked. "It was somewhere nearby, wasn't it?"

Xander was quiet for a long moment before speaking. "Yes. It was on Pall Mall."

"I'd like to see it sometime," she said, thinking of the crystal chandeliers and polished wood gleaming in firelight.

"I'm afraid it's long gone." He paused again. "There was a fire."

She let that information soak in. "That's too bad."

"Is it?" She could feel him studying her. "How can you stand to be here with me like this when you remember so much about being Eliza?" he asked eventually.

She shrugged, not sure if she would really be able to make him understand when he was so thoroughly convinced that she should be fleeing from him in horror. Tré had already tried to explain some of it, but perhaps a slightly different perspective would reach him where his friend's words had not.

"I grew up with the idea of reincarnation. It's part of the fabric of my culture and my religion. It's not a shock to me to discover that I've lived other lives. I understand the ways in which I both am and am not Eliza." She paused, choosing her words.

"Her life was tragic in many ways, but there was also joy in it. She found love. She experienced terrible poverty, but also spent time living in comfort and luxury. While it's true she turned a blind eye to the conditions in your mills, she did fight to right other social ills. And in the end, she was able to save someone she loved—even though doing so meant her death."

She heard Xander swallow before he spoke. "She should have been the one to survive. She was better than me. I should have been the one to save her, not the other way around."

Manisha turned her gaze away from the rays of weak London sunlight spilling over the edge of the horizon to look at him.

"Eliza had both light and dark in her soul, just as you did. Just as you and I still do today. Just as everyone does. But, in the same way that I am both the same person and a different person as Eliza, you are both the same man as you were then, and a different man. Now, answer me something."

"What?" His reply sounded guarded.

"How do you treat the people who work in your factories today? What are the conditions like?" She had a feeling she knew the answer, but she wanted to hear him say it.

"I… set up the largest of the production facilities in Romania, after consulting with Tré, who's from the region. Labor costs are cheaper there, so the company is able to offer generous compensation levels for the area without negatively impacting profits. There's also a research and development branch just outside London."

She nodded. "And they're well paid, too, I assume? What about the working conditions?"

"We hire an outside agency to police factory conditions and ensure that no one is tempted to cut corners as a way to inflate reporting numbers."

Manisha cocked her head at him. "So, are you going to make me say it, or can I safely assume that your intelligence is one of the things about you that *hasn't* changed?"

He was quiet for a moment. "Given the number of brain cells I've tried to destroy with illicit chemicals over the decades, I wouldn't presume to comment," he said. That fragile, hopeful look was back behind his eyes.

"Then I'll spell it out, just to be safe," she said. "You're not perfect, because *no one* is perfect. But you're also not the same man you were a hundred years ago. Now… Eliza loved that man. She died for that man. But here in the present, *you* are the one I was drawn to. Everything I've learned says that my wolf should have been drawn to my pack alpha. I should have mated Crank."

His eyes flared brilliant green, a wave of rage and denial that nearly bowled her over erupting from his end of the link. She smiled wryly.

"But I didn't," she said. "My wolf would have died before submitting to another male, because we'd already chosen *you*."

His hands closed on her upper arms as she continued to look over her shoulder at him, holding his gaze. At that moment, the morning sun reached their terrace, peeking through the gaps in the London skyline. Xander caught his breath as the hazy golden light illuminated his handsome face. It reflected in his green eyes as he looked out over the city with something like wonder.

"I keep expecting to wake up from this dream any minute," he said, his voice suspiciously hoarse.

TWENTY-THREE

Xander tore his eyes away from Manisha's earnest face to gaze out across the city he'd called home for far more than a lifetime. Sunlight spilled over the glittering skyscrapers clustered on the banks of the Thames and illuminated the historic buildings around Trafalgar Square, bringing cold glass and stone to life with a soft yellow-orange glow.

How pathetically symbolic it all seemed right now. Christ, look at him. He was in danger of turning into some second-rate Lord Byron, waxing lyrical over the sunrise.

But still, as it touched his deathly pale face with a warm caress, his eyes burned and prickled in a way that had nothing to do with vampire vulnerabilities to day-light. How was it conceivable that he was standing here with his hands wrapped around his soulmate's arms, looking out across the city at dawn?

The problem with things that were too good to be true was that they were generally too good to be true. As soon as you let your guard down and accepted them, something came along to pull the rug out from beneath your feet and dump you straight onto your arse. He'd learned that lesson a long, long time ago on what had turned out to be the worst night of his life.

Manisha was watching him watch the sun, but now she cocked her head at him. Of course, he realized. His shields had been utter shite since he'd awoken chained to a bike rack with werewolf blood running through his veins, so she had probably just heard every last word of his silent musings.

This was confirmed a moment later when she said, "Isn't it better to enjoy the good things while you have them, rather than spend a lifetime frozen in place, worrying that the rug will disappear?"

He looked down at her again, drinking in her beautiful features with the same intense gaze he'd spared earlier for the sunlit city behind her.

"I'm afraid I really wouldn't know," he said. After all, he'd devoted all his spare time and energy chasing fleeting oblivion—the very opposite of living in the moment. In fact, he was reasonably certain that he hadn't spent this much time focusing on strong emotions without fleeing into a chemical haze since the night a demon had torn his soul apart.

Predictably, the thought that came immediately on the heels of that one was, *Christ, I need a drink.*

"Yeah," Manisha said with a wan smile that reminded him just exactly how much she'd gone through in the past few weeks. "You know what? I think drinking right now is a plan I can get behind."

Berating himself for letting his admittedly numerous and deep-seated issues distract him from what *she* needed, he took a deep breath and tried to lighten the mood.

"God help me," he said. "I've just realized that I'll have to stop feeding from alcoholics and drug addicts now, since they can't give meaningful consent. I may need to rethink this entire plan."

She turned in his arms, facing him properly now with her back to the wall of the terrace. "So, you did a lot of that kind of thing before, I take it?"

He snorted. "You could say that. Though as coping mechanisms go, it's a fairly ineffectual one for a vampire, I'm sorry to say. Drugs barely work, and have no long-term effects at all. Which is probably just as well, since I really *wouldn't* have any brain cells left otherwise. Or, you know, a liver."

Looking back, he thought that perhaps the ritual involved in finding an appropriate victim and obtaining their blood had become as much a part of the distraction from his shitty life as the few minutes of resulting buzz. She nodded in understanding.

"But it does help for a little bit?" she asked, and that haunted look was still very much present behind her deep brown eyes.

He shook his head slowly. "I'm not sure how to answer that. I'm still here, and I haven't snapped completely. I suppose it must have done."

She pressed her hand flat against his chest. It was the same gesture she had used earlier in the bedroom, when she'd broken through his mental shields as though they were made of spun glass. He let her walk him backwards, maneuvering him around the table and chairs until the backs of his knees hit the edge of the chaise lounge. Another push, and he toppled into it, looking up at her five-foot-three-inch frame and feeling something start to unravel inside him.

"Stay here," she said, and disappeared into the flat. She emerged a few moments later, examining a bottle of *Sauvignon Blanc* held in her hands. "Since it wasn't refrigerated, can I safely assume this is wine and not plasma? Despite the super-classy screw-top?"

He looked at her curiously. "The wine rack is for guests. It's certified plasma-free, I promise. And it's a common misconception that all good-quality wine uses corks. Those meant to be drunk young often benefit from the airtight seal of a screw top. It helps keep them crisp."

She quirked a brow in acknowledgement. "Huh. Well… live and learn, I guess." She twisted the cap off and sniffed at the contents. "Right—give me a minute, here. It's been a while."

198

Xander watched in mild shock as she tipped the bottle back, her throat working as she swallowed. Perhaps it shouldn't be so surprising, since she still craved solid food as well as blood. But there were other considerations beyond the mere fact of her being able to swallow the stuff without it coming right back up.

"And here I had you pegged as a good little Buddhist girl," he said, trying not to focus too closely on the movement of her throat muscles and what it was doing to his libido.

She lowered the bottle, now about a quarter of the way drained. "You know, some advanced Vajrayana practitioners consider alcohol a valuable tool for assisting in the divestment of the ego," she said solemnly.

"And are you an advanced Vajrayana practitioner?" he asked.

At that, she huffed a breath of harsh laughter. "Uh… *no*. Not even close. Of course, I haven't always been a good little Buddhist girl, either. Between my periodic overindulgence in alcohol and my occasional trysts with boys as a teenager, I'm sure my parents frequently despaired of me."

"Shocking," Xander said in a gently teasing tone, even as the revelation of Manisha's minor bouts of adolescent rebellion made an almost overwhelming ache of fondness surge inside him.

She knocked back another few swallows of the wine and wiped a forearm across her mouth, the movement delightfully unguarded as she paced along the wall of the terrace, looking out over the city.

"They're gone now," she said quietly. "My parents, I mean. And I never had any brothers or sisters, so there's really no one left to disapprove, I suppose." She gave a harsh little snort of bitter amusement. "I think everyone assumes that I ended up as part of Sangye's retinue because I'm some sort of extra-devout, holier-than-thou Buddhist paragon. But, actually, it was because they needed a housekeeper when they arrived in India, I was looking for work at the time, and Jampa and I hit it off."

"Manisha…" he said quietly, feeling the fresh swell of distress building within her mind at the reminder of Sangye and his mother.

She threw the wine back again, swallowing several times, and when she lowered it her voice grew tight. "No one ever thought I'd end up being Sangye's last line of protection. Though if they had, they probably wouldn't have been surprised that I failed at it so spectacularly."

"*Manisha.*" He put more force behind the word that time, and she paused in her pacing, not looking at him as he continued. "We're not giving up on them, you know. Not on Sangye; not on Snag."

What started as a nod became a shake of the head, the sentiment behind it caught somewhere between agreement and disagreement. "I… I know. I know you'll try to find him. Them."

"Of course we will." He fought the urge to go to her, sensing that it was important to let her come to him instead. Though, that sort of psychological give and take was probably much subtler when the person you were with couldn't pluck thoughts straight out of your mind.

She shot him a faintly sheepish glance, the first hint of alcohol-fog becoming visible in her eyes, though her words were still clear and precise.

"Sorry. I guess I was trying to give you a chance to make your escape without it turning into a big drama," she said. "Because my wolf is on edge and I really, really need a break from thinking right now. So, if you're still here when this bottle is finished… well, things are probably going to degenerate into a repeat of the freezer incident."

… and just like that, Xander was hard as a fucking rock.

"Bloody Christ, Manisha. You don't need to finish the bottle if that's your end game. *Come here.*"

She looked immediately reassured, as if she were honestly still hung up on her perceived 'sexual assault of an unwilling vampire' from the other night. Still, she shook her head. "No, wine first. You didn't see how much alcohol the other werewolves could pack away." Her eyes burned into his, golden light kindling in their depths. "Believe me, if this bottle is going to serve two, we'll need all of it."

A noise rumbled up from his chest, the unfamiliar new presence of the wolf inside him rising and stretching in anticipation. "Oh, yes?" His voice went low and rough. "In that case, get your arse over here and you can finish it while I get that robe untied."

A wild, untethered look came over her face, her eyes flaring brilliantly. Xander knew his own matched them, burning green as his fangs pressed into the sides of his cheeks. To his utter relief, she walked over to him without hesitation and sank down, straddling him as he leaned back against the chaise lounge.

He reached along the bond, wanting his own reassurance that this was truly Manisha talking and not the booze. Her mind remained sharp and bright, the wine barely beginning to touch her control.

Told you. It's a werewolf thing, apparently, she said, and he couldn't stop the lazy smile that pulled one corner his lips back, revealing a hint of fang.

So you did, he returned. *But I'm sure you understand why I wanted to see for myself.*

"Yeah," she breathed. "Yeah, I get it." With that, she closed her eyes, and let him see *everything.*

Her memories of the distant past, of the love they'd shared before tragedy struck. Her utter relief at not being alone after the massacre at the warehouse. Her gratitude for his comfort and protection in bringing her back to his home to care for her when she was on the verge of physical and emotional collapse. How it had felt to drink his blood, and the jolt she'd felt upon realizing that not only wasn't he disgusted—he was taking pleasure from it. The blanket of warm contentment that had settled over her when he convinced her to shift form with him, and watched over her while she curled up to sleep as the wolf.

How every precious, fleeting moment of respite she'd experienced since escaping the werewolves had taken place in his embrace.

Right now, Xander wanted to wrap her up in his arms and never let go. He wanted to deliver Sangye to her unharmed, and spirit both of them away to some magical place where Bael could never touch them again. He wanted to drink from her veins. He wanted to feed their mingled blood right back to her, and fuck her until neither one of them could remember their own names.

Yes, she thought, sounding young and unguarded. *I want all that. I want to forget. Please... can't we both just forget for a little while?*

"Manisha, love," he said, cupping her cheek in his hand. "I am the world's foremost expert on forgetting for a little while. Now—why don't you get back to drinking, and we'll go on from there."

She did, and he immediately turned his attention toward doing everything in his power to distract her. Happily for him, she still wore only the terrycloth robe he'd draped around her after waking her earlier to speak to the others. Xander hooked a finger in the fold covering her left breast and drew it slowly to the side, his fingertip brushing along the olive-toned skin that was revealed, inch by inch.

Manisha wanted to forget, and Xander found that he wanted nothing more than to give her whatever she desired. If that meant giving himself permission for a few hours not to obsess over the darkness that surrounded them... if it meant not questioning how he had somehow gone from being a miserable sod to the luckiest man alive… well, so be it. She wasn't the only one who needed to set down the heavy weight on her shoulders for a bit.

Manisha went still as his finger trailed over the swell of her breast, a soft noise emerging from her lips. When the smooth globe was revealed in its entirety, she muttered something in Hindi and threw back the bottle, chugging the remaining contents without ceremony. Xander's smile grew wider as he allowed all the other problems swirling around them to fall away.

"Better now?" he asked, feeling through the bond as Manisha's muscles finally began to relax, the wine smoothing away some of the sharp edges of her thoughts. It probably wouldn't last any longer for her than it ever did for him, but he fully intended them both to be distracted for other reasons by the time it wore off.

"Promises, promises," she breathed, melting into him a little further. The bottle clattered to the terrace floor, glass ringing as it rolled a short distance and fetched up against a random piece of furniture.

TWENTY-FOUR

Xander closed his fingers around one end of the belt holding the robe shut at her waist and tugged, loosening the knot until the soft garment fell open, revealing more dusky flesh.

"One more thing," he told her in a low voice. "This is not, in fact, going to be a repeat of the so-called *freezer incident*. If you think I'm going to be done with you in mere minutes when we have *hours* to ourselves, then—closet 'bad girl' or not—you lack imagination."

She shivered against him, the tiny movement sending an answering frisson up his spine.

"I can't help noticing you're still sober," she said. "Why is that? I didn't chug an entire bottle of screw-top wine for my health, you know."

Good god. Could this woman be any more perfect?

A brief brush of thoughts confirmed that she was well aware of what she was offering, and also revealed a tangle of confused memories from the night of the full moon—his fangs sinking into her neck; the explosion of pleasure-pain that drove the wolf wild. That need to be held in place and marked by her mate, combined now with the newly risen vampire instinct to revel in blood.

Nature, red in tooth and claw? he thought. *Christ, Manisha, you're killing me, here.*

Bending her backwards, he dipped his head and caught a dusky nipple between his teeth, letting his fangs scrape along the tender skin around her areola without piercing it. Her flesh tasted as succulent as he'd known it would, and he marveled now that he'd ever found the smell of werewolf anything other than intoxicating.

Her head fell back and she groaned, the sound rushing straight to his cock. Xander sucked on the pebbled point, more of his control falling by the wayside as she arched, trying to press her breast harder against his mouth. The point of one fang slipped into delicate skin, a drop of blood welling up.

The taste exploded across his tongue, and even without the wine she'd drunk, it would have been pure ambrosia. He drew harder on her breast, not deepening the tiny puncture, but instead reveling in the slow tease of her blood squeezing out a droplet at a time. She let out a weak cry, her palms splayed against his chest. When he scraped a fingernail across the painfully hard point of her other nipple, her fingers curled into claws. The half-moons of her nails pricked his skin through the fabric of his shirt, waking every nerve.

His cock was trapped between them, and he hummed around her breast when she rolled her hips, trying to get friction. Xander let go of her nipple, ignoring her moan of disappointment as he lapped at the little dribble of blood that trickled down from the puncture he'd left.

It didn't heal immediately, making him cognizant of the fact that vampire and werewolf blood still interfered with each other in some ways. And while he had absolutely no problem with ending up covered in bites and claw marks at the end of this, he didn't want her to end up a bloody mess of wounds as well… even if that little sluggishly bleeding smear of red on her chest *was* driving him slowly insane.

Sometimes, he decided, the old clichés were still the best. With that in mind, he kissed his way up from her nipple to her collarbone, lifting one of his hands to tangle in the thick, waist-length hair he couldn't seem to get enough of, and lowered his other hand to cup her thigh.

The grip allowed him to ease her up from his lap until she was no longer rutting on him—and, more importantly, until he could get his fingertips against the slick heat of her center.

Jesus, Manisha, you're soaked, he observed silently, teasing her wet folds with light strokes up and down her length. Meanwhile, he nibbled his way up her throat, pausing over a thrumming vein that smelled and tasted like paradise. He let his fingers explore her sex while his lips and tongue explored the side of her neck, searching out the perfect place to strike.

She shuddered, trying to press onto both his fingers and his fangs at the same time. He kept both touches light, right up until the moment her grasping fingers clenched at his shirt and yanked it apart, popping buttons loose as she tore it open.

Well, all right, then, he thought. Though, in her defense, sometimes teasing really was overrated.

With a low hiss of warning, he dragged her head to the side and sank his fangs into her neck at the same moment he thrust two fingers inside her sex, pressing in to the third knuckle. Alcohol-infused blood flowed into his mouth, and tight heat clamped around his fingers. Manisha gasped raggedly, her hands tangling in the fabric of his abused shirt. Xander swallowed the heady liquid gushing over his tongue, feeling the feedback loop of their mental connection swell under the sensations they were both experiencing.

He stroked her pulsing inner walls, pulling out to circle her clit with slick fingertips before thrusting in again, reveling in the sensations coming through the bond. He tried to send back the exquisite feeling of her blood slipping down his throat; their life forces mingling.

Only when her dizzy climb reached its summit and left her poised on the edge of release did he drag up his battered mental shields, not wanting to spend in his trousers like a virgin the moment her climax hit. Even so, his cock twitched and throbbed almost painfully when her body went rigid, her walls fluttering around his fingers. He coaxed her through the orgasm, drawing things out as long as he could.

The flow of blood from her neck was slowing now, even as the alcohol in it started to hit him, quieting the endless confusion of circling thoughts that plagued him so much of the time. He pulled away from her throat and stilled his fingers inside her, enjoying the last weak quivers as her muscles worked around him.

She sagged into his embrace, and he steadied her, soaking up the boneless feeling of contentment flowing along the bond, mixing and merging with the buzz of blood and wine. Apparently, this was an effective way to spare his trouser fly the same tragic end his shirt had suffered, because rather than ripping it open, she fumbled at the closures with clumsy fingers.

"Need you," she murmured against his neck, making the fine hairs on his nape stand at attention. "Need more… need all of you…"

He slipped his fingers out of her warm depths and helped her get the damned trousers out of the way, lifting his hips enough to slide them down and free his cock without dislodging her from his lap.

Taking a bare instant to be thankful that he didn't generally bother with underwear, he lifted her hips and impaled her on his aching cock. Just as it had the morning after the full moon, the simple act of sliding into her body slotted something in his life into place, making him feel whole in a way he had never thought to experience again after the agony of his soul being rent in two.

Physical pleasure was a dim flicker of candlelight compared to the blazing bonfire of reunion with his soul's true mate.

Oh, yes. Her mental words were a sigh of relief. *Finally…*

They didn't even move. They just lay there, sprawled on the chaise lounge with her legs wrapped around him, and his arms wrapped around her.

"*Manisha,*" he breathed.

As he had suspected might be the case after he'd drunk so deeply from her, he felt her hunger begin to grow through the link. It started as a feeling of emptiness low in her belly that tangled with her banked sexual desire and grew into an ache. With his cock surrounded by her heat and her lips brushing the half-healed bite on his neck from her first feeding in the shower, the anticipation of what was to come was as much pleasure as agony.

He didn't try to rush her, instead rolling his head back to bare his throat to her as her lips and teeth toyed with the tender wound. Then and there, he decided that, as long as being some kind of fucked-up vampire/werewolf hybrid meant he could wear the marks of her fangs on his body for the rest of eternity, it was bloody well worth it.

Eventually, her hunger overcame her drowsy, post-orgasmic lassitude, and sharp teeth sank into his ravaged flesh. His hips jerked deeper into her of their own accord, and all thoughts of a lazy, hours-long shag flew away into the London morning. She ground against his lap and swallowed him down, taking back the blood he'd pulled from her earlier, and then some.

Her feeding was messy and wild—he could feel his blood dribbling down in ribbons from the place where her lips were fastened around his throat. Any human unlucky enough to stumble upon the scene would doubtless have been horrified. The two of them writhed together, Xander arching up to meet her thrusts while their upper bodies slid together, slick with blood. He managed to worm a hand in between them so he could palm the breast he'd nicked earlier, red staining his fingers as he pinched and plucked at her nipple.

He'd been absolutely right the first time she'd fed from him—the lightheaded feeling as she drained him really was sublime with his cock buried inside her.

"It's all yours," he said, eyes open and staring at the white clouds and blue sky above as the sun shone down on them. "Take all of it... all of me..."

In what seemed like no time at all, her movements grew desperate and her walls clamped around him. Release coiled hot and insistent at the base of his spine, exploding outward when she grunted against the abused skin of his throat and clamped her jaws into him *hard*.

Coming with her while his mental shields were down was almost too much—the London sky went hazy and dark, his brain losing the metaphorical arm-wrestling match over the remaining blood in his body to his pulsing prick.

Which only went to show that his body, at least, had its priorities firmly in the right place.

The feeling of fangs retracting from his neck brought him back to a modicum of awareness some unknown amount of time later. Manisha was a soft, sleepy weight against him. A low, pleasant hum like white noise suffused the bond, empty of everything except sexual afterglow.

The decision whether or not to move seemed to take on a deeply significant weight, and Xander eventually compromised by swinging his legs up so he was lying full-length along the chaise with Manisha draped over him like a blanket. She murmured some sort of wordless, approving noise and settled herself a little more fully onto him.

For the first time in longer than he cared to remember, Xander took a deep breath and slipped into a contented doze, without a single thought for anything but the present moment.

TWENTY-FIVE

Manisha awoke slowly to the feeling of rhythmic swaying. She curled into the strong arms holding her, and realized with drowsy curiosity that she was being carried bridal-style.

"Mmm... Xander?" she asked sleepily. "Wha's happening?"

Lips brushed her forehead. "A shower, followed by bed, I should think. How are you?"

She took stock. *Good,* she decided. *Don't want to have to face everything yet.*

All you're facing right now is a spray of warm water, he sent back. A mental curl of amusement brushed at her awareness. *Come now... did I say I was done with you yet?*

A lazy flush of desire rose from her belly despite what they'd done earlier. She relaxed, letting the wolf have control again. Content to set aside human concerns for a few more hours, or however long they had left before reality once more intruded. In the meantime, this fantasy world of luxury and sex would do... just fine.

Xander set her on her feet on the heated tile floor of the master bathroom. She let her robe slide down her arms, feeling dried blood flake on her skin. Xander busied himself running the water to just the right temperature, and she busied herself by coming up behind him and easing the shirt off his shoulders.

He let his arms drop so she could get it off, then he turned to face her. Still letting the wolf lead, she licked a stripe along the trail of mostly dried blood leading down from his throat to his chest, while her hands unfastened his trousers and slid them down. They pooled on the floor, and he stepped out of them.

He was well built without being muscle bound, she realized—beautifully proportioned with a smooth, hairless chest and defined arms and legs. His skin was strikingly pale even after the time they'd spent in the morning sun. She realized with a possessive lurch that his pallor was probably due to the fact that a good portion of his blood was currently running in her veins, not his.

"Finally got you properly naked," she said, looking him up and down with satisfaction, noting that blood loss hadn't stopped his erection from rising to half-mast already. "It took long enough."

A smile twitched at one corner of his mouth. "The wolf was naked last night. Don't be species-ist."

She tried to smile back, but even now, outside pressures were starting to swirl back in as she woke up properly.

"Oh, no," he said, opening the door and ushering her into the familiar steamy shower. "None of that, now. Soap. Shampoo. Cunnilingus. More shagging. Sleep."

That shocked a short laugh from her. "Bit sure of yourself, aren't you?" she asked, as he crowded her up against the wall.

"Not in the least," he replied easily. "I'm still expecting to wake up from this any minute, love. Which is all the more reason to take advantage while I can."

He poured soap into his hands, forgoing a washcloth in favor of sliding his palms over her upper body directly, lathering her shoulders, arms, and breasts with firm strokes. Manisha let her head fall back against the glass, relief flooding her as her mind once again went warm, pliant, and empty.

As it had the first time he'd brought her in here to wash the blood from her body, the sudsy water ran rusty for a few moments before growing clear. The tiny puncture on her breast was scabbed over, though it hadn't disappeared yet. The bite mark on her neck was still tender, and he washed around the edges carefully.

Apparently, however, being a werewolf and/or vampire was giving her a kink for pain, because the sting of soap against the fang marks drew a high-pitched whine from her throat, which tailed into a needy moan.

Xander breathed out sharply in response, his hands going still. "You know what? Fuck shampoo. Shampoo is vastly overrated."

And then he was crashing to his knees in front of her, dragging one of her legs over his shoulder and steadying her with a rock-solid grip on her hip to keep her upright. A moment later, his mouth was on her sex, and no teenage tryst with an awkward, fumbling boy had *ever* prepared her for this.

I should fucking well hope not, he sent along the link, his mental voice a growl. Manisha squeezed her eyes shut and panted. Hot water pelted her, running in rivulets down her body to the place where a cool tongue and sharp teeth methodically shattered her into a million pieces.

-o-o-o-

Xander made good on his promise to make her forget everything for a few hours. They had sex on the bed. They had sex in the kitchen. They had sex in the jetted Japanese soaking tub. They shifted into wolf form and had rough and dirty animal sex on his expensive Turkish rug... at which point Manisha discovered what knotting was and why it was basically the best thing ever.

By the time Xander finally tucked her against his side in the massive bed and pulled the elegant black and gray comforter over them, Manisha was one huge swirling muddle of happy, exhausted endorphins, and she slept the sleep of the dead—or should that be the *un-dead?*—for hours.

She awoke to find herself still wrapped around Xander, who was propped up against a pile of pillows drinking one-handed from a bottle of blood while she drooled all over his opposite shoulder.

"Evening, love," he greeted, and offered her the bottle once she'd peeled herself off of him enough to roll up on an elbow. "Breakfast?"

She took the bottle and drank from it, noticing on the first swallow that she was developing a decided preference for Xander's blood over bottled blood. She also noticed that while she was definitely hungry, it wasn't the same sort of mindless animal hunger she'd felt the last few times.

"You're already getting stronger," he said, presumably in response to her mental observations. "Gaining control."

"Hmm," she replied, not really up to much more conversation. Was blood going to be her new coffee now? The kick she needed before she could face the day or hold an intelligent conversation?

She drank some more and offered it back, but Xander waved her off, indicating he'd had enough. Shrugging, she tipped it up and let the last few swallows slide down her throat. When she was done, he took the empty bottle and stretched over to set it on the bedside table. When his green eyes returned to her, there was a hint of wariness behind them.

"Just to be perfectly clear and aboveboard, is this going to be the point when you realize what you've done and run screaming for the hills?" he asked.

She blinked at him. "Why?" she asked cautiously. "Are you hoping I will so it saves you having to do it? I get that it could be awkward since this is, you know, *your flat* and everything."

The tension ran out of his shoulders and he flopped back down, drawing her with him until she was once more curled up with her head on his shoulder.

"No," he said. "No, I definitely wasn't hoping for that."

It wasn't yet second nature for her to look inward and feel what was running through his mind, but it occurred to her once he'd spoken. Indeed, his relief across the bond was palpable.

"Okay, good," she said. "I've got nowhere to run and it's just about the last thing I want to do right now anyway." She swallowed. "This really is kind of awkward, isn't it?"

His hand came up to cradle the back of her head, stroking her scalp in a way that made her want to slide right back down into sleep. "I think it will stop being awkward if we can both accept that even though we're a mess, we'll be less of a mess if we face things together."

The tidal wave of relief that swamped her at the idea of letting herself become part of this bizarre vampire family of his took her by surprise. "I'd like that," she said, choking a bit on the words.

"Oh, thank god," he said in a rush, his voice a bit hoarse as well. He cleared his throat. "Well, then. The others will probably show up in an hour or so, and we'll plan our next move properly now that everyone has had a chance to rest."

She nodded. "Does that mean there's time for a quickie in the shower first?"

His huff of laughter was silent, but she felt his chest move beneath her cheek.

"Fucking hell, Manisha. If this is what positive karma looks like, I must have accumulated it when I was either too drunk or too stoned to remember afterward what good deeds I'd performed." He stroked a strand of hair back from her face and hooked it over her ear. "I expect there's time. And if there's not, the others will just have to wait on us. It's not as though I haven't been subjected to their near-constant shagging over the past few months. Turnabout, and all that."

She rolled into a sitting position, letting the sheets slide down. "Tomorrow, I want to try to contact my relatives in Swansea. Will you come, in case things go badly and I need to make them forget?"

His fingertips trailed over the tender place on her neck where his fangs had pierced her earlier. "Try to keep me away."

She smiled as he rolled onto an elbow, facing her.

"I should also talk to a few of my people privately about blood," he continued. "People from the company who I think we can trust. Starting with the pimply kid down in the IT department who's a conspiracy theorist. I bet he'll lap this story up with a spoon. I'd... like you to come with me for that, as well."

She smiled, the expression feeling genuine for the first time in days, if not weeks. "Do I look like someone who would miss the chance for a tour of a vampire-owned solar panel company?"

The corners of his eyes crinkled. "You look... *beautiful*. That's how you look. Now come on, love—stop being a layabout. There's a shower through that door with our names on it, and we'll have guests to scandalize before long."

Epilogue

(A silent conversation in the dark.)

Why did you surrender yourself to the demon, Elder?

Silence.

He'll destroy you.

Perhaps, child.

I'm so hungry. It aches…

Then feed.

But I don't want to.

You must.

Why? Why Must I?

For strength.

What about your strength?

Silence.

Elder? What about your strength?

My strength does not lie here. It resides elsewhere. When the time is right, I will have whatever strength I require.

Are you sure?

I am sure.

Rustling. Glowing eyes in the dark.

Yes. That's better. Feed now, child. Don't concern yourself with me.

End of Book Four

CIRCLE OF BLOOD, BOOK FIVE

LOVER'S ATONEMENT

R. A. STEFFAN & JAELYNN WOOLF

ONE

There was a special kind of clarity that came from knowing you were one tiny slip away from certain death. As a CIA undercover operative and former US Navy SEAL who'd completed multiple hazardous missions over the years, Chan Wei Yong had spent enough time walking along that razor's edge to recognize its dangerous caress.

Now, he stood at the back of the raised stage set up in front of the Buddhist Thean Hou Temple in Kuala Lumpur, Malaysia. Chan looked out over the assembled crowd as the monk standing at the front of the stage whipped them into a frenzy of anti-Muslim hatred.

"It is time for followers of the true religion to rise up! We must cleanse this city of the infectious parasites that have been sucking us dry for so long… this is our domain now, and we must claim what we deserve!"

Thunderous roars of approval accompanied the monk's words. The crowd stood in the torch-lit courtyard, naturally forming little clusters of people within the larger pattern of the mob. As the shouts died down, disgruntled murmuring remained audible under the speaker's booming voice. The onlookers almost seemed to sway together, as though mesmerized by the words pouring across the open space of the courtyard.

The natural reverberation from the temple and the surrounding palm trees magnified every word the monk spoke. It was a fascinating phenomenon that allowed him to speak powerfully to large groups without the use of electronic amplification equipment.

It also allowed Chan to record the assemblies discreetly from his place in the shadows, using the wire hidden his sleeve. He stood straight, his shoulders back—his dark gaze looking out from a stony face. Every now and then he moved his eyes over the assembled people, searching the crowd for anyone with malicious intent. He needed to maintain his cover, after all. And his cover right now was the role of a hired security man, paid to protect the self-proclaimed warrior monk, Tengku Asal.

As ever, the danger of possible discovery made Chan feel more alive, even with the knowledge that his death could fall upon him at any moment. He was focused. Centered. His attention, sharp and steady.

It might have been that same craving for danger which had kept him in the service of the Central Intelligence Agency for so long—and in the Navy SEALs, prior to that. It was as though risking his life made everything feel more real to him. More immediate. As long as he was risking his life, he could set aside his feelings of failure and self-loathing for all the shitty things he'd done in the past.

Focus on the moment. That was his motto these days. Because when you stopped worrying about the here-and-now and let your thoughts wander down the path of might-have-beens...

He blinked, bringing himself back to the present, the tightening of his lips the only sign that his focus had wavered momentarily. *No. I am not going down that rabbit hole tonight.*

Tengku's voice still rang out, whipping across the crowd. "*...and the Divine spirit within us will wash these lands clean with the blood of our enemies! I call on each of you tonight to fulfill your oath to me. Give yourselves in honor of the nation that we will build from the ashes! We will watch the bastard offspring of the evil that has overrun this country burn alive, and they will know death at our hands!*"

Chan very carefully held in the sigh that wanted to escape. Zealots were the same the world over.

Ten points for enthusiasm, he thought. *Minus several hundred for logic and rationality.*

He'd been deep undercover in Malaysia for almost eighteen months now, serving Tengku as his joint chief of security. Chan had moved up the ranks of the so-called Brotherhood of the Cleansing Flame thanks to an informant who'd vouched for him. Shortly after Chan was made co-chief of security, that informant had died of a mysterious illness. Chan would never know for sure, of course, but he strongly suspected poison. The man had seemed perpetually haunted and fearful whenever he and Chan met—as though he were always looking over his shoulder.

This life isn't for everyone. You have to watch your back every moment, and if you can't handle that, you have no business playing the game.

To be truthful, the informant's loss hadn't hit Chan all that hard. As cold as it sounded, it was simply one less loose end—one less person who might possibly blow his cover within the ranks of the Brotherhood. It saved him having to deal with the man at a later date, and now no one in Malaysia knew Chan's identity. His cover was deep enough to withstand almost any scrutiny... unless he fucked up, of course. Then all bets were off.

The Malaysian government might have known that the US had a man on the ground within the Brotherhood, but they could no sooner identify him than they could lay hands on Tengku. And Chan had no doubt whatsoever that the authorities would *love* to lay hands on Tengku. Unfortunately, they knew full well that he and his cult were gaining in popularity by leaps and bounds. At this point, with all the instability and political scandals going on in the region, taking Tengku could well spark rioting that would tear the country apart.

So, with few other options, the Malaysians simply watched and waited, hoping that Tengku's cult wouldn't continue to grow at its current pace—all their hopes riding on one unknown American agent in the midst of the nest of lunatics.

And didn't it just sound completely ridiculous when you put it in those terms? They couldn't even be bothered to embed their own damned spies in their own damned back yard... or at least, they hadn't done so as far as Chan knew. If nothing else, a bit more international cooperation here would lessen the load of paperwork Chan faced once he returned home. *If* he returned home.

"The government soldiers will soon be coming for us!" called a voice from the crowd, interrupting Chan's thoughts. "We must take care, my brothers!"

He gave the speaker a closer look and moved strategically forward, ready to protect Tengku if the guy made a move toward the stage. Almost everyone in the crowd was either a Chinese national or a naturalized Buddhist immigrant, including the man who had spoken.

"And even if the soldiers do not come, the Malay Muslims will fight to the death, just like their brothers in the Middle East!" the guy continued, gesturing with both hands.

"We will not bow to those swine," Tengku replied in a deceptively calm voice. "Come forward and join me, brother."

Chan watched as the man blanched, clearly not expecting to be called up to the stage. He shuffled forward and stepped onto the raised platform with Tengku, looking like someone who was abruptly and seriously reconsidering his life choices.

"What is your name?" The monk asked, placing a hand on the speaker's shoulder.

Chan could see the man swallow hard. "Loy Cho."

"Why do you doubt the cause, Loy Cho?"

Loy chewed on his lower lip, obviously sensing the danger in Tengku's voice. "I'm... merely concerned for your safety, Honored One, and the safety of all the Brotherhood."

Chan could tell Loy was lying through his teeth, but he did not speak. He moved closer to Tengku, ready to intervene if Loy tried to attack the monk physically.

"Such deception," Tengku purred. Slowly, he withdrew a dagger from his waistband. Loy jerked backwards even as Chan stepped forward, grasping his shoulders from behind to hold him in place.

"You will pay the price for your lack of faith," Tengku whispered. Menace radiated from him, palpable in the still night air. No one in the crowd moved or made a sound. They scarcely seemed to be breathing.

With a flash of the blade, Tengku ripped open Loy's shirt with the knife, nicking his chest superficially with the tip of the blade. The wound was not life threatening, yet blood streamed from the shallow gash.

The man gasped and tried to pull away. Chan tightened his grip and hissed for the man to remain still.

Tengku paced back and forth, a predator toying with his prey. He fingered the blade in his hands, tapping it gently on his palm. It left bloodstains on his skin.

Using the tip of the knife, Tengku flicked the shredded pieces of fabric away from the man's chest, exposing more of his flesh. The heat of fear was rising all over Loy's body, and Chan could feel sweat forming on his skin under his grip. Loy flinched away every time the knife was brought towards him.

"I think he is beginning to learn, don't you?" Tengku asked Chan.

Chan knew better than to respond. Instead, he maintained his flat stare at the leader, as any faithful security chief would do. Tengku smiled and shook his head.

"All work and no play, Chan?" he asked.

The western proverb was stilted and out of place in the Malaysian dialect of Mandarin Tengku was speaking, and Chan was too old a dog to fall for such an obvious ploy. He allowed a slight expression of confusion to pass across his features before they settled back into a blank stare.

"Oh, never mind," Tengku said with a wave of his hand. He turned back to his victim, who used the momentary interruption to speak.

"Honored One," he croaked, his voice harsh, "I will never doubt the cause again. I meant nothing by my questions, I was simply seeking to ensure that everyone remains safe. I hear rumors on the streets day and night; I thought I could serve you in this warning!"

The monk raised an eyebrow. "Rumors? And what exactly are the contents of these *rumors*, my conflicted friend?"

The man swallowed, and Chan could feel him trembling. "People speak of government crackdowns. They are saying that the police may start mass arrests in some of the Buddhist enclaves."

"What do you think, Chan?" Tengku asked. "Should we believe him?"

Chan stared into Tengku's eyes, his expression betraying neither worry nor any other emotion.

"Caution is always prudent," he replied, keeping his voice low.

"Well said," Tengku acknowledged. He turned back towards Loy, who was now sinking towards the ground as his knees went weak. Tengku raised the knife, and Loy let out a terrified squeak.

"Never question the goals of the Brotherhood again," Tengku said, and struck a crushing blow across the man's jaw with the hilt.

Chan felt the strike reverberate through Loy's body, but made no attempt to support him as he fell. Rather, he allowed the man to stagger out of his grasp and collapse onto the wooden platform. Another man, his hands raised in a gesture of peace, inched forward and grabbed Loy's arm.

"Respect to you, Honored One," the man quavered, his voice strained as he pulled his comrade off the edge of the stage and led him away, staggering.

The crowd parted and let the two men pass, recoiling as though they were diseased… as though their treachery might be contagious. Clearly, no one else wanted to incur Tengku's wrath today.

"No more doubt, my friends," Tengku insisted, his voice rich with persuasion.

With that, he lifted his hands in farewell and departed the stage. Chan followed a few steps behind him, scanning the crowd of people nearby. Tengku's entourage, or his henchmen as Chan preferred to think of them, followed as well. They smiled and waved, basking in the reflected glory from their fearless leader.

After Chan escorted Tengku safely to his quarters in the temple and ensured that guards were stationed to watch the door, he was ordered to return to the large building nearby, where the Brotherhood maintained most of their operations. The place had originally been a condominium complex one street over from the temple, though it had since been repurposed as an office building before being abandoned completely.

Chan had already reported its location to his US handlers. Should Tengku start making attacks on a larger scale, they were contemplating a joint mission with the Malaysian government to attack the facility, just as the unfortunate Loy Cho had tried to warn. A military operation so close to the historic temple grounds would no doubt incite outrage among the populace, but with luck, collateral damage would be minimal and there would be few civilian casualties.

Chan, of course, was in considerably more danger than most in the event of such a strike. He accepted this knowledge. He had come to terms with the idea of his own death years ago. Right after his divorce, in fact.

Ever since then, he'd found that living had lost quite a bit of its appeal.

Two

 amn it, Chan chided himself. This was not even *close* to a good time to rehash that particular part of the past. He tried to push the memories of his wife and daughter back down into the darkness, where they belonged. Nevertheless, as he walked along the dimly lit street, he couldn't stop his mind from replaying the memory of the woman he'd pledged to love, honor, and cherish climbing into a car and driving away forever. All because Chan had done something unforgiveable.

He shook his head sharply. *For better or worse, for richer or poorer, in sickness and health. Forsaking all others.*

What a goddamned joke.

The aftermath of the divorce was when he'd decided to accept a position with the CIA as an undercover operative. Because at least that way if he died, his benefits would go to his daughter and she would be well provided for by Uncle Sam. God knew that was a better future than he'd been able to manage for her on his own.

And if he lived…?

Honestly, Chan never considered that option too closely. It was probably only a matter of time before he was compromised—his cover blown during a delicate operation, to fatal effect. Why should he plan for a life well lived when he'd already destroyed every possibility of a happy ending?

That was the real reason he wasn't afraid of death. Why subject another operative to the most dangerous missions, when Chan himself was not worthy to walk the earth?

Focus, Chan. This is the kind of self-indulgent shit that leads to mistakes. He could practically hear his grizzled old CIA trainer speaking in his ear, giving him a hard shake of the shoulder for good measure.

He let out an audible sigh as the yellow lights of the complex came into view. Two of his men stood blocking the gate as he approached, but they immediately leapt back when they recognized him.

He'd trained the Brotherhood's guards to expect harsh punishment for every mistake. For a band of guerillas with no formal military background whatsoever, they were remarkably easy to mold. Several of them could have enjoyed very fruitful careers in their country's army, he suspected, had they not chosen the path of extremism instead.

"As you were," Chan murmured as he walked through the open gate. The two security guards nodded to him respectfully as he passed, then resumed their positions near the gate, watching the dark road leading into their base.

Chan had been informed that the Brotherhood had recently taken several more hostages, including one American reporter who'd been snooping around for information regarding recent terrorist bombings. Chan was confident that Tengku was behind the bombing attacks, but he knew better than to ask for outright confirmation. His job was merely security within the complex and the nearby temple. Any intel beyond the day-to-day running of the Brotherhood, he needed to seek out on his own — *discretely.*

He walked into the ground floor of the large building and made a right turn. There, he entered a dingy office with multiple computers crammed onto dated desks. He shut the door behind him, hearing the click echo all around the room. As he flipped on the light, he was startled to see another one of Tengku's lackeys sitting with his feet up on a desk in the corner, waiting.

Chan covered his reaction and betrayed no hint of surprise as he surveyed his co-chief of security with a steely stare.

Time seemed frozen for a moment before Chan broke the stillness. He pulled out his battered wallet and a ring of keys from his pocket, tossing them down on a nearby desk.

"You're here late," he observed as he sat down across from the other man.

"I've been waiting for you," his co-chief replied.

"What do you want, Pula? Just here for a pleasant midnight chat?"

Pula smiled, more of a sneer than a look of pleasure. "I wanted to brief you before I left. There are some new security measures that Tengku wants enacted."

"Funny," Chan replied in an icy tone, "I just left Tengku and he made no mention of anything like that."

Pula glared at him for a long beat. There was no love lost between the two of them, and Chan suspected that the entire point of having two security chiefs was so that they could keep an eye on each other. It was practically Rule One for cults—make sure everyone was spying on everyone else.

"I believe it is the wish of the Honored One that we address this project together," Pula said eventually. "I was given the information and instructed to pass it along to you."

"Right," Chan shot back, "so, get to it. What is this new plan, exactly?"

Pula massaged his chin with one hand, a thoughtful gesture.

"Tengku is beginning to fear that our ranks have been infiltrated," Pula finally said, his tone businesslike.

Chan did not react outwardly.

"Oh, really?" he asked Pula. "What gives him that impression?"

"The government often seems to be one step ahead of us. That is all I am permitted to say."

Chan shrugged. "That's true enough. I suppose it makes sense. Does he have any thoughts on who the traitor might be?"

Pula considered him again. "He's got a vague idea."

After several moments of silence where Chan looked at Pula expectantly, the other man finally continued, "We have a local arms dealer that we do business with sometimes. He's been off the grid for several weeks. The last time he met with the Brotherhood, he was given very generic information about some of our targets so that he could help us acquire the weaponry that would be most effective."

Chan raised an eyebrow. "Well, that was stupid. Surely Tengku would never…"

"*No*," Pula interrupted, his voice sharp. "Of course not. You should be whipped for even suggesting such a thing. This was a security breach by the low-level contact person who met with the dealer."

"So, you think this contact person could be the leak?"

Pula shrugged. "That's what Tengku believes. It's our job to tighten security within the ranks to prevent any further… *slips*."

"And the suspected mole has already been dealt with, I presume?" Chan asked, already knowing the answer.

Pula smirked. "He will no longer complicate matters."

Chan leaned back in his chair and cupped his hands behind his head. He felt his back pop in several places as he stretched tight muscles.

"Well, at least we aren't stuck dealing with a manhunt," he finally said shrugging his shoulders and trying to loosen up. He did not want his internal tension to alert Pula that anything was amiss.

"Agreed. This breach of security is to go no further, however."

"Understood," Chan said with a nod. "So, what is Tengku proposing?"

Pula quickly outlined a new plan that would further isolate the Brotherhood's prisoners and hostages. They would only have contact with a small number of trusted guards, and all supplies would be delivered to an off-site location before being brought in on the opposite side of the compound from the cells. The security of the hostages was now one of Tengku's highest priorities.

"So, any questions?" Pula concluded.

"No. That all seems quite clear," Chan answered.

It made perfect tactical sense, too, but inside his heart was sinking. This would make getting information even more difficult than it had been before. To date, Chan had been relying on loose-lipped cult members discussing rumors and plans. Tengku was a master at keeping any incriminating documents or other hard evidence close at hand. If that had been his only source of intel, Chan would have had to pry the information out of Tengku's cold, dead fingers.

Now there was an appealing mental image.

Chan chewed the inside of his cheek. He would have to contact his handler soon. He was overdue getting her a report on the status of Tengku's plans. The CIA was also hoping to learn the numbers and identities of the hostages.

Pula stood up with a grunt and headed toward the door of the office. Chan got up as well.

"You just got here. Where are you headed?" Pula asked, his voice growing suspicious.

"I make it a habit to do a security walk of the building every couple of hours. That way, I always know what's going on and where my men are. While they, in turn, realize that I might appear at any time."

"Ah," Pula replied with a knowing look. "Well, I'll leave you to it, then."

He left by the same door through which Chan had originally entered.

Sighing in relief, Chan walked quietly to the other door, which led to a large storage room. At the far end, there was a door opening onto a flight of stairs that led down to an old basement bunker. It was originally built as a storm shelter for the condominium residents, but it had become very useful to the Brotherhood as a prison for their most valuable hostages and dangerous enemies.

Chan pitied the poor souls who were kept down here. The ones held in the main part of the building had it bad enough, but these people? They'd been sent down here to disappear, he suspected. He'd spent an inordinate amount of time recently trying to figure out their identities without tipping off the Brotherhood that he was more interested than he should be.

Now, though, it was time to stop fucking around. He crept down the steps, exhaling silently each time one of his feet landed—an old SEAL trick that helped him move around without making a sound. The darkness in the hallway was absolute, so he flipped the light switch that he knew was located on his right side, from his previous expeditions down here.

The single bulb burned yellow in the center of the large space, casting a hazy light all around. The prisoners were held in small cells along the edges of the room. Iron bars formed the front of the cages. The sharp smell of fecal matter and decay hit his nose like an assault. Checking the gag response that threatened him, Chan narrowed his eyes and took inventory.

As a highly trained observer, Chan immediately began cataloguing basic information about each of the prisoners, along with any changes to their numbers. He recognized several of them from his previous trips. Some of them had been held here for months now. He'd gotten a few names during that time, but the basement was under constant surveillance, so he couldn't speak freely. Unless they volunteered the information while trying to wheedle him into letting them out or getting messages to their loved ones, it would be too suspicious for him to speak with them.

At the back of the room, a prone figure caught his eye. Since he'd joined the Brotherhood more than a year ago, that particular cell had remained empty. It seemed ominous to him that the figure inside did not stir in response to his approach as the others did. For the most part, his journey down the row of cells was met with blank stares and shuffling limbs. A few of the newer prisoners still maintained enough spirit to glare suspiciously at him, clearly fearing that they were about to be subjected to some new torture.

It disgusted Chan that he could do nothing to help them, but he knew that it was only a matter of time before the US and Malaysian governments got impatient and organized a raid on the warehouse, potential riots be damned. He tried to tell himself that when it happened, these people would be extracted safely and returned to their families.

On some days, he even believed it.

As Chan moved through the semi-darkness, he noted that the prone prisoner still hadn't moved a muscle. There was no sign of breathing, or any other suggestion of life.

Just great, all I need is someone down here dying on my watch, Chan thought. Despite his natural compassion, he was almost frustrated that this guy—whoever he was— couldn't have held on a little longer. *A few more weeks, and maybe you could have gotten out of this shithole, you poor bastard.*

Placing his hand on the cell door, he rattled the bars.

Nothing.

"Hey!" he called to the prisoner, who still made no movement.

"Wake up!" he said in an even louder voice.

The man's face twitched, the movement so slight Chan wasn't totally sure he'd seen it.

Fuck, I guess he's alive after all. Good.

Even so, the guy looked more like a goddamned mummy than a living person. Emaciated, as thin and ragged as if he hadn't eaten a solid meal in months. Frail. Covered in burns and odd scars. Chan flinched as the figure's head rolled toward him, skin stretched tightly over sharp bones like cracked parchment. Eyes pinned him, cold and distant, as ancient as the moon in the sky, but dark like night.

Those eyes chilled Chan's marrow, making him feel as though his legs had been paralyzed by the power of a mere glance.

What the – ?

Chan blinked several times, trying to mentally shake himself free of the hypnotic gaze. He opened his mouth to speak; yet no sound escaped him. The figure before him made no move, took no breath, and his lips remained pressed closed. Yet Chan heard a voice in his mind. The tone was deep and arresting, though he detected no malice in it.

Is it really you? The voice asked inside his head, sounding distantly curious. Those hypnotic dark eyes blinked once, slowly, before the voice continued. *How strange, and yet how terribly apt.*

Chan could no more answer than he could make his feet move. His legs and his tongue might as well have been paralyzed.

I have a message for you to relay, the voice continued. *I fear I will soon lack the strength to deliver it myself. I will give it to you, and then you will forget it until the time is right. Do you understand?*

Chan had undergone years of training in resisting psychological manipulation, and part of him thrashed under the weight of the hypnotic presence pressing down on him. But the rest lay quiescent, waiting to be told what to do—eager to hear the message.

"I… understand," he heard himself whisper.

Good, the voice murmured, *now, listen closely…*

THREE

"**D**uchess?" Abby whispered through the crack in the door.

Duchess, who had been checking email on her laptop in the spare room graciously offered to her by Mason's brother, glanced up and saw a pair of lips pursed next to the small gap. A faint smile tugged at one corner of the vampire's lips. She left the computer and crossed the room with silence worthy of a nightwalker, her feet making no sound on the bamboo floor. Before Abby could grow impatient enough to call again, Duchess was poised on the other side, gazing with veiled affection at the little fingers gripping the doorframe.

"Hello!" Abby whispered, even louder.

"Yes, Abby?" Duchess answered in a normal tone, right next to the child's ear.

Abby jumped and squealed in surprise before collapsing into delighted giggles. With the corners of her eyes crinkling from the smile she was suppressing, Duchess opened the door and allowed the light from the hallway to stream inside.

"It's very early, Abby," she observed, mock severe.

The small, dark haired child stood before her, looking faintly apprehensive in her pink pajamas. Her father's storm-blue eyes peered out from a tiny version of her mother's oval face.

"I know. But will you brush my hair?" Abby asked, producing a predictably pink hairbrush from behind her back.

Duchess let her features soften as she opened the door more fully.

"Of course I will, *petite oiseau*. Come and sit on the bed," Duchess answered. She stood back a step and allowed Abby to pass in front of her.

"You make your bed really fast every day," Abby observed. "I hate making my bed, but Daddy says I gotta."

Duchess glanced at her bed, which had not been slept in since she arrived. "It is a good habit to cultivate, even if it isn't very fun."

Abby made a noise in her throat that suggested she didn't think too much of Duchess' opinion on the matter, but she clambered onto the bed in question without further protest. Once settled, she sat expectantly with her legs crossed.

Duchess perched behind the little girl and gently brushed tangles out of her long raven locks, starting at the ends and gripping the hair so it would not tug. Before long, she was able to pull the brush through effortlessly with long, smooth strokes.

"How long are you staying with us?" Abby asked in a soft voice.

Duchess considered her words for a moment. "I'm not certain, *ma petite*. Until your parents get tired of us and ask us to leave, I suppose."

Or until the next crisis calls us away.

"They won't do that," Abby replied with supreme confidence. "They say that it's important to always make guests feel welcome."

Duchess chuckled and tweaked the girl's ear. "Well, until *you* get tired of us, then."

"No way!" Abby insisted, clearly offended.

Hurried footsteps passed along the hall outside the door. Duchess paused, sensing Mason's retreating presence. He was worried about something.

Abby, noticing nothing amiss, clapped her hands together and said, "Oh, good! Someone else is awake! It must be time to get up!"

Unfolding her legs, the little girl leapt off the bed in a single bound. She spun and held her hand out to Duchess, who laced their fingers together and allowed Abby to tug her out of the door.

The house was dim and silent, the sun only barely peeking above the horizon—not yet high enough to pass through the large windows. Duchess took a moment to enjoy the glittering beauty of Singapore beyond. It was refreshing to be surrounded by such brilliance, after the darkness they had experienced in Damascus and Haiti. Here, there was no outward sign of Bael's presence—so far, at least.

The reprieve was a relief for all of them, pouring much-needed life into their battered souls—even if Duchess was finding it increasingly difficult to be with the happy couples around her. When it was just Eris and Tré who had reunited with their mates, she and Oksana could sequester themselves to privately bemoan all the love floating around in the air. Now, though, she was starting to feel very alone in her aloneness.

Well, alone accept for Snag… assuming he still lives.

That sense of isolation pulled heavily on her, and for comfort she squeezed Abby's fingers. The little girl looked back at her and flashed a dazzling smile. She was missing two of her teeth, making her grin look lopsided, like a cheerful jack-o-lantern.

The warmth that spread through Duchess at the sight almost made up for everything else. Since she'd been barely more than a child herself, Duchess had adored children and dreamed of being a mother. Bael snatched that opportunity from her before it ever bore fruit, however. Even some four hundred years later, the pain of that loss was almost more acute than the loss of her soul mate.

And what did that say about her?

"Who's Uncle Mason talking to?" Abby whispered, tugging on her hand.

Duchess had been so lost in thought as they entered the kitchen that she barely noticed Mason having a tense conversation over the phone.

"What have the local authorities told you?" he asked, his tone grim.

Mason stared blankly at the cabinets, clearly not seeing them. He held the phone in one hand, while his other hand gripped the edge of the marble countertop, white-knuckled.

"And they could tell you nothing useful at all? There are no suspects? No clues?" he demanded.

"Abby, come away for a few minutes," Duchess said quietly, about to pull the child from the room.

Abby resisted, planting her short legs shoulder width apart and pulling her arm back. "No—Uncle Mason is upset. He needs me!"

"Let's allow him to finish his phone conversation in private, *petite oiseau*," Duchess murmured, but the little girl shook her head stubbornly.

"You don't understand," she retorted with a glare in Duchess' direction, "I'm his little bird. I can always make him smile. You'll see!"

Before Duchess could stop her, the small child had pulled her fingers from Duchess' grasp and hurried towards her uncle.

She took his hand and looked up at him.

"Uncle Mason," Abby whispered, shaking him.

He flashed her a brief, strained smile, but shook his head at her with a soft shushing sound, still listening to the rapid speech of the person on the other end of the line.

This is bad, Mason sent along the bond, a bit too loudly. Though his control of his recently acquired vampiric powers had improved immensely in the past few weeks, he still struggled to control his mental volume at times, especially when under pressure.

Mason, we aren't deaf, she replied in kind.

His eyes flickered to where she was standing in the doorway, and he sent back an apology. Chagrin briefly crossed his expression, but then he was once more focused on the phone conversation.

"I understand. No, I think the clinic is fine with a substitute physician. I'm sure, given the circumstances, that Doctors Without Borders will send extra help."

He listened again. "Of course. But keep me posted, okay?"

He chewed at the inside of his lip as the person on the other end spoke. "All right, Gita. Please take care of yourself and let me know if there's anything I can do to help from my end. We'll talk soon."

He hung up the phone and stared at it for a moment, his face blank.

"Uncle Mason, don't be sad. I can chirp like a bird!" Abby offered, smiling up at him.

Despite his obvious preoccupation, he smiled back and brushed her hair away from her face. "That makes sense, since you are my little bird. Now, though, will you fly away and find Oksana for me? I need to talk to her and Duchess for a minute."

Abby stuck out her lower lip. "Adult talk?"

"I'm afraid so, sweet thing," he said gravely, "but it shouldn't take long."

With a dramatic sigh, Abby shuffled away muttering, "That's what grown-ups always say."

After the little girl left the room, Duchess sat down at the table and lifted an expectant eyebrow at Mason.

He sighed and scrubbed a hand over his face. "So. That was Gita Belawan — my old partner. The one who took over the clinic in Haiti when I left," he said, and sat down next to Duchess. "She just got a call from the Malaysian authorities."

"Oh?" Duchess prompted.

"Her son, Haziq, has been kidnapped. He's a doctor in Kuala Lumpur."

Duchess' eyes narrowed as tension took root in her chest. "Kuala Lumpur. The same place we've been getting reports of religious unrest and escalating violence."

Mason nodded. "Yup. Spot on. I mean—there's always been a fair amount of civil unrest in that region. And while kidnapping isn't uncommon, it's usually drug-related. Not respectable professionals being nabbed off the street."

"Did the authorities have any idea why Dr. Belawan's son was targeted?" Duchess asked. "Or was it random?"

Mason sighed. "It's not clear. Maybe he offended the kidnappers in some way? Or they thought he'd be valuable? Hell, he may have just been in the wrong place at the wrong time. There's no way to know for certain right now."

"What *are* the authorities saying? What did they tell her?"

"Basically, they told her to sit tight. They suspect a particular group, and they're supposedly doing everything possible to recover the group's hostages, who they believe are still alive. Apparently Haziq is one of several that are being held right now by this... cult, or whatever you want to call it."

They were both silent for a moment. Duchess sent a tendril of thought across the bond to Oksana, questioning.

I'm listening, ti mwen, Oksana replied. *I'll be down in a moment — just let me get this blasted foot attached.*

Duchess gave an internal nod and spoke again to Mason. "Did the police say anything else specific about this group they think is holding hostages?"

"They did," Mason replied, sitting back in his chair. "Surprisingly, they're Buddhist extremists." He flickered a wry eyebrow. "I suppose there's something to be said for bucking stereotypes."

Duchess shook her head. "It's not unheard of. It might not get much play in the news media, but there are plenty of Muslims in Myanmar who would be happy to tell you about abuse by Buddhist militants."

"Good point," Mason allowed. "And I should know better, really. I had some colleagues in Myanmar, and I heard how much of a mess it was there for a while."

"Malaysia is majority Muslim with enclaves of Chinese immigrants, most of whom are Buddhist," Duchess mused. "It could be a similar dynamic. Cultural friction artificially magnified by the general slide into chaos."

Mason sighed and said, "Yeah. It could be. Seems like everything that was already bad is getting exponentially worse in the last few months."

"And now your friend's son is caught up in the mix," Duchess said, her voice fading away as she considered the situation.

"Just so," Mason agreed glumly. "Haziq Belawan specializes in pediatric medicine, of all the damned things. Just like his mum."

Duchess felt her blood burn. Always, it was the children these days. The children, and those who tried to protect and care for them.

"Savages," she whispered.

Mason nodded but did not speak. She could tell that the news was weighing heavily upon him, especially since they were very close to Kuala Lumpur. Close enough to get involved, in fact—should they choose to do so.

The sound of soft, slightly uneven footsteps caused her to look up. Oksana entered the room, and her grim expression confirmed that she'd heard every word of their conversation.

"Hey, sweetheart," Mason greeted. "I just got a call from—"

"Gita," Oksana interrupted, and sat down next to him at the table. "Yes, I heard. No offense, my love, but you were projecting so loudly that I'm sure any vampire within a five-mile radius could have heard you."

Mason frowned. "I've really got to figure out how to control that."

"You're better than you used to be," Duchess assured him. "Especially while you two are having sex… thankfully."

Oksana cleared her throat loudly. "Yes, *thank you*, Duchess." She shot Duchess a glare. "So. Kuala Lumpur. That's not very far from here. When do we leave?"

"Whoa, there. Aren't we getting a bit ahead of ourselves?" Mason protested, holding up a hand. "It's quite a jump from 'my friend's son was just kidnapped somewhere in a city of a million and a half people' to 'when's the next flight out?'"

"Is it really? Why? I mean… what else do we have to do?" Oksana inquired, angling her body towards Mason. She cupped her chin in one hand, the two seeming instantly lost within each other's gazes as they communicated silently.

Ah, and once again I am the third wheel on the bicycle, Duchess thought. She made sure to shield the dark observation, aware of how bitter such things made her seem. Besides, as much as the thriving couple-ness of everyone close to her turned her stomach these days, she truly did believe that no one deserved happiness more than Oksana.

She would not let her cold cynicism ruin her comrades' contentment so easily—and *certainly* not Oksana's contentment.

"All right. Fine," Mason said. "So, we're talking about a field trip straight into another hornets' nest. What precisely do we hope to accomplish by going? What's our plan?"

"Hostage recovery isn't nearly as challenging as humans make it out to be," Duchess said in a bland voice. She examined her manicured nails, making a show of it. "I daresay we can do a far better job of it than Malaysian law enforcement is managing right now."

Mason perked up for the first time since the phone call.

"You think we could really get him back? Well, I suppose Malaysian law enforcement can't change into mist or owls," he mused, getting into the spirit of things. "Which is hardly their fault, obviously. But you're offering to help? Even though it would still be dangerous?"

Duchess shrugged. "Dangerous? Against militant Buddhist *monks*? I'm reasonably certain we can handle them." She let her lips curve into a pointed smirk. "Even though you're still practically a newborn."

Oksana stifled a snort, covering her mouth.

Mason appeared mildly offended at the jab. "Yes, well—I am completely capable of changing form and feeding on my own these days, so you can dispense with the baby vampire jokes any time now." He gave Duchess a narrow look. "Christ. You're starting to make me miss Xander's subtle application of tact and diplomacy."

That riposte did manage to hit a tender spot, but Duchess only lifted a haughty eyebrow. "Mason, you *are* a baby vampire. You still shout half the time when you and Oksana are—"

"*Oh*-kay, I think that's enough of this particular conversation," Oksana interrupted. "I agree that we should visit Kuala Lumpur and see if we can be of any help with Gita's son. Duchess, you're the one who's been saying that some of the reports coming out of Malaysia were alarming, even before this happened—so let's go check things out."

"Agreed," Duchess said readily enough, experiencing a sudden surge of eagerness to be doing something more positive than sitting around, waiting for the next crisis to appear.

"Agreed," Mason echoed, a bit more hesitation in his tone. "But with the caveat that if this somehow turns into another *vortex of chaos*, as you two insist on calling it—we bring in more backup this time. I'm not in a hurry to see anyone else get knifed, shot, poisoned, staked, abducted, or turned into a werewolf if we can avoid it."

Oksana lifted a pointed brow at Duchess, who frowned at her.

It's a fair point, her friend sent.

"What are you implying, *mon chou*?" she asked aloud, her tone a bit sour. "Mason is the one who brought this particular crisis to our attention. It's nothing to do with me."

The vortices of violence and unrest seemed to form when one of them got too close to his or her lost mate; something that hardly applied in this instance.

Oksana's eyes narrowed. *You'd tell us, wouldn't you, ti mwen? If you sensed your mate nearby?*

Duchess' frown deepened. "I'll go contact the others and start arranging transportation for us," she said, ignoring the silent question. "Then we should speak to our hosts."

She could feel the others' eyes on her back as she rose and left the room.

-o-o-o-

An hour later, the three of them were sitting at the table again, this time across from Jackson Walker and his wife, Yi Ling.

"You really think this is a good idea, Mace?" Jackson asked, looking at his brother steadily. "You three just got out of one disaster zone. Yet you seem awfully eager to run straight into another one."

Mason shrugged, but his expression was dark. "Gita's a good friend, Jack. And we might be able to do something to get Haziq back safely to his family."

Yi Ling cocked her head. "We were hoping that you would stay here longer. But if your friend needs help, then you should try to help." Her bell-like voice was quiet, but Duchess sensed her lingering unease around them. And yet, Jackson's wife had been the consummate hostess during their stay—even going so far as to donate blood for them. Duchess could not help respecting her for that.

"Our sentiments exactly," Oksana said.

"Well… it sounds like your minds are made up," Jackson said. "For what it's worth, there are still a couple of blood bags in the freezer. You should take them with you, so you don't have to go all *'Interview with the Vampire'* on some poor, unsuspecting Malaysians while you're gone."

"That's very kind of you," Duchess said politely.

Oksana nodded. "We could keep them on dry ice, I suppose. We aren't planning on being there for very long, though."

Jackson sighed, the expression of worry sounding eerily like his brother's. "Well, I guess that's settled, then."

"The girls won't like saying goodbye," Yi Ling murmured, looking at Mason. "They've loved having you here."

Mason smiled. "Oh, I imagine we'll be back in a few days, Yi Ling. It's not that far away, and we're just going to go have a quick poke around. See if we can turn up anything the police have missed."

Jackson huffed, and Duchess got the distinct impression that he didn't believe a word his brother was saying.

Four

The three of them spent the rest of the day tending Mason's nieces. Apparently, Yi Ling had slowly been growing more comfortable with them, because she and Jackson took advantage of their last chance for babysitting services to sneak away for a day out. Duchess couldn't blame them; these days, quiet moments were hard for anyone to find.

"Duchess!" Abby called from the other room. "Me and Ming want some juice, please!"

"'Ming and I,' Abby," Duchess corrected. "What kind of juice do you want?"

"Papaya!" Ming answered in a bright voice.

Duchess stood and made her way into the kitchen, grateful for a few moments' escape from the happy-couple-bliss that surrounded Oksana and Mason like an aura. *Mon Dieu*, had she always been this twisted up inside, or was it a recent thing? She shook her head, irritated with herself.

Abby bounded into the room. "I have to have the purple cup today," she insisted in a solemn voice.

"Why's that, *petite oiseau*?"

"Because it's a purple kind of day," she answered simply.

"Right," Duchess murmured, and pulled down two cups.

"Lellow day! Lellow day!" Ming, the younger of the two girls, called out as she, too, entered the kitchen.

"She means 'yellow,'" Abby clarified, her tone communicating an air of long-suffering patience with her younger sister.

Duchess smiled at the antics of the two energetic girls, letting their carefree lightness chase away some of her own dark thoughts. After both had been satisfied with their drinks, they returned to the playroom, where Duchess encouraged them to parade past her in a variety of dresses and shoes obtained from both Yi Ling's closet and her own luggage. It was an eclectic fashion show and would no doubt have raised eyebrows on the runways of Paris—but it did ease the heavy weight that pressed down across Duchess' shoulders these days.

Later in the evening, once Jackson and Yi Ling had returned, the two girls clambered into Duchess' lap and demanded one last story before she left. Each night since they'd arrived, Duchess had spent a portion of the evening reading to Abby and Ming from a collection of Grimm's fairy tales.

She flipped through the pages, aided and abetted by the captivated girls. Finally, it was time for them to say their goodbyes. Through the curtained windows of the stylish but homey apartment, Duchess could sense that the sun's rays were sinking safely below the horizon. Soon, they would begin the journey to Kuala Lumpur.

"Please don't go," Abby begged, her small arms wrapped around Duchess' neck. "I don't want you to leave yet!"

Duchess caught herself before the unexpected ache in her chest could enter her voice. The small pain was sharp enough to take her by surprise. Sharp enough to make Oksana look at her with an expression of worry.

"Abby," Duchess answered, squeezing the little girl, "we will return another time. You must stay here and look after your little sister while we're gone."

"And Mommy and Daddy, too?" she asked, leaning back with wide eyes.

"Of course, *petite oiseau*. Your parents, as well," Duchess replied, passing the little girl into Mason's waiting arms. She hugged Ming next. The younger girl was obviously getting sleepy, sucking her thumb with drooping eyes. As soon as everyone had hugged everyone else, Duchess picked up her bag and departed with the others.

Despite her earlier appreciation for the restful break, she found that she was happy to leave the emotional surroundings. Everyone seemed to be on edge with this departure. Singapore's humid night air flowed over her cool skin as they exited the building, and she could smell several humans walking along the road nearby. It would take them hardly any time to travel by mist to Kuala Lumpur, yet Duchess felt strangely rushed.

A few moments later, Oksana and Mason followed her outside, slinging their bags across their backs.

"The girls certainly have the knack of tugging at your heart with those big puppy dog eyes, don't they?" Oksana said, looking troubled.

Mason chuckled, though he, too, looked less than pleased about leaving. "Oh, just wait until Christmas time. Abby practically has me convinced it's a moral imperative that I tell her what I got her in advance."

"That little girl will rule the world someday," Duchess said wryly, "assuming we can save it from the forces of evil for her."

"No doubt," Mason said. "I keep telling Jack that he's going to have to start saving for either an Ivy League college fund or bond money. I doubt there's going to be much of an in-between with that one."

Duchess couldn't help her small breath of amusement, as some of the tension in the air eased.

She hefted her bag and gestured for Mason to hand his over as well. They were traveling light, leaving most of their belongings with Jackson and Yi Ling. Still, there was a knack to transporting inanimate objects while in a shifted form, and although Duchess trusted Mason not to reappear on the other end of the journey wearing only his boxers and one sock, asking him to keep mental track of a knapsack full of clothing and incidentals was probably a bit much at this stage.

"Stay close to me, Mason," Oksana said. "I don't want you to get lost or separated."

"Try not to worry, sweetheart. I'll be fine," he answered, his voice low. "In fact, I'm rather looking forward to this—my first long-distance flight."

He bent to press a kiss to her lips, and when they were still lip-locked fifteen seconds later, Duchess cleared her throat.

"Dawn isn't *that* far off, you two," she pointed out, and felt a brief, unworthy flash of satisfaction at the twin expressions of embarrassment that flared through the bond.

"Right," Oksana said, breaking away from Mason and clearing her throat. "Yes. Traveling now."

Duchess shook her head and took a deep breath, pulling her life force inward with one sharp jerk. She felt the rest of her body follow and hurtled off into the night sky. Oksana and Mason streaked along behind her. She could sense their thoughts and essences more powerfully in this form, and she knew that something about her bond with Oksana had changed. She was so closely intermingled with Mason these days, that at times it was hard to tell them apart.

That should not matter to you. What business is it of yours? Duchess thought, irritated with herself. It took almost all of her concentration to shield her thoughts when in this non-corporeal form. Yet, despite this fact, it still felt as though a wall had risen between the two of them. The question she was unwilling to examine too closely was whether the wall was on Oksana's side... or on hers.

Duchess had a sudden—and rather farcical—vision of her and Snag holed up somewhere in a dark room, bemoaning their lack of mates like a pair of old maids. It was a disturbing enough mental image that she vowed to find as many random partners as possible for mind-numbing, meaningless sex and feeding just as soon as she had a free moment in Kuala Lumpur.

A few hours later, Duchess sensed light and life ahead of them. The capital of Malaysia was a massive city—one of the fastest growing metropolitan regions in Asia. She sought out a quiet, shadowed place near the outskirts where they would not be observed and led the way lower. With an outward pressure on her life force, Duchess burst into human form as she leapt lightly down to the ground. Oksana materialized right next to her an instant later.

With an *unff!* Mason popped into existence and tumbled into a heap on the ground. Unable to stop herself, Duchess let out a snort of laughter and shook her head.

Baby vampires are hilarious, she thought, making only a cursory effort to keep from broadcasting the observation. Mason, distinctly red in the face, scrambled to his feet. Duchess tossed him his rucksack, and he caught the bag awkwardly against his chest.

"Well, that was certainly humiliating," he said as he brushed himself off.

"Trynn was worse to begin with." Duchess offered the words like an olive branch, burying her amusement. "She still ends up flat on her face half of the time."

Oksana patted him on the back. "I'll tell you about Della's first attempt one of these days. That was... memorable."

Mason managed a rueful half-smile. "All right, you two. Consider my bruised ego sufficiently bandaged." He huffed. "At least my *actual* bruises heal in seconds, now. Come on—let's go. Hotel first, I assume?"

"Yes," Duchess agreed.

"Can you get contact information for Haziq's family from Gita?" Oksana asked. "That's probably the easiest way to start."

"I don't see why not," Mason said. "We're… what? Twelve hours ahead of Haiti? So, it should be afternoon there. I'll call her as soon as we're settled."

Despite the darkness, there seemed to be a large number of people out walking on the streets. The atmosphere was restless. Watchful. Something about it made Duchess' spine tingle. It reminded her of—

"Is it just me, or is anyone else getting flashbacks to that night in Port-au-Prince, right after the earthquake?" Mason asked, interrupting her thoughts.

Before either she or Oksana could reply, two men stepped out of the shadows of an alley, streetlights glinting off the steel blades in their hands. The pedestrians around them scattered, but it was immediately clear that she and her companions, with their obviously foreign features, were the targets. Both humans appeared to be of Chinese descent, a fact that was confirmed when the one on the left spoke with a thick Cantonese accent.

"Oy, *gweilo*," he snapped, his focus on Mason. "Speak English? Give us your money, or we cut up your pretty girls."

Mason blinked. "*Seriously*? No offense, mate, but you really have no idea what kind of shit you're about to step in."

Duchess was not in a great mood by this point, but she still recognized that teaching moments were important—especially for baby vampires. She stepped forward and knocked the knife from the hand of the would-be mugger on the right before grabbing him by the throat and slamming him up against the wall of the alley, where they would be hidden from casual view by other people on the street.

"Practice time, *Docteur*," she said, her eyes blazing into those of the human she was holding. He went very quiet, like a cornered rabbit. "The other one is yours."

She could sense Oksana poised nearby, ready to jump in like a hovering mother hen with one chick. To his credit, though, Mason didn't hesitate. She glanced quickly back at him, to see his eyes glinting like sunlight on blue steel.

"Right," he said. "Back into the alley, slowly. And you want to put that knife down now."

There was the briefest of hesitations, but then shuffling footsteps sounded and something metallic clattered to the ground.

"Good," Mason said. "Now, you and your friend are going to stop robbing people. If you need food or a place to stay, go to social services and ask for help."

Duchess managed not to roll her eyes. Barely.

"It doesn't really work that way, Mason," Oksana said. "You can't influence them to do things they don't want to, once they're away from you. You'd need Snag's kind of power for that."

Duchess dragged her captive around until she could glare at both muggers.

"Run away now," she snarled. "And forget any of this happened."

She let go of the throat she was holding, and both humans hared off like the flames of hell were licking at their heels. When they were gone, she raised an eyebrow at Mason.

"Not too bad. But don't overreach yourself."

Mason scrubbed a hand over his scalp. "I cannot count the number of times in my life when that ability would have come in insanely useful."

"Hotel?" Oksana asked, sounding as tired as Duchess suddenly felt.

"Hotel," she agreed.

They checked into the first place they found that didn't look like an utter shithole, and booked a double since that was what was available. It wasn't completely awful. There was a small bathroom adjacent to the sleeping area. The two beds were full sized. The room was dimly lit but seemed comfortable enough and free of insects.

Mason flopped face down on the far mattress without ceremony. "Ugh. I don't know if it's just the remnants of my humanity, or if I'm a terrible vampire, but I still get tired after dark," he said, speaking into the bedding.

Oksana perched at his side, stretching. She slid a hand up and down the length of his spine, and he made a noise like a contented cat. "Well," she said, "you spent your entire life going to sleep in the evening and waking up in the morning. Your biological clock is probably confused."

"Not true," Mason answered, the words still muffled. "My residency was almost exclusively at night. I was never lucky enough to land the day shifts."

"Then you don't have much of an excuse," Duchess said, "beyond the fact that you just flew three hundred-fifty kilometers in four hours."

"Yeah, you're probably right," he murmured. "I just need a couple of minutes to shut my eyes, and then I'll call Gita."

-o-o-o-

True to his word, Mason dragged himself up a short time later and called Gita, even though he still felt like he'd run here from Singapore on foot rather than flying. His old friend was relieved and more than a little thankful to hear that they were in Kuala Lumpur and planning on making their own investigations. She was also quick to give him every bit of contact information and background that might conceivably come in helpful, which he jotted down on a notepad next to the phone. When he was done, he gave into Oksana's pointed look and fed on some of the blood Jackson's wife had sent with them. Then, he sat down with the other two, so they could discuss their plan of action.

"I really want to get to know the city first," Duchess said, standing alone by the window and looking out at the pouring rain. The skies had opened half an hour previously and showed no signs of slowing anytime soon, despite it not technically being the rainy season. "That would be most helpful to me. I need to get a feel for the place."

Mason looked at her, aware that he was unsuccessful in keeping an air of skepticism out of his reply. "Um, all right. Well… while you're *sensing the city*, I'm going to talk to Haziq's colleagues at the hospital where he worked. Gita told me that he was abducted just after a shift, so maybe one of his co-workers saw something."

Maybe Mason just hadn't gotten used to Duchess' ways yet, but there were times when it felt like she was more *alien* than vampire. What did she hope to accomplish by wandering aimlessly through a city of a million and a half people?

Duchess pulled the notepad toward her with a manicured fingertip and frowned down at it. "You have the hospital's address here?" Her eyebrows went up. "*Mon Dieu, Docteur*—this is the sort of penmanship only a medical professional can get away with."

"Okay, you two, let's have a *bit* of peace on earth," Oksana interjected wearily. "At least in here, all right?"

Not wanting to put Oksana in an awkward position between his and Duchess' sniping, Mason smiled wryly. "Of course, sweetheart. Sorry, Duchess—I'm sure that getting a feel for the city is a good idea. And, yes, poor penmanship is an actual class in medical school. Hadn't you heard? They don't give you a diploma until you pass it."

Duchess looked at him for a long moment, and then sighed. "Forgive my short temper, both of you. We will find your friend's son, Mason."

Shortly before dawn, the three of them went their separate ways— Mason to talk to Haziq's coworkers, Oksana to meet with his family, and Duchess to seek out the militant Buddhist cult thought to be behind the kidnapping. This was actually the first time he and Oksana had been apart for any length of time since Haiti, he realized. He found that being away from her was... strange. Still, knowing that he had his new mental abilities available, Mason tried to subtly reach out and touch Oksana's mind as she left for the central part of the city.

He sensed her mental flinch and knew that, once again, he'd been too heavy handed. *Damn it.*

Her reply was soft and warm. *You're getting better at it, really,* she assured him from over a block away, and he could feel the smile in her mental voice like the memory of sunlight. *Just try to relax. It should be light and easy.*

Mason smiled despite himself. *Easy for you to say, sweetheart. You've been doing this for hundreds of years.*

The impression of an impish wink washed over his mind, and his smile grew wider. *Practice makes perfect,* she said.

It took Mason only a few minutes to fly to Haziq's clinic. Of course, he then made the mistake of returning to human form while still outside. Even though he was only a few steps away from the entrance, by the time he slipped inside, he was completely drenched.

Note to self: in future, fly inside as mist and change back to human form in a storage cupboard or something. Or else, bring along an umbrella.

With nothing else for it, he slogged up to the visitors' desk staffed by two nurses.

"Can I help you?" one of them asked in English as he approached. Her accent was very good, giving Mason the impression that she'd been raised or at least trained somewhere in the West.

"Yes, I'm Dr. Mason Walker. I'm a colleague of Dr. Belawan's mother. I was hoping to find someone to talk to about what happened to Haziq a couple of days ago."

The nurse's face grew troubled. She glanced at her colleague nervously and gestured for Mason to step into the hallway.

As he followed her through the doorway, he became aware of the thrum of her pulse beneath the skin of her throat. To his disgust, he felt a sudden urge to feed despite the bagged blood he'd had earlier. He pushed it away ruthlessly.

Not happening, he thought. Even after feeding several times from Jackson over the past few weeks, he wasn't sure if he would ever truly get used to the idea of drinking blood from humans. It had honestly been a relief when Xander had floated the idea of no longer hunting humans for blood, though he knew it further complicated their already complicated lives.

The nurse let the door swing shut behind them and glanced at him with anxious eyes.

"Why are you inquiring about Haziq?" she asked, clearly wary.

Mason's brow furrowed. "Do you know something about what happened?"

The woman pressed her lips together. "Answer me first. Why do you come here asking these questions?"

"I thought that would be obvious," he said. "He's a good man, and now he's been kidnapped."

But she continued to stare hard at him, as if expecting a different answer.

258

After a few moments of awkward silence, Mason rubbed the back of his neck with a weary hand.

"Look," he said, "it's like I just told you, I'm a friend of Haziq's mother. She's extremely worried and I thought that I might ask around, you know? In a hospital as busy as this, someone is bound to have seen something."

"And you think you can do something the police can't?" The woman demanded in a sharp voice.

Mason considered her for a moment. He couldn't read her mind like he could another vampire's, but pain and loss seemed to hang around her like a cloud.

"You cared for him," he said in a soft voice. "Didn't you?"

The woman looked away quickly, but not before Mason saw the tears welling in her eyes.

"Yes," she finally replied, "of course I cared for him. There's not a person in this hospital who didn't care about Haziq. He was an amazing doctor."

The woman turned away and walked towards a small, empty office. He followed her inside, and she flopped down in the chair behind the desk. She gestured for Mason to sit across from her.

"Tell me more about him," he prompted as he took the offered seat.

A single tear trickled down her face as she stared silently out the rain-washed window for several moments.

"Haziq was my friend. I came here through the American Peace Corps and fell in love with Kuala Lumpur. Even after my rotation was over, I opted to stay behind and work in this hospital. Haziq loved this place just as much. He always told me he felt more alive while helping the children here than he had anywhere else. He was a brilliant doctor; he could've made huge money in another country. He knew that, but he still chose to remain here with us."

"You're using the past tense a lot," Mason pointed out. "Do you mean to say you think he's dead?"

The nurse looked at him, moisture glistening in her eyes. "You don't?"

Mason shook his head. "No, I don't. I refuse to believe that's the case until I see incontrovertible proof. Right now, I'm looking into it under the assumption that he's simply missing."

"Then you should be commended for your hope, because the rest of us have none."

"Why do you say that?" Mason asked, not understanding how his friends and colleagues could have given up on Haziq so easily.

"The *Brotherhood*." The words were a whisper, even though they were alone in the small office. It was as though she thought invisible ears might still overhear them.

Mason had no such concerns. "The Brotherhood? That's the group the police think kidnapped him? What about them?"

"They're growing in size and strength every day. More and more people gather at the Thean Hou Temple every night to listen to the monks espousing hatred and violence. Any that oppose them are captured and killed. They hang the bodies from trees in the swamps outside the city as a warning. The police are too scared to stop them."

Mason felt a sinking feeling in the pit of his stomach. "Has anyone here seen Haziq's body?"

The nurse shook her head. "No, not yet. We can't bear to go look, but it's only a matter of time."

FIVE

"I am sorry to bother you during this difficult time," Oksana said, sitting on the small couch in the front room of Haziq's house. His wife, Jayda, sat ashen-faced in a chair across from her. With trembling fingers, Jayda handed Oksana a cup of tea on a delicate saucer.

"No, no," she murmured in lightly accented English, pausing to sip from her own cup. "I appreciate the company, believe me. Many of Haziq's friends and associates have been by, bringing me food and offering comfort."

Oksana could sense despair from the woman. It was clear she'd given up all hope, despite the police insistence that her husband might still be alive.

"You don't hold out hope of getting him back safely?" she asked Jayda.

Jayda gave her a brief, sad smile and brushed a tear from the corner of her eye. "No, not really. His colleagues think he angered the Brotherhood after he volunteered in the emergency room at the hospital. Several people had been publically tortured at a rally, and Haziq helped treat their injuries. Afterward, he wrote an editorial letter to the Star newspaper denouncing the growing religious violence. So… members of the cult took him from the parking lot as he was leaving work. There were several witnesses—it was obvious they wanted to make an example of him."

Her voice grew ragged on the last sentence, and she wiped her eyes again. Oksana sat back thoughtfully.

"That seems like a reasonable supposition, but I'm not so ready to give up on him. I'm trying to understand the impetus behind this cult. Can you tell me what else you know about them?"

Jayda swirled her cup, staring into the dregs seemingly without seeing them. "It is a bold group, and an angry one. How it started, I really can't say. It seemed like they simply exploded onto the scene overnight. One day it was whispers of a new religious group, and the next it was public torture and executions, extortion, terror... the cult's leaders are well versed in all the tactics of fear, it seems."

"Why do people follow them?" Oksana asked. "What do they hope to gain?"

"The monks shout aloud what some people have been whispering for a long time. They talk about change, which I suppose is needed, but I think they've been really effective at targeting a group that feels like they've been victimized. They paint a picture of revenge paired with new power and wealth. There are a lot of angry people in Malaysia—Chinese immigrants who feel disenfranchised and downtrodden by the Malay majority."

"There are a lot of angry people everywhere, these days. But that does sound like an effective way to throw gasoline on a fire," Oksana mused.

"It is," Jayda nodded. "The world today frightens me. I didn't know how we would be able to keep our children safe, even before this happened to us. Now, I have no idea what I'll do on my own."

"Maybe you won't have to do it alone," Oksana said quietly. "Tell me about the day Haziq was kidnapped."

Jayda sighed. "It was just a normal day, like any other. He left for the hospital early, while I left the children with their nanny and went to work for the morning. I got the call that afternoon. He'd been taken from the parking lot in broad daylight."

"Didn't anyone try to stop the abduction?" Oksana asked, surprised. She'd been imagining a nighttime snatch-and-grab operation. This daylight kidnapping in plain view of witnesses spoke to a whole different level of boldness.

"No," Jayda shook her head. "No one would dare. People are too scared. They're afraid they'd be next. It was sheer luck that someone even bothered to call the police."

"Did you talk to the police yourself? File a missing person report?"

"Yes, I filed one that same afternoon. It seemed very… *perfunctory*, though. I am certain they already know where and how he was taken. And that nothing will come of it."

"You think the police will ignore the report?"

"You misunderstand me," Jayda murmured, her eyes downcast. "I think they will do nothing because they believe he's already dead."

"They've said otherwise, though. Haven't they?" Oksana insisted. It was horrible to see the pain that Jayda was going through, yet Oksana could not give up hope so easily. She would not abandon Haziq if there was even the slightest chance that he was alive.

"Of course they would say that, to try to keep me from becoming hysterical during the interview." Her voice was bitter. "But no one comes back after being taken by the Brotherhood. Haziq is strong, but how can I bear to have hope when no one ever comes back alive?"

"If he's anything like his mother," Oksana replied, "then he's both smart and stubborn."

More tears spilled onto Jayda's cheeks as she looked at Oksana. "That is certainly true. But—"

Oksana cut her off gently. "So, believe that he hasn't given up and that he won't stop fighting. Don't give up on him, because I bet he'll never give up on you. Mason and I won't give up on him either."

Jayda gulped back a sob and set her cup down on the coffee table with delicate care. She stared without blinking at the ground for long moments, clearly trying to rein in her emotions.

"You remind me of him," she whispered eventually. "That's why we're here—because he refused to give up on this city. He said the hospital needed him, and he thrived on helping others."

"That same strength will carry him through this. I know it," Oksana insisted.

Jayda swallowed hard. "I hope you're right, Oksana. I really do. I'm… just trying to be realistic."

Oksana stood and placed her cup next to Jayda's. "I understand. You just worry about yourself and your children for now. Let us worry about finding Haziq and bringing him back to you."

Jayda looked at her. "Hope is a cruel mistress. I appreciate what you're trying to do, but you don't know how it's been around here lately. Bodies in the streets. People disappearing every single day and never coming back."

Oksana suppressed a shiver. She knew all too well about those things… and worse. Again, she wondered if Duchess was being straight with them about her sense of what was going on in Kuala Lumpur. Was it just the same general chaos that was spreading across the globe in a slow march… or something more?

Oksana reached over and gripped Jayda's hand, staring at her with a level gaze. "I do know how it's been, Jayda. And even knowing that, you have my word. My friends and I won't stop until Haziq is found and—spirits willing—returned safely to you."

A flicker of painful hope passed across Jayda's drawn features, and she squeezed Oksana's hand in return. "Thank you. Please, though… try to keep yourselves safe. The last thing Haziq would want is someone else getting hurt while trying to save him."

-o-o-o-

Duchess slipped into a small shop that was mercifully empty of customers. She could hear that the shop owner was just out of sight in the next room, but she did not call for assistance. She merely needed to get away from the sense of chaos swirling around in her head for a few moments.

Pressing her fingers to her temples, she tried to block out the feeling.

As she walked through the city, the undercurrents of turmoil and barely suppressed violence were eerily reminiscent of New Orleans and Haiti. That fact had implications she wasn't ready to examine too closely yet. She'd been eager enough to come here from Singapore, and she told herself it was because she was tired of cooling her heels—doing nothing of use besides watching the news reports.

Was she deluding herself, though? Had she been drawn here for a different reason? Duchess grunted in disgust as she tried to shake free of the cloud of clutching evil present on the streets of Kuala Lumpur.

"Can I help you?" the shop owner asked in Malay.

Duchess looked up, surprised by the man's approach. Such distraction from her surroundings was a bad sign. After spending several hours letting the city's aura permeate her awareness, it was clear her senses were rattled.

"Oh," she answered, clearing her throat. "No, just getting out of the rain."

Unfortunately, her speaking skills in Malay were not quite as good as her comprehension and reading skills, but apparently, she'd at least gotten the gist across. To back up her story, she brushed off water that had soaked her rain jacket.

The owner looked at her and raised an eyebrow.

"We don't often see tourists in this neighborhood," he said crossing to the counter. "Especially with the violence in this part of the city. You'd do well to find a safer place, or at least stay in a group with other people when you venture out."

Duchess took a long slow breath and managed to block out the rest of the chaos, concentrating only on the shopkeeper in front of her. He was middle-aged, but he'd obviously kept up his health and appearance. To her mild relief, she found that his thoughts were slow and calm, matching his speech. She could sense concern, but also a cloak of peace that seemed at odds with his dire warnings.

"I've heard about that, yes," Duchess admitted, feeling him out. "So far, I've been lucky, though. I haven't seen anything."

He nodded thoughtfully. "Hmm. Well, hopefully your luck continues."

Figuring that she might as well take advantage of a person who wanted to talk, she walked toward the sales counter, letting a bit of sensuality color her movements. The man maintained his pleasant and respectful demeanor… but he still looked at her with an appreciative eye. People *always* looked.

And where would I be if they didn't? she thought.

"My name is Duchess," she said in a low voice. She allowed some of her hypnotic force to bleed through into her words, making them impossible for him to ignore.

"It is my pleasure to meet you," the man responded with a slight bow of the head. His pupils dilated in the harsh, overhead strip lighting. "I am Raahim, at your service."

"Well, Raahim," Duchess said. "Maybe you could tell me what else I should do to stay safe in this city. I'm not looking for trouble."

Despite the mild daze she'd put him under, a faint smile tugged at his lips—as though he doubted her words. "Am I to take it that trouble often finds you, regardless?"

"Oh, yes," she answered. "Inevitably."

He nodded and leaned towards her over the counter, resting his elbows on the wood.

"Well, in that case, you should avoid crowded places after dark," he advised, staring straight into her eyes. "Especially the local mosques."

"Why?"

Raahim cocked his head. "The Brotherhood has taken issue with men and women of Muslim faith. Our places of worship are too often the targets of brutal attacks these days."

"Really? But Malaysia is majority Muslim. Why doesn't the government step in?" Duchess asked.

"The government fears escalating the tensions into full-blown civil war."

"Fools," Duchess breathed. As though one could look at the world and not understand that without action, things would only get worse as time went on.

"Perhaps they are foolish," Raahim said. "Or perhaps they are correct. As it is, though, things continue to escalate. One attack must always be bigger and more frightening than the last."

"How long has this been going on?"

"Long enough that many of our citizens are becoming numb to the violence. But recently, it has become much worse. One would think that the Brotherhood has lost all fear of reprisal."

Duchess nodded, allowing her long, blonde hair to fall over her shoulders in waves. Raahim's eyes followed the movement in fascination.

"Do you know anything more about it?" she asked, knowing that he was hers now, to do with as she wished. Somehow, the thought did not bring the same satisfaction that it might have brought in the past.

"I do not," he said. "I try to stay out of the politics and extremism—as much as one can these days. I'm a merchant. I simply want to do business and make an honest living."

She could sense that he was telling the truth. And—now that she had extracted as much information from him as she could—it was time to satisfy another need.

"I'm so grateful that you took the time to talk to me," Duchess said, leaning forward with one hand braced on the counter. "I'll try very hard to stay out of trouble—*I promise.*"

Raahim leaned forward as well, closing his eyes as she lifted her other hand to cup his cheek. He sighed in pleasure as her lips latched onto the skin of his throat, fangs extending to pierce the delicate flesh.

-o-o-o-

Some time later, Duchess reconvened with the others in their hotel room to exchange information. Both Oksana and Mason had been busy, taking advantage of the heavy clouds that kept the sun at bay. Between the three of them, a familiar narrative was beginning to emerge.

"… and Jayda is sure that his kidnapping has something to do with her husband's critical editorial piece in the newspaper, so it doesn't look like this was a random abduction," Oksana finished, leaning back in the wooden chair by the desk. "That's pretty much all I've got, I'm afraid."

"That jives with what Haziq's co-workers told me," Mason affirmed from his perch on the edge of the nearest bed. "This group is serious about dissuading anyone from speaking out against them. Now, don't get me wrong—I refuse to give up on him until I see proof that we're too late; that they've already killed him. But these are some scary blokes. It's obvious they don't shrink from murder for murder's sake."

Duchess had resumed her place at the window, staring out into the dark clouds that still swirled over the city. She was silent for a long time, reflecting on the information they'd gathered.

"I think," she said after a while, "that we need to go deeper."

Mason and Oksana regarded her, clearly waiting for her to elaborate.

Duchess looked straight at Oksana and said, "You aren't going to like my next idea."

Oksana sighed in resignation. "Really, *ti mwen*? You shock me."

"There is something more here than is visible on the surface. I want the head of this cult."

A finely swept black eyebrow lifted. "Of course you do."

Duchess lifted an answering brow, not backing down. "I need your help."

"Of course you do," Mason echoed.

Duchess turned a haughty stare on the two younger vampires. "I'm going to infiltrate the cult tonight. It may be a day or so before I can return. While I'm gone, I want you two to get as much information as you can about this *Brotherhood* from law enforcement officials."

"I told you, Jayda doesn't think they'll follow up on what she—" Oksana started.

Duchess shook her head. "I know, *ma petite*. But I still want you to try. Just because the police choose not to act, it doesn't mean they won't have other information that could be useful."

Mason glanced at his watch. "I suppose with the storm clouds overhead and the buildings being packed so closely together, we could go there now if we were careful to keep to the shadows."

Oksana gave Duchess a long, penetrating look. Finally, Duchess could sense her friend giving way.

I don't like this, Oksana said, for her ears alone.

I know you don't, Duchess replied in the same manner.

"Let's go then," Oksana said, and Mason nodded. The pair gathered a few things and turned to leave, opening the door and stepping into the hallway. Just before Oksana let the door swing shut, she paused to give Duchess a final, lingering stare.

"Don't make us have to come rescue you," she said, her tone deceptively light.

Duchess canted a tight smile in her direction. "Me? I wouldn't dream of it, *ma chère.*"

SIX

Night was finally falling, a relief even with the unrelenting cloud cover. Duchess found a deserted alley and solidified from mist into human form. Emerging from the shadows at last, she wandered the streets in the Brickfields neighborhood north of the Thean Hou Temple, where Mason had reported the Brotherhood held frequent rallies. The area had once been vibrant—a cultural center for the Indian and Ceylonese immigrants who had come to work in the late 19th-century brick-making kilns that supplied building materials for the city's explosive growth.

The Buddhist influence here was readily apparent in the large number of temples dotted amongst the Indian restaurants and spice shops. When she'd been here twenty years ago, it had also been home to the hundred-year-old historic YMCA building, several Christian churches of various denominations, and a mosque. The place had teemed with life, exuding that extreme vibrancy which seemed unique to the growing Asian mega-cities in the first decade of the twenty-first century.

Now, the vibrancy was muted under a layer of fear. Again, Duchess was reminded of New Orleans. Of Port-au-Prince. The knowledge lodged in the pit of her stomach, making her feel like she'd tried to swallow solid food rather than blood.

It was far from deserted, but the people around her were tense. A nearly palpable aura of distrust and anger choked the air. There appeared to be a growing current of pedestrians heading south, toward the Brotherhood's base of operations at the temple, so she melted into the groups of people and followed the crowds. A few around her shot nervous or hostile glances at her pale skin and hair, but in the emotionally charged atmosphere it was easy enough to let her power unfold around her, convincing them that they had been mistaken and there was nothing unusual in her being here.

The growing crowd spilled onto Jalan Permai road, dense buildings and gray pavement giving way to vibrant green as palm trees rose around them. The thick growth on either side of the road gave one the illusion of having been transported to another time... another realm. The road widened into a parking area choked with cars, motorcycles, scooters, and lorries, but still surrounded on all sides by trees and brush. The crowd rounded a bend in the road and the temple appeared, lit by torches, its facade and intricate pagoda roof done up in brilliant shades of red, orange, and white.

A raised stage had been erected near the base of the double staircase leading up to the entrance. Duchess slipped into the trees at the edge of the large courtyard and transformed into an owl. From a perch high up in the palm fronds, she surveyed the growing crowd of spectators, easily over a thousand strong with more pouring in every moment. She scanned her surroundings continuously, taking advantage of the elevated position and her enhanced sight and hearing.

A monk with the light of fanaticism in his eyes took the stage and began to speak. All eyes were on him, despite the presence of several other men hanging back in the shadows at the rear of the dais. Unsurprisingly, the monk's speech was soaked in violence, intolerance, and the lust for blood. Some of the people listening shifted restlessly, as though the rhetoric made them nervous or uncomfortable. But a majority of the listeners were clearly there to satisfy their own need for savagery, and the monk delivered it with obvious relish.

Enthusiastic shouts of agreement filled the courtyard, nearly deafening in their intensity. But then, Duchess became aware of something else tickling the edges of her mind. Familiar, but not. And it was shocking enough—once she realized what it was—to make her nearly topple from her perch. That brush of mental energy came from another vampiric presence.

A vampiric presence *that she didn't recognize.*

It wasn't Mason. It most definitely wasn't Oksana, who Duchess could recognize as easily as she recognized her own face in a mirror.

Another vampire? How was that even possible?

She concentrated all her mental power on the presence. No, it was not one of the others. Nor was it Snag. This was definitely a vampire she had never met before. She strained to understand the thoughts flickering at the edges of her awareness. They were confused, distant— filtering to her as though through a dense fog. Those thoughts sounded… very young.

And perhaps she had her answer. A young vampire… a *vampire child*. Of course.

Can you hear me? Duchess called across the mental connection.

Although this vampire had never fed from her and they did not have the same bond she had with the others of her coven, Duchess was certain he would be able to make out her words over such a short distance. There was no direct response, but Duchess thought his attention flickered in her direction. And the more closely she focused on his life force, the more certain she felt that there *was*, in fact, something familiar about the feel of his mind.

Roars and applause broke out in the watching crowd, snapping her focus away from the shadowy presence. Something was happening on the platform.

Still in owl form, Duchess flapped silently to a new vantage point closer to the raised stage, but remaining within the shelter of the trees. The warrior monk turned, and a small form emerged from the shadows behind him. It was the same presence she'd just felt.

A young boy stepped forward, draped in orange robes. He had a very slight build and round, Tibetan features. His head had been completely shaved to match the other monks'.

Sangye Rinchen. It had to be.

With his eyes closed, the child lifted his hands towards the sky.

He was silent, but the monk who had whipped the crowd into a frenzy cried, "We will usher in a new era of prosperity and power, once we rid this city and this nation of the worthless filth polluting it!"

The boy opened his eyes. They glowed brightly in the dark—burning like embers, flickering red in the night as he gazed imperiously over the crowd. Duchess could not look away from him. She was both captivated by his presence here and repulsed at his inclusion within this farce of a rally.

Why was he helping the Brotherhood, even tacitly? He was a *vampire.* Xander and his mate Manisha reported that Sangye had been starving himself in London, making him too weak to fight or escape his captors. But he was not weak now. Power nearly crackled from his slight form. Nothing prevented him from transforming into mist and disappearing into the night this very instant. And yet, he did not.

The monk began to speak again, further inciting the crowd's passion. The mob fed off the aura that radiated from the boy. He said no word, but his presence filled the courtyard like the electric potential of an approaching thunderstorm, and even Duchess was not immune. Yet her fascination had nothing to do with the violent rhetoric being spewed from the stage. It was all for the child. He was a study in contradictions—both young and old, familiar and strange, inexperienced and powerful.

Could he be the answer to all we seek? Or is he a fresh danger to us?

She desperately needed to talk to him. She had to get him alone, so she could find out what he was doing here, and how he'd come to be here. Because the last time any of their number had seen this child, he'd been in the company of Bastian Kovac, the demon Bael... *and Snag.*

Rushing in would be foolish. She was no reckless youth, to act without thinking. She knew nothing about the child's loyalties or even his mental state. Manisha thought he was the reincarnation of the Dalai Lama, but he was also a little boy—and he'd been whisked away by a demon and a sadistic madman. They'd had him under their complete control for weeks now. She had no way of knowing what they'd done to him... whether he would consider her a friend or a foe.

Common sense took over. She knew that he was aware of her presence, just as she was aware of his. She would try to learn more before seeking to confront him directly. If nothing else, there was still Haziq to consider—she'd learned nothing of use regarding his condition or whereabouts. Not wanting to risk drawing attention, Duchess concentrated and pulled her life force into a tight knot in her chest. She transformed into mist, which would free her to move around without detection.

The rally rose to a crescendo before finally winding down. The child disappeared inside a side door leading into the temple, while the speaker and most of his entourage embarked with considerably more pomp and fanfare.

Duchess circled, still in vaporous form, and spotted a man from the head monk's retinue who was moving in the opposite direction from the others, clear purpose in his stride. He pushed his way through groups of people and did not stop to cheer or clap as the others nearby did.

Under the circumstances, she decided she could do worse than finding out what his errand was. She materialized into human form in the shadows and slipped after him on silent feet. While her beauty normally drew quite a bit of attention, stealth had always been a particular talent of hers when she cared to employ it, and she did so now.

The man slipped into a large complex of buildings about a block from the temple. They were close enough that the sounds of the crowd were still audible behind them. Duchess slipped into a recessed area between two of the buildings, completely hidden in the darkness. With her sharp hearing, she could make out the low voices of two individuals standing in the doorway of the building in front of her.

Most of the older vampires had picked up a number of languages over the centuries, out of some combination of interest, practicality, and boredom. Duchess was no exception, and that hobby came in useful as she came within hearing range of the men's conversation.

"Any new orders?" one of them inquired in Cantonese.

"He wants us to move the new hostage to the far end of the compound," the man Duchess had followed replied. Although they were keeping their voices quiet, Duchess could tell that neither of them was particularly concerned about being overheard.

"I wish he'd make up his mind," the first man grumbled. "This guy is trouble and I'm tired of carting him around."

"Hmm. Got a fighter this time, eh?" the second man said, mild amusement coloring his voice.

"Seems like it. I don't know—I complain about him, but in a way it's kind of nice to see some spirit for once."

The other man chuckled. "Spirit? Don't get used to it. I doubt it'll last long in this place."

Duchess felt her expression sharpen. How many new hostages were the Brotherhood likely to have? Could it be Haziq they were discussing? That seemed like quite a coincidence, on the one hand, but on the other hand, it made sense that if a new prisoner was causing trouble, the cult leader might have him moved to a more secure place of confinement. It was certainly worth following up, since that was the reason she'd come here in the first place.

The two men turned and entered the building, still chatting as they disappeared through the open door. Duchess darted forward with inhuman speed to catch it an instant before it could close and latch behind them. Holding her breath, she reached out with her senses and found that neither man had paused to make sure the door locked properly. They were already moving deeper into the building.

When she was sure that the way was clear, she slipped inside and allowed the door to slip fully shut behind her. Following the receding sound of the humans' footsteps, Duchess moved along behind them cautiously, pausing at every door and junction to ensure she was not seen. The footsteps grew fainter and she paused in the hallway, listening intently.

A door opened and closed somewhere ahead of her, but it echoed strangely, making the location impossible to pinpoint. There was no movement, no voices, nothing to guide her any further. She continued in the direction she'd been going, so focused on detecting any movement in the distance that she didn't pay close enough attention to her immediate surroundings. She had only an instant to register the indrawn breath and the sound of a steady heartbeat inside the room she'd just passed, before a body exploded into action behind her. A metal bar flashed across her vision, settling under her chin with surprising speed and force. Before she could slip free, a strong tug on the bar jerked her backwards through the open door by her neck.

The pressure on her windpipe would have been immediately debilitating to a human. Even as a vampire, it was a struggle to overcome the long-buried human instinct to panic at the feeling of her trachea being crushed. With a movement too quick for the man to avoid, Duchess landed a solid elbow blow to her attacker's stomach and was rewarded with a satisfying *oof* sound as the air left his lungs.

As the man fought not to double over in pain, the pressure on her windpipe eased for an instant. Duchess swung her legs up and planted her feet on the wall next to the door. With all the force she could muster, she propelled her weight backwards, sending them both crashing to the floor.

The man lost his grip on the metal bar as they went down. Duchess took advantage of the reprieve to twist so that she faced her assailant. As his head slammed on the clay tile floor behind him, Duchess jerked away, freeing herself from the close-quarters grappling.

Her limbs were quivering with reaction from the surprise attack, but she pushed power into them from her center. With a snarl, she reached down and hauled the man up by his shirtfront. Her strength flowed around the room, the air crackling with electricity.

"Enough," she hissed, feeling her fangs lengthen.

The man smirked, his dark eyes narrowed. "Not quite."

Duchess cocked her head and as she blinked, he moved. A gun barrel materialized inches from her face.

Merde. He was fast for a human.

After a split second's calculation of her chances in a fight while healing from a bullet wound through the face, she released the fabric clenched in her hand and took one step back. His expression was cold as he planted his feet and rolled his neck, vertebra cracking. She widened her eyes, playing the frightened captive as she prepared to mesmerize him.

"That's better," he said in Cantonese. "Now, let's start with who you are and…"

He fell silent, staring at Duchess with a strange, blank expression sliding over his strong features. The gun, which had been pointed at the center of her forehead, dipped slowly towards the floor.

Duchess gaped at him, taken aback. She hadn't exerted her power, yet he was acting like someone else had taken control of his will.

"I have a message for you," he said in a distant monotone.

Her gaze sharpened. "Do you, indeed?"

He was staring blankly into the middle distance, like he could no longer see her standing right in front of him.

How interesting…

Duchess reached out mentally, hoping to get a sense of the man's mind, but all she met was a completely blank wall. It was as though he were deep in a trance, without a hint of thought or emotion leaking through. She could sense nothing from him at all.

His lips parted. "Sangye is not the Thirteenth," he said in a monotone. "Bael is attempting to draw the Angel out of hiding, but he does not understand."

Silence descended for a long moment after the flat, distant words faded away. Duchess raised her eyebrows, perplexed.

"Who told you to say that?" Duchess asked cautiously. There were an extremely limited number of people in the world who could have implanted such a message. The most obvious culprit was the boy Sangye. But… did he have the power and skill to do so? Did he even know about the prophecy? A hundred questions swirled around her mind as she stared at the blank-faced human before her.

"Who are you?" Duchess demanded. "How did you know to tell me this?"

The man's arms dropped to his sides, the gun held loosely in his right hand. He made no answer and didn't even blink.

Duchess let out a growl of frustration. "Oh, come now! You've got to give me more than that. What do you know of the Thirteen? What do you know of the Angel?"

He still gave no reply, continuing to stand as if turned to stone.

Duchess felt her temper crackle, anger rising at whoever would plant such a cryptic message in a random human cult member and provide no further useful information beyond a riddle. She reached out and grabbed the man's throat, intending to shake him out of his stupor. Her fingers touched the exposed skin above the collar of his long-sleeved shirt. A sensation like an electric current passed through her, jolting all of her senses and sending her staggering backward a step. She stared down at her offending hand like it belonged to someone else.

"No," she whispered, unable to say anything more as memories rose up like brackish floodwater, choking her.

-o-o-o-

"No!" she screamed into the darkness. "I will not serve you, demon! I will not kill the father of my child!"

"Marie, do as the creature says!" her beloved Bertrand cried, thrashing on the ground. His spine arched in agony. A terrible gurgling noise came from his throat, right before blood erupted from his eyes and ears.

She stood over her fallen husband, facing the dark cloud that shifted and swirled around them. Marie could see glowing eyes within the mist and the vague outline of a huge, monstrous form with the head of a toad. A scratching noise filled the air around her, like millions of spiders crawling over plaster walls. The putrid smell of the black fog made her retch.

"Please," Bertrand whimpered, his voice growing weak. "Please, Marie, you must save yourself. Think of our child. Please!"

Marie wrapped her arms around her swollen stomach, feeling their child moving inside of her. She stared down at the protruding bulge, trying to picture the child within her womb. She knew she'd need every shred of strength she could muster if any of them were to survive.

-o-o-o-

"No," Duchess repeated in horror, wrenching herself back to the present. "No, I can't. *I'm not ready.*"

SEVEN

Chan blinked back to awareness as a shock like touching a live power line jolted through him. The woman who had just grabbed him by the throat reeled away from him, looking horrified. Chan fell to his knees, leaning over to catch his breath, one hand planted on the floor. He grasped his chest with the other and tried to master the sudden nausea that threatened to engulf him.

"No," the woman breathed, the word barely audible. "No, I can't. *I'm not ready.*"

Chan was a highly trained CIA operative, and a battle-hardened military veteran. He wasn't about to be knocked on his ass twice in sixty seconds by a slip of a woman with golden hair and dark, fluttering lashes. He lurched upright, putting a few steps of distance between them, and swallowed several times to bring his stomach back under control. After a moment, his watery eyes cleared enough for him to see the blonde woman staring at him with an unnatural, electric blue gaze.

His breath caught. It wasn't the first time he'd seen a person's eyes glowing like laser beams. In fact, he'd just come from the stage, where the nameless Tibetan boy's red eyes had whipped the crowd into new heights of fanaticism. Chan had been able to convince himself, up until now, that the red glow was some sort of stage trick. But the actinic blue light shining from the eyes of the woman in front of him wasn't so easy to dismiss.

He could feel the power leaking from her as much as he could see it. What she had just done should be impossible—no way should this woman have been able to restrain him and lift him from the floor like a rag doll. Even though she was only a few inches shorter than he was, he easily outweighed her by 30 kilos.

And she was *unarmed*, for fuck's sake. How could she possibly have gotten the best of him? Despite his burning humiliation at having been taken down by an opponent who should have offered no challenge whatsoever, he couldn't seem to stop staring at her like some kind of drooling imbecile. Catching himself, he raised the gun again, and blinked. When had he lowered it?

The moment he did so, the glowing light in her eyes intensified. A gray haze settled over his thoughts, and he shook his head sharply—trying to clear the confusion in his mind. It made his wits feel dull. He brought his free hand up to press at his temple, forcing himself to focus.

"What just happened?" he asked in a tone that was supposed to be stony, but somehow emerged sounding bewildered.

The woman took a long, slow breath before answering. "I believe I'm the one who will be asking the questions."

He raised his eyebrows at her confidence, flicking a quick glance at the semi-automatic pistol just to reassure himself that, yes, he was still holding it, and yes, it was still pointed at her head. She continued to stand there, ignoring the weapon, her eyes burning even brighter. He opened his mouth to snap something… to demand she start acting like someone who was staring down the barrel of a loaded gun.

Somehow, the words tangled up in his brain before he could say them, and his mouth slid shut again. It was really much easier that way, since his brain felt like overcooked mush.

"Who are you?" she asked.

"Chan Wei Yong," he replied, giving her his real name without a single thought, blowing his cover as though it meant absolutely nothing. *What the…?*

"Why are you in Malaysia, Wei Yong?" she pressed, her voice growing low and smoky.

Chan took a moment to breathe. Two decades of intensive training on how to withstand interrogation techniques warred with his primal, deep-seated need to speak. He hung in the balance for a long, tense moment.

"I… I am here… operating in Kuala Lumpur… as a security chief for the Brotherhood of the Cleansing Flame."

"Is that why you're really here?" she asked conversationally, staring into his eyes.

Chan felt a stirring in his consciousness, an unfamiliar sensation. He struggled mutely for a moment before relaxing. Giving in. The words flowed from him as though someone else was speaking using his voice.

"No," he answered with a heavy sigh. "I am here as a deep undercover operative employed by the United States. I'm CIA."

The woman nodded. "Go on…"

Her voice was a purr. He wanted to curl up at her feet and listen to it all night long.

"I've been undercover for a long time," he said, the truth continuing to pour from him in a damning stream of verbal diarrhea. "So long that sometimes it's hard to remember who I really am anymore. There are… so many awful things I've seen and done in the name of maintaining my cover." He blinked. "I used to be one of the good guys. That's what they told me, anyway, but even back then it was bullshit."

"That must be difficult," she said, leaning against the wall by the door. Her arms were crossed over her breasts, her tense posture at odds with her coaxing tone.

"It's all I've known for a long time," he said, feeling more certain of himself now. "I'm a good agent, and I want to serve my country."

"I understand," the woman replied, and the weight pressing on his mind lifted.

Chan took a deep breath, almost a gasp. He looked around, his vision swimming. The woman was still standing a few steps away, staring at him with an expression he couldn't decipher.

"What are you doing to me?" he demanded, his voice barely more than a whisper. His fingers clenched convulsively around the gun. *Shit*. He'd just blurted out his deepest secrets, and the only way to put that information back in the box was…

He steadied his aim, appalled by the fine tremor making the barrel waver. The woman gave him a knowing look. Her eyes glowed again, and the world went wobbly. When it settled, she was in exactly the same place as before, but his hand was empty, and she held the gun next to her hip, pointing down.

"I'm not doing anything to you," she said. "How could I? I'm standing all the way over here."

"You…" He strained to get the words out. "You're doing something to my mind!"

"Try to relax," said the demon temptress.

This seemed patently unfair since she appeared anything but relaxed. Even so, Chan closed his eyes, struggling with the impulse to simply slide down the wall and go to sleep. He wanted to forget about his duties… his handler… and most of all, about the beautiful and terrifying woman in front of him.

"If you're the Brotherhood's security chief, they must trust you with their secrets," she observed.

At that, Chan was able to pry his eyes open. They appraised each other for a long moment before his mouth started running again, still without his approval.

"Not as much as you might think. I mostly learn details by snooping and talking to people behind the scenes. It's my job to gather intelligence and report it back to the US."

"Is your handler nearby?" she asked.

"No. I have a supply of burner phones that I use to contact my superior."

"And no one here suspects you?"

He waved his hand. "It's a cult. They're suspicious of everyone. But they have no reason to suspect me more than anyone else."

"What do you know about them? The leaders—what are their aims?" the temptress asked, moving closer to him in the room's low light. Her eyes still glowed in a way that made Chan's skin tingle with apprehension and, oddly, a growing desire. He felt more aware of his own skin than he had in a long time, even though he still felt like an invisible weight was pressing down on him.

Did she drug me somehow? What the hell is this?

Still, the words flowed like water. "Like all such groups, they started small—just a handful of angry, disenfranchised people coming together around an outspoken leader. The monk's name is Tengku Asal, and he is a very powerful speaker. Charismatic. The Chinese immigrants around here feel like they've gotten a raw deal from the government, and Tengku spews rhetoric about cleansing the area of the Muslim nationals."

The temptress nodded. "What about money? Nothing gets this big without deep pockets standing behind it."

He shook his head slowly. "I can't find any concrete information about their source of funding. I do know that the leaders meet frequently with wealthy businessmen from Beijing, but they're careful never to name names." Chan paused. "There's also some guy from Eastern Europe, but I haven't been able to get any info on him. He's basically a ghost, and Tengku is the only one who ever seems to have contact with him."

The woman twitched at his last words and Chan blinked at her.

"*Putain de merde*," she cursed under her breath. "This is all we need." She shook her head and addressed him again. "Enough about that. Tell me about the kidnappings."

"They capture people off the street. Sometimes at random. Sometimes political targets or opponents."

"What happens to these people?"

"It depends. Some are held for ransom. Others are tortured, starved, and eventually killed. The leaders try to get information out of those that they believe have connections."

"Do you know where the prisoners are being held?" The woman's voice held only mild interest, but her expression was that of a jungle cat scenting prey.

Chan struggled again, with exactly the same result as before—which was to say, none at all. "I can take you there now," he said in defeat.

Yes. Bring her to me. Hurry—my strength is almost gone.

The deep mental voice echoed inside Chan's skull, making the world go sideways for a moment. When he blinked his vision clear, he found that the woman had gripped his arm through his shirtsleeve and was squeezing hard enough to bruise.

"What was that?" she asked.

"It's nothing," he answered in a flat tone. "Let's go. I need to take you to see the prisoners now."

Her eyes narrowed, but she gestured toward the door. "Lead the way. I'll just hold onto your gun for you."

He fought his way through the mental fog long enough to ask, "Who are you?"

The woman paused, as though considering her answer.

"Duchess," she said, her expression very controlled. "You can call me Duchess."

Chan nodded, and led the way deeper into the building.

-o-o-o-

The journey through the sprawling condominium complex felt like walking through a dream. The world around him was surreal, everything seeming darker and more threatening than he ever remembered it being before. Even so, he led Duchess towards the prisoners with stealthy steps. She walked at his left shoulder, pausing at the exact moment he did, as if she could predict his movements before he made them.

His body felt sluggish... or maybe everything around him was speeding up? He couldn't really tell. He took them up the stairwell to the higher stories of the building that weren't being used for anything. These levels were deserted, meaning they could avoid prying eyes as they crossed to the other end of the complex—where the repurposed office area was located, with its hidden entrance to the basement level.

"Tell me more about the message you gave me," Duchess said once they'd left the more populated areas.

Chan looked at her. Pale moonlight filtered through the windows of the hallway they were traversing, bathing her features in silver.

Beautiful, he thought, only to berate himself a moment later. For fuck's sake... she was doing something to his mind. She had his fucking *gun,* while he was taking her to see the Brotherhood's most secure prisoners. And he was mooning over her because she was *pretty*?

Eventually, his brain caught up with her words. "Message?" he finally asked.

She gave him a searching glance. "You said, 'I have a message for you. Sangye is not the Thirteenth. Bael is attempting to draw the Angel out of hiding, but he does not understand.'"

"I don't know what you're talking about," Chan replied, frowning. "I… don't remember much after hitting my head."

"That didn't seem to keep your mouth from running."

Chan threw a dark look at her.

"You really have no memory of saying that?" she asked.

"I told you I didn't," he said, a bit sharply.

She was silent for a long time, clearly turning the information over in her mind.

"I wonder if he's here," she murmured. "It would make a sort of sense, since the boy is here."

"What are you talking about?" Chan asked, his frustration beginning to grow as his mind became clearer.

Duchess looked startled by his question, clearly not realizing that she'd spoken out loud. "Someone I'm looking for. That message—it sounded like something he would say. Which makes me wonder if he's the one who gave it to you."

"No one has given me any messages," Chan insisted, his voice growing hard even as uncertainty pricked at him.

Dark eyes, meeting his from a face that looked like it should belong among the dead, not the living. A deep voice emerging from lips that did not move…

"Suit yourself," she muttered. "There are people ahead of us. What are you going to tell them?"

They were approaching the atrium, with the ground floor offices beyond. It wasn't surprising that other people would be around. Guards patrolled the occupied levels of the building twenty-four hours a day, seven days a week.

"I'm not going to tell them anything," he replied. "They answer to me, not the other way around."

As they passed into the atrium, Chan thought he saw a smile pass across Duchess' face, but it was quickly masked by indifference. He turned his attention to the double doors ahead of them and pushed through. He approached the guards at a comfortable pace. Chan's men stepped aside as he nodded to them, allowing him to pass without question. Even so, he had no doubt that a report of his visit in the company of a female westerner would reach Tengku's ears. He turned towards the highest ranking of his men, prepared to offer some lie to account for her presence, when he realized with a start that she was no longer behind him.

He checked his surprise sharply, only his long experience with covering his reactions keeping him from gasping. His men looked at him expectantly, clearly thinking he was about to issue them some order.

He scanned the area discreetly and muttered, "As you were."

What the actual fuck? Was he finally losing his grip on sanity?

Chan didn't know what the hell to do, so he proceeded into the office as he'd originally planned. *Shit, shit, shit.* If he could just clear his head, he might be able to think properly and figure out what the hell was happening to him. He slipped through the heavy door, eager to get away from suspicious eyes. Pulling the door shut behind him, he turned to find Duchess standing right in front of him.

Years of practice covering his reactions be damned — he flinched hard at her unexpected reappearance, taking a step back. His back thumped softly against the closed door.

"What. The. *Hell*?" he demanded, lifting a hand to his head. "Where —? *How* —?"

"Practice," she replied, her tone making it clear that the topic was not up for discussion.

"*That's not an answer!*" he hissed through gritted teeth, not wanting to risk attracting the attention of the guards outside.

Neither was the reappearance of the eerie glow in her blue eyes, but a moment later he found himself leading her to the storeroom and the basement staircase beyond, with no memory of making the decision to do so. Duchess followed silently behind him. He opened the stairwell door and confirmed that the light was turned off, which meant no one was in the dungeon with the prisoners.

"There are no guards down here at the moment," he breathed, "but it's still a good idea to keep quiet."

"Is this where the prisoners are being kept?" she asked, peering into the darkness as though she could see right through it.

Chan blinked a few times. What the hell had he been thinking, bringing her here? He hesitated, his foot dangling over the edge of one of the stairs.

"I don't know why I brought you here," he said in a slow voice, his eyes unfocused. "What's... happening to me?"

"There was something you needed to show me," Duchess prompted, her voice infinitely reasonable. "One of the prisoners, perhaps?"

"Yeah," Chan answered in a haze. "Yeah, I think... that sounds right."

He led her down to the dungeon as though sleepwalking.

"Through here," he said as they exited the stairwell. The stench of filthy bodies and waste rose up to greet them. Duchess gasped sharply and stepped forward, moving with unerring steps to the cell holding the skeletal man with the dark, piercing eyes. His flesh was scarred and grey in the flickering light from a single bulb. He was still chained to the wall, lying on his back and resembling nothing so much as a preserved corpse.

Duchess' steps faltered, her hands gripping the bars of the cell as though she needed the support to remain upright. A small noise slipped free from her throat.

Chan leaned heavily against the moist wall. The damp seeped through his shirt, and he focused on the faint chill as he used all his willpower to try to fight off the wooziness that still assailed him. Around them, the other prisoners muttered and wept, but the figure chained in the cell was completely silent. No dark velvet voice spoke inside Chan's head; no piercing black eyes met his. Time stretched like melting taffy.

A blur of movement startled Chan from his reverie.

"Come on," Duchess hissed, grabbing his shirt and yanking him towards the stairs.

"What?" he asked, frowning at the way his voice slurred.

"Come *on*! Move your feet!"

"Where are we going?" he asked. Something in his mind snapped back into place like a rubber band, making him stumble uncharacteristically.

"Nowhere if you don't keep your legs underneath you," Duchess snarled.

Chan blinked and found himself at the top of the stairs, still being dragged along by the demon temptress.

"You know him, then?" he asked, jerking his head towards the captives. The movement nearly sent him careening back down the stairs as his balance wavered.

"We've got to get out of here," Duchess said, her tone urgent. "You're going to have to walk, it will look too strange if I carry you."

"What are you talking about?" Chan asked, bewildered. Her words sounded like they were coming from underwater. Or maybe he was the one that was underwater.

Pressure tightened in his chest.

They stumbled forward through the offices, bursting out to the atrium and past the confused looking guards. One of them shouted something, but Duchess sent him a hard glare, eyes glowing, and he subsided. The building's exit loomed ahead. Duchess hauled him through it, his limbs barely functioning enough to hold his weight.

"I will drag you the entire way if I have to," Duchess growled, "but this would really be easier if Snag hadn't mind-whammied you nearly into a coma."

"Uhh," Chan replied, trying to remember how to make his legs work. He drew on all his strength and pushed away from her, shaking like a leaf. His muscles burned. He took a few staggering steps before she was back under his arm, helping him along. Their bare skin brushed when she grabbed his wrist to steady him, making everything inside of him sing.

Closing his eyes for just a moment, Chan felt himself being guided across gravel. They were outside. The air in Kuala Lumpur was hardly what you'd call fresh, but it was much better than the musty basement where Tengku was holding his prisoners.

He lifted his heavy head and saw that guards were stationed around the gate to the complex as usual.

They'll never let us through, he thought.

Chan was wrong, however. The guards neither moved nor spoke as they passed through the open gate, Duchess still supporting his heavier frame. At any moment, he expected a shout to follow them, but not a sound could be heard except the quiet chirping of nighttime insects.

"How...?" he began, only to fall silent. It was taking every ounce of his concentration to flop one numb foot down in front of the other, over and over.

Duchess didn't answer, and he fell into an uneasy fugue state, his legs moving on autopilot. When he became aware again, they were inside an unfamiliar building, standing in front of a dark, wood-paneled door. Duchess pushed it open and tossed him unceremoniously over the threshold. He fell to the floor in a heap, distantly relieved that it was covered in plush carpet. As his awareness came into sharper focus, he heard a pair of surprised exclamations from elsewhere in the room.

"Duchess! What on *earth*?" A female voice asked.

A man crouched in front of him, his slate-blue eyes peering at him in concern. He lifted one of Chan's eyelids and brought up a cell phone. A bright light flashed in Chan's face.

"He's completely out of it," the man muttered, turning off the light. "What the hell did you do to him? I thought that we agreed about feeding from strangers…"

"I didn't feed from him," Duchess snapped.

"So, what happened to him?" the man asked. "Who is he?"

"Long story," his temptress muttered.

"*Duchess*—" The other woman's voice was sharp.

Chan peered at Duchess as she crouched next to him and lifted him by the arms. To his surprise, she was able to lift him easily, half-carrying him towards a bed. He felt himself being lowered onto the comfortable mattress and sighed in relief. Maybe if he could get a few hours of sleep, things would start to make sense when he woke up. Or, even better, he'd find out this had all been a dream. That would definitely work for him.

He smiled, feeling better about things now that he'd figured out this wasn't real. *Yeah, just a dream…*

"You're not going to be so happy about things in a minute," Duchess said grimly.

She straightened up, glaring at the other two people in the room.

"This is Chan Wei Yong," she said, and Chan twitched at the use of his real name. "He used to be my husband, Bertrand, in seventeenth century France. Now he's an American CIA agent on an undercover assignment inside the Brotherhood. I'll need you both to watch over him for the next day or two. Oh, and I also found out that they're holding the boy, Sangye Rinchen. Snag is there, too, but he made me promise not to rescue him yet."

The twin expressions of shock and increasingly strident demands for an explanation went unheeded.

"I'd apologize for this," she said, looking down at him with an unreadable expression. "But in the end, what would be the point?"

"Wait…" Chan began, wanting answers to at least some of the myriad of questions whirling inside his head. The rest of his sentence was lost as Duchess leaned forward and sank her teeth into his neck.

For a moment, he was lost in the sharp, shocking pleasure-pain of her bite. He gasped and arched, his body straining toward the demon temptress and away from her in equal measure. Deep suction drew his pulsing blood through the wound she'd just inflicted on him. His hazy thoughts grew hazier, lightheadedness making the room grow darker and lighter in time with his pounding heartbeat. She took and took from him, until he was certain he had nothing left to give.

He *burned*. His neck was on fire at the site of her bite and he jerked weakly, trying to sever the connection.

Chan felt her draw even more deeply from the wound at his neck, and the burning began to spread into his head and down his limbs. It was agony, but nothing compared to the feeling that rose in his chest. Something inside him was being ripped in two—the very fabric of his soul rending like torn cloth.

"Stop!" he tried to scream, but the word emerged as a nearly inaudible croak. The feeling of sedation was still lying heavy across his body, and he could only muster enough strength to lift his hands a few inches. They felt detached from his body, useless and numb.

Still, she did not yield. He tried to roll away, but she restrained him as easily as one might restrain a new-born kitten.

"No," he whispered, fire consuming him from the inside out.

Finally, she released him and stepped away.

"I'm sorry," she whispered. "I won't burden you with my presence after this, but for the sake of the world, it has to be done."

"*Ti mwen*, what are you *doing*?" The other woman implored. "You're giving him no choice!"

The reply was hard and cold as ice. "That's because there *is* no choice, Oksana. Don't you see? There is no choice at all—there never has been, for us."

Cool flesh pressed across his slack lips. The smell of copper assaulted Chan's nose, and thick liquid dripped into his mouth. The fire roared higher, demanding to be slaked with blood. Fresh stabs of pain erupted in his mouth as his canines lengthened and sharpened, digging into the flesh of his cheeks.

A few drops of the temptress' blood slipped down his throat, and all rational thought fled. He snapped his jaws around the offered wrist, tearing into pale flesh to get more of that sweet nectar. He drew it into himself in great, gulping swallows. He needed more… more… *more*… needed all the blood in her body… all the blood in the world. There would never be enough blood to douse the flames inside him.

This was hell. It had to be. When his movements grew weaker and more lethargic with every swallow, his mind sliding down to a place of blackness and torment, he was sure of it.

The last thing he heard was the temptress saying, "Look after him," in a voice scraped raw, as though she'd been screaming. A door opened and closed with a slam. After that, he knew no more.

EIGHT

Snag drifted in a state of unbeing, his mind far away from the wasted remains of his body, which was laid out in iron chains on the floor of the Brotherhood's dungeon in Kuala Lumpur. He had not moved a muscle since Duchess fled with her mate... had it been several hours ago?

No matter. He'd summoned a last burst of strength and ordered her not to intervene in his captivity. For the moment, he was exactly where he needed to be. The young vampire, Sangye, still required his help. Without drawing too deeply on his dwindling reserves, he reached out mentally and touched the connection between the two of them. The boy had sensed her presence earlier that evening. His skills were not so well tuned that he could identify Duchess specifically, but he'd felt another vampire nearby.

After her mate's unexpected appearance at the door of Snag's cell the previous day, he hadn't been surprised to find that Duchess was the one to stumble upon him. There was a hand at play here beyond mere happenstance—this much had become clear to him in the months since Tré found Della in New Orleans.

Israfael was finally waking from her long sleep.

Elder? Sangye's youthful voice pierced his musings. They were separated by distance—he a shackled prisoner, while Sangye played the part of Kovac and Bael's puppet. Yet the bond that he shared with the young vampire was strong, tying them together by necessity and blood.

Are you well, child? Snag inquired.

I am tired, Elder.

Snag sent what strength he could spare, which sadly wasn't much. *We must persevere. Withdraw into meditation and rest your mind, as you are able. You must maintain the strength to keep going.*

Snag felt the boy's hesitation. Snag had never fully explained the depths of his own power, knowing that the information would not be helpful to Sangye, and might be dangerous. It was knowledge that needed to be kept far from Kovac, and even farther from Bael.

I wish I had your courage, Elder, Sangye finally replied.

Courage is merely unwavering focus on one's goal, even when circumstances seem dire. You fed enough to maintain your strength until the monks return you to my side. Draw on the stores of energy you gained from me.

A pause. *What I am doing for the monks is wrong. Yet I cannot do otherwise.*

Despite Sangye's ancient soul, he was still a frightened boy who lacked practical life experience. He was respectful of Snag's guidance, but Snag knew he did not understand why they were going along with the ploys of their captors. Whereas Snag, a chess expert, was himself a master of ploys.

Patience, child. Your time will come to stand up for what is right, Snag counseled.

He felt Sangye sigh in weariness and allowed his own life force to swirl around the boy. It was all the comfort he had to offer.

The door at the top of the stairwell leading down to Snag's basement prison crashed open, and boot steps pounded down the stairs. He let his awareness flow back inside his physical shell as moans of fear erupted from several of his fellow prisoners. The humans kept here had good reason to fear the appearance of the guards. Cruelty was rampant.

With the exception of Snag, everyone in this place was expendable in the eyes of the cult leaders, at least to some degree. More than one had been dragged from the cells and had not returned. The rest were given only enough food and water to survive, and the stench of illness and rot in the basement was nearly overwhelming.

Fortunately for his fellow prisoners, it seemed as though Snag was to be the focus of attention for now, at least to start.

"You," a voice spat.

The voice did not belong to Bastian Kovac, the cult leader called Tengku, the man who was Duchess' lost mate, or any of Snag's friends, so it could safely be ignored. Snag might be encouraging the child Sangye to cooperate with their captors, but that was because he didn't yet know how Sangye's story would end.

He, on the other hand, was in no danger. Bael wanted him alive.

The door to his cell creaked open. A moment later, a hard boot impacted his ribs. Two of the bones cracked, and then immediately started to heal. The process was growing markedly slower these past days. After weeks of feeding Sangye, his body had nearly reached its limits. Once it finally did, matters would be simplified. In the millennia since his turning, the physical had always been little more than a distraction to him.

"Unless you are finally dead, you will show respect to your betters, Silent One," the guard growled. Another flurry of kicks followed.

The man was one of the many guards who patrolled the building where Snag and the other prisoners were being kept. A nobody, caught up in the imagined glory of something larger than he was. Snag let his eyes slip closed, trying to tune him out.

"Maybe you'd pay more attention if I brought you the head of that little freak child on a stake, eh?" A heavy boot landed on Snag's sternum, pressing down.

As abuse went, he supposed it would have been more effective on a being that still needed to breathe.

And as for the verbal threat, it probably would have been more effective on someone who didn't know how much the monk Tengku relied on his new pet vampire. Without Sangye, who would awe Tengku's followers with glowing eyes and an otherworldly aura?

Under Bastian Kovac's instruction, Tengku was engaged in a delicate balancing act with his two vampire prisoners. Snag's original plan, hastily conceived in the warehouse in London, had been to accompany the child and convince him to feed until he was strong enough to shift form and escape. Unfortunately, Sangye was naive and softhearted enough to be controlled by threats against Snag's life.

Tengku had convinced the boy that he would behead Snag the instant Sangye attempted escape, and no reassurance Snag gave him would move the child to ignore that threat. Snag, of course, could not leave a young boy alone in the hands of Darkness. And so, their slow dance of danger continued.

Now that Duchess was here — presumably still in the company of Mason and Oksana — the balance would not hold much longer. He only hoped that Sangye would come to understand his true power before it was too late. Snag could perhaps feed the child one more time, but it was quite likely that would be the end of his physical reserves. Once more, he would be relegated to the corpse-like state in which he had spent so much of his long, painful life.

He had faith that Eris and the others would know what to do when that happened, but it would mean the end of his usefulness in convincing Sangye of his power and agency. Tengku was using Sangye as a figurehead to awe the gullible, and Snag was counseling the boy to go along with that manipulation. Because, once the figurehead came to wield more influence over the cult's followers than Tengku did, that figurehead could step forward and wrest control from the warrior monk.

There was only one problem. The child feared that the moment he rebelled, it would mean Snag's death. Snag knew that was an unlikely outcome since the demon Bael had other uses for him, but Sangye refused to entertain even the slight risk.

Stalemate.

On the physical plane, blows and abuse continued to rain down on him until the bored guard grew weary of beating and yelling at an unresponsive body. He left, kicking the bars of another cell hard on his way out, making the poor soul inside cringe and cry out in fear.

Snag lay on the floor and waited for what would come next. He didn't need to wait for long before the skittering of thousands of invisible spider legs across his skin alerted him to the presence of the demon.

There was another reason Snag had encouraged Sangye to feed from him until his body hovered on the edge of complete shutdown. Snag purposely sank more fully into the physical, letting his body pull more of his dwindling energy reserves from his mind to repair the fresh damage done by the guard's boots and fists. Being a simple creature at heart, Bael assumed that additional pain and injury would weaken Snag's defenses against the demon's mental assault.

Fortunately for all of them, Bael was a foolish being in many ways—otherwise, they would have perished long ago. But Bael was incomplete, driven by what he lacked and unaware of what he truly needed. The demon thought to drive his opponent, the Angel Israfael, into the open by threatening the most powerful member of her Council. He sought to finish the job he'd been unable to complete millennia ago, by ripping the Light from Snag's soul while he perceived Snag to be weakened.

Foolish.

Snag let his body draw energy until his consciousness guttered to a mere ember, only dimly aware of Bael's shrieks of frustration as the demon clawed uselessly at the tiny flicker of life, unable to grasp something so small and insubstantial.

Again, a stalemate. And at least now, Snag could get some proper rest until they brought the boy back to drain the last few dregs of his blood. After that, the fight would lie in other hands than his. He only hoped the groundwork he'd laid would be enough to shape the outcome of the battle.

NINE

Duchess strode out of the hotel room as though the hounds of hell were at her heels, the door slamming behind her. It was wrenched open an instant later. The grip that tightened on her arm and spun her around before she'd made it a dozen steps was not that of a hellhound, however, but that of her closest friend.

Pity—she would have much preferred to face a spectral predator than the look of shocked disbelief on Oksana's face.

"*Duchess!*" Oksana said on a gasp. "What in the name of all that's holy are you *doing*?"

She should dissipate into mist and flee. She should fall into Oksana's arms and beg forgiveness for what she'd just done. She should—

She swallowed hard. "What does it look like I'm doing? I've just located the eleventh member of the Council, and turned him before the forces of Darkness could find him and kill him."

Oksana gaped at her, as though it had somehow escaped her attention before now that Duchess was an ice-cold bitch with no compunctions and no illusions about what her future was likely to hold. She felt a sudden, irrational desire for Xander's presence, which was ridiculous since she'd recently thrown Xander's heartfelt confession of his past sins in his face and more or less spit on him. If there was a way to burn a century-old friendship to the ground without uttering a single word, that was probably it.

She really hoped her friendship with Oksana wasn't about to go the same way.

Oksana blinked, and shook her head—a tiny movement that made it look like she was trying to shake her thoughts back into order. The grip on Duchess' arm relaxed from *bruising* to *steadying*.

"All right," she said, more calmly. "So, you've turned your mate. You've made it harder for Bael to move against him, and maybe it will help calm the vortex of chaos that was already forming around this place. Now come back inside and talk with him. It's clear he has no idea what's going on."

"No," she said immediately.

Oksana's hand tightened again. "Why? *Why*, Duchess?"

A gaping chasm opened in Duchess' chest. "Because he may be the reincarnation of my husband Bertrand, but we have no future together. My situation is not like yours, *ma petite chérie*."

It was the middle of the night, and the hotel hallway was deserted. One of the bulbs lighting it was about to go out—it flickered in an irregular pattern, in time with a faint electrical buzz. Oksana's other hand closed around Duchess' shoulder, and she used the grip to press Duchess back a step until her back met the wall with a light thump. Oksana looked up from her slight disadvantage of height, dark eyes kindling with small points of violet.

"It's time for you to tell me what happened to you, *ti mwen*," she said, very quietly. "In fact, it's well past time."

Duchess' chest caught on another shard of pain. She was older than her friend by the better part of two centuries and had the power to prove it—but to shove Oksana away and flee might well be the action that set their friendship aflame. She was old, yes… and strong. But she wasn't *that* strong.

"Bertrand was a musketeer under King Louis XIII," she began slowly, striving to keep her voice level and dispassionate, "and I was his wife. I was also a spy for the king's greatest enemy—his younger brother Gaston, better known as the Duc d'Orléans. Gaston had designs on his brother's throne, and at the time, the king had no heir. If Louis had died before his wife Anne bore him a son, the throne would have gone to Gaston."

Oksana did not speak or interrupt. Nor did she let Duchess go. Instead, she only nodded, listening avidly.

"My husband was a favorite of the king's," she continued. "He was both brave and courtly, with a pleasant demeanor and a sharp wit. As a favored musketeer, he had the king's ear, though I never knew him to use his influence for selfish or political means. Nevertheless, it made him a powerful figure at court."

Oksana's shrewd eyes widened in understanding. "He was powerful because he had the king's ear. But you were a spy for the king's brother. You had both Bertrand's ear and Gaston's."

Duchess nodded, her eyes growing distant. "Bael thought that if I were his puppet, I might be the key to bringing down the French monarchy. Had he been successful, it would have thrown all of Europe into chaos. Gaston was a fool, and quite possibly insane as well. His ascension to the throne would have been disastrous."

A frown creased Oksana's brow. "If he was such a threat to France, why did you agree to be his spy?"

A harsh breath of laughter choked her.

"For the coin," she said. "Bertrand gambled. He lost all our money at cards, and then some. We were about to—" She cut herself off, appalled at what she'd nearly let slip, and shook her head. "It doesn't matter. I... needed money to buy food and pay Bertrand's gambling debts. There were a limited number of ways for a woman to get that kind of money, and when one of Gaston's lackeys approached me with an offer, it seemed less onerous than whoring, so I accepted."

Oksana finally released her arms, taking a step back.

"I see," she said, no judgment clouding her tone. "But what I don't see is how that affects the current situation. You and Bertrand might have betrayed each other once, a long time ago, but Chan isn't Bertrand. He needs you now, even if he doesn't realize it yet. And, I'm sorry, Duchess—but you need him, too."

"No," she said simply. "Chan is an innocent pawn caught up in this war. Believe me when I say, I am the very last thing he needs."

I am the very last thing any man needs.

Oksana continued to look at her with those large, violet-lit eyes, and Duchess could feel the tentative brush of her thoughts, searching.

"There's more, isn't there?" she asked.

Duchess regarded her, silent and unmoving. Not replying. Eventually, Oksana sighed in defeat.

"Fine," she said. "Keep the rest of your secrets for now. But what are we supposed to do with Chan?"

Duchess only shook her head—she had no more answers to give.

-o-o-o-

Chan's darkness was shot through with crimson swirls of memory and confusion. Dimly, he was aware of his physical body. It still felt as though he were being torn open by red-hot claws, exposing the vulnerable flesh inside to devouring flames. He heaved and struggled, but the agony was not something outside of him... not something he could escape by moving.

There was nothing to be done except surrender to the oblivion gathering at the edges of his mind. As he sank deeper, he began to feel a gentle swaying beneath him, like he was seated on a moving surface. His awareness became more dreamlike, and he blinked, finding himself no longer in a dingy hotel room in Kuala Lumpur, but rather in the dazzling sunlight on the edge of a glade of trees.

He looked down and discovered that the swaying motion was due to the fact that he was on horseback, of all things. The animal was plodding along at its ease, one ear cocking toward him in a lazy movement.

"Bertrand!" a voice called.

Trotting hoof beats approached from behind and he turned, somehow recognizing the name as his own despite the fact that he'd never heard anyone address him that way in his life. As he watched, the man on horseback approached him, dressed in leather and linen from a bygone age. A sword hung at his belt, and an antique musket hung in a long holster at his mount's shoulder. A moment later, he recognized the face of his dear friend, Pierre, one of his brothers-in-arms in the service of the King's Musketeers.

"You started your journey early, my friend," Pierre admonished. "You should have waited for me."

"Aye," Bertrand said, shifting his tabard to cover the nearly empty coin purse hanging from his belt. "But I couldn't bear to see the knowing look on your face."

"Hmm... I take it your purse is considerably lighter than before we passed the Red Hen?" Pierre raised an eyebrow. "Why do you gamble so much, *mon ami*?"

"Why, for the thrill of victory, Pierre!" he blustered. "It is much like a battle, in that I must slay my foe. But at least at the card table, he merely walks away humiliated and poor, rather than missing a limb or dead."

"How very altruistic of you to spare your opponents' lives," Pierre replied, allowing their horses to walk side by side. The two geldings were stabled next to each other in the Musketeer garrison, and they sniffed noses in greeting. "Though were I a braver man, I might point out that your analysis assumes your foe is on the losing side."

Bertrand only grunted.

"I doubt Marie will allow you to participate in such escapades once your babe is born," Pierre continued idly, settling back in his saddle and pushing his blue cloak out of the way of the breeze.

"Ah, I have no worries there. My wife is a magician with the coin, even when I manage to hit a spot of sore luck," Bertrand assured his friend.

It was true, and one of the many reasons he adored Marie. Yes, he probably gambled too much. He considered himself to be both lucky and skillful when placing bets, but he was not immune to the occasional downfall. No mortal man was, after all. Lately, he'd been in an admitted slump. He'd hoped that by playing a few rounds with complete strangers in the village they'd just left, he would break his losing streak.

"At the risk of raising your ire, my friend, you and sore luck seem to be close companions these days," Pierre said. "Perhaps it's time to leave these youthful follies behind? You are about to have a son of your own. You're not getting any younger, and it's time to think of accumulating an inheritance for your heir."

"Inheritance… yes," Bertrand answered in a vague tone. Truthfully, he'd given almost no thought to laying down an inheritance for a son, because he was secretly hoping that Marie was carrying a daughter instead.

That might have been an unusual wish, he knew. Much emphasis was placed on producing strong sons to carry on the family name. Yet Bertrand had long ignored traditional customs in favor of pursuing his heart's desires. He was an unusually old Musketeer at the age of thirty-one, and he had only taken a wife within the last few years. He'd courted Marie in secret until finally saving up enough money for a suitable dowry to her father.

Old Monsieur La Fleche had been less than delighted to know that his daughter was marrying a soldier, even one in a regiment as prestigious as the musketeers. He'd hoped, perhaps understandably, for a suitor with a less hazardous job and more financial security, but he'd accepted the arrangement grudgingly after Marie had made her voice heard over the matter.

Rarely meek or mild, Marie was usually one to speak her mind and make her opinions known. This was another thing that Bertrand cherished about his wife. He'd never been able to stomach the simpering women at Court. He needed someone who was bold and courageous, who could match his fire with a blaze that both fed and sated his needs. Marie fit that requirement admirably, and he loved her for it.

He and Pierre rounded a familiar bend in the road that led to the musketeers' garrison. After another ten minutes of riding, they reached the stables—home at last after a grueling two-day journey. They'd been tasked with delivering a message to one of the King's cousins in an isolated palace more than a dozen leagues from Paris. The King had ordered them to guard the missive they carried with their very lives, if necessary.

Happily, the trip had been uneventful—almost surprisingly so. The message was delivered without incident, and they were able to return home at a more leisurely pace. One that even allowed for a game of cards or three in the village between the cousin's palace and their home environs of Paris.

After unsaddling their horses and turning them over to the stable boys, Bertrand and Pierre slung their belongings onto their shoulders and checked in with Monsieur de Tréville, the garrison's commander.

The grizzled old soldier nodded in satisfaction upon hearing of the letter's safe delivery. "Well done, lads. His Majesty has no more use for you today. Take the time to rest after your journey, and report for duty at mid-morning tomorrow."

They acknowledged the welcome orders and departed soon after.

"Drink?" Pierre asked.

Bertrand smiled and shook his head. "I think not. I'm going back to my apartments to check on Marie. She works too hard when I'm not there to make her rest. Why don't you find René and Jean Paul? Let them buy you a bottle and raise a glass for me."

Pierre gave him a knowing look and nodded, diverting his course towards a tavern frequented by members of the regiment.

Bertrand continued on, trying not to think about the lack of weight in his coin purse. He did feel a twinge of guilt about losing so much at the Red Hen, but he hoped that Marie wouldn't be too severe with him. Surely she wouldn't be upset—she always managed to come up with the money they needed.

Finally, he came within sight of their small set of rooms on the Rue Férou. He passed through the front door, but the inside was quiet except for the purr of the fat tabby cat Marie kept to discourage the mice. Bertrand continued to the enclosed courtyard at the back of the small building. He found his beloved standing with her back to him, hanging clothes to dry from the line stretched across the open space.

At the sound of his footsteps, she turned and smiled at him. Her blue eyes sparkled, and a few dark curls escaped her chignon, framing her porcelain features.

Bertrand felt a strange sensation, like he was being pulled from a dream. Something about Marie's face tugged at him. In his thoughts, it was framed by loose waves of golden hair, and her eyes glowed from within, emitting a strange, unearthly light. He shook his head sharply, dislodging the odd daydream and the sense of unease that came with it.

"You've returned!" Marie said cheerfully.

He smiled at her and pulled her into an embrace, her swollen stomach pressed between them.

"So I have, *mon coeur*," he replied playfully, slipping a pin from her hair so that it fell loose around her shoulders. "You should not be straining yourself so. Are you well?"

"Quite," Marie said with a laugh, and batted his hands away. "You worry too much."

Bertrand reached out and laid a palm on her distended belly, hoping to feel movement from their babe.

"Sleeping, I think," Marie commented, rubbing her sides. "Which is saying something, since I was up half the night with all the kicking."

Bertrand chuckled, wondering if a quick tumble in bed would help her relax enough to nap for a bit. He could push up her skirts and tunnel beneath them, kissing his way up her legs until—

Marie shivered, and glanced around, looking suddenly nervous.

Bertrand frowned. "Marie?"

She looked back at him, smiling widely. *Too* widely. "It's nothing," she said quickly.

"What's wrong? Are you certain you're well?" Bertrand pressed, laying a hand across her forehead to check for fever.

"Yes, of course," Marie said, sounding more herself. "It's silly. I keep feeling this chill breeze blowing over me, that's all. Let's… just… go inside."

Bertrand raised his eyebrows. Of all the excuses Marie could come up with to reassure him, that was perhaps the least effective. Ever since her pregnancy first started to show, she'd been overly warm regardless of the weather. For her to confess a chill when the weather was so balmy seemed somehow ominous.

"You're only making me worry more, you know," Bertrand accused, but he allowed himself to be pulled toward the back door.

All at once, a low, dark cloud rolling in obscured the blue sky. Bertrand whirled and looked up in alarm as curls of blackness descended into the courtyard. *Mon Dieu...* was there a fire in one of the neighbors' houses?

Marie cried out and tried to pull him inside, but Bertrand's feet were rooted to the ground. He could not lift them, nor tear his eyes away from the darkness hurtling in their direction. This was no smoke. In fact, it was nothing from the mortal realm. The fog shifted and thickened, suggesting horrible, demonic forms within. With numb fingers, Bertrand crossed himself and drew his rapier, knowing even as he did it that there was nothing for him to fight. Nothing that could be stopped with steel, at any rate.

His wife tried to call his name, only to collapse into harsh coughing as the fog rolled over them. It was foul, like vitriol. Bertrand felt his nose and lungs burn, the smell of sulfur making his eyes sting and water.

"Marie," he choked out, reaching for his wife through the heavy gloom.

He found her arm, which was cold to the touch and shook violently under his hand.

A voice like nails screeching across slate echoed within the courtyard.

"She has betrayed you," it crooned.

Bertrand looked around wildly, hoping for an opponent he could fight with blade or flintlock. He could see no one else, however, and was forced to conclude that the terrible noise was somehow coming from the cloud itself. Still, he had never been one to quail in the face of danger. Bertrand pulled himself up straight and extended his blade. He moved to stand in front of Marie, who gripped his shoulders from behind, her fingers like claws.

"I would put more faith in such a ridiculous accusation if the man who made it had enough courage to show himself," Bertrand taunted, struggling to keep his voice strong despite the acrid fog choking him.

Cackling laughter reached his ears—a sound that would not have been out of place in hell itself. The fog continued to swirl around them, but part of it grew denser, until it resembled the outline of a huge, misshapen man with the head of a toad.

Bertrand stared, feeling horror sinking into the pit of his stomach.

"As you can see, mortal, I am no man."

"*Mère de Dieu,*" Bertrand breathed, the words hoarse.

The dark mist was suffocating him, stripping the flesh from his throat. Marie—he had to get her away from here. He couldn't let her be harmed—

"This whore you are protecting has betrayed you, musketeer," sneered the demonic voice. "Have you not realized that she is a spy for your enemies?"

Bertrand felt Marie flinch hard, and he tried to shuffle her backward, away from the creature. If they could get inside…

The demonic voice laughed. "You think to escape me by hiding behind a wooden door? You cannot escape the truth. How do you think your slut pays for everything, when you gamble away your earnings faster than the king pays you?"

Bertrand was barely listening to the sense of the words, unwilling to entertain the ranting of a minion of hell. Yet in the back of his mind, pieces of a puzzle were falling together despite his intentions not to give the creature any heed.

The money. Marie's growing interest about the goings-on at Court, these last few months. Her occasional disappearances for an hour here or an hour there.

He shook his head, trying to clear it. This didn't matter. Bertrand might have felt a sting of betrayal with this realization, but it paled next to the threat standing before him. The threat to his wife and his unborn child.

"She has betrayed you, and the king you are sworn to serve," the creature hissed. "She seeks to put the Duc d'Orléans on the throne. Every bit of information you've let slip has been passed straight to him. She opens your correspondence and eavesdrops on your orders. You are a traitor to the crown because of her."

Suddenly a gust of wind crashed down on him like a blow from a giant fist. He fell under the onslaught, an unseen force dragging him away from Marie. The mist cleared, and he saw her lying on the ground a few steps away, her skin raw and blistered. She was screaming, clearly in agony. Her eyes glowed and her face was twisted like a wild animal in the throes of death.

"No!" Bertrand yelled, despite the wind sucking the very air out of his lungs. "Stop! Spare her and take me!"

The voice laughed cruelly. "You fool. Don't you see? She will betray you for the last time tonight... by taking your life to save herself."

"No!" Marie screamed into the darkness. "I will not serve you, demon! I will not kill the father of my child!"

"Marie, do as the creature says!" Bertrand cried, latching onto the promise of her being saved. He thrashed, his spine arching in agony. A terrible gurgling noise came from his throat, fresh pain erupting in his eyes and ears. Warm blood trickled down his face.

His vision blurred, and he could barely make out Marie standing over him, facing the dark cloud that shifted and swirled around them. A scratching noise filled the air, like millions of insects crawling. The putrid smell of the black fog was nearly overwhelming.

"Please," Bertrand whimpered, his voice growing weak. "Please, Marie, you must save yourself. Think of our child. Please!"

Marie wrapped her arms around her swollen stomach and stared down at the protruding bulge. When she looked up again, her eyes were glowing with a feral, demonic light. Her body slammed into him, his teeth cutting into his tongue under the impact. Blood trickled down his face as he spat, trying to clear his mouth enough to breathe, even though they were still surrounded by the choking fog.

Hands yanked his head back by the hair, and he felt sharp teeth, like a wild animal's, at his throat. He blinked blood from his eyes and saw darkness descend. From the scent of rosewater, he knew with a jolt that it was Marie's dark hair flowing around him. He could feel her swollen belly pressed against him as she pressed him into the ground.

"Marie!" he rasped. He didn't fight back or try to throw her off, afraid that he might hurt her accidentally.

Evil laughter rang through the courtyard. With trembling fingers, Bertrand reached up and gently brushed the hair away from her face, as he had done countless times before.

"Protect our child, *mon coeur*," he whispered. "*Please*. I don't care what it takes."

Sharp pain pierced his neck, and Bertrand felt his lifeblood spurting from the mortal wound even as his beloved wife tore his flesh wider with her teeth and lapped at the gore like a ravenous beast. Blackness gathered on the edges of his mind, and he slipped gratefully into oblivion.

TEN

Chan emerged from his dark dream, flailing for purchase in unfamiliar surroundings. Something— *someone?*—was holding him down, but he couldn't make out any details. The light hurt his eyes, and the emptiness inside of him hurt his chest.

"Where am I?" he croaked. "Let me up… *get off me!*"

"Calm down, mate," The male voice was Australian, and heavily accented. "You're safe, but I'm not letting you up until I determine whether you're lucid this time."

There was a light fixture above him, the yellow bulb responsible for the burning glare in his eyes. His entire body felt unbalanced and a dry, parching thirst made his throat burn. He groaned, panic urging him to struggle against the hand splayed over his chest.

"Easy," the man said. "I remember how it is. Lie back for a moment." Something about the man's voice, or maybe his aura, started to percolate through Chan's panic, and he relaxed. The hand gave him a final pat and pulled away. "There, that's better, mate. Sorry about that, just had to make sure you weren't going to do a runner on us."

Chan blinked his vision clear and coughed, trying to form words around the terrible need burning in his belly. "Where… am I?"

"A hotel room in the central city. You've been out of it for the last twenty-four hours or so."

Chan tried to scramble upright. "The last *twenty-four hours*? I've got to get out of here—"

"Yeah, sorry. Not happening, I'm afraid," said the man. "Why don't you rest for a bit, and then we can talk. My name's Mason, by the way, and—"

"You don't understand!" Chan snapped. He felt hot anger lick at his insides like flame, making the burning in his mouth more pronounced. "*I have to leave.*"

Fuck, what was wrong with him? He needed to overpower this man and get out of here. But his limbs felt uncoordinated, and his instincts shied away from the idea of attacking his captor. Which was ridiculous—the guy didn't hold himself like a fighter. Even disoriented as he was, Chan could have taken him down in a minute, but instead, something inside him wanted to roll over and show his belly like a damned puppy.

"Yeah, Duchess mentioned about you being CIA," Mason replied, frowning. "I'm afraid that's going to be a bit of a problem now."

Chan froze, trying to drag his memories into focus. "She told you I'm CIA?" He swallowed, his throat rasping like sandpaper. "That's... that's complete bullshit."

Way to sound completely convincing, there. *Not.* What the *hell* had happened to him?

The Australian gave him a look that could only be called condescending. "Whatever you say, mate."

Chan narrowed his eyes, trying to claw back the upper hand even though he felt like his sanity was holding on by a thread. Why was he so *thirsty*?

"So, I've been abducted and...drugged, from the feeling of it, by a strange woman called 'Duchess' who dumped me in a hotel room with you after concocting this fabricated story that I work with the CIA. And you expect me to just sit here? You're out of your damned mind."

Mason sighed. "I get that you're trying to maintain your cover, but you really don't need to. And, honestly, it's a bit late for that now. Like I said, you're not in danger, and frankly no one here is particularly interested in what government you work for."

Chan stared at him with a level gaze.

"Are you delusional, *mate*?" he asked with mock concern. Then his voice hardened. "Or just an idiot?"

The man's mouth flattened in an expression of mild irritation, right before a disembodied voice filled Chan's head — still with the same Australian accent.

Neither, actually — but thanks for asking.

Chan jerked back, as though doing so could somehow stop him hearing disembodied voices in his head.

"Yeah, telepathy," his captor said aloud. "I know, right? Impressive. Sorry if I shouted, by the way — I'm trying to get a handle on that."

Chan stared at him for a long moment. "You cannot be serious."

"Serious as a heart attack," the other man replied with a shrug. "And I say that as a medical doctor. Not that heart attacks are a concern for either one of us any more."

"You're a doctor?" Chan asked, still trying to drag his head back in the game.

"I'm a doctor in the same sense that you're a CIA agent," the guy said infuriatingly. "Which is to say, I was one."

"Then, *doc*," Chan said, laying on the sarcasm, "Maybe you could get me a glass of water after I've been out cold for a *full fucking day*? Because whatever that demon bitch drugged me with is making me burn up."

"Duchess didn't drug you," the man answered, sounding suddenly weary. "And believe me when I say, water won't help."

"Whatever," Chan forced past a throat scraped raw. "Rice wine sounds more appealing anyway."

The guy grimaced. "Yeah, voice of experience speaking here — that would be even worse. Look, I'm probably not the best person to explain this mess to you. I think I only drew the short straw because I'm the youngest.'"

Chan stared at him, trying to convey through his expression how very *done* he was with this conversation. When that didn't seem to work, he said, "Look. You're holding me here, doped up on god-knows-what. It's really very simple—you tell me what the hell is going on and let me go; or, fuck it. Just let me go and ignore the first part, if that's easier."

Again, Chan railed at himself for his seeming psychological inability to leap up, knock Doctor Outback unconscious, and sprint out the door like all his instincts were screaming at him to do. Helplessness wasn't a feeling Chan experienced very often, but it was one he really, really hated. A memory floated up, of him standing on the porch, watching a car drive away with everything he was supposed to care about inside—

No. *Fuck*, no. Not here, not now.

His captor huffed a frustrated breath. "I wish there was a way to make this easier, but you need to understand a few things before you get up."

"Oh, yeah? That might be easier if you'd answer any of my goddamned—"

"You're a vampire," the man interrupted in a flat tone.

Chan snapped his jaw shut, waiting for the punch line. When the Australian simply continued to stare at him without speaking, Chan gave an incredulous laugh that made his throat hurt even more than it had before.

"Riiiight," he replied, drawing out the word. "Okay—well, if that's all…?"

He started to get up, but found an unyielding hand on his chest again, an irresistible force behind it that held his mind in thrall as much as his body.

"You need to hear me out," his captor said mildly. "This isn't a joke."

"Thought you were supposed to be a doctor." Chan said, forcing challenge into his voice. "Didn't they cover the whole 'vampires don't exist' thing in medical school? Now, get your hand off me and out of my way. I'm leaving."

"Oddly, they didn't cover it, no," the man said, ignoring the last part. "I think the instructors sort of assumed it was a given. So, yeah, it was a bit of a shock for me, too. I was like you in that regard — comfortable in my beliefs. I thought I had my life mapped out... thought I could fill the gap inside me by risking my life for a noble goal. I volunteered in war zones. Figured if I could save enough kids' lives, the world would start to make sense. But it never did. Not until recently, at any rate."

Chan couldn't help the chill that ran through him. The words prickled uncomfortably at the part of him that pushed him to take dangerous assignments. The part that had sabotaged his marriage and destroyed his relationship with his child before it ever had a chance to start.

He was damned if he'd admit that out loud to this guy, though.

"Look," he said reasonably, "I'm sorry you had a difficult life, but I'm a *security guard*. You want to know why? Because they pay me for it. They pay me *really well*, in fact."

"Whatever you say, mate," his jailer answered, clearly not believing a word.

The Australian accented mental voice reverberated inside Chan's head once more, making him suck in a sharp breath. *I realize that nothing short of absolute proof will convince you of the truth, so let me just lay it out there for you.*

Chan's indrawn breath hissed between his clenched teeth as he tried to scuttle backward on the lumpy hotel bed mattress.

You felt a powerful connection to Duchess, the woman who brought you here. It was almost like an electric shock when your skin touched, right? That's because you knew her in a previous life. And I bet you've been dreaming about the distant past recently, am I right?

Chan blanched.

Duchess dragged you back here and drained your blood almost to the point of death. After which, she fed you vampire blood and turned you. You're like us, now. Dependent on human or vampire blood for nourishment. Sensitive to sunlight, which will burn your flesh. Capable of healing from most wounds. Soon, you'll gain the ability to shift form, and to communicate mentally, as I'm doing with you now.

"How?" He injected disbelief into the single word, but despite himself, he couldn't hold back his growing curiosity.

The doctor snorted. "The others will tell you I'm not the person to ask. I'm still getting the hang of it myself. Mostly, though, you just concentrate on the words you want to convey."

Unable to help himself, Chan concentrated hard for a moment. *Like this?*

The guy winced. "That's the ticket—although you were shouting at the top of your mental lungs just now. I suspect this is some kind of cosmic karma that the others would find completely hilarious."

Can you hear me now? Chan asked, trying to make it a whisper. Fascinated despite himself.

"Yes, and that was much better."

"Okay," Chan said cautiously. "What was your name again? Mason, wasn't it? Let's just say for one second that I believe you. I'm not saying I do, but just hypothetically speaking."

"Sure," Mason replied.

"You said I could heal really fast. So why do I feel like complete shit right now?"

"You need to feed again."

"What are you saying," Chan pressed. "I'm craving blood or something?"

The words were disbelieving, but as soon as he said them, a spasm of hunger cramped his stomach, nearly doubling him over.

Mason nodded sympathetically. "Spot on, I'm afraid. You can feed now if you want."

Chan looked at him, appalled. "This is insane. I can't drink *human blood*."

"Human or vampire blood. And, I'm sorry, but it's either that or starve yourself into a coma... assuming you don't lose control and go on a killing spree first. Blood is necessary for your survival. Most of us can't stomach human food anymore, and it does us no good anyway. The good news is, you can feed from one of us until you get used to the idea."

Chan shook his head slowly back and forth. "You said you just recently became a vampire?"

"Yeah, a few weeks ago."

"Why are you the one telling me all of this shit? Why isn't Duchess in here explaining things, since she's apparently responsible for this?"

"She's... busy elsewhere."

"*Busy*," Chan echoed, his voice flat. "Busy doing what?"

"Trying to learn more about the Brotherhood and their prisoners," Mason said, grim. "I'm sorry—you're right that she should be here."

"You do realize how far-fetched this all sounds, right?" Chan asked, massaging his forehead.

Mason snorted. "Preaching to the choir, mate. I know it's a lot to take in all at once, but you can't leave here without understanding what you'll be facing now. You're not human anymore, and until your new instincts are under control, you're dangerous to others."

Chan sat back and closed his eyes. The burn in his throat was getting worse, demanding much of his attention. He gripped his neck with his hand and tried to push the feeling away.

Yeah, Mason said silently, *you won't be able to push this away using willpower.*

"Stay out of my head," Chan growled.

"Sorry, mate. It becomes something of a habit after a while."

"Don't any of you have any privacy?" he demanded, a bit of panic starting to claw at him as the idea that this might actually be happening began to take root.

"You learn to shield," Mason said. "There's a way to block the others from hearing your thoughts, and you learn how to ignore background noise, but it takes practice. Again, I'm not an expert yet."

Chan huffed in annoyance and changed tack, focusing on the dream he'd been having right before he woke to find his world turned upside down. As he reviewed the details, he remembered that everyone — himself included — had been speaking French.

That's impossible, he thought. *I barely know enough French to ask where the toilets are.*

It's not impossible, Mason said.

Chan grunted in irritation, having forgotten that his thoughts were no longer private. He rubbed his hands up and down his arms, his skin feeling unnaturally cool beneath his fingers.

His mind was starting to slide down this rabbit hole without his permission, if for no other reason than the creepy-as-hell telepathy and burning hunger that was now nearly insatiable. Yet, he still felt like *him*. He didn't feel like a monster.

The more he focused on his body, though, the more he began to realize that there were subtle differences. He could hear footsteps elsewhere in the hotel, and he was sure they were made by a man wearing steel-toed boots. He could clearly hear the soft *shush-shush* of blood running through Mason's veins. He could smell that the other man must've had sex recently.

"What's your girlfriend's name?" he finally asked.

"I'm not sure 'girlfriend' quite covers it," Mason replied wryly. "But her name is Oksana."

Chan cleared his parched throat, trying to get himself under control. He realized with a jolt that he was fantasizing about sinking his teeth into Duchess' throat and drawing out her blood to soothe the burn inside him.

Mason stood up from his chair and moved to sit on the bed next to him. Chan shifted uncomfortably. It made him feel oddly vulnerable and off-balance, two things he didn't enjoy *at all*. Mason, by contrast, seemed perfectly relaxed.

Maybe he's used to this sort of thing from being a doctor.

"Yeah," Mason agreed. "Bedside manner is the same whether it's a scared kid on the bed or a pissed-off new vampire, as it turns out. Who knew? Now, you're going to feed from me before you start looking at that third-story window and thinking that jumping out of it to drain some random, defenseless human sounds appealing. I know you'd rather have Duchess here instead of me, but needs must."

Chan looked at him, alarmed. "Excuse me, *what*?"

"Consider it a blood donation. Odd as it still seems to me, I'm more powerful than you. You can't hurt me, but you're likely to kill a human. Feeding will ease your thirst and make you stronger. Vampire blood also has some rather startling healing properties."

Chan was starting to feel ever so slightly light headed. Just the idea of sating his bone-deep need made him salivate in anticipation. "How… would I go about doing that, exactly?" he managed.

"What do your instincts tell you?" Mason asked. He put a steadying hand on Chan's shoulder as Chan closed his eyes and panted, trying to keep control. Something sharp was poking the insides of his cheeks. His eyes flew open again, burning now like the rest of him.

"I want to bite you," Chan whispered, feeling disgust at himself rise as he tried in vain to control the overwhelming desire.

"You don't have to fight it," Mason said evenly. "Just go with your gut on this."

He proffered his arm. Chan took a sharp breath, sensing blood just beneath the surface of the soft skin at Mason's wrist.

This is wrong. This is so fucked up. This is wrong. This is wrong.

"It's all right, mate," Mason said reassuringly. "I'm offering, and it won't hurt me. This is natural, there's nothing wrong about it."

Before he could stop himself, Chan lunged forwards, sinking his teeth into Mason's wrist. For a brief instant, he was so horrified by his actions that he started to pull away, but then the first spurt of blood filled his mouth.

It was glorious. The burning in his throat and the terrible longing calmed almost immediately. Chan suckled at the wound he'd created like a babe at the breast, feeling a nearly palpable sense of relief. He hadn't recognized the terrible weight of weakness and exhaustion pressing on him until both began to fade. Life flowed into his limbs, strength returning to his grip.

He moaned like a cheap whore, beyond caring how it must have sounded.

"That's it," Mason encouraged. "You're doing fine. Just like that."

When Chan had drawn so much blood into his stomach that he felt he was about to burst, he sat back and allowed Mason's hand to fall from his grasp.

He slumped, scrubbing a hand over his face—not sure if he wanted a cigarette, or wanted to run screaming from the room. "*Shit.*"

Mason snorted. "Don't mention it." He rubbed at the gashes in his wrist, which healed in seconds right before Chan's eyes.

"That's... wait, *what*?" he asked, dumbfounded.

His erstwhile blood donor chuckled ruefully. "Yeah, it makes being a doctor feel a bit superfluous. If only everyone healed that rapidly."

"Doesn't that hurt you at all?" Chan asked, still straddling the knife's edge between fascination and repulsion.

"What? Feeding you?"

"Yeah."

Mason pondered the question a moment. "Not really. I've got a theory that something in vampire saliva acts like a drug. Being bitten can be... intense... but I wouldn't classify it as the kind of pain a human would feel while being bitten by a rabid dog or something. Mostly, I feel weaker and less energetic, because it's not just blood that you took from me. It's life force."

"*Life force*?" Chan grimaced. "Okay. That really doesn't sound good."

"I can get more, don't worry," Mason assured him. "Besides, it seems to act as some kind of social bonding thing for vampires. It's fascinating, really. They've all fed from each other over the centuries, either to heal injuries or because no other blood was available. As a result, they... well, *we*... have become very close."

The sound of a disturbance outside the room interrupted their conversation.

Chan leapt smoothly to his feet, his strange, helpless lassitude from earlier gone. Whether it was adrenaline or the blood he'd just consumed, vitality flooded his limbs; his body feeling almost like it was vibrating with energy.

"Oh, hell. Here we go," Mason muttered, wincing. "I wondered how long it would take for all this to kick off. Sorry, Chan... things might get a bit—"

He was interrupted by the hotel room door slamming open hard enough to ricochet off the wall behind it. A small woman with dark skin, a prosthesis where one foot should be, and eyes glowing violet dragged Chan's missing demon temptress into the room.

Duchess swung around, her teeth bared at the shorter woman. "Unhand me," she hissed, "before I forget that we're supposed to be friends."

Chan's eyebrows went up, and he cast a fleeting *what-the-hell* look at Mason. *Okay, then. What happened to 'we've all become very close'?*

The glance he got in return said Mason wasn't any happier about being here than he was, but his telepathic voice had a wry twist to it. *I'm guessing you never had any brothers or sisters growing up?*

Chan hadn't, but he was distracted by the supernatural catfight unfolding on the other side of the room. Energy crackled around the enclosed space, making his skin tingle. He couldn't seem to look away from the blonde woman poised like a predator only a few meters away from him. Heat pooled at the base of Chan's spine, and the twin prick of pointed fangs rasped once more against his inner cheeks.

Yeah, I know the feeling mate, Mason said, the words sounding like a mental sigh.

"It's been more than a day. I'm not going to sit by any longer and watch you do this to yourself," snarled the dark-skinned woman, whom Chan assumed was Oksana. She released her grip on Duchess with a sharp shove and positioned herself between the taller woman and the door.

Duchess appeared to be in full-on ice queen mode. She glared at Oksana with glowing eyes the same color as the blue inside a glacier. "I do not answer to you, *petite soeur*, and I never have," she bit out. "Don't presume to lecture me on what I should and shouldn't do."

The words were deadly, her anger calling to something broken and ugly that lived deep inside Chan's soul. It resonated, that sharp-edged fury.

"*Presume?*" Oksana echoed, incredulous. "Here's a news flash for you, *ti mwen*. You're stuck with me, and that means I will always tell you when you're acting like a psychotic bitch."

Duchess growled. Actually *growled*, like a feral animal.

Oksana did not back down. Instead, she crossed her arms, her posture belligerent. "And, in case you need it spelled out, *you're acting like a psychotic bitch right now.*"

"I'm leaving." Each word was bitten off. Duchess' chest and shoulders heaved with emotion, though her voice was stone. "And since none of you in this room can match me in power, you'd do well not to stand in my way."

Something irrational and desperate clawed its way up Chan's throat at the thought of Duchess disappearing again before he could talk to her properly—a tangle of resentment and desire; anger and need.

Don't go, he thought at her as hard as he could, the words caught between a plea and a demand.

She froze, her back to him, shoulders stiffening. He tried to reach out to feel her mind, but his thoughts bounced back as though they'd hit a solid steel barricade.

"You turned me into some kind of a monster," he said aloud. "I just guzzled blood from a complete stranger's wrist. I have the right to an explanation about *what the hell is going on.*"

Oksana still had her arms crossed stubbornly, but now she raised a pointed eyebrow at her friend.

Mason crossed his arms as well. "That's fair, Duchess. Wouldn't you agree?"

A weighty pause ensued before Duchess eventually broke it.

"An explanation," she said in a monotone, not turning around. "Very well. Ask me your questions."

Chan had so many questions that they threatened to tumble over each other as soon as he opened his mouth. Surprisingly, the first one that popped out was, "How the hell is it possible that I'm having dreams about you in French? I barely know any French!"

"You might not know it now, but you did four hundred years ago," Duchess replied, still in that flat tone.

He gaped at her. "What the hell is that even supposed to mean?"

Oksana's mouth was pressed into a grim line. It was she who answered. "You are the reincarnation of her husband, Bertrand, who died in the early seventeenth century. That's why you dream of France a long time ago, and why your skin sparks with energy when the two of you touch."

Shock suffused him. He hadn't told another living soul about the name others had called him in the dream—Bertrand. Unless… could he have been delirious after they brought him here? Perhaps he'd mumbled it while he was unconscious?

Ignoring the feeling that he was taking his life in his hands by doing so, Chan strode up to Duchess and whirled her around by the upper arm. She was wearing a sleeveless tank top over stylish trousers today, rather than the long-sleeved blouse he vaguely remembered from their first meeting. When his hand touched her skin, it was like touching a bare wire. He jerked back even as she flinched, her blue eyes blazing at him.

"Told you," Oksana muttered, but Chan couldn't spare eyes for her.

"What gives you the right to do what you did to me?" Chan demanded, anger finally trumping the other swirling emotions long enough to lend strength to the question.

"You were marked for death," she hissed, her eyes chips of ice. "I turned you into a vampire so you would be safe among us. *I had no choice.*"

"You had a fucking choice," he barked, his face inches away from hers. "You could have minded your own business and let me die like I—"

He managed to cut off the flow of words before he said *deserved*, but from the nearly inaudible gasp and the way Duchess' eyes flared with anger, he might have been less successful at cutting off his thoughts.

His schizophrenic emotions abruptly changed course again, making him want to needle her into unthinking rage rather than this cold, simmering resentment. Against his volition, he pictured himself snarling at the others to leave... slamming her against the wall behind her and ravaging her mouth with lips, tongue, and fangs.

Yeah, talk about a death wish. Where was this even coming from?

She continued to glare at him. "Sorry to disappoint you, but this isn't about you. And I don't have the time or the patience for anyone's self-sacrificing, suicidal *connerie.*"

Outside of his dream, Chan's fluency in French had deserted him, but she bit out the word in the same way he might have said *bullshit*. Oksana and Mason remained silent during the exchange, while Chan's anger flared higher.

"Not about me, is it?" he shot back, his tone going as cold as hers. "So, I suppose it's just a coincidence that in the dream, you were carrying my child when you killed me?"

The room went absolutely silent, even as Duchess' porcelain complexion paled to chalk. Before Chan could press his momentary advantage, Duchess shouldered both him and Oksana aside as though they were rag dolls before disappearing through the door, which slammed behind her.

ELEVEN

Duchess slammed the door closed and fled down the hallway, dissolving into mist without even bothering to check for the presence of human onlookers first. She swirled free of the choking confines of the building, emerging into the twilight. Even as vapor, an unbearable weight pressed down on her, threatening to crush her.

A modest park nestled a short distance from the entrance of the hotel, and she circled the deserted space. Away from any witnesses, Duchess rematerialized in human form and dropped to her knees near the base of a tree. She did not bow her head in grief, but stared hard at the waving branches and darkening sky above her, feeling nothing except an all-consuming heaviness.

Her entire existence, even as a vampire, had been different than the others'. Yes, they'd all lost their beloved mates, but Duchess was the only one who had suffered two inconsolable losses in that one horrible day. She had never managed to heal from either of those blows. Each wound constantly kept the other one festering.

She wanted answers. She wanted an explanation for this curse. Justification.

Why did Bael mark me? Why not the King? Why not Queen Anne?

But, no. Bael had been attracted to her potential. Her ruthlessness. He'd wanted her as his puppet, to use and discard like all his other soulless pawns.

Breath escaped her lungs in a painful gasp. Her fate was entirely her fault. If she had not chosen to be a spy to manage Bertrand's gambling debts, she never would have attracted Bael's attention They could have lived destitute and blissfully ignorant of the true depths of evil in the world. Maybe Bertrand would have stopped his gambling after their baby was born. Maybe she could have appealed to her father for additional financial support. Maybe she could have just sucked it up and sold her body to strangers to get by.

A familiar presence materialized at the edge of the small park. It was not the presence she might have expected.

Mason stood at the entrance, his hands in his pockets.

"You followed me," Duchess said, not making it a question.

He shrugged.

"You're becoming more powerful already," she observed, her voice sounding distant and detached, even to her own ears.

"Baby vamps have to grow up sometime, I suppose," he said mildly.

Duchess turned back towards the plants and flowers in front of her, half-hoping that Mason would eventually give up and return to the hotel. A vain hope, of course.

He lowered himself onto the soft, fragrant grass—close, but not too close.

"So. Do you want to talk about it?"

Duchess locked her thoughts down tightly. Her reply was cool. "What do you think, *Docteur*?"

Mon Dieu. All these centuries, and still, the pain was unbearable.

Mason twirled a blade of grass between his deft fingertips, his attention on the slip of green, rather than on her. "I think that's a heavy burden to carry alone for four hundred years."

Part of her wanted to unburden herself, to throw everything onto him and wait to see if he condemned her for it. *Dangerous*, said a little internal voice. *Not safe to give anyone that much power over what's left of your soul.*

"You know nothing about it. Nothing about what I did," Duchess said, the words trying to strangle her as she spoke them.

Mason did not reply—not even to nod. He merely continued to examine the leaf of grass. *Merde.* She'd seen professional interrogators use strategies that were less effective.

"I was a spy." Again, it felt like the words were ripped from her. "That's what attracted Bael's attention to me. I only did it for the money. I was pregnant, and I wanted to be able to get us out of debt, because Bertrand was an inveterate gambler."

This time, Mason nodded absently.

"I loved him. As a musketeer, he was disciplined in many ways, but there was also a kind of wildness to him. It was difficult to get him to take anything seriously, especially his gambling."

Duchess gathered her thoughts and took a deep breath. "Nevertheless, he was a favorite of the king. Louis talked to Bertrand, and Bertrand talked to me. Then I talked to Gaston, and Gaston—the simple-minded fool—listened."

"Bael thought you were a historical lynchpin," Mason said with unexpected insight. Though perhaps it shouldn't have been unexpected. Affable, Mason was. Unintelligent, he was not.

Duchess nodded bleakly. "That's why he wanted me, yes. He thought he could topple the French monarchy and destabilize the continent by using me. It was a good plan, as such things go. But as with all of us, Bael misunderstood. He underestimated the love Bertrand had for me. I think Bael assumed that he would forsake me when he learned of my betrayal. Many would have, I suppose."

A faint smile curved Mason's lips, but only for a moment. "He didn't, of course."

"No," Duchess answered, her gaze growing distant. "Bael might as well have accused me of accidentally overcooking his dinner, for all the reaction Bertrand showed afterward."

"He sounds like a good, though imperfect, man," Mason said.

"Yes," Duchess agreed. "I hated lying to him, but it was a different time back then. For him to *only* have a problem with gambling was such a minor thing. I thought I could manage the problems it caused. But I only succeeded in making bigger ones. Deadly ones."

"You survived, though. Love was your protection," Mason observed.

"Yes," Duchess breathed back, still staring at the plants dancing in the evening breeze. Twilight was giving way to darkness around them as they spoke. "The only protection that we can have against such a force, it seems."

"And now Chan is here," Mason prodded gently.

"Yes."

Mason sighed. "I think I'm beginning to understand the prophecy better now. At first, I wondered why you all didn't just grab some random people and turn them, if a group of thirteen vampires is all you need to take on Bael. But that's not it, is it? Xander was onto something. Maybe it's the love between soul mates that will be the deciding factor in this war."

Mère de Dieu, I hope not, Duchess couldn't help thinking.

"What?" Mason asked, turning towards her. His brow furrowed. "You don't think that love will protect us?"

Duchess met his eyes. "I hope it will protect the rest of you."

"But not you?"

She shook her head, the truth rising up, unstoppable. "Chan will never love me, nor do I deserve it."

Even to Duchess' own ears, it sounded bitter.

"How can you say that?" Mason asked. "He's your soulmate, Duchess."

Duchess chewed on her lip, debating on whether or not to tell Mason the rest of it. She suspected that Oksana already had an inkling, and if so, Mason would find out soon enough. So be it.

"Bertrand asked only one thing of me before I killed him." Her voice was barely more than a whisper.

"What did he ask from you?" Mason prompted, using that quiet doctor's voice.

She held his gaze, despite what it cost her. "He begged me to save our unborn child."

A satisfying flicker of pain passed across Mason's face.

There, Duchess thought. *Now you understand how abhorrent I am.*

"How far along were you?" was all he asked.

The phantom sensation of a baby kicking pricked at her memory, and she smoothed a hand over her flat belly—an unconscious gesture. "I was about eight months pregnant when Bael destroyed us."

Mason watched her with a steady gaze. His inner scientist must be intensely curious about the biology of what happened, but he said nothing, waiting for her to continue in her own time.

"My body wasn't able to hold onto her after I was turned," Duchess said. "She did not survive."

"You miscarried?"

"Yes," Duchess answered. "Bael fled after Bertrand willingly sacrificed himself for me. For *us.* I was left shattered and broken, writhing in agony as my newly turned body tried to heal. When I awoke, I found my daughter's tiny corpse on the ground next to me."

Mason nodded.

"I'm so sorry, Duchess," he murmured.

The anger that rose up in response to his quiet words was a relief, and she grasped it around her like a threadbare cloak.

"Save your pity," she snapped. "I don't deserve it. If you must spout platitudes to someone, direct them to Chan, who has been thrust into this war *again*. He is trapped in a situation he cannot escape because of the decisions *I* made."

"You weren't wrong to change him," Mason said, ignoring her jab. "You were absolutely right—Bael would have destroyed him as soon as he became aware of Chan's presence."

"You think I don't know that?" she snarled. "That's not the decision I mean! Because I chose to be a spy four centuries ago, I attracted Bael to us. I made us targets. It's my fault, and I wasn't even able to protect his child—the one thing he begged me to do! Now instead of resting in eternal peace with our daughter, he has been reincarnated into the *same battle*. He'll suffer *again* because of me, lifetimes later!"

"Maybe some of us would rather fight next to our loved ones than rest underground with the worms," Mason said evenly. "Even if those loved ones are convinced they betrayed us somehow in the past."

Duchess fell silent, her chest heaving.

"You can ignore what I'm trying to tell you about Chan," he continued, "but as a doctor, I can assure you that there was nothing you could have done to save your child. You were late term, and Bael destroyed your body as well as tearing your soul in two. Bertrand asked you to do the impossible."

"I killed both of them," Duchess retorted.

"*Bael* killed both of them," said Mason. "And for some reason, all of you seem to have difficulty with that concept. But Chan is not Bertrand. Maybe you'll do him the courtesy of letting him make up his own mind about what's going on."

"You don't know what you're talking about," Duchess said, low and angry.

Mason snorted. "Don't I?" He shook his head. "I think you and Bertrand were on this path long before you chose to become a spy. Much as it still pains me to talk about prophecies, this one was apparently set in motion millennia ago. We all just happened to get caught up in it."

Her throat started to close. "Go away," she whispered.

"Duchess…"

"Leave me alone!" This time, her words sounded like broken glass. "Don't presume to tell me how I should feel about Bael, my past, or this *prophecy*."

A brief pause, and Mason sighed, pushing himself to his feet. He inhaled, as though debating the merits of saying something more, but in the end, he pursed his lips and turned away, heading back in the direction of the hotel.

Duchess reinforced the shields that kept her thoughts from reaching the others. Her emotions were ablaze, trying to burn down those barriers and melt them into slag, but she would not allow that. She built up her defenses taller and stronger, refusing to let anyone see the depths of despair she'd sunk to now that the past had returned to exact its vengeance.

Alone in the balmy night air, she covered her face and wept with all the hopeless desperation of the damned.

Twelve

Chan allowed himself to be guided into a chair. Already, his burst of energy was flagging, buried under a growing sense of having done something truly heartless to a person he should have been trying to protect, rather than eviscerate.

He frowned at himself. *Where the hell had that come from?* The woman in question had just admitted to more-or-less killing him and bringing him back as some kind of B-movie monster. He'd drunk someone's blood, tearing mindlessly into flesh until the crimson liquid overflowed his mouth.

He was a fucking *vampire* now, and he was supposed to worry about the feelings of the vampire who'd bitten him? Chan shook his head, trying to clear his thoughts, and pressed the heel of his palm into his left eye socket until he saw starbursts.

He was peripherally aware of some sort of silent exchange between the Aussie guy, Mason, and his vampire girlfriend, before Mason said, "I'll go. She'll probably be expecting you to come after her."

The girlfriend—Oksana—nodded. Chan heard the door open and close as Mason left. There was a soft feminine sigh, barely audible, and then Oksana was dragging a second chair around to face his.

"You still have questions," she said.

Chan let his hand drop and pinned her with a pointed gaze. "You *think*?" he asked, laying on the irony with a trowel.

She sighed again and leaned back in the chair, crossing her left leg over her right. The graceful arch of her prosthetic foot tapped against her other shin in a thoughtful rhythm for a long moment.

"There's more going on right now than is visible on the surface," she began. "Your presence here... our presence here... it's not just random happenstance."

His jaw clenched. "Of course it's not random fucking happenstance. I'm here on a mission, which has now been blown all to hell thanks to your friend the ice queen. Lives depend on my ability to get intel on the Brotherhood in advance of any government move against them. But I guess that's been pretty well screwed now, hasn't it?"

The corner of Oksana's mouth turned down for an instant before she consciously smoothed the expression. It bugged Chan that someone who looked so unassuming could give off such an aura of power. She was attractive, yes, with striking Afro-Caribbean features and the smooth muscles of an athlete—but nothing about her should have said, 'I can rip your head off in one second flat and make sure no one ever finds the body afterward.'

Yet, just as Chan had been unable to attack Mason and make a run for it even though he'd had every chance to do so, he now found himself pinned by dark eyes lit from within by the hint of an unearthly violet glow. If anything, the sensation coming from her was far stronger than it had been with Mason, and it made his spine tingle with unease.

She spoke again. "We'll work to minimize the damage done by the Brotherhood—don't worry. We still need to find out what Snag is up to and get him and the boy out of there somehow."

Chan blinked. "Who or what is Snag? And... what boy? Do you mean the child the monks are using as a sort of figurehead to rile up the crowds?" He remembered the boy's glowing red eyes. "Oh, my god. The kid. Is he… a vampire as well?"

"Yes." Oksana's reply was grim. "His name is Sangye Rinchen. Both he and Snag are vampires, and we need to free them. But Snag ordered Duchess not to act yet, and we don't know why."

He'd… ordered her? When and how would that have happened? Unless…

"This Snag. Is he a creepy, skeletal bald guy who looks like he ought to be dead? Lots of scars on his body?" He had a confused memory of Duchess holding onto the bars on the man's cell like they were the only things keeping her upright. Neither of them had said a word to each other, but there was something else niggling at Chan's mind, just out of reach.

"Yeah." The word was flat. "That's him. You wouldn't know it to look at him, but Snag is the most powerful among us. We need to get him back, because there's a war coming."

He frowned. "The civil war that Tengku and the other monks want to start against the Malay Muslim majority? No offense, but I don't think vampires are going to be much help with that."

"No," she said. "No… that's not the war I mean."

Chan gave her a rueful grimace. "Then I'm afraid you'll have to be more specific. There seem to be quite a number of wars to choose from these days."

She arched a dark brow. "In fact, there's only one. The rest of what you see is only symptomatic of the underlying conflict."

He stifled a snort. "What… are you telling me vampires subscribe to some kind of deep state, Illuminati bullshit? Hate to say it, but I'm part of the so-called deep state, and we're lucky to get our 401(k) paperwork turned in on time. Global conspiracy is sadly beyond our reach."

"The war is between the Light and the Dark," she said, ignoring his sarcasm. "More specifically, it's a battle for control of humanity between the demonic force that originally turned us into vampires—killing those closest to us in the process—and an angelic force that has been in hiding or asleep since the balance was tipped several millennia ago."

Chan stared at her.

"You don't have to believe it," Oksana continued, sounding tired. "For now, you just have to be aware of it. There were six original vampires. Each of us wielded power or influence of some kind in the human world. Bael attempted to turn us into his mindless puppets by ripping the Light from our souls, making us slaves to his Darkness. But in each case, the person closest to us sacrificed their lives to save us from that fate. Rather than becoming soulless creatures for Bael to use as he wished, we became vampires instead."

Chan continued to stare. "This is batshit insane."

Oksana shrugged. "Like I said, you don't need to believe it based solely on my word. Just file it away for later, okay? Anyway, one of our number stumbled on a prophecy stating that Bael would someday be defeated by a council consisting of thirteen of his greatest mistakes. For a long time, we had no idea what that meant. Now, it appears that the prophecy refers to us, the six original vampires, along with the reincarnations of those who sacrificed themselves so we might live."

He tilted his head. "Six vampires and six people who supposedly died for them doesn't make thirteen," he pointed out, unsure why he was even playing along with this shit.

"No," Oksana said. "It doesn't. We're not certain about the thirteenth member. We thought it must be the boy, Sangye, but that was before you gave Duchess the message from Snag."

Irritation rose in him. "I keep telling you all, *no one gave me any goddamned message.*"

She shrugged a shoulder. "It's clear you don't remember it, but as I said, Snag is very powerful. Right after you met her, you told Duchess, 'Sangye is not the Thirteenth. Bael is attempting to draw the Angel out of hiding, but he does not understand.' So now we're not sure. There are other possibilities. Maybe it has something to do with the child Duchess lost when she was turned. Or maybe it's something we just haven't thought of yet."

Unwanted guilt pricked at him with the reminder of what he'd said to Duchess before she went pale and fled the room. Before he could chastise himself again for going soft on these psychotic head cases, Chan heard footsteps approaching in the hallway. Oksana looked up expectantly. The door opened, revealing Mason wearing an unhappy expression.

"How is she?" Oksana asked.

Mason heaved a breath and sat down on the bed. "About how you'd expect," he replied. "She… uh, she asked for some time alone."

Mason's eyes settled on Chan for a moment. Perhaps it was Chan's imagination, but his gaze seemed almost speculative. Before he could begin to wonder what Duchess had said to him, Mason turned his attention to Oksana.

"I don't know that we should try to wait for her," he said. "Maybe we should move forward on our own."

Oksana pressed her lips together. "Maybe."

"Chan?" Mason asked. "Could you lead us to the cult's hostages?"

Chan scratched the back of his neck and nodded. "It depends. I'm not sure if they will have revoked my security access after me being AWOL for more than a day. Are you intending to go after the boy? Or that other vampire?"

"Neither," Mason said. "Duchess says Snag doesn't want us to try to get him yet, although I for one have serious reservations about listening to him under the circumstances. Right now, though, we're searching for a human."

"Who?"

Oksana rose from her chair in favor of sitting next to Mason on the bed. The casual way he wrapped his arm around her shoulders made Chan's chest hurt a little, though he couldn't have said why, exactly.

"A friend of mine contacted me a few days ago to tell me that her son had been kidnapped," Mason said. "His name is Haziq Belawan—a pediatric doctor who works at a hospital in the area. That's why we originally came to Kuala Lumpur—we were looking into his disappearance, in hopes that we might be able to uncover something the police had missed."

"It was only when we started poking around that we stumbled on Snag and Sangye's presences here," Oksana added. "Not to mention yours."

"That seems like a hell of a coincidence," Chan observed.

"Not really," Oksana said, sounding tired again. "Although if we'd known we were about to get sucked into another vortex of chaos, we might have come better prepared."

Mason huffed in grim amusement. "Yeah—silly us. We just thought we were wading into your average, everyday morass of violence and strife."

"'Vortex of chaos'?" Chan asked, not entirely sure he wanted the answer.

"That's what we've been calling it when Bael's forces are centralized in one location," Oksana said, "which to date has always corresponded with one of our lost soulmates being found. It's like his power is funneling towards the person we're seeking. This time it was you."

He was right. He shouldn't have asked. Still...

"So you think all this shit with the cult and the political instability is because he was coming after me? That's bull. Why would he bother? I was already working for the bad guys," Chan pointed out.

"Thought you were working for the Americans," Mason muttered.

Oksana elbowed him. "We weren't sure if he'd become aware of you yet. This vortex is muddled, with Snag and Sangye thrown into the mix."

Chan fell silent and thoughtful again. That must be why Duchess had acted so ruthlessly and changed him into a vampire. She believed this so-called demon would discover his presence and try to destroy him.

So, maybe she really did think she was saving me, he mused. *Fucking hell.*

"Saving you, and preventing as much pain and suffering as possible by short-circuiting the vortex," Mason offered aloud.

"This whole 'you can read my mind anytime' thing is getting really old, really fast," Chan observed coolly.

Neither of them looked particularly abashed.

"You get used to it," Oksana said. "And if you don't like it... well, consider that motivation to perfect the art of mental shielding."

Something else had been bothering Chan, and he changed the subject in hopes of getting more sense out of them. "How did your pediatrician friend get tied up in all of this vampire shit?"

Mason's brow furrowed. "From what we've gathered, he made himself a target by speaking out against the Brotherhood in a newspaper editorial, after he volunteered for ER duty to treat some victims of the cult who'd been tortured. He was snatched from the hospital parking lot in broad daylight, not long after."

Chan thought back to the man that he recently restrained as Tengku sliced him open with a knife—Loy Cho. It would make sense that he and others like him would seek medical attention after escaping Tengku's temper. Chan could easily imagine the monk targeting any doctor brave or stupid enough to call him out publicly like that.

He sighed, overcome with the sobering realization that whatever happened from this point on, his old life was over. He'd worked for well over a year on this mission, and for what? He'd been due to check in with his handler almost two days ago. It was likely they were already working on the assumption that he'd been compromised somehow.

Little did they know. What the hell kind of operative couldn't go out in daylight and needed to suck on someone's vein to keep from starving to death?

This had been a dangerous mission from the beginning. He'd undertaken it with the full knowledge that it was under an NOC designation—non-official cover, meaning that the United States would disavow all knowledge of him if he were caught. They wouldn't attempt to extract him, or even recover his body. He'd agreed to that on day one.

At least this way, once they get around to declaring me missing, presumed dead, my pension and insurance will go to my daughter, he thought to himself. *She'll have everything she needs.*

His old life was gone. The life that stretched out before him was filled with uncertainty—if you could call being a vampire a *life*. He tried to tell himself that it was an opportunity to shed his old skin and start fresh, but he couldn't shake the sense that he'd failed his mission. He'd been placed in Kuala Lumpur to help bring peace back to the region.

"Maybe you can still help with that," Oksana said, breaking into Chan's thoughts, "but the stakes have gotten higher. Help us bring peace back to the world, and Kuala Lumpur is sure to follow."

"And in the mean time, there's Haziq," Mason added. "Not to mention Snag and Sangye."

Chan sighed. As he saw it, there were a couple of possibilities here. This bunch might be completely delusional. Or—and this was much more concerning—they might *not* be delusional. Chan had seen some seriously weird shit in the last couple of days. Enough to make him think that even if things weren't exactly as Mason and Oksana had lain out, there was still more going on in the world than he'd ever believed.

Right now, all they were asking of him was to help find Tengku's hostages and free them. That was something he'd been itching to do long before a demon temptress kicked his ass and drank his blood.

"All right," he said. "I'll do it."

As he spoke, the door to the room creaked open, revealing Duchess framed in the doorway. Her flawless makeup was gone, and her eyes were suspiciously red and swollen. The yellow glow from a streetlight outside peeked through heavy curtains hanging across the window. It illuminated her face with a strange glow, making her look like a statue of some pale, long-forgotten goddess of grief and vengeance.

"In that case," she said, "we'd better get started."

THIRTEEN

The next several hours were spent in planning. Much to her disgust, Duchess found it difficult to stay focused on the here and now as memories and emotions clamored for attention behind her tightly constructed mental shields. Chan and Mason were deep in discussion when Oksana moved closer to her in the dim environs of the room.

"How are you?" she asked, keeping her voice low.

"Never better," Duchess replied, deadpan. "Why do you ask?"

Oksana raised an eyebrow. "Goodness. That was certainly… *believable.*"

Duchess lifted a matching brow. "It's what you're going to get, *petite soeur*. Learn to be happy with it."

"You're still angry I dragged you back here. I get it, *ti mwen*. But you *cannot* avoid this situation forever."

"Watch me," Duchess bit back, her tone sharp. An instant later, she realized that the words were a precise echo of what Oksana had told her under similar circumstances in Haiti.

The sound of a throat being cleared interrupted the quiet but tense exchange.

"Chan has a proposal," Mason said. "Unfortunately, I'm a doctor, not an army general, so about all I'm able to offer up is some variation of, 'wow, that sounds really dangerous.' Which means you two will probably want to hear him out and offer more useful feedback."

"Probably so," Oksana agreed. She stood up, though her eyes remained on Duchess for a long beat before she turned her attention to the men. "Go on—run it by us."

"The problem is going to be firepower," Chan said, keeping his eyes averted from Duchess. "Unless you have a stash of weapons hidden somewhere, that is."

"Nope. What you see is what you get, I'm afraid," Mason replied.

"I'd figured," Chan murmured, something about his tone conveying that he thought they were being irresponsible by coming here without bringing along a small arsenal.

"We don't generally need heavy weaponry against humans," Oksana explained.

"As you might recall from our first meeting," Duchess couldn't help adding—petty though it might have been.

Chan flushed, the human reflex not yet subsumed by his new vampiric nature.

"Nevertheless," Chan continued, "It's a matter of logistics. Mason told me that a gunshot wound wouldn't kill one of us, but it could slow us down, requiring time for healing."

"Yes, that's right," Oksana replied. "Short of staking and decapitation, there's very little humans can do to us that would be fatal. But there's plenty that a group of well-armed humans with the force of numbers behind them might do to render us temporarily unable to function effectively—at least if we were in solid form."

Chan's eyes flashed. "Solid form? Explain that."

"It will take time and practice for you to master the skill," Duchess said, "but the rest of us can change form at will."

"Into what? Anything?" he asked.

"Into owls, or a vaporous cloud of mist that's unaffected by bullets," Oksana answered for her.

Chan frowned. "Vapor." His eyes met Duchess' for the first time since he'd started talking. "It's a bit muddled… but when I took you into the bowels of the complex, you disappeared when we got close to the guards, and reappeared a few moments later."

Duchess blew out an impatient breath before dematerializing long enough to swirl across the room and reappear by the window.

"Well, son of a bitch," Chan said. "That's certainly a game-changer."

"Yes," Duchess agreed. "Pity you'll be unable to make use of it, and that Mason is still in danger of leaving an impact crater whenever he tries to shift back into human form and land."

"Thanks for that," Mason murmured, giving her a sour look but not rising to the bait otherwise.

"This would still have been good information to have several hours ago," Chan said pointedly.

The worst part of it was, he was absolutely right.

"Suffice to say," Duchess began, "for three of us at least, getting in is not the issue. It's getting out with Haziq, Sangye, and especially, Snag."

Chan frowned. "I'll grant you Haziq. But shouldn't the vampires be able to sneak out in this vaporous form?"

"Normally, yes," Oksana said. "But something has kept Sangye from escaping in the weeks he's been held prisoner. Without speaking to him, we have no way of knowing if it's due to unwillingness or inability. After weeks as a vampire, he *should* have the power to transform, even if he's not skilled at it yet. But it's dangerous to assume things."

"Especially since the poor kid apparently spent the first couple of weeks starving himself rather than feed from any humans," Mason added grimly.

Chan looked taken aback. "Damn. Given how strong my cravings were when I first woke up, that's saying something for a kid that young."

Oksana rubbed her face. "We might have neglected to mention that Sangye is thought by many to be the reincarnation of the Dalai Lama."

Chan had been pacing restlessly as they spoke, but now he sat rather abruptly in the closest chair. "*What?*"

"Yeah, you heard right," Mason said. "Probably best not to think about that one too closely."

Chan shook his head slowly back and forth. "Uh… yeah, maybe not. Okay, so we can't count on the kid being able to poof himself out. What about your friend? Why did you say, 'and *especially* Snag'?"

"You saw him yourself," Duchess said. "He's nearly comatose—barely strong enough to move, much less transform."

"This mission is a logistical train wreck. You realize that, right?" Chan observed in a pleasantly conversational tone.

"Welcome to our world," Mason said.

-o-o-o-

In the end, they settled on a plan in which Duchess, Oksana, and Mason would sneak into the Brotherhood's complex as mist, while Chan flexed his new powers of mesmeric influence. It was risky since he'd had no real chance to practice the art, but Duchess figured it wouldn't take much to get him in. He was already a figure of authority over the complex guards; he would merely need to remind them of that fact. What they would do to get back out was considerably more nebulous at present.

There was one additional aspect that needed to be addressed before they left, and it was one Duchess fully intended to leave to the others.

"Oksana," she said, "feed Chan before we leave. I don't want him going for someone's vein at an inopportune moment."

Then, exercising the better part of valor, she left the room before anyone could say anything in response.

Half an hour later, the four of them were walking down the same road she'd taken to the temple on the night she'd found Snag and Chan. While there were a few people headed in the same direction, it wasn't the large tide she'd seen before. When they arrived in the large courtyard, it was clear that if there had been a rally the previous evening, it was long over. Not surprising, since it was well past three a.m.

They had intended to continue to the complex as quietly as possible; those of them who could do so changing form in the shadows of the trees that bordered the area. As the temple came into view, however, Chan called a halt.

"Something's up," he said. "That's way too much activity for this time of night. The temple should be shut up tight."

Duchess cast her senses outward, aware of Oksana doing the same. "Things inside seem rather… confused," she said. "And there's something I can't quite put my finger on —"

Chan's jaw worked for a moment, then he appeared to come to a decision. "I think we should check it out. If it looks like many of the guards are inside, we can take advantage of whatever is happening and try for the complex. But I don't like not knowing what's going on."

"Agreed," Duchess said. "Most of the activity feels like it's coming from the lower level. Is there a way leading directly into the basement?"

Chan indicated the west side of the ornate structure. "The side door behind the stage leads to the ground level, but there's a partially excavated underground area that can only be reached from a stairway inside."

Duchess met the others' eyes, confirming they were ready. She led the way into the shadows beneath the thick growth of palm trees nearby. Chan pulled the gun she had returned to him from his waistband and double-checked it was loaded.

"Let's do this," he said.

The rest of them transformed into mist and swirled above him, following as he walked with confident strides toward the side door. It was guarded, of course, and Duchess hovered, ready to act. Chan walked up to the guard, one hand raised in greeting. When he got close enough, the man's eyes widened, and he scrambled for his weapon.

"Stop," Chan said calmly, copper light kindling in his eyes. "You don't need to detain me. I'm the security chief. You should let me inside now."

The guard hesitated, shaking his head as though to dislodge an insect. A moment later, his shoulders relaxed, and he stepped to the side, opening the door so Chan—and the rest of them—could go through.

"These aren't the droids you're looking for," Chan muttered under his breath, once the door closed behind him.

Inside, the sounds of people could be heard from further ahead, but the entryway was clear. Even on this lower level, the architecture and decoration was stunning. The place exploded with color, open spaces broken up with alcoves defined by ornate columns and scrollwork. Prayer wheels lined one wall.

Chan led them deeper, only to dart into an alcove when a group of monks appeared at the end of the hallway beyond. Duchess and the others swirled around him, concealing themselves near the ceiling where few people bothered to look. Whatever had been grating on her senses earlier was getting worse, but she was distracted by a presence she had felt once before.

Sangye is nearby, she sent through the link.

I feel him, Oksana confirmed. *But there's something else…*

I think they may be keeping the boy here permanently, rather than at the complex. That was Chan, his mental voice clear but unpracticed.

The voices of the monks gathered in the hallway moved farther away, and Chan slipped out of his hiding place. They followed him to a door decorated in the same ornate style as everything else. This one was unguarded, and Chan frowned.

Too easy, he thought, and drew his gun, flipping off the safety before he opened the door one-handed and peered inside. As he'd described, it was a staircase leading down to a subterranean level, though even down here, the walls were brightly painted and clean, covered with decorations.

Duchess realized what was wrong an instant before Chan emerged into the open space beyond the foot of the stairs. She felt Oksana's jolt of distress at the same moment, but Chan was already striding forward toward the circle of monks surrounding a young boy and a withered figure lying on a stretcher on the floor.

"*Tengku,*" Chan snapped, and one of the monks straightened. Duchess recognized him as the charismatic speaker from the rally the other night.

The monk's mouth split into a sickening grin, and he reached for the hilt of a curved sword at his belt. Duchess and the others swirled into solid form just as Chan shot the monk through the heart. The man staggered back a step, but then he straightened, still grinning. He slid the sword from the sash around his waist, and stepped forward, lowering the blade to hover over Snag's neck.

"What the hell?" Chan hissed, staring at the bullet hole clearly visible through the center of Tengku's chest.

"*Undead,*" Oksana grated, her fists clenching at her sides.

"Bael has turned these people into lifeless puppets," Duchess explained, anger flooding her. "Your bullets won't stop them."

"And your friend's vertebrae will not stop my blade as I decapitate him," Tengku said coolly, staring them down with filmy, bloodshot eyes.

The child Sangye still crouched on the floor next to Snag, looking up at his captors with pleading eyes. "Do not do this," he begged.

Tengku didn't even spare him a glance, his eyes only for the vampires standing before him. The other undead monks stared blankly at them, awaiting orders.

"Your arrival is fortuitous," Tengku said conversationally. "The child will not feed."

Duchess itched to pull the dagger from the sheath at the small of her back and dart forward toward him, but that razor-sharp blade poised over the brittle length of Snag's neck held her back.

"Snag doesn't have a drop of blood left in his body," Oksana said in a reasonable tone. "Look at him. There's nothing there for the boy to feed on."

Tengku's head tilted in slow motion as he regarded her, the movement reptilian. "Then, as I said, your arrival is fortuitous. We will capture the most powerful of you, and the child may feed from a fresh vein. The rest of you will join our ranks, as you should have done long ago."

A sick feeling washed over Duchess as the monks' heads fell back in unison, their mouths opening soundlessly. Tengku lifted his arms, the sword still grasped in his right hand.

"We need to leave," Duchess rasped. "Get out now—"

But it was too late. Tengku laughed, the sound like cracking plaster. "Come, my Master. Your new servants await you!"

Black mist poured in from the edges of the floor and ceiling—a great weight pressing down on Duchess as Oksana and Mason cried out behind her.

FOURTEEN

Duchess tried to draw enough breath to shout again—to order the others to flee. But the suffocating weight of the blackness smothered her, eating at her flesh with that horrible vitriolic burn. Chan screamed, and a single thought of *'No!'* propelled her toward the place where he'd been standing.

Their bodies collided, and Duchess pressed him to the floor, covering him, for all the good it would do against an attack that was as much psychic as physical. She cast around; her telepathic senses feeling like they were submerged in murky swamp water. She could just about make out Oksana and Mason clinging together. Their love for each other was a faint globe of light pressing back against the darkness within the landscape of Duchess' mind.

They were hanging on—barely—but they were in no position to mount any real resistance. Snag's essence was so faint that she'd lost track of it as soon as Bael descended on them, and Sangye cowered on the floor, obviously terrified. The worst was Chan, though. Even trapped beneath her body, he was still screaming—clutching at his head and trying to throw her off.

Duchess was the strongest. It was her job to protect the others. She tried to place her mental essence over Chan's like a shield. For a moment, his struggles quieted, but then a cruel laugh echoed around the fog-filled space. Duchess cowered as Bael turned his attention on her, hating herself for the instinctive reaction, but utterly unable to prevent it.

You think to protect your worthless cur of a mate from the darkness that already lies within his soul? Bael cackled. *He is as good as mine. Go on — try to stop me from plucking free the tiny spark of Light remaining to him. I can hardly wait to see what happens when I reach inside* your *darkness.*

Duchess moaned as fingers tipped in greasy black claws tore into her essence, reaching unerringly for the cancerous tumor of guilt and grief that twined through her rent soul. *No, no, no,* she thought, feeling the fingers grasp at her soul and begin to tear. She was desperate for a lifeline... for someone to reach out a hand and save her, but Chan was too weak, Snag was nearly dead, Sangye was a young child, and Oksana and Mason were barely holding their own.

She would not drag any of them down with her.

Just as she feared Bael would overpower her and destroy the others, a dome of brightness mushroomed outward from the middle of the room, pushing back the black fog in its wake. It flowed over Duchess and Chan as she lay huddled over him, ripping Bael's grasping fingers free of her essence. The demon shrieked in anger, scrabbling for a hold on her soul, but the moment the light enveloped her completely he slipped loose, leaving her soul still anchored inside her chest.

Every square centimeter of Duchess' body ached and burned, but she pushed upright and looked around in confusion, seeking the source of her salvation. For a bewildering moment, she thought the dome of light was centered over Snag, but his life force was the same flickering ember it had been before. Then, her eyes moved to Sangye.

The boy knelt at Snag's side, his head bowed, and his eyes closed. The harmonics of the protective hemisphere of light matched her memory of the brief brushes she'd had with his mind.

He raised his head and opened eyes that glowed red with power.

"You cannot have them," he said quietly, his child's voice pure and clear.

Above them, Bael roared and battered at the edges of the light.

Filthy whelp! I will destroy them one by one for this! Bael's voice was incandescent with rage as the sound of millions of insect legs skittered over the dome. *Their blood will be on your head!*

For an instant, Sangye faltered, and the light around them flickered. What had been a solid shell became more like a web, allowing tendrils of Bael's power to slip through. The boy looked down at Snag, clasping his withered shoulder as though somehow drawing strength from the older vampire's presence. His small chest rose and fell rapidly, and after a moment, the light steadied.

"You would seek to destroy them whether I resisted your will or not," Sangye said. "Their blood rests on no one's hands but your own."

Sangye released his grip on Snag and crawled to Duchess, who was still huddled on the ground next to Chan. His eyes met hers, and she knew that Sangye had seen into her soul and understood what lurked there. He knew everything about her, including the centuries-old pain that had been threatening to overwhelm her from the moment Chan first appeared.

As Bael's power continued to coil angrily around the outside of the sphere, Sangye knelt next to Duchess and took her hand.

His fingers were small and thin against her palm, making her heart ache even more for the child she'd lost long ago. She'd always dreamed of holding that tiny hand in hers, just like this.

It is time to release this pain, Sangye said silently. *I see who you truly are, Marie de Duschéne. You were not at fault; this creature was. Your child has long been at peace. You should be at peace as well.*

Even with the others nearby, Duchess sensed that these words were for her alone. Tears welled up in her eyes, yet these felt different than the bitter ones she'd shed before. They no longer held the piercing sting of guilt and despair. These tears were... *cleansing*. They felt like a burden being lifted away; like rain clearing the filth that had been left behind.

Sangye reached up and brushed her face, wiping away the rusty moisture that clung to her cheeks.

"You have a chance to make things right again," he whispered. "Do that for me."

Duchess blinked up at him. She didn't know why she was so certain, but it was clear to her that Sangye was saying goodbye.

"What are you saying?" she demanded, gripping his small arm.

He did not answer, but instead rose to his feet. Her grip slipped free as though an irresistible force had simply pried open her fingers.

"Sangye!" she cried hoarsely, trying to rise only to fall back—still too weakened by Bael's attack to move.

He smiled for an instant, but still did not reply aloud as he gazed around at the others with a solemn look in his eyes. Silently, he walked over to Snag and knelt next him. Sangye closed his eyes and pressed a hand to Snag's forehead. As he exhaled, the dome of light around them contracted, as though some of the energy required to maintain it had been directed elsewhere.

As Duchess watched, it seemed to her that a bit of life returned to Snag's desiccated form. He no longer looked like a petrified fossil, but more like a leathery mummy. His life force flared momentarily and settled into a slightly stronger level. No longer a guttering ember, but now the tiniest of flames.

Sangye stood and walked towards the stairs. Tengku and the other undead monks backed away as though the power surrounding him was poisonous to them. With each step, the luminous dome grew larger, until they could not escape it.

"You will not win, boy," Tengku hissed, his back hitting the wall.

"I do not seek to win," the boy told him, before widening his gaze to encompass all the undead creatures. "Be free, all of you. Return to the circle of life, as it was meant to be."

The light slid across Bael's puppets, and they dissolved into dust that fell to the floor, forming half a dozen small piles. Sangye closed his eyes again, small brow furrowed, and the light around him exploded outward, streaking beyond the bounds of the underground room.

Bael shrieked and roared in rage, retreating before the blinding flash of pure and unconditional love. A crack like lightning split the atmosphere, and when it faded, the quiet left behind made Duchess' ears ring. Chan groaned and rolled into a sitting position, clutching a hand to his temple.

Sangye turned to look at them, the red glow in his eyes fading until only his natural brown was left behind. *Dawn is breaking outside,* he said through the bond. *The Brotherhood's followers are gathering, drawn by unnatural black fog in the sky over the temple. I must go now and speak to them.*

Duchess tried again to rise and could not. Sangye gave her another one of those soft, mercurial smiles before turning away and ascending the stairs to the main part of the temple.

I don't like this, Oksana sent, her mental voice sounding as weak as Duchess felt.

Duchess dragged herself forward, barely able to crawl. The stairs stretched upward like an unscalable mountain. She was too weak to stand; too weak to transform. All she could do was pull herself forward a few centimeters at a time. She was aware of the others following her in a similar state—all except Snag.

"Sangye, wait," she croaked, but he was already gone.

She reached the base of the stairs and began to crawl up them. The distant sound of a restless crowd reached her sensitive hearing. By the time she reached the top, a bit of strength was starting to return to her limbs. She staggered upright, using the doorframe for balance. The inside of the temple felt nearly empty—everyone was outside.

By staying next to a wall for balance, she was able to walk, after a fashion, retracing their path to the side door that led to the raised stage over the courtyard. She was aware of Oksana some distance behind her... Mason and Chan even further behind. Ahead, she could hear Sangye's clear, childish voice.

"*Brothers and sisters, you must change your path,*" he called. "*Do not believe those who counsel violence and bloodshed as a way to achieve your aims.*"

The crowd noises changed, from fear over the black fog roiling in the sky, to confusion over their figurehead's sudden change of message.

"*Evil came to Thean Hou Temple this night, drawn by the Brotherhood's message of hatred,*" Sangye continued.

Duchess stumbled forward the last few steps and threw open the door leading to the stage. Beyond, Sangye stood with his back to her, looking out across the assembled people. The shadow of the temple fell over part of the stage, sheltering it from the rising sun. Sangye stood near the boundary of the light, which crept closer nearly imperceptibly. Monks huddled on the temple steps and at the base of the stage, looking as confused and lost as the common people gathered beyond.

Oksana arrived, grasping Duchess' shoulder to help keep herself upright. "What's he doing?" she asked breathlessly.

Duchess shook her head, trying to pinpoint the reason for her growing sense of dread. He was just talking to them. It might be effective to sway at least some of those present—and they needed all such help they could get.

"That darkness took the leaders of the Brotherhood. It took Tengku. He and the others are dead now," Sangye said. "Hear me, brothers and sisters—if you give yourselves to the darkness, you will never again be able to stand in the light. I let the darkness take me. Now, I pay the price, so you may see and avoid the same fate."

Duchess frowned. Sangye's sweet mental voice wove through her mind, and Oksana drew in a sharp breath beside her.

Tell Kumari Sadhu not to grieve for me, he said. *If I am needed, I will return.*

Duchess opened her mouth to cry, "No!" even as she coiled her weakened muscles in readiness to spring forward and try to grab him. But a mental roar of anguish and denial from Snag made her stumble. Sangye stepped forward into the sunlight and burst into flame. The flare of agony through the bond sent her to her knees, Oksana falling beside her.

FIFTEEN

Screams erupted from the crowd, a deafening wall of noise that seemed to physically press Duchess backward. Sangye's small body fell to the stage in a heap, the flames burning brighter before gradually dimming, until nothing but ashes and bones remained.

She was only dimly aware of Oksana's fingers digging into her arm hard enough to bruise. There was a strange keening noise, as well—barely audible beneath the crowd's hysteria. Duchess only realized that it was coming from her when her throat started to ache.

"Why?" Oksana repeated, over and over. "*Why?*"

Mason stumbled to his knees beside Oksana, and Chan caught himself against the doorframe an instant later.

"What was that, what happened?" Mason demanded.

"Sangye is dead," Oksana whispered. "He immolated himself in front of the crowd."

"Oh, dear god, no," Mason said faintly, looking at the pile of smoking ashes with horror.

Duchess slapped her palm over her mouth to stop the noises coming out. The sick feeling of having allowed a child to die… *again*… erased the brief easing of her spirit that she'd felt after Sangye spoke to her. He'd spoken to her, and now he, too, was dead.

"Get yourselves together, you three," Chan said. "This is a delicate situation—we've got a hysterical mob on our hands."

He was right, of course, but that didn't stop an irrational part of her from wanting to snarl at him. How dare he be so logical when Duchess had just failed to save Sangye?

"Can I go out there if I stay in the shadows?" he asked, grim.

"Yes," Mason said. "But be careful. What are you—"

But Chan was already striding onto the stage.

"*Quiet!*" he roared in Cantonese.

A few of the people closer to the stage turned to look at him, and gradually, the realization of his presence on the stage spread through the crowd in ripples, until enough of them were focused on him rather than making noise that he could be heard more easily.

"Your leaders are dead! Tengku and the boy are dead!" he called. "The Brotherhood is collapsing, and government forces will come soon to pick over the bones! They will arrest anyone found here, and anyone speaking publicly in support of this dead cause. Leave here in an orderly fashion. Go home. Go back to your lives! Don't become embroiled in this kind of hatred. Look where it leads!" He pointed. "Those of you at the back, turn around right now and walk away. The rest, follow quietly as soon as the way forward is clear. *Now. Get. Out.*"

He continued to point an imperious finger over the crowd. Slowly, those at the back did as he'd ordered, retreating down the road that led to the temple parking lot and the city beyond. Duchess watched numbly as others followed, until the entire crowd was shuffling toward the exit, muttering and throwing uneasy glances at the stage bearing Chan, and beyond him, Sangye's sad remains.

Chan was trembling visibly when he returned to the doorway, his face pale and his eyes glowing coppery behind the irises. "Fucking hell," he muttered. "I've always hated public speaking."

Duchess knew she needed to pull herself together. She'd left a two-day-old vampire to deal with an unruly crowd alone, and even now, Snag lay defenseless in the temple basement. She made herself rise; relieved that at least her body was recovering from Bael's attack, even if her mind was still reeling.

"We need to prioritize," she rasped, barely recognizing her own voice. "We can't go anywhere until sunset, and then our goal needs to be to get Snag's body to safety."

"What about Haziq?" Mason asked, not sounding appreciably better off than she did.

It was Chan who answered. "I don't know where he's being kept, and Tengku—the obvious person to interrogate—is currently a pile of dust in the basement. If we try to search, we'd have to split up our forces to guard Snag as well. Duchess is right. We'll have to get him out of here and then return, maybe with the police."

"Agreed," Oksana said softly. "Mason?"

"Yes, agreed," Mason said reluctantly.

The sun's killing rays were creeping ever closer to the doorway where they huddled. Duchess gave a last assessing look outside, not letting her eyes linger on Sangye's remains for more than a couple of seconds. The sun continued to consume him… already flaky ash was wafting away in the morning breeze. Soon, nothing would remain at all.

On the steps leading to the main entrance of the temple, many of the monks whose humanity Bael had not taken were wandering around, looking lost, or else seated with their faces buried in their hands. There was no way of knowing whether the guards tasked with overseeing the complex where the hostages were held knew what had happened here. No way of knowing how they would respond if they did.

"We should shelter in the temple basement with Snag," Duchess said. "If any of the monks are inside, we can mesmerize them into guarding the door to the stairwell until sunset. They can send any guards away without arousing suspicion."

Chan nodded. "Once the sun is down, it shouldn't be difficult to hotwire a truck and transport Snag out of here on the stretcher. There are several vehicles in the parking lot used for shuttling supplies in and out."

"Come on, then," Mason said, hoisting himself to his feet. "I don't like the idea of Snag being alone down there for this long."

-o-o-o-

Chan glanced at his watch, relieved that their involuntary daylight quarantine was nearly over. The day had been surprisingly uneventful, the hypnotized monks guarding the door for them only having had to send away a handful of people who'd been searching for anyone high enough in the Brotherhood's food chain to give them orders in a convincing manner.

He slanted a glance at the six piles of dust decorating the floor across the room and wished he could have Tengku back long enough to shake some answers out of him.

Watching the monk laugh off a high-caliber bullet through the chest had unnerved him badly—there was no denying it. Though not as much as... whatever the hell had happened next. His thoughts still shied away from the vision of black fog choking the room, and icy, monstrous fingers shoving through his skin to get at the soft parts inside his mind. He recognized the memories as potential PTSD fodder, and for now he was more than content to let his mental defense mechanisms block them out.

But those monks. Oksana had called them *undead*, and Chan was uncomfortably reminded of the sensationalized news stories coming out of the Middle East. The so-called *zombie plague* that reputable sources still claimed was something to do with radiation sickness after the terrorist bomb in Damascus.

He wasn't so sure about that anymore.

His gaze cut to Duchess. She was curled in a corner of the room, allegedly resting, but even now he could feel her mental distress over what Sangye had done. Whereas Chan was almost more angry with the kid than upset. And maybe that wasn't fair. What he'd done was psychologically shocking enough that it had turned the crowd from zealotry to fear—enough fear that Chan had been able to use it to send them away. He'd tried to channel mental power as he spoke, but he had no idea how much of his success had been down to vampiric influence, and how much to garden-variety psychology.

As long as they left and didn't come back, he guessed it didn't much matter.

He stood and stretched. "Sun should be down," he said. "I'll go liberate a truck for us. Once we're loaded up, do we have a place to go? I doubt your hotel would look kindly on us hauling a half-mummified body into one of their rooms."

"I know a place," Duchess said, still hunched in her corner.

"Need any help with the truck?" Oksana asked.

Chan shook his head. "No, I've got it."

He left the basement, glancing at the blank-eyed monks as he passed, and exited the temple cautiously. The whole place still had an air of waiting for the other shoe to drop, and Chan vowed to make sure that it dropped just as soon as he and the others could get something organized.

The humid dusk closed around him as he went out the side door of the temple. The stage was empty—no trace remained of Sangye's ashes. Only a few people wandered around outside. He ignored them and made his way to the parking lot.

"Chan?" a sharp voice said, a figure emerging from between two vehicles. "You're not supposed to be here. What's going on?"

It was one of the guards—a man who had always struck Chan as more intelligent than some of his fellows. The guard paused warily, his hand going to his sidearm.

"Don't," Chan said, putting some power behind the word. Already, it was becoming easier. "Turn around and walk away. Tell no one you saw me."

Those wary eyes went blank, just as the monks' had done when Oksana told them to guard the stairwell. The man lowered his hand and wandered away without another word.

Dangerous, that kind of power.

When he was gone, Chan broke the window on one of the older trucks and unlocked it. The plastic cover on the steering column was cracked and brittle. He popped it off, breaking it off around the screws holding it in place. It took a moment to sort out the wiring harness in the dim light, but before long he'd isolated the battery, ignition, and starter wires. He pulled out a pocketknife and stripped the ends, twisting the ignition and one of the battery wires together, then sparking the starter wire against the other battery wire.

The engine turned over, coughing until he revved the gas pedal a few times. A sharp twist of the wheel disengaged the steering lock, and he backed the truck out of its spot. There was a low concrete divider between the lot and the temple courtyard, but nothing the twenty-inch tires couldn't drive over. He steered to the side of the building and backed up to the door.

Limo's here, he sent, and felt an acknowledgment a moment later. By the time he'd exited the cab and lowered the tailgate, leaving the truck idling, the others emerged with Snag's stretcher and a small escort of mesmerized monks.

They loaded up efficiently and sent the monks away with orders to forget what they'd seen. Duchess took shotgun, directing him into the city, to a neighborhood about a kilometer and a half away.

"Here," she said, pointing to an alley leading behind some shops.

He parked the truck and joined Duchess while the others stayed behind to guard Snag. She led him out of the alley and to the front door of what looked like a general convenience store, signs in Malaysian advertising newspapers, snacks, and hardware supplies in the windows, one of which was boarded up.

"You take me to all the nicest places," he couldn't help saying, and Duchess rewarded him with a glare.

A bell jangled as they entered. Inside a middle-aged man looked up from his magazine and blinked.

"Raahim?" Duchess asked, and the man's face dissolved into an expression that could only be called *soppy*.

What the hell? Chan thought, only remembering when he received a second blue glare that he was supposed to be trying to learn how to shield his thoughts.

"I did not expect you to return, *Puan*," the shop owner replied, still making doe eyes at Duchess in a way that raised Chan's hackles.

Duchess' Malaysian was halting, but serviceable. Her eyes glowed as she spoke. "Greetings, Raahim. My friends and I have found trouble after all. We need a quiet place to stay for a day or two. Will your storeroom suffice?"

Raahim's face lightened. "Of course! Please, make yourself at home. There is a door in the back opening onto the alley. I will give you the key."

"Thank you," Duchess said, gracing him with a small smile. "We'll meet you there."

Raahim was already rummaging for the key as the two of them left to get the others.

"Admirer of yours?" Chan asked tartly, berating himself for giving a shit.

"Lunch date," she retorted in a flat tone that didn't invite further conversation.

It took Chan a minute to parse that, but when he did, he bit his tongue. Evidently, Raahim had enjoyed 'grabbing a bite' with Duchess quite a bit more than he had.

Her eyes narrowed at him. "When you drink someone's blood, it makes it easier to influence them. He'll let us stay in his storage room and not even think twice about it."

She wasn't lying. Raahim didn't bat an eyelash at letting them bring a mummified guy on a stretcher into his nice, reputable store. Chan shook his head in mild amazement as the guy bustled around, setting things up for them in the back room without giving Snag a second glance… or even a first one. When they were settled, he left them to it without a word about compensation or time frame. And, thankfully, without anymore puppy dog looks in Duchess' direction.

"What's that saying about absolute power?" Chan mused.

"I know just what you mean, mate," Mason muttered back.

Sixteen

As soon as everything was settled in the cramped back room of Raahim's neighborhood store, Chan cornered the others.

"I want to get law enforcement moving on the compound while the cult is still in disarray," he said.

"Seconded," Mason replied immediately. "I don't like the idea of someone panicking and deciding to get rid of the hostages. Or abandoning them with no food or water, for that matter."

Chan nodded. "It's still a delicate situation. There were discussions underway about bringing military force into it, with some... international cooperation that I'm not comfortable discussing in detail despite the fact that all of you could probably pluck it from my mind if you wanted to."

"Was this military intervention imminent?" Oksana asked.

"No," he told her. "Though I'm totally out of the loop now, and I don't know what—if any—influence my disappearance and presumed compromised status will have on the decision-making process."

"So, if we can get ahead of the process by inserting civilian law enforcement, we can potentially de-escalate the situation, correct?" Duchess asked.

"Exactly." Chan ran a hand through his hair, idly noting that it needed a trim. Would his hair still grow now that he was a vampire? He shook off the odd thought. "Police action wouldn't have been practical before. Too many people ready to riot, and too many ready to rally around Tengku like some sort of martyr for the cause if he were arrested. But Tengku's dead, and not in a martyr-ish kind of way. My sense of things today was that the Brotherhood's back has been broken. It's just a matter of cleaning up the leftovers."

Mason raised a brow, probably at the idea of Chan considering the hostages 'leftovers,' but Duchess and Oksana nodded.

"There's just one problem," Chan said. "None of us have any standing with the police force. There's no reason they should take us seriously."

Duchess gave him a look that seemed almost pitying, which grated on his nerves more than it probably should have.

"You still aren't thinking like a vampire," she said.

His irritation flared higher. "Really? Wow. It's almost like I only became one a few days ago."

Oksana looked between them and sighed. "She just means that having credentials won't be an issue. You can influence whoever you speak with to shift you up the chain of command until you're talking to someone with the power to organize an immediate raid. Then you can influence that person to make it happen."

Chan stared at her. "You're right, I still don't think like a vampire."

"Apparently it takes a few decades to grow into that level of shameless audacity," Mason muttered.

Chan's lips twitched into a frown. "Look, if it'll get those hostages out, then fine. Let's do it. I know more details about the cult than the rest of you, so I need to go."

Oksana spoke up quickly, before Duchess had a chance to respond. "Mason and I will stay here and see if we can do anything for Snag. Since Mason's a doctor, it only makes sense, and I'd be more comfortable if I was here to watch over the two of them. I'll also try to contact Eris."

Duchess gave her a look that said Oksana was about as subtle as a two-by-four to the side of the head, and Chan couldn't disagree. But, whatever strange motivation Oksana had for trying to force them together, there was no logical reason to argue the plan.

"Fine," Duchess said. "We'll take the truck. I'll call you if we're forced to shelter somewhere from the daylight tomorrow."

-o-o-o-

It was shockingly easy to influence the police to do what they wanted, as it turned out. Chan was caught between being a bit awestruck by Duchess' ice-cold manipulation of the evening shift commander and being irritated with her ice-cold treatment of *him*.

She was locked down tight after her display of anguish that morning when Sangye had killed himself. Not a single thought or emotion leaked through the blank wall she'd erected around her mind. Chan tried to tell himself he shouldn't care. What was it to him if she wanted to treat him with contempt, like some kind of mute appendage following her around until she needed a piece of specific information about the Brotherhood?

It didn't matter. All that mattered was that the fat Kuala Lumpur police commander with the too-tight jacket straining across his belly was on the phone arranging for SWAT teams and uniformed backup. The guy didn't so much as blink when Duchess informed him in her slightly broken Malaysian that she and Chan would be leading the hostage recovery team, and that he would need to provide her with a gun.

Three hours later, they were jouncing along in a dark Kia Pregio van, part of a convoy headed for the old condominium complex held by the cult. They didn't speak, nor did the stony-faced assault force members, dressed in black and cradling their service weapons like swaddled infants.

Chan had already sketched out maps of the place, and the vehicles immediately split up to cover the main entrance of the building as well as the side entrances and the delivery dock. He wished he had a better idea of the status of the hired guards and mercenaries. Most of them must surely know by now that their paymasters were dead. Would they have left? Or gone on a rampage, looting the place and killing hostages?

It was tempting to send Duchess inside in vaporous form to do recon, but they couldn't afford to have too many members of the police teams see something impossible and freak out. It would be difficult to mentally influence them all without also making them too out-of-it to do their jobs properly.

So, they did things the old-fashioned way. As far as the rest of the team was concerned, he and Duchess were specialists from another department. He was armed with his Glock, and Duchess had a 9mm Makarov shoved into her waistband. They were leading the group storming the main entrance, near the offices where Chan had worked as co-security chief with Pula, and also near the secret entrance in the storeroom leading down to the converted storm shelter where Snag and the other 'dangerous' hostages had been held.

Half of the team covered their approach while he and Duchess led the other half through the unlocked glass doors. The offices were empty, raising Chan's hopes that the guards had fled. The light was on in the staircase leading down to the cells, though, and as they thundered down the staircase, Chan heard the unmistakable sound of a gunshot up ahead. A figure in paramilitary gear was moving methodically along the row of cells, shooting the prisoners as he went. He whirled at the approaching racket, giving Chan a good look at his face.

"*Pula*," Chan snarled, and charged him.

The assault team couldn't shoot Pula without risking the prisoners in the cells, but Pula had no such compunctions. He let off a wild shot that missed Chan but hit someone behind him, judging by the sharp cry of pain. The cry wasn't female—wasn't Duchess—so he ignored it, plowing into the larger man.

Pula slammed against the bars of the cell behind him, the breath knocked out of him despite Chan's comparatively slender build. He swept Chan's feet and they both went down hard. Chan's limbs had new strength after his vampiric transformation, but the downside of the increased power was that he no longer knew his own body. He'd need time to train and relearn his capabilities, but that was no help now.

This fight would come down to brute, animalistic strength rather than finesse. Before, engaging in such a fight with an opponent as big as Pula would have been suicide, but now, his instincts rose, whispering *prey*, and before long he had the larger man pinned with an arm across his throat.

"*You*," Pula choked. "Goddamnit, I *knew* you were a traitor, Chan."

Chan ignored the words. "Where are the rest of the hostages?"

"Fuck you," Pula spat.

Chan felt his eyes burn, and hoped that they were angled away from the assault team sufficiently not to be noticeable. "*Where. Are. The hostages*," he repeated, pressing his will against the other man's.

Pula's face went gratifyingly blank. "Tengku ordered them moved to the cellar under the rear storage building after you disappeared. He thought you would return and try to free them."

"Goddamn right," Chan said. "Where are the rest of the guards?"

"Most of them took off when they found out Tengku and the other leaders were dead," Pula continued in a monotone. "A few are in the temple. I came to kill the hostages since there's no one to guard them or feed them anymore."

Anger surged, and Chan pressed his forearm harder against Pula's throat. "And you didn't think to, I dunno, *release them* instead?" he asked incredulously.

"No."

"Fucker," Chan hissed. "Stay down and let the police cuff you."

With that, he rolled off the other man and rose to his feet, brushing his hands off in disgust.

"Do you know the location of this storage building?" Duchess asked.

"Yes, it's not far," Chan said. "Though if anything, it's even less fit for human habitation than this place."

She nodded. "Two of you secure this room. Three more deal with the wounded and begin removing the surviving prisoners for medical treatment. The rest, come with us."

Once they were organized, Chan led them out of the building. They skirted the side to the open area behind it, where a barn-like equipment storage building with a metal roof stood at the edge of a line of trees.

"I can hear heartbeats," Chan murmured as he and Duchess neared the building, guns drawn.

"Humans below ground, but none in the main building," she confirmed, too low for the police behind them to pick up. Louder, she said, "It looks like they're unguarded, but take care. Someone might still be lying in wait for us underground."

Chan wasn't intimately familiar with this structure, but he'd seen the lean-to against the south wall that presumably led down to the cellar beneath. He and Duchess approached it.

"Bolt cutters," he ordered, examining the padlock holding the latch closed. Someone passed him a pair and he holstered his gun so he could cut through the metal shackle and toss the lock aside. Several rifle barrels pointed into the darkness as he swung the cellar door open on creaking hinges.

"Police!" Chan called. "We've come to free you. If there are any guards down there, put down your weapons and come out with your hands up. You've got about a dozen rifles trained on you."

"There are no guards," a weak female voice called up. "No one has come to give us food or water in more than a day!"

Chan exchanged a glance with Duchess, who shrugged. A guard could certainly be threatening her to make her say that, but Chan didn't think any of the guards would have agreed to stay padlocked inside a dark, musty cellar with a bunch of desperate hostages.

"Give me a flashlight," Duchess ordered.

One of the officers handed her one, and she descended the steep staircase. Chan followed right behind, gun in hand.

At the bottom, they found about twenty people huddled in truly awful conditions. Moisture glistened on the moldy walls, and the floor was half mud, half rotted boards. Some of the hostages were chained, while others weren't. Several were blinking, squinting, or covering their eyes. It was clear that they hadn't seen light in a while.

Duchess took a step forward, further into the gloom.

"Haziq Belawan?" she asked.

Someone moved, and Chan followed Duchess' gaze to a young man who looked to be in his late twenties. His hair was disheveled and matted with dirt, but he appeared to be in fairly good health otherwise.

"Who are you?" he asked in a hoarse whisper.

"An acquaintance of your mother's," Duchess said. "She asked us to help the police find you."

Haziq gaped at them. He pushed himself up from where he was lying on a pile of rags and walked forward. He was filthy, skinny, and looked exhausted.

Chan sniffed the air around Haziq instinctually and somehow came to the conclusion that he had suffered no major ill from his time in captivity. He was weak, certainly, but would make a full recovery—at least physically. Chan had been held prisoner on a couple of memorable occasions in his life. He knew that a part of you could become lost while in captivity. It would be up to Haziq to come to terms with the psychological impact of what he'd experienced.

"We're getting all of you out of here and back to your families," Chan said to the others. Several looked at him fearfully, as though they didn't believe him.

"It's not a trick," he continued. "The police are right outside. Gather any belongings you have. We need to get moving."

It took a moment before anyone moved, and none did so until Haziq had pulled on his battered tennis shoes.

He wrapped his arms around tattered scrubs and stood shivering in the darkness despite the smothering heat. Slowly, several others got up and joined him in the darkness, following his lead.

"That's the idea," Chan approved. "Let's get out of this place."

When all the prisoners had gotten up and were prepared to leave their dungeon, Chan and Duchess led them out. They walked back down the mud hallway and then up the stairs. A few of the prisoners were so weak they had to be helped by others.

"Don't shoot!" Chan called to the police as they emerged, his hands in the air. "We're coming up with the hostages!"

Carefully, they pulled every person up and out of the muddy hole.

One woman trembled with fear, tears streaming down her streaked face. She blinked and turned her head away from the lights being held by police officers.

An older gentleman appeared to be only semi-conscious. Haziq had one of his arms slung around his shoulders and Chan came forward to help him.

"I think he has pneumonia," Haziq whispered, his voice hoarse. "We could barely get him to wake up in the last day or so."

"I'm glad we got here when we did, in that case," Chan replied, easing the gray-haired man up the rotting steps. "We'll get him help right away."

Hands reached out to them from above, pulling the man from their grasp. Chan looked around and saw a stretcher waiting nearby.

"What about the others?" he asked Haziq.

The doctor wiped his brow, smearing dirt from his hands across his sweaty face. Like the others, he squinted in the light from the flashlights. It was clear they'd been held in the dark.

"Um," Haziq replied, sounding tired. "Almost everyone has diarrhea, which is pretty typical under these conditions. We're malnourished and dehydrated, but other than that I'm not sure. One woman might have a broken wrist. She'll need an x-ray."

"You did good, doc," Chan insisted, clapping the man on his bony shoulder.

Haziq smiled vaguely. "Thanks, I think. Who are you, again?"

"My name is Chan. I actually don't know your mother, but I know Duchess."

"I'm afraid I don't recognize that name either, but thank you both for getting us out of that hellhole. How on earth did you get past the guards?"

Chan gave a rueful smile, figuring that 'we're supernatural badasses with mind-control powers' probably wasn't the most useful answer he could give.

"We brought lots of police with us," he demurred. "Besides, the cult is in disarray, and there weren't that many guards left."

"Sir? Are you in need of medical attention?" An officer interrupted, approaching Haziq with a concerned look on his face.

Both Haziq and Chan spoke at the same time.

"No, I'm not."

"Yes, he is."

Haziq turned an aggrieved eye towards Chan. "I'm fine, really."

"He at least needs to be evaluated," Chan answered with a shake of his head.

"No, what I need to do is get home to my wife. I can't imagine what she's been through the last few —"

Chan interrupted him. "We can get her to meet you at the hospital. Come on — tell me you wouldn't order someone else in your condition to be checked out medically?"

Duchess approached, having been helping some of the others into the backs of waiting ambulances.

"What's this?" she asked.

"Haziq thinks he's getting out of an ambulance ride," Chan explained, raising an eyebrow pointedly. Even though he'd only known the doctor for fifteen minutes, he could already tell that he was going to like the guy.

Duchess turned her best haughty look on the disheveled man. "Physician, heal thyself. Or we'll set your mother onto you."

Haziq sighed and ran his hand through his matted hair. He glanced skyward for a moment, as if for patience, and nodded.

"Fine… at least I can shower at the hospital and leave the mess behind for them instead of Jayda. These scrubs should probably be burned in the hazardous waste incinerator," he joked.

"That's the spirit. We'll ensure that your wife gets to the hospital," Duchess told him as they walked slowly towards the last of the ambulances.

Chan could tell that the adrenaline from being rescued was wearing off. Haziq's legs trembled and he stumbled over nothing before righting himself.

"Take it easy, now," Chan said, catching his elbow.

"We will ride with this patient," Duchess told the wide-eyed ambulance driver, who was wise enough not to argue. Instead, she merely gave a mute nod.

"Did you psychologically compel her to agree?" Chan asked curiously.

Duchess snorted. "Oh, no. That was my normal intimidating glare. She was just being smart."

Haziq let the EMTs settle him in the back.

"We'll be there soon," Chan told him. "Just take it easy — the hard part's over."

Seventeen

A couple of hours later, Duchess entered Haziq's hospital room, seating herself in the chair next to Chan's. The young doctor had been evaluated by emergency room staff and was admitted for fluids, re-feeding, and monitoring over the next few days. He was also being given a round of powerful antibiotics to treat his gastrointestinal issues. Aside from that—and somewhat remarkably— he'd emerged largely unscathed after his time as a prisoner.

"No IVs until I've had a hot shower," Haziq had repeated, over and over again. The nurses pursed their lips in disapproval, but finally gave him clearance to bathe.

"As long as you have an attendant help you!" one of them had called after Haziq's retreating back.

That had been roughly thirty minutes ago. Once he'd disappeared into the bathroom, Duchess excused herself to make some phone calls.

"I finally spoke to Haziq's wife," she said. "I let her know that we'd located him, and that he'd been admitted but was in reasonable condition. She'll be here soon."

"As middle-of-the-night phone calls go, I imagine that was one she was happy to receive," Chan replied, rubbing his face with his hands. Duchess made note of his clear exhaustion, but did not comment on it.

"I could tell I woke her from a sound sleep," she said instead. "She seemed fairly confused for a moment, but she was wide awake by the time we hung up."

Right on cue, rapid footsteps could be heard in the hallway. At nearly the same moment, Haziq opened the bathroom door.

He was unrecognizable as the same man that they'd pulled out of the cellar. No longer caked with dirt, his hair was clean and damp, standing on end from where he'd tried to dry off with a towel. A hospital robe was tied loosely around his body.

With a bang of the door, Jayda burst in looking around wildly. "*Haziq!*"

Haziq made a low noise of relief, and the two fell into each other's arms. Jayda hurled herself against him with enough force that he staggered backwards a step, his back thumping softly against the doorframe of the bathroom.

Duchess stood and jerked her head at Chan, motioning for them to leave and allow the two some privacy.

"Oh, my beloved... let's get you into bed," Duchess heard Jayda whisper as they walked out. Both of them were weeping openly with the joy of being reunited. Duchess refused to acknowledge the hard lump that tried to lodge in her throat as the door swung shut behind her with a soft click.

Chan sank into a chair in the hallway, his expression tense. Duchess followed suit after the barest moment of hesitation. She felt unsure of herself in a way that she hadn't in centuries—off balance and out of her element.

"What's wrong?" she asked, when Chan's expression of disquiet deepened.

"I'm... not entirely sure," he replied, running his hand over his face. "But I'm not really feeling my best, all of the sudden."

She examined him more closely, a thread of fresh worry worming its way through her. He looked pale, and a fine sheen of sweat covered his forehead.

"I don't know what the problem is," he continued. "Probably just tired. I don't think I'm very good at this whole *being a vampire* thing yet."

Duchess glanced along the hallway, making sure there was no one nearby.

"You need to feed," she said. "You're pale, and your hands are shaking."

Chan grimaced. She could tell that he was still deeply uncomfortable with the concept. "Maybe that's it. How should I know?"

"You know when anything human with a pulse starts looking irresistible," Duchess said dryly. "Some of the others describe it as a burning thirst, but for me, it was always more like hunger. It seems to be a little different for each of us."

Chan pondered this. When he finally spoke, his voice was grim.

"Yeah, I can kind of see both. I feel like I haven't had anything to drink in days. Parched."

"Like dehydration?"

"Yes. But also… predatory. Which is distinctly disconcerting when I'm stuck in a hospital with a bunch of sick and injured people."

Duchess nodded in understanding. "It won't always become so intense, so quickly. Though I must say, I'm impressed by your self-control as a new vampire."

"What's that supposed to mean?" he asked with a frown.

Duchess gave him a pointed look. "You haven't gone after anyone's throat yet."

"Oh," Chan replied, looking taken aback. "That's… a common issue, is it?"

"Don't worry. I wouldn't allow you to hurt anyone," she reassured him.

Duchess was well aware that as a freshly turned vampire, Chan's instincts would be commanding him to hunt. It was a very difficult position to be in—stuck between the remnants of one's humanity and the instinct of a vampire to seek blood.

A dark-haired nurse emerged from one of the nearby patient rooms. She was young and very pretty, with long hair tied back into a high ponytail. Chan's eyes snapped up, his nostrils flaring as his attention focused on her. Copper light kindled in his dark brown gaze.

To her surprise, Duchess felt a bristle of irrational jealousy. She quashed it immediately, appalled at herself. She had no claim on Chan. Aside from preventing unfortunate accidents while he was still a slave to his hunger, it was none of her business who he chose to feed from. What was it to her? It didn't matter whose neck he decided to latch his lips over, biting through soft skin as his victim moaned in a combination of shock and ecstasy.

Hypocrite, accused the voice of self-loathing that lived inside her. *How many nameless, faceless men and women have you bedded and bitten to make the pain go away over the centuries?*

A growl escaped her throat. She managed to cover it — poorly — with a cough.

The sound drew Chan's eyes away from the nurse and back to her. He looked guilty, as though he'd been caught in some wrongdoing.

"Shit... I think I'm in trouble. I may need a bit of backup, here." The coppery glow was still sparking in the depths of his irises. His tongue played over his teeth as though checking for sharp points.

"What do you mean?" she asked, distracted by the small movement.

"I shouldn't be thinking about hunting, especially at a time like this. We just got all the hostages back and--"

Duchess dragged herself back to the present concern. "It's only instinct."

"It's still an instinct that I'm not about to indulge *inside of a fucking hospital*," he hissed, low enough that no one else would overhear.

She opened her mouth to reply, but the door to Haziq's room opened, revealing Jayda.

"You don't have to sit out in the hallway like you've been banished," she said, her face radiating happiness. The relief emanating from her was palpable.

Duchess rose and gave her a gentle hug. "How are you doing?"

"Much better now," Jayda replied sincerely.

"How is Haziq?" Chan inquired, looking through the open door. The glow was gone from his eyes, and Duchess marveled again at his willpower in the face of a new vampire's hunger.

"Why don't you come in here and ask me in person?" Haziq's voice called.

Chan huffed in amusement, despite the tension still coiling in his shoulders. The three of them reentered the room, and Duchess' eyes fell on the frail man lying in the hospital bed.

"I'll need to fatten him up," Jayda observed, plumping his pillows behind his head.

Haziq turned an aggrieved eye towards his wife. "My weight is just fine, thank you. Before all this happened I needed to lose a few pounds anyway."

Jayda rolled her eyes and mock whispered, "That's what he keeps saying, but I don't believe him."

"I'm hurt, dearest. You can trust me on these things—I'm a doctor!"

"A very *stubborn* doctor," Jayda shot back.

Everyone chuckled, even Haziq.

"Well, I can't deny that," he admitted wryly.

"Other than being stubborn and in need of fattening, how are you, truly?" Duchess asked. After so much darkness and fear over the past months, it would be a relief to contact his mother Gita with some good news.

Haziq's face clouded over, his smile fading. "I've been worse, but I expect I'll still need a few days to recover. We survived—that's the important part. I hope that the others you took out of the cellar are okay."

"We haven't received any reports to the contrary," Duchess assured him, figuring that he didn't need to know right now about the prisoners the guard had shot in the complex basement.

Haziq nodded, but he didn't seem satisfied. "I wonder if I'd be allowed to visit them?"

"You can talk to the police about that. I expect they'll be here in the morning to interview you about your experiences." Chan explained.

Jayda made a noise of protest. "So soon? My husband needs his rest!"

"I don't disagree," Chan assured her, "but they'll want to get as much information as possible so they can make arrests and post charges."

"I want these barbarians off the streets," Haziq insisted, a fire burning in his eyes.

"Well," Jayda hedged, "I suppose it's necessary, then. But I will insist to the hospital staff that he needs to take it easy until he's completely recovered."

"And so you should," Duchess said, inclining her head. "Has anyone spoken to Gita yet?"

"I tried to call her on the way to the hospital, but she didn't answer," Jayda said. "I'll try again now."

She dialed and held the phone to her ear, smiling when someone picked up on the other end. Without a word, she handed it to Haziq.

"Hello, *ibu*," he said fondly. "I'm safe."

Then, he winced a bit and pulled the phone away from his ear, as Duchess made out a cry of "Haziq!" from the other end, followed by a rapid-fire torrent in Malaysian. Haziq lapsed into the same language, and Duchess could just about follow as he reassured her repeatedly that he was being treated and nothing was seriously wrong with him. Then he switched back to English.

"Two of my rescuers are here right now," he said. "I'm not sure if you know them?"

More words from the other end, and Haziq covered the microphone. "She wants to talk to you."

Chan waved the phone toward Duchess, since he and Gita had never met. Not that Duchess knew her terribly well, either, but they'd at least spoken a few times in the days after Mason had been turned in Haiti. Gita knew who she was, and, more importantly, *what* she was.

"Hello, Gita," she said. "I'm pleased we could bring you some good news today."

"Duchess?" Gita asked. "Is everyone else safe, too? Mason, and Oksana?"

"We're all fine," Duchess assured. "And Haziq will be soon."

"Allah be praised," she breathed in relief. "I can't ever repay you for what you've done. When I found out he'd been taken, I feared the worst."

"You don't owe us anything," Duchess said. "As it turns out, we needed to be here for… other reasons." She very carefully did not let her eyes slide to Chan. "It's good that we could help get Haziq back at the same time."

"Nonetheless," Gita said, "if any of us can do anything to help you, we will. I spoke to both Jayda and Haziq about you, though I'm not certain how seriously either of them took me. Mason told me you would be searching out sources of voluntarily donated blood. Do you have such a source in Kuala Lumpur?"

"No," Duchess said.

"Let me talk to Jayda, then. And thank you again, from the bottom of my heart. I'll speak to Mason as soon as I can and thank him as well."

Duchess gave the phone back to Jayda. She spoke to Gita in Malaysian, her expression growing uncertain as the conversation drew out. Haziq, listening to Jayda's end, gave Duchess and Chan a speculative look. After Gita finished speaking with Jayda and shared a few more words with her son, she ended the call.

Jayda met Duchess' eyes uneasily. "These things Gita says about you. Are they true?"

Duchess let her eyes glow with inner fire for a moment. "They are. You have nothing to fear from us, though."

"But… you do need blood?" Jayda asked.

Duchess felt Chan stiffen beside her. She hoped that he still had control of his growing hunger.

"We do," she said calmly. "But we can procure it from other sources if necessary."

There was a beat of silence, and Haziq asked, "How long since you last donated, dear?"

Jayda thought about it for a moment. "A little over two months. Maybe nine weeks?"

He nodded. "All right. Here's what I propose. There are bags and catheters in this room. No one will think anything of it if one goes missing. I'm too weak to give blood, but I'm perfectly qualified to draw some from Jayda for you if she's willing."

Duchess looked at Jayda, awaiting her decision.

Jayda swallowed. "Just a normal blood draw? Yes, I can do that."

"Thank you," Duchess said. "It's immensely helpful."

Chan was, if anything, wound even more tightly than before. "I think it might be best if I waited outside," he said.

"We'll both wait," she said, not wanting to leave him alone with his cravings increasing. She ushered him out, and he leaned against the wall, running a shaking hand over his face.

"Shit, Duchess. I'm not sure I can hold on for fifteen minutes while he sticks her," Chan said. "As soon as you started talking about blood, I felt like I was going to lose it. Can you—I don't know—mesmerize me into calming the fuck down for a few more minutes, or something?"

She looked at him in concern. His trembling was growing worse, and light was glinting in the depths of his eyes. "That won't work on you now that you've been turned," she said, running through options.

There was no doubt that she could restrain him if need be, but not without making the kind of scene that would necessitate a fair amount of damage control inside a hospital. They did have another option—one that wouldn't have been her first choice, but was undeniably the logical thing to do. She sighed. "Stay here for a moment."

She stuck her head back in Haziq's room. "We'll be back in fifteen minutes or so."

Haziq waved a hand in acknowledgement and went back to swabbing Jayda's arm with disinfectant.

"What are you doing?" Chan asked as Duchess took his arm. His eyes flared brighter.

"Come with me," she said, and dragged him into the first room that didn't have a heartbeat inside, closing the door behind them.

He was starting to get that feral look a vampire got right before they lost control and lunged for the nearest vein… which was all right, she supposed, since the only veins nearby were hers.

"Feed from my wrist," she ordered. "You've done that before from the others, have you not?"

His lips pulled back, revealing fangs beneath. Rather than answer, he leapt at her, crowding her against the closed door. She snarled back, letting her greater power press against him—not liking the idea of him tearing into her flesh like it was some kind of ravishment.

Or liking it a little too much, suggested an unhelpful inner voice.

He was growing in strength already, but nowhere near the levels of someone who'd walked the earth for more than four hundred years. The violence of his attack diminished, and he stood poised barely a step away, panting with need. His fiery copper gaze rested on her jugular with clear longing.

"The wrist," she reminded him sternly, and extended an arm.

He continued to stare at her neck with blatant avarice, but after a moment he grasped her arm and his fangs sank into the thin flesh over her pulse. His eyes fluttered closed in utter bliss as her blood welled up, pouring into his mouth. He was lost in his hunger—probably wouldn't remember this at all once he came back to himself.

At least, she certainly hoped that was the case, because then he wouldn't remember the small, needy noise she made as he suckled at her blood, the bond flaring between them. He wanted… so much. And she could feel him. *All* of him. It wasn't supposed to feel like this. It hadn't felt like this when he'd drunk from her after she turned him… had it? No, then her guilt had kept her from feeling anything deeper. Now, though, it seemed she could do nothing *but* feel.

When he finally pulled away, his physical need temporarily sated, it was all she could do to slam her mental shields down on the confusion of hope and fear and want and need swirling between the two of them. The abrupt jolt of the cut connection seemed to bring him back to the present. He blinked rapidly, his eyes returning to their normal deep mahogany.

"What… just…" he began, but she cut him off.

"You waited too long before feeding," Duchess said in clipped tones. She pulled her arm back, and Chan let it slide free of her grip. "Come on," she told him. "I need to go refill. Then, we're leaving."

EIGHTEEN

Roughly an hour later, the pair returned to the store-room inside Raahim's shop, where the others awaited them. The sun would rise soon, but humanity's pre-dawn lassitude had allowed them to pass easily through the nearly deserted streets of Kuala Lumpur. Chan kept throwing Duchess veiled glances, making her skin tingle even as she schooled herself not to respond.

He had no way of understanding the complexities that lay between them. All he knew of her was a few dream images and a single, devastating lucky guess about her pregnancy. Her centuries of mental torment were not his fault. By contrast, his current circumstances and the upheaval of his life were completely her fault. Feeding him had been a mistake—no matter that she'd worried for the safety of the humans in the hospital at the time. For his *own* safety, she needed to keep Chan firmly at arm's length. He was a good man, but she had never been a good woman. She would only destroy him—even more than she already had.

They entered the storeroom's back door to find that Oksana and Mason had been busy. Some effort at cleaning had been undertaken, and Snag now rested on a simple pallet bed raised slightly off the floor. He was as still and deathly looking as before, his eyes closed and his flesh sunken.

"Any luck?" Mason asked immediately, hope lighting his pleasant features.

Duchess reached for a smile. "Yes, we retrieved him, along with the other hostages. Haziq is at the hospital right now with Jayda. It will take some time for him to recover, but they think he'll be fine. He's already talked to Gita."

Oksana grinned and closed the distance between them to pull Duchess into a hug.

"That is wonderful news!" she said. "I'm so glad to hear that."

Mason sagged in relief. "Oh, thank goodness for that. I can't thank you enough. Both of you." He rose as well, crossing to grasp Chan in a heartfelt handshake before clasping Duchess' shoulder.

"His wife seemed over the moon. Nice to get front-row seats to a happy ending for once," Chan said. He walked over to the cot, looking down at Snag with cool pity in his eyes. "Any change with him?"

"No," Oksana said, as she and Duchess joined him. "I'd hoped he'd continue to improve after Sangye injected him with some of his life force." Her voice grew sad at the mention of the young vampire who'd immolated himself to save them, and Duchess felt a painful stab at the reminder.

"By all conventional measurements, he's dead," Mason said grimly. "If I didn't have your assurances that he'd survived a similar state before, I'd say it was hopeless."

"He spent thousands of years like this and recovered," Duchess said.

"At least whatever Sangye did was enough for us to get him out of there without his body crumbling to pieces," Chan murmured, studying Snag's sunken face. "Maybe that was what he told the poor kid to do?"

Duchess and Oksana shared a look before turning simultaneously towards Chan.

"What do you mean?" Oksana asked.

Chan shrugged. "Well… he supposedly gave me a message to give to you, right?"

"Yes," Duchess said cautiously.

"Maybe he did the same for Sangye."

Oksana's eyebrows drew together as she said, "You think Snag planned this entire thing?"

Chan shrugged again. "Anything is possible, I guess. I don't know the guy, but I just find it oddly coincidental that he came back enough to make it easier for us to get him out. Either we were incredibly lucky or…"

"Snag arranged it in advance," Mason finished for him.

Duchess recalled the mental flare of anguish that had seared through the bond when Sangye died. "He certainly didn't plan what came next," she said in a low, angry tone.

Oksana shivered. "No. That much was obvious."

"Manisha's going to be gutted over losing Sangye, poor woman," Mason said. "Xander, too, I expect."

The vampires all stood in silence, staring at the eldest among them, who remained as deathly still as ever.

"So, how do you fix this?" Chan asked, gesturing to Snag. "Just give him a whole bunch of blood?"

"I have no idea," Mason admitted. "His swallowing reflex is non-existent in this state. We tried giving him our blood, but we just can't get it into him in any kind of quantity. I'd be inclined to try it intravenously — or maybe subcutaneously, since all his veins are collapsed. But I'd rather hold off until I can consult with the expert in the field. Snag's completely out of it right now, for all intents and purposes."

"He didn't seem all that 'out of it' when he was screwing with my mind and implanting strange messages," Chan pointed out.

"No, he definitely maintains some awareness," Duchess said thoughtfully. She moved forward and laid a hand on top of Snag's head. His skin was disconcertingly cool and dry, very much like one of his mummi-fied Egyptian contemporaries. Yet as she closed her eyes, she could still sense his life force deep within him. It was faint and flickering, but it was definitely there.

"He's still in there," she concluded.

A bell-like chime broke the thoughtful silence, and Duchess looked around.

"That'll be Eris," Oksana said. "We can't get a decent voice connection, so he's been blowing up my phone with texts." She gave Mason a speaking look. "Excuse us for a few minutes. The signal might be stronger at the front of the shop."

Mason looked momentarily confused, but then he glanced at Duchess and Chan, and his expression cleared. "Oh. Right. I'll… uh… just go see if Eris and I can come up with anything useful in a hundred and six-ty characters or less. Back in, um… a while?" he offered before backing out of the door leading to the main part of Raahim's shop.

"Smooth," Chan observed.

"Not really one of Mason's strong points," she conceded, "though he does have several other admirable qualities."

Chan wandered over to a set of shelves and leaned against it, crossing his arms. "Interesting," he said. "So it's not a generalized contempt for all things male, then? Just me, in particular. Aside from allegedly being the reincarnation of your long-dead husband, what exactly did I do to piss on your cornflakes?"

"You didn't do anything," she finally answered in a soft voice. "You're the victim, here."

He snorted. "Tell me something I don't know. There I was, just minding my own business, trying to infiltrate a militant Buddhist cult run by undead zombie monks, then all of a sudden, I'm caught up in a battle for heaven and earth. You know, I've signed up for a lot of crazy shit over the years, but I didn't sign up for *this*."

Duchess nodded, picking at a frayed piece of stitching on her sleeve. She knew he was right. "I did what I had to do to protect you."

"I know you *believe* that. But how is this protecting me?" His words were sharp, but there was genuine curiosity in his tone.

Duchess sighed. "Bael will try to destroy you, either way. He intends to prevent the formation of the Council of Thirteen. At least as a vampire, you're tougher. Harder to kill. And… you're with us, now."

Bitterness filled her voice towards the end. She couldn't help but turn away as terrible memories from the day she was turned rose up in her mind.

"That doesn't explain why you seem to hate me so much. Especially since I've done nothing to you," Chan pointed out.

"I don't hate you, but you should—"

"I should what?"

"You should hate me. You have every right," Duchess said.

Chan frowned. "Why? Because you killed whasisname? Bertrand?"

Duchess could feel her anger rising, coming to her defense. Its return was a considerable relief. "Is that not enough?" she snapped. "But, *non*, that is only the beginning. You are far better off staying as far away from me as possible. I'm a cold, selfish, angry bitch."

Chan pushed away from the shelves, straightening. "Yeah, I already got that part, thanks. The thing that seems to escape you is that in comparison to me, you look like a fucking saint."

Thinking back over her long and checkered history as a vampire, it was quite likely that Duchess had, in fact, fucked a saint at some point. She debated telling him that just to shock him, but he spoke again before she could.

"So... you acted to save me from the devil, without asking first if I wanted to be saved. And now, here we are, bickering like an old, married couple over the mummified not-corpse of a guy who can quite possibly hear every word we say. Now what?"

The sarcasm in his voice dripped between them like acid.

"Now, nothing," Duchess said coldly. "I've told you. Do yourself a favor and stay away from me. I've already torn your soul apart. Come too close, and I'll corrupt what's left of it."

Chan laughed. In fact, he kept on laughing—choked guffaws that eventually made him collapse into the chair Mason had vacated when they arrived, holding his stomach.

Duchess stared at him as though he'd gone mad.

Eventually, he got control of himself, slumping forward in the rusty folding chair with his elbows propped on his knees and the heels of his palms pressing into his eye sockets.

"*You'll corrupt me,*" he echoed, and laughed again—the sound edged with something harsh and ugly. "Oh, that's rich. Seriously, you have no idea how funny that is."

"I certainly don't find it as amusing as you appear to," she said in an icy voice.

He sat back, looking her straight in the eye. "I was married, you know. To a truly good and loving woman."

All the air left Duchess' body, in a single, irrational rush of *who is this woman, and how do I find her and kill her?*

"Yeah, it's true," Chan said, meeting Duchess' shocked gaze with his tired one. "You know what happened? I cheated on her. I left her to go on deployment while she was pregnant with my child, and while I was gone, I banged random women that I met in bars. Then I got caught. One of my buddies told Janette what I was doing—as well he should have. I destroyed her life and the life of my unborn daughter. How's that for some cosmic irony? And I'm supposed to be an upstanding member of the armed forces, living my life beyond reproach. Serving my country and my family with dignity, fidelity, and honor, *blah, blah, blah.*"

He trailed away, looking up and shaking his head at the ceiling. "If you had any concept of what I've done to the people I was supposed to protect and cherish, you'd have let the fucking demon have me, and thanked him afterward for the public service."

Duchess could find no words. She'd tried to listen, but her brain had latched onto the phrase 'I was married,' and gotten stuck there. A surge of territorial jealousy threatened to overwhelm her as she imagined him holding another woman. Loving another woman.

This is insane. Was Bael possessing her somehow? Had she lost her mind? She'd given up any claim to the heart and soul of the man in front of her when she'd failed him in a muddy Parisian courtyard, surrounded by hanging laundry and the stink of evil. Had she not filled the empty years since his death with as many meaningless sexual trysts as possible? Had she not told him only moments ago to stay away from her, or risk what was left of his tattered soul?

This logical line of thought did nothing to quash the swell of bitter envy she now felt toward this woman she'd never met. Everything inside of her had been ripped open by his words, left glistening and bleeding in the sun.

She realized that she'd been standing in silence for too long and Chan was staring at her. Slowly, the rest of what he'd said percolated into her consciousness, and she blinked, the red rage of jealousy receding.

Oh.

It was obvious he expected a harsh response to his secret.

"Your wife and daughter," she said, forcing the words to emerge evenly, rather than as a hiss. "Do they still live?"

His eyes snapped back to her.

"Of course they're still alive! And they have the good sense to live their lives *without me*, which is something you might want to think a bit harder about."

She narrowed her eyes. "If they're alive, then it appears you have a considerably better track record in marriage than I do."

"*Fuck*. Listen to this shit. This is just *perfect*," he growled. "There's nothing you could say to make me forgive myself for what I did to my wife. I don't love her. I never loved her. I'm incapable of love. I don't deserve to be saved, and I *don't* deserve happiness."

"Neither do I," Duchess retorted.

They stood in the quiet, dingy storeroom—staring at one another without blinking, trapped in silence. A tentative knock shattered the strained atmosphere, and a moment later, Oksana and Mason returned. Oksana looked from one to the other of them, her dark eyes missing nothing.

"Eris is going to travel somewhere with better phone coverage. Then he'll try again to contact us so we can talk properly," she said, choosing to ignore the lingering miasma of emotional carnage in the room. "We should try to get some rest until then. We're safe enough here, and it's not like Snag is going anywhere."

Chan snorted. "Yeah. Sure. Makes sense. First rule of an operative—take your rest where you can get it." His voice was flat and distant. "Someone let me know when anything interesting happens."

With things by no means resolved, Duchess found an unoccupied corner and allowed herself to slide down the wall until she was seated on the floor. Wordlessly, she furled her aura and locked her mental shields down tight, suddenly aware of just how exhausted she was after the events of the past few days. Since it was the only escape available to her within the confines of this cluttered room, she turned her thoughts inward and let them drift, hoping for the respite of sleep.

Even if the nightmares came, it would still be better than trying to untangle the bad dream that was her current reality.

NINETEEN

Duchess awoke a short time later from dreams of red, red blood and the bottomless rage of a mother's loss. She rolled into a crouch, fangs bared and eyes burning, but the vision of that muddy, seventeenth-century courtyard littered with the corpses of her husband and daughter faded an instant later. In its place knelt Oksana, one hand resting on Duchess' shoulder and unwanted sympathy lighting her dark eyes.

"*What?*" Duchess demanded, before her friend could say anything Duchess might regret.

For a moment, Oksana appeared to debate whether or not to comment on the manner of Duchess' awakening, but fortunately, she thought better of it.

"Eris finally got through," was all she said.

Duchess blinked, and her surroundings came into focus, along with the previous night's events. "Oh," she mumbled. "*Très bien.*"

Oksana rose and offered her a hand up. The others were gathered around a wooden crate they'd been using as a makeshift table, though Chan hung back a couple of steps. Oksana's mobile phone lay face up on the rough surface.

"I've got him on speaker," Oksana said, "but we wanted to wake you before we waded too far into things."

Duchess shook off the remainder of her grogginess and joined them around the crate. "*Bonjour*, Eris."

404

"Good, you're awake," came the tinny and faintly static-riddled reply. "Duchess, I need you to tell me exactly what message Snag left for you. Word for word."

One of the others might have berated Eris for his lack of social graces, but Duchess had little use for such pleasantries. She pushed her hair out of her face and pulled up a chair, settling into it.

"He said, 'Sangye is not the Thirteenth. Bael is attempting to draw the Angel out of hiding, but he does not understand.' The first part is straightforward enough, if somewhat difficult to credit. The second part is characteristically cryptic, unless you have some insight I lack."

"Nothing concrete enough to be useful," Eris replied. "Though we'd better hope he was right about the boy."

Mason frowned, his brows drawing together angrily. "That's a six-year-old child you're talking about, mate. One who burned himself to death out of some misguided attempt to save the rest of us—"

Eris cut him off. "Yes. He was a young child. And now he's a dead child, so if he was, in fact, our thirteenth member, then we have a rather serious problem, don't we?"

Oksana put a hand on Mason's shoulder as she spoke. "I've been thinking about that, Eris. The council is supposed to be made up of thirteen of Bael's greatest mistakes. But Bael turned Sangye purposely—he wasn't a mistake. At least, he wasn't until he sacrificed himself to thwart Bael's attempt on us at the Thean Hou Temple."

Eris was silent for a moment. "It's a fair point," he said thoughtfully. "As for the part about drawing out the Angel, with luck we'll have the chance to ask Snag for clarification directly, now that you've got him back."

"We've tried several times to give him blood orally," Mason reported in a flat voice, having apparently brought his temper back under control. "But, not to put too fine a point on it, his body is a mummified husk. He can't swallow, and if I tried to massage his throat I think I'd just end up pulverizing it. How exactly did you manage it the last time?"

"With a great deal of patience." Even over the cellular connection, Eris' grim tone was evident. "It took me almost a hundred years of squeezing a few drops at a time into him."

Mason's mouth opened and closed a couple of times, and Chan's eyebrows shot up.

"A hundred… *years*?" Mason echoed. "You might've mentioned that up front, Eris. We don't have that kind of time!"

Oksana met Duchess' eyes briefly, her thoughts brushing along their shared bond.

"Oh! That's right…" Duchess said. "Eris, Sangye was able to inject Snag with some of his life force without using the medium of blood. We perceived it as a sort of white light surrounding the two of them."

"It was enough to rouse him from a petrified state to how he is now, so we could move him without his body being in danger of shattering," Oksana added. "But I couldn't puzzle out the mechanism. I'd have no idea how to replicate it."

"I might," Eris said. There was a weighty pause. "I think you'd better bring him home."

"Home," Duchess repeated, surprised. "*His* home, you mean? To Cairo?"

"To Saqqara," Eris clarified. "To the place where I found him. We may have to make a final stand soon, and I can't think of a more appropriate place than where it all started."

"You think the war is starting now," Oksana said, sounding faintly shell-shocked. "Why? What's changed?"

"With the addition of Duchess' mate, Snag remains the only one of us not to be reunited," Eris said.

Duchess felt Chan stiffen more than she saw it. "Her *mate*? What the hell is that supposed to mean?"

Eris did not appear to have heard him as he continued, "If Bael wishes to act to prevent the council's formation, it will have to be soon. Snag is vulnerable right now. We need to regroup and start planning our defense."

Duchess tried to focus on logistics, but her thoughts were still tumbling like leaves tossed by the wind. "Getting Snag to Egypt will be a challenge. It's going to take some creative planning."

"What resources do you have there?" Eris asked. "I can transfer additional money if you need it, or Xander can."

Mason spoke up. "I can try to arrange for medical transport by air." He paused, rubbing at his forehead. "It will be difficult, though. It takes a ridiculous amount of resources, and there will be plenty of questions about who he is, what's wrong with him, and so forth. For obvious reasons, we can't let any other medical professionals near him unless we mesmerize them immediately afterward."

"Can you do it, though?" Eris asked.

Mason sighed. "Maybe. I can try calling in some favors through Doctors Without Borders. If nothing else, Gita owes us pretty big right now for helping free her son."

"Very well," Eris said. "Let me know what you come up with. In the mean time, I'll organize things on this end."

After a brief round of goodbyes, Oksana ended the phone call. "If nothing else," she said, "it will be a relief to be back together. If we're going into the end game, we should face it as a group."

Duchess had to fight not to let her eyes stray to Chan, who was still standing a short distance away from the others. It took a few moments to identify the tight feeling in her chest as the first stirrings of panic, and a few more to realize that it was in response to the idea that Chan might run for the hills the first chance he got, now that the immediate crisis had been resolved.

A mobile phone rang, but not the one sitting on the crate. Mason rummaged in his pocket and came up with the device, answering it.

"Gita," he mouthed by way of explanation, as someone spoke excitedly on the other end.

When the torrent of words finally stemmed, Mason smiled and said, "I'm just relieved we could help out, Gita. I can't take credit, though—it was Duchess and another friend of ours who finally got the police moving and found where the hostages were being kept. Yes… yes, that's right… I'll pass it on for you, don't worry."

Another heartfelt spate of words.

"Actually," Mason said, "There is something I could use help with. We've got one casualty who's in bad shape, and we need to get him back to his home in Egypt if it's at all possible…"

Mason pointed at the phone and then the door into the main part of the shop, which Duchess took to mean he wanted to get Raahim's input on something to do with the logistics. He and Oksana left a moment later, leaving Duchess alone with Chan again. Given what tended to happen when they were alone, this was perhaps not the wisest course of action. It was, however, a chance to ask him the question that she needed an answer to.

She must have looked uncomfortable, because he studied her warily for a moment and asked, "What is it?" in a guarded tone.

Castigating herself internally, she flipped her hair over her shoulder and turned to study the contents of the shelf nearest her. The affected nonchalance felt like a flimsy act even to her. For the dozenth time in the last twenty-four hours, she wondered what in hell's name had happened to her. This uncertain, emotional creature wasn't *her*. Was it?

"You heard Eris earlier," she said, still not looking at him. "We'll be rejoining the others soon in Egypt."

"Yes," he replied, still sounding cautious.

"I understand that you have no reason to want to be anyplace near me, but the simple fact is that you'd be much safer with the group," she said, pleased with how reasonable that sounded. "You've already experienced what Bael intends for all of us, and how impossible it is to fight him alone. Only together do we stand a chance."

"Of course I'm coming," he said, sounding confused.

She was already framing her next argument, so it took a moment for the sense of his words to penetrate. She whirled to look at him. "You are?"

"Well… yes?" He was giving her a strange look. "I mean… I feel like I'm starting a new TV series by watching the season finale, but I'm not a complete idiot. I think I've picked up the gist, which is that even if you and I would tear each other apart if we got too close, I'm still part of this council, or whatever. We're all that stands between the world and that *creature* from the temple. And your guy on the phone thinks the big battle is kicking off soon, right?"

He's not leaving.

The words reverberated through her mind, and she tightened her shields before they could escape and possibly echo across his thoughts. He wasn't leaving. Maybe all hope wasn't lost.

Now he looked even warier. "Assuming the others are on board with me tagging along. Or, did I read this wrong?"

"No," she said quickly. "You didn't read it wrong."

"Well, that's a relief," he said. "All of my bridges have been pretty thoroughly burned."

She frowned. "What do you mean?"

Chan laughed. It was a low, pleasant sound, and Duchess cursed herself for enjoying it.

His expression turned wry. "It's not like I can call up the CIA and say 'Oh hey, it's me! Sorry I've been out of touch for days after my check-in deadline. The good news is that the militant Malaysian cult has been defeated and their leader destroyed, sort of. The bad news is that I've been turned into a vampire!'"

She winced. *It had to be done*, she reminded herself.

"They wouldn't believe it, of course," he went on, "but I imagine they'd still have operatives coming after me with orders to eliminate quicker than you could say 'national security threat.'"

"I'm sorry," she said, knowing that he deserved far more than that.

He shrugged. "Honestly, I always expected this gig to result in my death sooner or later. I told myself that at least that way, my little girl would get my government benefits and insurance. Now she'll get them—once the powers that be get around to declaring me dead, anyway—but I still get to walk around and maybe make a difference in the world after all."

He'd said before that he was incapable of love, but listening to him talk about his daughter, she wanted to cry, '*Liar!*'

Instead, she asked, "Your little girl. Do you have contact with her?"

His face and posture had relaxed as they spoke, but now he closed off like a blast door slamming down. "No. And I suppose there's not much chance of that changing now."

He was probably right about that—another wound laid squarely at Duchess' feet.

"Well, then," she said quietly, "let's see what we can do about making sure she still has a world to grow up in."

Oksana poked her head in a moment later. "Hey, you two. We came up with a new plan."

"Oh?" Chan asked, moving towards the door. As he passed by Duchess, his arm brushed against hers. They both froze at the thrum of electricity, but Chan shook it off first, pasting on a neutral expression.

"It was Gita's idea," Oksana said, "though she has no idea how helpful it was."

Mason was still on the phone, jotting notes on a scrap of paper on the counter while Raahim looked on with mild curiosity.

"Mm-hmm," he said. "Yes. Absolutely. We can make sure to get that done tomorrow. Yeah. No problem. Thank you so much, we really appreciate it."

He hung up the phone, quirking a lopsided smile at the others. "We're set for transport, assuming no one was banking on traveling first class."

"I'm impressed," Duchess said, meaning it.

Chan clapped Mason on the shoulder. "Ditto. So, what's the new plan?"

"It was going to take the better part of a week to arrange for medical transport," Mason said. "So, I might or might not have made it sound like Snag was nearly on his death bed, in hopes of hurrying things along a bit."

"Emotional manipulation?" Chan asked, a hint of amusement peeking through his stoic facade.

Mason let out a rueful laugh. "These days, some of my closest friends are sociopaths—just ask Xander when you meet him. Maybe it's starting to rub off."

"You're a mad genius Australian man, my friend," Chan teased.

"*Anyway*," Oksana interrupted, "Gita mentioned that it was a sad state of affairs when it's quicker and easier to find a cargo plane to transport a dead body than to get medical transport for someone who was still alive. At which, point, a light bulb went off above Mason's head, and he started calling around to the various airlines. There's a cargo plane leaving from the Kuala Lumpur International Airport at eleven p.m., and assuming we can make all the arrangements by then, we're on it."

Duchess' eyebrows rose at the elegance of the plan. "Are we indeed? Well played, *Docteur.*"

Mason shrugged. "We just need to get a coffin so we can store Snag's body inside of it. Then we take the cargo plane to Mumbai, and Eris can find us a flight to Cairo from there."

Chan let out a small, choked noise, and the others looked at him. "Sorry," he said, his voice sounding a bit strangled. "Is it in really bad taste that I find it hilarious you're going to transport a vampire inside a coffin?"

Mason looked confused for a moment before his eyes widened. "Oh. Bloody hell. I didn't even make the connection."

"If we're lucky," Oksana said, "Eris will find a way to revive him, and Snag can give you that flat, thousand-yard stare as punishment for laughing at him when he was down."

"Just don't dress him in a dark, red-lined cape before you put him inside the thing," Duchess offered wryly. "It's a very good plan, though."

"Thanks," Mason said. "All we need to do is let Eris know so that he can get working on the connection from Mumbai to Cairo. With luck, we can be in Saqqara within forty-eight hours."

"Do you think it will be hard to find a coffin on short notice?" Oksana wondered.

"These days?" Chan replied, growing sober once more. "I really doubt it."

In the end, it was relatively simple. Since they were confined to the shop due to the bright sunlight, Duchess used her mental powers to convince poor Raahim to help them obtain the needed item. Fortunately, both she and Oksana still maintained the habit of carrying a large amount of whatever the local currency happened to be, whenever they traveled. She pressed a fairly obscene amount into Raahim's hand and sent him on his way.

"That mind control thing is still more than a little disturbing," Chan said as he watched the shopkeeper go.

"At least I'm not asking him to commit a crime," she said carelessly. "I'll even let him keep the change."

"It's more the loss of free will aspect," he said. "Maybe I'm just hard-headed."

Without even thinking, Duchess said, "You always have been, yes."

Chan went still, giving her a thoughtful look.

"I'm starting to regain some of those memories, I think," he said. "Or maybe they're just dreams. But it's still really hard for me to believe in reincarnation."

She glanced at him through her lashes, wishing she'd kept her mouth shut. "Haven't you been living among Buddhists?" she asked carelessly, as though it didn't matter.

"Yes. But it goes against everything that I've always believed," Chan admitted. "I've never been a religious man, so I have a hard time with the whole demons and angels thing, too."

"Even after what you experienced in the temple?"

"Call me the CIA's own Doubting Thomas, I guess," Chan replied with a shrug.

"What do you remember from the past?" Duchess asked, still unable to stop the words flowing.

Chan drew his eyebrows together, as if concentrating.

"It's very hazy. But I remember riding a horse — something I've never done, by the way. And I remember you. Your hair was black."

Duchess lifted a brow.

Oksana snorted. "It could be worse. You should have seen her blue period."

She scowled. "It was the nineteen-eighties, *mon chou*. Blue hair was practically *de rigueur*."

Chan smiled, then sobered. "I remember the dark cloud surrounding us. But that part's more difficult to bring into focus."

She tilted her head, watching him carefully.

"Imagine you were trying to remember something when you were really drunk or had been hit in the head," Chan said. "It's like the memories are there and I can kind of see them, but I can't draw the images up clearly in my mind."

"You aren't missing much," Duchess answered in a dark voice.

"I didn't figure I was," Chan agreed.

Silence fell between them, but it was a more relaxed sort of silence than what had come before. Perhaps, Duchess thought, they would be able to forge a truce of some kind. Perhaps they could simply exist in their separate spaces, without constantly grating against each other's sharp edges.

Perhaps one day, thinking about him marrying another woman—fucking her and siring a child by her—would not make Duchess want to tie him to a bed and mark him from head to foot.

By mutual accord, the four of them returned to the storeroom in hopes of grabbing more rest while Raahim acquired what they needed. A few hours later, Duchess' sharp ears caught the sound of the front door being unlocked and the bell chiming as someone entered. A knock sounded on the storeroom entrance, and Raahim stuck his head in, smiling amiably.

"I have arranged for your coffin. It will be delivered to the rear door of the shop in an hour or so. My condolences on your loss," he said, giving them a small bow.

"Thank you," Mason replied. "You've been exceedingly helpful."

Raahim nodded and withdrew.

"Remind me to leave a big wad of money in the till for him before we leave," Mason added.

"Done," Oksana agreed. "Though I do hope the coffin delivery service in this city is prompt. I'm eager to be on our way."

Twenty

Chan had never given much thought before to what it would mean not to be able to tolerate daylight. While the group's travel plans went surprisingly smoothly, he couldn't deny a sense of nagging anxiety that a delay or breakdown might leave them exposed to the sun. And while Chan had long been inured to the idea of his own death, going out in a blaze of frying flesh while horrified onlookers screamed their lungs out wasn't quite what he'd envisioned for his final moments.

The others seemed positively blasé about the concept of travel, however, so he tried to take his cue from them.

"There's usually a shadow somewhere that you can huddle in," Oksana said cheerfully, "if worse comes to worst."

They arrived in Mumbai a couple of hours before dawn, fleeing the sun's slow rise as they flew west. Eris had arranged their connecting flight for that evening. After a brief discussion, they left Snag's coffin in the airport's care and booked a hotel room rather than camping out at the gate.

Chan had an uncomfortable feeling the decision was because of his strange lethargy, which seemed to grow worse as sunrise approached. He wasn't used to being the weak link in the chain—the one who needed accommodation.

"Don't give it a second thought, mate," Mason said. "If it means I'm not the baby vamp of the group anymore, I'm all for it."

Chan slept like the dead… or perhaps, like the undead. He awoke to Duchess' hand on his shoulder, a hum of power washing along his nerves even through the material of his cotton shirt. He must have slept the day away. No light slanted through the gaps in the curtains, but Duchess' eyes flared ice blue before she pulled her hand away and moved back a step.

"Mason bought you a suitcase and some basics for travel," she said, a throaty note to her voice that made his stomach tighten. "Clothing, toiletries—that sort of thing."

With a mild jolt, Chan realized that he'd walked away from every single possession he owned in Kuala Lumpur except for the dirty and sweat-stained clothes he was currently wearing. If he'd had an emotional tie to anything left behind, it probably would have been upsetting… but he didn't. His quarters at the complex had been as sterile and devoid of personality as a jail cell.

"Oh," he rasped, still waking up. "Clean clothes? That was nice of him. Do I have time for a shower?"

She nodded, and he stumbled to the *en suite*, turning the water on as cold as it would go. It took him almost ten minutes to realize that only part of the burning inside him was due to his unwanted and completely inappropriate sexual desire. The rest was hunger.

Shit.

When he emerged a few minutes later, wrapped in a towel, the other three were deep in conversation.

"I think I need to feed," he blurted, not wanting to be stuck in an airport full of innocent people if the cravings got worse. He had a ridiculous flash of being trapped on the plane, ripping the cabin door off its hinges and drinking the pilot dry while the aircraft plummeted from the sky.

Oksana glanced at Duchess and raised an eyebrow that almost looked challenging. "Sorry, no help here, I'm afraid. I've sworn off hunting, and I still need to feed Mason."

Mason shrugged, with a *'what can you do?'* gesture.

"Duchess refilled at the hotel bar while you were asleep, though," Oksana continued. She was still gazing unblinkingly at Duchess, who returned the look with a flat stare.

Chan didn't want to examine the surge of—*jealousy?*—he felt at the idea of Duchess wrapping her arms around some bland businessman in a dark corner of the bar... pressing her mouth to his throat...

"Your high-beams are on, mate," Mason said.

It took Chan a minute to parse the cryptic observation, at which point he realized the burning in his eyes must mean they were glowing in the room's dim light.

Double shit.

He blinked rapidly, hoping that was the magic formula for getting rid of the telltale glow. "Unless you want me savaging some poor loser at the airport, come with me," he growled, and grasped Duchess by the arm, pulling her into the bathroom.

He closed the door behind them and realized a moment later what a bad idea it had probably been. Her scent filled the small room; her eyes flashed with wariness. Goddamn it, she was more beautiful than anyone had a right to be after a day spent stuck in cargo planes and hotels.

His hunger must be affecting his brain-to-mouth filter, as well, because when he opened his mouth, what tumbled out was, "Did you feed from a man or a woman?"

Her haughty eyebrow made him want to pin her against the door and repeat the question right up against her ear. *Fucking hell, what was wrong with him?*

"Since I've bedded so many of both that I long ago lost count, does it really matter?" she asked.

The knowledge that if she wanted to, she could flex her power and throw him off like an annoying fly gave him the courage to succumb to his earlier temptation. Her back thumped softly against the door, her eyes still blazing at him.

"No," he murmured against the pale shell of her ear. "It doesn't matter."

He nuzzled the sweet-smelling skin at the hinge of her jaw and trailed his lips downward, bloodlust rising. When he struck, it was purely on instinct, his fangs piercing tender flesh until the nectar beneath welled up. *God.* It was a hundred times worse than when he'd fed from her in the hospital—or a hundred times better.

She gasped, her hand coming up to fist in his hair. He growled and clamped down harder, his instincts urging him to fight if she tried to drag him away. But she didn't. She merely held him there, his scalp tingling where her grip on his hair pulled against it.

Long moments of blood-fueled bliss passed before she hissed, "*Enough.*"

The power she'd held in check before unfurled, forcing his inner beast into submission. He sagged against her, pulling his fangs free and lapping at the dribble of red trickling down from the twin wounds. By the time he pulled back enough to see them, they'd already closed over.

Even so, she looked… debauched. Wild, for all her new pallor. Chan's cock throbbed beneath the towel, which was in danger of sliding free of his waist. He grabbed it and backed away, unable to look away from her heaving breasts until she spoke, drawing his eyes back to her face.

"Be ready to leave for the airport in twenty minutes," she said, and left the bathroom, closing the door behind her.

-o-o-o-

The flight to Cairo went as smoothly as the flight to Mumbai had, though Chan and the others passed it in far more comfort than the stripped-down cargo plane had offered.

"For such a frail creature," Mason grunted as they shoved Snag's coffin into the back of a rented truck, "he certainly weighs a lot."

"It must be all that ageless wisdom," Oksana quipped, slamming the dented tailgate shut.

"Or possibly the sheer volume of ornamental metal on this casket," Duchess opined. "Perhaps I should have been clearer when mesmerizing Raahim that he did not need to spend all of the money I gave him buying the most ornate coffin available."

Chan glanced at his watch. "Are you sure we can make it to this place we're headed before dawn?"

Duchess smiled, showing a hint of fang. "As long as absolutely nothing goes wrong between here and there."

Oksana gave her a quelling look. "Don't listen to her. It'll be fine. It's not far—less than fifty kilometers, and Eris says the roads aren't bad. There's plenty of time."

"And the likelihood that someone will stop us and start asking questions about the dead guy in the back of the truck?" Chan pressed, still feeling that the others were treating this expedition too cavalierly.

"Middling," Mason said, not sounding concerned. "Which might be a problem for someone without the ability to hypnotize humans into believing everything is just fine."

Chan managed to rein in his skepticism, knowing that even after what he'd seen and done in Kuala Lumpur, he still wasn't thinking like a vampire. He climbed into the cab with Duchess, while the other two piled into the truck bed with the coffin. As it turned out, his insight had been all too keen and before they had traveled more than twenty-five kilometers, they came upon a road-block.

Duchess slowed sedately to a stop and lowered the driver's side window. Chan was glad of his passable grasp of Arabic as the uniformed soldier approached, flashlight in hand.

"Vehicle check," he said. "What's that in the back?"

Two more guards approached the truck bed, shining lights on the casket with its shiny silver accents.

Duchess didn't so much as blink. "It's lumber for the archaeological dig in Saqqara," she said in the same language, her eyes glowing. "Nothing to worry about."

Chan glanced in the rearview mirror and saw the other guards straighten in momentary confusion. He caught a flash of violet... a flash of cobalt blue. Oksana and Mason, their eyes burning in the night.

"This is nothing to worry about," the soldier next to Duchess' window parroted. He stepped back and gestured the others away from the truck bed. "Please pull forward."

"You're too kind," Duchess muttered, already closing the window as she pulled away from the barricade.

"I don't think I'll ever get used to that," Chan said, shaking his head. "But it's fucking useful as hell."

"There are compensations for being a bloodsucker," Duchess said grimly, "though they may be few and far between."

The process was repeated twice more with only minor variations. Within an hour of leaving the outskirts of Cairo, the truck was pulling onto the dusty, sand-covered roads beyond the western edge of the Nile flood zone. Behind them lay palm trees and buildings; ahead was the Western Desert, silent and devoid of life.

"That was abrupt," Chan observed, his newly enhanced night vision allowing him to take in more of his surroundings than he would otherwise have been able to. The line of demarcation between livable and lifeless was unexpectedly stark.

"The Nile's waters spread so far, and no further," Duchess said philosophically as the truck bounced over the desert roads. "Beyond that, life must be imported, subject to heavy tariffs in the form of both time and effort."

"Yet this is where your friend wants us to gather?"

Duchess adjusted her grip on the steering wheel. "So it would seem. I'm certain he has his reasons."

His attention shifted abruptly to a flat area in the distance before them. "People up ahead," he said tersely. "Several of them."

"Yes, I know. It's Eris and the others."

He looked at her. "And you're sure of that because…?"

She tapped her temple with a manicured fingertip. "Because I can sense them. Just as they will be able to sense us."

He made an effort to relax his tense posture. They closed the last few hundred meters and pulled into what appeared to be a parking lot for tourists visiting the site. A large sign reading 'Closed for Renovations' in English and Arabic partially blocked the entrance, but several trucks were parked there—some with large trailers attached. A couple of smaller cars completed the mix. Their truck's headlights swept across a group of six people watching their approach.

Duchess parked the vehicle between two of the other trucks and turned off the headlights, killing the engine. Chan let himself out of the cab in time to see Oksana vault from the bed. Her prosthetic foot didn't slow her down in the least as she jogged toward the others. Duchess followed at a more leisurely pace.

Chan hung back a ways, watching the reunion without inserting himself into it for now. Mason stayed back as well, and Chan was oddly grateful not to be the only one playing odd man out.

Oksana went first to a small woman with waist-length black hair and sad, dark-brown eyes. "Manisha," she said, hugging the sad-eyed woman tightly, "I'm so, *so* sorry."

Manisha nodded against Oksana's shoulder, returning the embrace for a long moment before drawing away. Oksana turned immediately to the tall, brown-haired man standing next to her and embraced him as well. Meanwhile, Duchess strode over to the other two couples, no sentimentality evident in the reunion as they immediately fell into intense conversation.

"Fire and ice, those two women," Mason muttered next to him. "Typical. C'mon, mate—we might as well run the gauntlet now, so we can get the patient unloaded and under cover before sunrise."

The tall man and the short, dark-haired woman Oksana had embraced were already walking toward them.

"Ozzie, old chap," said the man, in the urbane tones of a BBC voiceover, "good to see you. You've not met Manisha properly yet—Manisha… Ozzie."

"Manisha," Mason said, taking her by the hand. His other hand came up to cover hers. "Please accept my sincerest condolences. I'm so sorry we weren't able to prevent this." His eyes flickered to Chan's. "Manisha and Sangye were acquainted before they got drawn into this mess," he said by way of explanation. "Xander, Manisha, this is Chan Wei Yong."

"Hello," Chan said, still unsure of where he stood within this odd group.

"Hello," Manisha said, accepting his offered hand. "Welcome to… well… *here*."

He shook Xander's hand next, meeting the cool, assessing gaze.

"American, eh?" the British vampire asked. "Well, I suppose Della turned out to be all right, so we'll try not to hold it against you."

"If it's any consolation," Chan said, "the US would probably deny any knowledge of my existence at this point."

Xander released his grip and gave Mason a brief clasp on the upper arm before turning back to the main group, who were approaching. "Ah, here come the others. This is Tré, Della, Eris, and Trynn," he said, pointing out each of them in turn.

Chan filed the names and faces away, used to committing such details to memory. Tré was dark-haired and Slavic, with unusual silver eyes and the bearing of a natural leader. Della was a short, curvy woman with wild waves of chestnut hair and a mole that brought to mind old photos of Marilyn Monroe. Trynn was a slender, suave woman—tall and a bit boyish with cropped black hair. Eris had a nose, chin, and cheekbones straight from ancient Greek statuary, with a dark and wavy shoulder-length mane. His eyes skimmed over Chan for a bare instant before settling on the coffin in the truck.

"Chan," said the leader—the one called Tré. "You are welcome in our family, such as it is. Don't hesitate to ask for whatever you need." His accent carried strong hints of the Black Sea.

Chan needed oh so many things, but they weren't the sorts of things one got for the asking. "Thank you," he said. "Right now, though, I think what we all need is to get this friend of yours under cover before the sun comes up."

"Quite right," Eris said.

Xander helped Chan haul the heavy coffin forward. While his fight with Duchess had disavowed him of any idea that the women here were weaker than he was, a quick look around showed that he, Xander, Tré, Eris,

Trynn, and Mason would be the best match in height to carry the casket funeral-style, on their shoulders. They hefted it up and followed Della's lead toward the dark silhouette of the ancient monument.

The indigo sky was beginning to lighten to navy in the east, a low wash of red at the horizon. Chan craned around as much as he was able to take in their incredible surroundings. The ten of them entered the column-flanked grand hallway that led into the site. Chan knew about as much as most westerners probably did about the pyramids at Giza, which were located not far from here. Still, the age of this place was like a palpable aura.

The high stone walls breached by this single entrance weren't familiar to him, but the broken tetrahedral shape of the Step Pyramid within rang a few bells. It was supposed to be ancient—far older than the other pyramids, if his schoolboy memory served. It was certainly damned impressive, even in the murky pre-dawn light.

It was not to the pyramid that they went, however. Other structures dotted the huge, enclosed space, including a handful of tents. Some of the stone constructions were small; some were massive, like the two-story tall barrier topped by carved cobra heads that loomed before them. Stairs led up to the top—uncomfortably narrow for six people and a coffin. Once at the top, an even narrower staircase led downward, disappearing below ground level.

"The South Tomb," Eris said. "That's where we're set up.

TWENTY-ONE

reat, Chan thought, eyeing the switchbacks on the precarious stone staircase with misgivings. They picked their way down it slowly, and his eyes adjusted to the deeper darkness in seconds. At the bottom, he could make out artificial lighting down a tunnel leading away from the landing at the base of the stairs.

"We've got some solar panels set up, along with a bank of batteries for electricity," Xander said by way of explanation. "Mostly, the lights are for the donors, but it really does get quite dark down here at night—even for vampires."

"Donors?" Chan asked.

It was Della who answered. "Humans who tagged along to voluntarily supply us with blood. That's who's in the tents up top. Xander's got some... connections with people who were willing to help us out."

Chan frowned. Vampires had human groupies who followed them around to offer free meals? That was news to him. Although Oksana *did* say something back in Mumbai about having sworn off hunting...

"Oh-*kay*," he said, drawing out the word.

"I've set up a cot in the tomb where I originally found Snag," Eris said. "It seemed an appropriate place to put him."

And hardly morbid at all, Chan thought, only remembering that he was surrounded by people who could read his thoughts when both Mason and Xander snorted quietly in amusement.

The tunnels were cool and dusty, the floors worn smooth by the passage of time. Chan caught glimpses of artwork on the walls—sand-scrubbed friezes and carvings, some still with paint clinging to them, the colors leached by dim light. The place was far larger and more maze-like than he would have guessed, not that he'd ever given much thought to the layout and spaciousness of underground Egyptian tomb structures.

Eventually, Della led them into a decently sized room with the promised cot set up in the center. It had its own halogen bulb strung up from the ceiling, throwing light over the stunning murals that decorated every inch of the three unbroken walls. Chan had a confused impression of gods and humans, horse-drawn chariots, lions, hippos, oxen, even crocodiles... all carefully detailed with brilliant pigments that had stood the test of time remarkably well.

Wow. He supposed that if you had to spend centuries stuck in a tomb, there were definitely worse ones available.

"Set him down here," Eris said, and they lowered the casket onto the stone floor next to the low cot.

Eris cracked the seal and opened it, pausing to let out a slow breath as he looked down at the figure resting inside. "Oh, my foolish friend. I'd hoped never to see you like this again."

Della tangled her fingers with Tré's, squeezing hard. "He looks dead," she whispered.

"As close to death as our kind is capable of from natural means," Eris said. "But his soul is still clinging to the husk."

In Kuala Lumpur, Mason had suggested placing Snag on a sheet inside the coffin, so they could use it to lift him out more easily. Chan, Eris, Duchess, and Trynn each grasped a corner and used the cotton material as a sort of sling, easing his body up and onto the cot without jostling him.

"Jesus, Snag," Trynn muttered. "What the hell were you thinking?"

Mason spoke next. "Eris, you said you had an idea that might help him recover without taking a century to do it. What did you mean by that?"

Eris stroked his jaw, which was shaded by a couple days' growth of stubble. "You said it yourself. It's life force that he needs. Blood is merely the medium of transfer. The last time I did this was more than sixteen hundred years ago. I was young then, and alone."

"But now, you're much older, and there are ten of us," Trynn said. "Are you saying we all need to feed him?"

"Yes and no," Eris replied—somewhat unhelpfully in Chan's opinion. "As the doctor said when we spoke before, his physical condition limits how much blood we can get into him right now."

"Ah," Mason said, with the air of someone experiencing a revelation. "You're saying we all need to feed *you*, and you'll try to transfer life force to him. You're the oldest, right? The most powerful, except for him?"

"Yes," Duchess replied for him. "Eris, then Tré, then myself, followed by Oksana and Xander."

Chan frowned. "But Sangye was a new vampire, right? And he was just a kid. Yet he was able to do this life transfer thing somehow…"

"He was an old soul, with a greater than usual awareness of his past lives," Duchess said. Both she and the woman Manisha looked very pale and sad at the mention of the boy. "He'd also consumed Snag's blood and life force to very nearly the last drop."

Tré approached the cot, looking down at the mummified figure lying on it. "If you think this has the best chance of working, Eris, then it's what we will do," he said.

428

"How's the human donor situation?" Oksana asked. "It's been some time since I fed, and Mason has been feeding from me."

"We have a dozen people," Xander said. "I'll admit I didn't expect us to be channeling all our power into a mummy, but we won't keel over from starvation in the next few days, at least."

"How'd you swing this thing with the donors, anyway?" Mason asked.

Xander shrugged. "I paid a quiet visit to the IT department at HelioTeque. One of the kids there is a conspiracy theorist. He ate up our story with a spoon. Turns out he runs a website for other... shall we say, *like-minded individuals*. Several of them volunteered to help us in exchange for proof of the existence of paranormal phenomena, plus an all-expense paid expedition to view the archaeological wonders of Saqqara."

"I don't think I've ever been a *paranormal phenomenon* before," Trynn muttered. "I'm still on the fence about it, honestly."

"It's blood, freely given," Xander said. "And I'm afraid at this point, beggars can't be choosers."

Chan wanted to dig a bit further into the whole blood donor thing. Several of the others apparently thought *not hunting hapless humans for blood* was a pretty big deal. Yet Duchess appeared to have no compunctions whatsoever about drinking from random passersby like Raahim and the nameless patron at the hotel bar in Mumbai. Now wasn't the time to press her on it, obviously, but he still felt a bit better knowing that there were people available who were giving their blood voluntarily.

"So, are we ready to do this?" Xander asked. "You want us in shifts, Eris, or all at once?"

"All of you," Eris said. "Though it remains to be seen how much life force I can contain at once."

True to his obvious status as *de facto* leader, Tré nodded and stepped forward. "Start with the oldest among us," he suggested, and offered Eris his wrist.

Mason had done the same thing for Chan, but it was still strange to watch—an oddly intimate exchange as Eris bared glistening fangs and sank them into Tré's vein. Eris' eyes glowed gold, and Chan felt power sizzle through the enclosed underground space. Duchess offered herself next, but the expected burn of jealousy didn't materialize in Chan's chest. These people gave off too much of an aura of family for that—even though their backgrounds spanned the globe, not to mention several millennia.

Also, it hadn't escaped him that he was in the presence of four very obvious couples. Except for the half-dead vampire lying on the cot, everyone here had found the person they'd lost, as Duchess had once lost Bertrand. He couldn't deny the taste of bitterness that rose to the back of his tongue upon realizing that only he and his golden-haired temptress appeared unable to get their emotional shit together.

Eris worked his way through the group one by one. In his turn, Chan proffered his left arm, unsure what to expect after his singular—and life-altering—experience with being bitten. It didn't help that by this point, getting within arm's reach of Eris made it feel like static electricity was skittering along his skin, leaving gooseflesh in its wake.

Screw the solar panels—they could've stuck an electrical plug in the guy and run the lights off *him*, as much juice as he seemed to be channeling right now.

Fangs slid into his flesh. He felt them—of course he did—but it was nothing like the burning agony he'd experienced as Duchess had destroyed his humanity. He was aware of the pull, a deep draw that tugged not just at his blood, but also at his life. At the same time, he became more attuned to the man whose lips were clamped to his wrist. He felt Eris' fear for Snag, his determination to succeed in healing him, his worry over the coming war, and his deep sadness over the loss of a brilliant, innocent child who should never have had to worry about sacrificing himself to save others.

He could feel the other vampires, too, perhaps because Eris had drunk from them as well. All of them were determined, yet painfully aware of the odds stacked against them.

Eris pulled away, and Chan watched the wounds in his wrist seal over as though they'd never been there to begin with. The only lingering effects were a growing fatigue and a nagging emptiness in his stomach. His lips thinned—being drained probably meant he'd need to feed again soon, and no doubt the sun was rising over the desert above their heads. For now, he drew on his years of practice in self-discipline and set the hunger aside.

The only vampire remaining was Trynn. Rather than taking her wrist, Eris pressed a kiss to her lips and drew her head to the side. His fangs pierced her neck, and a small noise escaped her throat that sounded far closer to ecstasy than pain. Chan shifted in place uncomfortably as desire washed through the newly expanded link, twining with his growing hunger. It took every goddamned iota of his willpower not to let his eyes drift to Duchess, who now stood propped against the wall next to the doorway.

When he was done, Eris rested his forehead against Trynn's for a moment before straightening. He sank into the chair that Della had dragged in and arranged next to the cot.

"This is far more life than I can use, old friend," he murmured. "Perhaps it will be of more help to you." With that, he ripped into his own wrist with his teeth. Blood spurted—Chan could only imagine that he must be filled to bursting after drinking from nine other vampires. The thick red liquid dribbled between Snag's jaws, with his lips stretched into a mummy's rictus grin. Only a tiny amount went into him before it overflowed, dripping down the parchment-like skin of his cheeks. Eris's wound was already healing, though. He laid the palm of his other hand over the withered skin of Snag's forehead, his eyes slipping closed. Chan guessed he was trying to replicate Sangye's trick of willing strength into him.

"Let him work, everyone," Duchess said. "This will no doubt take time."

"Yes," Tré agreed. "The rest of us should feed and rest while we have the chance."

"I'm staying," said Trynn. "I'll let the rest of you know if he needs more blood from you."

TWENTY-TWO

Duchess fed from a human girl named Shay, replenishing her strength in anticipation of what was to come. Tré and Della took the four of them who had just arrived on a quick tour of the underground space. Duchess had been to the Giza plateau many times, but had never made the trip to the Saqqara necropolis until now. It was an impressive site, though one she was not in any condition to fully appreciate at the moment.

The underground system of tunnels and rooms stretched over a much larger area than one might expect. It had been thoroughly cleared and restored by archaeologists over the last several decades. The condition of some of the artwork was truly exquisite. It was also perfect for their purposes. Meters of stone and sand blocked the unforgiving desert sun above. There was plenty of room for all eleven of them.

Xander had obviously been busy in the day or so between his arrival and their showing up with Snag. He, Eris, and Tré had convinced the guards that normally patrolled the site to take an indefinite vacation. Soon after, truckloads of supplies had started arriving from HelioTeque—enough for the humans camping in the compound above to survive in relative comfort while the vampires below had a safe and private place to lick their wounds and devise some sort of strategy.

Eris' description of a final stand was all well and good, but the truth was that if Bael and his undead forces descended on them right now, they would have no defense. The attack at the Thean Hou Temple had proven that clearly enough.

At the end of the impromptu tour, Della pointed to two small rooms a short distance apart, both of them near the end of the tunnel they'd been exploring.

"Oksana, I've got you and Mason in this one," she said. "Some of the guys from up top already brought your luggage down. Duchess, you and Chan are in that one."

Duchess paused, drawing breath to demur, only to be cut off by Tré's uncompromising mental voice in her head.

No, he said. *I don't know what's wrong between the two of you, Duchess. And I don't have to know, if you'd prefer it that way. But you need to fix this. I won't go into a battle with one of my generals waging war against her own troops.*

The words had clearly been directed to Duchess alone, since none of the others reacted. She pressed her lips together, a trapped feeling washing over her that she didn't like one little bit.

Mind your own business, Tré, she managed.

Chan was looking at her warily, and she knew she'd been silent too long. He opened his mouth to say something, his brow furrowed.

She interrupted him before he could. "I need to talk to Xander," she said. "I'll be back later."

With that, she spun and headed in the direction they'd come, following her mental sense of him. This was another discussion she dreaded, but facing it was marginally less daunting than facing Chan alone in a small room again, especially after the bathroom incident in Mumbai. As avoidance strategies went, this was at least one which would accomplish something that needed to be done anyway.

She arrived at a closed door, feeling Xander's presence in the space beyond it. Not all of the rooms had doors on them, but it appeared Della had chosen the ones that did for their sleeping quarters. The door in front of her opened before she could lift a hand to knock. Instead of Xander, however, she was met by a less-than-pleased looking Manisha, blocking the opening as she met Duchess' eyes with a hard, brown gaze.

"What do you want?" Manisha asked in a flat, unwelcoming tone. She was dry-eyed, but grief had cut deep furrows in her pleasant features.

Xander appeared behind her, his hands closing over her shoulders. "Manisha. Love. You can lower your hackles. It's all right."

Manisha's eyes didn't stray from Duchess' or soften in the least. "It's not all right. I'm not in a good place right now, Duchess, and I'm certainly not in the mood to stand around while you pass judgment on the man I love. So, again, what do you want?"

Duchess' heart ached at seeing this tiny woman who was obviously drowning in her own grief standing in front of Xander like an attack dog, ready to defend him against a vampire with many times her strength.

"Nothing that will hurt him," she replied honestly.

Manisha lifted her chin. "You've already done that."

"Only after I hurt her, Manisha," Xander said, and guided her back by the shoulders, opening the door the rest of the way. "Come in, Duchess. Let's talk."

Duchess eased inside, leaving the door open. The room was empty except for a mattress on the floor and a couple of pieces of luggage stowed neatly in the corner.

"I've nothing to offer you by way of hospitality, I'm afraid," Xander said. "Not so much as a chair, though I could probably find one without too much effort."

She waved him off. "You needn't play host with me. I've come to apologize. I can do that while standing."

Manisha had retreated to the corner, where she now perched on one of the upright suitcases with the air of someone waiting for an excuse to throw Duchess out.

"Apologize for what?" Xander asked, sounding tired. "You didn't do anything wrong."

"I judged you," Duchess said, "just as Manisha said."

Xander ran a hand through his hair, mussing it. "Judging someone for ruining the lives of hundreds of people, out of nothing but greed? Including the lives of young children? You shock me, Duchess."

He'd changed, she realized with a faint jolt of unease. She hadn't appreciated how much until she was here, able to feel him through the bond. Xander had always been quicksilver, sliding away from anything that struck too close to the bone. Deflecting. Misdirecting. Now, though, he stood before her, shields down, waiting for her to say whatever she needed to say. Was this what Manisha had done for him? What *love* had done for him?

"I walked out on you," she tried again, when the silence threatened to stretch too long. "I should have stayed."

"I'm all right, Duchess," he said. "Well… perhaps not *all right*. But I'm better than I was. You're worrying me right now, though."

"I'm fine," she said faintly, thinking *no, stop — this is not how the discussion was supposed to go.*

"No one here is fine," Manisha said, and the bitterness in her voice was unmistakable.

"Your pain is bleeding all over the link," Xander said. "I was debating cornering Oksana and trying to shake some information out of her. I still can, if you'd prefer me to take that approach."

The ache that had taken up residence in Duchess' undead heart unexpectedly sprouted tentacles and tried to strangle her. Her head swam, and without realizing it, she slid down the frescoed wall into a heap, covering her face with her hands.

"*Whoa*, now," Xander said, his voice coming from much closer now. Through the gaps in her fingers, Duchess saw him crouch in front of her, lifting one hand but pausing before it made contact with her skin. Even Manisha rose from her perch in the corner and came nearer, sitting on the edge of the mattress.

"I don't... know what to do, Xander," Duchess found herself saying. "What do I *do*?"

Xander's hand closed the final distance and wrapped around her wrist, drawing it away from her face and tangling their fingers together. A fresh wave of guilt at taking his attention away from the person who truly needed it swamped her. Her shields were in tatters; she was broadcasting all over both of them, she could tell—

"Don't be daft," Manisha said, her earlier hostility gone... replaced by what sounded like exhaustion. "I might be angry, but you did apologize, and anyway, you're family."

"Just so," Xander agreed. "Now, will you tell me what's wrong? Your mate is here. He's safe. You found him, but you're sitting curled up in a ball in my room, instead of being with him. What happened, Duchess?"

She still couldn't talk or even draw breath properly, but in a moment of weakness, she let everything flood the bond in a tangle of terrible hopelessness. Her betrayal as a spy... Bertrand's last plea... her dead baby... Chan, confessing to his marriage and its ugly end...

Silence reigned for the space of several heartbeats, deep and smothering.

"Duchess..." Xander began tentatively, a wealth of compassion coloring his rich voice.

"Sounds like you two are perfect for each other," Manisha said, cutting across him. "So, what's the problem?"

Xander craned to look at her. "A little diplomacy here, love?"

Manisha came over and sat against the wall a few inches away from Duchess. "To hell with diplomacy. If one of you had done all sorts of bad stuff, and the other one was a paragon of virtue, then *fine*. Maybe it's a problem." She shrugged. "But if you've both got horrible track records, then you're on even footing. So come clean with him, stop avoiding him, and agree to start fresh."

"But—" Duchess began.

"But nothing. Get over it," Manisha said mercilessly. "There's more at stake here than your desire to castigate yourself for something that happened hundreds of years ago. People have died, and more of them are probably going to die in the coming weeks. You're alive. So is he. What more do you *want*?"

Duchess covered a wince.

"You're no more used to being put in your place than I am—are you, Duchess?" Xander murmured, still holding her hand. "But please take my word that having someone around to take you down a peg as needed does a world of good."

"I hardly recognize you anymore, *mon ami*," Duchess said, staring at their entwined fingers. "You or Oksana."

He snorted. "I can't speak for the snack food addict, but I'm the same rat bastard I've always been, I assure you." He gave her hand a final squeeze and let it go. "Sometimes, though, it does help to see myself through someone else's lens. It's a very nice lens—I'm becoming quite fond of it. Now, though, I need you to tell me one thing. Mind you—I already know the answer. I just want to hear you say it aloud before I kick you out, so Manisha and I can get some rest."

"What's the question?" Duchess asked.

"Chan. Do you care about him?"

"Yes," she rasped. "Of course I do. He's my soul-mate, Xander."

He nodded, a ghost of a smile tugging at one side of his mouth. "There. Wasn't that simple? Now stop cluttering up this dead Egyptian person's perfectly nice floor and go talk to him."

TWENTY-THREE

Chan was easy enough to find. He was in the room Della had shown them earlier. He was also asleep, with a newborn vampire's aversion to the daylight hours. After a moment's hesitation, Duchess lowered herself to sit cross-legged next to the mattress, watching him.

He was… so different now.

Or perhaps not. The differences were skin deep—his square-jawed Asian features housing a soul that had gravitated unerringly to the elite military force of his day. He reveled in risk-taking, he was fiercely independent, and he scoffed at personal danger. He was willing to give up his life for his daughter if he thought that would serve her better than continuing to live.

Dark brown eyes blinked open, meeting hers. His hand twitched toward a weapon that wasn't there, only for awareness of his surroundings to return an instant later. Copper highlights glinted in the depths of his gaze.

"I've been a fool," she said. "Ask me anything you want, and I will answer. Then tell me about your wife and daughter. I want to know everything."

Wariness flitted across his handsome face.

"Why?" he asked. "What's changed since you went high-tailing it out of here earlier?"

She chewed her lower lip, a nervous habit she hadn't manifested since before steam engines had been invented. "I went to speak with an old friend, and his lover ripped me a few new and richly deserved orifices."

He blinked.

"Okay."

Silence settled over the room.

"So… questions?" Duchess prompted.

"Uh… right." He seemed to flounder for another moment, before settling on, "The others. They all seem so… nauseatingly happy. Are we just the only fucked up ones, or…?"

It was almost funny, how closely the question echoed her mental moaning back in Singapore.

"I suppose you could say there are degrees of emotional damage," she said. "Some of them have rather serious issues. And all of us that you might call the original vampires are guilty of murdering our soulmates in their previous lives."

He nodded. "But they all got over it somehow, apparently."

Duchess nodded thoughtfully. "Perhaps gaining absolution helped them. Their reincarnated lovers are all disgustingly noble and altruistic people. It is, as you say, rather sickening at times."

He pillowed his head on one lean-muscled arm and raised an eyebrow at her. "Not a fan of altruism, huh?"

"Or nobility. It makes me uncomfortable."

Chan let out a low snort. "Maybe you and I aren't completely doomed after all."

The stab of hope she felt at his words was completely ridiculous… probably.

"No more doomed than the world at large, perhaps," she allowed.

Chan winced and rubbed his stomach absently with his free hand, as though it pained him. She frowned at the gesture.

"You need to feed," she realized.

"Yeah," he agreed. "I can keep a lid on it for a few more minutes, though. That said, I'm not sure you should let me near any of the human groupies quite yet.

I don't want to hurt anyone, or scare them off, for that matter."

The low flutter in her belly as she contemplated the alternative should not have been unexpected, but it still made her catch her breath. "Feeding from Xander's groupies will… not be necessary," she managed.

The copper glint in his eyes flared, but as promised, he kept himself under control.

"Okay, questions," he said, as though reminding himself. "So, did spying in seventeenth century France pay any better than it does now? Because, yeah, the benefits may be pretty good, but the salary sucks."

She wavered, caught between the assumption that he was needling her and the idea that he might simply be trying to lighten the mood. Instinct urged her to react defensively—slam down the barriers and retreat, or launch a retaliatory attack.

Stop, she ordered herself. *Forge a new path, or risk following the old path over the edge of a cliff.*

"That's a sore subject," she said carefully. "I'm certain you can understand why."

"Okay. Sorry. Poor choice of topic," he said, sounding just as cautious. "But you have to understand, I don't give a rat's ass whether you were working for the king of France, or the king's brother, or Cardinal… what's his name? Cardinal Richelieu."

Her brows flew up as genuine outrage suffused her. "*Richelieu*? That snake? As if I would *ever* have soiled myself by working for the Red Bishop!"

Chan laughed aloud—the rich chuckle she'd heard only a handful of times before. "*God.* This is so strange. For me, these people are characters in old novels, or maybe history books. It's hard to wrap my brain around the idea that they were your contemporaries."

She let her outrage drain away, unable to stop her own breath of amusement.

"Once again, though," he continued, "you need to realize—I don't care that you were spying because your gambling addict of a husband lost the household savings on cards. Aside from feeling kind of bad that you were stuck in that situation in the first place, I mean. Because... newsflash. *I'm. A. Spy.*"

She paused, trying to fit the idea that he wasn't outraged by her betrayal of Bertrand's trust into the puzzle that was her relationship with him.

"Maybe so," she said eventually. "But you were spying because you wanted to lend support to your lawfully elected government. You didn't betray those close to you with your choice of career. You weren't spying *on them.*"

In an instant, his expression went flat and controlled, the light in his eyes dimming.

"No," he said in a voice gone suddenly hoarse. "I wasn't spying on them. I was cheating on them."

"Tell me," she said softly.

Chan swallowed hard, his Adam's apple bobbing. He looked away, as though wavering over whether or not to tell her.

Trust me, she begged silently, unsure if he would be able to hear the plea.

A shudder wracked him, and he dragged in a slow breath. "I've never..." He trailed off and swallowed again. "People know about it, of course. Far more people than I wish knew about it. But I've never just... *told* someone. About the whole mess, I mean. You know?"

She nodded.

"I married Janette right out of high school. Neither of us was ready. I think she loved me, but from my perspective she was just... convenient, I suppose. People expected me to marry her, so I did. God, that sounds every bit as awful as it actually was." He shook his head. "I went straight into the Navy at eighteen. Worked my way up the ranks and got accepted into the SEALs. And the whole time, things between us got worse and worse. I resented her. Convinced myself she was holding me back.

"After SEAL training, I started getting regular deployments. It was so easy to pay for prostitutes in some random, war-torn shithole, in hopes that I might find with them what I never found with her. In between, I'd come home and try to make things work. She was on birth control; neither of us expected her to get pregnant. But she did, and she was about three months along when I shipped out to Afghanistan.

"I tried to talk myself out of doing any more stupid shit after that. But while I might've been part of an elite unit, I was a goddamned coward at heart. I didn't want to be with her anymore, but I was too much of a hairy ball sack to do the right thing and leave honorably. It wasn't three weeks before I was trawling bars, sleeping with anyone female who'd have me.

"Problem was, this time all of the guys in my unit knew Janette was pregnant. A buddy of mine—Ridley—finally had enough of me treating her like shit. He told her everything. Guess I was lucky he didn't try to have me brought up on charges at the same time. But anyway, Janette waited until I got home and asked me straight to my face if it was true or not. I… couldn't lie to her. She walked out the very next day."

Duchess weighed saying *I'm sorry*, but it would have been a lie since she really wasn't.

Instead, she said, "I've spent far more than a single human lifetime fucking my way through the great cities of the world. If I was going to drink from them, I fucked them first. If I wasn't going to drink from them, but I was bored or the clamor of my thoughts was too loud, I fucked them anyway."

His jaw worked for a moment, but then he shook his head and sighed. "Not the same," he said. "You weren't married."

"No, but I'd already deceived my husband in a different way, as we've discussed before. We both betrayed our spouses."

He lifted a shoulder in what might have been a shrug. "Maybe so."

"What happened next?" Duchess pressed. "Janette left, and then…?"

He sighed. "There was an ugly divorce proceeding. I didn't protest the custody arrangements or the child support amount. My parents did the right thing and took Janette's side in the matter. They haven't spoken to me in almost four years. Janette and Ridley got married less than a year after she left me, and he's been raising Courtney as his own daughter. He adopted her when she was three."

"Do you ever see her?" Duchess asked, wistful.

"I was granted visitation rights during the divorce proceedings. But… I took the CIA job not long after." He closed his eyes, and his voice grew choked. "I've been in Kuala Lumpur for nearly eighteen months. I haven't seen her in all that time, and now…"

"Wei Yong," Duchess whispered.

"Now I guess I won't ever see her again."

He rolled to his feet—pacing… agitated. She rose as well, blocking him with a hand splayed over his chest. His eyes were wet.

"Right now," she said, "we have to fight to make sure she still has a world to grow up in. One free of darkness and terror."

He froze, caught by whatever he saw on her face.

"Your eyes," he breathed, and she realized that rusty tears had welled up and overflowed while he was speaking.

"Vampire tears," she said, her voice grown husky. "Yours are the same."

He wiped at his cheeks in surprise, looking at the moisture clinging to his palm. "*Shit.*"

The word emerged broken. It was the most natural thing in the world to wrap her arms around him and pull him to her. He was trembling as he returned the embrace, his spine curving to bring them level. She was a decently tall woman, and he was not an overly tall man, so his lips ended up even with her ear. He breathed in, a ragged sound that reminded her of his growing need for blood.

"Feed," she whispered. "It's all right. Draw strength from me."

He groaned and slid his fangs into her throat, bending her backward in his hold as blood welled from her neck and into his mouth. The position pressed her body against his from breasts to knees, and there was no mistaking the feel of his hardening length against the crease of her thigh.

How often had she held humans like this, either before or after a seduction? Yet she had never been in this position herself… never felt the pull of blood drawing along the length of her body to tug at her sex, or the feeling of strong arms supporting her. She let her head fall back, baring herself to Wei Yong's fangs, and gave into the sensation with no thought of the past or future—only the present moment.

He fed from her until a faint feeling of dizziness started to tickle the edges of her awareness. Even when he pulled back, he didn't release her completely. One arm still wrapped around her back, supporting her, but his other hand caressed her throat, fingertips sliding over the healing punctures.

"It didn't help," he said hoarsely. "I… want more. I want *you*."

Something clicked into place in Duchess' thoughts, making her wonder how this whole thing could possibly have felt so complicated before. "Then have me."

But he shook his head, his hands falling away as he eased her upright, to stand under her own power. "I don't deserve happiness," he told her. "I don't deserve any second chances."

"Neither do I," she said without hesitation. "But we still need to save the world. Would it be so bad if... we tried to do that together? We can always run away from each other later —"

His hands clasped her shoulders. "What happened to Bertrand and your baby wasn't your fault. My sins are worse than yours," he argued.

She shook her head. "You're wrong. They're not. You don't know all of my sins yet."

"I don't need to," he said. "Duchess —"

She placed a finger over his lips, stilling them. "No." Something heavy tore free inside her; an anchor she'd been using to keep from being dragged into the past. "Not Duchess. Call me Marie."

"*Marie*," he whispered, and kissed her.

TWENTY-FOUR

She'd kissed so many people over the endless years since Bael had taken her life away—and yet, the moment his lips touched hers, her soul recognized him. He kept the kiss light, just a shade beyond teasing. So different then the demanding pull of his mouth on her neck just moments before.

Rather than frustrate her, the slow seduction of his mouth unknotted her muscles one by one, as all the tension she'd been carrying for weeks… for months… for *years* began to unravel and slip away. As long as he was kissing her, she didn't have to fight him. She didn't have to run, or hide, or protect her battered heart and torn soul.

All she had to do was kiss him back.

When he pulled away enough to rest their foreheads together, his undead heart was galloping like a racehorse. She splayed a hand over it, feeling the rhythmic thump against his ribcage. His chest rose and fell rapidly, and she couldn't help the smile that curved the corners of her lips.

"Except for talking, you don't really need to breathe anymore, you know," she told him.

He huffed, and tightened the grip he still maintained on her shoulders. "Tell it to my body. My head is swimming."

She lifted a hand to cup his cheek, daring herself to meet his eyes and really *see* what lay beneath. For so long, sex and seduction had been another wall she'd built around herself. A role she'd played.

Femme fatale, vampire edition.

Wei Yong's gaze was deep and dark, but lit from within by the light of his growing arousal. Beneath it lay a sea of hope and turmoil, guilt and determination. He didn't look away, even when the words *what you're doing right now terrifies me* echoed across the deepening bond to her.

I need to see, she answered in kind. *I need to see you seeing me, or I'll never believe it's real.*

"I've built a life around not being seen," he murmured aloud. "What's hidden under the surface is too awful."

"That's what I'm counting on. Otherwise, you'd never want me," she said, and kissed him again.

He made a low noise and crushed her body to his, kissing her again, the earlier control he'd shown snapping. Her lips parted, and he took immediate advantage of the opening, his tongue sliding in to tangle with hers. He dueled her with all the skill Bertrand had once shown with a rapier—a single-minded opponent bent on conquest. And for once, she was eager to be conquered.

In all her meaningless liaisons, she had made it a point never to cede control to another. Whether there was one person in her bed or half a dozen, she was always *le capitaine*, leading the troops.

Something of her thoughts must have shone through the bond. "I am so completely okay with that," Wei Yong said against her lips. "But maybe not right this minute."

"Another time," she agreed, breathless despite her earlier chiding about not needing to breathe. "This… is about something different."

"Yes," he said, walking her backward until her back thumped against a wall covered with priceless ancient artwork. "It is."

Her short-sleeved cotton shirt buttoned in the front, and his fingers attacked it with purpose. Lips followed, running over each new centimeter of exposed skin. When the shirt fell open, hanging to the sides, he straightened. His eyes lit upon the front clasp of her bra.

"Whoever designed this is officially my hero," he said, popping it so her heavy breasts spilled out.

Her head thumped back as his lips closed around a nipple, drawing it to a point—teasing with tongue and teeth.

"Practicality is important," she managed, arching as she felt his fangs lengthen.

He divided his attention between her breasts until desire started to make her dizzy, then pulled away long enough to strip his utilitarian black t-shirt over his head and throw it aside. Her trousers and underwear followed. Finally, he shoved his pants and briefs down his hips before crowding against her, dragging her wrists together and pinning them over her head with one large hand.

Yes, she thought as he used the other to hitch her left leg up, wrapping it around his hip.

"Sorry," he rumbled, "I know it's too fast, but I swear I'll make it up to you afterward."

In fact, a rough fuck against a wall was the polar opposite of the carefully orchestrated scenes she usually used for distraction… and it was exactly what she needed. She gasped as his hard length breached her, sliding inside to the hilt. Her eyes slid closed, and her mouth fell open.

"*No*," he ordered. "Look at me. I have to see you. I have to know you really want this. Want… *me*."

Dragging her eyes open in that moment of vulnerability was one of the hardest things she'd ever done—but once she had, she couldn't have shut them again if she'd tried. His expression was raw. It was the look of someone who didn't really believe this was happening, and she had the awful feeling her face reflected the same thing.

Then, he began to move.

After the first few slow thrusts, his movements grew hard, almost brutal. Daring her to look away... to shrink from the ugliness inside him. She bared her fangs, not backing down, using his tight grip under her left thigh as leverage to wrap both of her legs around his waist.

With only his strength and the weight of the wall at her back supporting her, she kept her gaze locked with his and flexed her hips, angling him even deeper with every stroke. Everything burned—her eyes... her heart... her throbbing and greedy *chatte* clutching at his hard flesh with every stroke. Her aching nipples rubbed against his smooth chest as he screwed her into the wall, her wrists still pinned overhead.

The grind of his pelvis drove her ever closer to release, and her mouth watered with the sudden desire to bite him as they both came.

"No," he growled. "Not now. Look at me. I need to watch you."

She didn't want him to see her final barriers crumble. But if she closed her eyes or looked away, it would mean she couldn't see *him* fall apart.

"I will if you will," he said breathlessly, in response to her unraveling thoughts.

His hips snapped forward, hitting her in just the right way to take her over the edge. Ecstasy slammed over her like a breaking wave, and she fought to keep her eyes open even as they blurred with tears of long overdue catharsis. His face twisted, but he, too, resisted the urge to hide himself away as he groaned and spilled inside her.

I see you, she thought. *I won't run away if you don't.*

He released her wrists in favor of wrapping his arm around the small of her back. Gravity pulled them down the wall in slow motion, leaving them in a tangled heap on the floor.

"Not going anywhere," he murmured into her hair.

-o-o-o-

Somehow, they roused themselves enough to make it across to the mattress on the floor, shedding the rest of their clothes as they went. Chan was fairly convinced that Mason had been wrong before and heart attacks weren't out of the question even for vampires, given what the organ in question seemed to be doing inside his chest right now.

Could it really be this simple? Agree that they were both terrible people who'd made bad decisions, hurting those they loved, and move on from there... together? He rolled onto an elbow, looking down at the golden temptress who had destroyed his life and maybe—*just maybe*— redeemed it in a single stroke.

"I want to taste every part of you until you're calling out my name and begging for my cock," he said. "And then, I want to fuck you again. I want to keep doing those things over and over until I can convince myself this is real."

She blinked luminous blue eyes up at him. "I want your mouth on me. I want your flesh inside me, so I know this isn't some dream that I'll wake up from... only to find that I'm alone again."

He nodded slowly. "How long do you think those things will take us?" he asked.

Her hand stroked over his temple, settling to cup his cheek. "I don't know. Forever might just about do it."

Chan almost wanted to weep again, but he swallowed the lump growing in his throat and rolled on top of her instead. "Forever sounds good," he whispered against her ear, and started kissing his way down her body, making certain to cover every square inch as he went.

Epilogue

A brisk knock at the door roused Chan from the most peaceful stretch of sleep he'd enjoyed in years. It creaked open a moment later, and Oksana poked her head in. She ran a practiced gaze over the rumpled bedding on the mattress, not to mention the single sheet that was doing a wholly inadequate job of covering Chan's and Duchess' — *Marie's* — naked bodies.

His blonde temptress jerked awake beside him, scrambling somewhat inelegantly into a sitting position. Her hair was a wild mess, half-covering her face. Oksana grinned at the two of them, slow and evil.

"About damned time," she observed, before sobering. "Now — get dressed. Things are happening. And not just down here in the tunnels."

"Is it Snag?" Marie asked.

Oksana raised an eyebrow. "Snag, plus the small matter of at least a couple of hundred people from Saqqara village who've come to see what's going on."

Marie tensed. "Are they hostile? Likely to cause problems for the donors, or us?"

"Apparently not," Oksana said with a shrug. "Just curious. The kids topside have been talking to them as best they're able, since none of them speak Arabic. Xander and Manisha have also been keeping an eye on things, since they're both sun-proof now."

"Sun-proof?" Chan asked. "What do you mean?"

"Ah, right," Oksana said. "I forgot you didn't know that part. They're both part werewolf, as well as being vampires. So, they shift into wolves rather than owls or mist, and sunlight doesn't burn them."

"That's… handy, I suppose," he managed.

"Very," Marie agreed dryly. "Now, *mon chou*, please stop standing in our doorway exuding smugness, and let us get dressed. We'll be right there."

Oksana's grin returned, wider than ever. "Oh, but I've earned this smugness, *ti mwen*. You've been positively unbearable for weeks now."

With a final cheeky wink at Chan, she left and closed the door behind her.

After they'd pulled on enough discarded clothes to be presentable, Chan asked, "Do you think this means Snag's awake?"

Marie stilled, her gaze turning inward. "Not yet. But his mind is beginning to stir."

She twisted her hair into a loose knot, pressed a quick kiss to his lips, and the two of them hurried through the maze of tunnels toward the chamber where they'd taken the coffin. It appeared they were the last to arrive. The room was full of vampires—all staring toward the figure on the cot, with Eris slumped in the chair beside him.

It was Eris who caught Chan's attention first. Not to put too fine a point on it, the man looked like shit. His hand still rested on Snag's forehead, but where he'd been crackling with life and power when they left him early that morning, he appeared severely drained now. His Mediterranean features had taken on a gray cast, and his gold-flecked eyes were sunken. Those observations distracted Chan from scrutinizing the form on the bed more closely—at least until Marie drew in a sharp breath at his side. He glanced at her, and then followed her gaze to Snag. Or… to the guy lying on the cot previously occupied by Snag's mummified body, at any rate.

What the *hell*?

The man on the bed appeared to be in his forties, with striking Middle Eastern features and deep-set eyes. A dense fuzz of freshly grown black stubble covered his skull—except at the temples, where it was silver-gray. The shadow of a beard hugged his jaw. Winged eyebrows drew together as Chan watched, mesmerized. The man's eyes flickered under closed lids, like someone in REM sleep.

"Is that really him?" Chan whispered, thinking, *how could it be, though*?

"It is," Marie said, low and shocked. "*Mon Dieu*. I can feel him. He's waking up."

Indeed, Eris slid his hand away just as those piercing eyes opened, glowing with bronze light. Snag sat up, even as Eris sagged.

"*Dóxa to theoí*," Eris murmured, embracing the newly regenerated vampire in obvious relief.

Trynn piled on from Snag's other side, half-kneeling on the edge of the cot to get to him. Snag's expression appeared mildly quizzical at being sandwiched between the pair. After a moment's pause, he lifted his arms to encircle both of them carefully, as though he'd nearly forgotten how to touch other people in such a way.

Most of the others crowded forward, though Chan hung back near the door with Marie.

"Snag," Tré said in relief.

Snag blinked up at him, a thoughtful movement.

Menkhef, he said, the word echoing along the mental bond.

"Menkhef?" Eris asked in confusion, as he and Trynn eased back from the three-way embrace.

Snag brushed Eris' pale cheek with his knuckles and smiled fondly—a nearly imperceptible curve of the lips that was gone almost as soon as it appeared.

It is my name. Perhaps there is finally a worthy reason to take it up again. He examined Eris closely for a moment, and his expression settled into a frown. *You have over-exerted yourself on my behalf. You must feed.*

"Here—we've got him," Oksana said, as both she and Tré moved forward to offer their blood. Eris drank gratefully from both of them.

Trynn continued to stare at Snag—*Menkhef?*—in something like awe. The newly awakened vampire was looking at his hands and arms as though he'd never seen them before; turning his hands this way and that as he examined flesh that was now filled out and free of scars. Chan could feel the thrum of power rolling off him—not the cracking overload that Eris had been carrying around after feeding from all of them, but more like a cocooning blanket that enveloped the room in warmth.

Xander crossed his arms, eyes raking the newly imposing figure as he rose from the cot. "If you'd asked, we could have chipped in with a group blood donation long ago, old chap."

Menkhef tested his legs cautiously and straightened to his full height, his molten bronze gaze meeting the younger vampire's.

It was not yet time.

Xander raised an eyebrow. "It might have saved lives," he said, and though his tone was mild, his expression was hard.

It would not have. Regret tinged the commanding mental voice. He turned to Manisha, Xander's sad-eyed mate, and gathered her hands in his. *Sangye's death lies on my conscience,* he told her silently. *I thought I could shape events to my liking, only to fail in the worst possible way. It was not my lack of power at issue, but my lack of vision.*

Manisha swallowed, and Chan could see rust-colored tears overflow her eyes. "You tried. At least you went with him—you didn't leave him alone with the monsters."

Menkhef bowed his head in acknowledgement. He lifted it, meeting her shiny gaze once more. *He had a message for you, alsghyr. He said, 'Tell Kumari Sadhu not to grieve for me. If I am needed, I will return.'*

At that, Manisha's face crumpled into lines of abject grief, and a sob rose from her throat. Menkhef let her hands slide free as Xander gathered her into his arms. She burrowed into his chest, weeping. Xander's eyes were also suspiciously bright.

Chan felt an ache through his bond with the woman next to him, and knew that she, too, felt responsible on some level for the boy's death—despite what Menkhef had said. He suspected she wouldn't welcome any overt display from him right now, but he tangled his fingers with hers in support, and she squeezed back tightly.

The mood in the room was sober as Menkhef spoke once more. *It is time for us to move out of the shadows— metaphorically, if not literally. Humans are gathering above, at the foot of Djoser's great pyramid. Stand with me as I speak to them and warn them of what is to come.*

Chan turned and looked into Marie's brilliant blue eyes, feeling as though they were standing on the cusp of something. She returned his gaze with a mixture of grief and stony determination.

-o-o-o-

As the sun slipped below the western horizon, an imposing figure climbed the steps leading from the South Tombs to the cobra-head wall overlooking the grand courtyard and the massive pyramid beyond. The man wore only a death shroud, the white cloth wrapped around him like robes.

The people assembled below gasped in shock as they took in the two massive wolves flanking him, matching his measured pace like well-trained guard dogs. A shorter man with inscrutable Asian features and a military bearing followed him, walking next to a woman with eyes the color of the sky and hair like spun gold.

The rustle of wings heralded the arrival of a pair of yellow-eyed owls that soared to a perfect landing on the man's outstretched arms. A moment later, swirls of fog descended to coil around the group, solidifying into four more striking figures—two men and two women. A hush spread over the watching crowd, the air humming with expectation.

The man in the death shroud spoke no word, but his mental voice rolled over the assemblage, filling every mind with its rich timbre.

My countrymen, he said. *The end of the world is nearly upon us. The war that is coming is a war of the spirit — not of the body. Each of you will be called to join it, for good or ill.*

He paused, the silence so complete that not even the sound of breathing marred it. His ageless eyes looked down at the faces below, as though committing each one to memory. Eventually, he spoke again—a final question.

Ask yourself now, children — which side will you embrace? Love… or hate?

End of Book Five

CIRCLE OF BLOOD BOOK SIX:

LOVERS' VICTORY

R. A. STEFFAN & JAELYNN WOOLF

ONE

The entrance to the ancient Egyptian compound of Saqqara was simultaneously claustrophobic and overwhelming. It was narrower than Amy had pictured, but the fluted stone columns rising on either side of her loomed like giants in the shadows. She hoisted her backpack more comfortably on her shoulders and slanted a glance at Elijah, feeling a sudden bout of nervousness.

"I can't believe you used to come here for work every day," she said. "Why on earth did you give it up?"

Both she and her husband boasted the title of 'Doctor' before their names, but in Elijah's case, it was a PhD in Archaeology to go along with his Master's in Cultural Anthropology. To say that Amy's doctorate was a little more mundane was putting it mildly.

Elijah shot her a sideways glance, his mahogany eyes flat and expressionless, as they so often seemed to be these days. "It's a pile of dusty rocks and sand, Ames. When you've picked through a few dozen places like this for weeks at a time under the desert sun, they start to lose their appeal," he said. His jaw worked, a tendon standing out under his dark skin. "Which isn't to say I'm thrilled about a bunch of hippies camping here and destroying the place. The regular tourist crowds are hard enough on historical sites."

Back home in Pennsylvania, Elijah was a professor at West Parklands University. For the first few years of their relationship, he had been passionate about going on digs all over the world, and he'd been part of the team working on the restoration of the very site they were walking through. These days, Amy was lucky to get her husband to take her out for dinner and a movie.

She suspected he was suffering from clinical depression and had been for some time, but on the handful of occasions she'd brought it up, Elijah had brushed her off. And lately, things in the world at large were becoming so hopelessly whacked that the idea of badgering someone into therapy because they no longer felt fulfilled by their job seemed… shallow, somehow.

Not to mention the fact that if he did submit to getting help, any psychologist worth his or her salt would want to drag Amy in as well for joint counseling. Which… wasn't something she was in much of a hurry to do.

Hypocrisy for the win.

So, instead, here they were—half a world away from home, hanging out with the hippies while rioting and border wars flared in countries around the globe. She ran a hand over her belly absently.

"Let's just get inside the complex and check things out," she said, painfully aware that Elijah had only agreed to this trip to humor her. From the look of things, he was regretting the decision more and more by the minute.

"Yeah. Okay." His tone was flat, but a moment later, his fingers brushed hers. She tangled their hands together gratefully, the creamy white of her skin contrasting with the rich dark brown of his.

They'd always been a study in opposites. Amy's genes came straight from Ireland—she was pale and freckled with curly red hair and green eyes. Elijah was more than a head taller than her, a devastatingly handsome black man with close-cropped hair and an athlete's build. Indeed, he'd been a marathon runner when she'd first met him—another passion of his that had fallen by the wayside over the years.

Coming here to Saqqara had become a strange obsession for Amy. In the last few weeks, reports had started appearing on the internet—communes spontaneously popping up at spiritual and cultural sites across the world. She couldn't really explain her desire to come to this place; certainly, there were several other sites closer to their home. Maybe it was because Saqqara had been the first such enclave to appear. Maybe it was because Elijah had been here before.

Whatever the case, something about the gathering of people at Saqqara called to her. It was totally irrational, but a part of her mind insisted that here, she and Elijah might find the part of their lives that had been missing. The part that was slowly destroying them with its absence.

She stifled a snort. She could almost hear Elijah saying, *"Don't be ridiculous. All you'll find here is an increased risk of skin cancer and, if you're not careful, a bout of gastroenteritis."*

Bright light made Amy's eyes water as they reached the end of the claustrophobic stone corridor and stepped into a massive, open esplanade.

Amy's eyes widened at the sight beyond. It was completely different than what she had expected. Overwhelming, like the first time she saw the ocean as a child. Seeing places like this on television or in books simply couldn't convey the awe-inspiring size of them.

"This is... *wow*. Amazing." She placed her hand above her eyes, shielding them from the glare of the unforgiving desert sun. Her gaze took in the wall of the southern tomb, a row of cobra heads carved along the top as though standing guard over the space below. To their right, some distance away, stood the step pyramid. "Oh, my god. This is *so damned cool*. How tall is that thing?"

"Sixty-two meters. About two hundred feet," Elijah said. His attention wasn't on the pyramid or the cobra head wall, however. It was on the incredible bustle of human activity filling this ancient place. "So many people," he whispered, shaking his head. "This was a terrible idea."

Amy winced, and tried to cover it. Who knew five words could hurt so much?

She whirled on her husband and pulled her hand free from his, schooling her voice to stay low and even. "You said you'd try. Thanks *so much* for the ten minutes of effort you just expended. It must have been excruciating to endure."

A frown drew his brows together. "I didn't mean coming here. I meant... *this*." He gestured at the space filled with tents and portaloos and solar panels and power cables and people. "Look at it! These idiots could ruin all the work archaeologists put into restoring this place."

Relief combined with a momentary feeling of sheepishness deflated her bubble of anger. Damned if she'd show it, though.

"Well, it doesn't look like they're ruining it to me," Amy said stubbornly. She returned her gaze to the crowd of people gathered in the shadow of the pyramid. The atmosphere was peaceful as they chatted amiably or rested against the rough stone. "Besides, I think it's wonderful, all these people coming together. Standing up for something."

"Couldn't they have stood up for something while staying at—I don't know—a convention center, or a hotel or something?" Elijah muttered. "They could have gone to the Luxor in Vegas if they thought the whole 'pyramid' vibe was so important."

"No, it wouldn't be the same," Amy said, taking in the aura of peace that covered the ancient site like a comforting blanket. "There's something about this place, don't you think? It feels... powerful, yet calm."

Elijah blew out a breath. "Sorry—I don't feel anything but annoyed. They're turning this site into a joke. I mean, come on. Portable toilets at the base of the oldest pyramid in Egypt?"

She stopped herself from asking if he'd rather the people here used the sand dunes as a great big human litter box instead. Bickering wouldn't help the situation. It never did. God knew they'd tested *that* theory often enough over the past few years.

"There's still something about it," she insisted. "Something I can't quite put my finger on." She took a deep breath of the hot dry air and let it out slowly, closing her eyes. "It feels like... like a weight's been lifted from me. Like something inside me is lighter. Everything just seems... familiar. You have to at least admit that."

She opened her eyes to find Elijah looking down at her with a raised eyebrow. "Yes, I admit—it's familiar. That's probably because I've been here before."

Amy wrinkled her nose at him, coming to terms with the fact that this trip wouldn't be as smooth and easy a feat as she might have hoped. *Please, let this excursion not have been the stupidest idea I've ever had,* she prayed to whatever ancient gods might be lingering around this place.

Her plaintive prayer was interrupted by the approach of a lovely olive-skinned woman. She looked Indian, or perhaps Pakistani. Her waist-length black hair hung in a silken wave down her back, and her hazelnut eyes were depthless, full of a haunting sadness.

Still, her gaze was direct and assessing as she looked them over. She lifted her chin and offered them a brief, soft smile that didn't touch her grief-filled eyes.

"My name is Manisha," she said. "Welcome to the Saqqara necropolis."

TWO

From the moment Elijah stepped onto the tarmac at Cairo's airport, he'd had this strange sense that something pivotal—and potentially devastating—was about to happen in his and Amy's lives. It wasn't his damned depression talking, either. At least, he was fairly sure it wasn't. An off-kilter pressure had taken root within his chest, and as much as he tried to ignore it, there it continued to sit like one of the ancient sandstone blocks from Djoser's pyramid.

Maybe it was a ridiculous thing to think, but the woman who'd appeared to greet them at the entrance to the esplanade looked like someone carrying around a similar weight, despite her pleasant smile as she greeted them in lightly accented English.

Amy smiled back and reached out a hand. "Nice to meet you. I'm Dr. Amy Carpenter, and this is my husband, Elijah."

The woman—Manisha— shook hands with Amy and lifted her eyebrows. "Americans, eh? Where in the States are you from?"

"East Coast. Pennsylvania, to be specific," Amy said. "My husband is actually an archaeology professor. He's been here on digs before."

His wife's smile lit up her green eyes. She always sounded so proud of Elijah's accomplishments, even though he'd not added all that many since they got married and he stopped making career moves.

"Very good. So you know the area, then?" Manisha asked.

Elijah cleared his throat. "A bit, yes. Though I have to say I've never seen the place looking quite like this before," he muttered, his scowl returning as he once more took in the controlled chaos around them.

Manisha did not appear to notice his testy tone. "There are many people here seeking refuge from the upheaval in the world, and they need access to the basics like power, water, and sanitation. We're using composting toilets and recycling as much of our graywater as we can capture. The solar panels are a way to access the earth's resources without putting more strain on it."

Elijah pursed his lips.

"You disagree with that?" Manisha raised an eyebrow in mild challenge, or possibly amusement.

His irritation surged. "No. It's just… this place. It's an irreplaceable historical site."

"We understand that. Don't worry, Dr. Carpenter. When the threat to the world has passed, this site will be restored to its previous condition."

"'The threat to the world,'" Elijah echoed flatly.

The woman still didn't rise to his bait. "Just so. As I was saying, many people have come to Saqqara seeking refuge from the upheaval around them. We're happy to have you and your wife, but there are rules you must adhere to in order to keep peace amongst the visitors."

Beneath his tension, Elijah felt terrible. After all, he had promised Amy he would make an actual effort during this trip and yet something about the place still felt… disquieting.

Disquieting? That's the best you can come up with? Great. All those years of higher education certainly paid off, didn't they? Elijah let out a sigh, shaking his head at himself.

If he wasn't careful, his attitude was going to ruin everything. This trip obviously meant a lot to Amy, and he *had* made her a promise. The least he could do was be here for her instead of expending his mental effort on irrational, non-existent emotional perceptions. He wasted enough energy on that kind of shit at home.

Elijah loved his wife more than anything in the world. Still, he couldn't seem to shake the feeling that something bad loomed on the horizon—that leaving Pennsylvania and coming here to Saqqara wouldn't be the refuge Amy was seeking. It felt more like jumping from the frying pan straight into the flames of hell.

Stop, he admonished himself once more, growling silently at his apparent inability not to act like an asshole. Elijah had no intention of losing his wife, damn it. Not now. Not ever.

Yes, strange things were going on around the world, but nothing supernatural like the panic-mongers had started saying. Science and reason could explain everything that was happening, from the riots to the radiation sickness, and he was confident he could prove that to Amy as well. He just needed to *talk* to her instead of arguing or sniping at her.

He rubbed at the stubble that had begun growing on his chin. He'd not had the chance to shave since leaving the states. Maybe he could use time here to revive his career? And perhaps save his marriage at the same time. But the sad truth was, it would take science and reason to save the world, not hippies and whatever new age, feel good crap Amy was hoping to find in this place.

"Rules?" he said, recalling himself to the conversation. "Of course. That makes sense. You'll have to excuse my lack of manners. I'm afraid I'm pretty jet-lagged."

The look that Manisha gave him was a bit too penetrating. A bit too knowing. It only added to his sense of being off-balance, and his jaw clenched.

"I was saying that you and your wife may move freely around the encampment, speak to others and get a feel for the area," she said. "Some come here only to decide it wasn't what they were expecting, so we suggest you take a day or two before determining whether you'd like to stay longer or not."

Amy and Elijah hadn't really discussed how long they planned to stay. This was likely due to Elijah's reluctance to discuss much of anything these days, especially when it was almost certain to end in a fight. Manisha made a good point, though. And if Elijah still felt this irrational sense of foreboding after getting more of a feel for the place, it could be an easy way out for him.

"That's a good idea, right, Amy? We'll give it a day, and decide then if we want to stay longer?" Elijah looked to his wife, who was already showing signs of disappointment.

"I suppose." The smile that had briefly graced her full lips faded.

The emptiness that seemed to have taken up permanent residence in Elijah's stomach grew deeper. No matter how hard he tried, he felt like a perpetual disappointment to his wife. He reminded himself again why he'd come here in the first place… to try and save their marriage.

"I'm not saying I definitely want to leave tomorrow," he said. "I made you a promise, after all."

Amy's eyes rose to his, and the tentative smile returned. "Thank you."

"Well, then," Manisha said. "You're free to find a shady space and set up camp. Many people here speak English. We only have a few rules. No stealing. No violence. People come here seeking refuge from the dangers outside. They don't need any more drama than they're already experiencing. Treat others as you'd like them to treat you; common courtesy is expected by all."

"That's no problem," Amy said. "If everyone could abide by those rules, we wouldn't be in this mess in the first place, right?"

If everyone could abide by those rules, humanity would be a very different species than it is, Elijah thought, but kept his mouth shut.

"Very true," Manisha replied. "We have tents set up over there." She pointed at a pair of large, colorful tents at the far end of the esplanade. "You will find food and water inside, and further down, behind the green tent, sanitary facilities. Please, make yourself at home, Amy. Elijah." She extended her hand first to Amy, then to him. When he took it, her grip was cool and firm as she continued, "If you need anything, ask around. Someone will point you in the right direction."

With a final sad smile, she moved past Amy and Elijah to meet more new arrivals entering the compound behind them.

"Thank you, Elijah," Amy said quietly. "I know you don't really want to be here, and I do appreciate your efforts."

"I made you a promise. I'm going to keep it." Elijah grasped her hand in his again, and she let him.

With a deep breath, he took another slow look around the area. There were many smaller tents set up in addition to the large ones Manisha had pointed out—close to a hundred lined up in the shadows of the archaic walls, he thought. Most appeared occupied, their inhabitants likely waiting out the brutal daytime desert temperatures.

Elijah wondered if the solar panels were hooked into a battery system to give the place nighttime lighting. In fairness, solar panels did make a good amount of sense in a land where the sun was so unrelenting. If they had to make alterations to meet the needs of the visitors here, solar energy was probably the least invasive way of doing so.

"Let's stake out a spot," Amy suggested, pulling Elijah along the stone-lined walkway by their joined hands. After a few minutes, they found a suitable place in a somewhat shady area and set up camp.

It had been years since Elijah had camped in conditions like these, and Amy wasn't usually the outdoorsy type, so it wasn't something they were used to doing together. That was part of the reason why it had surprised him so much when she expressed interest in coming here in the first place. He wondered if, after a day or two of roughing it in hundred-degree heat, Amy might be ready to return to their comfortable house back in the States. They'd spent so much time planning their dream home and having it built after they got married. Who would have thought once they finally moved in, everything between them would start to fall apart?

THREE

After setting up their tent, Amy suggested that they check out the food and water situation, then rest in the shade until things started to cool off a bit.

We could rest now," Elijah countered, eyeing her drawn features. "We've still got plenty of bottled water and energy bars in the packs."

Amy shaded her eyes and peered at the afternoon sun, then glanced at her pale arms, which were already starting to redden despite the sunscreen she'd applied. "I guess so," she said. "I do want to explore later, though."

"Aren't you tired?" Elijah asked, as they pulled out drinks and settled in the shade by the tent. "You didn't sleep much on the flight, I thought you might want to nap until nightfall."

"Yeah, I'm definitely a bit frazzled," she admitted, "but I'm also way too wired to sleep right now, I'm afraid."

Elijah made himself as comfortable as he could, opening the bottle of water and chugging half of it. He thought of all the places he'd rather be than here in the desert, hot as hell and sweating like a sinner in a summer revival tent.

Amy was looking around the place with an expression of fascination, clearly excited to be here despite her fatigue. Meanwhile, Elijah could barely peel the scowl off his face. Sometimes, it felt like that scowl had been permanently etched into his features for the past three years.

Coming back to this site was not having the effect on him Amy had probably hoped it would. All Elijah felt right now was a sort of dull self-loathing at everything he'd failed to accomplish in recent years, both in his professional and personal life.

You gave this up, said the ugly inner voice that delighted in pointing out his shortcomings. *And for what?*

After he'd married Amy, he went on a few digs—both here in Egypt, and elsewhere. When he came home, though, Amy always seemed distant. Elijah eventually decided to give up archaeological expeditions in favor of spending more time with his wife. It worked—for a while, at least.

Then Amy started pulling away again. She'd find all of these different causes to volunteer for. Charity events. Things that were undeniably noble, but that took her away from him.

While Amy was out trying to make a difference in the world, Elijah became more closed off. He'd stopped writing papers, and for a university-level professor in the sciences, that was a problem. An academic who didn't do research had little chance of climbing the professional ladder. Fortunately, he'd already gotten tenure shortly before they married… but the warnings still came. Given the way academia was changing, he was skating on thin ice after years of career stagnation—tenure or no.

The thought of doing some research while he was here had crossed his mind. In fact, that's how he'd managed to get time off to come in the first place—by convincing the head of the archeology department he'd have a research project ready to publish in the spring semester.

It could well be his last chance to avoid losing his job. And that was another thing he really didn't want to tell Amy.

Elijah sat, silently cataloguing the damage he'd done to their future. Predictably, the more he stewed, the more irritated and emotional he got. He glanced at Amy sitting beside him. The enchanted expression on her face as she watched their surroundings just made him feel worse. Following her gaze, he tried to figure out what, precisely, she was staring at.

Across the esplanade from them, a woman who looked to be about nineteen sat between two young men, her arms linked with each of theirs. They were laughing. Talking. Happy.

Two men, both doting on the girl like she was the only woman in the world.

How the hell could they all be so happy when the world was falling down around them? Didn't they *get it*? There were no happy endings in this life.

Amy was still watching them, her features growing wistful. Something about it made a hot, hard lump rise in Elijah's chest. Weren't things hard enough for just two people? He tried to rationalize it. The trio obviously wasn't blood-related, but they could be college buddies. Maybe the guys were gay and she was just their friend. Maybe they were competing for her, and things would turn ugly once she chose between them. Maybe—

"What's wrong?" Amy was staring at him now, rather than the laughing threesome. Whatever she saw on his face made her narrow her eyes. Her lips thinned.

Elijah looked around at all the people. The place really did look like a hippie camp. What the hell had Amy been thinking that made her want to come here?

His thoughts overflowed into words without his conscious decision. "Look at this place. Amy, this is crazy. Seriously. Why are we here?"

He hated the hurt that rose behind her green eyes, but her voice was tight and angry. "We're here because you *agreed to come*. You said we could make a retreat. Get away from the world for a bit. How many times are we going to have this argument?"

"Do you even understand how hard it was for me to take time off?" The words were still coming, like a dam had been breached and was crumbling under the weight behind it. "I haven't published a paper in *two years*. Dr. Stevens said... if I don't publish before the year is out, he's going to replace me, Amy."

"What?" Amy's expression morphed into shock. "You could lose your job?"

"Yeah." Elijah stared down at his hands gripping the water bottle tightly. "Do you have any idea how much this trip is costing us? What if things really do start to fall apart around us? We put thousands of dollars into this trip—a big chunk of our savings is gone, and for what possible benefit?"

Amy's face settled into taut lines, pale beneath her freckles. "For us. Our marriage. What's that worth to you?" She scooted back a bit, crossing her arms over her chest in a self-protective gesture that made Elijah ache as she continued. "We have a baby on the way. Do you want to be a part of your child's life? Because there are times I'm really starting to wonder if you do."

His heart started to pound, defensive anger flaring. "*Every single time*, you have to bring up the baby. Nice." He swallowed hard. "Yes, we have a child on the way. I think you're the one who forgets that, not me. If you were really concerned about this child, you wouldn't have dragged us halfway across the globe to the middle of nowhere in a Third World country! What if something goes wrong? And your practice? You're abandoning it for god knows how long."

"Don't bring up my job, Elijah. My partners have things well under control. Besides, *I'm not the one about to get fired*."

Amy's brow was furrowed, her chest heaving with her attempts to maintain control of her temper. Elijah knew that look, and right now, he didn't care. No matter what he did, it would never be good enough. Whatever choice he made, it was always the wrong one.

"Why can't I be enough for you, Amy?" Elijah asked, his voice flat. "I gave up my career ambitions to spend more time with you, only for you to disappear into your charity work. I mean, helping strangers is great and all, but it sure as hell shows where your priorities lie. Namely, *not with me*. And now here we are, hanging out at the Saqqara Woodstock festival with a pair of fiddles while Rome burns around us. God, I'm such an *idiot*."

His voice had risen as he spoke. He ran a hand over his face, only to find that he was shaking. Amy had already opened her mouth to say something angry or hurt or both, but the words seemed to lodge in her lungs as she looked past him. Elijah followed her gaze, and found that the woman from the happy hippie trio was approaching them with clear intent. She plopped down a couple of feet away without invitation, sitting with her legs crossed and her arms resting on her knees.

Elijah stared at her, struck as mute as Amy had been—hit by a combination of anger at having been interrupted and embarrassment at being caught having a private argument in a public place.

"Hi, I don't think we've met," said the young woman, whose tanned, faintly boyish features were topped with an unruly mass of brown hair. "I'm Shay. Is everything okay over here?"

Amy and Elijah flickered a glance at each other, embarrassment gaining the upper hand over ire.

"Um... yeah," Amy said, red rising to her pale cheeks. "Sorry. Just a bit of a private disagreement."

"Sure, I get it," Shay said, no judgment in her tone. "It's just that you guys were getting kinda loud. Lots of people here sleep during the day, to escape the heat and because most of the interesting stuff happens at night.

We try not to disturb the informal siesta time if we can avoid it. Know what I mean?"

Elijah scrubbed a hand over his scalp, berating himself for needing etiquette lessons from a college kid. "You're absolutely right to say something to us. This was my fault, and I apologize."

Shay smiled. "No need for apologies. I just thought you two might want to know about the unofficial nap time."

She rubbed absently at her left forearm. The movement drew Elijah's eye, and he noticed a path of needle tracks on the paler skin near her elbow. Shay followed his gaze, a strange smile tugging at her wide mouth.

"Problem?" she asked, her tone one of amusement.

Elijah realized how rudely he was staring, and immediately tried to backpedal. "Er… sorry, it's none of my business," he muttered.

The smile widened.

"You think I'm a junkie." Shay blinked at him, and made an attempt to pull her expression into something more neutral. "Wow, you really are new here, I guess?"

Elijah glanced at Amy, who clearly shared his confusion, before turning back to face Shay. "Yes… we just got here an hour or so ago. Like I said, though—it's none of our business."

"For fuck's sake, dude," she said, and her tone was almost pitying now. "Did you two do any research *at all* before you came out here? I'm not a user. *I'm a donor.*"

FOUR

Amy stared at Shay, trying to keep up with the conversation despite her jet lag and roiling emotions after Elijah's bombshell about his job. A *donor*? What the hell was that supposed to mean?

"You know… a *blood donor*." Shay was looking at them like she was starting to think they were both mentally deficient. "For the people here who need it more than we do."

Amy blinked, and a connection clicked into place in her overtired brain. At the same instant, a sinking feeling settled in her stomach. There were, broadly speaking, two kinds of reports to be found online about the peace communes popping up around the world—and about this one in particular.

The first type of story came from the news media, which reported factually about the existence and locations of the various groups camping at historical and spiritual sites. These reports were mostly couched in terms that made the places sound like long-term protest rallies, kind of like the Occupy movement that had briefly gained traction when Amy was younger. There were occasional interviews with people staying at the communes, usually short and carefully edited to convey sound bites about standing up for peace and love in a world gone mad with hate.

The second type came from dodgy websites and internet forums. They showed up in the first few pages of search results for things like 'Saqqara commune' and 'world peace protests.' Amy had stumbled across several of those when she'd gotten curious about the main-stream news stories. She'd skimmed them, rolled her eyes, and dismissed them as being the fevered imaginings of a bunch of crazy basement dwellers and fundamentalists.

Those kinds of forums were full of murmurs about cults. Whispers about demonic influence and unholy rituals. About… *blood* rituals. Brainwashing. Powerful figures drawing in unsuspecting, innocent people for their own nefarious purposes. Things that had seemed so at odds with the rational, idealistic people being interviewed on TV that Amy had scoffed and mashed the 'back' button, rolling her eyes at the seedy underbelly of the internet with its endless trolls and conspiracy theories.

Suddenly, they seemed less crazy. Holy crap. Had they been right? Had *Elijah* been right? Had she done something monumentally stupid, and dragged them both into danger? But Manisha seemed so nice… and she'd talked about them checking out the place for a day to decide if they wanted to stay or not—

Amy's mouth opened and closed a couple of times before words came out. "You… take part in *blood rituals?*"

Shay scoffed. "Seriously, lady. I'd hardly call sterile needles and IV bags a *blood ritual*. You're being a bit over-dramatic. Have you been reading the fundie forums online or something? Fire and brimstone, devil-worship, and all that shit? Look. You've only just gotten here. It's pretty clear neither of you have a clue what's going on in Saqqara, and all the other places where people are gathering together to fight the darkness. Maybe you should just chill here until tonight, and then you can see for yourself."

By this point, Elijah had a faintly glazed look on his face, somewhere on the spectrum between *what-the-ever-loving-hell* and *oh-god-please-kill-me-now*.

"Why wait until tonight?" he asked. "Is that when the orgies and the virgin sacrifices kick off?"

And just like that, Amy was pissed at him again.

Shay laughed, bright and clear. "Not hardly, dude. That's when the vamps come out of their catacombs." She wiggled her fingers dramatically.

"Vamps? As in *vampires*?" Amy said faintly, half-convinced Shay was just messing with them now to get back at Elijah for his sarcasm.

The pitying look was back on Shay's face, though. "Vampires… blood donors. You see where I'm going with this?" She shook her head. "Don't worry, hon — it turns out they're actually the good guys. Like I said, just hang out for a few hours until everyone starts waking up. Don't take my word for it."

With a final cheery smile, Shay scrambled to her feet and turned her back on them, heading away toward the two men she'd been talking and laughing with earlier. Covering a wince at what she expected to see on Elijah's face, Amy turned to look at him. He didn't look angry, though — just tired.

"I know. I *know*," he said. "I gave you my word, and I'll keep it… within certain limitations. We'll stay until the floorshow kicks off tonight and you can see from yourself that this whole thing is a farce. Unless there's some indication that we're in danger — then we're out of here. No debate, Ames. It's not just you and me anymore."

With that, he placed a hand over her stomach, fingers splayed protectively. Tears pricked at the back of Amy's eyes, and she cursed the pregnancy hormones playing merry hell with her emotions and moods.

"All right," she whispered. "If it's all a trick, or if anything alarming happens, we'll leave right away."

-o-o-o-

Far below the milling humans in the compound, the vampire Menkhef sat silently in the chamber where Eris and Trynn slept. He regarded the entwined lovers over hands laced meditatively beneath his chin, keeping watch over more than just his two friends. The catacombs of the South Tomb were still much the same as they had been over the course of the three millennia he'd been buried here. Yet there *were* differences—and not just the ones wrought by the passage of time.

Many of the rooms and corridors still boasted the intricate artwork carved and painted by artists whose bones had long ago crumbled and turned to dust. Now, though, artificial lighting powered by the energy of the unforgiving desert sun illuminated the Stygian tunnels, revealing brilliant colors that still clung to the stone in many places. Even mortal eyes would be able to appreciate every fine line and elegant detail in the corridors and tombs, lit as they were by glowing yellow bulbs.

Human archaeologists had returned to this house of lost souls over the past few decades, clearing away both its resting bones and the ravages of time. They had restored it, in many ways, both aboveground and below. Now, his fellow vampires had gone further, altering Saqqara's very nature by changing it from a necropolis for the dead to an acropolis for the living—a haven for those who clung to the Light in the face of approaching Darkness. In addition to electricity, Xander and the others had also brought in medical equipment for the sterile removal of blood from willing human donors, mattresses for sleeping, and chairs for sitting... including the chair he himself now graced.

The tomb that had once imprisoned him now offered respite from the sun's killing rays. It had become both a refuge and a stronghold.

Menkhef had chosen, without much thought, to claim for himself the same room in which the Pharaoh Qahedjet had once buried his mummified, comatose body. Perhaps that had been a mistake. Certainly, he often seemed to find excuses to be elsewhere, as he had done this day.

Eris and his mate Trynn had wisely decided to claim one of the larger galleries as a sleeping place—one centrally located among the maze of passages snaking beneath the esplanade dominated by the Step Pyramid of Djoser. Menkhef himself did not sleep... had not slept in longer than he could remember. Instead, he cast his mind outward throughout the walled complex, standing watch against the dark forces gathering around them while also blanketing the area with an atmosphere of serenity that the humans would find calming.

It was because of this mental openness that he had become aware of Eris' disturbed slumber, some hours ago. He knew well that—even weeks after the fact—his oldest surviving friend was still rattled by Menkhef's apparent surrender to the demon Bael and his deathlike condition when the others had finally found him. Eris had drained himself to dangerous levels in his determination to revive Menkhef over the course of days rather than decades.

His friend's gamble had paid off, restoring Menkhef to levels of power and vitality he had never before experienced. It was still vaguely discomfiting to catch glimpses of himself in a reflective surface and see the form he'd held on the day Bael had turned him, rather than the wizened and skeletal creature he'd become for so long afterward.

Nonetheless, Menkhef regretted the toll that the past weeks had taken on those he held dear. Perhaps coming here to reassure Eris with his presence through the bond as he slept had merely been selfishness masquerading as compassion... but at least Eris and his mate slumbered more peacefully this way.

Watching them curled together in such quiet contentment was piercingly bittersweet, and despite

Menkhef's recent rejuvenation, he found himself feeling tired beyond measure. But none of the others were powerful enough to blanket so many worried humans with an aura of serenity… and how would Menkhef seek out sleep after so long forgoing it, anyway? He wouldn't even know where to start.

Besides, the point was moot; there was far too much to do right now. New humans were arriving almost every day, and with them, new swirls of conflict and fear. Some of them left soon after they arrived, unable to face the truth, while others stayed. Xander and Manisha watched over the aboveground part of the complex by day, but Menkhef and the others made a point of ascending to greet the newcomers once the sun went down each evening.

As it was going down now. After a final few seconds spent in quiet contemplation of Trynn and Eris, Menkhef rose and left the room. Outside, he focused his attention on the bond he shared with the others and sent a mental wake-up call along it, before preparing to ascend from the tunnels to the dry sands and the waiting humans above.

FIVE

Elijah sat propped against the cool stone of one of the faux buildings that made up Heb Sed Court at the southeast edge of Djoser's pyramid, his arm curled around Amy's sleeping form at his side. The ancient Egyptians had built an entire city in miniature inside this complex, but since it was meant for the dead, the houses and monuments weren't real. There were no rooms inside the structures—they were solid stone throughout.

In the world of the dead, appearances suffice, one of the older Egyptologists had quipped when Elijah had been here on a dig a few years ago. It was true enough. Corpses had no use for real buildings—not when fake ones were enough to drive home their wealth and power to the awestruck peasants they'd left behind.

Amy's breath puffed warm and wet against his collarbone. He settled her more comfortably against him as he watched the shadows lengthening into evening. Tired and jet-lagged, she had fallen asleep despite the tension between them... despite their disturbing conversation with the young woman, Shay.

Elijah had become a pathetic enough figure these days that he wasn't above soaking up this unexpected tender interlude. Moments like this didn't come around much for them lately. Amy was always busy with work or some charitable event she'd been hosting or organizing, while Elijah taught his classes. He'd even started teaching some at night once Amy's schedule grew so full that she never seemed to be home anyway.

The truth was, Elijah missed his wife. He had the feeling that a lot of his depression was due to the distance growing ever wider between them. He hoped she wasn't purposely using her career and all the charity work she did outside her practice as an excuse to stay away from him, but after so long, he was really beginning to wonder.

Her work was important to her, though, and his life was humiliating enough without him constantly sniping at her for daring to try and make the world a better place for others. Especially for those less fortunate than they were. So, he endured the lonely nights and the lonely weekends, telling himself he was being selfish and shallow for resenting her absence. If he repeated it to himself often enough, maybe it would eventually start to stick, right?

Elijah wondered if this trip was Amy's way of trying to make things up to him, ill conceived though the idea might have been. She probably thought bringing him back here, to a place with so many fond memories, would have some kind of positive impact on him. So far, it hadn't. Not really. Sure, he'd enjoyed digging up historical artifacts and helping restore the step pyramid from the ravages of time when he'd been here before. Back then, it had been fascinating work—but none of that mattered now.

What did matter at this very moment, was that his wife—the beautiful, intelligent woman he still loved more than life itself—was here, lying trustingly in his arms, setting all of her worries aside for a few fleeting hours of rest. He didn't want to waste a second of it. He'd hold her like this for as long as she'd allow it.

After another hour or so, the strange new world inside Saqqara's necropolis began to stir. The sun was setting, and scents of something cooking outside stirred Elijah's hunger, eliciting a rumble loud enough to wake the dead from their underground tombs.

The dead, and also his wife.

Amy's eyes fluttered open, and she glanced up at Elijah, whose left arm was still wrapped around her waist.

"Hey," he said, offering her a tentative smile. "Did you sleep well?"

The answering drowsy curve of her lips lacked the wariness it might have had if she'd been fully awake. The sight of it warmed him more than the beating sun had managed earlier. Why could they never seem to hold onto these fleeting moments where everything became simple again?

"Very well, especially under the circumstances," she replied in a sleepy rasp. "What time is it?"

Elijah tugged his phone out of his pocket with his free hand, but it had died. He wondered with a pang of uneasiness if he'd be able to charge it here. He'd have to ask someone. "I'm not sure—my battery's dead. I'll have to dig out my watch. The sun's going down, though. You hungry?"

"Starving." She rolled up enough to kiss him, and the look of almost painful affection on her face was one he'd missed desperately. She didn't say anything further because she didn't have to. Neither did he. If they started talking about anything of substance, they would probably ruin things again by fighting, and he wasn't ready for that yet.

Instead, he leaned down and pressed another brief kiss to her chapped lips. "Something smells good. Probably not gourmet fare, but definitely good enough to eat. Let's go see about feeding that baby of ours."

Elijah rose to his feet as Amy sat up the rest of the way, yawning and stretching her arms. The movement showed off the toned lines of her body beneath her loose cotton shirt. She peered up at him with the sweetest smile on her face as she caught him looking. And for one fleeting moment, Elijah believed — irrationally — that everything was going to be okay.

"Come on, Ames. Let's see what passes for dinner in the desert." He winked, holding out his hand to her.

She accepted it, allowing him to help her to her feet, and then her nose wrinkled.

"Oh my god, I need to pee." She snorted, settling one hand over her belly. "Damned hormones. I'm barely even showing! How bad is this going to be five months from now?"

Something hit Elijah in the gut as he pictured her heavy with their child. It was part panic, part longing, and part... something else. He covered it quickly.

"Bad enough that I'm glad I'm a man, for sure," he said lightly. "Come on, let's find you a portaloo." He took her hand and they ventured out of their tent, heading through the compound toward the makeshift lavatories Manisha had pointed out to them when they arrived.

After they were done using the facilities and washing up, they met up again and followed the scent of cooking food to a huge red and white striped tent. Outside it, a line was already forming. Elijah and Amy stood amongst other visitors waiting their turn for food.

Under a canopy near the back, three people were manning propane cook stoves, covered with various large pots billowing steam into the dry, greedy air. The scent of spices and herbs was tantalizing. While standing in line, Elijah dug discreetly into his wallet. Despite the rules against stealing, there was no way to know what kind of people might be paying attention to the resources they had brought with them. He felt as though he should be more worried than he actually was. Despite the air of calm serenity around them, there was no point in flashing cash around.

Amy's gaze wandered over their surroundings, analyzing everything — the people, the tents, the way things were set up. Elijah followed her gaze, beginning to wonder with real interest who was behind this setup. Somebody had invested a hell of a lot of time and money into it, and people generally didn't do that unless they planned to get something tangible out of their investment.

"How much do you think the food costs?" he asked, trying to start a conversation that wouldn't devolve into sniping. Maybe keeping things light was the best course of action. They'd had a nice afternoon despite the disturbing conversation with Shay earlier. Why rock the boat?

Amy shrugged. "No idea. If it's too high, maybe we can hike into the village tomorrow morning and pick up supplies there."

The line moved up two more paces, and an older woman standing in front of them turned to look at them. "The food is free here. It costs nothing for guests of the compound."

Elijah blinked at her. "Seriously?"

She tilted her head, as though surprised by his disbelieving tone. "Yes."

The woman's face was deeply wrinkled and tanned by the sun. She had clearly been here a while. She wore sandals and light clothing in the Egyptian style. Thick, grey streaks highlighted her brown hair.

She seemed happy. Easy inside her skin.

"How do they pay for all this?" Elijah asked. Surely he couldn't be the only person suspicious of this place. After all, any intelligent person knew that nothing came free. And judging by the resources around them – solar panels, expensive tents, food and water – someone was paying through the nose for this operation. It couldn't possibly be for no personal gain.

"I'm not certain. But nobody pays here—not for anything." The woman continued. "Though the organizers do encourage long-term visitors to volunteer their time and help keep everything running smoothly."

Elijah tried to keep his expression neutral, even though his bullshit detector was tingling at full-strength now. This couldn't be what it appeared. Nothing so seemingly altruistic ever was.

Stop, Elijah admonished himself. He'd promised Amy they would stay at least until the show later, to find out for themselves what was really going on here. And honestly, he couldn't deny a growing sense of curiosity now, especially regarding Shay's story of the mysterious figures at the center of this gathering. If they were the ones funding this thing, what was their angle?

Because it sure as hell wasn't blood farming for vampires. No way. Would they all be like that Manisha woman who had greeted them when they arrived? Unassuming and normal? And if they were—if nothing alarming happened—what then? Elijah's sixth sense had been urging him that this trip was bad news since they'd arrived, but now he was getting sucked into it, wanting to play amateur detective and figure out what was going on.

Maybe that's how they get you, his paranoia offered helpfully.

"Manisha said they use recycled graywater to grow vegetables here," Amy mused, still looking around with obvious fascination. "I'd like to see what they're doing with the gardens."

As Amy and Elijah waited in the line for food, volunteers standing at a long table were spooning scoopfuls of rice, beans, and cooked vegetables onto plates. They accepted a pair of generous servings once they reached the front of the queue, and Amy politely thanked the server. A kindly old man at the end of the table smiled, handing them each a cold bottle of water along with some napkins and utensils to eat with.

Outside the tent, the level of conversation and ambient noise grew noticeably. Something was happening.

"Sounds like the show is about to start." Elijah tipped his chin to a small area of seating set in front of the food tent. "Let's find a place to sit before the commotion gets out of hand."

The noise echoing among the archaic stone structures rose to a surprising din. Most of the people sitting at the nearby tables abandoned their meals and rose to their feet, craning to look toward the center of the esplanade.

As he and Amy moved to set their plates down, a ragged cheer rose around them. Amy gasped, and his attention flew to her. She was staring not at the crowd, but above it, her mouth forming into a round *oh* of surprise.

"What is it?" Elijah asked, trying to follow her gaze to whatever had caught her attention.

"Elijah… have you ever seen anything like that in your life?" Her voice held a note of pure amazement, and her eyes were wide as her hand closed around his upper arm, holding tight.

Then he saw them. Beautiful owls were circling the esplanade overhead — at least half a dozen, maybe more.

Owls.

Several different species.

In the middle of the desert.

That was definitely not something he'd ever seen before while staying here. Sure, there were owls in Egypt, but he'd never witnessed so many different kinds in one small area. Wild animals should have wanted nothing to do with an excited crowd of humans in a confined area. And they would never behave as though they were putting on an intricate aerial ballet for the onlookers. Had the people here been… feeding them, or something?

As he watched with the same stunned fascination as Amy, the avian predators took turns swooping down amongst the crowd in a manner that seemed almost... *playful*. He and Amy stood staring at the sky, their food forgotten on the table next to them. Eventually, the owls disappeared one by one, diving too low to be seen over the sea of heads, and not returning

Elijah narrowed his eyes, searching the skies for the missing birds.

"Okay. That was... weird." He scratched his chin.

The crowd's open glee subsided into quiet murmuring now that the show appeared to be over. Elijah started to turn to Amy, but a swirl of cool breeze broke through the sudden stillness. His gaze fell on a curling cloud of thick, white vapor as it rolled into an open area a few yards away from where they were standing. Any words he might have been about to say died in his throat.

Amy tightened her grip on Elijah's arm and moved closer to him, tension coiling her muscles. "What the hell is that?"

He glanced down at her pale features, but her eyes went wide and she pointed toward the center of the mist. *Fog machine*, he started to say, only to have his breath catch in his chest as the vapor appeared to pull into itself, condensing into solidity in a way that just didn't happen in nature.

The solidifying form stepped forward, taking on human shape even as swirls of mist trailed behind it, like it was being poured into existence from the thin desert air. Elijah nearly stumbled back a step as he attempted to convince himself this wasn't real. Things like this didn't happen outside of movie special effects. This was just an illusion orchestrated to pull them further into... whatever this crazy place turned out to be.

The last wisps of vapor disappeared into the now very solid form of a man. He looked... real. Undeniably real and present—confirmed when several people in the crowd hurried forward and touched him.

The figure stood like a statue of some ancient pharaoh, brought to life by the energy of the people surrounding him. His chiseled features, straight nose and high cheekbones were pure Egyptian royalty—the real deal, right down to the kilt-like linen *shendyt* belted neatly around his waist.

Next to Elijah, Amy stared shamelessly as though unable to look away from the man's dark eyes and full lips. Of course, as soon as Elijah followed her gaze, he was caught again as well, that pit inside his stomach which had opened the moment they'd touched down in Cairo growing ever deeper.

Grab Amy and run, or your lives will never be the same again, said a voice inside him.

And yet, his feet remained rooted to the sand, his eyes glued to the figure that had materialized from thin air in the middle of the crowded concourse. The people surrounding the man weren't mobbing him, exactly, but they were certainly eager to be close, like he was some kind of god to be worshipped.

"This is… unreal." Amy stared at the scene in awe, sheer wonderment in her demeanor. "Tell me you're seeing the same thing I'm seeing…"

A searching glance at her face showed that Amy had definitely drunk the Kool-Aid, and Elijah had to suppress a shiver despite the heat. He returned his attention to the man greeting the people around him, clasping shoulders, laying a hand on their backs briefly in greeting before moving on to others.

Obviously, Amy wasn't the only one around here who liked the taste of Kool-Aid. Holy shit.

The mystery man's expression was calm—unruffled and cool as he made his rounds through the crowd. He nodded occasionally but did not speak, though the people approaching him frequently spoke to him.

And... now he was coming straight toward Elijah and Amy.

Caught between several conflicting impulses, Elijah made an abortive move to place himself between Amy and the enigmatic figure. His feet were glued in place, though. His gaze, trapped by eyes which had looked nearly black before, but now kindled with an inner glow the color of molten bronze. Impossibly, a deep voice rolled through Elijah's mind even though the man's lips hadn't moved.

Do not fear. You are both welcome in the stronghold of Saqqara.

Again, Elijah felt that he should move or protest as the man lifted an elegant, long-fingered hand to brush a lock of hair back from Amy's face with a gossamer touch... but the moment was already past. Then, the same hand closed fleetingly over the junction of Elijah's neck and shoulder, surprisingly cool where it brushed his skin.

Now, more than ever, we must hold fast to the things that are important, continued the silent voice. *Do not allow the Darkness to steal away your Light.*

A look of wistfulness flickered across that carved-stone face as he looked between the two of them.

"What—" Elijah began hoarsely, but the man had already moved onto the next knot of people, leaving him and Amy gaping at a broad, well-muscled back.

SIX

Amy stared unblinkingly at the receding figure who had just spoken directly to her soul without uttering a single word aloud. He might as well have run a blade through her heart and left her bleeding out on the sand—all of the things she possessed and all of the things she lacked pouring into a messy red puddle at her feet.

She realized she'd been holding her breath and gasped sharply for air, her chest burning. The ragged sound drew Elijah's attention, breaking him free from his earlier paralysis. His handsome, dark-skinned face blurred oddly in her vision, like she was looking at him through a window lashed by rain. Callused palms cupped her face.

"Ames, you're crying." He sounded struck, like the same invisible knife had slipped between his ribs, too. "What is it?"

"He's right," she said, everything suddenly becoming clear even as her vision continued to blur with saltwater. "Oh god, Elijah... he's right. What have we been doing to each other?"

Elijah shuddered, though his hands remained gentle on her face, like someone holding delicate glass.

"I love you, Amy. Still. Forever and always, I never want to lose you, or god forbid, give you up. Ever." His voice was hoarse. "You have to know that, don't you?"

"*Elijah.*" Amy swallowed hard, and tried to blink her eyes clear enough to see his expression properly.

He leaned down, pulling her into his arms, holding her tightly to his chest as he used to do so long ago... like he could shelter her from the whole world with his body. "We need to find someplace quiet to talk, sweetheart."

"Okay. Bring the plates," she added as her stomach rumbled, reminding her of her baby's need for food.

Elijah chuckled, though it sounded a bit watery. "Of course." He grabbed their plates and led Amy through the esplanade toward their tent, searching for a quiet place where they could finally clear the air, years after they should have done.

It was telling that Elijah hadn't said a word about the impossible nature of what they'd just seen and experienced. Amy might not have been the hard-core skeptic that Elijah was, but she knew the moment she really stopped and thought about the last few minutes, she would have to make some serious decisions about what was and wasn't part of her worldview. Right now, though, talking about their future—and their past—was more important to her.

She was a bit surprised that it seemed to be more important to her husband, too.

He led her past groups of people clustered around musicians, and others who seemed to be listening to storytellers. There were kids here, she realized with a jolt. People had uprooted their whole families to come to the middle of the desert and do... what? Were they hiding from the darkness, or confronting it?

Elijah led her away from the crowds to a corner of the walled complex that was nearly untouched by the electric lighting—a ledge beside a staircase that led down to one of the lower chambers of the tombs.

"Here." Elijah sat along the ledge and patted the masonry beside him. "Let's sit here."

Amy sat beside him, her eyes still damp.

He stroked her face again. "Please, eat. We'll talk right afterward."

She nodded, taking a few moments to eat the vegetables and rice on her plate, then downing her bottle of water. She took a napkin, dabbing at the salty tear trails on her cheeks. Then she leaned back, letting her gaze roam upward.

"Wow, would you look at those stars," she breathed. The dark desert sky was awash with millions of pinpricks, the Milky Way clearly visible as a streak above their heads. "It really is beautiful here. I can see why you loved coming. I wish I understood why you stopped traveling to digs."

The air was cooling rapidly now that the sun was down. Amy ran her hands over her upper arms in an absent rhythm, staying silent while Elijah struggled to organize his thoughts.

"You were gone a lot," he said eventually, "working after hours. I thought if I gave up my research, you'd stay home more." Elijah scrubbed at his chin. "It was stupid. I see that now. We'd started growing apart long before then. But when I was gone on digs all the time, you found ways to cope. It's my fault, really. You got involved in your charities because I abandoned you, but by the time I came back, it was too late. You'd already pulled away."

Amy sat beside him, quietly contemplating his words.

This conversation had been a long time coming. They'd both been lazy with their marriage. She knew she was lucky he still cared enough to even want to save it. If it weren't for the baby, she thought he might very well have left her already. Fate had given them a second chance to fix things, and she was determined to make it count.

"You're not to blame," Amy said, laying her hand over Elijah's on the warm stone ledge. "We both are. I complained a lot when you traveled. I didn't appreciate how dependent your career was on it."

He snorted. "Only because I never explained it to you properly. I told myself I didn't want to worry you, but it was more a case of not wanting to face the choices I was making. Being a college professor is tough these days, but it's not the only thing I can do, Ames. I could always go back and teach high school again."

She frowned. "No, Elijah. You love university teaching. I would never ask that of you."

"You don't have to ask." He set his hands on her belly. "I'd do it for us. For our family. Whatever the answer is, we'll figure it out together."

She covered his hands with hers, knowing that in a few short months, he would be able to feel the baby move when they did this.

"Thank you for bringing me here," he continued. "That man, whoever... whatever he was... he was right." Elijah swallowed. "And so are you."

Another tear overflowed. It ran down Amy's cheek as Elijah reached up, wiping it away with the base of his thumb.

"Don't cry, baby. Please, just listen. I got depressed, that's all. And if I'm being honest, maybe a little jealous. It felt like you were moving on without me."

Amy swallowed the lump that was forming in her throat. "I never meant for that to happen. This is my fault, too."

"I'm not trying to place blame. When I gave up research, I think I expected you to give up your charities. But that was completely selfish of me. I was wrong." He pushed a curl of red hair off Amy's shoulder. "I know why you did it. Truth is, I felt it too. Something important was missing in our marriage. It still is, to be honest. I'm not naive, I know this trip can't be a cure-all, and I have no clue what will fix things for good. What I do know is that I'm still completely, *crazy* in love with you. I'm committed to our marriage, no matter what." He held her cheeks, gazing deeply into her eyes. "Our family is worth fighting for."

Amy made a small noise in her throat and surged forward, kissing her husband deeply before pulling back enough to rest their foreheads together. "I love you, Elijah. I don't know how to fix things either, but please—never doubt how much I love you."

He nodded, and she felt the pull of the small motion against her skin where he still pressed against her.

"Come on," he said, pulling back a little. "Let's go back now. You look exhausted, and I know I am."

He took her hand and led the way back to their tent, dropping off their dishes and cutlery at the mess tent on the way. Once there, they shuffled inside and closed themselves off from the rest of Saqqara, zipping the door shut. Amy curled up in Elijah's arms, feeling a tiny flame of hope that this would be the first step of many toward a better future. It wasn't the solution, and there was certainly more work to be done, but maybe the conversation they'd just had marked a new beginning for their family.

"I do love you Amy," Elijah said as he settled her into his embrace. "I'd give anything to have all the answers, but I don't. All I can do is promise that I'll be right here beside you for as long as you'll have me."

"That's forever, Elijah," Amy whispered. "Now sleep. Whatever else is missing in our lives, you and this baby are my family, and I *will not* let us fail. That much, I swear."

The arms around her tightened, and Amy squeezed back just as hard.

SEVEN

"I'm not sure I've ever seen you this distracted during a game before, my friend," Eris said. "And after more than sixteen hundred years, that's saying something."

Menkhef dragged his attention back to the marble chessboard, realizing with some surprise that his king was in check. Across the room, Trynn looked up from her book, raising an eyebrow as she straightened from her sideways slouch in the chair.

"Don't tell me you're going to beat him?" she asked, sounding intrigued.

Eris snorted. Menkhef narrowed his eyes at her—a quelling expression. He quickly moved a castle to remove the check, casting an eye over the remaining pieces to reassess the state of the game as Eris moved his knight in reply.

"I doubt there's much danger of that," Eris said in a dry tone.

"Well, you shouldn't have tipped him off to what was happening," Trynn observed with some asperity. "What the hell kind of strategy is that?"

Eris' wash of amusement across the mental connection was a balm. "Probably a poor one. But I'm more interested in the reason for his woolgathering than I am in the fleeting satisfaction of a stolen win. Aren't you?"

"Hmm. Fair point." Trynn's sharp eyes pinned Menkhef. "So, spill. What's got your knickers in a twist this morning, Snag? I thought things had been going pretty well the last few days."

It was a reasonable question, even when couched in such flippant terms. There was no reason his thoughts should keep returning to the unhappy human couple who'd arrived the previous day, seeking answers to all the wrong questions in this faraway place. Though it was out of character for him, he allowed his impressions of the pair to leak out through the bond—from their desperate love to their desperate unhappiness, and their understandable fear for the tiny new life they nurtured against the backdrop of an uncertain future.

Trynn stared at him in surprise after the unaccustomed outpouring, her book lying forgotten against her knees. Pages slipped past the restraining finger she'd laid over the edges, losing her place. Abruptly, she came to her senses and stopped the cascade of paper, blinking at him across the length of the room.

"Thinking of getting into the marriage counseling game?" she asked, clearly taken aback by the strength of his reaction to the unlikely couple. "No offense, but I'm not sure it really suits you."

Unsurprisingly, Eris was watching him with a more insightful expression, absently twirling a white pawn he'd taken earlier back and forth between his fingers. He cocked his head. "You're a tight-lipped bastard, my old friend, but I hear the things you don't say as well as the things you do. Be patient for a little while longer, and I'm certain what you lost will be returned to you, just as it was returned to the rest of us."

Menkhef arched an eyebrow, his face giving away nothing as he slid his bishop diagonally across the board. *Mate in seven*, he sent, effectively closing the conversation before it could turn to things he wasn't ready to discuss, even with people he cherished as much as he cherished these two.

-o-o-o-

Despite his exhaustion, Elijah spent a long time staring into the darkness inside the tent. Amy had once again fallen asleep almost immediately, only the occasional small noise or movement as she dreamed marring the stillness of her body. He spent the time thinking, re-treading familiar territory regarding their marriage troubles without reaching any new conclusions.

It was a relief beyond measure to have things out in the open—to know that Amy wanted to work things out as much as he did. Maybe he shouldn't have doubted that in the first place, but one thing he'd learned the hard way over the past few years was that depression could whisper all sorts of lies into your ear and make them sound perfectly believable. Now, though, relieved or not, he wasn't willing to sit by while the two of them slid right back into the quicksand.

There had to be an answer.

But what, exactly, was the question? They'd both used language about feeling like something was missing in their lives. Elijah frequently found himself thinking that he wasn't enough for Amy. Something inside him was convinced that no matter what he did, it would never fill the gap. Whether he was a career-driven ba-dass or a stay-at-home domestic dad, he didn't think he'd ever be able to erase that searching, faraway look from her eyes—the look that said, 'I need something more.'

After their talk, he was starting to understand that her seeming desperation to fill every moment of every day with activity was her way of trying to deal with whatever need she had that he wasn't meeting. Or may-be it wasn't to do with him at all? Turning his focus toward his own unmet needs was surprisingly uncom-fortable. He made himself do it anyway.

It was far too easy to fall into the trap of thinking he was only unhappy because Amy was unhappy and be-coming ever more emotionally distant toward him. Was that the whole truth, though? If she woke up in the morning to become the perfect, emotionally attentive wife… if she gave up her charities and focused on their relationship… would he magically become a happy and fulfilled person?

No, he thought with brutal honesty. No, he wouldn't. The answer was obvious when he stripped away all the bullshit and really thought about it, because he had never in his damned life been a happy and fulfilled person.

He had experienced moments of happiness. He had experienced moments of fulfillment. But from adolescence onward he'd always yearned for something both unreachable and indefinable. Something… *missing*.

And so he'd come full circle.

There was no question that Amy had filled an empty place inside him. From what she'd said tonight, he'd filled an empty place inside her, too. But their rough edges rubbed up against each other, grating together rather than sliding into place like puzzle pieces. In many ways they were too alike. In others, so different that they often seemed to have nothing in common.

A few months ago, before Amy got pregnant, Elijah had been convinced that she was about to leave him. He started having dreams of seeing her in another man's arms—hazy images that haunted him even after he woke up. The biggest problem was, it wasn't necessarily jealousy that tortured him afterward. For weeks, he obsessed over the dreams, indulging in several clandestine internet searches he really wasn't proud of before coming to the conclusion that he had an unwanted and extremely humiliating cuckolding fetish.

In what was probably their ugliest marital fight to date, he'd snapped, "Well maybe we should have an open marriage and start seeing other people!" in response to something she'd said that had pissed him off.

Good god, he couldn't even remember now what the argument had originally been about. How utterly ridiculous.

Not that it mattered—he might as well have slapped Amy across the cheek, from her reaction. She'd physically staggered back a step, the blood draining from her face until it was chalky.

"You... want to see other women?" she'd whispered hoarsely.

Frustration had kept the words coming despite the warning signs. "I thought you might want to see other men, since I'm obviously not good enough for you!"

The blood that had left her cheeks returned to color them bright red, and her eyes snapped fire as she'd hissed, "If you want to get rid of me so badly, hire a fucking lawyer and serve me with divorce papers, damn it! I won't be your castoff leftovers!"

It was the first time either of them had used the 'D' word, and the pain lurking behind Amy's anger ensured that Elijah never brought up the idea of alternative lifestyles again. Not long afterward, they'd hit a slight thaw, and fate combined with faulty birth control brought a new twist into their lives. Elijah was damned if he'd rock the boat—not when that boat now held a child with Amy's bright green eyes and his tight curls... or whatever other combination of traits their genetics happened to produce.

The noises of happy people outside were starting to fade when fatigue finally began to pull him down toward sleep. He fought it, knowing that he still had no good answers, no fresh ideas. He dreaded the thought of slipping straight back into the mess they'd been wallowing in for the past couple of years.

They needed a fresh perspective. They needed... *they... needed...*

Elijah's eyes slipped closed, the stuffy confines of the tent giving way to an arid landscape of dreams.

EIGHT

The sun was disappearing behind the swaying palm trees on the western bank of the Nile when Heqab returned from an afternoon spent training new archers to shoot from the back of a chariot. Several people greeted him as he approached the edge of the village, but he restricted himself to brusque nods in return.

Passersby would see only the Captain of the Guard, hurrying from the training grounds to his evening duties in the royal household. And that was exactly what he wished them to see. They did not need to know precisely what those duties entailed—or, more to the point, they did not need to know that it wasn't duty hurrying his feet toward the palace, but desire.

As was usual in the weeks since Heqab's oldest friend had extended him a shockingly unusual offer, the palace was deserted when he arrived. The scribes, servants, and supplicants had all been sent away with the setting sun, leaving the building quiet and peaceful as golden light slanted through the reed coverings hanging across the western windows. It was hot inside the stone structure. The red blocks were slow to absorb the sun's rays in the morning, but they were also slow to give up the baking heat they had absorbed once evening came.

Heqab moved through the sparsely furnished rooms until he reached the open courtyard at the building's center. There, an artful arrangement of ferns and small trees gave the illusion of a secluded glade, the greenery combining with the fresh air to make the surroundings feel noticeably cooler. He stopped at the entrance, resting a hand on the sandstone pillar next to him to steady himself as the now familiar feeling of this being a dream washed over him.

A divan with polished legs carved in the forms of lions sat in the shade of a date palm at the far end of the courtyard. It was not the fine workmanship of the low couch that held Heqab's gaze, however. It was the people resting on the cushions. The nomarch—ruler of the local principality and Heqab's dear friend since childhood—reclined on the divan with his queen resting against his chest as he hand-fed her figs. His dark eyes held nothing of their usual penetrating ruthlessness; instead, he watched his wife with such depths of affection that Heqab caught his breath.

The small sound must have reached the pair, because Nebetta's gaze flickered to him and held. She very deliberately swallowed the morsel of fruit she'd just nibbled from her husband's fingers, and a smile graced her luscious lips.

She was stunning, with large, brown eyes, long black hair plaited into dozens of tiny braids, and sumptuous curves. Her regal bearing hid a mischievous twinkle that very few people got to see, and she employed it now, stretching in her husband's arms until the loose linen *kalasiris* she wore slid lower on her torso, baring one breast to his hungry eyes. Then she winked at him.

Her husband lifted a winged brow and followed her gaze to where Heqab was standing. A touch of a teasing smile curved one corner of his full mouth.

"Good evening, Guard Captain." His voice was deep and commanding, though the overly formal greeting carried the same hint of fond teasing as his expression. "We were starting to think you found the company of your recruits more stimulating than ours."

Heqab wrested himself free of his momentary paralysis. *This was real. They wanted him here—it wasn't a dream.* He affected a lazy grin, examining his ragged fingernails for a moment as though the sight in front of him didn't affect him right down to his marrow.

"*Really*, Your Excellence... if my recruits stimulated me half as much as our queen does, I suspect there would be immediate rioting within the barracks." He made sure to inject a note of tartness into the words, and was rewarded by a rich chuckle in counterpoint with Nebetta's light laughter.

"I suspect you're quite right about that," said the nomarch, his voice still tinged with real amusement.

Nebetta grinned at him as he pushed away from the stone column he'd been leaning against and sauntered toward them. "Politeness dictates I ask how your day was," she said, "but I find myself much more interested in a kiss. Menkhef has been teasing me terribly while we waited."

As though to illustrate, Menkhef cupped Nebetta's naked breast, his thumb tweaking the dusky point of her nipple. She made a low noise and arched like a cat, the movement sending an arrow of lust straight to Heqab's groin.

"My day was fine, my Queen," he managed, his flesh hardening almost painfully beneath his belted linen *shendyt*. "But I suspect it's about to get even better. Remind me to thank our esteemed ruler for his efforts in keeping you... entertained... in my absence."

Nebetta's eyes grew heavy-lidded, and Heqab started shedding clothing and leather armor as he went. His words hadn't been meant as fatuous diplomacy... merely the truth. As he drew near the divan, the smell of Nebetta's arousal tickled his nostrils. He'd learned over the past weeks that his old friend had a penchant for drawn-out love play—one that meshed rather well with Heqab's own tendency for not beating around the bush.

So it was that he had no guilt whatsoever in dropping to his knees, dragging Nebetta toward him until her loose skirt ruched around her thighs, and burying his face in her sex. She'd asked for a kiss, after all. She hadn't specified *where*.

The noise she made was wholly gratifying, though it made the ache in his cock grow almost unbearable.

"Brute," she managed, her tone of accusation not terribly convincing.

He smiled against her flesh, dipping his tongue deeper to taste the pulse of wetness that belied her feigned outrage, making her shudder. Meanwhile, Menkhef gathered a handful of her dark braids and used the light grip to turn her gaze up to his.

"This is what you get for agreeing to take a soldier as a lover, my beloved," he observed, his voice a rumble of warm decadence. "Soldiers conquer."

He lifted his free hand and rubbed over Nebetta's lower lip with the pad of his thumb. Heqab dragged his tongue up the length of her slit, lapping roughly at the nub of her pleasure. She gasped, letting her husband's thumb slide into her mouth, her soft lips closing around it and her eyes fluttering closed. Heqab groaned against her sensitive flesh at the sight, and the vibration was apparently too much for her—she writhed, her body growing taut between them the instant before her hips jerked, signaling her release.

Watching her, Heqab knew exactly what he wanted this evening. He continued to nuzzle her sex, drawing out her pleasure until she was a limp, shivering mess between them. With a glance at Menkhef, he rose and manhandled her spent body into position so she was kneeling on shaky legs at the edge of the divan, giving him a fine view of her rounded buttocks as she faced her husband.

Menkhef was still sprawled against the divan's backrest, his legs parted, one bare foot resting on the floor. Nebetta attacked the clasp of his belt with unsteady fingers while Heqab slid the loose folds of her linen skirt up to drape over her lower back, baring her to him. She finally defeated the closure of her husband's *shendyt* belt and dragged the fabric out of her way. His prick sprang up, as hard and ready as Heqab's.

Nebetta already looked debauched, and that was *before* she leaned forward, the lips that had closed around her husband's thumb now closing over the head of his cock instead. Heqab couldn't hold back the growl that rumbled up from his chest. His hands closed around Nebetta's hips, fingers gripping tight enough to leave marks. He sheathed himself inside her dripping passage with a single unforgiving slide, not stopping until his sac slapped against her folds.

She cried out around the hard flesh in her mouth, and Menkhef's head fell back, a huff of breath escaping his lungs as his much-vaunted control finally started to slip. It thrilled Heqab anew each night simply to realize that he was wanted here… but it thrilled him even more to know that he could reduce both the nomarch and his queen to the status of writhing, wanton animals.

He pulled back slowly and thrust into Nebetta's welcoming heat again, driving her forward onto her husband's cock. Menkhef gathered her braided hair away from her face with a shaky hand, letting Heqab set their rhythm. For long minutes, only the sounds of flesh on flesh and Nebetta's low moans broke the stillness of the courtyard as the evening darkened around them.

Surprisingly, Menkhef was the first to break, arching in silent release as he spilled his seed down Nebetta's throat. Her choked keening noise and the feeling of her inner muscles clamping around Heqab's cock as she came caused the heat coiling at the base of his spine to explode outward. His vision went white as he spurted his essence as deep inside her as he could get. When he had nothing more to give, he half-collapsed over her back, catching himself with one hand on the edge of the divan to keep his weight off her.

His softening prick slid free of her welcoming depths and they both shuddered. Nebetta sagged into her husband's embrace, while Heqab managed a marginally controlled sideways slide onto the ground, twisting so that his back leaned against the edge of the low couch, even with Menkhef's hip.

A slender, female arm draped around him from behind, soft fingers splaying over the center of his chest where his pounding heartbeat was gradually returning to normal. He let his head fall back on the cushions, eyes closed, soaking in the touch. A smile tugged at his lips as Nebetta's fingers curled in his dark chest hair and tugged playfully.

"After being drowned with so much seed at once," she said, her voice sounding fucked-out and throaty, "I'll be lucky if I don't fall pregnant with twins."

Heqab's smile grew wider, even though he couldn't be bothered to move yet. "You'll birth a pair of godlings, and throw the Pharaoh Qahedjet into palpitations," he murmured.

A larger hand closed over the juncture of Heqab's neck and shoulder, the fingers strong and callused. "If that happens, they will have need of a strong guardsman to watch over them," Menkhef said, his voice rich and soothing. "Fortunately, I know just the man for the job."

NINE

Amy awoke with a familiar form spooned around her back. What had become considerably less familiar over the past couple of months was the morning wood nestled between her ass cheeks as Elijah's warm breath puffed against the back of her neck. Her body reacted before her mind had a chance to catch up, tightening in pleasant anticipation at the prospect of sex after going well over two months without.

For all she knew, the last time they'd made love might well have been the time she unexpectedly got pregnant. Shortly afterward, their brief relationship thaw had chilled again, and a few weeks after that, she'd come down with morning sickness that stubbornly refused to confine itself to the mornings. Later they'd been planning—and fighting about—this trip, and suddenly it had been more than ten weeks since she'd gotten any action.

If that was about to change in the next few minutes, was she really okay with the idea of getting it on inside a flimsy tent surrounded by people in dozens of other flimsy tents? Elijah made a low, male noise in his chest. He flexed his hips, rutting against her from behind, and she decided that, yeah, she kind of *was* okay with it at this point. The arm he'd slung over her waist shifted, his hand closing around her hip and pressing her against his hard length. Her pussy throbbed, getting on board with the program immediately.

Hot damn. Whatever dream he was having, Amy was woman enough to admit that she was jealous as hell right now. Going with the moment, she wriggled her hips, increasing the friction and causing his fingers to tighten over her hipbone. Just as she was trying to figure out the most efficient way to start shedding clothes in such a confined space, Elijah froze, going very, very still behind her.

An instant later, he shuffled back, putting a careful inch of space between them, and her stomach sank in disappointment. Bracing herself for rejection, she rolled onto her back so she could see him.

"Elijah? You… uh… you didn't have to stop on my account…"

The expression on his face halted her in her tracks. He looked… guilty. There was no other word for it. His face had gone positively gray beneath the rich mahogany of his skin. Why would he be guilty about a sex dream? Unless—

Unless he'd been dreaming about another woman. Not *her*. Not the harpy he was married to who constantly fought with him and snapped at him and dragged him halfway across the world when he didn't want to go. Her stomach churned.

His eyes darted around, as though searching for an escape route. "It's…" he started, only to cut himself off and begin again. "There are too many people around, that's all. Someone will hear us."

He's lying, her internal bullshit detector pronounced with certainty.

She tried to laugh off the awkward moment. "Yeah. Um. I guess you're right. Last thing we need is Shay unzipping the tent and sticking her head in to tell us we're being too loud, right?"

His answering smile looked tight and uncomfortable, but relief rolled off him in waves. "Right," he agreed. "We wouldn't want to interrupt people's *siesta time.*"

At that, she became aware of the world beyond the stifling atmosphere of tension inside the tent. It was light outside, the bright desert sun illuminating the interior through the fabric and driving the temperature up.

"Geez," Elijah said, scrubbing a hand over his scalp as though to brush away whatever had just happened between them. "We must have slept ten hours straight. We should, uh, go see if they're still serving food. You need to eat regularly."

Amy tried to let the weird interval go. Even if Elijah had dreamed something that would legitimately make him feel guilty, it's not like you could hold someone to account for the random images that popped up in their heads when they slept. God knew, she'd had her share of weird sex dreams over the years, including ones where she was having sex with more than one guy at a time. She'd be a hell of a hypocrite if she went all judgy on her husband for getting some illicit action while he was asleep.

Besides, he was right about all the people who might hear them, and he was right about her needing to eat. She also felt more than a little gross after twenty-four hours in the same clothes, and desperately wanted to clean herself up. The urge to pee rose to join the growing litany of reasons why having sex right now was a bad idea.

Pregnancy was weird—what with the cravings for strange foods, the roller coaster of swirling emotions, and losing control over body functions she'd always taken for granted. On the positive side, her previously underwhelming boobs had grown three cup sizes... maybe someday she'd even get to enjoy that fact.

Amy looked forward to the day she would feel their baby move inside her. All her friends said four months, so hopefully it wouldn't be too much longer. She smiled, rubbing her belly for a moment, saying good morning to her unborn child. A much-needed sense of peace fluttered inside her chest, settling. Even with the momentary strangeness between her and Elijah this morning, after their talk last night the fear of having to raise her child without its father was fading away.

Today would be a fresh start, she decided. For all three of them.

"That was a better night's sleep than I expected considering we're camping in the desert," she said, forcing positivity into her tone. "Though I may have to make a run for the portaloos before I tackle breakfast. Coming?"

"Yep," Elijah confirmed, easing through the tent flap and reaching his hand out for hers. She took it and he helped her out of the tent, zipping it up behind them. Then he handed her a bag.

"Do I have all the items I'll need so I can clean up?" she asked.

"Yes," he gestured at the bag. "That's the restroom bag."

Amy nodded as she slung it over her shoulders.

"Want me to carry it?" he asked.

"Nah, I'm good." She smiled. "Let's go—I'm starving. Not to mention, dying to clean up. I feel pretty disgusting at this point."

They walked from their tent to the food stations at the edge of the esplanade where they'd witnessed the strange events last night. It was probably closer to lunchtime than breakfast now, but the smell of cooking food still lingered in the air. Perhaps they were serving brunch instead.

Amy's stomach started rumbling more ferociously the closer they got to the food. "Would you get me a plate?" she asked. "I need to go wash up first. I wonder what kind of amenities they have here?"

"Probably decent ones given the money someone appears to have spent on this place," Elijah said. "They might even have portable showers."

"In the desert?" Amy asked skeptically. She narrowed her eyes, curious how they'd even get showers out here.

"They could have brought in water tanks from Cairo. There are all sorts of possibilities. You'd be surprised the things people come up with in situations like this."

She shrugged. "I guess I would at that. Okay, I'll be back as quickly as I can."

Amy leaned in and gave Elijah a soft kiss, relieved when he didn't tense up or pull away. Then she walked the short distance to the ladies' area. Behind a privacy section marked off with hanging sheets, she did indeed find two portable showers. Elijah had been right; there was a good-sized water tank on wheels positioned just outside.

Beside a row of five port-a-potties was a makeshift cleaning station. There was a sign stating in several languages that if anybody needed soap, toothbrushes or toothpaste, they could get items in the medical tent, which was a red tent near the food station. That seemed very kind of them. Amy was more impressed now than ever by the generosity of whoever was funding this camp. They truly seemed to care about the people here.

Fortunately, though, Amy and Elijah had come prepared. Elijah—an old hand at traveling to remote places—knew exactly what they'd needed to bring along.

Amy used one of the port-a-potties and briefly considered trying out one of the showers, but there was a line for both of them. She didn't feel like waiting that long, so she used one of the three portable sinks that had small hoses attached, running from the water tank, she assumed. She dug into her bag and pulled out a bar of soap and a washcloth, then used the running water to wash herself, head to toe, as best she could. Next, she pulled out her toothbrush and toothpaste.

They had brought some dry shampoo along, not knowing if they'd have facilities for washing hair. She used the dry shampoo then picked out her tight red curls. Her hair was still going to be a disaster, but under the circumstances, who cared? She pulled it all up and twisted it into a messy bun. Problem solved.

Afterward, Amy felt somewhat more human. She put all her things back in her backpack and was on her way out of the cleaning station when she bumped into Shay, the teenager from the day before.

Shay smiled widely. "Hey, girl. How's it going? Did you find everything you needed?"

Her brown hair was pulled back in twin braids, and her tanned skin was starting to peel. Amy still had to fight a faint flush as she recalled the way she and Elijah had been fighting when Shay first approached them, but it didn't seem that the young woman held it against her.

"We're good," she said in reply. "Thanks. I think we're all set. Just going to get some food and then decide what we're doing today."

Shay nodded sagely. "Cool. You two gonna stick around for a while, then? I saw you talked to Snag last night."

A frown of confusion wrinkled Amy's forehead. "Snag?"

Shay tilted her head, birdlike. "Yeah, you know. The vamp. Mister 'Walks-Like-an-Egyptian?"

Understanding dawned. "Oh. Uh… yeah. Sort of."

"Right. They call him Snag because of his…" Shay made a vague gesture toward her mouth, wiggling her finger up and down. "Anyway, are you staying?"

Amy blew out a breath. "I think so. For now, at least. Last night… definitely gave us some things to think about."

"I just bet it did." Shay grinned at her again. "Well, I'll leave you to it. Don't forget your sunscreen—your shoulders are starting to burn already. Have a good one!"

With a cheery wave, she departed, leaving Amy feeling like she'd been assaulted by a bubbly tornado. Amy shook her head and took off toward the food tents. Elijah was at one of the picnic tables nearby, two plates of food in front of him. As soon as she approached, he handed her a bottle of sunscreen.

"Be sure to put on plenty. You don't want to burn. Drink plenty of water today, too. Sunstroke would be terrible in your condition."

Amy smiled, taking the sunscreen and slathering everywhere she could reach with the lotion. "Get my back?" she asked, handing him the sunscreen and perching on the bench.

"Of course."

She held her hair up, and he smoothed the sunscreen over her back... or at least what was bare above her tank top. Elijah rubbed the lotion in with long, firm strokes, making her wish once again that he hadn't had his little freakout session in the tent earlier. She closed her eyes, appreciating the love and care in the slide of his fingers. Even with the false start this morning, something between them had changed for the better—she could feel it. She smiled at the thought.

Elijah's touch was surer. His words were softer. She could feel the weight of constant worry beginning to lift off her shoulders.

"There you go," Elijah said with a final caress across the back of her neck. "Now, eat something. I can hear your stomach growling."

She blushed—whether due to the brush of his fingertips or his words, she wasn't sure. They used napkins to wipe the slippery suntan lotion off their hands and dug into the food, which was a slightly different variation of beans and rice with vegetables and interesting spices. It was really rather good, and Amy thought she might have to look into some Middle Eastern recipes when they got back home.

When his plate was empty, Elijah cleared his throat as though unsure of what he was about to say. She raised her eyebrows at him, still chewing—urging him to go ahead.

He fiddled with his napkin and met her eyes. "I thought maybe I could take you exploring around the area later today. It's not as hot as it was yesterday, and there's more to see around Saqqara than just the Step Pyramid." He shrugged. "I mean… we're here anyway, so…"

She swallowed her mouthful of food. "I'd love that, Elijah. Would we need to find a car or get a taxi or something, though?"

Elijah shook his head. "No, I shouldn't think so. As long as we keep covered up and you continue to apply sun block with a trowel, it's all accessible on foot without too much problem." His enthusiasm grew at her receptive response, his hands moving as he spoke. "You saw how close Saqqara village is to this place? We could go into town long enough to pick up any supplies we need, and then there's a museum right on the boundary between the Nile floodplain and the edge of the desert."

She rested her elbows on the table next to her empty plate, growing intrigued. "A museum? Really? With artifacts and mummies and things?"

He nodded, his eyes glinting. "Yep. They've got a Ptolemaic mummy unearthed by Zahi Hawass, and part of the statue of the Pharaoh Djoser that came from this very complex. The inventory rotates in and out, but I think they've got a really impressive collection of tomb objects, too."

"I would absolutely kill to see that," Amy said, thrilled at the idea of a day spent exploring ancient art and history with her archaeologist husband.

A smile split Elijah's face. "Then, if there's time, there's also the Headless Pyramid and the Mastaba of Mereruka, both within half a mile of here with decent roads leading right up to them. Or we could do that another day—"

Her smile grew to match his. "This is going to be brilliant! I didn't even really think about all the things we could sightsee while we were here. And I've got the next best thing to a native guide! Okay, let's start by hitting the museum. Honestly, I think we're okay for supplies, since they seem to pretty much be providing everything we need here. So let's skip the village for now, and if there's time we can hike out to one of those other places you mentioned." Her brow crinkled. "Why do they call it the Headless Pyramid, anyway?"

She could tell he was warming to his subject. "It's more a place where a pyramid used to be, at this point," he said. "Picture the gap where a tooth used to be after someone pulled it out."

She wrinkled her nose at him. "I'd rather not," she said wryly.

He laughed. "Sorry. Basically, the superstructure is lost to time. It's gone. But the entrance to the underground tunnels and galleries is still there, and archaeologists have been excavating it in a serious way since 2008."

"Oooh." Amy waggled her fingers. "A ghost pyramid. Spooky."

Elijah's smile grew a bit frayed at the edges. "I'm guessing there's more woo-woo stuff going on right here than there will be at the unoccupied dig sites," he muttered.

It was clear he was still having significant issues with what they'd seen and experienced last night—not that Amy could blame him. Rather than risk falling back into a spat about what was going on here with the...

supposed vampires… she moved the conversation along to practicalities.

"So, how about we hang out here for a few more hours until the sun gets a bit lower. We can nap, or chat with people—whatever, really. Then we'll hike out to the museum, and go from there?"

His expression cleared again. "Sure, babe. Whatever you want. This is your rodeo—I'm just along for the ride."

"Then we have a plan," she said, leaning forward to give him a peck on the lips. "I can hardly wait."

TEN

Elijah tagged along while Amy chatted with random people in the complex, reminding her every so often to reapply her sunscreen and drink more water. Despite the weirdness of the place, she seemed right at home here. The people they talked to ran the gamut from obvious new age hipster types to folks so normal that he wouldn't have given them a second glance in everyday circumstances.

They were on the receiving end of an additional smattering of crazy talk about supernatural creatures and a war between good and evil. But there were plenty of others here who seemed to be in roughly the same boat Amy was in—caught up in a questionable logic loop.

The world is crazy, and I need to do something.
This is something.
Therefore, I need to do this.

Elijah's air of detached superiority would be a lot easier to maintain if he hadn't watched a guy materialize from smoke and heard him speak telepathically inside his mind last night. For now, he was dealing with what he'd experienced by compartmentalizing it, which basically meant pretending it hadn't happened.

Even though it totally had.

He blew out a silent breath in frustration. In all fairness to Mister Wannabe Pharaoh, what he'd said had helped them with their problems. At least, it seemed to have done so. He and Amy had talked. Properly. They'd gone the better part of a day without fighting—more than that, they were *getting along*. Bonding. Enjoying each other's company.

A flush rose to Elijah's cheeks as he remembered how he'd started to *enjoy Amy's company* that morning in the tent, and he was glad that his dark skin hid it. That had rattled him, and he didn't think he'd done a very good job of hiding just how badly.

Fucking dream, he thought, only to blush harder as the unintentional double entendre registered.

The dream had been different this time, in a way that was completely and utterly devastating on several levels. First, it had gone on longer than in the past. Always before, he'd dreamed of walking in on Amy in another man's arms, and felt the sight making him horny as hell when he should have been angry, jealous, and hurt. It had only ever come to him in short fragments — abbreviated scenes with no context.

He'd always assumed it meant Amy had left him. It never occurred to him that he was supposed to join her and her lover — *her husband?* — like he'd done in the dream last night. Why would it? While it wasn't as though he'd never heard of alternative lifestyles, he'd always figured most swingers just paired off and did their thing in private with whatever partners they chose. This had been… something different than that.

He wished he could remember what they'd talked about in the dream, but the details had started to fade the moment he'd awoken to find himself grinding his dick against Amy's ass. There was a definite feeling of surreality to the whole thing. He was pretty sure the woman in the dream had borne no resemblance whatsoever to his red-haired, freckle-faced wife. But it had still somehow been Amy, without question.

Conversely, he really wished he *didn't* remember the man in the dream so well. Before, he'd always been a cipher. A faceless image for Elijah's mind to torment him with. Last night, the face had been the same one that poured itself into existence from a cloud of vapor, like some kind of high-end CGI special effect. Mister Wannabe Pharaoh, walking straight from his waking hallucinations into his dreams.

Fuck.

He needed to stop obsessing about this. It was a dream. Dreams were weird; that was kind of the point of them. This particular one probably said something really twisted about his current mental state, but... hey. Big surprise there, right?

Still, subconsciously wanting to have a threesome was probably less screwed up than getting off on your wife having an affair. Or at least it would have been less screwed up if he'd dreamed about getting it on with two women instead of his wife and another man. Another man who was her husband inside the dream, while Elijah had been—what?

They'll have need of a strong guardsman to watch over them. Fortunately, I know just the man for the job.

The snippet of dialogue flitted through Elijah's mind without context, and he shook his head, trying to rattle it loose.

He was fucking losing it, and he needed to stop. Things were going well right now. He couldn't afford to mess that up. They were going to go see some cool and interesting artifacts together, and even with all the people around, Amy had seemed pretty into the idea of having sex before Elijah had his little meltdown and ruined it. Maybe she'd be in the mood when they got back and went to bed.

Now, the sun was no longer pounding down on them from above. They'd retreated to the tent to rest for a while during the worst heat of the day, and Amy had dozed a bit. She stretched now, yawning widely.

"Hey, can we head out now?" she asked in a drowsy tone, unzipping the tent opening to peer outside.

"We sure can," he agreed readily. "Let's get kitted out and do it."

Her answering smile was as bright as the desert sky. "This is going to be *awesome*."

He couldn't help smiling back, his earlier broodiness falling by the wayside as he looked forward to showing her some of the fruits of his colleagues' labors. Maybe someday soon, he would join them again in unearthing and restoring humanity's history. God knew, it was past time. The tentative hopeful feeling that had crept into his soul over the past day lifted its head again, making him feel lighter.

"You look like a kid contemplating a trip to the candy store," she accused, smirking at him.

He grinned back and splayed a hand over her belly where her shirt had ridden up, picturing a bouncy toddler with caramel skin running through aisles of sweets. "So do you," he shot back. "Now put on some more *SPF gazillion* and grab a long-sleeved shirt. I'll get your sun hat."

She stuck her tongue out at him, playful in a way he'd missed terribly in recent years, and they organized themselves for their mini-expedition. When they were ready, he hefted the larger of the packs—full of bottled water, more sunscreen, a compass, and some energy bars—while she took the lighter one. They headed toward the towering columns of the Grand Entrance, waving cheerily to a couple of people they'd chatted with earlier.

Instead of the Indian woman, Manisha, there was a tall white guy with brown hair and striking green eyes a similar shade to Amy's lounging on a folding chair near the colonnades. Those piercing eyes raked over both of them, assessing them with a single glance.

"Leaving us already?" he asked in an upper crust British accent.

Elijah stared right back, some of his earlier misgivings creeping in again. "Would it be a problem if we were?"

An eyebrow arched. "Not at all," he said, the mildness in his tone not reaching his green gaze. "We merely like to keep track of how many people are staying here at any given time."

"'We'?" Amy echoed, stepping forward until her upper arm brushed Elijah's. "So you're another one of the... organizers?"

"Indeed I am," said the man, still unperturbed. "Necessity dictates that Manisha and I manage gate duty during the daylight hours. We tend to switch off around midday so we can each get some rest."

"You're aware that some of the people here claim you're vampires." Amy's voice was challenging, and Elijah was caught between wanting to cheer her on and wanting to cringe at the awkwardness of bringing something so ridiculous into the open.

The man snorted. "Of course I am."

"And are you?" Amy pressed. "A vampire, I mean?"

"Among other things, yes."

"Vampires don't exist," Elijah blurted, unable to stay silent after the matter-of-fact declaration.

"So one might assume," the man said. "And don't even get me started on werewolves or zombies."

Elijah blinked. "That's..." he began, only to flash back to the news reports about crowds of shambling 'survivors' after the bombing in Syria.

"Ridiculous?" the man finished for him. His lips stretched into a smile that bared pointed fangs for the space of a heartbeat, and his green eyes glowed with an actinic inner light for a moment before fading to normal. "Yes, quite so. Now... once again. Are you leaving us?"

Elijah's pulse thundered against his ribcage as a jolt of adrenaline shot through him—an instinctive fight or flight response to the presence of… what? A predator? A monster? Or… some kind of clever illusion?

Amy's voice was shaky, but she didn't back down as she said, "N-no. I came here to try and make a difference. I'm not leaving until I have more answers."

The man's expression sobered. "An admirable sentiment. Very well—I gather you're just heading out on a day trip, then?"

She nodded, and Elijah finally found his tongue. "Yes. Sightseeing for a few hours at the Imhotep Museum and possibly a couple of the closer dig sites. I'm a professor of archaeology. I've been out here before in a professional capacity."

The man's brows rose. "Archaeologist, eh? You should chat with Eris sometime. He used to be a tomb robber, and he probably lived through half of the stuff you've dug up. Him and Snag. Er, I mean *Menkhef*. I still can't get used to that." The last sentence was a barely audible mutter.

Elijah opened his mouth, but he wasn't sure what to say to that, so no words came out.

"Anyway, it sounds like you're well equipped to manage a short hiking expedition," the guy continued, waving a careless hand toward the exit from the complex. "We generally counsel people to be back by dark. The desert is an unforgiving landscape. That was true even before the world started going batshit insane."

"I know my way around the area," Elijah said. "We won't do anything unsafe."

The man's lips pulled into a pleasant smile, and this time there was no hint of pointed teeth. "Cheers. Have a lovely afternoon, both of you."

ELEVEN

The column-flanked entryway was no less impressive on the way out than it had been on the way in yesterday, but Amy was too focused on the conversation they'd just had to pay much attention to it. The British guy… he'd had fangs. Like… *proper fangs.*

"It could have been another trick. But what's their game?" Elijah muttered, as though reading her mind. He was clearly as rattled as she was, if not more so.

"Elijah… we watched a man materialize right in front of us. In the middle of a crowd, no less—not on some stage like an illusionist or a magician in Las Vegas."

"This stuff is impossible," Elijah said, still sounding dazed. "You've got a background in the sciences just like I do, Ames. You *know* it's impossible."

"I know what I saw," Amy shot back. "You saw the same thing or you wouldn't be so freaked out right now."

He was silent for a moment before he shook his head almost angrily. "This place is fucking mental. I swear I'm getting to the bottom of things before we leave."

That's the spirit, Amy thought. *Stubbornness for the win!*

"I'm on board with that," she said.

He let out a frustrated sigh. "At least they seem to be telling the truth about letting people leave if they want to. Let's just go and enjoy the museum. We can worry about the rest later."

She nodded, trying to put the unsettling revelations aside in favor of this opportunity for bonding time. "Sure. How far away is it, anyway?"

The mid-afternoon sun was at their backs as they emerged from the covered entrance. Elijah pointed east, toward the line of green visible in the distance. "It's right on the edge of the Nile floodplain. Barely half a mile."

They headed off, and Amy was immediately grateful for her sunhat even in the slanting afternoon light. Before long, an attractive sandstone building landscaped with palm trees became visible, and less than fifteen minutes later, they were walking up to the shaded portico covering the tall double doors of the entrance.

The place seemed deserted, but for all Amy knew, that was normal. After all, this was a fairly remote area next to a tiny village. From what Elijah had described, Saqqara mostly housed workers who assisted in area digs. The pop-up commune they'd just left probably represented the most excitement this place had seen in millennia.

Elijah grasped the handle of one of the big doors and tugged, but it remained stubbornly closed. He tried the other — same result.

"That's odd," he said.

Amy frowned. A sign next to the doors listed the opening times in English and Arabic, and the place wasn't due to close for two hours. "Did we miss a sign about it being closed for renovations or something?"

"No, we didn't. This is the main entrance — if it's closed, it should say so." Elijah gave a final tug on the doors and stepped back. "Well, then. So much for the first part of my romantic date idea."

She laughed. "Best laid plans, right? We're really close to the village here, aren't we? Why don't we walk to the nearest shop that sells cold soda and ask if they know anything about when it's going to reopen?"

"Might as well." Elijah shrugged and shot her a crooked smile. "But, *soda*, Ames? You know that stuff will rot your teeth, right?"

"Smartass." She poked his arm in retaliation for the old joke. "Which way?"

He caught her hand, lacing their fingers together. "The village is literally right behind the museum. There used to be a sort of general convenience store a few blocks away, when I was here before. Newspapers, snacks, gasoline—that kind of thing."

"Perfect," she said, and let him lead her back to the road abutting the museum parking lot. "You know, it seems kind of odd that the lot is totally empty. Shouldn't there at least be security guards on duty? There's valuable stuff here, after all."

"Yeah, there should be. Who knows, though? They could have walked or biked to work from the village." He gave her hand a squeeze. "We'll see if anyone knows what's up. A lot of the people here speak at least a bit of English or French. It helps them find work at the dig sites."

As they walked into the greener area of Saqqara village, they found it was also surprisingly empty.

"Good lord, this place is like a ghost town. I thought you said people lived here?" Amy asked, surprised.

"Uh… they do?" He posed it like a question, sounding suddenly unsure. "I've never seen it so deserted. Everyone seems to have closed up shop and gone home."

"Okay, that's a little creepy."

He chewed on his lip for a moment. "Let's head toward the store. If anything seems dodgy, we'll go back."

Amy nodded in agreement despite the nagging feeling growing inside her that this whole excursion had been a really bad idea. They held hands as they walked down the empty street. The low brick and stucco buildings lining the pavement on both sides were all closed and sealed up tightly. The sense of foreboding lingered in her chest, becoming more difficult to ignore the longer they walked through the deserted town.

"Hey, look over there!" Amy pointed ahead of them. A few blocks away, a group of people was moving down a side street, heading away from them.

"Finally!" Elijah said with relief. "Huh. Maybe there's a festival or some kind of religious holiday going on today. That could explain why all the shops and the museum are closed."

He studied the pack of people. The ones in front were turning down another side road that would soon take them out of sight.

"Hello there!" he called. Several of the people near the back of the group halted and turned toward them, but did not answer. "*Bonjour?*" he tried next, in hopes that any of them spoke French.

The group stayed still—staring at them, but apparently not interested enough to respond to the greeting. After a few tense moments, they turned and continued on their path, disappearing around the corner of a building.

Amy let out a nervous laugh. "Okay. *That* wasn't unsettling or anything. I guess the creepy Egyptian gang members don't want to be our friends today." She tightened her grip on Elijah's hand. "Can we, uh, leave now, please?"

He continued to stare after the group for a long moment before shaking himself free of his short reverie. "Yeah. Sure thing, Ames. I have no idea what that was about, but we can go check out the mastaba, at least. That way the afternoon won't be a complete write-off. It's within reasonable walking distance, and the roads should be well marked. There's some extraordinary artwork inside the interior chambers, and I brought a flashlight with extra batteries so we won't be in the dark."

"Sounds good. Let's get going—this place is seriously starting to creep me out." Amy didn't relinquish her grip on Elijah's hand. The excitement of sightseeing had worn off, replaced with an irrational certainty that bad things were about to happen. It was ridiculous. So what if the museum and shops were closed? Like Elijah had said, it was probably the Egyptian version of a bank holiday.

In a place as small as this, they must just close up everything and gather someplace centrally located to do their thing. The group they'd seen could have been heading toward the local mosque or community center or whatever, and maybe none of them spoke English or French. They probably didn't want to deal with a couple of clueless foreigners when they were late to... wherever they were going. That was totally normal, right?

The weight in her chest grew heavier.

A stiff, heated breeze gusted past them, carrying with it traces of sand, dry air, and a faint, rotting stench that turned Amy's stomach sour—roadkill, maybe. Faint as it was, she couldn't help but notice. It was probably down to her pregnancy. Hormones seemed to have heightened all her senses recently.

Amy swallowed against the nausea, contemplating the reason why so many people had flocked to the peace enclaves in the first place. She usually felt safe with Elijah—it was one of many things she loved about him. He was tall and intimidating enough that most people wouldn't mess with him. He also gave off a sort of vibe when he was with people that he cared about—one that said no one had better mess with them, or they'd answer to him. She'd jokingly called him her silent bodyguard on more than one occasion.

Right now, she appreciated that feeling more than she could say, but it still wasn't enough to stop the creeping dread rising inside her. She clung to Elijah's hand, following him back to the museum and the desert beyond.

TWELVE

For Menkhef, meditation had never been a particularly effective balm. Perhaps it had something to do with spending millennia aware of his surroundings while being unable to move or interact with the outside world in any way. Perhaps it was because during much of that time—and the centuries that followed—his sanity had been… *intermittent.*

Whatever the case, meditation wasn't a skill he had nearly as much experience with as most people might assume, and it also wasn't a skill that was proving to be of much help to him now.

Ever since coming across the unhappy married couple the previous evening, he had been beset by memories best left forgotten. Normally, he avoided the nightmares of his distant past via the simple expedient of not sleeping. It had always struck him as an elegant solution, despite Eris' occasional pitying looks when the subject came up.

Now, whenever his focus wavered, visions of corrosive black smoke and the screams of loved ones pricked at the edges of his awareness. By rights, after more than four millennia, the look of devastation on Heqab's face as he stood over Nebetta's broken body with a spear pointed at Menkhef's heart should have faded under the ravages of time.

Yes, the demon's sibilant voice had crooned, the dark fog swirling ecstatically around them. *Kill your ruler, insect, and die for it. Kill him and make him mine!*

Menkhef remembered stalking forward until Heqab's spearpoint pricked his chest, blood trickling from the wound in a thick, red rivulet. Bloodlust would have driven him to impale himself on the wooden shaft, if that was what it took to reach the thundering pulse of the man on the other end with his fangs, but the spear clattered to the ground before the point could slide between his ribs. Heqab followed its trajectory an instant later, crumpling to kneel next to the bloody corpse of the woman they'd both loved.

"I cannot kill you," he said, his voice scraped raw by grief and the bitter acid of the fog. "I will not kill you, Menkhef... not even for this. I beg of you—don't make me live with that decision for another moment."

Heqab's right hand had rested on the still place between Nebetta's breasts where her heart had beaten mere moments before—a tender gesture. It was sticky with the blood from her torn throat. Menkhef fell upon the man who had been his closest friend and companion since boyhood, with no thought for anything beyond slaking the terrible, burning thirst that clawed at his body like a thousand ravenous jackals. Warrior that he was, Heqab uttered no cry as Menkhef's fangs sank into salty skin, coppery ambrosia exploding from the jagged tears in his neck.

Menkhef blinked, pulling himself free of the sucking pit of the past... yet again. Around him, the tomb in which the Pharaoh Qahedjet had sealed him swam into focus, the painted carvings blurred by time. An electric bulb threw harsh yellow light around the chamber.

His lips thinned. Fortunately, his mental shields had sprung up out of habit as visions from the past rose inside him. Even so, his preoccupation interfered with his duties toward the souls in his care—both those above in Djoser's pyramid complex, and those hiding with him in the depths of the South Tomb.

Unacceptable.

He was supposed to be watching over them, not wallowing in bitter memory. Perhaps he was not giving the humans enough credit, with his insistence on projecting calm over the area. Yet now that their minds had become receptive to his, he could all too easily flood them with his nightmare of death and loss should his shields slip at an inopportune moment.

Not to mention the effect it would have on his fellow vampires if they realized that he was weakening. He'd been surprised on a very deep level at the way the others had deferred to his leadership after Eris drank from them and used their combined powers to revive him from his state of near death. Even Tré, who for centuries had led and forged the vampires into a cohesive group, merely stepped back and focused his efforts on organizing Menkhef's vision for this place and the others like it around the world.

That was true leadership—a fire in which Menkhef, too, had been forged at a young age. The life of a true leader was steeped in service, not tyranny. A true leader ate only after the lowest of his followers had eaten; slept only once those in his care were safe and protected; never sent another to do something he was not himself willing to do.

In life, he had not always been such a leader to his people… though he had striven to act in their best interests to the extent that his imperfect nature allowed. In undeath, he had hidden behind a cloak of guilt and madness for longer than many civilizations existed—but now, the moment of truth was upon him.

He merely had to avoid being brought low by a bare moment's interaction with a pair of humans, for the sole reason that they reminded him of his lost mates. When he'd touched them, he had allowed himself an instant of foolish hope. But, truly, what were the odds that Heqab and Nebetta would be reborn after four millennia to marry each other and conveniently present themselves before Menkhef, right above the tomb where he'd been buried?

No spark of connection had flared along his nerve endings when he touched them. They were merely a troubled couple, drawn to a faraway place in hopes of finding answers. Perhaps the ones he'd offered would make a difference to them in some small way.

He hoped so. For whatever reason, their brokenness called to his on a very deep level.

A sense of worry not his own brushed the edges of the bond he shared with the other vampires, and he lowered his shields to feel it more clearly. It was Chan Wei Yong, the young man he'd so recently utilized to deliver a message in Kuala Lumpur. Duchess' mate.

I think I need some help here. The worry grew deeper, tinged with a flash of real fear. *It's Marie.*

A quick image of Duchess staring into the distance, her blue eyes glazed and unseeing, flitted across Menkhef's awareness. Now the others' concern joined Chan's. Menkhef rose smoothly from the mat on which he'd been kneeling and swept out of the room, transforming into mist and swirling through the maze of corridors separating his tomb from the quarters Duchess and Chan had claimed.

He arrived to find that Oksana and Mason had beaten him here. The physician knelt at Duchess' side and gently turned her face toward the light. Her eyelids were fluttering now, eyes rolling up until only the whites showed. Menkhef probed at her shields, but her mind was far away, locked down tight.

"How long has she been like this?" Mason asked, peeling back one of her eyelids with a frown.

Chan stood a step away, tension coiled in his spine, his arms crossed tightly in front of him. "I'm not sure. I went to get us a couple of blood bags from the storage unit, and when I got back she was unresponsive. I tried calling her name and shaking her, but I didn't want to get more creative without knowing what the hell's happening to her."

Oksana had hung back, standing close to the door. She, too, looked as tense as a drawn bowstring. "She's in a trance. A deep one. I can't even feel her right now."

Tré's deep voice came across the link. *Do you want the rest of us to come, or stay out from underfoot?*

I will deal with her, Menkhef assured. *Stay alert.*

"Can you jolt her out of it, Snag?" Oksana asked.

Mason glanced up from his examination. "Since you're the most powerful, you might as well try. Medically, I'm at a loss—we didn't cover psychic vampire trances at uni."

Menkhef focused his power and crashed through the reflective wall around Duchess' thoughts. Visions pulsed through the breach, passing from her mind to his. At the same moment Menkhef saw what had pulled Duchess' awareness away from her body, she startled awake, returning to consciousness with a gasp.

"The undead," she whispered. "They're coming."

-o-o-o-

Menkhef's failure to police his own mind had resulted in a breach that could easily have had devastating consequences if Duchess' own well-developed mental powers had not sensed the approach of Bael's undead forces. As the other vampires gathered for a council of war, he cast his awareness outward—beyond the confines of Djoser's complex to the surrounding landscape.

There, as Duchess had seen, lay a dark stain where the inhabitants of the nearby village had been not half a day before. Some of the local residents had already come to the step pyramid upon learning of the vampires' presence. Many others had remained in the town, not wishing to sleep in tents in the desert when their comfortable homes were such a short distance away.

With luck, some would have fled, and others might have escaped Bael's mindless minions by hiding. He mourned those that had been lost with a deep ache of regret and a sense of failure.

"You couldn't have known," Duchess said. She was seated on the mattress she shared with her mate, hugging her drawn-up knees. "There was no way to foresee when and how the Darkness would rally to engage us. We've been here for weeks with no sign of them."

The room was crowded with all eleven vampires inside. It was not yet dusk, but Xander had left some of the trusted humans from his business in London to watch over things aboveground while they discussed strategy. Duchess, Chan, Oksana, and Mason were seated on the room's bare mattress while the others stood at intervals along the walls.

Tré's mate Della crossed her arms. "Does this mean the person you lost is nearby, Snag?" she asked. "Did the undead come because they sensed your proximity to your mate?"

Eris saved him from having to come up with an answer to a question that could not be answered. "Speaking as someone who's spent the last several centuries being regularly trounced at chess, this feels more like an endgame than a vortex of chaos to me."

"It's true that things have been unexpectedly peaceful until now," Tré agreed. "And it's not as though Bael could have failed to notice where we've been holed up."

"Yeah, we're kind of the opposite of a secret at this point," Trynn put in. "Kovac can't have missed all the chatter online about the enclaves."

"Speaking of which," Tré continued, "we need to contact the other locations and warn them that the undead may be moving on them as well."

"Already on it," said Xander. "The satellite link is holding, so I've got Shay on a group Skype with Madame Francine in New Orleans, Mama Lovelie in Haiti,

Trynn's old boss Mandy in Canada, Mason's brother in Singapore, and HelioTeque's VP in London. Between them, they'll disseminate the information to the other locations."

"Which leaves one very important question," Manisha said softly. "What are we going to do when the undead show up here in force?"

"Fight them," Chan said simply, not moving from his position crouched next to Duchess with his arm around her shoulders.

It will not be so simple as that, Menkhef sent, the tiredness that had plagued him for days now returning in force.

"Then what exactly do you suggest, sir?" Chan retorted, his military background and hawkish response to the approaching threat reminding Menkhef for a piercing, painful moment of his long lost and much beloved captain of the guard.

For now, reconnaissance, he said evenly.

Eris crossed his arms, meeting Menkhef's gaze with his gold-flecked one. "But first, a bit of sharing and caring. Della asked you about your mate, and your failure to answer is no longer acceptable. The time for secrets between us is fast coming to a close, old friend."

Menkhef held Eris' eyes for a long moment, reluctantly examining the motivation behind his lack of transparency regarding a subject that affected all of them. Allowing a small measure of the tension in his shoulders to loosen, he met the others' eyes one at a time.

The Council has thirteen members, he reminded them pointedly.

Xander raised an eyebrow. "We're aware," he said, his voice as dry as the dusty landscape above them. "And we thought that Sangye was our odd vampire out, but then he died." Next to him, Manisha gave a minute flinch, and he wrapped her hand in his. "Though, mind you, Duchess told us you'd already said that he wasn't the thirteenth, so…" He trailed off, and blinked. "Oh." He blinked again. "*Oh.* You have got to be *kidding.* Bloody hell, Snag. *Really?* I didn't think you had it in you."

"Where's a decoder ring when you need one?" Della asked. "Someone spell it out, please?"

Eris was still holding Menkhef's gaze, unwavering. "When Bael came for him, our taciturn friend had not one lover, but two."

Della's eyes went wide. "You had a *harem*? Was that even a thing in ancient Egypt?"

I did not have a harem, he replied evenly.

Trynn gave him a shrewd look. "But when Bael came, two people sacrificed for you; not just one. Is that why you're so powerful?"

I do not know, he told her truthfully. *Whatever the case, the point is moot. There is no indication that either of those I lost is nearby. I have made a point to greet all newcomers as they arrive. I have touched all of them, and never felt the flare of the bond that the rest of you have experienced.*

"Do you think the two of them somehow found each other across their reincarnations?" Manisha asked quietly. "Do you believe they're together somewhere?"

He paused for a long moment. *I hope so.*

"All right," Tré said, interrupting the heavy atmosphere. "While this is undoubtedly important information to have, for now we need to focus on the immediate threat."

"I'll shift into wolf form and sneak into the village to see what's happening," Manisha said.

"*We'll* shift into wolf form and sneak into the village to see what's happening," Xander corrected without missing a beat. "You're not going alone, and since we're the only ones who can do it before the sun goes down I suppose it makes sense."

Manisha nodded, not arguing.

"That will leave the complex essentially unguarded for more than an hour until the sun goes down," Chan pointed out. "Xander, can your people topside handle that?"

"Yes," Xander said. His eyes flicked to Snag. "Though it would be useful if you could start pumping out the mental happy juice again. You've been… a bit on edge the past few hours, and it's coming across through your powers, old chap."

Menkhef nodded, well aware that he had shirked his self-appointed responsibilities.

"There's another option," Della said. "Could we fit all of the humans down here in the tunnels? It might be safer for them when…" She swallowed. "When things start to get ugly."

Tré's mouth twitched down. "It might. Or it might trap them with nowhere to retreat."

"If we can't protect them, they'll be dead either way," Chan said bluntly. "I've seen what this creature—this *demon*—can do, and if he gets to them, being in a tunnel isn't going to make a blind bit of difference versus standing on open ground."

"We'll go and get a better idea of what we're up against," Manisha said. "That should help when it comes to planning a response."

Tré nodded, his gaze taking in both her and Xander. "Go. But I want you both to stay out of sight and maintain mental contact the entire time."

"We should inform the humans of the danger," Duchess said. "At least let them know not to leave the compound. We could give them the choice of coming down here or staying aboveground, where they can try to flee if need be."

"Xander," Tré began, "do we know if all the people here are currently accounted for?"

"All but two of them are," Xander said. "Two individuals and a family of four left this morning—

hopefully they all went straight to Cairo and avoided whatever happened in the village. But there was a married couple that left to sightsee at the museum and the local digs a couple of hours ago. They were a fairly distinctive pair—a tall back man and pale, red-haired woman."

A chill of unease washed through Menkhef's chest, and Xander gave him a surprised look.

Search for them while you are out, he managed, pressing down on the irrational reaction.

"We will," Manisha said, her dark eyes shining with concern for the innocent humans.

"Of course," Xander agreed. "I'll brief Shay and the HelioTeque employees about what's happening on our way out." His green eyes sought Menkhef's again. "Remember to think calm thoughts, old man."

It was Tré who answered him. "Thank you, *tovarăș*. Be careful—both of you."

Xander gave his friend a nod and a tight smile before following Manisha out of the crowded room.

THIRTEEN

When nothing else weird or unsettling happened after they left the village and headed back into the desert, Amy gradually started to relax. The Mastaba of Mereruka was every bit as amazing as Elijah had made it sound. It, too, had been deserted, but unlike the museum no effort had been made to bar access to the interior.

The outside might have been a bit underwhelming, but once she'd passed through the entrance to Mereruka's tomb, her breath had exited her lungs in a shocked gasp. The chambers were a landscape of statues and artwork that brought a long-dead world back to vibrant life. By the time they'd made the rounds and left the place, Amy felt like she had slipped back in time to a land both simpler and more complex.

She could practically feel the sway of a fishing boat beneath her feet… hear the clash of battling chariots… the scratch of a scribe's stylus… the low chanting of priests conducting a religious ceremony. Unbidden, the bronze-lit eyes of the mysterious man who'd greeted them at the pyramid complex swam before her vision. His high cheekbones, his straight nose, the strong jut of his chin, and the touch of gray at his temples combined to awaken an ache in her chest that made no sense.

He'd been an impossibility, true. Materializing from a swirl of fog, as out of place in the modern world as could be, but perfectly suited to his timeworn surroundings in the shadow of the step pyramid. Even so, they'd only interacted for a handful of moments. Why should she be any more fixated on him than on the strikingly handsome green-eyed Brit who'd flashed a vampire's fangs at them before wishing them a pleasant afternoon?

And why the hell was she focused on *any* other man right now when this was her chance to finally make things right with the guy she loved more than life itself? Elijah should be the center of her attention today, not some creature who might well drink human blood the same way she guzzled Dr. Pepper. She firmed her grip on Elijah's hand, dragging her attention back to the present and the tumble of stone blocks ahead of them.

Elijah pointed with his free hand. "That's it. The Headless Pyramid. We should have time for a quick look around and still be able to get back before dark."

She tilted her head at the gap in the desert landscape. "Okay… I'll admit this is almost the opposite of what I was expecting."

He chuckled. "I tried to warn you. Missing tooth, remember? This is what happens when you take the pyramid away and leave behind only what was hidden beneath it."

Indeed, what was left was a sunken pit with random piles of stone blocks resting here and there. A couple of areas were fenced off with wooden boards, and as they got closer, she could see that those safety fences surrounded dark holes in the ground.

"What happened to the rest of it?" she asked. It was interesting to be able to see the tunnels and shafts that would normally be hidden from view by the stone superstructure of a pyramid, but it was also a bit disconcerting.

Elijah shrugged. "Good question. My guess is that someone in the distant past wanted to save time and money by reusing the dressed stone for another building project, and they were willing to risk their gods' wrath to do it."

"Makes sense," Amy allowed. "Bronze Age recycling, right?"

He laughed again, a sound Amy didn't hear nearly often enough these days. She let the last of her tension from earlier slip away and just enjoyed the evening. The sun was slipping low in the sky, the temperature growing cooler as it did. She pulled off her sunhat and folded it up, jamming it in her back pocket. The faint breeze felt divine against her sweaty scalp.

They still had many things to face. Elijah's depression, the threat to his job security, her pregnancy... not to mention the small matter of the world falling apart around them. Right now, though, she was in an amazing location with someone she loved, under a wide blue sky turning to shades of scarlet and magenta in the west. She let Elijah guide her down a ramp-like structure made of rubble and packed dirt that led into the excavated area where the pyramid had once been.

They didn't have the equipment to explore the deep shafts leading down to the underground tomb areas, and looking at the dark pits behind the makeshift fences, Amy didn't think she would have wanted to, regardless. But Elijah led her around and pointed out the remnants of the original structure, and she found herself getting wrapped up in his obvious enthusiasm for a subject close to his heart. Whatever else happened, she vowed there and then that she would convince him to start going on digs again.

The lower edge of the brilliant orange sun had just touched the horizon when Elijah stilled beside her, looking back toward the ramp they'd used to enter the site. She frowned and followed his gaze, only to find a group of people dressed in the kind of loose, white clothing favored by the natives approaching.

They were... *shambling*. There was really no other word to use.

"Are those the same people we saw in the village earlier?" she asked slowly.

Elijah's hand tightened around hers, the grip almost painful.

"Ames," he said very deliberately, "please tell me the heat's getting to me and I'm seeing things."

She looked more closely at the figures, a trickle of cold dread twining through her chest until it felt like it might choke her. The people approaching the edge of the pit were gray-skinned, with sunken features. Some of them looked blind, their eyes milky and unseeing. Others had… limbs missing. Grotesque, unhealed injuries that should have been debilitating… if not deadly.

"Elijah." Amy's voice was a hoarse croak as panic slammed into her. "We need to get out of here."

The tendons in Elijah's jaw stood out, flexing in agitation as he threw a quick, searching gaze around their surroundings. Amy did the same, the fine hair at the back of her neck prickling as she confirmed what they both already knew. The… *things*… were blocking their only means out of the excavated pit. Aside from the ramp, everything else was smooth earth and stone, easily eight feet high and with no obvious hand- or footholds.

"*Shit*," Elijah hissed under his breath, moving to place Amy behind him.

"We have to get away from them," Amy whispered, all the sensationalized news reports from Syria flooding into her mind.

Elijah released her hand and stooped to pick up a loose chunk of rock about twice the size of his fist. "See if you can find a place to climb out," he said as the first of the creatures stumbled down the ramp, its fellows following close on its heels. "Maybe you can pile up some rubble to stand on or something. Don't let them get close to you. It doesn't look like they move very fast."

Amy's heart pounded with terror. The breeze wafted a horrible stench of rotting flesh across her face, nearly making her gag.

"Go!" Elijah barked, and she tore her legs free from their paralysis.

It was hopeless—she knew that before she'd even started. They had a clear view of the walls of the pit, and any rubble large enough to be useful for climbing out would also be too heavy to move. Nonetheless, she started a quick, systematic survey of the outer walls, throwing nervous glances over her shoulder every few seconds to check on Elijah.

He was trying to talk to them—backing slowly away from their advance as he spoke to them in English, French, then Spanish. It was obvious even from across the length of the pit that there was nothing behind those dead, filmy eyes, however. Nothing except bloodlust, at any rate. One of the creatures reached a ragged hand toward Elijah, making Amy gasp with fear on his behalf. Elijah knocked it away violently and hurled the large rock he was holding at its head.

The blow was a direct hit, and the thing staggered—only to right itself, unfazed by a blow that should have rendered it unconscious at the very least. Amy swallowed a sob of fear and started praying, still searching feverishly for some means of escape for them.

"Get out however you can and *run*, Amy!" Elijah called. "Don't wait for me!"

Oh hell no, was her only thought as the dozen or so creatures ranged around Elijah and started driving him backward—driving him toward one of the open shafts, with its rickety wooden safety fence. They were *toying with him*.

Ignoring his barked order, she grabbed a couple of heavy rocks and threw them at the advancing creatures, scooping up more as she ran toward them. They were losing the light, making the uneven, rock-strewn footing ridiculously dangerous, but the thought of what might happen if they got too close to Elijah and overwhelmed him lent her feet wings.

"I told you to go!" Elijah shouted as she reached him, real fear audible in his voice for the first time as he clenched his jaw and grabbed the largest rocks he could lift, hurling them at the nearest zombies.

"Not happening," she grated, trying to help him hold back the advancing tide with her smaller missiles.

It wasn't working.

A frantic glance found that they were nearly backed up against the rickety fence with a yawning black chasm beyond. Just then, the eerie, unexpected howl of a wolf broke the tense silence, echoed a moment later by a second. They sounded close.

The creatures surrounding them paused, looking around as if in confusion, their milky eyes scanning the deepening dusk. Two large, gray, four-legged blurs burst into the pit and plowed into the fight, ripping and tearing at anything within reach.

Amy screamed in surprise at the sudden carnage, the sound torn from her throat. The giant wolves continued to attack the undead monsters surrounding her and Elijah, and she wasn't sure whether to be more frightened now, or less. Her answer came a moment later, when one of the zombies armed with a broken length of wood slammed it into the side of Elijah's head, sending him crashing through the flimsy barrier around the excavation shaft.

Amy shrieked *"No!"* and dove after him, grabbing his forearm with both hands as he hung by his fingertips from the dusty edge of the drop-off.

FOURTEEN

The sun was slipping under the horizon above the South Tomb. Menkhef was aware of its passage even without being able to see it—tied as all vampires were to its fiery push and pull. He allowed the knowledge to slide over the surface of his consciousness in favor of concentrating on the blanket of calm that he, Eris, and Duchess were attempting to maintain for the humans above them.

Menkhef cast another part of his mind farther across the desert and the fertile Nile valley east of them, unwilling to make the same mistake twice by focusing too much on the compound. The details were unclear; too much of his attention was taken up by other things to see all that he wished to see. Still, he could tell that the undead were moving… but not *en masse*. Not yet.

Several of the other vampires were here, offering their life force through the bond to help bolster the three with the greatest psychic abilities. Mason had gone to speak with the young human woman who'd been communicating electronically with the other enclaves, but he entered now, his aura grim. Menkhef drew enough of his awareness back to his body to open his eyes and focus on the physician.

"Those creatures are massing around all of the other worldwide locations as well," Mason said, his voice tight with worry. "They're not doing anything aggressive yet—just gathering nearby—like a bloody noose tightening."

"Things are coming to a head," Oksana said, sounding just as tense.

Mason paced, his arms crossed. "We need a better plan than this. None of the other enclaves have vampires to keep the people calm in the face of rampaging zombies. There will be panic."

Tré's deep voice was calm, but sober. "If we don't gain some sort of edge for the final battle, panic will be the least of their problems. There will be a slaughter."

Mason rounded on Tré, his fists clenched. "My brother is running one of those enclaves, Tré. My *baby nieces* are there!"

Enough, Menkhef said calmly, letting power flow through the bond. *The stakes are the same no matter where our loved ones shelter. Bael will not rest until the entire world is broken beneath him. Not unless we defeat him first.*

Mason turned the glare towards him. "Not helping, mate," he said through clenched teeth.

Before the pointless argument could continue, Xander's mental voice cut sharply across the link. *Snag! We found your missing humans. Eleven undead are attacking them at an excavation site half a mile northeast of the complex. We're going in, but we need reinforcements right the fuck now!*

A mental map of the area appeared in Menkhef's head, and he was on his feet instantly, pinning the others with his eyes.

Oksana, Chan — with me, quickly. Tré —

Tré nodded his understanding. "The rest of us will watch over the compound. Go."

Menkhef did not spare a reply, instead transforming into mist between one breath and the next, streaking toward the entrance to the tomb complex and the desert above. He quickly outdistanced the two younger vampires, speeding toward the location of the tomb that had once belonged to the Pharaoh Menkauhor.

The sense of foreboding that had plagued him since learning that the human couple had wandered from the complex returned in force, becoming a nearly all-consuming need to be at the site of the battle *now*. The desert landscape flew past in a blur as he pushed himself to the limit.

He crossed the kilometer or so separating the two sites in mere moments. Ahead, his sense of the undead pricked at his awareness, their twisted wrongness acting like a beacon as sure as any lighthouse. He materialized in the open pit where the battle was taking place just in time to see one of the unnatural creatures strike the dark-skinned human man, sending him crashing through a flimsy barrier and into the open shaft beyond.

The woman screamed and dove after him, all thoughts of defending herself forgotten in her desperation to reach her husband. Menkhef lunged into the midst of the confusion, batting away two of the creatures before they could grasp her. He was aware of Chan and Oksana arriving and joining the fight as Xander and Manisha's wolves continued to tear at whatever attackers they could reach.

Menkhef reached out for the sense of the humans' minds and found the man dazed from a head wound, wavering on the knife's edge of consciousness. He wouldn't be able to pull himself up, and the woman wouldn't be able to hold onto him if his grip on the crumbling edge of the shaft slipped.

Judging that the others could hold back the remaining undead for a few moments, Menkhef dematerialized and swirled into the open shaft. Centering himself, he wrapped his vaporous form around the man's body, transforming it into the same incorporeal form long enough to transport him away from of the excavation area.

Behind them, he heard the woman scream, "Elijah!" as she felt her husband's arm dissolving within her grasp. The noise would draw more of the undead toward her. Menkhef placed the man on the ground a short distance away and swooped back into the pit, swirling past the creatures threatening her and plucking her away to safety as well.

He materialized them next to her husband. She staggered on unsteady legs, her eyes darting wildly from him to the man's crumpled form. *"What—"* she began in a high-pitched, frightened voice.

Menkhef eased her down to a seated position, steadying her with one hand. With the other, he reached to tilt the dark-skinned man's face to one side, intending to examine the wound at his temple. As though a circuit had connected the instant he touched both of them at once, a powerful shock barreled through Menkhef's body, sending him reeling backward to land unceremoniously on his rump in the sand.

-o-o-o-

Menkhef knew his mouth was hanging open. The man—*Heqab, the man was Heqab!*—stirred, and the woman—*oh, my Nebetta!*—stared at him, wide-eyed. Menkhef stared right back at her, dumbfounded.

"My heart," he whispered, voice hoarse from long disuse. His eyes tore away to look at the man. *"My soul. After all this time…"*

Before either of them could respond to such a ridiculous declaration from someone they would consider a complete stranger, Chan jogged up, grim-faced.

"We're too exposed here," he said without preamble, and just like that, the moment snapped like a broken thread.

"Yes," Menkhef agreed, and suddenly he was not acting like the most powerful vampire in existence, but rather like a fool sitting on his backside in the dust, staring at a pair of humans with his jaw hanging slack.

Chan looked between the three of them warily. "Can... these two travel, sir?" he asked slowly, as if to an imbecile.

Through the bond, Menkhef could feel Oksana, Manisha, and Xander's curiosity. He tamped everything down, shaping it into a hard, burning ball, and drew heavy layers of practicality over it.

I will transport Heq—

He cut himself off and tried again. *I will transport the man. The rest of you can escort the woman back on foot. She is uninjured, but shock is a possibility.*

Oksana and the two wolves joined them, a quick visual sweep assuring Menkhef that any injuries they'd sustained while dispatching the undead were superficial. He first met Oksana's eyes, and then Xander's lupine gaze, aware of the picture he must present, but relying on whatever regard they might hold for him after their years of camaraderie.

"Guard her from harm at all costs," he begged them in hoarse tones.

Snag, Xander's mental voice began, but Menkhef cut him off.

"*All costs,*" he repeated.

Xander's furry head cocked in consternation, but Oksana laid a hand on the wolf's shoulder and he subsided.

"We have her," Oksana said. "Go. We'll join you soon."

Relief at the younger vampire's understanding flooded Menkhef, and he nodded. He pushed himself up from the ground on shaking arms and legs, giving the red-haired woman a final, lingering look. Then he gathered up the dazed man at his feet and swirled a cloak of power around them both, disappearing into the rapidly cooling desert night as fast-moving vapor.

FIFTEEN

"Elijah!" Amy cried as her husband disappeared right before her disbelieving eyes. Fresh panic flooded her and she cast around, her eyes sliding wildly over the pretty black woman, the Asian man, and the two wolves — *wolves!* — arrayed around her.

"What. The. *Hell!*" she shouted, each word louder than the last.

The Asian guy frowned, glancing from side to side as though he expected more zombies to appear out of nowhere and jump on them. The wolves looked restless as well. Amy staggered upright from her undignified sprawl in the sand, nearly toppling over when her legs didn't want to hold her.

The woman stepped forward as though to steady her. Amy stumbled backward, out of reach, and locked her knees to stay upright. Her gaze was drawn to the prosthesis where the woman's left foot should be, but she dragged her eyes back up to meet the dark ones looking at her with sympathy.

"*Somebody start talking,*" she grated, glaring at the others and trying to pull her shit together. "Where's my husband? *What's going on?*"

"Your husband is safe," the black woman said quickly, a pleasant Caribbean accent coloring her words. "Our friend is transporting him back to the pyramid complex. It's a much faster method of travel than walking would be."

Amy pressed the heel of her hand into her eye socket, remembering a confused sense of being whisked through the air, out of the excavation pit—her surroundings a formless blur.

"This is insane," she whispered.

The man and the woman exchanged a glance, as though they were somehow conversing silently.

The woman met Amy's eyes again, giving her a smile that was doubtless meant to be reassuring. "It's all a bit complicated, I'm afraid. Right now, we should probably concentrate on getting you back to safety." She indicated the man. "This is Chan Wei Yong. He and the wolves are going to look after you. With this foot of mine, I'd only slow you down walking on sand. It makes more sense for me to do aerial surveillance and make certain nothing nasty is waiting for us between here and there."

"Aerial surveillance?" Amy echoed weakly.

"That's right." The woman smiled again. She truly was lovely, and something in Amy wanted to trust her as she continued, "Chan, have you got this?"

"We're good," Chan said curtly. "Go ahead. We'll stay here until you circle back and give the all-clear."

"Okay," said the woman, looking at Amy again. "Now, don't be afraid…"

With no more warning than that, her slender body warped and changed, reality twisting until a small brown owl with white flecks on its wings stood balanced on one leg in the sand where she had been an instant before.

Amy stared at the bird, her mouth hanging open and her eyes as wide as dinner plates. She watched as the dark owl flapped its wings, launched itself upward, and took off into the dark sky above her head.

"*Oh…* wow." Amy saw the bird swoop ahead of them, scouting for danger. Her mind had gone suddenly numb, as though it was pretty much done with the whole 'accepting input from her senses' thing today. "Yeah, okay. I think I'm really losing it this time." She reached for her ponytail, pulled it out, and ran shaky fingers through her tangled hair.

So… *yeah.*

Experiencing a psychotic break was quite a bit different than how she'd imagined it would be, she mused. It was a lot trippier, for one thing. Because… owls? *Seriously?*

It wasn't just owls, though. She frowned at the huge canines standing guard nearby. "Are those werewolves?" she asked Chan matter-of-factly.

"Sort of," Chan said.

She nodded. "Right. The, uh… the vampire guy back at the compound said not to get him started on werewolves or zombies. I guess I can see why now."

"Xander, you mean?" Chan pointed to one of the great beasts. "That's him, actually. Technically, he's a vampire who got bitten by a werewolf."

The other wolf growled.

"Oops, sorry." Chan moved his pointing finger. "*That's* him. I have kind of a hard time telling them apart until he growls at me. The other one is Manisha. She's a werewolf who got bitten by a vampire. Like Oksana said, it's… a bit complicated."

Amy stared at them, feeling a bit dizzy now as her adrenaline started to crash. "Uh-huh. I can see that."

Chan glanced up at the owl, which had circled back to them. "It looks like the way ahead is clear. Let's get you back to your husband."

With those words, Amy's fragile shell of calm shattered, and she wavered on her feet. Chan's hand darted out and steadied her by the upper arm.

"Whoa… you sure you're all right?" he asked.

"No," she said faintly.

He nodded, his features set in an expression of understanding under the silver light of the rising moon. "Okay, that's fair enough. But can you walk?"

"Yes." If it meant she could get to wherever the impossible pharaoh guy had taken Elijah, she'd fucking walk if it killed her.

"Let's go, then." Chan didn't let go of her arm, though his sharp eyes scanned the surroundings as he led her away from the grisly excavation site. "This place won't stay secure forever."

The wolves flanked them, the one on her left walking close enough that its fur brushed her leg occasionally. It was beautiful, with a silver pelt and black-tipped ears. Her free hand landed on the thick fur of its shoulders before she realized she'd reached out to touch. Gold-brown eyes flicked up to meet hers with the same soul-deep sadness Amy had seen in Manisha's on the day they'd arrived in Egypt. She caught her breath, but the animal had already returned to scanning the desert around them for threats.

The stench of rotting corpses still swirled around her. It was in her hair, on her clothes. She tried putting it out of her mind, but that was impossible.

She glanced at Chan, needing distraction. "Are you a vampire too, then?"

"Yes," Chan answered as they continued along the dusty road leading to the compound.

"So, can you turn into an owl?"

"Yes."

"And that weird… vapor thing? Can you do that?"

"Yes."

"In that case, if you're worried about more zombies coming, shouldn't we go back that way instead of walking?"

He shot her an inscrutable look. "Believe me, I would if I could. But apparently Menkhef is the only vampire powerful enough to transport other living beings that way. I can barely manage to keep track of my clothes and small inanimate objects."

"So he's that most powerful vampire. Got it."

She wondered why some of them called him Snag and some of the called him Menkhef. Menkhef certainly sounded like a good name for a vampire that looked like he should have his own pyramid somewhere.

Snag… not so much.

For the remainder of the journey, Amy kept her questions to herself. They spent the next twenty minutes or so trudging through the sandy desert. At least, Amy trudged. Chan strode with graceful, confident strides, and the wolves padded over the sand on silent paws. Amy didn't see much of the owl—just the occasional dark silhouette in the sky ahead of them.

She let out a silent breath of relief when they arrived at the grand entrance to the step pyramid complex. Amy followed Chan as he led her to what Elijah had called the South Tomb. They ascended a set of stone steps leading to the top of the wall studded with stone cobra heads, and then down into the catacombs below.

At first, Amy couldn't help but shiver at the idea of entering that dark world. She was surprised to find LED bulbs strung overhead, pushing back the stifling darkness to reveal intricate carvings and paintings on the walls. If she hadn't been a complete wreck over Elijah and the horror of the last hour, she might have taken a moment to appreciate them. As it was, her thoughts raced in frantic circles. Was Elijah okay? Could she trust these people?

Because… they weren't people. They were vampires, and werewolves, and apparently fucking *zombies* existed and were trying to kill them all. She was still on the fence about the whole 'psychotic break' thing, not least because it was a lot less scary than believing what she'd seen was real.

And then there was the man. The one who had tilted her world on its axis with a handful of silent words, barely more than a day ago. He'd looked straight at her after rescuing them from certain death and called her his heart; then he'd looked at Elijah and called him his soul. What did that mean? His eyes, when he'd said those things...

She shivered again. He'd touched them both, and a jolt of pure power ran through her. She'd never felt anything remotely like it in her life.

"Here we are," Chan said. He stood at the entrance of a chamber and ushered her inside.

It was surprisingly large. She barely had a chance to take in that fact, along with the basic medical setup and the presence of other people, before the figure on the cot in the center of the room grabbed her attention.

"*Elijah!*" She rushed to his side, tears welling up in her eyes.

A sandy-haired man with slate blue eyes stood beside the cot. He was placing an IV needle in Elijah's vein, the flexible plastic tube attached to a hanging bag of fluid.

Red fluid.

"Is that... blood?" Amy tensed, her protective instincts rushing to the fore. "What are you *doing*? He hasn't lost any blood, and you don't even know his blood type!"

The man gave Amy a reassuring look that was wholly ineffective. "In this particular case," he said in a pronounced Australian accent, "the only thing I need to know about his blood type is that it's human."

He straightened from the IV as red started flowing through the long tube toward Elijah's arm. "I'm Dr. Mason Walker. Your husband suffered a severe head wound, but it just so happens, you're in luck. You happened to be in the same neighborhood as a bunch of vampires."

"What are you *talking about*?" Amy demanded, her muscles tense as she debated whether to spring forward and drag the needle out of her husband's vein.

Just as she decided to do it, the supposed doctor's eyes flared with an inner light, and her brain went foggy.

"Give me a few moments to explain the situation," the doctor said calmly, and Amy felt that calm spread through her as well. "I'm sorry to influence you like this, but I promise it's only for a minute, and only to ensure that your husband gets the care he needs as quickly as possible."

"What's… going on?" she asked, much more reasonably this time. "I don't understand."

"Vampire blood has extraordinary healing properties in humans," the man told her, still in the same soothing voice. "Your husband took a bad blow to the skull and was showing signs of bleeding on the brain. In human medicine, that kind of thing takes some serious medical firepower to treat that I don't have access to out here, but I do have access to something even better."

"Vampire blood?" Amy echoed blankly, feeling on some level like she should be way more freaked out right now than she was.

"That's right," the doctor said. He gestured to a corner, and Amy was surprised to see their rescuer skulking like a shadow, unmoving and silent. "Menkhef here donated a pint for him that will have him as good as new in no time. Look. You'll be able to see as it starts working."

Amy followed his pointing finger and gulped. The side of Elijah's head was a mess of swelling and bruising, his eyes swollen shut and his features on that side practically unrecognizable. A wash of gray encroached on the edges of her vision as she realized that the blow might easily have killed him.

"Easy," the doctor told her, and another wave of calm pushed back on the hysteria. "Look closer."

She swallowed hard and looked closer. As she watched, the swelling seemed to recede, the progress slow but detectable to the naked eye.

"Just give his body a bit of time to repair itself," the blue-eyed man continued. "He'll be fine. My word on it."

SIXTEEN

Elijah struggled to move—to regain awareness of his surroundings and *wake the hell up.* He needed to make sure Amy was all right. Something really, really bad had happened, and then something… else… had happened, and now he couldn't seem to make his brain function, much less the rest of his body.

For a few moments, it had felt like he was moving, a sweeping feeling of vertigo joining the pounding ache in his head and the sense of being stuffed to the gills with cotton wool. Then the dizzy sensation of flying—or maybe falling—subsided. Without even that much feedback from the outside world, he lost his grip on anything resembling consciousness. Between one moment and the next, disorientation became black nothingness—a smooth, untouched canvas to act as the backdrop for strange fever dreams.

-o-o-o-

Heqab looked up as the skinny messenger boy scurried through the confusion of sparring military recruits. His small body darted between the larger, heavily muscled ones raising clouds of dust in the late afternoon light as they clashed in simulated battle. He skidded to a halt in front of Heqab, breathless, his small chest rising and falling rapidly.

"Captain!" the child piped in a high, clear voice. "The nomarch orders that you join him at the palace for a private meeting when the sun touches the trees over the western bank of the Nile!"

Heqab covered a sigh, a flash of irritation furrowing his brow before he smoothed it. He had much to do today, and would have preferred not to waste the last of the precious daylight in some endless strategy meeting with Menkhef that could have been scheduled later in the evening. Sometimes, he felt that the ruler of the Nome of the Northern Sycamore was inclined to take advantage of their boyhood friendship, presuming on his time in a way that he would not have done with an older and more experienced commander.

Or… it might have had more to do with the fact that Heqab folded like a sodden rag to every single such request. His old friend had not ascended to the governorship of a prefecture without being both charismatic and persuasive.

"Very well," he told the boy, resignation coloring his tone. "Tell the nomarch that I will join him at the appointed time."

The messenger nodded, wide-eyed, and hared off again—avoiding the training soldiers as deftly as he'd done on the way in. Heqab's eyes followed him for a few moments, thinking the lad might be useful in the infantry in a few years.

Trying not to let speculation about the subject of the upcoming meeting distract him, he turned his attention back to the task at hand—teaching a dozen raw conscripts how to string a bow without putting their own eyes out during the process. Or putting out anyone else's eyes, for that matter.

Menkhef probably wanted to talk more about the rumblings from the pharaoh's court, whispers that Qahedjet intended to consolidate his power over the dozens of small administrative districts running up and down the length of the Nile. The pharaoh had always been the ultimate ruler in the region—a god made flesh—but in practice, the nomarchs had been seizing more local power for themselves for many years now.

Heqab dragged his focus back to the present just in time to stop one of the would-be archers from using a knot to secure his bowstring that would have slipped loose the first time he tried to nock an arrow. He told himself firmly that he would find out what Menkhef considered so important soon enough.

The afternoon slipped by in a haze of heat and blazing sunlight. At intervals, Heqab shaded his eyes as he gauged the progress of Ra's chariot across the sky. As it approached the western horizon, he wrapped up the day's training and headed off for his summons. He was sweaty and covered in dust, but he decided not to bathe before presenting himself at the palace.

Let that small act of defiance communicate my opinion on having my workday cut short, he thought dryly. It wasn't as though Menkhef would take any great offense over the minor slight from his childhood companion. Frankly, he'd probably find it amusing.

Heqab stalked up to the palace entrance, where he was met by a servant who bowed low and immediately ushered him toward the central courtyard. That was a relief, at least—the day had been a brutally hot one, and the last thing Heqab needed was to be stuck in a stuffy stone room, baking like a clay pot in an oven. The servant indicated the table set in the middle of the shady space, and bowed again before withdrawing.

Heqab followed the direction of the gesture with his eyes. He halted abruptly, surprise and another emotion he didn't care to examine freezing him momentarily in place. Three chairs were ranged around the low table, which was piled high with fruit, bread, meat, and cheese. It wasn't the feast that gave him pause, however; it was the woman seated in front of it with Menkhef.

Nebetta. The nomarch's consort.

The woman Heqab had loved since he was barely old enough to wield a spear.

Menkhef swirled his goblet of wine, drawing Heqab's attention away from dangerous territory. The nomarch raised a tolerant eyebrow, his lips twitching faintly with what might have been amusement.

"I wasn't aware that we had commissioned a new statue for the entrance of the courtyard," he said mildly, still with that faint teasing gleam in his eye.

Heqab felt blood rise to his face, relieved that his dark skin hid the flush. He forced himself forward, cursing his callow reaction to Nebetta's unexpected presence.

"And I wasn't aware that you would be providing enough food for the entire regiment, Your Excellence," he retorted. "I didn't realize I was supposed to invite them along."

The smile tugging at Menkhef's lip grew wider for a moment before he hid it behind the mask of a ruler. Heqab approached the table and stopped a few steps away, bowing at the waist.

"My queen," he said respectfully, all hints of banter gone.

"Captain," she replied in her warm, honeyed voice, making no attempt to hide her pleasure at his presence. "Thank you for coming on such short notice."

"I wouldn't dream of ignoring such a summons," he said immediately.

In truth, Nebetta would not have been considered a queen by most in the Kingdom of Egypt. She was the wife of a nomarch—an administrative governor. While all three of them hailed from noble families, they were hardly royalty in the pharaoh's eyes. In both Menkhef and Heqab's eyes, however, Nebetta was royalty. For Menkhef, it was because he intended to establish his own dynasty with her in the Land of the Northern Sycamore —a dynasty to rival the pharaoh's. For Heqab, it was because she had always ruled his heart from afar.

Many times over the past few years, Heqab had wondered at the fact that his poorly hidden yearning for the nomarch's consort had not resulted in his banishment from the land he called home. As far as he could tell, it hadn't even put strain on the friendship that bound him to his ruler—for all that their friendship was now hidden under the duties of soldier and leader.

Perhaps it was because Heqab had never allowed his behavior to become unseemly. Perhaps it was because he loved Menkhef, too, and Menkhef knew it. As lads, they'd been joined at the hip, close enough in station not to raise eyebrows with their friendship, but both acutely aware of the paths already laid out for their lives.

As soon as Menkhef had reached his majority and attained the position of regional governor, it became clear that Nebetta would be his and not Heqab's. He'd never once rubbed Heqab's face in that knowledge, and in some ways it had been easier to watch her marry someone Heqab cared for so dearly. Especially since Heqab knew that Menkhef loved her with every bit as much passion as he did.

Heqab could not overstate his gratitude toward Menkhef for allowing his unrequited longing to remain in the shadows, unremarked—for bringing it into the open would surely ruin him

"Sit, old friend," Menkhef said, gesturing to the empty seat at the table. Gracious, as always, and with a look in his dark eyes that said he knew something Heqab didn't.

Heqab sat. "Thank you. Now, what did you wish to speak with me about?"

"Eat first," Menkhef insisted, waving a lazy hand at the food. "I may not have the entire army here to deal with this embarrassing amount of food, but that only means I need to make full use of the one soldier I do have."

Heqab flickered an eyebrow that communicated his opinion of being put off in such a way, but he started loading fruit and cheese onto a copper dish without comment. It had been a trying day even if it had also been an abbreviated one, and he hadn't eaten anything since a chunk of unleavened bread dipped in oil late that morning.

Nebetta kept up a stream of pleasant conversation on light subjects as they ate, putting him at ease like she always did. Menkhef was his usual charming but inscrutable self, and before Heqab knew it, his stomach was full, his wine glass was empty, and he was far too sated and relaxed to want to discuss military strategy or — gods forbid — political strategy.

The servant who had shown him in returned with two others to clear away the detritus of the meal. Menkhef halted the young man with a glance and said, "Take the food back to the kitchens and put it away. Then dismiss everyone for the evening, yourself included, Sef. I desire to speak to the captain in private."

"Yes, Your Excellence," the servant said immediately. "I will see to it at once."

Heqab frowned, curiosity rising to war with his pleasant state of drowsiness. The other two continued to chat about nothing for a few more minutes, until Sef returned and bowed to the nomarch.

"The others are leaving now," he said. "I will follow and secure the door on my way out."

"Thank you," Menkhef said calmly, and waited until the sound of fading footsteps disappeared, leaving the building in eerie silence as the light faded into dusk above the courtyard.

Heqab expected Menkhef to ask Nebetta to leave as well, but he made no move to do so. Unease began to war with the curiosity running rife inside his mind. Unable to contain himself any longer, Heqab turned to his ruler. "Forgive me," he said, "but I had assumed you wished to speak about the rumors coming from the pharaoh's court. Was I mistaken?"

Menkhef smiled, but Heqab thought he could detect a hint of tension in the expression. "In a manner of speaking, you are correct," he said cryptically. "We do wish to speak with you about the implications of Qahedjet's power grab, but not in a... military capacity."

The 'we' made Heqab's brow furrow in confusion. As far as he knew, Nebetta had never involved herself in her husband's political machinations. Not in any sort of active role.

"I... don't understand, Your Excellence," he hazarded, looking between them.

Menkhef's eyes flicked to Nebetta for a moment, the small physical manifestation of nervousness doing more to disquiet Heqab than anything that had come before. Menkhef did not display uncertainty. He decided to do something and did it without a second thought. To Heqab's further shock, it was Nebetta who spoke next, rather than her husband.

"Menkhef and I wish to establish a ruling line for this land," she said in her low, decadent voice. "The pharaoh does not know what the land of the Northern Sycamore needs. Nor does he much care. The people need their own rulers, and without a dynasty in place, there will be too much uncertainty about the future."

Heqab knew this already. He looked between the two of them, feeling like someone had thrown him into the Nile without a rope during the spring floods.

"And... you wish to discuss some aspect of this with me?" he asked.

Nebetta blinked her large eyes. "I have not yet fallen pregnant."

The sense of being buffeted by an unpredictable current grew stronger, and he floundered for any sort of suitable response. "You are young yet, my queen. It signifies nothing—"

"It signifies that after more than five years of marriage, I have been unable to give my queen a child," Menkhef said evenly, and Heqab's attention swung back to him.

It took him even longer to formulate a reply to that. "You… are the nomarch, Menkhef. No one would protest if you took a second wife to bear you children."

He had to force himself not to look back at Nebetta, unsure if she would be hurt by the suggestion. It was true that polygamy wasn't common in Egypt, but it wasn't totally unheard of among the upper classes. In a case like this, it wouldn't raise eyebrows, even though something inside Heqab burned on Nebetta's behalf at the implication that she somehow wasn't good enough.

"It is true," Menkhef agreed, still in that calm, even tone. "No one would protest. However, all of the female members of Nebetta's family old enough to do so have borne several healthy babes in short order, while my mother only ever birthed me… and died while doing so. A second wife will no more be able to provide us with a child than Nebetta has been able to… if the problem lies with me.

Heqab stared at him, dumbfounded. Menkhef blinked at him.

"Have I shocked you?" His voice grew dry. "Your mouth is hanging open in a thoroughly unappealing manner, Captain."

He snapped it shut, and considered before answering, "Yes. You've shocked me. In twenty-six years of life, I have never heard a man admit that his wife's failure to bear children might be his fault."

Menkhef shrugged. "Then those men are fools. I care nothing for the perceived slight to my manhood. All that interests me is solving the problem. My wife comes from a family of fertile mother-goddesses, and I come from scorched and barren earth. It seems clear enough."

"But why tell me this?" Heqab asked, at an utter loss as to why he was even here. "In what way can I possibly help with this situation? I'm a *soldier*, Menkhef."

"You love her," Menkhef said simply, and Heqab's thoughts solidified into marble.

A moment later, there was a loud clatter, and he realized he'd leapt to his feet, sending his chair crashing to the ground behind him. He pointed a shaking finger at the nomarch.

"I have never once shown the least impropriety toward our queen, Menkhef," he ground out, anger and mortification flooding him at having his scandalous secret dragged into the open without warning. Why would Menkhef lull him into a sense of security for *years*, only to betray him like this in front of *Nebetta herself*? "I have never wavered in my loyalty to you—not *once*! Yet you would bring me here to… *what*? Accuse me?"

"Husband." Nebetta's soft voice cut through Heqab's distress. "You are making a terrible mess of this."

Heqab's frantic gaze flew to her, his chest heaving as wildly as the little messenger boy's had been earlier. He had a terrible feeling that his emotions were as clear in his eyes as if a scribe had inked them on papyrus for the world to see.

"Why did you call me here?" he whispered, not even sure which one of them he was addressing anymore.

"You love Nebetta," Menkhef said again, still infuriatingly calm. "You also love me. Your allegiance has never been in question, old friend. We have watched for years as you put aside your feelings in the name of duty and loyalty. And for that, we love you back with equal ferocity."

Heqab fumbled behind him for the overturned chair and righted it so that he could half-fall into it. "*I don't understand what you're saying to me.*"

Nebetta rose, graceful and regal as always, circling the table to stand next to him. She took his right hand in both of hers and lifted it to her cheek. "Before my beloved Menkhef is forced to take a second wife, I would have you as a second husband."

Heqab looked up at her with a lifetime's worth of longing, his palm burning where it touched the smooth silk of her flawless golden skin.

"It doesn't work that way," he whispered hoarsely.

"I cannot offer you public acknowledgement," Menkhef said quietly. He hadn't moved, but his eyes watched them both with aching fondness. "I cannot offer you true fatherhood in the eyes of the people, should Nebetta bear children. But, on my life, I swear that should you accept our plea and join us in our bed, you will always be welcome there. I will name you my family's personal guard rather than my army's captain, and you will have access to your children day and night as their protector."

Something caught in Heqab's chest, a choked noise emerging as he pictured children with Nebetta's beautiful eyes laughing and shrieking with joy as he taught them to shoot a bow and arrow or hunt with a spear.

"I…" he began unsteadily. "I don't…"

His hand was shaking where it rested against Nebetta's cheek, and so was the rest of him. Menkhef rose smoothly from his chair, approaching him from the other side.

"Don't make your choice tonight. Give us your answer only when you are ready, old friend," he said.

A hand closed around the back of Heqab's neck, and Menkhef pulled him into an embrace. Heqab felt himself caught between the two them. Held there, wordless, his heart lurching wildly inside his chest.

"Know that you are the only one I would ever trust with this, Heqab," Menkhef continued. "The only one I would ever ask. We don't seek this solution at any price. Only at your pleasure."

-o-o-o-

Much later, Heqab lay alone in his hut on his straw-stuffed sleeping pad, staring into the darkness at the thatched roof above him. Menkhef had told him not to make his choice tonight, but in reality, there was no choice at all. His oldest friend had just asked him to claim the woman he'd loved as long as he could remember, and give her children to rule a kingdom.

What answer could there possibly be, besides *yes*?

SEVENTEEN

"**I** don't care if the bruising is going down! This is still *completely fucking insane*! He *needs* to get a CT scan, and he needs to be seen by specialists!"

Elijah winced as the outside world intruded on his dreams, Amy's shrill and slightly hysterical sounding words jolting him back to the present.

"He really doesn't, you know," said an unfamiliar male voice.

Wait. That was weird. What the hell was Hugh Jackman doing here?

He tried to pry sticky eyelids apart, but it was as though he'd forgotten how. It felt like there were a whole lot of things he should be worrying about... but, as ever, when Amy was upset, everything else faded to unimportance.

"Ames?" he croaked, finally managing to peel one eyelid open.

All sound in the area ceased, and then Amy cried, "*Elijah!*" and practically flung herself into his arms. He lay flat on his back, holding her against his chest as she sobbed, and tried to remember how to make his brain cells work.

"Are you all right?" she choked out after a few moments. "Are you in pain?"

He paused, taking stock. A hazy vision of a creature from his darkest nightmares swinging a heavy wooden board at his head flickered before his eyes... a sound, dull, but deafening as it connected, and then, confusion.

Elijah lifted a hand from Amy's shoulders to gingerly prod at the side of his skull. The skin felt faintly tender and stretched, like an old bruise, nearly healed. "Not… really?" he hazarded, because while it didn't in fact hurt, something told him it really, really should have.

"Give it another few minutes, mate," said Hugh Jackman. "You'll be good as new, promise."

He blinked, managing to get both eyes working this time. He was on a cot in a dimly lit room with stone walls. It was cool, but the atmosphere was stuffy in a way that was familiar from his days working in subterranean dig sites.

"Are we underground?" he asked, more memories starting to trickle in.

"Yes," Amy said, her voice more controlled and less terrified now. "We're under the… South Tomb? Is that right?"

"That's correct," Hugh Jackman confirmed.

Elijah dragged his eyes from Amy to the source of the Australian accent. Not Hugh Jackman after all, but a well-built, sandy-haired man with blue eyes and a professional demeanor. "What happened?" he asked. "How did we get here?"

"What's the last thing you remember?" the Aussie asked.

Elijah frowned, and couldn't even feel the bruising on his head this time. "There was… a courtyard, and… a table, piled high with food. Menkhef wanted to see me—"

A sharp indrawn breath came from the shadows at the back of the room, out of Elijah's line of sight.

Amy's brows drew together in worry. "Elijah? What are you talking about?"

He blinked, the memory sliding away as more pressing images crowded in. Saqqara. The Imhotep Museum. The group in the village. The Headless Pyramid—

"The zombies. Holy shit. Amy, are you all right?" His eyes flew to her, searching for injuries.

"I think it's coming back to him now," said a dry British voice. He recognized the man who'd spoken to them when they left the compound, lounging by the doorway with his arms crossed. The Indian woman, Manisha, stood next to him, watching Elijah with interest.

"I'm okay," Amy reassured. "Just a few scrapes and a wrenched shoulder."

"Manisha. Xander," said the Australian. "Go let the others know he's awake, and that everyone needs to bugger off for a bit."

"Come on, love," said the Englishman. "It appears our presence is surplus to requirements."

"We'll let them know, Mason," Manisha said.

When they were gone, the Australian gestured Amy back so that he could get at Elijah's arm. Elijah hadn't even noticed the I.V., he'd been so wrapped up in what was going on around him. It led to an empty bag hanging nearby, traces of red visible inside.

"Is that a blood transfusion?" he asked, wondering how badly he'd been hurt. Surely it couldn't have been too awful since he felt pretty darned good right now, all things considered.

"It's a *vampire* blood transfusion," Amy said tightly, and pressed her lips together in an unhappy line.

Unease trickled down Elijah's spine. "*Excuse me?*"

"From what I understand, you were unconscious for most of the interesting parts of Chan and Oksana's explanations," the man name Mason observed mildly. "But, yes, we're vampires. I'm also a doctor, as it happens, and I gave you a pint of Menkhef's blood to heal you. You suffered serious head trauma and it was the safest way of ensuring there was no permanent damage. Vampire blood is basically a miracle cure for humans."

Menkhef. There was that name again.

But he needed to prioritize. There were too many crazy assertions being thrown around, and while his head might not be spinning from a concussion, it was whirling nonetheless. "Amy...?"

Amy perched on the edge of his cot. "I don't know what to tell you, Elijah. You remember the zombies. Do you remember the wolves showing up?"

Her words brought images in their wake, and feelings, too. The sudden realization that what he had thought was reality was only a comforting illusion. The absolute fear upon realizing that Amy's life was in danger and he wasn't strong enough to protect her.

"*I told you to run,*" he accused in a hoarse tone.

She shrugged and took his hand between both of hers. "Yeah, sorry. That was never going to happen. Not unless you ran with me." She cleared her throat, trying to bring her emotions under control. "Anyway, the wolves showed up and started tearing into those... *things*... attacking us. A few minutes later, three more people appeared and joined the fight. They say they're vampires, and I believe them, Elijah. The things I saw —"

"Amy," he said softly.

She shook her head. "One of the creatures hit you, and you tumbled into an open excavation shaft. The man—the one we met that first night—he rescued you and flew you to safety somehow. Then he came back for me. The vampires fought off the zombie things, and he flew you to safety while the rest of us followed on foot."

Elijah squeezed her fingers as she cradled his hand in hers. "As long as you're safe."

She squeezed back. "Your head... that thing hit you so hard. I was afraid you'd die." Her voice quavered, and she swallowed hard, steadying it. "They said their blood could heal you, and almost as soon as the IV was attached, the swelling started to go down. I tried to argue that you still needed proper medical care... and then you woke up. You're sure you're okay now?"

It was… one hell of a story. But to discount it completely would be to call Amy a liar, and Amy *wasn't* a liar. He touched his head again with his free hand. It felt completely normal now. With a deep breath, Elijah swung carefully into a sitting position, not releasing his grip on Amy.

"Yeah," he said, in some surprise. "I actually feel… fine. A bit thirsty, I guess."

"Not for blood, I hope?" Amy joked weakly.

The Australian chuckled. "It doesn't really work that way. To become a vampire, you have to be drained to the edge of death before drinking vampire blood. That's…" His eyes slid to the shadows at the back of the room. "… a conversation for another time."

Both Elijah and Amy followed his gaze in time to see a tall figure step into the light. Elijah's breath caught, dream images once more blurring with reality as that face from the distant past emerged into view. He couldn't look away, even when the doctor spoke again.

"You should be fine now," he said, "but I'd still like you to take it easy for a few hours. Get something to eat and drink. I'd tell you to sleep, but… I'm afraid that may not be in the cards for any of us. I'll leave you to speak with Menkhef, but if you need me, he can call for me, or you can. Just give a yell. I'll be nearby."

The doctor tidied the medical equipment out of the way and paused, shooting the mysterious figure in the corner what looked like a significant glance before leaving the three of them alone. Silence reigned for several moments as Elijah tried to reconcile the conflicting images whirling inside his mind.

Menkhef, brushing a strand of Amy's hair back as he told them not to let the Darkness steal away their Light.

Menkhef, rising from the remains of an ancient Egyptian feast to embrace him like a brother after granting him his fondest wish.

Menkhef, leaning over him in the desert, his worried face blurring beneath the dizzying pain of a concussion.

Menkhef, reclining on a carved wooden divan in an ancient courtyard, his head thrown back in ecstasy as the woman they both loved writhed between them, crying out as she came.

Elijah's heart kicked hard, like a surprised mule driving its heels repeatedly into his chest. Beside him, Amy stiffened. Her green eyes narrowed, pinning the man who now haunted both Elijah's dreams and his waking world.

"Explain," she demanded, nearly spitting the word. *"Explain all of this to us."*

Menkhef did not move closer; he merely inclined his head, his chin rising.

"I will," he promised. "And I am sorry for what you will learn."

EIGHTEEN

Amy gripped Elijah's hand like a lifeline, glaring at the vampire who had saved them only to disappear into the shadows immediately afterward without a word of explanation. She didn't know why she was suddenly so angry—at herself, at the vampires running this place, at Shay and her cheerful acceptance of the madness around them...

At Elijah, for trying to convince her to leave him behind during the attack. At the world, for not making sense. Okay, maybe she did know why she was angry. But, *by god*, she was finished with this shit. She was getting answers, and she was damned well getting them *now*.

"Explain," she spat. "*Explain all of this to us.*"

Elijah was frozen next to her, though she could feel his pulse galloping. The vampire barely moved, only regarding them with dark eyes.

"I will," he promised. "And I am sorry for what you will learn."

He was so... damned... *beautiful*, standing there like some ancient work of art, and it only made her angrier. How dare he look so fucking tragic as he was promising to explain things, like he knew the story they'd been thrust into wouldn't have a happy ending. She opened her mouth to snap, *Stop apologizing and start making sense!*—

And then a freight train slammed into her thoughts and steamrolled her into the ground.

A confused tangle of images and feelings plowed into her consciousness in no particular order. *So many.* Far too many to belong to a single person. Far too many to fit inside her brain at once. Her skull would crack under the pressure any second now, four thousand years of history spilling onto the dusty stone floor…

The pressure eased, another mind surrounding hers—helping her sort through the swirling tornado of memories and drag them into some kind of coherent narrative.

She was inside Menkhef's memories. The tornado was his life, unfolding before her. She watched him grow up in an ancient land, loving Heqab as a brother and falling in love with Nebetta. *Me*, she thought. *That's me! I remember those dreams… I remember this place! Heqab… Elijah… I remember you now!*

She watched as Menkhef married Nebetta. Watched him mourn their lack of children as the years went by. Until one day, he made a suggestion and Nebetta's eyes lit up with hope, her overflowing love nearly spilling from her skin, it was so radiant. Soon after, they had Heqab with them, and Nebetta bore her two lovers a girl and a boy—perfect and beautiful and *theirs.*

For more than ten years, Menkhef lived a life far better than any mortal deserved, watching his family grow and his land prosper. Until one day, a dark evil descended on the palace and turned him into a ravening monster. He killed Nebetta and when her blood wasn't enough, he killed Heqab, too. It still wasn't enough, but the priests and the warriors came, casting spells and tangling him in heavy fishing nets until he was too weakened and injured to get free.

Then, the priests ordered him dragged before his hated enemy, the Pharaoh Qahedjet, and turned him over as a gift to prevent war. Qahedjet kept him in a stone cell and forced him to fight animals in the arena. Despite the burning thirst for blood, he refused to drink from humans, surviving on animal blood until even that comfort was taken away. Eventually, too weakened from starvation to heal from his injuries, he fell into a coma and Qahedjet had him entombed below Djoser's pyramid.

The millennia that followed were slow torture... until one day, the sound of tools chipping away at stone gave way to a shaft of dusty torchlight and the first breath of fresh air to enter the small chamber since the pharaoh's stonemasons had sealed it.

There you are, came a pleasant voice, echoing in their thoughts. *I thought I heard you whispering to me. Looks like I'm not alone after all... though I'll confess I feel a bit odd talking to a petrified mummy. Let me figure out how to get you out of this place, and we'll go from there.*

The grave robber's name was Eris, and he had the patience of Osiris. After decades of drinking Eris' blood a few drops at a time, Amy watched Menkhef grow strong enough to finally rise from his bier... though he was not precisely sane. Happily, Eris did not seem particularly bothered by the fact that he was mad, and the centuries passed much more quickly with company.

Especially once chess was invented.

More time passed, and they found other creatures like themselves—all damaged and bleeding inside, cursed to replenish themselves by making the humans bleed in turn. Still, Menkhef refused to feed from any but Eris, and even then, only seldom. Eris shared his blood willingly enough, but Menkhef knew he became complicit in Eris' need to hunt humans, each and every time he drank from him.

The others were obsessed with discovering why the Darkness had raped them and left them cursed to exist in a shadowy half-life. Eventually, Eris discovered an ancient prophecy regarding a council composed of thirteen of the demon Bael's greatest failures that would rise up to defeat him. They waited and watched, but no more vampires appeared, and together they were only six, not thirteen.

Still, Menkhef refused to feed more than was absolutely necessary, but even on the verge of constant starvation, his powers grew year by year. Eventually, the vampires found Della—the reincarnation of the woman who had sacrificed herself to save one of their number from Bael's damnation.

And Menkhef alone realized what the Council of Thirteen represented. Six vampires. Seven reincarnated mates. The key to holding back the wave of Darkness threatening to eat the world.

But only if they were strong enough to step into the Light.

-o-o-o-

The tidal wave of memories subsided, and Amy's knees gave out. She crumpled to the floor, tears streaming from her eyes, vaguely aware that Elijah had followed her down, his hand still linked with hers.

"It can't be true," she whispered.

The man she'd loved almost five thousand years ago moved to crouch silently next to her, forming the third point of a triangle with the man she'd loved since she was twenty-one. His dark eyes shone with pinpricks of molten bronze. Beside her, Elijah shifted his grip on her hand, lacing their fingers together. With his other hand, he reached out and gripped the vampire's upper arm.

"It's true, Amy," he said, sounding like something inside him had cracked open, spilling out its contents. His gaze moved to Menkhef's and held. "I remember you. *Jesus Christ.* I *dreamed* you. I dreamed... this."

The vampire lifted a long-fingered hand, hovering an inch above Amy's skin for a moment before lowering it to rest lightly on her forearm. Electricity thrummed between them, raising every tiny hair on Amy's body and pulling a gasp free from her lips.

She jerked away from both of them, scuttling backward until her shoulders hit the sandstone wall behind her. "Oh my god. Oh my god, *oh my god*. I can't do this. It's too much—"

Elijah's hand fell from the vampire's arm. He looked nearly as shell-shocked as she felt.

I would not ask it of you on my own behalf. The mental voice was calm. Composed and deep, but sad beyond measure. *I am not the same person I was then, and neither are you. If neither one of you wished to grace my presence ever again, I would understand.* His chest rose and fell. *But that does not negate the responsibility we hold as the final battle for humanity draws near. Bael is coming for the world, and the Council is the only thing standing in the way of the oncoming Darkness.*

She swallowed, her dry throat clicking. "But… we're here. All thirteen. Right? Isn't that what you supposedly need?"

His look of sadness grew deeper, but to her surprise, it was Elijah who spoke.

"The others are all vampires."

A strange kind of panic gripped Amy by the throat. The last couple of days had been so… surreal. People turning into owls, or wolves, or mist. Teenagers with needle tracks on their arms from giving blood donations to vampires. Zombies overrunning an innocent town full of people. Elijah's life-threatening head wound, healing right before her eyes in a handful of minutes.

But there was something more real and immediate than any of those things. Something more important than the craziness swirling around them, threatening to drag them under.

"I can't do this. I'm pregnant," she said, wrapping an arm around her belly.

"I know," Menkhef said aloud. "That is why I said I was sorry."

Elijah climbed to his feet slowly, and the vampire rose to match him.

"I don't understand," Elijah said, in a tone that made it clear he expected Menkhef to make him understand pretty damned fast.

One of our number was with child when Bael attacked and turned her, centuries ago, he said in their minds. *The child… did not survive her turning. While the circumstances are different, I cannot guarantee that the results would not be the same.*

Amy made a small noise in the back of her throat and wrapped her other arm around her middle, holding her belly. Elijah seemed to grow three inches taller. He squared up to Menkhef, his hands clenching into fists at his sides.

"Get out," he growled. "*Now.*"

Menkhef only bowed his head in acknowledgement, his body dissolving into vapor before their eyes and swirling away. Elijah whirled and met Amy's eyes, his own expression devastated as Amy's body began to tremble. She curled up against the wall and hugged her midsection harder.

NINETEEN

The last thing Menkhef wanted to do right now was speak with the others. Unfortunately, circumstances were arrayed against his personal preferences in the matter. Ancient and broken he might be, but he was not so broken that he would allow his selfish desire to withdraw into himself to further endanger those under his protection.

His fellow vampires were waiting for him in the largest gallery of the underground tunnel system, where those with well-developed mental powers were still attempting to spread calm and spiritual light over the complex. He materialized silently, steeling himself to face them.

Tré had been seated facing Della, his hand on her face as he borrowed her young, untempered power to bolster his own telepathic abilities. Upon Menkhef's arrival, he lowered his fingers from her temple and opened his eyes. Serious silver-gray met and held Menkhef's gaze. The others recalled at least part of their attention to their surroundings—and the imminent confrontation brewing.

"The undead are massing around us," Tré said. "We may have very little time left. If we are to have any chance to save the humans, we need to complete the Council before it's too late. You must turn them now, Menkhef."

"No," Menkhef said simply.

Tré rose to his feet. "There's more at stake than your feelings on the matter, or theirs. I'm sorry, but if you won't do it, I will."

Menkhef let the others' thoughts filter into his mind through the bond. Della, Trynn, and Manisha were troubled by Tré's words. Chan seemed unsurprised. Oksana, Mason, Xander, and Duchess were shielding heavily. From Eris, he felt compassion, but no sense of whether the second most powerful vampire would support Tré's position or oppose it.

"No," Menkhef repeated mildly. "You will not turn them without their permission. I will not allow it."

Xander rose to stand next to Tré. "I know what you're thinking, Snag," he said. "We can't play the good guys while we're acting like the monsters. I *do* understand—truly. But you must also be aware that we're both out of time and out of options. The final two members of the Council are right down the hall. Will you stand by while Bael's forces crush every person in every one of our enclaves around the globe, when the possible means to stop him is waiting mere meters away?"

"The woman, Amy, is pregnant," Menkhef said, in lieu of a direct answer.

Duchess swore on a sharp breath and surged to her feet. Oksana made a noise of pain, and Xander closed his eyes, chin dipping sharply as though he'd been struck. Tré's silent resolve wavered only for an instant before steadying, but it was now laced with heavy regret.

To Menkhef's surprise, it was Mason who recovered first. "I'll talk to her. Do you know how far along she is?"

"Two months, or perhaps three."

Duchess hugged herself. "I'm coming, too. Tré, if you try to act before we have a chance to speak with her, I'll side with Snag against you."

She was still shielding strongly, her words tight and flat. Menkhef thought she would seek to dissuade

Amy from risking her child, but he made himself let go of his fears and expectations regarding what might happen in the coming hours. It was suddenly a far more difficult thing to do than it had been in the weeks since he'd come to the conclusion that the Angel Israfael was influencing things as the final battle approached.

Apparently, it wasn't so easy to trust in Her power when the lives of those he cherished hung in the balance.

"Go," he told Duchess and Mason. "I will remain here. My presence would only complicate matters further."

Duchess raised a sharp brow at Tré, who paused before giving a minute nod of acquiescence. Once the pair had left, Menkhef turned his back on the others and settled into a seated position on the stone floor, intending to once more lend his mental aid in calming and protecting the people above them.

In almost five thousand years of living, clearing his mind of worry for his mates was one of the hardest things he had ever done.

-o-o-o-

Elijah held Amy tightly against his chest. Panic was still thrumming through his veins like ice water. In the space of an hour, his world had been turned upside down; his rational beliefs upended and set on fire. But one thing remained the same as it always had—in the end, Amy and the child she was carrying were the only things that truly mattered to him. He'd failed to protect them at the Headless Pyramid. They would have died if…

He gritted his teeth. It was still almost physically painful to say the word, or even to think it.

Amy and their baby would have died if the *vampires* hadn't shown up and saved them.

But no matter what the cost, Elijah would protect them now. God help him, he just had to figure out how to do it first. How did you protect someone during an apocalypse?

"We could make a run for it," he said against Amy's hair.

"Where would we run?" she croaked. "Elijah… Saqqara is overrun with the living dead, and a demon is coming to take over the world."

He wanted so badly to be able to say, *don't be ridiculous*. But they'd both seen the truth of it; relived it in gory detail. Felt the burn of bitter, acrid black fog and the agony of Menkhef's soul being ripped in two. Maybe Elijah should have scoffed anyway. Dismissed what they'd experienced as a hallucination or some kind of bizarre brainwashing. But he couldn't do it. The truth was wound through the depths of his soul like the roots of an ancient tree. He swallowed hard, a question burning in his chest.

"Did you dream about him, too, Amy?" he asked. "Did you dream about the past—about the three of us together in Egypt?"

She stilled in the circle of his arms. "I dreamed. But it was always hazy. I couldn't recall the details afterward." They were both silent for the space of several breaths before she spoke again. "Is… that why you told me last year that you thought we should see other people? Because of the dreams?"

He stiffened, but she tightened her grip on him, keeping him from pulling away.

"Elijah. Is that why?" she pressed.

His heart was pounding, pride and humiliation urging him to put her off. To keep his secret. But how would keeping his secret help them now? They could well be about to die, overrun by monsters or destroyed by a vengeful demon. Did he really want to go out perpetuating a lie with the woman he loved—even a lie of omission?

"Yes," he said quietly. "I dreamed of you in his arms. And I should have hated it. I should have been enraged by it... but I wasn't. I was... relieved. I loved seeing you with him, and you were so *happy*."

She was holding onto him so tightly he thought she might leave bruises as she said, "When I dreamed, I couldn't remember much. But sometimes I remembered that I'd been dreaming about loving two men at once. Two men who both loved me, and who cared about each other as well. When I woke up from those dreams, I felt like the luckiest woman on earth." Her chest hitched. "I told myself it was just a stupid sex fantasy. I didn't want to say anything to you about it. I knew you already felt like you weren't enough for me."

"We're both idiots," he murmured into her hair.

She nodded. "I need you to know, Elijah—I never had any desire to start sleeping around or to find another man. It's just, in the dreams, it felt like we were finally..."

"Complete?" he finished.

She paused, mulling the word over. "Yeah. Yeah, that's it. It's like we fit together—the three of us. Stronger with each other to lean on than we ever could have been apart."

"Jesus, Ames," he whispered, cradling her close. "I just hope we have a chance to figure all this out."

A light knock on the door had them breaking apart, the realities around them returning with a vengeance. It creaked open a moment later to admit the Australian doctor and a pale, beautiful blonde woman with a haunted expression lurking behind her china-blue eyes.

"May we come in?" the doctor asked.

Amy hastily scrubbed her palm across her cheeks, as if that would somehow hide the evidence of her tears. "Yes," she said, and glanced at the empty hallway behind them. "Where's—?"

"Menkhef seemed to think his presence might be a distraction," the guy replied. "This is Duchess. She was eight months pregnant when the demon Bael turned her, several hundred years ago. She wanted to speak with you both."

Shit. She must be the one he'd spoken about. No wonder she looked so haunted.

"Okay," Amy managed, her hand creeping to her belly.

"So, talk. Menkhef said turning into a vampire might kill our baby," Elijah said, focusing his attention on the blonde woman. "That means it's not happening. If any of you try to get to her, you'll have to go through me first."

Even as the words passed his lips, new panic rushed through his veins like ice water. He recognized the sheer impotence of the threat. These people could transform themselves into other forms; they had fought off undead creatures that Elijah had been completely powerless against. If they turned on him and Amy, he didn't see any way the two of them could possibly save themselves, and that knowledge ate at him.

"It's true," Duchess, the female vampire, said in a rich French accent. "I miscarried my daughter after the demon attacked me."

The doctor looked between Elijah and Amy, his expression serious. "I want to give you some additional context, here," he said. "This demon wasn't trying to turn Duchess into a vampire. He was trying to turn her into an undead puppet by ripping out half of her soul and destroying it. To aid in that, he thought nothing of destroying her body in the process."

Next to him, Amy shivered, and Elijah thought he saw an answering shudder go through Duchess as well.

"What Bael did to the original vampires in his quest to bend them to his will was brutal beyond all telling," the doctor continued. "No late-term fetus could have been expected to survive that kind of traumatic injury. I want to make it very, very clear that being turned by another vampire is a completely different thing, and I can tell you that from personal experience."

Elijah snaked an arm around Amy's shoulders and held her close against his side, still watching the pair warily.

The doctor sighed. "I can't say it wasn't a traumatic process, though in my case I was already dying—so my experience wasn't exactly typical. But at its most basic, with a healthy human, it involves being drained of blood almost—but not quite—to the point of death. After which, ingesting vampire blood in turn triggers the change."

"What are you getting at?" Elijah demanded. "Because I already made it very clear that the answer is *no*."

"What I'm getting at is this. As a medical professional, nothing about the process is necessarily fatal to a first trimester embryo. The female body goes to surprising lengths to protect the contents of the womb during sudden physiological shocks, and this particular shock need only last a few moments. I'm not convinced that being turned by a powerful vampire who was going to purposeful lengths to make the process as gentle as possible would necessarily cause a miscarriage."

"But it might," Amy said flatly.

"Yes," Duchess replied. "It might."

"It might. But from what I've seen," the doctor said, "Menkhef would expend the last iota of his power to make sure it didn't. And he's the most powerful vampire there is, by quite a large margin."

Elijah's arm tightened around Amy's shoulders, and his voice was hard. "For a doctor, you seem to have a definite bias in this discussion. Shouldn't you be counseling against a procedure that obviously has serious risks, instead of going to such lengths to downplay those risks?"

Up until now, the Australian had remained an affable figure, soft-spoken and calm. But at Elijah's words, his face and tone went stony, while his eyes flared with an inner glow like sunlight on gunmetal.

"I'm going to be blunt, here, Dr. Carpenter—because frankly, we don't have time to beat around the bush," he said. "I've spent my adult life volunteering pediatric medical services in war zones because I care about saving kids. At this moment in time, my brother and his family are running an enclave similar to this one in Singapore. He has two daughters. They're three and five years old. And right now, they are surrounded by an army of walking corpses massing in readiness to attack them—just like the army of walking corpses massing around this compound as we speak."

Elijah's stomach turned over, but he didn't allow it to show on his face as the man continued.

"You two saw those creatures up close. I want you to stop and think very carefully about what they could do to a young child. What they will do to *my nieces* if we don't find a way to stop their attack." A muscle ticked in his square jaw. "I'm sorry that you are forced to face the possibility of losing your unborn child. But your child is not inherently more important than my brother's children, or any of the other untold millions of children who will become prey to Bael's Darkness if we can't stop him, right here and now. Tell me, how long do you think your unborn child will survive when those zombie creatures overrun us?"

Amy was crying again, soft sobs hitching her chest where it pressed against his side.

"*Docteur*," Duchess interrupted softly. "That's enough."

The Australian's flashing eyes turned to her. "You know I'm right about this, Duchess. It's a chance for survival for all of us—this unborn child included—versus no chance at all. Tré knows it. Oksana and Eris know it. Menkhef seems to be the only one who doesn't see it that way."

"He sees more than any of us, I suspect," said the blonde vampire, very softly.

An idea started percolating through the layers of Elijah's mind as the pair spoke. It was still half-formed — terrifying in both its simplicity and its uncertainty.

"I want to talk to Menkhef," he said, before he could second-guess himself. "Get him in here now."

Amy lifted startled eyes to his, a question in her face. Tear tracks left pale streaks through the dust that still dirtied her face after the horror they'd experienced at the Headless Pyramid. He set his jaw, trying to ready himself for what he was about to do.

Duchess' eyes grew distant for a moment before meeting his again. "He's coming."

Elijah swallowed against the dryness of his throat. If the vampires decided to turn on them, as a human, he could do nothing to protect Amy. They were far too strong for him to resist. But if he were a vampire himself…

Menkhef slipped silently into the room, his countless centuries of age showing clearly in the set of his shoulders and the lines around his eyes.

"Turn me," Elijah said, before he could lose his nerve.

Amy gasped and whirled on him. Menkhef raised an eyebrow.

"I won't let you turn Amy," he continued quickly. "But… maybe twelve vampires will be enough for your Council. And… well, if it's not enough, once we see that turning into a vampire is truly safe, then we might reconsider things."

That last part was a lie, but if it sweetened the deal enough to convince Menkhef to turn him first — to make him strong enough to protect her — then his conscience could go to hell. He just wished that Menkhef would stop looking at him with such a depthless expression. An expression that said he knew Elijah better than Elijah knew himself, and that he could see right through him.

"Elijah, no!" Amy exclaimed, grabbing his bicep. Her grip was so tight that her fingernails pricked at his skin, leaving little half-moon indentations in his flesh.

"Ames," he said, meeting her eyes. "Please… just this once, you *have* to trust me."

She opened her mouth as if to argue more, but the words seemed to get caught in her throat. Nothing emerged. He grabbed her free hand and pressed it to the side of his head… the place that had been bruised and shattered before being miraculously healed with vampire blood.

"Think, Amy," he said. "I'll be safer as a vampire than I ever was as a human. I can protect you better that way, from whatever comes next. You, and our baby."

Amy bit her lower lip, chewing at it until he feared she might draw blood.

Very well. Come to me, Menkhef said inside Elijah's mind, still giving him a look that said he knew exactly what Elijah intended, but would give him what he asked for regardless.

Elijah took a step toward him, only to find Amy still clinging to him, her feet set and unmoving. "Amy…" he began.

Menkhef swept the other two vampires with a look. "Leave us," he said softly.

They left, though Duchess paused in the doorway, sending a last, troubled look over her shoulder at Amy. When they were alone, Menkhef turned back to them.

I will not allow the others to change either of you against your will, he said silently, before his gaze narrowed to Elijah alone. *Do you still wish to proceed?*

The words gave him pause, but only for an instant. They were telling in many ways. Elijah even believed them. But it changed nothing. Whether he was protecting Amy from the other vampires or from the undead, he could do it better as a vampire himself.

"Yes," he said, and Amy made a pained noise of denial that pierced his heart like an arrow.

Menkhef approached her and cupped her tear-stained cheek tenderly. "*Hayati*. My heart. Will you trust the two of us to try to keep you safe? You, and the life you carry inside?"

And just like that, Menkhef became complicit in Elijah's plan to protect Amy, rather than being an adversary. The change was so natural and seamless that Elijah might have missed it if not for the way something settled into place inside his chest, the world reorganizing around him until everything made sense for perhaps the first time in his entire damned life.

"He won't hurt me, Ames," Elijah said. "You know he won't."

Menkhef closed his eyes briefly before meeting Elijah's. "Would that it were true, my brave guardsman. I *will* hurt you, though. I will rend your spirit until it tears down the middle, even though it pains me as if it were my own spirit. I can only promise that you will emerge stronger and more powerful on the other side, just as you desire."

Amy stepped away from Menkhef's touch and pressed a hand over her mouth, her body trembling.

"Do it," Elijah said.

As you wish. A heartbeat later, strong hands turned him until Menkhef was standing with his chest to Elijah's back. Power sparked along his nerves at the touch of Menkhef's hands, distracting him as his head was eased to one side. Fangs sunk into the tender skin of his bared throat, and the world whited out around him, descending into flame.

TWENTY

Amy didn't think she'd ever cried so much in her damned life… or been so scared. The feeling of helplessness was the worst thing she'd ever experienced. She couldn't save Elijah, she couldn't save herself, and no matter what decision she made in the end, she might not be able to save her baby.

A wife and mother's worst nightmare, tied up with a neat black bow and placed on a silver platter.

Trust me, Elijah had said, his dark eyes burning into hers with more intensity than she'd ever seen in him. But how could she trust anything or anyone when her husband was writhing in obvious agony, his lips open in a silent scream. She wanted to leap forward and try to wrestle him out of Menkhef's arms, but what if the distraction interrupted whatever the vampire was doing somehow, and Elijah simply died?

Who was she kidding, anyway, thinking she had a chance in hell of overpowering a being so old and powerful that he'd watched the pyramids being constructed? Elijah asked her to trust him—but she didn't trust *this*. She didn't trust *any* of this.

It's almost over, hayati, came the deep voice in her mind, layered with warmth and reassurance. She wanted to scream at him to keep his mind on what he was doing, damn it—but her breath was locked in her chest, her lungs burning as she held her breath, waiting for it to be done.

Finally, Elijah slumped in the strong arms holding him, his eyes rolling up until only a sliver of the whites showed. His face was gray; his lips tinged blue. Amy shuddered, pressing a hand to her mouth. Strong arms lifted him onto the medical cot where he'd so recently lain unconscious.

Her eyes were drawn to the molten bronze glow in Menkhef's eyes, and a moment later, to the red dripping from his fangs. One of them was slightly maloccluded, the professional part of her mind noted distantly, the vicious point displaying a few degrees of buccal torque.

He met her eyes over Elijah's unmoving body. *Not long now.*

Still the words were calm and reassuring. She wondered with a chill if he was influencing her somehow — making her stand here, silent and compliant, while he drank her husband's blood.

No, hayati. You feel only the aura that the others are spreading across the complex to try and hold the Darkness at bay. I will not overpower your will, just as I will not allow your humanity to be taken without your consent.

She thought of the Australian doctor, Mason, and of his baby nieces in Singapore.

"Not even at the cost of innocent lives?" she whispered.

He looked... so old, in that moment. Fresh tears spilled over Amy's cheeks.

Your humanity does not belong to me. It is not mine to barter for other lives, he said. *Perhaps if I were a kinder person, I would steal that choice from you and make it my own. But I cannot. Once I do so, the Darkness inside me wins.*

He looked down at Elijah, and Amy shivered as he tore into his own wrist, blood dripping from the jagged wound to splatter against Elijah's slack lips. For long moments, nothing seemed to happen... but then, Elijah's tongue darted out, tasting the red liquid. His eyes opened, and they were glowing. Amy caught her breath sharply as he grabbed Menkhef's arm and pulled it to his mouth, lapping and sucking at the gore, burying his teeth into flesh to widen the wound.

Amy didn't want to look… couldn't look away. It was primal, and ugly, and if it hadn't been for Menkhef's air of calm serenity as Elijah tore into his wrist with feral intensity, she was pretty sure she would have collapsed into screaming hysterics.

"All is well," he said aloud, though she wasn't sure which one of them he was speaking to.

Elijah continued to swallow the blood flowing from Menkhef's veins, until his movements grew slower and less coordinated, as though he were growing sleepy. Eventually, Menkhef eased his head down to the pillow and touched his forehead as though in benediction.

"Rest now, my guardsman," he murmured, and Elijah's eyes slid shut. With Elijah once more lying silent and still, he lifted his eyes to Amy's. "It is done."

Amy stared at Elijah's body for long moments. "He's not breathing," she whispered hoarsely.

"He no longer needs to," Menkhef said, sounding infinitely weary. "Come. Sit with him. But you must heed me when I warn you to back away. He will not be able to control his hunger when he first awakes."

That sounded… ominous. But she cautiously approached the cot and sat in the chair they'd pulled up to it for her earlier, when he'd been injured. Amy took his hand in hers. It was cool to the touch, and his complete stillness was more than a little disconcerting. But she'd seen him wake up and drink blood, just like they'd said he would. Menkhef had assured her that he was all right—that the transformation was successful.

Elijah was a vampire now.

"Did it work?" she asked. "Did making a twelfth vampire change anything?"

Menkhef's eyes went distant in the way she'd come to understand meant he was exercising his mental powers—seeing and hearing things she couldn't.

"There is no change," he said eventually. "The un-dead are still massing around the walls."

She was disappointed, but not surprised. "What are they waiting for? Why don't they attack while it's dark?"

Menkhef lifted a shoulder in an elegant half-shrug. "The enclave is protected by vampires. It will be far more strategically advantageous for them to attack after the sun is up."

"So we have a few more hours." A few more hours for her to torture herself with an impossible choice — the safety of her baby, or the safety of everyone else. Menkhef had been right earlier. It would have been kinder for him to take the choice out of her hands. Right now, she wasn't sure if she loved him or hated him for refusing to do so.

He watched her with an expression that said he knew exactly what she was thinking, and she had to look away, her eyes returning to Elijah's slack features. "You're certain he'll be okay?" she asked, aware of what a ridiculous question that was under the circumstances.

"He is arguably safer now than he was before," he replied.

She swallowed, trying to hold any further tears at bay. God knew they hadn't done her any good up to this point. "I suppose that's something, then," she said.

-o-o-o-

Several times over the course of the night, Menkhef urged her to leave the bedside and stand across the room by the door. Moments later, Elijah would awake and try to lunge for Amy's throat before she even had time to draw breath. She'd screamed the first time, but even before the shrill sound exited her lungs, Menkhef had already blocked Elijah with a hand splayed over his chest, pressing him back onto the bed as invisible energy crackled between them, raising the hairs on Amy's nape.

Mason had come in earlier that night with a cooler full of what Amy later learned were blood bags full of donations from humans like Shay, who had volunteered to feed the vampires. Each time Elijah regained consciousness, animalistic in his hunger, Menkhef fed him blood from the bags until he subsided into sleep again.

Above them, dawn was approaching. Amy had tried to distract herself as the hours passed by intermittently peppering Menkhef with questions about the past. He'd answered her every time, not shying away from her inquiries, but she got a sense that he was distancing himself from his answers. He replied with facts, but not emotions. Memories, but not the feelings associated with them.

"What happened to Nebetta's children?" she asked, remembering that with Heqab's help, she had eventually borne a boy and a girl.

"I do not know," he said, his eyes not lifting from Elijah's face, peaceful in sleep.

"They didn't die when Bael came for you, though?" she pressed.

"I did not kill them in my bloodlust," he told her, and she wondered how much his continued detachment was costing him.

"That's good, right?" she said. "They escaped, and went on to live their lives."

"Perhaps. Or perhaps the pharaoh hunted them down. If he found them, he would have had them executed or sold into slavery to ensure that my line could not continue, and that my lands would once again be under his control."

Her heart sank.

"No," came a faint rasp from the bed. Elijah's eyes opened, but they weren't glowing with unthinking bloodlust this time. "I'd arranged for the servant, Sef, to hide them if anything ever happened to all three of us. He took them upriver to another village, where they were to be raised as commoners by a family I knew. Sef was loyal — the pharaoh would never have been able to find them." He frowned. "I mean… Heqab did those things. Weird. Everything's running together in my head."

"Elijah?" Amy asked tentatively, hope swelling in her heart now that he seemed to have come back to himself.

"Amy?" He blinked up at her. "What happened? Are you all right?"

"I am now," she said, and watched as everything seemed to come back to him at once.

His nostrils flared. "I'm… really thirsty. I feel like I'm burning up."

Menkhef had grown silent and still when Elijah spoke about the past… about the children. But he roused himself now, leaning forward. "Feed from me, but try to maintain control this time. My blood will give you more strength than human blood, and I fear you may have need of that strength soon."

He offered his arm upturned, and Elijah's gaze caught on the blue-green roadmap of veins beneath the skin. His eyes kindled with a coppery glint, and fangs poked out from his gums as Amy watched in fascination. He took the offered wrist and dragged his gaze up to meet Menkhef's for a moment before he bit into it, drawing on the blood that welled up.

"I never knew what became of Iahmesu and Ehsret," Menkhef mused quietly as Elijah drank. "By the time Eris found me in my tomb, three thousand years had passed. If our children had survived to adulthood, any of their descendants would have been more than a hundred generations removed from me. Perhaps I could have searched and found some fragment of record about them. But I decided, in the end, that not knowing was preferable to finding that they had died young, or lingered in cruel servitude."

"It sounds like they had the same chance at life as any person has," Amy offered, picturing the two young children spirited away to a new life by a trusted servant. "Why not believe that they went on to be happy?"

Elijah forced himself to release Menkhef's wrist, and Amy watched as the twin wounds closed over in seconds. Menkhef cupped his cheek—a fleeting caress.

"Even in death, you watched over them," he mused. "I should not be surprised by this."

Elijah looked uncomfortable. "Not me. Heqab."

"His soul is yours," Menkhef said, the words stated as fact.

Reincarnation. Amy had never been all that religious, and she could barely wrap her brain around it even now. Could it be true that this whole situation—this whole war—hinged on the sort of love that drew lost souls to return over and over to the living world, searching for their missing pieces?

Suddenly, the underground room felt claustrophobic.

"Elijah, are you all right now?" she asked, bringing his knuckles to her lips and kissing them.

"I'm not sure *all right* is the word," he said. "But I feel like myself again, at least. My mind isn't burning any more."

She nodded. "I need to get out of these tunnels for a few minutes." She looked to Menkhef. "Is it safe?"

He smiled, but it was a sad expression. "No. It is precisely as dangerous as it would be if you remained here. Go, *hayati*. If you need help, call, and we will come."

Elijah tangled his fingers around hers, holding her in place as his eyes shot to Menkhef. "None of the other vampires will try to take matters into their own hands if she's alone?"

Christ. She was such a wreck right now, the thought hadn't even occurred to her.

Menkhef held his gaze evenly. "They will not. I have spoken with them, and we have an understanding in place. I trust each of them with my life. More importantly, I trust them with *your* lives."

She frowned. "You spoke with them? But you never left this room, and neither did I."

I do not need to leave this room to speak with them, nor they with me, he said inside her mind.

"Oh. Right. Still working on getting my head wrapped around that part—sorry." Amy thought of the way he'd barreled into the fight at the Headless Pyramid like a creature possessed, knocking undead creatures away from her like bowling pins and whisking her and Elijah away to safety. Even so, there was no real guarantee that one of his friends wouldn't take matters into their own hands. A tiny, unworthy part of her couldn't help thinking if they did, it would save her from having to make the impossible choice that faced her.

Elijah's brow furrowed, his expression unhappy, but not as worried as before. "I can see his memory of the conversation in my head. He... told them that turning you against your will would jeopardize the battle, and they believed him. They agreed not to."

"That's good enough for me." She kissed Elijah's hand again, though he looked troubled as she let his fingers slip free.

"Don't go far," he begged. "Come back the instant you sense trouble."

"I just need some air," she assured him. "I won't be long."

She could feel both of their gazes on her back as she left the room. She'd been more worried about Elijah than about paying attention to her surroundings when she'd arrived, but it wasn't too difficult to follow the line of hastily strung bulbs back to the landing, where steep stone steps led up toward the light.

At least, it *should* have been light outside. It was well past dawn by now, but the illumination was murky, and gusts of wind carried stinging dust through the compound. She climbed to the top of the imposing cobra head wall, wondering if there was a storm coming. Even in the Egyptian desert, there must be storms sometimes, she supposed. When she looked up at the sky, however, her breath caught as memories from another life bubbled up.

The sky roiled with thick, oily black fog. Not clouds, but something far worse. The memory of watching that smothering vapor descend into the courtyard of Menkhef's palace—burning her like acid as it swirled around her body—made her choke on a cry of dismay.

The demon was here, circling their desert refuge like a vulture circling prey.

TWENTY-ONE

Amy was so distracted by the horror floating above them in the sky that she didn't realize she wasn't alone on the windblown stone parapet at first. A woman she'd only noticed in passing when she'd stumbled in from the desert, desperate to get back to Elijah, stood at the end of the wall. Wild chestnut curls whipped around her face in the breeze, her loose white clothing billowing as she looked out across the compound spread out below them.

Amy moved to join her, suddenly wanting to be close to another person in the face of the Darkness looming over them, despite her earlier desire for a few moments of solitude. She looked down at the tents and other detritus of human occupation. From this height, it all looked hopelessly delicate—like a child's toys that might be knocked over and smashed at any moment.

The people who had come here to escape the wrongness creeping over the world were gathered in the open space, facing a low stone plinth. Three people sat cross-legged on the raised stone—a woman with two men flanking her. Amy looked closer, and thought she recognized Shay and the two guys she'd been talking and laughing with the afternoon when she and Elijah had first arrived. The three appeared to be leading the crowd in a chant, or maybe a prayer. Xander and Manisha stood watchfully at the back of the group, eyes scanning their surroundings for approaching danger.

The woman on the parapet next to Amy spoke without turning to look at her, eyes fixed on the seething sky above them. "Five hundred years ago," she said, "that creature tried to destroy the man I loved right in front of me. I didn't let it happen then, and I'm not going to let it happen now."

A lump formed in Amy's throat.

Another figure joined them on top of the wall—a striking man with black hair and silver eyes. Those startling eyes swept over Amy, sadness and resolve behind them. He stepped forward and wrapped the woman in his arms from behind. "Together, *draga mea*. We will face the battle together. All of us—stand or fall," he said in a calm, resolute voice. "Now, come away, please. It is not safe for you in the open with the sun already up. This kind of Darkness is no refuge for us."

"Just a minute more..." the woman said, and turned her head to meet Amy's eyes. "Is your husband okay now, Dr. Carpenter?"

Amy nodded uncertainly. "I... think so. He woke up a few minutes ago and seemed more like himself."

"That's fast," the beautiful vampire said. "He must be a strong person to have recovered so quickly."

"Stronger than me," Amy whispered, mortified to realize that fresh tears were welling up in her eyes.

Compassion flitted across the woman's lovely features, and she slipped free of her partner's arms to close the distance between them. To Amy's surprise, the vampire drew her into a tight embrace and rubbed her back soothingly.

"I somehow doubt that," she said.

"Why?" Amy managed.

"Because you're Snag's mate. Menkhef's, I mean. And I can't imagine him going for some kind of fading flower—now, or four millennia ago."

Amy squeezed her eyes shut, tears slipping free as she did. She realized, then, how close the vampire's teeth were to her neck, and again the irrational desire for the woman to *just fucking do it* and make it someone else's responsibility flashed through her thoughts.

"I'm scared," she admitted, as though that fact should come as a surprise to anyone at this point. "I am scared out of my goddamned mind right now, and it's all on me. *All* of it. I want so fucking badly to make the wrong choice, but I *know* it's the wrong choice." She looked up at the sky, not pulling away from the other woman's embrace. "I know what that creature is. I *re-member*. I don't want to risk my child by letting Menkhef turn me. Though if I don't, I'll probably die during the battle, and then my baby will die with me. But... if we did somehow escape... if we survived, how could I even think about bringing an innocent life into a world ruled by that sadistic, horrible *thing*?"

She was weeping again, barely able to get the words out around her sobs.

The female vampire didn't try to shush her... didn't try to tell her what to do or offer meaningless platitudes. She just held her. The silver-eyed man approached them quietly and put a gentle hand on Amy's shoulder. Amy looked up at him, her vision blurred with tears.

"I don't have an answer for you," he said. "But I've known Menkhef for almost six hundred years... or rather, I *thought* I knew him. I have seen him protect those he cares about. I have seen him sacrifice for the innocent. But in all that time, I have never before seen him burn with such love for someone. Much less, *two* someones. Whatever choice you make, he will exert the last ounce of his power to protect you—and to protect the life you carry inside."

She already knew the right answer. She'd known the answer ever since the moment she truly accepted that Bael was coming to destroy the world. "I have to go," she rasped. "Let me go, please."

The woman's arms loosened, and the man's hand fell away.

"We'll come with you," said the female vampire. "We may not be able to do much, but we will damned well make sure that *nobody* faces this battle alone."

Amy nodded, the tiniest thread of comfort weaving through her panic upon hearing those words. She let the pair lead her back into the catacombs of the South Tomb, where they brought her unerringly to the room where Elijah and Menkhef were waiting. Elijah lurched to his feet when he saw the two vampires with her, his eyes flaring the color of molten metal.

"It's all right," she told him, knowing that she probably looked anything *but* all right, with her red, puffy eyes and cheeks wet from crying. "Elijah… I'm so sorry. But I can't condemn our child to a world where Darkness has overcome the Light. I just… can't do it."

"Amy! Are they controlling your mind?" Elijah demanded, still glaring daggers at the pair standing behind her. "*What did they say to you?*"

"They said that Menkhef would try to protect us no matter what choice I made." She swallowed hard. "And I choose to join the Council and fight." Her eyes slid to Menkhef, pleading. "Please, just… try to save my baby."

Menkhef rose to stand next to Elijah.

I will. The words echoed in her head.

"Amy, *no,*" Elijah whispered.

She bit the inside of her cheek until her traitorous emotions calmed enough that she could speak without her voice trembling—but the words were still some of the most difficult she'd ever uttered. "I'm sorry, Elijah. I love you, but just as Menkhef couldn't make this decision for me… neither can you. I understand what's at stake, and I choose the risk."

Menkhef met the silver-eyed man's gaze over her shoulder. "Time is short. I need you, Eris, and Duchess." His expression went distant for a moment, presumably as he contacted the others. Then his deep eyes settled on Amy. "Come here, *hayati.*"

She unlocked her knees by force of will and walked on shaky legs to the cot Elijah had vacated, settling on its edge. Elijah sat next to her and wrapped an arm around her shoulders.

"Do you forgive me?" she asked tremulously, looking up at her husband's face.

A harsh rush of air escaped his lungs. "Amy. I love you. There's nothing you could do that would make me stop loving you."

It wasn't exactly an answer, but she couldn't bring herself to press the issue. Menkhef gathered her hands between his. Though his skin was cool, she felt the hum of power along her nerves like tiny flames.

You must understand what you ask of me, hayati. I will have the strongest among us try to cushion the life inside you from danger with their power. But to ensure that I harm your body as little as possible, I must drain you slowly. In doing so, I will extend the agony of your soul being rent in two.

She'd relived Menkhef's turning at Bael's hands; felt what it meant to have one's soul torn into pieces. She'd watched Elijah writhing in pain, his mouth open around a cry too large to escape his lungs.

"I understand," she said. It didn't matter. All of her fear was tied up on behalf of others right now. She couldn't spare any for herself, but… "Will it hurt my baby the same way?"

One of Menkhef's hands untangled from hers to rest over her womb, still and grounding. "No. I will not touch your child's soul, my heart. Only yours."

A faint fluttering hitch vibrated against her side where Elijah was pressed against her—the feeling of someone ruthlessly forcing back tears. She leaned into him, squeezing closer against the curve of his body, and his arm tightened around her.

Other vampires arrived—an olive-skinned man Amy hadn't seen before, along with the Australian doctor, Duchess, and the black woman who'd helped rescue them from the zombies and then turned into an owl. Oksana, Chan had called her. Duchess looked as pale as a ghost, and she balked in the doorway. Her eyes slid over Amy and away, as though she couldn't bring herself to make eye contact.

"I can't do this, *grand frère*," she said. "I'm sorry. I know you've asked almost nothing of me over the centuries, but this task is beyond me. Forgive me."

"I'll act in her stead," Oksana said. "I'm not as old or as powerful, but when Mason was dying, I was able to wrap my life force around his and keep it from flickering out until help came. I know what to do."

Menkhef nodded. "I understand. I am sorry to have asked this of you, my sister. Oksana, your help is most welcome."

Duchess managed a tight nod in return before more or less fleeing the room. The man with dark Mediterranean features—who by process of elimination must be Eris—looked grim.

"We have an additional problem," he said. "I can sense Bastian Kovac's presence nearby."

"I am aware," Menkhef said, his features going stony with anger for an instant so brief, Amy wasn't totally sure she'd seen it.

"One crisis at a time," said the silver-eyed man. "Xander and Manisha are keeping watch above. They'll let us know as soon as anything happens."

"Who's Bastian Kovac?" Amy asked, more for distraction than anything else.

"The man behind the bombing in Damascus, among several other unsavory things," Eris said. "I suppose it was inevitable he'd be tied up in the endgame somehow."

Amy shuddered, thinking of the awful news reports about the terrorists' suitcase nuke. Elijah's arm tightened around her protectively.

"Are you ready, *hayati*?" Menkhef asked, his expression back in its smooth, unruffled lines.

"What the hell kind of question is that?" she asked, an odd feeling of detachment beginning to creep over her. "No, I'm not. Now, can we please do this before the world ends?"

He nodded, and his eyes flickered to Elijah's. "She will need my blood for strength, but she will need yours as well, for the love behind it."

Elijah glared at him. "I'd give the last drop of my blood to keep her safe," he grated out.

"I know," Menkhef said. "I promise you—while we live, she will never lack for blood."

Despite her fear, a lump rose in Amy's throat. She choked it down and let them position her lying back in Elijah's arms, cradled between his thighs with her head resting against the crook of his shoulder. Menkhef stood next to the cot on her right side, and the three vampires he had asked to help him protect her baby stood shoulder to shoulder on her left.

Oksana placed her hand over Amy's womb. Eris and the silver-eyed vampire covered it with theirs. All three closed their eyes. Amy couldn't feel anything where they touched her, but the hairs on her arms stood up, her skin prickling into gooseflesh.

"I love you," Elijah said, the choked whisper sounding broken against the shell of her ear.

"I love you, too. It—" She had to stop and swallow to steady her voice. "It'll be okay, Elijah. It has to be."

Menkhef lifted her right arm as though it was made of the finest glass. She refused to squeeze her eyes shut like a frightened child at the dentist's office, instead watching his face as he cradled her forearm. His eyes glowed with that strange inner light, and the points of fangs erupted as his lips drew back.

Her odd detachment had apparently returned, because she once again noticed the slight malocclusion of the left one.

"Did you know I'm an orthodontist?" she asked in a faraway voice. "I could totally fix that fang for you if… well… if we manage to live long enough to get back to civilization. And, you know, if the world doesn't end in a fiery apocalypse first." She trailed off, vaguely aware that she was babbling to distract herself from what was happening.

He paused, a look of painful fondness crossing his regal features. *I will keep it in mind*, he replied silently, pressing a kiss to the sensitive skin stretched over her veins. He cast a final, meaningful look at the three vampires huddled on her other side… and struck.

Amy gasped, bracing, but the pain of the wound was hidden under a sense of burning warmth that seemed to radiate outward from Menkhef's bite. The intense sensation hovered on the cusp between pleasure and discomfort. She was shocked and a bit mortified to find fire igniting in her belly. She squirmed in Elijah's arms, trying not to feel such a thing while three near-complete strangers were pressing their hands over her lower abdomen.

A moan slipped free from her lips, though she hoped it could credibly be ascribed to pain rather than… anything else. Elijah's arms tightened, and he let out a harsh breath that puffed against her temple. The burning sensation crept up her arm to her shoulder, and eventually flooded into her chest. Any question of it not being painful fled, and her heart stuttered before picking up the pace in a fluttering frenzy.

Lightheadedness swept over her, the room narrowing to a tunnel before turning gray around the edges, then red. She started to buck and struggle in earnest, but the hands holding her arm steady might as well have been iron bands. Elijah made a harsh sound and buried his face against her hair, but his arms around her didn't loosen.

"Careful, Snag," an Australian voice cautioned, though the words sounded like they was coming from underwater. "Take it slow now."

Agony erupted behind Amy's heart and lungs, unlike anything she'd ever experienced. She thought she screamed, but her hearing seemed to have gone away at the same time her vision closed in, until only impenetrable blackness remained. She panicked, certain that the demon had come for them… that it was too late. They would fall before its power, helpless as it pierced them with filthy claws and ripped out their humanity, leaving them as soulless puppets like the ones that had attacked her and Elijah.

Her throat hurt with the force of screams she couldn't hear, but then the sense of something vital being torn from her eased. Time slowed to a crawl, the fiery pain not receding, but not growing any worse, either. She tried to focus on the reasons she had to hang on, but her mind had been reduced to animal instinct. She would have bartered anything to make it stop—torn off a limb, thrown her loved ones to the wolves, all of it without a second thought.

An all-encompassing need was growing inside her. It was a thousand times worse than the most terrible drug addiction she could imagine. It wasn't just that if she didn't get what she needed, she would die. If she didn't get what she needed, the fucking *world* would burn.

Madness threatened—rose up to swallow her—and just as it was poised to devour her whole, the sweetest ambrosia that had ever existed dribbled between her lips. She roared, all her senses exploding back to life as she lunged for the source of the rich nectar. Arms fell away under the force of her struggles, and an instant later her teeth were latched onto cool flesh, ripping and tearing, desperate to make more of that nourishing liquid appear.

"*Amy!*" The choked cry came from behind her, but she ignored it.

She prepared to fight any attempts to pry her loose from her prize, but none came. A strong hand cradled her head in place, holding her lips to that source of salvation.

It's all right, hayati. Feed now, and deeply.

The mental voice was a cool wash of comfort, but it didn't touch the raging need inside her. Only the liquid pouring into her mouth and down her chin could do that. As the desperate craving began to ebb, she became aware of a second figure pressed against her back, sandwiching her between two tall forms. A rumble shook free from her throat, and she arched like a cat between them, rubbing her body with abandon as though she could mark both of them for her personal use.

When the flow of ruby blood from her first prize slowed to a trickle, she twisted, sliding sharp fangs into flesh the color of fine chocolate rather than dusky gold. Her new conquest groaned, a hard length sliding against her belly as his hips flexed.

"Fucking… *Christ*," he said, and she felt the strangled curse vibrate against her lips.

Drowsy lassitude slid over her as her sated stomach stopped screeching like an angry beast. She sagged, still held between the two strong men as her fangs slipped free from raw flesh.

"How is the child?" a hoarse voice asked from behind her, sounding exhausted beyond measure.

She knew something about the question was terribly, *life-changingly* important, and she tried to focus on the answer. It was no use, though, as weakness pulled her consciousness into the depths of a dark, endless ocean.

614

-o-o-o-

Amy was still floating when a different voice penetrated the cocoon of cotton wool surrounding her thoughts. This one was female, melodic, like a thousand bells chiming in harmony.

Wake, my child, it said, and Amy felt a sensation like a mother's hand stroking through her tangled and sweat-soaked hair. *You are needed. I will lend you strength to keep the blood-hunger at bay for now.*

Power not her own flooded through her body, bringing vitality to rubbery muscles and clarity to her decimated thoughts. Amy lunged upright, the stone room where she'd been turned into a vampire swimming into focus as memories slotted into place like puzzle pieces. A hand closed on her shoulder, the weight of command behind it keeping her from leaping off the blood-spattered cot she'd been lying on.

It wasn't blood she was after, though. "My baby?" she asked, her hands flying to her belly.

She was peripherally aware of the vampires around her exchanging looks of surprise, but then Elijah was there, cupping her face, pressing his lips to her forehead.

"Still alive," he whispered, and the world started turning again.

The Australian doctor approached cautiously, as though braced for her to go for his throat at any moment. "We can still sense the fetal life force, and with the benefit of vampire hearing, I was able to confirm with a stethoscope that the heartbeat is elevated but stable. That's not a guarantee that your body will be able to carry to term as a vampire, and it's definitely not a guarantee that any of us will be alive tomorrow to find out one way or the other. But for now, your baby is alive."

She sagged with relief.

"That being said," the doctor continued, "you're supposed to be out cold for hours, and mindless with hunger for at least the better part of a day." His slate blue eyes sought Menkhef, who was standing by the side of the cot. "Any thoughts on why that's not the case?"

Amy swallowed against the dryness of her throat. "There was a voice in my head. Female. She said I was needed and she'd lend me strength."

Before any of the others could respond, Duchess appeared in a hurry, slapping a palm against the doorframe to halt her momentum. Her expression was tense. "Xander says come quickly. Something's happening."

The general rush for the door was halted an instant later, when the same voice that had spoken to her before echoed through the stone chambers of the South Tomb, clear and beautiful.

I have come to you, my children. I hear your call, and I am here. But the final confrontation is almost upon us. If you are to prevail, you must first step into the Light.

TWENTY-TWO

Menkhef steeled himself to face this final battle in the face of his growing exhaustion, unwilling to seek nourishment from either his fellow vampires or the humans above when doing so might weaken them at a critical moment. He reached out to Israfael, trying to communicate, but gods and goddesses had never shown much interest in the thoughts of their game pieces. There was no response.

At least She had seen fit to spare Amy the aftermath of her turning. His two long-lost mates clung together for strength, just as it should be. If nothing else, Menkhef would carry with him the memory of holding Amy between his body and Elijah's after the worst of her torment had eased, but before her fangs had slid free from his throat. That sweet, fleeting moment would serve as his talisman through whatever came next.

He had his suspicions as to what that might be. If he was wrong, it seemed very likely that they would fall to Bael's creatures—becoming meat for the undead. And if he was right, they might well fall prey to their own natures, instead.

He needed to stay strong for just a bit longer.

"Come," he said, shaping his voice into something calm and commanding despite the burn of fatigue pulling at his bones.

Their group met Xander and Manisha at the entrance to the tunnels. They were ushering dozens of humans into the dubious protection of the tomb—many of them carrying small children or helping the elderly and infirm.

"That's it," Xander was saying, his voice determinedly calm. "Pardon the dust and gloom. Make yourself at home—several of the rooms have chairs and mattresses. And don't worry; this place has been here for more than forty-seven hundred years. It won't be going anywhere today."

Menkhef transformed into mist and swirled past the crush of humanity, aware of Tré and Eris doing the same behind him. They materialized next to Xander and Manisha. The young woman motioned them to one side of the tunnel with a jerk of her chin while her mate continued to reassure the people hurrying past.

"Something's happening in the sky," she said. "It started about five minutes ago. Beams of light are randomly breaking through the dark fog. It's not sunlight. The rays are coming from every direction and they're blinding, both to us and to the humans. As soon as we saw them, we brought everyone who wanted to come down here. The rest are sheltering in their tents, though the wind has picked up considerably in the last few minutes so I don't know how safe they'll be there."

"You did well," Tré said.

Xander joined them once the last of the humans had disappeared into the catacombs, and the other vampires came as well, once the way was clear.

"So," Eris said, eyeing the shifting patterns of light and shadow beyond the tunnel entrance with misgivings, "do we think stepping into the Light was meant as a literal directive, then?"

"Ah. You all heard the voice, too?" Xander asked, a wry twist entering his voice. "That's a relief. I thought maybe I'd finally cracked."

"We heard it," Eris confirmed, putting an arm around Trynn when she came to stand at his side. "The question becomes what we plan to do about it."

Xander took a deep breath and exchanged a look with Manisha. "It seems relatively straightforward from where I'm standing," he said. "As one of the least combustible people here, I'll volunteer to go out and check the UV rating."

"You mean *we'll* volunteer," Manisha said in a tone that brooked no opposition. "Your Victorian chauvinism is showing, my love."

Tré shook his head. "That will not be necessary, *tovarăș*," he began. "I should be the one —"

Menkhef did not allow him to finish. "I will go. Shield yourselves, and help the youngest protect their minds from whatever befalls me. If I survive, reopen the link and follow me one at a time."

"No, *wait*—" The voice was Amy's, and Menkhef met Elijah's eyes for the briefest of moments. As though they were in complete accord, Elijah nodded and took Amy's shoulders, gently restraining her from trying to come after him. Her eyes were full of such fear for him that it brought an ache to Menkhef's chest, but she subsided in her husband's grip, biting her lower lip in distress.

He let his gaze slide over the others, pausing last on Eris and Trynn.

"My old friend," Eris asked, "are you certain about this?"

"In the end, it seems I am certain of very few things," he replied truthfully, and strode out of the tunnels, mounting the stairs that led upward toward the light.

His instincts cringed from the crazy patchwork of blinding brilliance in the sky above, cutting swathes through the oily black mass of Bael's power. A quick mental scan of the surroundings beyond the walls showed undead numbering more than a thousand massed beyond the entrance, led by the only being in recent memory who had succeeded in rousing Menkhef to feelings of murderous hatred.

The black stain of Bastian Kovac's crippled soul stood ready to march his Dark troops into this fragile enclave, bringing horror to those who'd come seeking shelter and refuge. Still, Menkhef could make no move against his old enemy until Israfael's will had been done.

He stepped into the dazzling light, and burned.

Yet his body was not destroyed by Israfael's light. Rather than coming from his flesh, the agony came from within — from the darkest parts of his soul being illuminated for all to see. Every moment of hatred or despair. Every decision that caused innocents pain. Every werewolf who'd ever suffered because Menkhef had drunk from an innocent animal to sate his thirst. His failure to protect Sangye Rinchen, an innocent victim of Menkhef's own hubris. Every instance where his tendency toward secrecy and silence had placed his friends in danger.

His mental walls crumbled in the first instant, and he fell to his knees at the top of the cobra head wall, clutching one hand to his chest. He could sense the others experiencing his worst transgressions right along with him.

We can't shield against this, my friend, came Eris' warning. *We'll stand with you, though. Your darkness is ours, and all your sins toward us — if sins they truly were — are forgiven.*

Menkhef had never sought absolution in all these long and hopeless years. To do so had always felt as though it would somehow minimize the scope and breadth of his wrongdoings, both in his human life and after his turning. For this final battle to hinge on his ability to do just that seemed a cruel irony.

And he was so tired.

You're a good man. You were a good man in Egypt and you're a good man now. The feminine mental voice was unpracticed—both unfamiliar to him, and somehow better known to him than his own reflection.

His precious heart, lost for so long, and now found again.

There's a reason Heqab and Nebetta loved you more than they loved their own lives. A different voice. Male. And just as familiarly unfamiliar.

His noble soul—his guardsman—still watching over that which he held dear, so many millennia later.

Menkhef curled forward until his forehead rested on the cool sandstone of the parapet, letting the Light burn through him and illuminate every crevice... every dark nook and cranny left festering in the hidden corners of his injured spirit. And when it was done, the terrible scorching exposure of it eased, leaving him shaky. Lighter. Parts of him burned away to nothing.

We're still here. Eris' voice, filling his mind like a warm breeze.

Not going anywhere. Trynn, that time—stubborn and steadfast as ever.

Are you all right? Amy's unpracticed voice, thready with fear.

And... he was.

The Light had not destroyed him. His friends were still here.

Join me, he told them, rising on unsteady feet.

Eris strode up from the tomb—his oldest friend, and his savior twice over. The younger vampire cried out in pain as the Light shone into him. Menkhef steadied him, lending him strength as Israfael exposed every selfish and greedy impulse of the former tomb robber. Every grave he'd ever desecrated in the pursuit of art and money. Every display of impatience and short temper. Every unworthy impulse. Every drop of blood stolen from an unsuspecting mortal.

When it was over, Eris leaned heavily on him for a moment, head hanging and face pale. The others followed, joining them one by one.

Trynn, with her arrogance and her burning, bone-deep hatred for Bastian Kovac, the man who had tortured her mate nearly to the point of death.

Tré's scorching—and largely irrational—sense of failure in his self-imposed duties of leadership. His certainty that left up to him, the war against Bael would have been lost. His ruthlessness. His zeal in hunting humans for blood during the early decades after his turning.

Della's unspoken guilt over having allowed her parents to believe she'd died during the violence in New Orleans.

Oksana's deeply rooted self-loathing for the monster Bael made her—a loathing that had led her to punish her body by forcing food and drink into it over the centuries, despite the unbreakable curse that only allowed her to consume blood without pain.

Mason's sense of having abandoned the children in Haiti he'd sworn to care for. His sickening fear over having placed his brother's family in danger by convincing them to open an enclave in Singapore—an enclave now surrounded by an undead army poised to strike them down.

Xander's continued guilt over the suffering he'd allowed in his London factories during the Industrial Revolution—children exploited to line his own pockets with money.

Manisha's feelings of worthlessness after being unable to save a young boy she'd considered to be under her care. Her fervent wish that she could have been the one to die in Sangye's place.

Elijah came forward reluctantly. Menkhef could feel his uncertainty about the reception he was likely to receive from this tight-knit group… this unlikely family of choice. He gasped as the burning Light illuminated his desire to give up — on *everything*.

On his career. His marriage. And, in the depths of night when his terrible despondency of the spirit was at its worst... his desire to give up on his own life. To end things permanently.

The revelation threatened to shatter Menkhef's frail and battered heart. He and Eris caught Elijah as his body sagged. Eris eased back after a moment, and Menkhef turned the support into an embrace, feeling Amy's love for her husband crash through both their minds like a runaway chariot team.

No more despair, Menkhef silently assured the shaking man. *We'll make a new world, my guardsman — right here, right now. A new start for both of you.*

Wetness trickled into the dip of his collarbone, and he knew that should he look down, he would find rust-colored tears pooling there.

Amy rushed toward them, and they both caught her when Israfael's power shone on her horror at herself for having willingly risked her unborn baby's life... her belief that her impossible decision made her unfit to ever be a mother or a wife to anyone.

"No," Elijah rasped, pressing her between them as he'd done after Menkhef turned her. "It makes you the bravest and most selfless person I've ever met. I love you so much it hurts."

"I thought you'd never forgive me," she sobbed. "I thought you'd never even want to look at me again."

"No, Ames... no, no," Elijah crooned, murmuring against her hair as they both wept openly.

Menkhef closed his eyes against all the pain that this long war — this endless chess game between gods — had wrought in the world. The other vampires were also embracing each other; grasping hands and wiping away each other's tears. Only Chan and Duchess remained behind.

Go, he heard Duchess tell her mate, a terrible desolation behind the word.

Chan hesitated before mounting the steps reluctantly, like a man walking to the gallows. Oksana and Mason broke apart from the others to meet him, and supported him when the Light tried to drive him to the ground. He shuddered as his darkest secret was dragged into the open—infidelity, continuing even after his human wife had fallen pregnant. She had discovered it, and left him. He'd barely had a chance to know his own daughter.

She remarried, mon coeur, came Duchess' mental voice. *And if he was your friend, it must mean he's a good man. You told me he loved your daughter like she was his own. He raised her as a father should—he even adopted her. Your infidelity freed Janette from an unhappy marriage to you, and allowed her to find happiness with another.*

Chan collapsed to his knees, covering his face with one hand as Mason and Oksana followed him down. They sat with him quietly as he gasped like a man surfacing from drowning, Duchess' words finally forcing him to see his actions from a different perspective.

Duchess stood alone now at the mouth of the tunnels, that bottomless sense of desolation from earlier leaking through gaps in the mental shield she was trying to hold around her innermost self. Menkhef frowned as she started up the stairs, step by slow step, as though being dragged forward by a rope tied around her waist. He let his arms fall away from Amy and Elijah, whose emotions were finally calming as they continued to hold each other.

Menkhef's eyes met first Oksana's, and then Xander's. Both looked as worried as he felt. They rose and headed to meet Duchess, Oksana leaving Mason behind to support Chan as he recovered.

My sister, Menkhef sent, trying to reach her through the heavy barrier she was struggling to maintain, *you *must let your walls crumble. You are not strong enough to resist the goddess' pull; you will only cause yourself more pain by resisting Her.*

The Light reached Duchess at the same moment Xander and Oksana did. She gasped, her face set in hard lines, wisps of steam sizzling from her skin as she fought not to let the beam penetrate into her soul, leaving it to ravage her flesh instead.

"*Ti mwen!*" Oksana cried, as she and Xander tried to shelter her with their bodies. "Don't fight it! You'll hurt yourself!"

"Duchess," Xander murmured, "*don't do this.* No matter what it is, it's not worth your life."

Chan was struggling to his feet, his own pain forgotten as he tried to get to his mate. Duchess cringed back, refusing to meet his gaze—only Oksana and Xander's grip keeping her from tumbling right back down the stairs she'd just ascended. Chan skidded to a halt, stark fear on his face.

"Marie—no." His voice was a bare croak. "I don't care what it is. Please, you have to believe me. Whatever it is… *I don't care.*"

Alarmed, Menkhef strode across to join them as the faint smell of burning flesh wafted across the parapet. He pushed close and took Duchess' face in his hands, his dark eyes boring into her distraught blue ones.

"Stop," he said softly, "we will not allow you to sacrifice yourself out of fear. *Let us in.*"

She squeezed her eyes shut to avoid his gaze, but her shields cracked nonetheless, pain spilling out through the gaps like blood. All at once, he could see her secret shame in the harsh Light of Israfael's power.

"My Darkness will break the Council," she whispered.

"It will not," Menkhef promised her. "Tell us now, and be free of it."

Her chest shook with sobs as she choked, "In the months before he sacrificed his life to save my soul from Bael… when Bertrand had gambled all our money away and first forced me into a life of treason, spying for the king's brother, I…" Her throat closed up until the words were almost inaudible. "I wished him dead. I thought… if he were killed on the king's business… I would get his pension, and I could marry again, or perhaps return to my father. My baby would not be born into poverty and constant fear, with a spy for a mother."

Menkhef wiped her tears away with his thumbs, and eased out of the way as Chan enveloped her in his arms, rocking her.

"I wished you dead, Wei Yong," she sobbed into his neck, "and then, I killed you."

"I told you," he said hoarsely. "I don't care. It's in the past, and I don't care about any of it, Marie."

Duchess clung to her mate with all of the desperation that she'd been holding inside for four centuries, and the Light no longer burned her skin. Menkhef felt the others' support swirl around her through their bond, and added his own to the mix.

When her shuddering tears subsided, the thirteen vampires gathered together, standing shoulder to shoulder as they looked out across the pyramid complex and the desert beyond. Above them, the Light grew stronger, more beams breaking through Bael's swirling Darkness as Israfael's chiming voice rolled over the courtyard.

Now you understand the nature of the final battle, my children. It was never a battle at all.

Menkhef felt confusion echo through the bond, and realized that the others still hadn't solved the puzzle. This was confirmed a moment later, when Xander raised a quizzical brow and said, "Er… that might be something of an optimistic conclusion, actually. The understanding part, I mean."

The ground rumbled, bits of stone shaking loose from the pyramid and rattling their way down to the bottom.

"Also the 'not a battle' part," Trynn muttered under her breath.

The atmosphere sparked with electric potential, and Menkhef narrowed his eyes as the makeshift barricade that Xander, Manisha, and the humans had tried to erect across the compound's only entrance exploded outward in a shower of wood and stone.

Bastian Kovac stood framed in the gap, power sizzling around him and Bael's undead army at his back.

Well, *bugger*," Xander observed. "Now things are going to get *really* interesting."

TWENTY-THREE

"Stand with me," Menkhef told the others, "But make no move toward violence. The fate of the world depends on it."

Then, knowing that the time for secrecy and silence was long past, he let his conclusions about Bael, the Angel, and the war they'd been waging flow freely through the bond. Shocked silence reigned for a long moment before Eris breathed, *"Oh,"* and Xander murmured, "Right. Bloody hell—of *course* they are. Son of a *bitch*."

"We're with you," Tré assured Menkhef. "It's time to end this."

Menkhef lifted his chin and led the way down the steps from the top of the cobra head wall to the esplanade below. He walked toward Bastian Kovac with steady strides, allowing no hint of weakness to show in his bearing.

Bael's lieutenant radiated power. It crackled around him like a dark halo as he led his army into the complex. Menkhef continued forward to meet him, his comrades arrayed behind him. Sparks erupted between the two groups as their auras clashed. Kovac raised a hand, calling his undead forces to a halt, and Menkhef stopped as well, the other vampires in perfect synchrony with him.

Bael's creature—the being that had tortured Menkhef's oldest friend and destroyed an entire city with fire and poison—tilted his head, regarding him across the short span separating them.

"So," he said in his heavy, Eastern European accent, "you have found your thirteen bloodsuckers and formed your council. Yet you appear to have gained no new powers... acquired no new strength. I will take the utmost pleasure in making you watch as my Master's army rapes and consumes the fragile humans cowering in their tents and hiding in your underground tunnels like rats. Then, I will take just as much pleasure in personally finishing what I started with that one—" His eyes flicked to Eris. "—and repeating the process until each of you have watched your mates suffer, then perished yourselves."

Trynn made a sound like a snarl, but both Menkhef and Eris whipped mental power around her before she could lunge for Kovac. He could feel her trembling with rage, but she controlled herself, not making a move toward their old enemy.

Menkhef turned all of his attention back to the creature in front of him, and let a faint smile spread across his features.

"There will be no battle today, I fear," he said mildly.

Bastian frowned.

"Perhaps not, nightcrawler," he said, baring yellow teeth. "After all, from where I'm standing it looks more like a slaughter than a true battle."

Menkhef only raised an eyebrow. "Then you should focus less on what is in front of you, and more on what is above you. Israfael is not warring with Bael. She is merging with him. They are two parts of the same being—a universal force that was in balance until it was catastrophically split into two pieces, millennia ago."

Since that time, the dark part—Bael—had been leaving a trail of victims suffering the same agonizing wound he himself had suffered... the Darkness and Light inside them torn asunder. A broken creature lashing out, repeating the horrors of its past in unspoken—perhaps even unconscious—desperation to understand its own pain.

"Lies!" Kovac spat. "My Master would never join with a creature so sickeningly weak and saccharine! You seek only to delay the inevitability of your own demise."

Menkhef felt a wash of pity for the broken puppet before him.

"Indeed? Ask yourself why your *master* did not order you to lead your forces into our domain while we were weakened by Israfael's Light," he suggested, still in the same mild tone. "Ever since Bael realized the true meaning behind the prophecy, he has not sought our destruction directly. He has sought us as test subjects—beings suffering the same injury he suffers. Souls divided into Light and Dark."

Eris stepped up to Menkhef's side, undaunted as he faced his former tormenter. "Don't you *see*, Kovac? He couldn't use you, or any of his other undead puppets. Your soul is torn, but you don't seek to repair the damage. Instead, you revel in it. Only we vampires have sought some means of repairing the injury done to us—some way to make ourselves whole again. And with the return of our lost loved ones and our acceptance of our own Darkness, we have finally succeeded in healing."

Kovac's lips curled back in a snarl. "Fabricated drivel!" he spat. "Bael is perfect in his Darkness. He will destroy this cloying Light and rule the world! I will stand at his right hand, and finally receive everything I deserve!"

Trynn came to stand on Eris' other side, her narrowed eyes cutting through Kovac as though he were nothing. "Somehow," she said, "I very much doubt that."

Her gaze rose to the sky, and Kovac's followed it, as though he couldn't help himself. Above them, the Light and Dark were swirling together, merging and joining into a breathtaking dance of shadow and brilliance. The wind rose higher, whipping at them.

"No," Kovac said. "*I refuse to believe it.* My Master would not betray me in such a way..."

But the maelstrom of color and shadow was whirling even faster now, condensing and shrinking as the two forces canceled each other out.

"D'you think?" Trynn asked sweetly. "Because it kind of looks to me like he would."

Kovac growled and pulled an iron dagger from its sheath, the undead creatures at his back shifting in readiness to attack. Menkhef tilted his head, appraising the man who had roused him to vengeful bloodlust by harming those he cared about.

"Bastian Kovac, servant of Bael," he said, the words quiet but utterly sincere. "I forgive you."

At the same moment, the last of the dark clouds marking Bael's presence dissipated into nothingness, as the reunified force that had been split into two halves for so long disappeared from the mortal realm with a crack like thunder. Disbelief spread across Kovac's features as he realized that his idol had, in fact, abandoned him, followed by terror as he understood exactly what that meant for one whose only tie to the living world was the Darkness inside him.

A scream of rage tore free of Kovac's chest as his connection to his creator snapped. His flesh split and peeled, both he and the undead creatures under his command crumbling into dust before the vampires' eyes. The iron dagger clattered to the ground, abandoned. Wind gusted around the esplanade, blowing the powdery remains of Bael's army away to join with the desert sands.

There was a beat of absolute silence.

It was broken by Xander's sharply indrawn breath. "*Shit...* the sun! The rest of you need to get under cover *right now—*"

Indeed, the sky above them was now clear and blue. The sun was a fiery yellow orb above the eastern wall of the compound, visible to the right of the pyramid. But the light did not burn their flesh. Instead, Menkhef felt it like a warm caress on the side of his face. He closed his eyes, savoring the sensation of the rays against his skin.

Our gift in exchange for your faithful service, came a melodic, androgynous voice, sounding paradoxically both distant and achingly immediate. *You have stepped into the Light, and it can no longer harm you.*

"Oh. Good. That's good…" Menkhef murmured, as the crushing exhaustion he'd been holding at bay finally demanded its moment. A quick mental check ensured that Amy and Elijah were unhurt, standing a few steps away from him in the golden sunlight. Satisfied by that fact, Menkhef was only vaguely aware of his knees giving way. He was out cold before his body hit the ground.

TWENTY-FOUR

Six days after the world failed to end, Amy sat next to the familiar medical cot in the underground tomb at Saqqara, staring at strongly sculpted features that seemed ageless and ancient even in repose. She'd been doing a lot of that over the past several days—sitting here, watching Menkhef's motionless form, sometimes holding his hand and sometimes rising to pace restlessly around the stone chamber, her thoughts churning in endless circles.

He wasn't even breathing, damn it. And yeah, yeah, the others had reminded her repeatedly that as a vampire, he didn't need to breathe. But, well, it was the *principle* of the thing, all right? No one should be that... *still*.

Elijah wandered in, stretching, and came up behind her chair to place his hands on her shoulders and press a kiss to the top of her head. "Break time, Ames. I'll take over until sunset. Any change this morning?"

She shook her head. "I don't think so. Though... I was trying to concentrate earlier like Eris showed us, and I think maybe I felt him dreaming. It was hard to tell. I could have been imagining it, or maybe sensing someone else's thoughts instead of his."

Elijah sighed and dragged a second chair next to hers, dropping into it. He leaned forward, resting his elbows on his knees, and cocked his head at the figure on the bed. "You know, old man," he told the unconscious form, "when most people say they're so tired they could sleep for a week, they *don't mean it literally*. It's absolutely crazy out there. I expect the others could use your help with some of this shit."

"Any news worth passing on from the past few hours?" Amy asked.

Elijah brightened. "Yes, actually. We finally got a satellite link to Singapore. Mason's brother and his family are okay." He sobered. "They had about a dozen injuries and two deaths at the enclave—the wind blew down a large tent with some people inside, and there was a married couple who tried to make a run for it before the final battle. The pair of them ended up walking right into a group of zombies. But... given that there were almost a thousand people sheltering there, it could have been a lot worse."

"Yeah," she agreed. "It could have. Thank god Mason's nieces are all right—and his brother and sister-in-law, too." She shivered, unable to help herself. The married couple who'd died... it could have been her and Elijah. They'd come so close. Hanging onto survival by their fingertips—quite literally—before rescue had come in the form of the vampire lying on the cot before them.

The aftermath of the *battle-that-wasn't* had been a confusing tangle of relief that they'd somehow survived—that they'd somehow *won*—and terror when Menkhef had crumpled to the ground like a marionette with its strings cut. Eris and Trynn were closest; they'd been the ones to grab him and keep his skull from bashing into the dusty stone of the esplanade. Amy and Elijah had lunged forward the moment they saw his knees buckle. Amy thought she might have cried out some kind of denial at the feeling of Menkhef's mind folding in on itself and disappearing from her awareness like an old-fashioned TV monitor powering off.

She'd snarled at Eris and Trynn—a feral, animal noise that seemed to rise from nowhere. An instinctive, gut deep reaction to seeing someone cradling that broken form who *wasn't her or Elijah*. She was still more than a little mortified, thinking back on it, but neither Trynn nor her mate seemed to have held it against her. Eris had done something with his mental power that snapped her back to a more rational sort of awareness, keeping her from doing anything truly awful like trying to tear them away from Menkhef physically. Elijah skidded to his knees next to her an instant later, his hands closing around her shoulders convulsively.

"What happened, what's wrong with him?" he snapped, having evidently been more successful than she was at holding onto to little concepts like *language* and *asking reasonable questions*.

She was distantly aware of the other vampires gathering around them in a half circle, looking on with concern.

A horrible realization slid into Amy, and her hand flew to her mouth. "It was me, wasn't it?" she said, her voice coming out high and reedy. "I drained him. I drank too much of his blood and weakened him!"

Trynn actually snorted. "Yeah — no offence, kiddo — but get over yourself. I've seen him drained, and this isn't what it looks like. Eris, what the hell has he done to himself this time?"

Eris freed one hand and placed it on Menkhef's forehead, his expression growing distant as he concentrated. Amy held her breath, and noticed a moment later that Menkhef wasn't moving *at all*. As in, his chest wasn't rising or falling. He wasn't breathing.

"Is he — " she began, having to force the words past paralyzed lips.

"Sleeping," Eris interrupted mildly. "He's sleeping."

"Are you fucking kidding me?" Xander asked, as a general relaxation of tension swept through the group.

Mason squeezed past her to crouch near Menkhef's shoulders. "Just normal sleep? You're certain, Eris?"

Eris removed his hand and sat back on his haunches. "I'm not certain that *normal* is the applicable word, since to my knowledge, he hasn't slept in more than sixteen centuries. But, yes, he's merely resting in the arms of Morpheus. In the temporary way, I hasten to add—not the permanent one."

Around them, the humans who had been sheltering from the clash of otherworldly forces were creeping out of their tents and emerging from the tunnels, blinking in the bright morning light. Amy was reeling, her mind pulled in a dozen different directions. She and Elijah had been pulled into this close-knit cadre of individuals during the worst kind of crisis imaginable. She'd seen their innermost selves exposed, and they had seen hers. She'd learned that her husband had contemplated suicide and—god help her—she'd never even known about it.

She had no idea what state the world was in beyond the walls of the complex. Undead monsters had ravaged Saqqara village the previous night. Had the same thing happened around the world? Were her parents okay? Were Elijah's? Her friends? Her coworkers? Her clinic back in Pennsylvania? Would her baby survive to term, now that she was a vampire?

More than anything in the world, she wanted to collapse into hysterics in Elijah's arms. She swallowed hard, and craned to look over her shoulder at the silver-eyed vampire, Tré, who'd led his friends for centuries with courage and honor, all while thinking himself completely unworthy to do so.

"What do we do now?" she asked. "I want to help."

Tré met her gaze with perfect understanding… the sort of understanding that usually only came from being family, or through close friendship forged by the fires of shared danger.

"I need you and your husband to take shifts watching over Menkhef while he recovers," Tré said. "Mason and Oksana, check for injuries among the humans and treat them if necessary. Xander and Manisha, we need to find out what's happening elsewhere in the world. See if the satellite connection is still working, and find out what you can. Eris, Trynn, Duchess, and Chan — with the attack on Saqqara village, it's likely our supply chains for food and water are broken. We'll need to acquire both from whatever sources you can find nearby. See if the village is habitable. We may need to move these people there to simplify things. Della and I will coordinate from here and lend aid as needed once we have a better idea of what's happening outside the walls."

Everyone nodded, and Eris glanced between Amy and Elijah. "Need a hand getting him to a bed?"

Elijah eyed Menkhef's tall form for a moment. "I could probably manage him in a fireman's carry, but I doubt it would be very dignified for either of us," he said uncertainly.

"We'll get a stretcher," Mason said. "You're sure my skills aren't required, Eris?"

"He truly is just sleeping," Eris reassured. "Albeit quite deeply."

Mason shrugged. "After sixteen hundred years, I guess he must've needed it. Back in a tick."

Mason returned with the promised stretcher, and they moved Menkhef down to the catacombs again. Amy hurried ahead and pulled the bloody bedding off the cot where she'd been turned into a vampire mere hours ago. Once Menkhef was settled, Mason gave her and Elijah an assessing look and returned with a couple of bags of blood.

Even through the plastic, the smell was enough to overcome Amy's instinctive aversion to the idea of drinking human blood in the space of a heartbeat. Maybe the Angel hadn't been lying about sparing her the mindless bloodlust of her turning, but she still fell on the bag with ravenous hunger, aware that Elijah was doing much the same.

Self-consciousness didn't return until the bag was empty and she realized that she had torn it open so she could turn it inside out and lick up the last traces from the plastic. Mason had already left to check on everyone else, but Eris was still there with them. He took the torn bags, only asking, "More?" without a trace of judgment in his tone.

Amy tried to listen to her stomach before answering. The ache was gone, so she said, "No, thank you... I think I'm all right now. Elijah?"

"I'm good," Elijah confirmed. "No lingering urges to jump on anything with a heartbeat."

Eris nodded solemnly. "Then I'll leave you to watch over him. Can you still feel the link between us?"

Amy flushed, remembering all she'd seen and felt from the others along the strange mental bond. Gamely, she attempted to look inside herself, not entirely sure what she was looking for. Something in her mind vibrated like a plucked violin string.

"You felt that?" Eris asked. "That's the bond. Now try to reach me along it."

Hello? Amy thought tentatively, focusing intently on that odd inner connection.

Very good, Eris replied in the same way. *Elijah?*

Amy felt Elijah's attempt to speak through the bond much more clearly and immediately. *Yes, I hear you.*

"Well done," Eris said aloud. "It is likely that Tré and Della will be nearby, at least for the next several hours. But if you need something and can't easily find one of us, call along the bond and someone will come."

"Okay," Elijah said. "Good to know. Thanks."

Eris smiled, though there was a certain amount of tension behind it. They were all feeling it, Amy knew, and would be until they found out more about the state of things in the world at large. Eris reached a hand down to brush the tousled black strands of Menkhef's hair from his brow. This time, Amy saw it for what it was—a brother's love—and her protective instincts stayed quiet.

Eris seemed to pause as though debating whether to say anything more. When he did, his voice was quiet. "Look after him for me, please. I know that your circumstances are complicated, and only the three of you can decide how you wish to move forward. But... although he may not show it outwardly, he needs you both. *Badly.*"

Amy's eyes were drawn to Elijah's, where she saw the same uncertainty that was almost certainly reflected in her own. She drew breath to speak, only to pause, not knowing what to say to Eris' words. But when she dragged her eyes away from her husband's, Eris was already gone.

"There's time now, Ames," Elijah said softly. "It's all right. Somehow, we'll figure it out."

They'd stayed with Menkhef and talked. For *hours*.

They talked about Elijah's terrible admission—that he'd considered suicide and never told anyone... never sought help.

"Do you still feel that way?" Amy asked him, her voice quavering.

He took both her hands in his. "No, Ames. As soon as you got pregnant, I knew I could never go through with it. And now—even though it seems crazy with everything that's happened—I feel different, somehow. I feel... *hope*. I have no idea what's going to happen next, but somehow, for the first time in years... I want to find out."

She closed her eyes in relief, only to open them a moment later so she could stare into his. "Good. Because, Elijah? If you died, I'd just find you again when you were reborn and start over. Look around us. Look at what we've seen in the past couple of days. It turns out that for true love... *death is not the end.* And, realizing that? Well... I think it's just changed our lives forever."

He'd kissed her, with a passion she hadn't felt from him in years. If they'd been alone, she would have started tearing clothing off of him there and then. A deep-buried part of her whispered that she should do it anyway… that Menkhef wouldn't mind. But newly animalistic vampire instincts or no, going from a thoroughly vanilla marriage—and in recent months, a largely sexless one—to doing the nasty while locked in a room with an unconscious man was a step too far.

Okay, it was *several* steps too far.

But, *damn*. That kiss. When they pulled back in favor of resting their foreheads together, Elijah's hand tangled in her messy curls, they were both breathing hard.

"Vampires don't need to breathe, *my ass*," she whispered.

And then they were chuckling; snickering like two teenagers trying not to get caught while making out in the shadows, the laughter completely inappropriate for the circumstances, the surroundings, and the topic of conversation.

"I love you, Amy," Elijah said once they'd regained control. "I won't leave you, and I want you to be happy, even if *happy* doesn't end up looking like either of us expected it to look. I don't know what's going to happen now. I don't know if vampires can teach university classes or run dental clinics, or if those things will even exist in whatever the world has become now. But it's time for both of us to stop compromising with our lives. It's time for us to figure out what we want, and make it happen."

"I like that," she told him, still resting her head against his. "I like that a lot, Elijah. No more compromising. No more *scraping by*. It's time to live now."

Six days later, she still felt the same way, even though there were so many things hanging over them. Her body was still clinging to the pregnancy, but there were no guarantees. Neither of them had been able to contact their families yet. Menkhef still hadn't woken up. Daily life had become a near constant struggle to make sure that the humans in Saqqara had safe food, water, and shelter until some sort of transportation and communications infrastructure was up and running again. And yet, like Elijah, she felt hope for the future.

Humanity was in a sort of collective worldwide shock in the days since skies across the globe had gone dark with swirling black fog, and the undead had marched on the living. Only a tiny fraction of the population had fled to the network of enclaves set up at spiritual sites around the world. The rest had done what people always do, pretending nothing was wrong until the crisis showed up on their doorstep.

And it had.

Saqqara had not been the only place where the undead had attacked en masse. The geographical pattern was sporadic, but from what they'd been able to determine through the spotty news reports and satellite phone contacts, any area near an enclave had become a hunting ground for the zombies to increase their numbers in preparation for the final confrontation.

Eris hypothesized that Bael thought the show of force threatening Israfael's most devoted supporters would help draw Her into the open. It was sobering to think that by offering a refuge for people seeking the Light, they had indirectly placed the humans around them in heightened danger. Amy had been struggling these past days to reconcile her hatred of a creature that had caused so much pain and death in the world with the understanding that Bael was damaged on a fundamental level.

Was being damaged somehow supposed to make it all okay? As the reported death toll rose and the full scope of what had been done to the world became clearer, it sure as hell didn't feel okay.

Outside of the enclaves, the undead hadn't been the only agents of chaos. When things started to go sideways, terrorists and other malcontents had come crawling out of the woodwork, adding to the violence and destruction. Riots had broken out in most major cities when the sky went dark, and something about the power raging in the sky had played havoc with power grids and communications systems. Even a week later, the only reliable methods for reaching far-flung areas were satellite and ham radio.

Amy decided that the only thing to do was to narrow her focus to what she could personally influence, and work on that. The alternative was to fret and agonize and waste energy on things that might or might not have happened. She was sick with worry over her friends and family in the United States, but she couldn't do a single thing to help them until phone and internet service was in better shape.

She could help with things in Saqqara, though. She could work on her relationship with Elijah. She could make sure Menkhef wasn't alone while he rested and healed from whatever had made him collapse. So that's what she did.

She and Elijah instituted a sort of informal shift system. For roughly a third of the day, he went out to lend whatever aid was needed at any given moment—hauling loads of food, scavenging fuel to run the generators that powered the water pumps in Saqqara village, manning the shortwave radio, maintaining the solar panels, and so forth and so on.

Then he would come back to Menkhef's chamber and spell her so she could sleep for a few hours on the mattress they'd jammed into the corner of the room. She would get up and do the same for him, and when they'd both gotten enough rest to be functional, she'd leave Elijah alone with Menkhef and venture out to do her own stint of volunteer work. So far, the most excitement had come when a middle-aged man who'd been staying at the complex got a tooth abscess, and she'd had to do an extraction with minimal access to medical supplies.

With Elijah safely back for the day and noon nearly upon them, tiredness washed over Amy like a gentle tide. She was finding it harder to stay awake during the height of the daylight hours now that she was a vampire, though the others assured her the effect would fade with time. She yawned widely, and Elijah shot her a crooked smile.

"Get some rest, Ames," he said.

A different sort of yearning hit her. "Will you sit with me for a while?" she asked, feeling a bit shy even though it was ridiculous to feel that way. "Hold me while I sleep?"

Elijah's eyes darkened, only to be lit up a moment later with glowing pinpricks of copper light. "Always," he said.

She leaned across and kissed him, feeling her eyes burn with their own inner light. It was almost as though they were courting again—reveling in the slow seduction of kisses and caresses, but holding back from more. She'd thought about bringing it up; making use of their seemingly newfound willingness to communicate like actual adults. But she hadn't.

Truth be told, she was enjoying it too much to want to analyze it to death, at least for the moment. It would be another thing entirely if their intimacy was still restricted to necking like teenagers a month from now, but this stage of their rekindling relationship felt to her like something that had a distinct end date. When Menkhef woke up, everything would change. How it would change, she still had no idea. But that was the event that would shake up the puzzle pieces inside their box. It was anybody's guess how those pieces would fit together afterward.

Amy let Elijah lead her to the mattress in the corner. It was a bit cramped with both of them on it, but she wasn't about to complain. She took the side nearest the wall, while he stuffed a battered pillow behind his shoulders and arranged himself in an easy sprawl, half-propped against the wall at the head of the makeshift bed.

With her cheek resting on his chest, her leg slung over his, and his hand stroking up and down her arm, she let herself exist completely in the moment, all of their other cares and concerns falling away. She knew those cares would still be there later, when she was ready to pick them up again.

"Jus' for a few minutes," she slurred, sleep already tugging at her.

"Sleep, Ames," Elijah said, his voice a low rumble against her cheek. "I can see the cot just fine from here if he starts to wake up, and I can't think of anywhere else I'd rather be right now than holding you."

Amy made a sleepy noise, and burrowed closer against him.

TWENTY-FIVE

In the dream, Amy was in Menkhef's palace in Ancient Egypt, but when she caught a glimpse of her bare arm, her skin was its usual pale expanse of freckles rather than Nebetta's rich, golden brown tones. She was pressed between two bodies, her head lolling to the side in wanton abandon as lips and teeth worried at the tender skin of her neck from behind.

"You have no idea what you do to me, *hayati*," murmured the deep voice that had worked its way into the depths of Amy's soul in the short time before its owner had departed into the darkness. But Menkhef was not sleeping now. He was in front of her, his lips brushing the shell of her ear as he spoke.

The teeth that had been nipping a line down the side of her throat paused, and her husband's familiar low chuckle puffed against her skin, making gooseflesh rise.

"I know exactly what she does to you," Elijah said, his chest pressing against her back. "She does the same damn thing to me. She always has."

Elijah's hand slid up to cup Amy's breast through the loose fabric of the shirt she was wearing. At the same time, he bit down on her neck, and her belly clenched as she felt the slide of razor-sharp fangs through skin. Menkhef made a small noise as though he'd been punched, and a second set of fangs pierced her neck on the other side. Her blood sang between them, base lust dragging a high-pitched, keening cry from her lips. She arched, trying to get *more more more*, and—

—a hand closed on her shoulder, shaking her gently from sleep.

"Ames, honey?" Elijah's voice held a thread of worry. "Come on, now. Wake up, you were having a nightmare."

She swallowed hard and blinked up at him, feeling her body still pressed up against the length of his in more or less the same position as when she'd drifted off.

"No," she rasped, her voice sleep-heavy and roughened by lust. "I really, *really* wasn't."

She tried to send her focus along the internal bond. Her connection with Elijah had seemed intermittent and unpredictable since Menkhef collapsed, as though he was the link they needed to reach each other properly. It must have done the trick, though, because Elijah's eyes widened, and he made a sound not dissimilar to the one Menkhef had made in the dream.

"*Jesus, Mary, and Joseph,* Ames," he said, "You're killing me, here."

She rolled upright and slung a leg over him, straddling her husband's lap so she could watch his face more closely. "You mean that," she said cautiously, not exactly a question, but not quite a statement, either. "It really doesn't bother you? It doesn't make you… angry, or disgusted with me?"

He pulled one of her hands away from his shoulder where she'd been using him for balance, and pressed her palm to his cheek instead—holding it there beneath his strong fingers. With the other hand, he grabbed her hip and slid her forward until she was centered over the hard, throbbing length of him.

"What do you think?" he asked, the same vulnerability she was feeling mirrored in the depths of his eyes.

"I don't know whose dream it was, Elijah," she whispered, feeling lost.

"What do you mean?" he asked, still cupping her hand against his cheek. Still holding eye contact.

646

"I mean," she said hesitantly, "this wasn't a memory. It wasn't Heqab and Nebetta, pictures from the past. It could just be... my stupid sex dream, you know? My subconscious getting its rocks off because you've been driving me crazy in all the best ways this past week."

Elijah's brows drew together. "I still don't understand. So what if it was just a stupid sex dream?"

She bit her lip, trying to put her worries into words. Her eyes wandered to the cot in the center of the room for a moment before returning to Elijah. "In some ways, we know everything about this man. But in others, we don't know him at all. He's so... distant, and unreadable, and just because we know how he felt about Nebetta and Heqab, it doesn't mean we know how he feels about *us*. He was kind to us. He protected us as best he could—he saved our lives and kept the other vampires from turning us before we were ready. He managed to keep our child alive when he changed me. But... what if we're building up this big... thing... inside our heads that doesn't really exist?"

Elijah slid her hand down to his lips so he could kiss her palm. "I don't think we are, Ames. When I walked up those stairs from the South Tomb and the Light hit me..." He trailed off for a moment, clearing his throat. "When he caught me afterward and held me up... the way he spoke to me in my mind... well... I don't think that's the kind of thing you fake, just to be nice to someone."

But she only shook her head. "He also told us he wasn't the same person he used to be, and neither were we. He said if neither of us wished to be in his presence ever again, he'd understand."

Elijah just continued to watch her, his expression open and unguarded. "When he wakes up, I guess we'll just have to ask him."

When he wakes up.

"And when will that be?" she wondered bleakly.

-o-o-o-

The following morning, while Elijah was out doing who-knew-what in the neighboring village, Shay wandered in and made herself comfortable on the extra chair by Menkhef's bed.

"Um… hi?" Amy said, taken by surprise at the unexpected visit.

Shay smiled. "Hey, girl. Trynn said you needed to talk to me."

Amy blinked. "She did? I'm sorry, Shay—I don't know where she got that idea. I didn't say anything like that to her."

The other woman huffed a breath of amusement. "No, babe, you misunderstand. She didn't say you *asked* to talk to me. She said you *needed* to talk to me."

A bit of irritation crept in, though Amy tried to keep it out of her voice. "About…?"

"Relationships, I expect," Shay said matter-of-factly.

"*Excuse* me?" Amy nearly squeaked. "I'm sorry, but where do you—or Trynn, for that matter—get off inserting yourselves into other people's relationship issues without being asked?"

Shay only shrugged. "I get the impression that vamps aren't good with the whole *having boundaries* thing. A few people may have intimated over the years that I have a similar problem, so here I am, ready and willing to answer questions about having open and consensual relationships with more than one person at the same time."

With a jolt, Amy flashed back to the day of their arrival in Saqqara—resting in the shade with Elijah, only to have her eyes drawn to a trio of people laughing and talking nearby.

Shay must have seen the memory dawn, because she said, "Yup. *There* it is. I thought you'd remember eventually. You were practically slicing us open with invisible laser beams, you were staring at us so hard that day."

Shay's wide mouth was still quirked in a smile, but that didn't stop embarrassment from burning its way up Amy's neck to her cheeks. All of her irritation and defensiveness drained away, like a plug pulled in a bathtub.

"Oh, my god," she said, scrubbing a hand down her face. "I am *so sorry*, Shay. Both for then and for just now."

Shay snorted. "It's all right, on both counts. Believe me when I say that when you're part of a bisexual poly trio, you get used to people staring at you pretty fast. And for what it's worth, Trynn totally *is* meddling — but only because you so obviously need the help."

Amy took that on board for a moment or two before replying, "Okay... but I'm afraid I really have no idea what she expects me to ask, or want to talk about."

"Maybe you just need someone to say, 'Hey, polyamory is a real thing in the world and people do it all the time'?"

A short bark of laughter slipped past Amy's control. "Oh, wow. I can't believe I'm actually having this conversation. Holy shit." She ran a hand over her face. "Right, so how much do you know about my life? Or maybe I should ask how much Trynn knows about my life... only I'm not sure I want the answer to that."

Shay cocked her head. "The vamps have been trying to fulfill a prophecy involving a Council of Thirteen, and the first eleven consisted of five obvious couples, with one really sad-looking guy left over. Then you and your husband show up and end up getting turned, after which you're both here watching over Super Sad Guy more-or-less around the clock for days on end." She huffed in amusement. "Rocket science, it is not."

At that moment, Amy really wanted the ability to sink straight through the stone floor, and she vowed to pester one of the older vampires to get serious about teaching her to shift form into mist as soon as possible. On the other hand, it was also kind of a relief to have someone to talk to about this subject. Someone besides Elijah, that is.

"Well," she admitted, "when you put it like that…"

"Yup," Shay agreed. "So, first question. Is your husband on board with this, or is he freaking out?"

Amy scrubbed at her eyes, trying to get all the scattered bits of her brain corralled in one place. "He seems… surprisingly on board with it, to be honest."

"Cool. Next question. Are *you* on board with it?"

Amy met her eyes squarely. "Shay—I have absolutely no fucking clue."

"Okay. Arguments against?"

Amy took a deep breath. "I'm scared that Elijah isn't really as on board with this as he seems."

"So you think he's lying?"

She shook her head adamantly. "No, it's not that. You know vampires have a kind of… telepathic thing with each other, right? I can tell that he really feels that way."

"So you're projecting, or maybe using him as an excuse to avoid looking at your own feelings?"

Ouch. "Uh… yeah. Maybe so."

"Right. Next objection?"

Amy thought for a moment. "What will other people think?"

Shay grinned. "That you're weird, possibly going to hell, and probably into all sorts of kinky sex shit. Now, tell me—are you honestly more worried over what people will think about you being with two men, as opposed to what they'll think about you *being a vam-pire?*"

"Fair point," Amy mumbled.

"I'd say so. Next objection?"

Amy's eyes slid to Menkhef's face, peaceful in repose. "We have no idea how he really feels about us. He's… not exactly an easy one to read, and that's when he's *awake.*"

"See, now — that's a valid objection. So, wait for him to wake up and ask him."

Amy wrinkled her nose. "Now you're starting to sound like Elijah."

Shay shrugged, a 'what can you do?' gesture. "Moving on. Arguments in favor?"

Amy sighed. "Elijah and I suck at being married on our own, and we've had dreams about him. Somehow that doesn't seem like a very good foundation for a serious relationship. Or even a seriously *weird* relationship."

Shay hummed thoughtfully. "Hmm, yeah. Maybe not. Still… the poor guy. I feel for him, you know? Stuck here all by his lonesome, while his other vampire buddies are happily paired off."

She reached out a hand as though to brush Menkhef's hair away from his forehead. Before the intent to move even registered in her mind, Amy had the other woman by the wrist, fangs erupting into points and her eyes burning in that way she knew meant they were glowing with an unearthly green light.

Shay met Amy's eyes with a very pointed — and a very *knowing* — look.

"*Oh my god.*" Amy realized what she was doing and dropped Shay's wrist like it had suddenly become red hot. She stumbled back a step, nearly falling over her upturned chair as she tried to put distance between herself and the defenseless human she'd just grabbed.

The defenseless human in question wriggled her fingers to restore the blood flow and tilted her head meaningfully. "Uh-huh. Thought so. Are you gonna make me spell it out, or have you got the memo now?"

"I've got the memo now," Amy said in a tiny voice. "Thank you, Shay."

"Don't mention it, babe," Shay said kindly. "If you're hungry later, I think Jason and Monique are on tap tonight. And if you get tired of waiting on Mister 'Walks Like a Pharaoh' over there—" She hooked a thumb at Menkhef. "—you might try the Prince Charming routine on him. You never know, right? If nothing else, he probably won't be expecting it."

To Amy's complete shock, Shay gave her a friendly hug on her way out—evidently unfazed by Amy's Bride of Dracula impersonation only moments before. Amy hugged her back gingerly. When she was alone again, she righted the chair and sank into it, her mind finally ditching its fruitless hamster wheel in favor of careening off in new directions... exploring new possibilities.

TWENTY-SIX

That evening when Amy went outside to help the others for a few hours, she made a point of tracking Trynn down. The other woman was at the Imhotep Museum, trying to hook the computer system there into a satellite phone link that had seemed to have a decent data connection earlier in the day.

Deciding to take a page from the other vampires' directness, Amy plopped down in a chair across the desk from where Trynn was scowling at her monitor screen and cleared her throat.

"Just a sec," Trynn muttered, not looking up as her fingers flew across the keyboard. "I need to finish this up and then devise some sort of terrible payback for Xander and that pimply IT kid of his. 'Why don't you just devise a protocol to let the computer systems piggyback on the satellite phone connection?'" She parroted in a decent impression of a British accent. "'Then maybe we can get a fast enough internet speed to be useful.' Because, *hey*, sounds simple, right?"

She continued to grumble at a lower volume while Amy sat waiting, her lips pursed to keep them from twitching. Eventually, Trynn sat back and stretched, cracking her knuckles.

"Any luck?" Amy asked.

Trynn's mouth twisted down. "Everyone and their dog who still has access to power and a working sat-phone is trying to use this link at once. Getting data through in either direction is like trying to pour molasses through a pinhole." She sighed. "So, what can I do for you? There isn't really anything here at the museum that would benefit from a second person, though I think Eris and Oksana were planning on moving more of the solar panels over here later."

"I talked to Shay," Amy said without preamble.

Trynn leaned back in her chair, finally giving Amy her full attention. "Oh, yeah? How'd that go?"

"I grabbed her by the wrist and flashed fangs at her when she tried to touch Menkhef," Amy said.

A furrow formed between Trynn's eyebrows. "Well, I did warn her your instincts might still be a bit heightened."

Amy's voice turned rueful. "I think she was counting on it."

Trynn's expression smoothed out. "No real harm done, then?"

"One of the legs on my chair is loose now, since I shoved it over. And I… might've left a bruise on her arm, though she didn't say anything about it, if so."

A shrug. "Could've been worse."

"She said you sent her," Amy said.

"Yup."

"Why? Why not come yourself?"

Trynn examined her for a long moment, as though choosing her words. "I'm not sure how much I could have helped you. I don't know Jack about dating multiple partners, and I have kind of a deep-seated *oh-god-no* reaction when it comes to picturing Snag romantically. I mean, er, picturing *Menkhef* romantically."

Amy scowled. "What's that supposed to mean?"

Trynn threw up her hands in the universal gesture for peace. "It's not supposed to mean anything. My mind just doesn't really want to go there. He's… well… he's *Snag*. That's all."

Amy stared at her, thinking of the stunningly statuesque specimen of male beauty currently resting on the cot in the South Tomb, silver hair streaking his temples, and tiny crows feet at the corners of his eyes. *Are you crazy, girl?* she thought in disbelief, before realizing that she didn't actually *want* other women lusting over Menkhef.

Or thinking about him in a romantic context.

Or, y'know, looking at him.

Shit.

Trynn laughed, and Amy covered her face with her hand and groaned as she remembered that Trynn could probably hear every one of those thoughts.

"Don't worry about it," she said kindly. "Here's the thing. You're still thinking like a human."

"Up until a week ago, I *was* a human," Amy pointed out.

"Yes," Trynn agreed. "And now you're a vampire. You're sitting there thinking, 'I barely know this crazy ancient Egyptian dude; how am I supposed to date someone who watched the pyramids being built?'"

"Er… yeah. Kind of?" Amy agreed.

"But that's the thing. You're not dating him, Amy. You're *mated* to him. You and Elijah both, I guess, and that's the part where Shay can be more helpful than I can."

"What does that even *mean*, though?" Amy asked, a plaintive note creeping into her voice.

Trynn met her gaze evenly. "It means your instincts go crazy at the thought of another woman so much as looking at your men. It means the idea of walking away, of being without them, makes you want to panic and tear the world apart with how wrong that is. It means that without them, you can never be a whole person. And without you, they can never be whole, either. It means that in the end, even death wasn't enough to keep you apart."

A lump rose in Amy's throat, trying to choke her.

Trynn's smile was lopsided and wistful. "Yeah, you understand what I mean. I can tell. Why don't you take the evening off and go back to the South Tomb? I'll let the others know. It's past time for the old scarecrow to wake up and help you and Elijah get this stuff figured out."

Amy nodded slowly, and rose.

"Why do some of you call him Snag?" she asked, aware that it was a non sequitur.

Trynn let out a low laugh and raised a finger, indicating her left canine. "Snaggle tooth, get it?" Her eyes crinkled at the corners. "I nearly lost my shit when I found out you were an dentist. You three need to get this worked out, because my life will *not* be complete until I've seen what Invisalign for vampires looks like."

Amy tried to swallow choked laughter for a moment before giving up and letting it out. The tension shattered, and she wiped wetness from her eyes. "Right. If I needed additional motivation, I guess I've got it now. Thanks for that—*I think*."

The other woman grinned. "All part of the service. Now get out of here, and let me plot my revenge on uppity Brits who have no appreciation for the complexity of cross-platform programming."

"I'm going," Amy said. "When Menkhef wakes up, I'll let him know that you're angling to get him in my dentist's chair."

"You do that," Trynn said, and turned back to her code.

Amy left the museum and centered herself, intending to take the fast way back to the complex. She was a complete dunce when it came to transforming into mist, but she'd managed her owl form a few times now without anything disastrous happening. She closed her eyes, taking mental inventory of the clothes and personal items she needed to keep track of, and focused on becoming her avian avatar.

A moment later, she pushed off clumsily, flapping upward into the evening sky. The South Tomb was only moments away by air, as long as she avoided the distraction of scurrying mice and other tiny night creatures along the way. She fluttered back to earth on top of the cobra head wall, unwilling to test her flying skills in the narrow tunnels below. Another transformation, followed by a quick check to make sure she was still fully clothed, and she was jogging lightly down the stairs leading underground.

Elijah looked up in surprise when she appeared in the doorway and entered, closing the door behind her on creaking hinges. He rose to meet her, giving her a warm kiss before he spoke.

"Everything okay, sweetheart? I didn't expect you back for hours yet."

"Nothing's wrong," she assured him. "I'm just done with waiting for answers. I want to try something."

He looked at her curiously. "Try what?"

"The Prince Charming routine. Shay suggested it this morning."

"The… what, now?" Elijah gave her an odd look.

Amy huffed. "Sleeping Beauty? Prince Charming?" He still looked blank, and she rolled her eyes. "*I'm going to kiss him,*" she spelled out. "Assuming… you're okay with that?"

The words trailed off in a question.

Elijah stared at her. "Amy, since I've indicated on multiple occasions now that I find the idea of you having sex with him hot, I think you can take it as read that I'm not going to freak out over the idea of you kissing him."

She swallowed her embarrassment over doubting him yet again, when he'd clearly been signaling all along that he was open to exploring… whatever this turned out to be. *Projection,* Shay had called it.

So, was Amy really ready to do this?

Yes, she decided. Yes, she most certainly was.

"Sorry," she told Elijah. "That's my nerves talking. Up until now, this was all theoretical… but shit's about to get real, I guess."

"I think it's past time," Elijah said mildly.

She kissed him again, pouring all of her feelings into the slide of lips, and he returned those feelings a hundredfold.

"Love you, Ames," he said when he pulled back. A smile quirked his sensuous mouth as he continued, "And if you kiss him like that, he'd have to be a dead man not to respond."

Something fluttered low in Amy's stomach. "God, I love you so much," she said. "No matter what else happens, I'll always be yours. You know that, right?"

He ran his fingertips down her cheek. "We'll be each other's. I get that now, Amy. I understand what it means. Love's not a zero-sum game."

She pressed her face into his hand like a cat, closing her eyes for a long moment as she let those words sink in. "Yeah," she agreed.

Elijah nudged her toward the cot, and by unspoken agreement, they perched on opposite sides of the mattress—Amy on Menkhef's right, and Elijah on his left. Amy stared down at his still features for a long time, tracing them first with her eyes, and then with the tips of her fingers. He was so… fucking… *regal*. It made him seem unapproachable. It also gave her a nearly overwhelming urge to muss him up a bit. To do something that would break through that cool reserve. She leaned down, teasing his lips with the faintest brush of hers.

Something stirred in the back of her mind—quiet and deep.

She kissed him again. It was like kissing a statue… right up until the moment when the statue kissed her back. A tiny movement; the merest slide of cool skin against hers. But that depthless presence inside her head roused further, coming slowly to life after long days of quiescence.

Amy closed her eyes, sinking into the mental connection even as she sank deeper into the kiss. A hand threaded into her curls and fisted, the gentle tug on her scalp zapping down the length of her spine like a lightning bolt and drawing a mewl from her lips. For a moment, she thought it must be Elijah, but she knew the feel of Elijah's hands.

This wasn't him.

Want spiraled higher, lengthening Amy's fangs. She was still unpracticed at managing the dangerous points, and the edge of her tongue rasped over the right one, opening a small wound. Menkhef made a low, male noise that did very interesting things to Amy's libido, and then he was holding her in place with both hands, demanding entrance to her mouth and tempting her tongue to explore his.

He sucked on it, drawing on the tiny cut… pulling her blood into him. The sensation made her toes curl, and she realized that she was grasping his shoulders so tightly that her fingernails were in danger of breaking his skin and drawing blood in turn. Deliciously wanton visions of tearing her mouth away so she could lick up every last drop threatened to unravel her control and distract her from the most important fact.

It had worked. He was awake.

Menkhef had risen to a seated position as they kissed, never relinquishing his grip on her or easing the exquisite ravishment of her mouth. Amy didn't think she had the strength of will to try and stop him, either. Especially not when she was getting echoes across the bond from a bottomless well of desire and raw need lurking in that powerful, ancient mind.

It was the kind of need that could devour someone whole, and leave them feeling grateful afterward for the opportunity to be consumed. So, it was honestly a disappointment as well as a relief when Elijah said, "Hey, old man. You know that's my wife you're kissing, right?"

Menkhef froze, his powerful aura furling up like a great bird of prey folding its wings. He pulled away from Amy's lips very carefully, his grip in her hair loosening.

Elijah's lips twitched as he continued, "Because I thought you might want to know, she loves it when you bite her lower lip. Though, mind you, I haven't tried it with fangs yet."

The tension in Menkhef's frame eased incrementally, and his brows drew together in something that looked like consternation.

"Guardsman," he said mildly, "are you *teasing me*?"

Elijah nodded. "Yup. And if you don't want it to become a regular thing, you'll probably need to work on your reaction—because right now it's priceless. So… welcome back. How are you feeling? Shall I get Mason in here to take a look at you?"

Menkhef blinked, as though he were just now cataloguing his surroundings and putting everything together in his head. His hand slid out of Amy's hair completely, and she tried not to mourn the loss. There were things they needed to discuss first. Questions that needed answers.

"I am… well," Menkhef said slowly, sounding like a man who also had questions he wanted answered.

"You've been asleep for seven days," Amy said, cringing a bit when it came out sounding like an accusation. She continued in a gentler tone. "We were worried."

His dark eyes softened. "It was not my intention to worry you." His brow twitched. "Nor was it my intention to sleep for seven days. That is… new."

"Hmm," Elijah said, leaning back to brace a hand behind him on the mattress. "Maybe try doing it in moderation on a more regular basis, rather than once every… what was it? Sixteen hundred years?"

"Sound medical advice," Menkhef said, the words emerging distinctly dry. "Perhaps Mason's presence will not be necessary after all."

"Lots of things have been happening since the battle… or whatever you want to call it," Amy said, bringing the conversation back to more somber territory.

"Yes," Menkhef said, sobering immediately. A light caress inside her mind drew Amy's attention to the mental link. "May I see?"

She nodded, and felt a deft touch slide through her memories of the past week, and Elijah's, as well. It didn't take long.

"You've done well," Menkhef said quietly. "All of you. I regret that my incapacity took you and your husband away from more important tasks."

"The others had it under control," Elijah said. "If they'd needed more from us, we would have worked something out. But everyone in Saqqara who needs it has food, water, shelter, and sanitation. Honestly, until communications recover, there's not a lot more we can do."

"Some of the others have been discussing going into Cairo to check things out, since it's not far from here," Amy said. "Now that you're awake, they'll probably want to move forward with that plan."

He nodded. "Logical."

"And speaking of the others, we should let them know you're all right," Elijah added.

"They are aware," Menkhef said. "I've asked them to give us privacy for a bit longer. There are… things we must discuss."

This was the moment, and Amy felt nervous butterflies gather in her stomach. She shot a glance at Elijah, who somehow appeared far more sanguine than she felt.

"Yes," she said. "We have questions." But that wasn't exactly right. "Well, okay—to be more accurate, we have *a* question."

"Then ask it," Menkhef said evenly.

She took a deep breath, steeling herself. "There's been this huge buildup about… fated mates, finding each other across different lifetimes and being reunited to live happily ever after. But… the whole time Elijah and I have been grappling with that—coming to terms with it—we've had no way of knowing if you even want that kind of happily ever after. No idea what it would look like if you *did* want it. You loved Nebetta and Heqab. But that was more than four thousand years ago. You told us that we're all different people now. Your friends just seem to assume that it doesn't matter… that we can somehow slide in and fill the space left by lovers who died in the ancient past. The question is—would you even want us to try?"

Her palms itched with nervousness. She clenched her hands into fists, wondering when she'd become so invested in Menkhef's answer to the question. Hadn't she been the nervous one? The uncertain one?

Menkhef reached out to cradle her face, his expression falling into lines of long-felt yearning. "*Hayati*," he said, "After the kiss you just shared with me, you really need to ask me this?"

"Told you," Elijah murmured.

"Okay," Amy said, relief and nervousness and excitement for the future singing in her veins like wine. "Okay, so—we're doing this. I have no idea how we even start, but let's *do* this."

Elijah laughed, and Menkhef smiled like the sun coming out, tucking a wayward red curl over Amy's ear.

"Maybe we should start simply," Elijah said. "Is that hunger I can feel through the bond, old man? You haven't had any blood in more than a week."

Menkhef shrugged the question off. "It can wait; it's not important."

Elijah held his gaze, a sad smile playing around his lips. Amy couldn't look away from the two of them—handsome, and kind, and principled, and… hers?

"It *could* wait," Elijah said patiently, "but there's no earthly reason why it needs to. It's true that you shouldn't drink more than a mouthful from Amy, because of the baby. But I'm right here. I'm topped up on blood bags… and I'm offering. I can always refill later."

"He can, you know," Amy said, her heart swelling until she thought it might burst. "I heard through the grapevine that Jason and Monique are on tap tonight."

"See? There you have it," Elijah said cheerfully.

Some deeply felt emotion passed across Menkhef's face, and he drew Elijah forward with a hand cupped around the nape of his neck. "My guardsman," he said quietly, and rested his forehead against the crook of Elijah's shoulder for a long moment. "Always concerned with the needs of others, rather than your own."

Elijah, too, looked like he was fighting some strong emotion, and Amy felt an echo of what had passed between the two after Elijah emerged into Israfael's Light.

"Not anymore," he said. "Not when I can look after both at once."

"Good." With that single word, Menkhef gently tipped Elijah's chin back and slid his fangs into chocolate-colored skin, sealing his sensuous lips over the twin wounds and drinking deeply.

Elijah's eyes fluttered shut. Longing swept through Amy like wildfire, and she realized that there was no longer any rational reason to deny herself. She shuffled across the bed to kneel at Menkhef's side. Once there, she kissed her way up Elijah's shoulder and sank her fangs into the other side of his neck. He gasped, his arm snaking around her to hold her tight against him as the cool delight of his blood spilled into her mouth.

She wasn't truly hungry, and didn't draw on the wounds to pull more from him—but hunger wasn't the point. As his blood flowed into both of them, the bond between them flared. She felt what they felt; knew what they knew. The truth of their connection flooded her, along with their mutual commitment to move forward and forge a new life in this uncertain future.

The three of them had seen a prophecy fulfilled against all odds. They had survived an apocalypse and confronted the depths of their own souls. After weathering all of those things and emerging alive to tell the tale, facing the future together was nothing to fear.

EPILOGUE

Al Ghorab Stables, Cairo, Egypt – one year later

Amy hummed in satisfaction and leaned back against the well-muscled chest behind her. The arm wrapped around her ribcage to steady her gentled its hold as she let her head fall back into the cradle of a strong shoulder.

The bedroom was quiet except for the soft slide of skin on skin. Lit only by the glow of the moon slanting through the wall of west-facing windows, it was a silver-limned oasis, tastefully if sparsely furnished with rich wood and sumptuous fabrics. The house sat on a dozen or so hectares of land at the western edge of the Nile floodplain, just beyond the southern reaches of the Cairo Metropolitan Area.

It was set back from the road, nestled among irrigated pastureland, with opulent stables off to one side. Menkhef had purchased the property nine months ago, stating that he'd always enjoyed working with horses and had not had the opportunity to indulge the passion since he'd been a young man. He'd acquired a small but select band of Arabian broodmares, along with a promising young stallion boasting bloodlines that harkened back to the earliest written breeding records.

It gave him something to do, he said, while she and Elijah were traveling back and forth to the United States to sort out their affairs. Amy had been thrilled. She'd been horse-crazy as a teenager, scrimping and saving every penny she could for riding lessons at the local barn. Now, on the days when she wasn't busy volunteering her dental services to the underprivileged in and around Cairo, she could often be found sneaking out for an hour to ride her fiery chestnut mare, or just to work in the barn, surrounded by the smell of hay and leather.

Elijah had given notice at his old teaching position in Pennsylvania, and landed a new post at the American University in Cairo, an English language institution with a well-respected archaeological program specializing in Egyptology. He'd returned to his first love—field research. But now, his digs were practically on his doorstep, an easy commute from their home overlooking the Western Desert.

And together, they lived.

The pace of their lives these days was busy, but not frantic, and for perhaps the first time in her life, Amy was at peace. She had everything that she needed. She knew why she was here, and how she could help make the world a better place with her presence.

Even though Menkhef—stubborn bastard that he was—still hadn't let her straighten his maloccluded canine.

But that was all right. Everyone needed fresh goals to aspire to… and besides, that particular snaggle tooth had kind of grown on her over the past year.

Lips nuzzled the sensitive skin beneath Amy's ear, and she shifted restlessly in Menkhef's lap. The movement jostled his hard length buried inside her, pressing against the spot on the front wall of her passage that made her inner muscles clench deliciously. Her breath huffed out, the rest of her body feeling soft and liquid after nearly a half-hour of his unhurried attention to her pleasure.

Her Egyptian lover was inhumanly patient in all things, and definitely in the matter of sex. She lived for the moments when she could pierce his much-vaunted control. Those moments were rare, but they could be volcanic in their intensity.

Tonight, she knew, would not be such a night. They were all feeling lazy, and their time right now was not unlimited. So, she was content to let the boys have their fun, and reap the benefits with a happy and grateful heart.

"Touch her," Elijah said from his comfortable sprawl in the chair next to the bed, where he was watching the show. "Make her come again."

As they always did, her husband's low-pitched suggestions ratcheted up her simmering desire, heating it to the boiling point. Knowing he was watching—knowing he was enjoying the show, getting off on her pleasure—it did things to her. Powerful things.

Menkhef slid one hand over her breasts, trailing it upward to rest over the arched expanse of her bared throat. It was a silent admonishment not to move—to remain pliant and loose in his embrace while he shattered her. She moaned, making no effort to lift her head from where it had fallen back to rest on his shoulder.

His other hand smoothed over her belly, fingers trailing past neatly trimmed pubic hair to delve into her folds and circle her clit. With a feeling like the tide coming in, her pleasure rose. Her muscles fluttered around his thick shaft, and he rolled his hips in an easy rhythm beneath her. He could have pushed her into a climax in mere moments, but even in this, he drew things out until she thought she might go mad.

She was considering the merits of shamelessly begging for mercy by the time the hand holding her throat tipped her head to one side. His fangs pierced her flesh, sliding deep. She cried out softly and came hard around his cock, the climax going on for so long that she wasn't sure if she was lightheaded due to blood loss or orgasm exhaustion. Menkhef made an animal noise against the tender skin of her neck and came right along with her, drinking her blood in deep swallows as he did.

When they both came back to themselves and Amy dragged heavy eyelids open, it was to find Elijah watching them intently, one foot resting on the edge of the bed as he fisted his cock with slow, firm strokes.

"Nuh-uh," she said groggily. "Hands off. That's mine."

She was slurring a bit, but Elijah only smiled at her. He made a point of sliding his fist along the heavy length a few more times before letting his hand fall away.

"Greedy," he accused fondly.

She smirked, and pointedly turned her attention back to Menkhef, craning her head around until they could kiss, even though the angle was a bit awkward. She could taste her own blood on his tongue, and his as well, after he purposely scored his lip so she could suck on it. She carried on until she heard Elijah shift restlessly in his chair, and then broke away with a final tender brush against Menkhef's soft smile.

Amy slid free of his body and prowled toward the edge of the bed, her movements loose and sloppy with relaxation. The chair Elijah was sitting in had no arms, which made it easy to crawl into his lap, facing him, and impale herself on the impressive erection he'd been teasing her with earlier.

The feeling of being split open by a fresh, straining cock while her nerves were still oversensitive and singing from fucking her other lover had quickly become one of Amy's favorite things in life. She growled and wrenched Elijah's head back, not being gentle as she tore into his neck and rode him hard.

Elijah's hands grasped her buttocks, strong arms lifting and lowering her onto his hot length as she drank him down. He came first, helpless beneath her onslaught, and the feel of it through the bond triggered her as well. It was like an earthquake—deep and far-reaching, leaving her slumped boneless in Elijah's arms.

Mere moments later, fussing noises came from the baby monitor on the bedside table, and Elijah chuckled into her hair. "Timing like an orchestra conductor," he murmured.

Amy snickered into his neck, just relieved that the unhappy cries hadn't started ten minutes ago.

I have her this time, Menkhef sent along the bond, already reaching down next to the bed to retrieve a pair of loose sleep pants. Amy let her silent thanks flow back to him, and kissed Elijah deeply before easing off of his body. He gave her ass a final companionable squeeze and lifted one hand to his mouth, yawning deeply.

"This is going to be a long day," he observed, and stretched. "Worth it, though."

Amy watched the play of muscles in moonlight with appreciation. "Definitely worth it," she agreed.

After cleaning up quickly and donning a robe, she returned to find Menkhef back in the room, cradling Neqaba against his bare chest as he looked down at her with a soft expression on his ageless features. His black hair had grown out until it fell over his shoulders in raven waves, and Amy took a moment to appreciate the picture he made with their daughter.

To appreciate what her life had somehow become.

She settled herself against the headboard of the bed and accepted the warm, squirming bundle into her arms. Neqaba squalled in distress, but it took her only a moment to realize where she was and latch onto Amy's nipple. Amy cooed to her and stroked her fingers over Neqaba's dark curls, wondering if it were possible to overdose on happy endorphins from breast-feeding while still high on mind-blowing sex and drinking blood.

Elijah chuckled and settled next to her on the bed. "Probably not," he said in response to her unaired musing. "But if you feel like volunteering for a more in-depth study, I'm happy to participate."

She wrinkled her nose at him.

"How long until the others get here?" she asked, rather than replying to Elijah's teasing. "For some reason, I seem to have completely lost track of time. No idea how that happened."

"Two hours or so," Menkhef replied, perching on the edge of the bed to watch their child nurse.

Amy yawned. "Okay. Two hours—that's doable. I definitely need a shower first, though. And frankly, so do both of you."

Elijah drew breath to say something, and she cut him off.

"*Separate* showers. Or the two hours suddenly becomes way less doable," she said sternly

Elijah shot Menkhef a rueful look. "Oh, well. You can't say I didn't try."

-o-o-o-

Eris and Trynn were the first to arrive that morning—unsurprising, since they, too, maintained a residence in Cairo. Trynn freelanced, plying her computer skills to several clients including Xander's company, HelioTeque. Eris had dusted off a couple of academic degrees and attached himself to Al Azhar University, one of the oldest institutions of higher learning in the world. He and Trynn were relatively frequent visitors to the house, and one or both of them usually had a virtual chess game going with Menkhef via email at any given time.

Tré and Della were next, with eleven-year-old Allison in tow. While both Amy and Elijah's immediate families had escaped harm during the events a year ago, Della's family had not been so lucky. Her mother had survived, and Della had sought her out shortly afterward to let her know she was still alive and explain what had happened. Della's estranged father had been killed, however, as had her aunt and uncle—Allison's parents. The little girl had been injured badly, but survived. Della and her mate had taken her in immediately upon finding out about the tragedy.

Manisha and Xander showed up shortly thereafter. They were living in London, to no one's very great surprise. Manisha was pursuing an advanced psychology degree with an eye toward trauma counseling, while Xander continued to expand his renewable energy company. Amy had learned that while all of the original vampires held a fair amount of personal wealth accumulated simply by virtue of investing money over the course of several lifetimes, it was Xander's company that allowed them to truly not have to worry about anything. He distributed the profits freely among his friends, seemingly unconcerned that none of them except Trynn contributed to the business in any meaningful way.

The final group to arrive was a boisterous one. Mason, Oksana, Duchess, and Chan had traveled together from Haiti, along with Oksana and Mason's brood of adopted Haitian children. There were four of them—all boys—ranging in age from seven to sixteen. The youngest, Cristofer, looked at Mason in particular with hero-worship in his eyes, and the oldest, Eniel, had always seemed to have wisdom far beyond his years. *An old soul*, Oksana would observe with a smile, ruffling his hair.

Mason and Oksana had returned to the island to continue Mason's previous work, this time with private funding that allowed them to get the resources they really needed. Amy was a bit in awe of the pair—they were making a tremendous difference for the war-torn country's orphans and child soldiers.

Duchess and Chan had been helping them for the past several months. What had started out as a way to stay busy and be productive while they decided on a long-term plan had, Amy suspected, become their passion as much as it was Oksana and Mason's. She was glad; Amy liked the idea of them being together. This was such an odd, close-knit group—it only seemed right that they would gravitate together, the same way Eris and Trynn had gravitated toward Cairo.

After hugs and greetings had been exchanged, Amy made sure that all the children were fed and had a chance to freshen up. Then Elijah sent them to the stables to greet the horses under the watchful eye of Ahmed, the farm manager.

Menkhef had set up tables and chairs on the east-facing patio, a pleasant space enclosed by a low stucco wall, and partially covered by an overhead trellis from which hung a riot of flowering vines. A faint wash of pink and orange was just starting to tint the sky above the horizon, heralding dawn's approach.

They made themselves comfortable in the cool predawn, easy together as only people who truly understand each other can be.

"It hardly seems as though a year has passed," Xander mused, leaning back with his ankles crossed in front of him.

"Speak for yourself, mate," Mason said wryly. "I hardly feel as though I've had time to stop and breathe in the past twelve months."

"Which is just the way you like it," Oksana said.

Mason shrugged and didn't deny it. "Maybe so." He smiled at Amy, who held Neqaba cradled in her arms, sleeping soundly. "How's the sprog doing these days, Amy? Looks like she's growing by leaps and bounds."

Amy couldn't help the radiant smile that blossomed on her face. "She's doing well, Mason. Healthy and happy, thanks to you."

Amy had been on tenterhooks through her entire pregnancy; terrified that something would go wrong.

Neqaba had clung to her vampire mother's womb tenaciously and been born without incident, only to suffer terrible colic and slow weight gain afterward. Amy had discovered ahead of time that her milk was tainted with blood in the same way that vampire tears and other bodily fluids were, so they'd made the decision to put Neqaba on formula immediately. It had been Mason who'd realized that Amy's milk might be exactly what her daughter needed, and to everyone's surprise and relief, the tiny infant had thrived on the pink-tinged liquid her breasts produced.

No one knew exactly what Neqaba was… vampire, human, or something in between. To their knowledge, there had never been another baby like her. As far as Amy was concerned, though, as long as she grew up healthy and happy, it didn't matter. She was Neqaba. She was Amy's daughter. The rest could take care of itself.

"I'm glad to hear it," Mason said, still gazing at the little girl with a fond smile.

Amy smiled as well, trailing a fingertip over Neqaba's soft cheek.

Many things had changed. The world a year after Israfael's final confrontation with Bael was a place experiencing both lingering trauma and burgeoning hope. The official death toll had eventually come in at almost two hundred seventeen million people worldwide, a figure that was both heartbreaking and impossible to truly grasp.

Aside from Della's family members, the vampires had mourned the loss of Mason's elderly mother in Australia, Elijah's faculty supervisor at West Parklands University, a friend named Madame Francine in New Orleans, and several of Xander's employees in both London and Romania.

It had been so random, and so utterly, completely pointless. For months, Amy had worried that the worst parts of human nature would take over, plunging the world into dark times. But while there were certainly moments of darkness, more people seemed to have gained a new appreciation for life and love after the terrifying months when Bael gained sway over the world.

The destruction and death had decimated the economy, but people were building it up again—making better decisions and looking toward a brighter future. As a group, the vampires had made a valiant effort at keeping a low profile, occasionally by means of a bit of hypnotic influence aimed at reporters or other humans who got too close or too pushy. As time went on, the public's attention moved to other things, as it is wont to do.

"Look. The sun's coming up," Chan said quietly.

By unspoken accord, Amy rose with the others and went to stand by the low wall bounding the eastern edge of the patio, Neqaba still asleep in her arms. Menkhef stood at her left side, and Elijah, at her right. The others joined them, standing shoulder to shoulder as the first sliver of brilliant orange light illuminated the horizon, brightening the eastern sky from navy blue to turquoise.

The fiery orb slid higher, bathing them in liquid warmth that turned everything gold. Amy watched as Menkhef closed his eyes, lifting his face toward the glowing rays. Elijah's arm slid around her waist, pressing her against his side.

Ahead of them, a new day dawned.

finis

Thank you for reading *Circle of Blood*. If you enjoyed this series, R.A. Steffan and Jaelynn Woolf have another collaboration titled *The Last Vampire*.

To discover more books by this author, visit www.rasteffan.com

www.ingramcontent.com/pod-product-compliance
Lightning Source LLC
Chambersburg PA
CBHW071955190726
48293CB00001B/27